OCTOBER Dreams

A CELEBRATION OF HALLOWEEN

OCTOBER *Dreams*

A CELEBRATION OF
HALLOWEEN

EDITED BY
RICHARD CHIZMAR
AND
ROBERT MORRISH

RoC
A ROC BOOK

ROC
Published by New American Library, a division of
Penguin Putnam Inc., 375 Hudson Street,
New York, New York 10014, U.S.A.
Penguin Books Ltd, 80 Strand,
London WC2R 0RL, England
Penguin Books Australia Ltd, Ringwood,
Victoria, Australia
Penguin Books Canada Ltd, 10 Alcorn Avenue,
Toronto, Ontario, Canada M4V 3B2
Penguin Books (N.Z.) Ltd, 182–190 Wairau Road,
Auckland 10, New Zealand

Penguin Books Ltd, Registered Offices:
Harmondsworth, Middlesex, England

Published by Roc, an imprint of New American Library, a division of Penguin Putnam Inc.
This is an authorized reprint of a hardcover edition published by Cemetery Dance Publications.
For information address Cemetery Dance Publications, P.O. Box 943, Abingdon, MD 21009.

First Roc Printing, September 2002
10 9 8 7 6 5 4 3 2 1

Printed in the United States of America

PUBLISHER'S NOTE
Some of these are works of fiction. Names, characters, places, and incidents either are the products of the authors imaginations or are used fictitiously, and any resemblance to actual persons, living or dead, business establishments, events, or locales is entirely coincidental.

Contents

For Ray Bradbury,

October Dreamer Extraordinaire

The Black Pumpkin

Dean Koontz

1

The pumpkins were creepy, but the man who carved them was far stranger than his creations. He appeared to have baked for ages in the California sun, until all the juices had been cooked out of his flesh. He was stringy, bony, and leather skinned. His head resembled a squash, not pleasingly round like a pumpkin, yet not shaped like an ordinary head, either: slightly narrower at the top and wider at the chin than was natural. His amber eyes glowed with a sullen, smoky, weak—but dangerous—light.

Tommy Sutzmann was uneasy the moment that he saw the old pumpkin carver. He told himself that he was foolish, overreacting again. He had a tendency to be alarmed by the mildest signs of anger in others, to panic at the first vague perception of a threat. Some families taught their twelve-year-old boys honesty, integrity, decency, and faith in God. By their actions, however, Tommy's parents and his brother, Frank, had taught him to be cautious, suspicious, and even paranoid. In the best of times, his mother and father treated him as an outsider; in the worst of times, they enjoyed punishing him as a means of releasing their anger and frustration at the rest of the world. To Frank, Tommy was simply—and always—a target. Consequently, deep and abiding uneasiness was Tommy Sutzmann's natural condition.

Every December this vacant lot was full of Christmas trees, and during the summer, itinerant merchants used the space to exhibit Day-Glo stuffed animals or paintings on velvet. As Halloween approached, the half-acre property, tucked between a supermarket and a bank on the outskirts of Santa Ana, was an orange montage of pumpkins: all sizes and shapes, lined in rows and stacked in neat low pyramids and tumbled in piles, maybe two thousand of them, three thousand, the raw material of pies and jack-o'-lanterns.

The carver was in a back corner of the lot, sitting on a tube-metal chair. The vinyl-upholstered pads on the back and seat of the chair were darkly mottled, webbed with cracks—not unlike the carver's face. He sat with a pumpkin on his lap, whittling with a sharp knife and other tools that lay on the dusty ground beside him.

Tommy Sutzmann did not remember crossing the field of pumpkins. He recalled getting out of the car as soon as his father had parked at the curb—and the next thing he knew, he was in the back of the lot just a few feet from the strange sculptor.

A score of finished jack-o'-lanterns were propped atop mounds of other pumpkins. This artist did not merely hack crude eye holes and mouths. He carefully cut the skin and the rind of the squash in layers, producing features with great definition and surprising subtlety. He also used paint to give each creation its own demonic personality: Four cans, each containing a brush, stood on the ground beside his chair—red, white, green, and black.

The jack-o'-lanterns grinned and frowned and scowled and leered. They seemed to be staring at Tommy. Every one of them.

Their mouths were agape, little pointy teeth bared. None had the blunt, goofy dental work of ordinary jack-o'-lanterns. Some were equipped with long fangs.

Staring, staring. And Tommy had the peculiar feeling that they could *see* him.

When he looked up from the pumpkins, he discovered that the old man was also watching him intently. Those amber eyes, full of smoky light, seemed to brighten as they held Tommy's own gaze.

"Would you like one of my pumpkins?" the carver asked. In his cold, dry voice, each word was as crisp as October leaves wind-blown along a stone walk.

Tommy could not speak. He tried to say, *No, sir, thank you, no,* but the words stuck in his throat as if he were trying to swallow the cloying pulp of a pumpkin.

"Pick a favorite," the carver said, gesturing with one withered hand toward his gallery of grotesques—but never taking his eyes off Tommy.

"No, uh...no, thank you." Tommy was dismayed to hear that his voice had a tremor and a slightly shrill edge.

What's wrong with me? he wondered. *Why am I hyping myself into a fit like this? He's just an old guy who carves pumpkins.*

"Is it the price you're worried about?" the carver asked.

"No."

"Because you pay the man out front for the pumpkin, same price as any other on the lot, and you just give me whatever you feel my work is worth."

When he smiled, every aspect of his squash-shaped head changed. Not for the better.

The day was mild. Sunshine found its way through holes in the overcast, brightly illuminating some orange mounds of pumpkins while leaving others deep in cloud shadows. In spite of the warm weather, a chill gripped Tommy and would not release him.

Leaning forward with the half-sculpted pumpkin in his lap, the carver said, "You just give me whatever amount you wish...although I'm duty-bound to say that you get what you give."

Another smile. Worse than the first one.

Tommy said, "Uh...."

"You get what you give," the carver repeated.

"No shit?" brother Frank said, stepping up to the row of leering jack-o'-lanterns. Evidently he had overheard everything. He was two years older than Tommy, muscular where Tommy was slight, with a self-confidence that Tommy had never known. Frank hefted the most macabre of all the old guy's creations. "So how much is this one?"

The carver was reluctant to shift his gaze from Tommy to Frank, and Tommy was unable to break the contact first. In the man's eyes Tommy saw something he could not define or understand, something that filled his mind's eye with images of disfigured children, deformed creatures that he could not name, and dead things.

"How much is this one, gramps?" Frank repeated.

At last, the carver looked at Frank—and smiled. He lifted the half-carved pumpkin off his lap, put it on the ground, but did not get up. "As I said, you pay me what you wish, and you get what you give."

Frank had chosen the most disturbing jack-o'-lantern in the eerie collection. It was big, not pleasingly round but lumpy and misshapen, narrower at the top than at the bottom, with ugly crusted nodules like ligneous fungus on a diseased oak tree. The old man had compounded the unsettling effect of the pumpkin's natural deformities by giving it an immense mouth with three upper and three lower fangs. Its nose was an irregular hole that made Tommy think of campfire tales about lepers. The slanted eyes were as large as lemons but were not cut all the way through the rind except for a pupil—an evil elliptical slit—in the center of each. The stem in the head was dark and knotted as Tommy imagined a cancerous growth might be. The maker of jack-o'-lanterns had painted this one black, letting the natural orange color blaze through in only a few places to create character lines around the eyes and mouth as well as to add emphasis to the tumorous growths.

Frank was bound to like *that* pumpkin. His favorite movies were *The Texas Chainsaw Massacre* and all the *Friday the 13th* sagas of the mad, murderous Jason. When Tommy and Frank watched a movie of that kind on the VCR, Tommy always pulled for the victims, while Frank cheered the killer. Watching *Poltergeist*, Frank was disappointed that the whole family survived: He kept hoping that the little boy would be eaten by some creepazoid in the closet and that his stripped bones would be spit out like watermelon seeds. "Hell," Frank had said, "they could've at least ripped the guts out of the stupid dog."

Now, Frank held the black pumpkin, grinning as he studied its malevolent features. He squinted into the thing's slitted pupils as if the jack-o'-lantern's eyes were real, as if there were thoughts to be read in those depths—and for a moment he seemed to be mesmerized by the pumpkin's gaze.

Put it down, Tommy thought urgently. *For God's sake, Frank, put it down and let's get out of here.*

The carver watched Frank intently. The old man was still, like a predator preparing to pounce.

Clouds moved, blocking the sun.

Tommy shivered.

Finally breaking the staring contest with the jack-o'-lantern, Frank said to the carver, "I give you whatever I like?"

"You get what you give."

"But no matter what I give, I get the jack-o'-lantern?"

"Yes, but you get what you give," the old man said cryptically.

Frank put the black pumpkin aside and pulled some change from his pocket. Grinning, he approached the old man, holding a nickel.

The carver reached for the coin.

"No!" Tommy protested too explosively.

Both Frank and the carver regarded him with surprise.

Tommy said, "No, Frank, it's a bad thing. Don't buy it. Don't bring it home, Frank."

For a moment Frank stared at him in astonishment, then laughed. "You've always been a wimp, but are you telling me now you're scared of a *pumpkin?*"

"It's a bad thing," Tommy insisted.

"Scared of the dark, scared of high places, scared of what's in your bedroom closet at night, scared of half the other kids you meet—and now scared of a stupid damn pumpkin," Frank said. He laughed again, and his laugh was rich with scorn and disgust as well as with amusement.

The carver took his cue from Frank, but the old man's dry laugh contained no amusement at all.

Tommy was pierced by an icy needle of fear that he could not explain, and he wondered if he might be a wimp after all, afraid of his shadow, maybe even unbalanced. The counselor at school said he was "too sensitive." His mother said he was, "too imaginative," and his father said he was "impractical, a dreamer, self-involved." Maybe he was all those things, and perhaps he would wind up in a sanitarium some day, in a boobyhatch with rubber walls, talking to imaginary people, eating flies. But, damn it, he *knew* the black pumpkin was a bad thing.

"Here, gramps," Frank said, "here's a nickel. Will you really sell it for that?"

"I'll take a nickel for my carving, but you still have to pay the usual price of the pumpkin to the fella who operates the lot."

"Deal," Frank said.

The carver plucked the nickel out of Frank's hand.

Tommy shuddered.

Frank turned from the old man and picked up the pumpkin again.

Just then, the sun broke through the clouds. A shaft of light fell on their corner of the lot.

Only Tommy saw what happened in that radiant moment. The sun brightened the orange of the pumpkins, imparted a gold sheen to the dusty ground, gleamed on the metal frame of the chair—but did not touch the carver himself. The light parted around him as if it were a curtain, leaving him in the shade. It was an incredible sight, as though the sunshine shunned the carver, as though he were composed of an unearthly substance that *repelled* light.

Tommy gasped.

The old man fixed Tommy with a wild look, as though he were not a man at all but a storm spirit passing as a man, as though he would at any second erupt into tornadoes of wind, furies of rain, crashes of thunder, lightning. His amber eyes were aglow with promises of pain and terror.

Abruptly the clouds covered the sun again.

The old man winked.

We're dead, Tommy thought miserably.

Having lifted the pumpkin again, Frank looked craftily at the old man as if expecting to be told that the nickel sale was a joke. "I can really just take it away?"

"I keep telling you," the carver said.

"How long did you work on this?" Frank asked.

"About an hour."

"And you're willing to settle for a nickel an hour?"

"I work for the love of it. For the sheer love of it." The carver winked at Tommy again.

"What are you, senile?" Frank asked in his usual charming manner.

"Maybe. Maybe."

Frank stared at the old man, perhaps sensing some of what Tommy felt, but he finally shrugged and turned away, carrying the jack-o'-lantern toward the front of the lot where their father was buying a score of uncarved pumpkins for the big party the following night.

Tommy wanted to run after his brother, beg Frank to return the black pumpkin and get his nickel back.

"Listen here," the carver said fiercely, leaning forward once more.

The old man was so thin and angular that Tommy was convinced he'd heard ancient bones scraping together within the inadequate padding of the desiccated body.

"Listen to me, boy...."

No, Tommy thought. No, I won't listen, I'll run, I'll run.

The old man's power was like solder, however, fusing Tommy to that piece of ground, rendering him incapable of movement.

"In the night," the carver said, his amber eyes darkening, "your brother's jack-o'-lantern will grow into something other than what it is now. Its jaws will work. Its teeth will sharpen. When everyone is asleep, it'll creep through your house...and give what's deserved. It'll come for you last of all. What do you think you deserve, Tommy? You see, I know your name, though your brother never used it. What do you think the black pumpkin will do to you, Tommy? Hmmm? What do you deserve?"

"What *are* you?" Tommy asked.

The carver smiled. "Dangerous."

Suddenly Tommy's feet tore loose of the earth to which they had been stuck, and he ran.

When he caught up with Frank, he tried to persuade his brother to return the black pumpkin, but his explanation of the danger came out as nothing more than hysterical babbling, and Frank laughed at him. Tommy tried to knock the hateful thing out of Frank's hands. Frank held on to the jack-o'-lantern and gave Tommy a hard shove that sent him sprawling backward over a pile of pumpkins. Frank laughed again, purposefully tramped hard on Tommy's right foot as the younger boy struggled to get up, and moved away.

Through the involuntary tears wrung from him by the pain in his foot, Tommy looked toward the back of the lot and saw that the carver was watching.

The old man waved.

Heart beating double time, Tommy limped out to the front of the lot, searching for a way to convince Frank of the danger. But Frank was already putting his purchase on the backseat of the Cadillac. Their father was paying for the jack-o'-lantern and for a score of uncarved pumpkins. Tommy was too late.

2

At home, Frank took the black pumpkin into his bedroom and stood it on the desk in the corner, under the poster of Michael Berryman as the demented killer in *The Hills Have Eyes*.

From the open doorway, Tommy watched.

Frank had found a fat, scented decorative candle in the kitchen pantry; now he put it inside the pumpkin. It was big enough to burn steadily for at least two days. Dreading the appearance of light in the jack-o'-lantern's eyes, Tommy watched as Frank lit the candle and put the pumpkin's stem-centered lid in place.

The slitted pupils glowed-flickered-shimmered with a convincing imitation of demonic life and malevolent intellect. The serrated grin blazed bright, and the fluttering light was like a tongue ceaselessly licking the cold-rind lips. The most disgusting part of the illusion of life was the leprous pit of a nose, which appeared to fill with moist, yellowish mucus.

"Incredible!" Frank said. "That old fart is a real genius at this stuff."

The scented candle emitted the fragrance of roses.

Although he could not remember where he had read of such a thing, Tommy recalled that the sudden, unexplained scent of roses supposedly indicated the presence of spirits of the dead. Of course, the source of this odor was no mystery.

"What the hell?" Frank said, wrinkling his nose. He lifted the lid of the jack-o'-lantern and peered inside. The inconstant orange light played across his face, queerly distorting his features. "This is supposed to be a *lemon*-scented candle. Not roses, not girlie crap."

❋ ❋ ❋

In the big airy kitchen, Lois and Kyle Sutzmann, Tommy's mother and father, were standing at the table with the caterer, Mr. Howser. They were studying the menu for the flashy Halloween party that they were throwing the following night—and loudly reminding Mr. Howser that the food was to be prepared with the finest ingredients.

Tommy circled behind them, hoping to remain invisible. He took a can of Coke from the refrigerator.

Now his mother and father were hammering the caterer about the need for everything to be "impressive." Hors d'oeuvres, flowers, the bar, the waiters' uniforms, and the buffet dinner must be so elegant and exquisite and drop-dead perfect that every guest would feel himself to be in the home of true California aristocracy.

This was not a party for kids. In fact, Tommy and Frank would be required to remain in their rooms tomorrow evening, permitted to engage only in the quietest activities: no television, no stereo, no slightest peep to draw attention to themselves.

This party was strictly for the movers and shakers on whom Kyle Sutzmann's political career depended. He was now a California State Senator, but in next week's election he was running for the United States Congress. This was a thank-you party for his most generous financial backers and for the power brokers who had pulled strings to ensure his nomination the previous spring. Kids verboten.

Tommy's parents seemed to want him around only at major campaign rallies, media photography sessions, and for a few minutes at the start of election-night victory parties. That was okay with Tommy. He preferred to remain invisible. On those rare occasions when his folks took notice of him, they invariably disapproved of everything he said and did, every movement he made, every innocent expression that crossed his face.

Lois said, "Mr. Howser, I hope we understand that large shrimp do *not* qualify as finger lobster."

As the nervous caterer reassured Lois of the quality of his operation, Tommy sidled silently away from the refrigerator and quietly extracted two Milanos from the cookie jar.

"These are important people," Kyle informed the caterer for the tenth time, "substantial and sophisticated people, and they are accustomed to the very best."

In school, Tommy had been taught that politics was the means by which many enlightened people chose to serve their fellow men. He knew that was baloney. His parents spent long evenings plotting his father's political career, and Tommy never once overheard either of them talking about serving the people or improving society. Oh, sure, in public, on campaign platforms, that was what they talked about—"the rights of the masses, the hungry, the homeless"—but never in private. Beyond the public eye, they endlessly discussed "forming power bases" and "crushing the opposition" and "shoving this new law down their throats." To them and to all the people with whom they associated, politics was a way to gain respect, make some money, and—most important—acquire power.

Tommy understood why people liked to be respected, because he received no respect at all. He could see why having a lot of money was desirable. But he did not understand this power thing. He could not figure why anyone would waste a lot of time and energy trying to acquire power over other people. What fun could be gotten from ordering people around, telling them what to do? What if you told them to do the wrong thing, and then what if, because of your orders, people were hurt or wound up broke or something worse? And how could you expect people to like you if you had power over them? After all, Frank had power over Tommy—complete power, total control— and Tommy *loathed* him.

Sometimes he thought he was the only sane person in the family. At other times, he wondered if they were all sane and if he was mad. Whatever the case, crazy or sane, Tommy always felt that he did not belong in the same house with his own family.

As he slipped stealthily out of the kitchen with his can of Coke and two Milanos wrapped in a paper napkin, his parents were querying Mr. Howser about the champagne.

In the back hallway, Frank's door was open, and Tommy paused for a glimpse of the pumpkin. It was still there, fire in every aperture.

"What you got there?" Frank asked, stepping into the doorway. He grabbed Tommy by the shirt, yanked him into the room, slammed the door, and confiscated the cookies and Coke. "Thanks, snotface. I was just thinking I could use a snack." He went to the desk and put the booty beside the glowing jack-o'-lantern.

Taking a deep breath, steeling himself for what resistance would mean, Tommy said, "Those are mine."

Frank pretended shock. "Is my little brother a greedy glutton who doesn't know how to share?"

"Give me back my Coke and cookies."

Frank's grin seemed filled with shark's teeth. "Good heavens, dear brother, I think you need to be taught a lesson. Greedy little gluttons have to be shown the path of enlightenment."

Tommy would have preferred to walk away, to let Frank win, to go back to the kitchen and fetch another Coke and more cookies. But he knew that his life, already intolerable, would get far worse if he didn't make an effort, no matter how futile, to stand up to this stranger who was supposedly his brother. Total, willing capitulation would inflame Frank and encourage him to be even more of a bully than he already was.

"I want my cookies and my Coke," Tommy insisted, wondering if *any* cookies, even Milanos, were worth dying for.

Frank rushed him.

They fell to the floor, pummeling each other, rolling, kicking, but producing little noise. They didn't want to draw their folks' attention. Tommy was reluctant to let his parents know what was happening because they would invariably blame the ruckus on him. Athletic, well-tanned Frank was their dream child, their favorite son, and he could do no wrong. Frank probably wanted to keep the battle secret because their father would put a stop to it, thereby spoiling the fun.

Throughout the tussle, Tommy had brief glimpses of the glowing jack-o'-lantern, which gazed down on them, and he was sure that its grin grew steadily wider, wider.

At last Tommy was driven into a corner, beaten and exhausted. Straddling him, Frank slapped him once, hard, rattling his senses, then tore at Tommy's clothes, pulling them off.

"No!" Tommy whispered when he realized that in addition to being beaten, he was to be humiliated. "No, no."

He struggled with what little strength he still possessed, but his shirt was stripped off; his jeans and underwear were yanked down. With his pants tangled around his sneakers, he was pulled to his feet and half carried across the room.

Frank threw open the door, pitched Tommy into the hallway, and called out, "Oh, Maria! Maria, can you come here a moment, please?"

Maria was the twice-a-week maid who came in to clean and do the ironing. This was one of her days.

"Maria!"

Naked, terrified of being humiliated in front of the maid, Tommy scrambled to his feet, grabbed his pants, tried to run and pull up his jeans at the same time, stumbled, fell, and sprang up again.

"Maria, can you come here, please?" Frank asked, barely able to get the words out between gales of laughter.

Gasping, whimpering, Tommy somehow reached his room and got out of sight before Maria appeared. For a while he leaned against the closed door, holding up his jeans with both hands, shivering.

3

With their parents off at a campaign appearance, Tommy and Frank ate dinner together, after heating up a casserole that Maria had left in the refrigerator. Ordinarily, dinner with Frank was an ordeal, but this time it proved to be uneventful. As he ate, Frank was engrossed in a magazine that reported on the latest horror movies, with heavy emphasis on slice-and-dice films and with lots of color photographs of mutilated and blood-soaked bodies; he seemed oblivious of Tommy.

Later, when Frank was in the bathroom preparing for bed, Tommy sneaked into his older brother's room and stood at the desk, studying the jack-o'-lantern. The wicked mouth glowed. The narrow pupils were alive with fire.

The scent of roses filled the room, but underlying that odor was another more subtle and less appealing fragrance that he could not quite identify.

Tommy was aware of a malevolent presence—something even worse than the malevolence that he could *always* sense in Frank's room. A cold current raced through his blood.

Suddenly he was certain that the potential murderous power of the black pumpkin was enhanced by the candle within it. Somehow, the presence of light inside its shell was dangerous, a triggering factor. Tommy did not know how he knew this, but he was convinced that if he was to have the slightest chance of surviving the coming night, he must extinguish the flame.

He grasped the gnarled stem and removed the lid from the top of the jack-o'-lantern's skull.

Light did not merely rise from inside the pumpkin but seemed to be *flung* at him, hot on his face, stinging his eyes.

He blew out the flame.

The jack-o'-lantern went dark.

Immediately, Tommy felt better.

He put the lid in place.

As he let go of the stem, the candle relit spontaneously.

Stunned, he jumped back.

Light shone from the carved eyes, the nose, the mouth.

"No," he said softly.

He removed the lid and blew out the candle once more.

A moment of darkness within the pumpkin. Then, before his eyes, the flame reappeared.

Reluctantly, issuing a thin involuntary sound of distress, Tommy reached into the jack-o'-lantern to snuff the stubborn candle with his thumb and finger. He was convinced that the pumpkin shell would suddenly snap shut around his wrist, severing his hand, leaving him with a bloody stump. Or perhaps it would hold him fast while swiftly dissolving the flesh from his fingers and then release him with an arm that terminated in a skeletal hand. Driven toward the brink of hysteria by these fears, he pinched the wick, extinguished the flame, and snatched his hand back with a sob of relief, grateful to have escaped mutilation.

He jammed the lid in place and, hearing the toilet flush in the adjacent bath, hurried out of the room. He dared not let Frank catch him there. As he stepped into the hallway, he glanced back at the jack-o'-lantern and, of course, it was full of candlelight again.

He went straight to the kitchen and got a butcher's knife, which he took back to his own room and hid beneath his pillow. He was sure that he would need it sooner or later in the dead hours before dawn.

4

His parents came home shortly before midnight.

Tommy was sitting in bed, his room illuminated only by the pale bulb of the low-wattage night-light. The butcher's knife was at his side, under the covers, and his hand was resting on the haft.

For twenty minutes, Tommy could hear his folks talking, running water, flushing toilets, closing doors. Their bedroom and bath were at the opposite end of the house from his and Frank's rooms, so the noises they made were muffled but nonetheless reassuring. These were the ordinary noises of daily life, and as long as the house was filled with them, no weird lantern-eyed predator could be stalking anyone.

Soon, however, quiet returned.

In the postmidnight stillness, Tommy waited for the first scream.

He was determined not to fall asleep. But he was only twelve years old, and he was exhausted after a long day and drained by the sustained terror that had gripped him ever since he had seen the mummy-faced pumpkin carver. Propped against a pile of pillows, he dozed off long before one o'clock—

—and something thumped, waking him.

He was instantly alert. He sat straight up in bed, clutching the butcher's knife.

For a moment he was certain that the sound had originated within his own room. Then he heard it again, a solid thump, and he knew that it had come from Frank's room across the hall.

He threw aside the covers and sat on the edge of the bed, tense. Waiting. Listening.

Once, he thought he heard Frank calling his name—"Tooommmmyy"—a desperate and frightened and barely audible cry that seemed to come from the far rim of a vast canyon. Perhaps he imagined it.

Silence.

His hands were slick with sweat. He put the big knife aside and blotted his palms on his pajamas.

Silence.

He picked up the knife again. He reached under his bed and found the flashlight he kept there, but he did not switch it on. He eased cautiously to the door and listened for movement in the hallway beyond.

Nothing.

An inner voice urged him to return to bed, pull the covers over his head, and forget what he had heard. Better yet, he could crawl under the bed and hope that he would not be found. But he knew this was the voice of the wimp within, and he dared not hope for salvation in cowardice. If the black pumpkin *had* grown into something else, and if it was now loose in the house, it would respond to timidity with no less savage glee than Frank would have shown.

God, he thought fervently, *there's a boy down here who believes in you, and he'd be very disappointed if you happened to be looking the other way right now when he really, really, really needs you.*

Tommy quietly turned the knob and opened the door. The hallway, illuminated only by the moonlight that streamed through the window at the end, was deserted.

Directly across the hall, the door to Frank's room stood open.

Still not switching on the flashlight, desperately hoping that his presence would go undetected if he was mantled in darkness, he stepped to Frank's doorway and listened. Frank usually snored, but no snoring could be heard tonight. If the jack-o'-lantern was in there, the candle had been extinguished at last, for no flickering paraffin light was visible.

Tommy crossed the threshold.

Moonlight silvered the window, and the palm-frond shadows of a wind-stirred tree danced on the glass. In the room, no object was clearly outlined. Mysterious shapes loomed in shades of dark gray and black.

He took one step. Two. Three.

His heart pounded so hard that it shattered his resolve to cloak himself in darkness. He snapped on the Eveready and was startled by the way the butcher's knife in his right hand reflected the light.

He swept the beam around the room and, to his relief, saw no crouching monstrosity. The sheets and blankets were tumbled in a pile on the mattress, and he had to take another step toward the bed before he was able to ascertain that Frank was not there.

The severed hand was on the floor by the nightstand. Tommy saw it in the penumbra of the flashlight, and he brought the beam to bear directly on it. He stared in shock. Frank's hand. No doubt about its identity, because Frank's treasured silver skull-and-crossbones ring gleamed brightly on one slug-white finger. It was curled into a tight fist.

Perhaps powered by a postmortem nerve spasm, perhaps energized by darker forces, the fisted hand suddenly opened, fingers unfolding like the spreading petals of a flower. In the palm was a single, shiny nickel.

Tommy stifled a wild shriek but could not repress a series of violent shudders.

As he frantically tried to decide which escape route might be safest, he heard his mother scream from the far end of the house. Her shrill cry was abruptly cut off. Something crashed.

Tommy turned toward the doorway of Frank's room. He knew that he should run before it was too late, but he was as welded to this spot as he had been to that bit of dusty ground in the pumpkin lot when the carver had insisted on telling him what the jack-o'-lantern would become during the lonely hours of the night.

He heard his father shout.

A gunshot.

His father screamed.

This scream also was cut short.

Silence again.

Tommy tried to lift one foot, just one, just an inch off the floor, but it would not be lifted. He sensed that more than fear was holding him down, that some malevolent spell prevented him from escaping the black pumpkin.

A door slammed at the other end of the house.

Footsteps sounded in the hall. Heavy, scraping footsteps.

Tears slipped out of Tommy's eyes and down his cheeks.

In the hall, the floorboards creaked and groaned as if under a great weight.

Staring at the open door with no less terror than if he had been gazing into the entrance of Hell, Tommy saw flickering orange light in the corridor. The glow grew brighter as the source—no doubt a candle—drew nearer from the left, from the direction of his parents' bedroom.

Amorphous shadows and eerie snakes of light crawled on the hall carpet.

The heavy footsteps slowed. Stopped.

Judging by the light, the thing was only a foot or two from the doorway.

Tommy swallowed hard and worked up enough spit to say, *Who's there?* but was surprised to hear himself say instead, "Okay, damn you, let's get it over with."

Perhaps his years in the Sutzmann house had toughened him more thoroughly and had made him more fatalistic than he had previously realized.

The creature lurched into view, filling the doorway.

Its head was formed by the jack-o'-lantern, which had undergone hideous mutations. That peculiar pate had retained its black and orange coloring and its gourdlike shape, narrower at the top than at the bottom, and all the tumorous nodules were as crusted and disgusting as ever. However, though it had been as large as any pumpkin that Tommy had ever seen, it was now only about the size of a basketball, shriveled. The eyes had sagged, although the slitted pupils were still narrow and mean. The nose was bubbling with some vile mucus. The immense mouth stretched from ear to ear, for it had remained large while the rest of the face had shrunk around it. In the orange light that streamed out between them, the hooked fangs appeared to have been transformed from points of pumpkin rind into hard, sharp protuberances of bone.

The body under the head was vaguely humanoid, although it seemed to be composed of thick gnarled roots and tangled vines. The beast appeared to be immensely strong, a colossus, a fierce juggernaut if it wished to be. Even in his terror, Tommy was filled with awe. He wondered if the creature's body had grown from the substance in its previously enormous pumpkin head and, more pointedly, from the flesh of Frank, Lois, and Kyle Sutzmann.

Worst of all was the orange light within the skull. The candle still burned in there. Its leaping flames emphasized the impossible emptiness of the head—how could the thing move and think without a brain?—and invested a savage and demonic awareness in its eyes.

The nightmarish vision raised one thick, twisted, powerful, vinelike arm and thrust a rootlike finger at Tommy. *"You,"* it said in a deep whispery voice that called to mind the sound of wet slush pouring down a drain.

Tommy was now less surprised by his inability to move than by his ability to stand erect. His legs felt like rags. He was sure that he was going to collapse in a helpless heap while the thing descended upon him, but somehow he remained on his feet with the flashlight in one hand and the butcher's knife in the other.

The knife. Useless. The sharpest blade in the world would never harm this adversary, so Tommy let the knife slip out of his sweaty fingers. It clattered to the floor.

"You," the black pumpkin repeated, and its voice reverberated moistly throughout the room. "Your vicious brother got what he gave. Your mother got what she gave. Your father got what he gave. I fed on them, sucked the brains out of their heads, chewed up their flesh, dissolved their bones. Now what do *you* deserve?"

Tommy could not speak. He was shaking and weeping silently and dragging each breath into his lungs only with tremendous effort.

The black pumpkin lurched out of the doorway and into the room, looming over him, eyes blazing.

It stood nearly seven feet tall and had to tilt its lantern head to peer down at him. Curls of sooty black smoke from the candle wick escaped between its fangs and from its leprous nose.

Speaking in a rough whisper, yet with such force that its words vibrated the windowpanes, the thing said, "Unfortunately, you are a good boy, and I've no right or license to feed on you. So.... What you deserve is what you've got from now on—freedom."

Tommy stared up into the Halloween face, striving hard to grasp what he had been told.

"Freedom," the demonic beast repeated. "Freedom from Frank and

Lois and Kyle. Freedom to grow up without their heels pressing down on you. Freedom to be the best that you can be—which means I'll most likely *never* get a chance to feed on you."

For a long time they stood face to face, boy and beast, and gradually Tommy achieved complete understanding. In the morning, his parents and brother would be missing. Never to be found. A great and enduring mystery. Tommy would have to live with his grandparents. You get what you give.

"But maybe," the black pumpkin said, putting one cold hand upon Tommy's shoulder, "maybe there's some rottenness in you too, and maybe someday you'll surrender to it, and maybe in time I'll still have my chance with you. Dessert." Its wide grin grew even wider. "Now get back to your bed and sleep. Sleep."

Simultaneously horrified and filled with strange delight, Tommy crossed the room to the doorway, moving as if in a dream. He looked back and saw that the black pumpkin was still watching him with interest.

Tommy said, "You missed a bit," and pointed to the floor beside his brother's nightstand.

The beast looked at Frank's severed hand.

"Ahhhh," said the black pumpkin, snatching up the hand and stuffing that grisly morsel into its mouth.

The flame within the squashy skull suddenly burned very bright, a hundred times brighter than before, then was extinguished.

A Moonlit Night With Rats

Elizabeth Engstrom

I grew up tortured. Literally. The only girl with five older brothers, I was alternately experimented upon, humiliated, and continually put in harm's way. I was also cherished and protected as only five big brothers can do.

As a result, I grew up hoydenish. I envied my brothers' physical prowess, their lithe grace, the easy way they handled snakes, guns and beer. I tried to be just like them.

But I wasn't. I was a girl. Plump, uncoordinated, easily scared, not at all athletic. When we were little, my mother always made them take me with them. I loved it; they hated having a little sister tag along, and they tortured me for it.

I loved that, too, in a way.

The Halloween when I was thirteen—too old for Trick or Treating, too young for the beer busts—two of my brothers, the two closest to my age, the two most vicious, got together with two of their friends in our back yard. I was inside, getting the candy ready for the neighborhood kids, looking out the patio doors at them with envy, as they lounged around on the lawn furniture in their sweatshirts and jeans. I had budding breasts and lank hair and was so self-conscious I didn't even want to look at those brothers, because they were always teasing me. And doing it in front of their friends.

Just at twilight, as the doorbell began to ring and our little dog barked every time as if it were a fresh surprise, Rob, my fifteen-year-old brother came in and asked me if I wanted to go out with them that night. Suspicious, I asked where. "To the dump," he said. "to shoot rats."

"With them?" I asked, pointing at his friends who were watching us through the window.

"Yeah," Rob said. "Van wanted me to invite you."

"Why?"

Rob shrugged. "Figure it out."

Did Van like me? I was staggered by the thought, and hammered by the implications. "Sure," I said. "I'll go." I looked outside, and Van smiled at me. He didn't seem so bad. I grabbed my jacket and handed the bowl of candy to my mom. "I'm going out with Rob and Christian," I said, then didn't wait for her questions or her protests. I'd learned how to handle the parents by watching the brothers.

Van opened the back door of Mike's beat up black Chevy for me, and hopped in next to me. Rob got in the other side, and my other brother Christian got in the front with Mike, and we took off.

We had always gone to the dump when we were kids; it was within bike riding distance, and it had awesome scavenging potentials. One time I found a perfect antique oil lamp, but the boys broke the glass. One time they came home with a shoebox full of green snakes and they smuggled it past Mom into the basement. The next day, the box was empty, and they threatened me with death if I told. I never did.

I hadn't been to the dump in years.

It was full dark by the time we parked, and Mike handed around a six-pack of Foster's. I sat quietly in the back, feeling the heat of Van's body next to me, listening to their easy laughter and smelling their testosterone. I drank the beer, which tasted mighty fine, but it wasn't long before the inevitable happened.

I had to pee.

I waited until the squirming point, hoping that one of the other boys would have to go first, and instead of listening to them talk and laugh, I concentrated on how I would go about the act. If I tried to go too far from the car, they'd pull around and shine the headlights on me. Or something equally as humiliating.

Eventually, I figured it out. I nudged Rob and had him let me out, and I pulled a tissue from my jeans and squatted right at the rear of the car, my hand on the trunk. I figured I would be safe there. But I was wrong.

No sooner had I got my pants down, than the car started up and gravel spit at me and they were off, their laughter ringing in my ears like demon shouts from hell.

Van didn't really like me, I realized, this would just be a good Halloween prank. Dump the kid sister at the dump.

I finished peeing, and then used the tissue to blow my nose. I found an old mattress to sit on while I weighed my options. I'd wait for them until I didn't want to wait any more and then I'd walk home. It wasn't that far.

But my heart was broken. So I sat on that old mattress and cried for a while first.

They didn't come back. Of course they didn't come back. And I sat there until I began to like it. The dump had a certain majesty in the Halloween moonlight.

During the day, the place was hot, it stank, and was filled with noisy, screeching seagulls. But at night, on this night, I could barely smell it, and its strange landscape shone silvery in the moonlight. I could see the rats, big as beavers, rustling through the plastic sacks. I stomped my feet at them if they got too close, and once they found out that I moved, they seemed content to leave me alone.

I spent a lot of time sitting on that nasty old mattress, until long after I was sure the little ghosts and goblins had finished ringing the doorbell and making Chika bark. I thought about my family, my friends, my brothers and their friends. I thought about my approaching womanhood, and realized that I could decide what kind of a woman I would be, and that the options were endless. I didn't have to be a tomboy, I didn't have to be ashamed of my breasts or my klutzy ways. I didn't have to be able to jump over barbwire fences, I didn't have to pretend delight in the killing of little furry things. I could try a few things, like earrings and lipstick, things that had intrigued me but which also had intimidated me. That girlie stuff seemed to come so easy to some.

When I sat down on that mattress, I was the tortured plaything of a bunch of bullies, and when I stood up, I felt as though my life had become my own. I felt adventurous in a completely different way.

And when I heard footsteps on the road, and identified the silhouette as Van's, I didn't hide and throw things at him as was my first impulse. Instead, I stood up and walked toward him. He had left the others in the woods and walked all the way back to the dump to see if I was all right.

By the time we reached my house, he was holding my hand, and I felt poised on the brink of Self.

My personal year begins and ends on Halloween; that is when I make my New Year's resolutions; that is the season when I take risks and plan for the future. I first met my husband on Halloween. It is also the day I send greeting cards to my wonderful brothers (now that they're grown) and sit for a few minutes every year and wonder whatever happened to Van. I wonder also if he has a special affinity for that day as well, because as sure as I grew up that night surrounded by rats, so did he.

Lantern Marsh

Poppy Z. Brite

The marsh brooded on the outskirts of town. We children sometimes played there during the day, poling flat-bottomed boats through the dark water choked with swamp hyacinth, stranding ourselves on any of the hundreds of tiny islands. By day the marsh was a place of filtering, shifting patches of sunlight, cypress and live oak bearded with Spanish moss, velvety brown cattails that would burst into clouds of white snow if you smacked them against the back of your friend's head, and unfounded rumors of quicksand pools full of skeletons and treasure.

At night, the lanterns took over.

Our parents forbade us to go into the marsh at night. Usually this rule needed no enforcing, but at one time or another, most of us had worked up enough courage to creep to the edge of the marsh with a group of friends, stare for a while at the bright globes of light hovering over the water, and then run away as fast as our legs could carry us. Later, we would laugh and call one another fraidy-cat, but not until we were back home in somebody's warm, well-lit room. After all, no one really knew what the lanterns were—our science teachers dismissed them as swamp gas, but hardly anybody believed that—or what they could do, if in fact they wanted to do anything besides hover and shimmer, be beautiful luminous ghosts.

We had lived in the town named after this marsh all our lives.

❋ ❋ ❋

Our first encounter with Mr. Prudhomme—and the first indication I had that Noel was perhaps not entirely sane about the marsh—took place on a Halloween afternoon when we (Noel, Bronwen, and me, Phil) were all ten years old. School had let out early that day. By some obscure tradition, Halloween in Lantern Marsh had always been a big occasion for the kids—maybe just because there wasn't really much for us to do the rest of the year—so the schools scheduled a half-day or canceled altogether.

The three of us were walking down the town's main street, enjoying the tangy autumn flavor of the air. This was the Deep South and Halloween often felt more like August, but this year we were having a decent cool season. Bronwen and I were talking about the costumes we were going to wear that night. Noel, who never went trick-or-treating, walked silently along beside us, hands shoved in pockets, thinking his private thoughts.

Suddenly he stopped in his tracks and stared across the street. "Look—look—there he is!"

We were used to Noel's intense reactions, but this time we had no idea what he might be reacting to. "Who?" I asked.

Noel jerked his head toward a shop door on the other side of the street, where a tall red-haired man stood talking to the shopkeeper. "That's George Prudhomme, the guy who runs that building company—Marshwood Development. He's a fucking bastard."

"Noel!" said Bronwen.

"Well, he *is*! He owns half the land the marsh is on. Last year, right after Halloween, he told my mother I'd been trespassing on his land. I didn't even go into the marsh, I was just watching the lanterns like I always do, but she bawled me out anyway. This year I told her I was going out trick-or-treating with you guys."

Noel had lived with his mother for seven years, ever since his father left for parts unknown. She was a big, ruddy woman who always smelled of cigarettes, and she frightened me and Bronwen a little, but she and Noel had negotiated an uneasy peace.

"Why *don't* you come out with us?" I said. "Seems like that'd be a lot more fun than watching those old lanterns again." Although I knew the lanterns were magic to Noel, I couldn't conceive of not wanting to go trick-or-treating. The idea of coming home at the end of the night empty-handed, with no laden plastic bag into which you could stick your face and breathe the odor of all kinds of candy mingling....

But Noel just shook his head.

Bronwen tucked a scrap of yellow hair behind her ear as she looked across the street at Prudhomme. "That man wants to hurt you, Noel."

I looked at her, puzzled. Why had she said that? But the red-haired man was beckoning to Noel. Bronwen clutched at Noel's arm. "Don't go!"

"It's OK, Bron. He can't hurt me here."

Noel crossed the street and stood in front of the big man, fists on hips, dark shaggy head thrown back, looking ridiculously small. Prudhomme said something to him, and Noel shook his head *no*. After a moment or two, Bronwen and I relaxed—it looked like they were just going to have a conversation after all. But then Noel began to shout.

"You can't do it, you dirty *shit*! I know you can't, because you only own half of it! And if you ever try, I.... I'll kill you! I swear I will!" Prudhomme stared obliquely down at him. When Noel turned and ran back to us, I saw that his features were contorted with rage, close to tears. Without waiting to see whether we would follow, he started off down the street, his back held stiff and straight. We hurried after him, not knowing what else to do.

When we caught up with him, all three of us strode along in silence for several minutes. Then Bronwen, always the peacemaker, touched Noel's shoulder and asked, "What did he say?"

Noel scowled. "He told me to stay away from the marsh tonight, like he always does if he sees me around Halloween. But I don't care what he says. He'll never know—he's too scared to go near the marsh on Halloween night. And he ought to be scared, too, because I bet they hate him as much as I do."

They? He meant the lanterns, I realized. Though I knew how they obsessed him, I'd never known that he believed they could love or hate.

But this realization was overshadowed by another. "That's not what made you so mad," I said.

Noel gazed at me. The expression on his face now was more fear than fury. "He said—he said someday he was going to fill in the marsh!" His lips trembled and he bit at them, swallowing hard. Finally he cried.

And well he might, for Noel had lived at the edge of the marsh all his life. His house was closer to it than any other in town. Ever since Bronwen and I had made friends with him in the first grade, we had been familiar with his fierce hatreds and equally fierce loves, his wild plans that always seemed to work, the mixture of sadness and rage that always seemed to linger just below the surface of his eyes...and his utter refusal to go trick-or-treating on Halloween night. Instead he would sit for hours at the edge of the water and watch the lanterns as if they were his own personal light show. On Halloween, he claimed, they were at their most spectacular. Spirits could visit the living world on Halloween, and Noel had always thought the lanterns were spirits. There were hundreds of the great glowing balls, and more mirrored in the dark water. They darted and showered sparks and made the whole marsh glow, and most of us had grandparents or other older relatives who'd assured us that anyone foolish enough to go into the marsh on the spirits' night wouldn't come out again. Noel brushed off all these warnings. He didn't go into the marsh on Halloween; he only wanted to watch. He was never able to explain this to the satisfaction of me and Bronwen, who loved our conventional, costumed Halloween as much as any other kids. It took us a few years to realize that Halloween was a time of magic for Noel too, magic far more potent than ours.

❋ ❋ ❋

After the night's adventures, we crept to the edge of the marsh with the taste of candy in our mouths and the smell of burning pumpkin flesh still trailing behind us. Bronwen was a yellow-haired gypsy rattling loads of costume jewelry. I was a black-masked bandit marred by my mother's strips of orange reflecting tape. We would never have gone alone to the marsh on Halloween night, but knowing that Noel would be there, we felt protected somehow.

"Noel?" I whispered into the darkness.

Something white rose up behind a tree. Bronwen gave a little shriek, but the flapping shape said "Ssssst!" and waved us over. When we got to him, I saw that Noel was in costume, presumably to fool his mother. He was dressed all in white, with white smudges of makeup smeared around his dark, dark eyes. If the spookiness of the marsh itself hadn't scared off any intruders, Noel might have.

Bronwen held out an extra bag heavy with candy corn and miniature chocolate bars. "We brought you some."

Noel accepted the bag like a prince and gave us one of his rare smiles. "Thanks." He considered us for a moment and apparently found us worthy. "Do you want to see them?" I hesitated, but Bronwen nodded.

Noel led us to his spot behind the tree. I looked into the depths of the marsh and saw nothing. Bronwen glanced off to the left and said *"Oh!"*, enthralled. For there they were, the hovering, darting colored globes. They drew closer as we watched. Depthless black water reflected them back a hundred times over, rippling and shimmering. Their pale light spilled between the trees, bathing our faces; tiny lanterns danced in Noel's eyes. For the first time I knew that he wanted to join them, whatever the price of that joining might be. But he had always been adamant about looking after his mother, who would be alone without him. For now, at least, he would have to content himself with these nighttime glimpses.

We watched the lanterns dance for what felt like hours, until I heard my mother calling me home from blocks away.

✻ ✻ ✻

Eventually Bronwen and I graduated from trick-or-treating to costume parties at our friends' houses. Noel, though, still spent his rapt nights at the edge of the marsh each Halloween. He and George Prudhomme glared at each other when they met in the drugstore or the

Central Park Cafe, but as far as I knew, no more words passed between them. We moved up from elementary school to the county consolidated junior high, where Noel's strangeness was judged less acceptable by kids who hadn't known him most of his life. Noel refused to even try to act normal, and so he was tormented. "The three C's of adolescence," he said to us more than once, "clothes, cliques, and cruelty." But he answered the teasing with sarcasm or indifference. Being ignored only made his tormentors angrier, and if he had to, Noel would fight. He usually won, too; Noel was skinny but wiry, and he clawed at his opponents with a mad abandon that usually kept them from challenging him twice.

By the time we got to high school, most people left Noel alone. He would never be accepted, but acceptance wasn't something he needed. More and more often, instead of going to the pep club meetings or basketball games that had captivated us earlier in our teens, Bronwen and I would join Noel in his room after school to listen to the Beatles, the Doors, Jimi Hendrix. We were learning that we didn't need acceptance either.

The three of us, now as close again as we had been in childhood, decided to form a band. Bronwen could play the guitar a little, and I began to get interested in drumming, something I'd previously practiced on the edges of desks and dinner tables. My parents bought me a used set, good enough to start out on, for fifty dollars. Noel needed no instrument. He had a high wail of a singing voice, huge and soulful and strangely beautiful. Our name, of course, was the Lanterns. We played at a couple of school dances, doing mostly Beatles and Stones covers but also a few songs Noel had written himself. We weren't well-received by the dance crowds, and after our first two gigs we were replaced by another garage band that played fifties hits and beach music. Noel didn't care. He had never been concerned about performing in public anyway, especially to a high school audience; he had only agreed to it because the idea excited me and Bronwen.

We didn't play any more gigs, but the Lanterns lasted through the summer after our high school graduation. Then Bronwen and I went to the state university, and Noel, who was planning to major in music, went to a small liberal arts college about a hundred miles away from Lantern Marsh. His mother wasn't happy to see him go, but as he had received a full scholarship, she could do nothing to stop him. At the state school, Bronwen and I met crowds of new people, but we always came back to each other. Noel wrote us long letters about learning to play guitar and piano (which he liked) and the atmosphere at his college, elite and self-consciously eccentric (which he claimed to dislike, but even he had to admit it beat high school). I bought a secondhand green Volkswagen Bug. Bronwen got her ears pierced. Things went smoothly until our fall break, when we were pleased to find out that Noel would be coming home at the same time we would.

Driving home, I gave half my attention to Bronwen and half to worrying about my bald tires. My parents had offered to replace them while I was home, but I wasn't even sure they would last out the trip. As we approached Lantern Marsh, my worry was interrupted. Bronwen gasped and craned forward in her seat. "Phil—look!"

We were entering town by a road that went past a far edge of the marsh. The marsh was still there, of course; but it was changed, weakened. Instead of a line of cypress and oak, I saw stumps, red mud, bulldozers and dump trucks. A large patch of land had been filled and cleared. A billboard announced in foot-high red letters:

FUTURE SITE OF
MARSHWOOD MALL
A PROPERTY OF MARSHWOOD DEVELOPMENT

At home, my father confirmed my fears. "George Prudhomme bought the rest of the marsh. Shame to tear it up if you ask me, but it wasn't making the town any money. People say he's having the whole thing filled in to build a new shopping center with a double-decker parking lot. You used to have a friend who liked the marsh, didn't you, Phil?"

When I called Noel's house, his mother said he wouldn't be home until the next day. Her voice on the phone was little more than a faint wheeze, and I wondered if she was thinking of what Prudhomme's plans might do to her son. Bronwen had gone out to dinner at the Three Lanterns Steakhouse with her family. My mom had fixed a welcome-home meal of pork chops, mashed potatoes, and strawberry shortcake, all my favorites. I wasn't able to enjoy it much. My parents could tell I was worried, but they thought it must have something to do with school. Of course I wasn't thinking about school at all. I was wondering what in the world we were going to say to Noel tomorrow, and whether it would do any good.

❋ ❋ ❋

As it turned out, we didn't have to break the news to him. His bus had come into town by the same road we'd used, so he already knew. His mother looked awful when she let us in. She'd always been a fleshy woman, and still was, but now the flesh seemed to sag off her bones. Her color was high and unhealthy-looking, as if she'd been running a fever. "He's in his room," she told us. "Hasn't hardly been out since he got here."

Bronwen knocked on the door. "Come in," said Noel hollowly.

He was sitting in the dark. Well, not quite; he had put his red light bulb in the bedside lamp. It cast a bloody glow over the room but offered little illumination. Noel's eyes were nothing but dark hollows in his angular face.

"What are you going to do?" Bronwen asked, putting her hand on his arm.

"Kill Prudhomme," he said without fervor. "Nine years ago I told him I'd kill him if he ever tried this. Now I've got to do it."

This made me impatient. "Come on, Noel. You can't kill Prudhomme. What would that accomplish? You'd go to jail and the mall would get built anyway."

Noel nodded. I wasn't sure he'd heard me, but he already knew the truth of what I said. He stared at a poster on the wall behind Bronwen and me, Jim Morrison in his Lizard King pose. "What am I going to do, you ask? I'm going to sit here and watch Prudhomme tear up the marsh. Maybe they'll be able to stop him, maybe not. If I could join them, I'd damn well stop him."

"You mean the lanterns?" Bronwen asked timidly. But we all knew what he meant. Noel had always wanted to join the lanterns, to become one with them, but his mother would be alone in the world without him. Now I wondered if even that would be enough to keep him here.

He lay back on his bed. "Listen, I need to think. Can you leave me alone for a while?" We nodded and left silently. It was the first time Noel had ever sent us away.

The next afternoon, as I was leaving the house, my father stopped me with a stricken look on his face. "Have you talked to your friend Noel?"

"Not today, but I was just going over there."

"You won't find him at his house."

"Why not?"

Dad sighed. "Phil, Noel's mother died last night. She had a stroke, was gone right away. Noel called 911, but when the ambulance got there, they couldn't find him. No one's seen the boy since."

A thought nudged me. With exams right before the break, I'd lost track of dates.... "What day is this?"

"The thirty-first," my father said, and I couldn't believe I'd forgotten.

"BRONWEN!" I yelled, still half a block away and glimpsing her yellow hair through the foliage that masked her front porch. Soon we were running toward the marsh where it came closest to Noel's house. We hunted up one of the flat-bottomed boats we hadn't used since we were twelve or so. Awkwardly, too heavy for the boats, we poled through the edges of the marsh calling Noel's name. He could be anywhere, but I wanted to find him before nightfall. Because now, with his mother gone, there was nothing to hold him here.

It felt as though we covered miles of the marsh, sometimes poling and sometimes just letting the boat drift, starting with hope at every bird-sound and frog-ripple. As the sky between the trees deepened into twilight, our courage failed. We dragged the boat back up onto solid ground behind Noel's house. Blocks away, we heard the shouts of early trick-or-treaters.

Something white rose up behind a tree.

"I came to say goodbye," said Noel. As he had been years ago, he was dressed all in white. There were no theatrical smudges of makeup around his eyes this time, just dark circles of exhaustion. He'd been up all night, I could tell. "I knew you'd come here, but I can't stay long. I couldn't go without saying goodbye."

"Don't go," I said.

"You know I have to."

He leaned toward Bronwen and kissed her lips. Then he turned to me, and I hugged him as hard as I could. I might have been able to hold him back at that moment, but I didn't try. I let him go. "Goodbye, Bron....

Phil," he whispered, and his voice broke just a little on my name. Then he stepped into our little boat and, standing easily, pushed himself away from the land. He was far better at it than we had been, shifting his weight with the water. He knew this marsh so well.

Soon the boat was invisible through the moss-fringed trees; we could just make out the white form of Noel guiding it between the shadowy hummocks of grass. The lanterns flickered in the distance. We could tell when Noel reached them, because they began to dance. Their colors grew brighter, as if disturbed at the intruder in their midst. Bronwen's hand tightened on my arm, and I covered it with my own.

Noel began to sing to the lanterns.

At first his voice reached us like a thread of leftover summer breeze, faint but sweet. Then it grew stronger, and though I couldn't make out the words, I knew Noel had penned them himself. His voice was hoarse and high, more gorgeous than ever. In it was the Arcadian splendor of the marsh and its spookiness, the joy it had brought him and the anguish he felt at losing it, the pure golden glory of the lanterns themselves. It was a tribute and a plea. We could see his tiny form in the distance, the lanterns surrounding him, weaving around him, dancing to Noel's song. "Now! Now! NOW...." I heard him shriek, and the lanterns suddenly grew brighter than we'd ever seen them, so bright we could not look at them. We turned away, shielding our eyes from what might have been a small supernova in the heart of the marsh. When we looked back, the blinding light had vanished. Noel and the lanterns were gone.

No one in town expected to see Noel again. They figured he'd either gone back to his arty school or drowned in the fabled quicksand of the marsh on Halloween night, and no one outside of our tiny circle much cared. But a week later, just before Bronwen and I were due back at school, Lantern Marsh discovered that one of its more solid citizens had gone missing. The police wouldn't do anything for twenty-four hours, so Marshwood Development organized its own search party; rumor had it that things hadn't been going well at the company, and perhaps they were nervous. They had reason. Before the day was out they found George Prudhomme hanged from the heavy limb of an oak tree in the middle of the marsh, his thick neck stretched by hemp, his red hair shivering in the wind.

Some tried to call it murder and blame it on the vanished Noel; there were plenty who recalled his hatred of the man. But his foreman at the company said Prudhomme had refused to go into the marsh for days, and the pharmacist revealed that he'd filled a prescription of strong sleeping pills for Prudhomme. General consensus was that the man had been afraid of something.

And who could they blame for the bulldozer whose engine suffered irreparable, impossible rust damage overnight? Or the fire that broke out at the offices of Marshwood Development, nearly killing a file clerk? Prudhomme's vice president told the local newspaper, "We're superstitious, but we're not stupid either. Marshwood Development has sold the entire parcel of land to the federal government to be turned into a wildlife sanctuary. It's a beauty of a tax writeoff." My father, an accountant at the paper, told us the man had actually said "a wet dream of a tax writeoff," and my mother nearly choked with laughter at the dinner table.

As for me and Bronwen—well, on the night before we had to return to school, we took a walk along the deserted main street of the town. We passed the doorway where Noel had shouted at Prudhomme, the drugstore where we had read horror comics and eaten ice cream, the school where Noel had taken his torment like a Stoic. We deliberately avoided Noel's empty house and the marsh near it. But as we were about to turn down the street that would return us home, Bronwen stopped and tilted her head. “Listen,” she said.

We both listened. We stood together on the dark street corner and listened for a long time, until a cold wind began to run its fingers under our collars. Bronwen shivered and tucked her arm under mine. We went on our way, not speaking of what we had heard on the corner.

Far away, from the direction of the marsh, we had heard faint strains of eerie, lovely music.

Nicknames

A Hallowe'en Reminiscence

Rick Hautala

Times have changed.

Kids don't use nicknames the way my friends and I did when we were growing up. At least it seems that way. When I was a kid living in Rockport, Mass., just about *everyone* had a nickname. There was Skippy "Cunna Lips" Munroe ("Skippy" was a nickname for Sandford, so he got double duty), Ronnie "Dead Eyes" Emerson (later immortalized as the name of my son Aaron's first rock band), Bob "Mustard" McIsaac, Bill "Dime's Worth" Williams, Phil "Kat" Degagne, Dana "Dots" Johnson, Mike "Grass" Powers (which had also been his father's nickname, so he was "Little Grass" and his father was "Big Grass"), and so many others. It seemed as though you weren't really "in" unless you had some kind of nickname. Mine, as was my brother's, was the fairly unimaginative but serviceable "Hauty," usually pronounced "Howdy." Hence my e-mail address.

A short sidebar:

In college, I loved digging into the derivation of words and phrases. Still do. I discovered that the word "nickname" comes from the Middle English an *"ick"* name, which essentially means an *"also"* name. Anyway, back to the story.

Another thing that there seems to be fewer of these days is what we call local "characters." You know, the town "drunk," the village "idiot," the "gimp" or crippled kid (who had probably been stricken with childhood polio or something even worse). In these p.c. times, such "characters" don't seem to be around as much, and they certainly don't have the social status they once had. Everyone's been mainstreamed, and we *certainly* don't call people "drunks" and "retards" and "cripples" anymore. We were heartless and unenlightened back then, and often cruel in our nicknames and characterizations of people.

One of the village "nuts" in our little town was a guy named Johnny Caffrey. He'd stop just about anyone on the street and ask if they wanted to hear his chicken imitation. Whether they wanted to or not, he would immediately begin to cackle and flap his arms around. We had other town "tards," notably "Saf" Stevens, but Johnny was the best, the most versatile and visible even though he made me and my friends feel really uncomfortable whenever he was around. We were always afraid he might flip out or something. We didn't know better.

That was one of the "functions" (for want of a better word) of these oddballs and misfits: to strike a bit of fear and wonder into all of us who thought we were "normal." "There but for the grace of God...." We didn't know then what we know now—that "normal" is a relative term. Back then, it was an absolute.

The scariest guys in town, though, were the town drunks. Some were stone cutters from the local quarries, which were still in business, but most of them, it seemed, were the fishermen and lobstermen from the wharves—a place my mother told me to avoid so, naturally, I went down there often. I'm not sure why or how our town qualified to have so many notable "town drunks." Maybe it's simply because we were a coastal community, and fishing and lobstering are *damned* hard jobs that call for extreme measures when looking for an outlet or, as folks call it, "blowing the stink off."

Sure, there are still plenty of alcoholics in every town. The problem is, most of them are doctors and lawyers. But like I said, times have changed, and there no longer seem to be groups of men who hang around the wharves or stagger through town loaded to the gills, ranting and cursing at...well, practically everyone, including the local cops who either drove them home or carted them off to the tank to sleep it off.

The town drunks all had their nicknames, too. There was "Peanut," "Honey," "Mickles," "Hobble," "Chick" and plenty of others. (You'll notice that I don't use their legal first names because I didn't know them; they were adults, and I was just a kid. I don't use their last names because I don't want to hear from their surviving relatives' lawyers.) All of the town drunks are long-since dead, mostly from alcohol-related diseases, accidents, or (in a few cases) suicide. Then again, drinking to excess *is* a form of prolonged suicide, just like smoking cigarettes.

I'm not saying that I miss them...Well, yes. Yes, I *am* saying that I miss them. They added local color and humor and an element of danger to my childhood. They were basically harmless fellas, I suppose, but we kids were scared to death of them...terrified, in fact. The dangers ranged from foolish and laughable (like the boiling hot summer day when "Mickles" ranted and raved about the heat while he hosed down the outside of his house to cool it off inside) to dangerous and scary because we were *positive* if any of them ever caught us alone in the woods they'd kill us...or *worse!*

They presented us with a sense of real danger, and that's why I want to tell you about the Hallowe'en night I had a life-threatening run-in with a couple of these old fellas.

Another sidebar:

The word Hallowe'en should have the apostrophe between the "e"s because it's a contraction of the words "hallowed" and "evening" which, in Elizabethan times, was contracted to "e'en," as in "Good e'en." Being the evening before All Hallows Day, we got "Hallow e'en." Of course, like many things—almost always for the worse—we've corrupted the word to Halloween. Man, I *hate* losing traditions!

I lived out in the country. Rockport was and still is a beautiful seacoast town, although there are now at least one if not two or three houses between each house that was there when I was growing up. We've lost our baseball field, our sliding hill, and most of the woods we played in. But long before I was born, especially in the summer, artists and photographers would flock to Rockport like seagulls to the town dump...before it became a "sanitary landfill and reclamation area." My parents' house on Stockholm Avenue was in a *really* rural area known as Pigeon Cove—the part of Rockport that not many artists or tourists ever visited. We had dirt roads, cow and horse barns, chicken coops, old fishing sheds along the wharf, large fields and pastures, gardens, old sheds, and lots of woods and blueberry swamps and "Indian" caves to play in. When I was in grammar school, there were actually two brothers who occasionally rode the family mule to and from school, leaving him tied to the bicycle rack with some grass and a bucket of water during class. It was a wonderful bucolic life, especially in retrospect.

Of course, on Hallowe'en night, my friends and I would do the traditional stuff. We'd dress up in costumes (I favored Zorro if, besides a black mask, cape, and hat, Zorro favored blue jeans, a Rockport Little

League T-shirt, and scuffed Keds sneakers), go "trick-or-treating," and go to church or school-sponsored Hallowe'en parties. (Yes. We had a local church that held an annual Hallowe'en party. Try getting away with *that* in these p.c. days!) As we got older, we'd play more elaborate tricks...some of them so mean and dangerous that today they would easily garner a police record if not actual jail time.

I think I was in sixth grade when the following incident happened. I'd been out trick-or-treating with some friends, and we got the brilliant idea that it would be fun to "bomb" passing cars with the little green apples from some of the trees on our street. We hit cars with snowballs in the winter, so what was the difference?

(Did I mention that we weren't the brightest batch of kids?)

Anyway, we hid in the shadows along the side of the road, armed with a handful or two of knobby, worm-eaten green apples as hard as small rocks. Whenever a car would go by—which wasn't very often—we would nail it, usually by bouncing an apple or two off the side panels or hubcaps, if our aim was true.

But I had the brainstorm that it'd be even better and funnier if we dropped the apples from the trees onto the passing vehicles. My friends weren't so sure about that one, so I was the only one who scrambled up into an old maple tree whose branches overhung the road. With my jeans pockets bulging with green apples, I was ready.

It wasn't long before a car went by, and I timed it just right so the first apple I dropped—I didn't even have to "wing" it hard—hit the roof of the car with a resounding *thump*. The only proof that I had frightened the poor driver (and that *was* our intention) was a quick flicker of brake lights as he reacted to the sudden *thump* on the roof of his car. Satisfied, I watched the car continue down the road, the driver none the wiser that Zorro had struck.

My ears prickled when I heard the approach of my next intended target. A loud sputtering and backfiring of exhaust filled the night. Looking up the road, I saw an old pickup truck, swaying around the corner by Old Man Nevala's house. My friends immediately scattered when they heard the raucous laughter and shouts of the passengers. They knew it was some of the local fisher- and lobstermen returning from the wharves. Even at a distance, it was obvious that they had been "celebrating" Hallowe'en and were drunk on their asses.

But I wasn't worried.

I was Zorro the Fox, dressed all (or mostly) in black, lurking above the road in the trees, hidden from them. I'm sure the palms of my hands were sweating as I gripped the green apples, preparing to throw. The headlights swung around the corner like prying searchlights as they momentarily swept aside the darkness along the roadside. I panicked, wondering if the light might illuminate me in the trees, but I felt safe. I was, after all, Zorro the Fox!

My friends had long since vanished, scattering into the darkness as the truck rumbled toward my hiding spot. My friends knew not to mess with these guys, but I waited...and waited, wanting to time my shots for maximum effect. I saw the dark silhouettes of several men in the bed of the pickup truck, swaying back and forth, laughing and shouting and waving their bottles around as they went. (How long could someone do *that* these days without getting pulled over?)

I waited...and waited until they were just about under my tree before releasing my barrage. Green apples rained down on the roof of the truck like huge hailstones, and I felt a rush of exhilaration when I realized that I scored several direct hits. It even looked like one apple bounced off the head of one of the guys in back.

What happened next wasn't according to plan. I saw the bright red flash of brake lights and heard the harsh, ripping skid of tires on the dirt-coated asphalt. That always happened when the driver reacted to the sudden *thump* of apples on the roof. That was my proof I had gotten them.

Only this time, the brake lights stayed on until the truck skidded sideways to a lurching stop.

In a flash, the drunken lobstermen spilled out of the truck, cursing loudly as they scattered in all directions, trying to find the culprit or culprits who had the gall to nail them.

I panicked, no longer feeling safe and "invisible" up in the tree. More like a "treed" raccoon. These guys were so raging mad and drunk that I *knew* they would kill me if they ever caught me. With my thin, black Zorro cape flapping behind me, I fell as much as leaped out of the tree and landed in the rocky, overgrown field beside the road. One or more of the drunks must have seen me, and they started yelling as they gave chase. I'm positive that they were flinging curses at me, but I was too terrified at the time to recall precisely what they said other than threatening to kill and skin me if they ever caught me.

And I knew they'd do it.

So I hit the ground running.

I remember twisting my ankle on an unseen rock, but it wasn't enough to drop me or even slow me down much. The men from the pickup were after me, but they were so drunk they tripped and stumbled in the darkness while I lit out across "Willow" Johnson's pasture and into the bordering woods. I had the strength of my youthful legs and pure terror pushing me on. Besides, I was dressed like the night, as Zorro, so I eluded them easily.

Crouching in the woods, panting heavily and dripping with sweat in the chilled night air, I listened as the fishermen finally gave up, climbed back into the truck, and drove off. I had escaped with my life, but I knew that it might not be over yet. If any one of them had caught even a glimpse of me, I knew they would have recognized me. In the morning, a phone call to my father to report what I had done would earn me a whipping.

One last sidebar:

Yes, this was back in the days when "strappings" and "beltings" were the common and accepted disciplinary punishment for me and all of my friends. I didn't get many. Just enough. My fear of punishment made me behave or at least make sure neither my parents nor any other adults ever caught me.

There's not much more to tell.

This is really just an incident from my life, not a story. But to this day it remains vivid in my memory. I'm sure the fear I felt that Hallowe'en night fuels some of the stories I write. And when I think about it, I miss the childlike innocence of those days. I wish I had a better memory. Maybe that's why I write fiction, to try to bring it all back.

But there is one thing I do, for sure, and that's encourage my kids to create and promote the use of nicknames among their friends. It's one of those little things that adds character to ordinary life.

Happy Hallowe'en.

A Condemned Man

Steve Rasnic Tem

Back then, for me, it was all about masks.

For Halloween, sure, but I'm also talking about day-to-day. This all started with the perception that people seldom said what they really felt about anything. I wasn't sure why, but apparently there was something impolite about frankness, and politeness was something we took pretty seriously in my part of the South. The only person I knew whose face invariably expressed whatever passed through his head was the town's retarded fellow who sat on a bench by the drugstore when he wasn't out with his burlap sack collecting roadside treasures. Whether he was angry or happy or sad you could always tell by the expression—or expressions—painting his face, and so as a child I got the idea that that was one sign of brain damage—you lost your mask.

I also came to believe that success or failure in life might be measured by how one handled one's mask. Steve McQueen, Robert Mitchum—they were born with wonderful masks, or maybe they grew them, I didn't know for sure. But in any case they handled them brilliantly—they appeared to have that coveted ability of *controlling* how other people felt about them, because of their mask. I would have given anything for that. I had an extremely difficult time figuring out how other people saw me—it's still not one of my major talents—much less knowing how one might control that perception. No one I knew had that power, although a couple of the more popular kids had a taste of it. They knew a little about handling the mask, wearing the body, saying the right things, modulating the tone, revealing just the right amount of feeling and no more. They even seemed to know the rudiments of altering that mask to fit the circumstances.

Fat kids, ugly kids, had the additional burden of a mask that rarely responded to what they wanted to project. Clearly, some masks were such that it was almost impossible to determine who was wearing them.

So putting on a mask, I thought, was a wonderful thing. If I could have gotten away with it—I think I would have worn one all the time.

I grew up in southwest Virginia, at that place where Virginia elongates into a point (a friend of mine used to say "it's where Virginia kicks Kentucky in the ass.") One of the poorer counties in the country. So Halloween wasn't something you spent a lot of money on. (I remember watching a *Beverly Hillbillies* episode in which the trick-or-treaters at one house were given plastic Jack-o-Lanterns full of treats. I was astounded, calling my brothers in to see how they celebrate Halloween at rich people's homes.) In our town treats were cheap candy at best, at worst hard pears from the last harvest of the year from the trees in people's own yards—I broke a tooth or two before I learned better. You could buy a mask at the five and dime for a dollar or so—I didn't see a full costume for sale in our town until I was almost out of high school. So every year the challenge became picking a mask that you could cobble up a matching costume for with little or no money.

Of course there were those universal costumes that kids with no money (or time to spend on preparations) have made for decades: hoboes and ghosts. My brothers and I were hoboes five or six years running when we were little—carrying a stick with a kerchief full of rags tied on (My mother kept referring to it as a "bindle stiff"—I thought she was saying "bend, 'lil sniff" which I figured was the way two smelly hoboes were supposed to greet each other, so all night long I was bending over and sniffing which must have looked *quite* odd.) Of course, since we were identical hoboes every year during that time and we rarely strayed far from our street, everyone knew exactly who we were. "Hey, Fred—it's them nice Rasnic boys from down the street. Drop a couple of extry pears in their pokes."

Being a ghost was spookier, and it was harder to figure out who was under that sheet. But when the sheet shifted the eyeholes didn't line up right and you could kill yourself tripping down semi-rural streets with few lights. One year my little brother insisted on wearing a sheet which was particularly lame since it had a big flowery border around the edges. But my other brother and I could not dissuade him, and had to take turns holding his hand so that he wouldn't get killed. In any case my mother felt he was safer in white. We were never allowed to wear dark costumes at Halloween because of an apocryphal incident some fifteen years before when a five-year-old dressed in solid black got away from his mother, ran out in the street, and was run over by a car.

Certainly there isn't a lot to that story but it creeped me out then and it creeps me out now. In part it is because the story was such a perfect container for my mother's obsessive worries and fears, and in part because of a *Life* magazine photo from those years which I just could not get out of my head: a small shoe with a dirty sock lying on a dark highway, and nearby a woman on her knees on the pavement, her face split with a kind of grief I'd never imagined before.

Southwest Virginia was rather isolated from the rest of the world at the time. Now I realize that we didn't have all that much, but at the time we certainly didn't feel poor. And it felt like we lived in the safest place on the planet. What we knew about the outside world came from *Life* and *Look* and *National Geographic* magazines, TV sitcoms, and the *CBS Evening News* (Douglas Edwards when I was small, then Walter Cronkite came along when I was just beginning to realize how big the world outside those mountains must be.) The first national newscasts I have memory of were only fifteen minutes long—I remember my dad saying that it was a good length for a news program, because "that's about all the bad news a man can take in one day." The outside world seemed to be all about bad news.

Which isn't to say that my friends were angels, of course. Halloween pranks could turn rather destructive, particularly out in the farm communities: trees cut down to block the roads, furniture and equipment hung from telephone poles, farm wagons hauled up on top of barn roofs (the exact mechanics of this particular prank seemingly as mysterious as the building of the pyramids), fields and brush set ablaze. Fewer parents allowed their kids to participate in trick-or-treating. Some years Halloween was practically shut down because of the pranking.

But something the outside world *did* have was color, and mystery, and a large number of people who had not known me all my life and would not recognize me behind a mask. The fact that a mask might work so much more effectively in that world was both exciting and terrifying. So at a certain point I started spending painful hours sewing and constructing in an attempt to make decent Halloween costumes for myself, costumes which in some twisted way reflected what I imagined of the outside world: a convict with hand-painted stripes and wounds, a two-headed snake whose narrow body was almost impossible to walk in, a succession of elaborate robots consisting of batteries and lights mounted to extremely uncomfortable cardboard boxes, "HelpMan" (my brother was "HelpBoy") who despite his name was solely out there to cause trouble, and a variety of criminals and thieves. The best thing about all of these costumes, I thought, was that I did not feel compelled to speak with them on. Back then even saying "trick or treat" to an adult or a stranger was extremely difficult for me.

The last year I went trick-or-treating, I had no intentions of going. I don't remember exactly why—it wasn't as if I had better things to do with my time. It seemed the rest of the world was well into the 1960s, but as far as Southwest Virginia was concerned it was still '55 or so—my dad still had his Chevy BelAire from that year and it didn't seem outdated in our little town. I still wore my hair in a flat top, having graduated up from a "burr" approximately two years previous (Although I had always thought of it as "Brer" because Brer Rabbit's hair was real short on top between his ears in this storybook I'd had since childhood—it's a wonder I ever learned English at all).

My friends had stopped going out on Halloween the previous year, but I only saw my friends at school. My brothers were going, of course, but they were going to dress up as baseball players or something equally uninteresting. I was a big kid, and I knew I was going to look weird out there begging for candy, and I would feel humiliated if anyone recognized me this year of all years, but something perverse in me suddenly wanted to go, at the last minute, a few hours before dark. It's an affliction I have to this day—sometimes when I'm convinced I'm going to have a terrible time at some event, it makes me want to go that much more.

It was too late to think up anything special. I rummaged through my drawers and pulled out an old checked shirt, some brown corduroys worn to the shade of attic dust. I didn't have a mask, and we were out of old sheets. I did find a foul, yellowing pillowcase on the floor of my closet. I cut three holes and slipped the thing on. It was too loose—the holes shifted around. I found a graying piece of cotton rope, and with an idiocy perhaps only another boy could appreciate I used it to tie the pillowcase to my neck. Not too tightly, of course. After all, I was thinking, *I'm not an idiot*. Then I was complete, a combination of two old standbys, hobo and ghost.

Just before I went out I was looking at myself in the mirror, and recognized where I'd seen this image before, in that bible of the outside world, *Life* magazine. With the exception that my hood had holes, it looked like what the guest of honor at a lynching might wear. I knew these things still happened, or had recently happened, in parts of the South, a South I did not know. Despite that, however, I knew there were people in my county, people with ordinary-looking faces, normal masks, who were capable of much the same. Looking in the mirror creeped me out then, which made me think that finally, this year, I had really succeeded with a costume.

Just as I expected, people were a little cold when I came to their door that year. A few even mumbled that it was a shame, a big boy like me out getting kids' candy like that. Normally comments like that would have sent me scurrying home. But it was obvious no one could recognize me. They didn't have a clue. I sang "Trick or treat!" sweetly, just like the little kids, at each house. And even if they were unhappy about me coming, they still gave me candy. I wasn't sure why—I guessed it was just southern hospitality at play. I used to think that if someone came to my grandfather's house to murder him, he'd first offer them cold milk and biscuits.

At one door a woman asked me somewhat sourly, "So what are you supposed to be?"

Without hesitation I answered, "a condemned man." There followed a profoundly uncomfortable silence, as if she didn't know what to say to a statement like that. I've received that same reaction more than a few times over the years.

Now, I didn't know I was going to say that—it just popped out. And as I thought about it, it didn't seem quite accurate—certainly by the time you've got that hood over your head and the rope around your neck you're at least one baby step past condemned. But I still liked the sound of it, and used the phrase at least twice more that Halloween, and each time I was pretty sure the people at the door didn't know what the hell I was talking about, which to tell the truth was a fairly liberating thing.

Then toward the end of the night I had the disorienting experience of passing by a mirror in someone's front yard: as I was approaching the steps I passed myself coming away from the steps. Then I stopped and looked very closely, because of course there was no mirror. The other me had stopped as well to stare.

I was terrified, my skin rippling with chill, a particular form of anxiety attack I was more than pleased to grow out of a few years later (although I certainly didn't think of it in those terms in my late adolescence—back then it was merely my skin trying to peel itself from the bone). The other me didn't say a word, but his fists were clenched, as if he were ready to beat the mask off me.

But then he ran, and I didn't see him again. Later I would realize that although the checkered shirt was of similar color, it wasn't *exactly* the same color, and I thought the pattern might have been different. The pillowcase hood looked much the same, but the rope was brown twine, I think, rather than my gray cotton.

But he had been about my size and build, and it was simply amazing to me that anyone would have come up with that exact combination of disguise. I wondered if he, too, had called himself "a condemned man." I wondered if he had had any better response from our neighbors behind their doors. And I wondered about what *they* must have been thinking, seeing two apparently identical boys, boys too big for Trick-or-Treating, wearing such odd, vaguely-disturbing outfits.

Most importantly, I hadn't a clue who this fellow was behind the mask, and I never found out, although we had to have gone to the same school—hell, there was only the *one* school, and I knew everybody, absolutely everybody in it, and I couldn't begin to guess who this could have been.

It really creeped me out. It creeps me out still.

Conversations In A Dead Language

Thomas Ligotti

After changing out of his uniform, he went downstairs to search the kitchen drawers, rattling his way through cutlery and cooking utensils. Finally he found what he wanted. A carving knife, a holiday knife, the traditional blade he'd used over the years. Knifey-wifey.

First he carved out an eye, spearing the triangle with the point of his knife and neatly drawing the pulpy thing from its socket. Pinching the blade, he slid his two fingers along the blunt edge, pushing the eye onto the newspaper he'd carefully placed next to the sink. Another eye, a nose, a howling oval mouth. Done. Except for manually scooping out the seedy and stringy entrails and supplanting them with a squat little candle of the vigil type. Guide them, holy lantern, through darkness and disaster. To me. To meezy-weezy.

He dumped several bags of candy into a large potato chip bowl, fingering pieces here and there: the plump caramels, the tarty sour balls, the chocolate kisses for the kids. A few were test-chewed for taste and texture. A few more. Not too many, for some of his co-workers already called him Fatass, almost behind his back. And he would spoil the holiday dinner he had struggled to prepare in the little time left before dark. Tomorrow he'd start his diet and begin making more austere meals for himself.

At dark he brought the pumpkin out to the porch, placing it on a small but lofty table over which he'd draped a bedsheet no longer in normal use. He scanned the old neighborhood. Beyond the railings of other porches and in picture windows up and down the street glowed a race of new faces in the suburb. Holiday visitors come to stay the night, without a hope of surviving till the next day. All Souls Day. Father Mickiewicz was saying an early morning mass, which there would be just enough time to attend before going to work.

No kids yet. Wait. There we go, bobbing down the street: a scarecrow, a robot, and—what is it?—oh, a white-faced clown. Not the skull-faced thing he'd at first thought it was, pale and hollow-eyed as the moon shining frostily on one of the clearest nights he'd ever seen. The stars were a frozen effervescence.

Better get inside. They'll be coming soon. Waiting behind the glass of the front door with the bowl of candy under his arm, he nervously grabbed up palmsful of the sweets and let them fall piece by piece back into the bowl, a buccaneer reveling in his loot...a grizzled-faced pirate, eye-patch over an empty socket, a jolly roger on his cap with "x" marking the spot in bones, running up the front walk, charging up the wooden stairs of the porch, rubber cutlass stuffed in his pants.

"Trick or treat."

"Well, well, well," he said, his voice rising in pitch with each successive "well." "If it isn't Blackbeard. Or is it Bluebeard, I always forget. But you don't have a beard at all, do you?" The pirate shook his head shyly to say "no." "Maybe we should call you Nobeard, then, at least until you start shaving."

"I have a moustache. Trick or treat, mister," the boy said, impatiently holding up an empty pillow case.

"You do have a nice moustache at that. Here you go, then," he said, tossing a handful of candy into the sack. "And cut a few throats for me," he shouted as the boy turned and ran off.

He didn't have to say those last words so loudly. Neighbors. No, no one heard. The streets are filled with shouters tonight, one the same as another. Listen to the voices all over the neighborhood, music against the sounding board of silence and the chill infinity of autumn.

Here come some more. Goody.

Trick or treat: an obese skeleton, meat bulging under its painted-costume bones. How unfortunate, especially at his age. Fatass of the boneyard and the schoolyard. Give him an extra handful of candy. "Thanks a *lot*, mister," "Here, have more." Then the skeleton waddled down the porch steps, its image thinning out into the nullity of the darkness, candy-filled paper bag rattling away to a whisper.

Trick or treat: an overgrown baby, bibbed and bootied, with a complexion problem erupting on its pre-adolescent face. "Well, cootchie coo," he said to the infant as he showered its open bunting with candy. Baby sneered as it toddled off, pouchy diapers slipping down its backside, disappearing once again into the black from which it had momentarily emerged.

Trick or treat: midget vampire, couldn't be more than six years old. Wave to Mom waiting on the sidewalk. "*Very* scary. Your parents must be proud. Did you do all that make-up work yourself?" he whispered. The little thing mutely gazed up, its eyes underlidded with kohl-dark smudges. It then used a tiny finger, pointy nail painted black, to indicate the guardian figure near the street. "Mom, huh? Does she like sourballs? Sure she does. Here's some for Mom and some more for yourself, nice red ones to suck on. That's what you scary vampires like, eh?" he finished, winking. Cautiously descending the stairs, the child of the night returned to its parent, and both proceeded to the next house, joining the anonymous ranks of their predecessors.

Others came and went. An extraterrestrial with a runny nose, a smelly pair of ghosts, an asthmatic tube of toothpaste. The parade thickened as the night wore on. The wind picked up and a torn kite struggled to free itself from the clutches of an elm across the street. Above the trees the October sky remained lucid, as if a glossy veneer had been applied across the night. The moon brightened to a teary gleam, while voices below waned. Fewer and fewer disguises perpetrated deception in the neighborhood. These'll probably be the last ones coming up the porch. Almost out of candy anyway.

Trick or treat. Trick or treat.

Remarkable, these two. Obviously brother and sister, maybe twins. No, the girl looks older. A winning couple, especially the bride. "Well, congratulations to the gride and broom. I know I said it backwards. That's because you're backwards, aren't you? Whose idea was that?" he asked, tossing candy like rice into the bag of the tuxedoed groom. What faces, so clear. Shining stars.

"Hey, you're the mailman," said the boy.

"Very observant. You're marrying a smart one here," he said to the groom.

"I saw you were, too," she replied.

"Course you did. You're sharp kids, both of you. Hey, you guys must be tired, walking around all night." The kids shrugged, unaware of the meaning of fatigue. "I know I am after delivering the mail up and down these streets. And I do that every day, except Sunday of course. Then I go to church. You kids go to church?" It seemed they did; wrong one, though. "You know, at our church we have outings and stuff like that for kids. Hey, I got an idea—"

A car slowed down on the street, its constabulary spotlight scanning between houses on the opposite side. Some missing Halloweeners maybe. "Never mind my idea, kids. Trick or treat," he said abruptly, lavishing candy on the groom, who immediately strode off. Then he turned to the bride, on whom he bestowed the entire remaining contents of the large bowl, conveying a scrupulously neutral expression as he did so. Was the child blushing, or was it just the light from the jack-o-lantern?

"C'mon, Charlie," his sister called from the sidewalk.

"Happy Halloween, Charlie. See you next year." Maybe around the neighborhood.

His thoughts drifted off for a moment. When he regained control the kids were gone, all of them. Except for imaginary ones, ideals of their type. Like that boy and his sister.

He left the candle burning in the jack-o-lantern. Let it make the most of its brief life. Tomorrow it would be defunct and placed out with the other refuse, an extinguished shell pressed affectionately against a garbage bag. Tomorrow...All Souls Day. Pick up Mother for church in the morning. Could count it as a weekly visit, holy day of obligation. Also have to remember to talk to Father M. about taking that kiddie group to the football game.

The kids. Their annual performance was now over, the make-up wiped away and all the costumes back in their boxes. After he turned off the lights downstairs and upstairs, and was lying in bed, he still heard "trick or treat" and saw their faces in the darkness. And when they tried to dissolve into the background of his sleepy mind...he brought them back.

II

"Ttrrrick or ttrrreat," chattered a trio of hacking, sniffing hoboes. It was much colder this year, and he was wearing the bluish-gray wool overcoat he delivered the mail in. "Some for you, you, and you," he said in a merely efficient tone of voice. The bums were not overly grateful for the handouts. They don't appreciate anything the way they used to. Things change so fast. Forget it, close the door, icy blasts.

Weeks ago the elms and red maples in the neighborhood had been assaulted by unseasonable frigidity and stripped to the bone. Clouds now clotted up the sky, a murky purple ceiling through which no star shone. Snow was imminent.

Fewer kids observed the holiday this year, and of the ones who did a good number of them evidently took little pride in the imagination or lavishness of their disguises. Many were content to rub a little burnt cork on their faces and go out begging in their everyday clothes.

So much seemed to have changed. The whole world had become jaded, an inexorable machine of cynicism. Your mother dies unexpectedly, and they give you two days leave from your job. When you get back, people want to have even less to do with you than before. Strange how you can feel the loss of something that never seemed to be there in the first place. A dwarfish, cranky old woman dies...and all of a sudden there's a royal absence, as if a queen had cruelly vacated her throne. It was the difference between a night with a single fibrillating star in it and one without anything but smothering darkness.

But remember those times when she used to...No, *nihil nisi bonum.* Let the dead, et cetera, et cetera. Father M. had conducted an excellent service at the funeral home, and there was little point in ruining that perfect sense of finality the priest had managed to convey regarding the earthly phase of his mother's existence. So why bring her now into his thoughts? Night of the Dead, he remembered.

There were no longer very many emissaries of the deceased roaming the streets of the neighborhood. They had gone home, the ones who had left it in the first place. Might as well close up till next year, he thought. No, wait.

Here they are again, coming late in the evening as they did last year. Take off the coat, a sudden flash of warmth. The warming stars had returned, shining their true light once more. How they beamed, those two little points in the blackness. Their stellar intensity went right into him, a bright tightness. He was now grateful for the predominant gloom of this year's Halloween, which only exacerbated his present state of delight. That they were wearing the same costumes as last year was more than he could have hoped.

"Trick or treat," they said from afar, repeating the invocation when the man standing behind the glass door didn't respond and merely stood staring at them. Then he opened the door wide.

"Hello, happy couple. Nice to see you again. You remember me, the mailman?"

The children exchanged glances, and the boy said: "Yeah, sure." The girl antiphonied with a giggle, enhancing his delight in the situation.

"Well, here we are one year later and you two are still dressed and waiting for the wedding to start. Or did it just get over with? At this rate you won't make any progress at all. What about next year? And the next? You'll never get any older, know what I mean? Nothing'll change. Is it okay with you?"

The children tried for comprehending nods but only achieved movements and facial expressions of polite bewilderment.

"Well, it's okay with me too. Confidentially, I wish things had stopped changing for me a long time ago. Anyway, how about some candy?"

The candy was proffered, the children saying "thaaank yooou" in the same way they said it at dozens of other houses. But just before they were allowed to continue on their way...he demanded their attention once more.

"Hey, I think I saw you two playing outside your house one day when I came by with the mail. It's a big white house over on Pine Court, isn't it?"

"Nope," said the boy as he carefully inched his way down the porch stairs, trying not to trip over his costume. His sister had impatiently made it to the sidewalk already. "It's red with black shutters. On Ash." Without waiting for a reaction to his answer he joined his sister, and side by side the bride and groom walked far down the street, for there didn't seem to be any other houses open for business nearby. He watched them become tiny in the distance, eventually disappear into the dark.

Cold out here, shut the door. There was nothing more to see; he had successfully photographed the encounter for the family album of his imagination. If anything, their faces glowed even brighter and clearer this year. Perhaps they really hadn't changed and never would. No, he thought in the darkness of his bedroom. Everything changes and always for the worst. But they wouldn't make any sudden transformations now, not in his thoughts. Again and again he brought them back to make sure they were the same.

He set his alarm clock to wake himself for early mass the next day. There was no one who would be accompanying him to church this year. He'd have to go alone.

Alone.

III

Next Halloween there was a premature appearance of snow, a thin foundation of whiteness that clung to the earth and trees, putting a pallid face on the suburb. In the moonlight it glittered, a frosty spume. This sparkling below was mirrored by the stars positioned tenuously in the night above. A monstrous mass of snowclouds to the west threatened to intervene, cutting off the reflection from its source and turning everything into a dull emptiness. All sounds were hollowed by the cold, made into the cries of migrating birds in a vacant November dusk.

Not even November yet and look at it, he thought as he stared through the glass of his front door. Very few were out tonight, and the ones who were found fewer houses open to them, closed doors and extinguished porchlights turning them away to roam blindly through the streets. He had lost much of the spirit himself, had not even set out a jack-o-lantern to signal his harbor in the night.

Then again, how would he have carried around such a weighty object with his leg the way it was now? One good fall down the stairs and he started collecting disability pay from the government, laid up for months in the solitude of his home.

He had prayed for punishment and his prayers had been answered. Not the leg itself, which only offered physical pain and inconvenience, but the other punishment, the solitude. This was the way he remembered being corrected as a child: sent into the basement, exiled to the cold stone cellar without the relief of light, save for that which hazed in through a dusty window-well in the corner. In that corner he stood, near as he could to the light. It was there that he once saw a fly twitching in a spider web. He watched and watched and eventually the spider came out to begin feasting on its prey. He watched it all, dazed with horror and sickness. When it was over he wanted to do something. He did. With a predatory stealth he managed to pinch up the little spider and pull it off its web. It tasted like nothing at all really, except a momentary tickle on his dry tongue.

"Trick or treat," he heard. And he almost got up to arduously cane his way to the door. But the Halloween slogan had been spoken somewhere in the distance. Why did it sound so close for a moment? Crescendoing echoes of the imagination, where far is near, up is down, pain pleasure. Maybe he should close up for the night. There seemed to be only a few kids playing the game this year. Only the most desultory stragglers remained at this point. Well, there was one now.

"Trick or treat," said a mild, failing little voice. Standing on the other side of the door was an elaborately garbed witch, complete with a warm black shawl and black gloves in addition to her black gown. An old broom was held in one hand, a bag in the other.

"You'll have to wait just a moment," he called through the door as he struggled to get up from the sofa with the aid of his cane. Pain. Good, good. He picked up a full bag of candy from the coffee table and was quite prepared to bestow its entire contents on the little lady in black. But then he recognized who it was behind the cadaver-yellow make-up. Watch it. Wouldn't want to do anything unusual. Play you don't know who it is. And do not say anything concerning red houses with black shutters. Nothing about Ash Street.

To make matters worse, there was the outline of a parent standing on the sidewalk. Insure the safety of the last living child, he thought. But maybe there were others, though he'd only seen the brother and sister. Careful. Pretend she's unfamiliar; after all, she's wearing a different get-up from the one she wore the past two years. Above all don't say a word about you know who.

And what if he would innocently ask where was her little brother this year? Would she say: "He was killed," or maybe, "He's dead," or perhaps just, "He's gone," depending on how the parents handled the whole affair. With any luck, he would not have to find out.

He opened the door just far enough to hand out the candy and in a bland voice said: "Here you go, my little witch." That last part just slipped out somehow.

"Thank you," she said under her breath, under a thousand breaths of fear and experience. So did it seem.

She turned away, and as she descended the porch steps her broom clunked along one step behind her. An old, frayed, throwaway broom. Perfect for witches. And the kind perfect for keeping a child in line. An ugly old thing kept in a corner, an instrument of discipline always within easy reach, always within a child's sight until the thing became a dream-haunting image. Mother's broom.

After the girl and her mother were out of sight, he closed the door on the world and, having survived a tense episode, was actually grateful for the solitude that only minutes ago was the object of his dread.

Darkness. Bed.

But he could not sleep, not to say he did not dream. Hypnagogic horrors settled into his mind, a grotesque succession of images resembling lurid frames from old comic strips. Impossibly distorted faces painted in garish colors frolicked before his mental eye, all entirely beyond his control. These were accompanied by a series of funhouse noises which seemed to emanate from some zone located between his brain and the moonlit bedroom around him. A drone of half-thrilled, half-horrified voices filled the background of his imagination, punctuated by super-distinct shouts which used his name as an excuse for sound. It was an abstract version of his mother's voice, now robbed of any sensual quality to identify it as such, remaining only a pure idea. The voice called out his name from a distant room in his memory. *Sam-u-el*, it shouted with a terrible urgency of obscure origin. Then suddenly—*trick or treat*. The words echoed, changing in sense as they faded into silence: *trick or treat—down the street—we will meet—ashes, ashes*. No, not ashes but other trees. The boy walked behind some big maples, was eclipsed by them. Did he know a car was following him that night? Panic. Don't lose him now. Don't lose him. Ah, there he was on the other side. Nice trees. Good old trees. The boy turned around, and in his hand was a tangled web of strings whose ends extended up to the stars which he began working like kites or toy airplanes or flying puppets, staring up at the night and screaming for the help that never came. Mother's voice started shouting again; then the other voices mixed in, becoming a foul babbling unity of dead voices chattering away. Night of the Dead. All the dead conversed with him in a single voicey-woicey.

Trick or treat, it said.

But this didn't sound as if it were part of his delirium. The words seemed to originate from outside him, for their utterance served to disturb his half-sleep and free him of its terrible weight. Instinctively cautious of his lame leg, he managed to wrest himself from sweaty bedcovers and place both feet on the solid floor. This felt reassuring. But then:

Trick or treat.

It was outside. Someone on the front porch. "I'm coming," he called into the darkness, the sound of his own voice awakening him to the absurdity of what it had said. Had the months of solitude finally exacted their strange price from his sanity? Listen closely. Maybe it won't happen again.

Trick or treat. Trick or treat.

Trick, he thought. But he'd have to go downstairs to be sure. He imagined seeing a playfully laughing shape or shapes scurrying off into the darkness the moment he opened the door. He'd have to hurry, though, if he was to catch them at it. Damn leg, where's that cane. He next found his bathrobe in the darkness and draped it over his underclothed body. Now to negotiate those wicked stairs. Turn on the hallway light. No, that would alert them to his coming. Smart.

He was making it down the stairs in good time, considering the gloomy conditions he was working under. Neither this nor that nor gloom of night. Gloom of night. Dead of night. Night of the Dead.

With that odd sprightliness of cripples he ambled his way down the stairs, his cane always remaining a step ahead for support. Concentrate, he told his mind, which was starting to wander into strange places in the darkness. Watch out! Almost took a tumble that time. Finally he made it to the very bottom. A sound came through the wall from out on the front porch, a soft explosion it seemed. Good, they were still there. He could catch them and reassure his mind regarding the source of its fancies. The labor of walking down the stairs had left him rather hyperventilated and unsure about everything.

Trying to affect the shortest possible interval between the two operations, he turned the lock above the handle and pulled back the door as suddenly as he was able. A cold wind seeped in around the edges of the outer door, prowling its way past him and into the house. Out on the porch there was no sign of a boyish trickster. Wait, yes there was.

He had to turn on the porchlight to see it. Directly in front of the door a jack-o-lantern had been heaved forcefully down onto the cement, caving in its pulpy shell which had exploded into fragments lying here and there on the porch. He opened the outer door for a closer look, and a swift wind invaded the house, flying past his head on frigid wings. What a blast, close the door. Close the door!

"Little buggers," he said very clearly, an attempt to relieve his sense of disorder and delirium.

"Who, meezy-weezy?" said the voice behind him.

At the top of the stairs. A dwarfish silhouette, seemingly with something in its hand. A weapon. Well, he had his cane at least.

"How did you get in here, child?" he asked without being sure it really was a child, considering its strangely hybrid voice.

"Child yourself, sonny. No such things where I come from. No Sammy-Wammies either. I'm just a disguise."

"How did you get in?" he repeated, still hoping to establish a rational manner of entry.

"In? I was already in."

"Here?" he asked.

"No, not here. There-dee-dare." The figure was pointing out the window at the top of the stairs, out at the kaleidoscopic sky. "Isn't it a beauty? No children, no anything."

"What do you mean?" he inquired with oneiric inspiration, the normalcy of dream being the only thing that kept his mind together at this stage.

"Mean? I don't mean nothing, you meany."

Double negative, he thought, relieved to have retained contact with a real world of grammatical propriety. Double negative: two empty mirrors reflecting each other's emptiness to infinite powers, nothing canceling out nothing.

"Nothing?" he echoed with an interrogative inflection.

"Yup, that's where you're going."

"How am I supposed to do that?" he asked, gripping his cane tightly, sensing a climax to this confrontation.

"How? Don't worry. You already made sure of how-wow-wow...TRICK OR TREAT!"

And suddenly the thing came gliding down through the darkness.

IV

He was found the next day by Father Mickiewicz, who had telephoned earlier after failing to see this clockwork parishioner appear as usual for early mass on All Souls Day. The door was wide open, and the priest discovered his body at the bottom of the stairs, its bathrobe and underclothes grotesquely disarranged. The poor man seemed to have taken another fall, a fatal one this time. Aimless life, aimless death: *Thus was his death in keeping with his life*, as Ovid wrote. So ran the priest's ad hoc eulogy, though not the one he would deliver at the deceased's funeral.

But why was the door open if he fell down the stairs? Father M. came to ask himself. The police answered this question with theories about an intruder or intruders unknown. Given the nature of the crime, they speculated on a revenge motive, which the priest's informal testimony was quick to contradict. The idea of revenge against such a man was far-fetched, if not totally meaningless. Yes, meaningless. Nevertheless, the motive was not robbery and the man seemed to have been beaten to death, possibly with his own cane. Later evidence showed that the corpse had been violated, but with an object much longer and more coarse than the cane originally supposed. They were now looking for something with the dimensions of a broomstick, probably a very old thing, splintered and decayed. But they would never find it in the places they were searching.

Gary A. Braunbeck

In 1974, when my little sister Gayle was barely four, she came down with a severe case of the flu on Halloween and couldn't go out trick-or-treating. Being the sensitive, compassionate, stand-up pearl of a human being that I am (even at 17, I was a little angel), I volunteered to go out and beg for her.

I put on the most tattered clothes I could find, donned a ratty old dark wig of my mother's, pasted on some garishly long false finger nails and painted them black, then hastily and foolishly used black nail polish to make up my eyes in the same manner as Alice Cooper (circa the *Killer* days). I went out and begged on behalf of my sister, and found that people were impressed with not only my selfless humanity, but my costume, as well (damn, but did I look good!); as a result, I was given tons of extra treats to take back to my sister, who was overjoyed at the results.

Then I discovered something.

The glue I had used to attach the nails was of the Super variety, so the nails weren't coming off any time soon; nor was the black nail polish I'd used on my face. Scrub as I did, none of it was coming off.

So I went to school the next day (this was a staunchly Catholic school in the early 70s, when gestapo tactics were still employed by many of the teachers) and found that the nuns were none too pleased at my appearance. I was banished to a desk in the hallway for the remainder of the week, where I had to endure some of the most humiliating treatment from my fellow students during class changes.

It was only toward the end of the day, right before school let out, that a bright spot appeared on my oh-so-bleak horizon. Father Metzger, the youngest priest at St. Francis, came strolling through the hall and caught sight of my terrible visage.

"Hey, Alice," he said, giving me the "thumbs-up" sign. "*Under My Wheels* kicks ass!"

Then we both laughed.

That was the day I discovered that God dug Halloween. It's been my favorite holiday ever since.

Jack Ketchum

When Halloween, 1970 rolled around I was twenty-four years old and still very much a hippie and crashing with my friend John Wexo in sunny Laguna Beach, California. (Remember crashing?)

I have notes on this so it's easy to recall. That night I got the notion that what we should do was to reverse the order of things trick-or-treat-wise. So Paula and John and I went out and bought fresh-cut flowers and salted mixed nuts and bagged the nuts in plastic-wrap along with thin-cut strips of typed paper (remember typing?) on which we'd written quotes from Camus and Abbie Hoffman and Mark Twain and a bunch of other people. Myself included. Sort of a homemade fortune-cookie type thing.

Then we put on masks—mine was a da-glo skeleton—-and went door-to-door handing out the flowers and the nuts.

Wouldn't accept a thing.

We pretty much upset everybody one way or another. John is six-two and that sure didn't help any. But mostly we upset them in good ways.

Most were smiling by the time we left and some even seemed genuinely touched by the gesture. One old woman, whose husband almost closed the door on us when we first told him we were there to give him something, actually blessed us. Teenagers goofed on the whole thing. Only one guy seemed really scared of us. And he was bigger than John.

But the best thing was that on three occasions children answered the door, little kids, astounded by this weird adult departure from the rules and delighted by it. One boy's eyes went wide as we handed him his flower and when he said thank you, and all the while he slowly closed the door, all three of us had the feeling that this little fella was really *thinking* about it. Hard. That probably he'd ask questions. That maybe he'd remember it.

We went home and drank hot hard cider and listened to the Song of the Humpbacked Whale.

Haunting.

Yesterday's Child

Thomas F. Monteleone

Scott Fusina sat in his living room, thinking of the best way to kill himself.

It was Saturday afternoon and his television blathered on about a classic shoot-out between USC and Notre Dame. Scott was considering a classic shoot-out too; between the side of his head and the little .22 caliber he kept in the drawer of his night-table....

His thoughts rushed about madly, connected only by tenuous causes and effects. Trish, his wife, hated him, and was sleeping with another man. Deanna, his ten-year-old daughter, also hated him because she believed he deserted her. And to complete the feminine conspiracy, his mother was totally disgusted with him, claiming that he was the prime cause of her angina.

Considering everything else, it was no surprise that his once-envied position as the top salesman at Providential Mutual Life was fading like the color in a cheap T-shirt. The thought of going out and hustling life insurance made him want to vomit. He just didn't give a damn about his job or anything else in his life, not even his friends—who were lately treating him like he had leprosy.

He had heard that your married friends avoided you when you were going through a particularly nasty separation or divorce, and it was true. They did it because they unconsciously feared that what was happening to you might be infectious, that it might happen to *them*. And so they stayed away.

Nothing seemed to be important any longer. Nothing mattered, and he wondered whether pills might be easier than a gun. The thought of actually holding that cold metal up to his head and pulling the trigger....

His thoughts were interrupted by a knock at the door, and for a silly instant he fantasized it being his wife and child coming to ask him to come home.

Such foolish dreaming was quelled as he opened the door to discover a more-than-middle-aged woman stationed outside the entrance to his second-floor apartment. He could not speak, and simply stared at her.

"Hello," said the woman gingerly. "I'm Emma Dodson from the Sudbrook Park Neighborhood Association, and we would like to know if you would be interested in volunteering for our Block Watch Program."

"Your *what*?" Scott was barely listening to her.

"Just temporarily, of course. We need some extra people to watch the streets tonight while the children go trick-or-treating in the Park." That was what all the residents of the neighborhood called the little suburban enclave— "The Park." Its tree-shaded streets were lined with 30-room mansions of a century past, many divided into fashionable apartments like the one he'd recently taken.

"Tonight?" Scott seemed stunned by the revelation. "Is tonight Halloween?"

Emma Dodson smiled. "Yes, it is, young man. Slipped your mind, did it? I'll bet you even forgot to buy some goodies for the kids...."

"Oh...yes, I *did* forget...."

She looked at him quizzically, then brightened. "Aren't you Marion's boy?"

"Uh, yes, I am...do you know my mother?"

Emma smiled. "Oh yes. I remember her walking you around the Park in a stroller more than thirty years ago. Time goes by, doesn't it?"

"Yes, I guess it does...." Scott was barely aware of talking to her. His mind seemed filled with important thoughts.

There was a moment of awkward silence before Emma pressed him again. Would he be interested in taking up a station on a nearby street corner to help ensure that no harm came to the children of Sudbrook Park?

He heard himself saying yes, as though listening to a conversation in a distant room, and Emma handed him a photocopied map of the neighborhood, using a pencil to mark off the place where he would be expected to stand between 6:00 and 8:00 p.m. that evening.

"You do have a flashlight, don't you?" asked Emma.

"Yes, I think so...in my car, I think."

She smiled, thanked him, and eased herself down the stairs to the sidewalk. Possession of a flashlight and having a mother who'd lived in Sudbrook Park was apparently enough of a qualification Scott was not a pervert or child molester, and good material for Trick-or-Treat Block Watching.

After a simple, microwave, cooking-pouch dinner from Stouffer's, Scott prepared for his evening's responsibility. Actually, he was grateful for the assignment. It was helping to get his mind off his great problems, and as long as he felt as though he had something to do, suicide seemed like only a possibility, rather than a certainty. Not the most encouraging prognosis, he knew, but at least it was something, right?

Wearing jeans, a flannel shirt, and a light jacket, he looked younger than his forty-one years as he exited the apartment. Down the outside staircase on the side of the old house, he noted that it was already growing quite dark. His landlord, who lived on the first floor, had already turned on his porch light—a sign that trick-or-treaters would be welcome.

Scott did not need Emma Dodson's map; he knew Sudbrook Park intimately. Walking to his assigned corner, memories of his youth in this neighborhood slowly crept back to stand like a waif at the doorway to his mind. It was a quiet residential area with streets vaulted by 100-year old poplar, oak, and chestnut trees. The gnarled giants towered over the Park's Victorian houses, cloaking everything in the earthy colors of Autumn.

Autumn. His favorite time of the year.

Scott had been living in such a terrible depression for the last eight weeks that he had almost been oblivious to everything. So much so, the passing of the seasons had been like the footsteps of strangers beneath his windows.

But Autumn was no stranger to Scott. From his earliest years, he had loved it as a special time. A time when the blistering heat-death of summer finally faded, when the evenings seemed to linger, and the woods blazed with spectral color. When you could rake enough leaves into piles taller than your head, and smell them burning in someone's back yard; when there was mist at morning and fog at twilight; when the moon seemed somehow fuller and bigger as it sailed against the blue aisle of the night.

Arriving at his "post," Scott peered up and down the tree-choked lane. Across the intersection, a street lamp defined a small cone of light sharply edged by the darkness beyond. A memory flashed into his mind: riding his big red Schwinn bike down to this corner to intercept the Good Humor Man every night at about this time. Unlike so many people he'd known, he had enjoyed a happy childhood.

So how the hell did he grow up to be so miserable?

He had moved back to his old neighborhood after Trish threw him out because he felt the need to be in the midst of comfortable, familiar surroundings during such a traumatic chapter in his life. Thomas Wolfe had instructed us, in a long, long book, that you can't go home again, and Scott wondered how axiomatic that notion might be.

Dusk crept through the streets like a predator, stealing the color and shape from everything it passed. Darkness filled in all the missing spaces as the moon began to rise. Jack-o-lanterns glowed and grinned from front porches and picture windows, and as though on cue, he heard the advancing vanguards of the kids, ready to launch their raiding parties for a few pieces of candy.

Flicking on his flashlight, Scott announced his presence to any who approached, identifying himself as a symbol of safety to the children of the Park. He watched them shamble past him in ragged little groups, up one walk, down another, cutting across lawns and almost crowding each other off some of the small front porches and landings. The cool night teemed with their unique sounds: rustling paper bags, rapid footsteps, and endless cries of "trick-or-treat!"

The pageantry of the evening made Scott think of his own childhood, and how Halloween had always been so grand to him. He remembered how he'd loved to create a new costume each year, and how he'd started planning it by the end of August, usually. A pirate, a space man (they didn't call them "astronauts" back then), a mummy, a cowboy, a robot...he had been a succession of cinematically-inspired images, but every one of them handmade with love and care.

Things were different now, he could see.

Almost all of the kids paraded past him in cheap ready-made costumes that you could find in any K-Mart and Woolworth during the month of October. Made from the flimsiest synthetic materials, they were usually just black coveralls with some Saturday morning cartoon character's picture appliqued across the chest. The accompanying mask was usually a one-dimensional, micron-thin shell of plastic with florescent paint hastily applied. Any connection between these "costumes" and something creative was purely accidental, and wholly unlikely.

But worst of all, the costumes weren't scary.

Scott smiled as two little kids passed him, one dressed as a woman named "Xena," the other a skeleton. The former, judging from the breast-plate-picture, was a shameless rip-off of Robert E. Howard, while the latter's chest resembled an illustration page from an anatomy text.

Whatever happened to those neat old skeleton suits with the bones painted down the arms and legs, front and back, and the rubber masks that covered your whole head so that you *really looked* like a skeleton? Whatever happened to wigs and greasepaint, and rags and old clothes?

These thoughts soughed through him like a breeze, long and warm and slow. He noticed the moon was high in the trees now. It still appeared to be a bloated sphere of pale harvest-orange, but it would be casting off the color as it continued its journey skyward. Memories reached out for him like opened window curtains touched by the nightwind. The smells and sounds of the evening seduced him, carrying him into the mist of a time long ago, but not forgotten. He found himself longing for the innocence and the industry of childhood, forgetting the fears and terrors that nightly accompany most kids to their beds. At this point in his life, for Scott Fusina, being twelve years old again seemed like a great idea.

He smiled at the notion as he detected movement in his peripheral vision. A flash of dull whiteness, kiting through the darkness like a wind-blown piece of paper. Turning quickly, he spun about to see...nothing. Nothing there.

But I'd have *sworn* there was....

For some reason, the experience made him edgy, and more than slightly paranoid. He scanned the darkness beyond his post, beyond the pale zone of the street lamp, but saw nothing. He could hear the laughter of trick-or-treaters on the next street over, but his own territory was desolate and quiet.

Again, the night breeze reached out to him with a long, slow touch. There was a warmth in the air, like the breath of an unseen creature, and it smelled of crisping leaves and carved-out pumpkins. Turning his head, Scott looked up the street.

That's when he saw the figure step from the shadows. It moved with a dark grace, as though materializing from the essence of the night. Although the sudden appearance startled him, he could see by the small stature of the figure it was just a kid in a costume. Scott started to relax. But he could see that this was no ordinary costume. A K-Mart special this was not. No, he thought as he watched the figure stride closer, there was a unique look to this costume...a *familiar* look.

The figure was dressed in the red and white regalia of a British Revolutionary War soldier, complete in most details from the brass buttons to the muslin-wrapped boots. He wore a full-flowing riding cape, which fell gracefully away from his broad shoulders.

But above the shoulders there was...nothing.

Scott smiled as he watched the Headless Horseman approach. True to Washington Irving's tale, the figure carried a brilliant jack-o-lantern under his arm—a surrogate head in search of his real one.

It was a beautiful costume—as good as the one Scott had created when he was ten years old...just like *this* one.

The Headless Horseman stopped perhaps ten feet distant, half-embraced by the shadows.

Just like this one. The thought echoed through his head as Scott studied the work of the costume. Wasn't that red jacket the same one he'd found in Aunt Maude's trunk? And wasn't that cape the one he'd made from one of his mother's tablecloths?

A chill passed through him like a point of cold steel. The Headless Horseman stood before him, silent and somehow defiant.

"Who *are* you?" asked Scott, his voice croaking.

A pause. Then, from within the depths of the costume: "You *know* who I am...."

"Do I?" Scott had a terrible urge for a cigarette, wishing for an instant that he'd never given them up.

The costumed figure placed the jack-o-lantern on the sidewalk, and with a few quick, practiced moves, unfastened the breast buttons of his jacket. The false chest and shoulders fell away to reveal the thin, angular face of a pre-adolescent boy. Dark hair fell across even darker eyes, which gazed at Scott with strength of the years which bound them together.

"This is impossible...." said Scott weakly.

"Perhaps," said the boy, shrugging artfully. "But that doesn't matter now, does it?"

"But *how*....?" Scott still protested with shocked confusion.

The boy tilted his head. "Don't know. But look, here we are. Let's just accept it for what it is...it simply *is*."

"Oh man, this is crazy.... I must be nuts!"

"Not yet, but you're on your way," said the boy.

"What're you doing here?" asked Scott. "How can this be?"

"This night always is, and I am always here...."

"What do you want with me? Why are you doing this to me?"

"For starters, you're doing to yourself. To *both* of us." The boy almost grinned. "You were missing me, calling out for me...."

"No I wasn't," said Scott. "This is crazy!"

"Maybe I should start with a few questions."

Scott laughed. "You sound like a cop!"

"What happened, Scott? What happened to all the dreams we had?"

"I don't know...gone, I guess."

"Dreams are never really gone...they just change their names to things like 'crazy ideas' or maybe 'regrets'."

"Maybe you're right...."

Scott nodded as he remembered being ten years old and dreaming of being an architect, and how he built miniature houses out of balsa wood in his basement workshop. In that instant, he recalled so many things. They flashed through his memory like cards thumbed through a deck: the first guitar he bought for ten bucks, his collection of E.C. horror comics, his Gilbert chemistry set, the microscope, the motorbike he tried to make from the old lawnmower, and so many other projects conceived out of boundless energy....

"Do you remember when you made the mummy costume? How it started to unravel in the big parade, and how you wouldn't give up trying to 'fix it,' right up until it was too late?"

"Right up until I reached the judges stand with only a few strips left...."

Scott smiled at the memory. He hadn't thought about it in thirty years. "Yeah...and what about the tree house I built out in Smith's woods...?"

The boy nodded solemnly. "Or the jungle riverboat, or the soapbox racer...it was all great stuff, always *will* be great stuff. We had something *special*, remember? And somewhere along the way, you've let it get away from you...."

"You wouldn't understand...it's different when you grow up. You have to have responsibility...."

"Yeah, sure...I know all about it: credit cards and mortgages and that kind of stuff." The boy paused, then stared deeply into him. "Listen, do you really like selling life insurance?"

"No, I hate it. I've *always* hated it.

"Then why do you do it?"

"It's a good way to make a lot of money, I guess."

The boy snorted. "*Nobody* grows up dreaming to be an insurance salesman."

Scott nodded. "I've always hated it."

"And maybe yourself too? For doing it?"

Looking up at the boy, Scott nodded. "Well, maybe...."

"Then I'd say it's time to quit, wouldn't you?"

"Yeah, maybe...."

"And what about this Trish? Do you really still love her? Did you ever?"

"I...I don't think so. It was all a mistake—a mistake I never wanted to admit." Scott looked down at his shoes, feeling very embarrassed.

"So admit it *now*. Really, is all this kind of stuff worth killing yourself for?"

Scott shook his head. "No, I guess not."

"Don't try to live for *any* of them," said the boy.

"What?"

"Haven't you learned yet—the world doesn't like dreamers?"

"What?" asked Scott.

"Most people don't want us seeing things differently than them. It's too uncomfortable, too scary."

"Man, you are right about that!" said Scott, starting to feel better.

"That's why you can *never* try to please them."

Scott nodded. "So young to be so wise...."

"I'm as old as you."

Scott smiled ironically. "Yes, I guess you are."

The boy hunched down and picked up his jack-o-lantern. "Listen, I gotta go now."

"So soon? We just got started."

"No, I think we're okay now."

The boy turned, began walking off into the shadows. Scott watched him move with an easy grace, a confident stride. It was an infectious kind of swagger.

"Hey!" called Scott, just as the figure reached the outer zone of the street lamp's glow. "Wait a second!"

Turning, the boy looked at him. "Yes?"

"I just wanted to tell you how much I liked your costume. Nice job. Really beautiful."

The boy smiled. "Thanks. But wait till you see the one I've got planned for next year...."

"You're right," said Scott. "I remember it...it was the best of them all!"

AFTERWORD

Okay, so here it is sixteen years later since I wrote that story, and it looks like old Ray and Rod[1] really had a nut-grip on my sensibilities during that period of my writing. Actually, they still do, but I've learned to keep them out of the sun more than I did back then. Bad for the complexion, to say nothing for the verbiage.

But seriously, folks (*Tap! Tap!...is this thing on?),* I do have a few observations to add to this piece.

Within it, you can find some autobiography, some bullshit, some heartfelt memories, and yes, even a bit of a message to any of the younger dreamers out there who might stumble across these pages. I did grow up in a neighborhood like the one above, and I did have a magical childhood, mostly of my own devise because I had no brothers or sisters. Halloween was my favorite holiday and I faced the challenge of making my own costumes with the same resolve as Newton divining the calculus. (And I've created a kindred mutant in my daughter, Olivia, who's best-est holiday is also Halloween, and who can't be kept out of a homemade costume.)

But I was never a depressed, suicide-contemplating wimp like our protagonist for several reasons—(a) I have always loved myself, and wouldn't want to deprive any of you the joy of knowing me; (b) I have always been way too busy; (c) I never forgot how to laugh—at myself as well as everybody else; and (d) I've never lost the power to be a fuzzy-headed dreamer.

The part about how most people resent folks like us is probably a lot truer today than it was when I wrote it, because we are spinning ever deeper into a maelstrom of homogeneity to a bottom-place where individualists might be considered a bit unstable or even...dangerous.

And we can't have that, can we?

Yeah, we can...and we always will.

Because the tragedy of life is not that we die, but rather what dies within us while we still live.

Because of people like me and people like you, and the children we teach and inspire, we won't be letting things like curiosity and wonder and imagination be dying out anytime soon.

Dream on, my friends.

[1] Bradbury and Serling for all of you too young or too numb-headed to remember or recognize the reference to two of my formative influences.

Zombies

Hugh B. Cave

It was a Halloween in the fifties and I was in Haiti, where I lived for the best part of five years. During that time I turned out a book about that land of poverty, mystery and voodoo called *Haiti: Highroad to Adventure*, about which the renowned novelist, Kenneth Roberts, wrote to the publisher, Henry Holt: "If there was anything about Haiti that I didn't read (when I was writing Lydia Bailey) either in French, or English, or in diaries, I couldn't find out about it; and Cave's *Haiti* seems to me to stand head and shoulders above all of them in its vivid depiction of the land and the people." Also, based on those years in Haiti, I wrote a double book-club selection called *The Cross on the Drum*, and novels such as *Black Sun*, *Legion of the Dead*, *The Evil*, *The Evil Returns*, *The Lower Deep*, and enough shorter tales for magazines like *The Saturday Evening Post* to make up a Doubleday collection called *The Witching Lands: Tales of the West Indies*.

On the morning of that particular Halloween I happened to be talking—in Petionville, where I lived then—with two Haitian men who had just returned from a village in the mountains, and when they mentioned zombies I was instantly all attention. I had been hearing about zombies for years but never seen one. Had they actually seen a zombie?

Yes, they said, they had. In fact, they had seen several.

"Can you take me there?"

They said they would.

We left in my jeep, one of four that I wore out exploring that rugged Caribbean country in the years I lived there. From Petionville we climbed the steep, winding road to Kenscoff. Then, with one of the two Haitians sitting on the hood to keep the vehicle's front tires on the road, so steep was it, we toiled up the unpaved road to the mountain settlement of Furcy. The Haitian peasants are fond of saying in their Creole, "Deye morne ge morne," which roughly means "Beyond the mountains are mountains." Our destination—reached only on foot—was a sort of valley between peaks, several miles ahead.

As we walked, I asked questions. "Tell me, something. What does a zombie look like?"

"Like you and us, m'sieu."

"And you believe they are dead."

"Dead but alive."

The Haitian—at least the Haitian peasant—believes in two kinds of zombies. One is a person to whom a certain poison is administered. He seems to be dead and is buried. Removed from the grave, he is administered a drug that restores life but leaves him with a damaged mind, so that he can be used as a servant or laborer. The other kind is a dead person returned to life by a kind of sorcery practiced, usually for money, by *bocors*.

The ones I encountered that afternoon were working in fields carved out of the lower slope of a mountain. Fields of cabbages, turnips, sweet potatoes, yam vines climbing a forest of slender poles. My companions explained that the vegetables, when harvested, were taken to the capital and sold there.

But oh, the odor!

The zombies—if zombies they actually were—wore only trousers, mostly black trousers. Otherwise they were naked. And the air on that mountain slope was—well, in a story I wrote later about the events of that day, I described it as the acrid stench of bat-guano in a wild cave I had once explored in Kentucky, or the stink of a pig farm I had once visited.

Obviously, the dozen or so men working in this field never bathed.

Well, I would have given almost anything for a camera at that moment, but my guides had warned me not to carry one. "The people who own these farms know how to make zombies," they had said. "If we meet and talk to them, do not eat anything they offer you, and do not try to take photographs, whatever you do!"

I asked now if I might talk to these "zombies" or whatever they were.

"You may try," my companions said. "And they are able to communicate somehow among themselves, but not in any way you will understand."

I tried, and they listened. But my guides were right; when they responded I could not understand them, though by this time I had been in Haiti often enough to speak Creole fairly fluently.

So, without meeting the owners of the property—who my guides assured me were just ordinary peasant farmers—we eventually departed.

Later I turned this into a short story which was published originally in the English magazine *Fantasy Tales*, edited by Stephen Jones and David A. Sutton, and has since been reprinted four times in various collections or anthologies. *Fantasy Tales* won many awards for its excellence. In this story, called "A Place of No Return," I used an arrogant, know-it-all Ivy League anthropologist as my leading character, and had him hire a Port-au-Prince taximan to take him to the zombie farm. There, after offending the farm's bocor owner, he is fed a poisoned chicken and turned into a zombie himself.

The story ends as follows:

They formed a line. The man with the whip forced Carter into it, and someone thrust a hoe at him. The whip cracked and the line trudged out of the shelter, along a path to the fields.

As it halted at the work site, Carter looked about him, aware that his mind was slowly becoming incapable of thought. He was receiving only impressions, and even those were now fragile and fleeting. In the golden dawn light the mountains all around him were part of a terrifying world in which he was a prisoner or slave. Deye morne ge morne. He was uncountable miles away from the home he would never see again.

By tomorrow would he even remember it?

Happy Halloween!

The Whitby Experience

Simon Clark

"I won't be long."

"Don't be. The pizza will be ready in twenty minutes."

"Red or white?"

"Go crazy: buy both. We're on vacation, aren't we?"

"Don't forget to lock the door."

"Afraid Dracula will get me?"

"Lock it, Ingrid."

"OK; now, do you remember the way to the supermarket?"

"Roughly."

"Don't get lost; those little streets are a maze out—"

"Ingrid, trust me. I'll be fine."

"OK. Get a move on. I'm going to put the pizza in now."

"Oh, there's just one more thing."

"What's that?"

"When I come back and you open the door for me?"

"Yes?"

"Be naked for me."

"Fat chance, mister."

"Aw...." He grinned, looking every inch a mischievous little boy. "This is a second honeymoon, isn't it? The kids are with grandma; the dogs are with Uncle Bob; work's a million miles away, and I'm feeling as raunchy as a—"

She found herself grinning back at him as he stood there at the turn in the stairs. "Be back in fifteen minutes." She adopted a sexily husky voice. "And you'll see what this old girl can do."

His eyes flashed. "Just watch me move." With that he went down the stairs two at a time.

"Oh, Ben," she called down after him. "Try and remember the scented candles."

His voice came softly back up to her, promising that he would. A moment later she heard the door of the apartment block shut far below. For a moment she leaned over the banister, looking down through the twists and turns of the stairwell, half expecting him to come running back up the stairs to say he'd forgotten his wallet or simply to kiss her and suggest they forget pizza in favor of slipping under the bedclothes. But a silence quickly settled on the stair, she couldn't even hear muffled TV sounds or voices from the other apartments below.

She was at the point of returning to the apartment, when she noticed what appeared to be a brown ball resting on the banister maybe two or three floors below. A misshapen ball set with two pieces of glass that....

Eyes.

"I'm sorry," she said startled. "I was just looking for my husband."

God, she sounded a total idiot, she realized, apologizing to the old man who looked up at her. But the truth of the matter was that his sudden appearance like that, gazing up with those glass-splinter eyes had startled her. Feeling more idiotic, she gave him another smile, then backed through the apartment door before closing and locking it.

The poor old guy had probably heard the two of them calling up and downstairs and simply come out to see what all the noise was about. No doubt permanent residents here must have had a belly full of here-today-gone-tomorrow vacationers who tramped up and down the steps calling to one another, playing music too loud, leaving sand all over the stair carpets and generally behaving like inconsiderate slobs.

Still with a twinge of guilt Ingrid went through into the lounge to look out of the window. She thought she might catch sight of Ben as he headed off in that long stride of his toward the seafront before cutting off to the supermarket, where it lay in a tangle of narrow streets and ancient cottages. But no. The mist that had been seeping in off the ocean all day had thickened so much she couldn't even see their car parked on the road four stories below. It now looked as if their apartment floated on a lake of streaming white.

Through the glass she heard the soulful call of the foghorn. Being a city dweller the sound was alien to her; gravely mournful, too. She couldn't escape the notion that she heard some primeval creature that lay dying on the shore as it called to its long lost mate.

The booming cry came again; a dark rhythm embedded with such a ghostly resonance it bordered on the funereal. She shivered. Now, alone in the apartment for the first time since her arrival, it suddenly became a grave and lonely place, where empty bedrooms were haunted by shadows that might—

"OK, enough," she told herself firmly as her imagination began to slide insidious little movements into the corner of her eye. "Dracula's hardly likely to come popping out of the closet, is he?"

Even so, she quickly turned on every light in every room, before returning to the living room where she switched on the TV. All channels were blank. Great...now the set was on the fritz. But they'd been watching it not ten minutes ago when they'd ran the fruits of their harem scarem camcorder work from the last few days. The video camera was still plugged into the TV; so instead of having to sit on the sofa listening to the mournful call of the foghorn she hit the 'play' button. First came a jogging shot of the village of Staithes just a few miles north of Whitby. Little more than a rock shelf on the sea's edge, it was home to a few dozen cottages and a couple of inns that were achingly picturesque. An October sun shone brilliantly on red tiled roofs; flocks of seagulls wheeled, crying raucously; fishing boats bobbed in the estuary. Ingrid smiled at the TV screen as Ben's face appeared, "Have you heard the local legend, Ingrid?" he was saying in his best Boris Karloff impression yet: "Ingrid, dear. On the last Friday of October those terrible...those dreadful hell birds come down and carry off the first blonde lady they see...."

Then came shots of Whitby: the ancient abbey on the cliff that had been ruined even further by a few stray shots from a U-boat in World War 1. After that, the church of St. Mary's surrounded by a graveyard full of headstones weathered into fantastically weird shapes. More views: the famous 199 steps that cascade down to the old town where streets are so narrow it's a struggle for a single car to pass between the rows of tiny sixteenth century cottages; the Banwick Arms with its whale bone rafters; the marvelously named Town Of A Magic Dream coffee house where Jim Morrison painted the 'Crazy Horse' ceiling mural of counterculture legend; then across the River Esk to Whitby's more modern half, complete with Woolworth's, the Gothic storefront of The Dracula Experience (displaying the cape that Christopher Lee once wore) and a gaggle of amusement arcades full of flashing, honking slot machines.

Ben had insisted on videoing her standing outside the house on Royal Crescent where they were staying over Halloween weekend.

They'd chosen the apartment by sheer chance at the tourist office. Soon they discovered that a hundred years or so before the house had played host to a famous guest. Ingrid watched the TV as her own face filled the screen. Off camera, Ben was asking her to get closer to the plaque. Now she watched her own blonde-framed face smile back into the camera. "It's too high."

"Stand on tip-toe."

"Can you get it in now?"

"Just...wait, the top of your head's covering the bottom half."

"This better?" She'd lowered her head a little.

Now, comically standing on her head like a blue crown, was the wall plaque:

WHITBY CIVIC SOCIETY
BRAM STOKER (1847-912)
AUTHOR OF DRACULA STAYED HERE
1890-1896

"My God, does it get any better than this?" Ben's voice soared from the TV as he filmed the inside of the apartment. "Bram Stoker dreamt up Dracula here. We're even sleeping in the great man's bedroom. *Jesus. Just look at the view."*

Smiling, Ingrid dueted her own voice from the TV: "But it's changed a bit since then."

"Just a bit," Ben said zooming the camera through the open doorway to reveal the hi-fi, TV and modern artwork on the walls. "Nice décor. Post modernist minimalist, would you say?"

"Absa-bloody-lutely."

A wavering shot of the square windows accompanied by Ben's Karloff voice. "Bram Stoker climbs the fifty eight steps to his apartment where he gazes out to the ghost-rich sea and thinks: I know I'll write a story about a foreign gentleman who goes round biting people on the neck. He shuns daylight, detests garlic—"

"Pizza...damn, he'll be back any minute."

"—the only way to kill him is to hammer a chunk of wood through his evil old heart. Little did he know—"

Ingrid stabbed the 'off' button then went through into the kitchen where she slid the pizza into a now smoky oven. Great, a second honeymoon and your husband will come back to find you reeking of cooker-smoke.

She went to the bedroom where she sprayed herself with scent, checked her long, curling blonde hair, then gave it a jet of hairspray to make sure it stayed in place. "There, thirty-six years old and still a beauty." She smiled into the mirror meaning the compliment in a faintly jocular way. But she did feel good, and if she were honest she looked good, too; her blonde hair shone, her eyes sparkled, her face glowed from a superabundance of Whitby fresh air, good food and—don't cha' know it?—a whole heap of good loving. This 'second honeymoon' as they jokingly called it, made her look years younger. She'd just added a touch of lipstick that was a knowing, lascivious red when she heard the knock on the door. Smiling, she remembered her promise. In a second she slipped off her clothes, then padded barefoot to the door.

Lay naked on the kitchen table and murmur, 'Supper is served.'

She smiled even more broadly at the mental image. *Maybe later, girl....* She slipped back the bolt then turned the handle ready to pull open the door to see Ben's surprised face.

But, what if it's the old man with those tiny glittery eyes?

"Good point," she murmured to herself. Slipping the chain back on, she opened the door an inch, making sure her body was well hidden behind it.

A good job, too.

She looked out onto an empty landing; craning her neck, she saw an equally empty staircase, too, with the brown wooden stair-rail backing its way into darkness below. For a moment she thought she saw a shadow moving through the gloom. "Ben...Ben? Is that you?" Confused, she tried to see at either side of the door without opening it any further. Cold air slid up from the darkness to make her shiver so much her skin puckered into goose flesh.

No. There's no one there. But who knocked on the door?

A knock came again. She started so much her forehead bumped against the doorframe.

"Ben?" The darkened stairwell gobbled up her whisper. Hell, it didn't take a genius of observation to tell there was no one down there. Who'd creep about in the darkness anyway, when there were light switches on every landing?

Again came a sharp tap of knucklebone on wood. Following that came a moment's absolute silence before the sound of the distant foghorn shimmered its way up the stairs like a ghost.

Confused, she shut and locked the door. Maybe it was a bird under the eaves, or maybe air in the pipes...she'd only just pushed the rationalizations through her head when the knock came again—impatient, demanding: *let me in.* She went into the kitchen where the cooker made faint clicking sounds, but those were nothing like the sharp raps on wood she'd heard. Pulling back the curtain, she looked out onto the expanse of rough grass, which provided a parking lot for the apartments. Through the mist, she made out fire escapes at the back of the buildings.

"Idiot," she hissed with relief. Ben must have crept up the fire escape for some reason, for some foolish romantic reason she hoped. The tapping came again; this time she hurried through into the bathroom where the fire escape door exited onto the escape itself. "Idiot, idiot," she whispered, amused. Would she find him there with roses as well as the wine?

She shot back the bolts and threw open the door that swung with a startling shriek of seldom used hinges. Running icy fingers over her naked body came the night air, heavy with sea damp and smell of brine. Immediately, the foghorn cried louder than ever now she was outside.

No Ben. No nobody. Nothing—but mist curling its tendrils round the ironwork of the open-air staircase. Good grief. What the hell's happening? Who was tapping on the doors then running away? Anyone would think it was....

But, damn it, *it was!* Suddenly, she expected to hear the call of 'Trick or treat?' After all, this was the last day of October. Britain celebrated Halloween, too. Come to that, they'd celebrated it as a religious festival for thousands of years, long before Christianity had washed up on its shores. But why hadn't those Whitby kids done the 'trick or treat' ritual first before knocking on the door and running away? She had no candy but she could have paid the little tykes off with some coins.

Arms across her naked breasts, she retreated into the bathroom and partly closed the door with just her head out in the cold night air. "Hello?" she called. Then waited a moment, listening for children's voices, or a cry of 'Trick or treat.' All that reached her, however, was the near supernatural lowing of the foghorn. Suddenly irritated she called down, "You'll break your stupid necks running up and down these steps in the dark."

With no answering shout; not so much as a 'Shut up, you stupid cow,' from the kids, whoever they were, she shut the door and rammed home the bolts.

She'd no sooner done that than a rap sounded on the door to the landing.

"Damn kids," she hissed. Once more she went to the door, but a flash of her naked body in the hallway mirror changed her mind about opening it straight away. She waited for a moment. Then the second the knucklebone sounded again she called out, *"Ben? Is that you?"*

No giggles. No 'Trick or treat?' Nothing. Damn well nothing. Blast them. And here I am running around the place in my birthday suit, she fumed.

As she went to the bedroom to get dressed she heard the sharp rap on the fire escape door. This time she ignored it.

❋ ❋ ❋

Twenty minutes later, the pizza had reached a perfect golden brown; cheese bubbled and the aroma of its spices filled the room where Bram Stoker had gazed out the window and dreamed his dark dreams.

Ten minutes later its crust began to burn. Annoyed, she yanked it from the oven catching her hand on the hot metal interior. *Damn....* The pizza flipped off the tray to land face down on the carpet.

Well, this was turning out to be a perfect evening.... Ben's gone walk about; the local Whitby kids are tormenting the hell out of me; the carpet's just gone and got itself a cheese shampoo—what next? For the next minute or so she busied herself scraping the goo from the carpet and dumping the whole lot in the trash. Maybe they should have eaten out as she suggested anyway, but Ben had to suggest a romantic evening in. Romantic, my foot; he'd either taken a scenic stroll round fog-bound Whitby or had been tempted into one of the pubs for a beer.

Result? One ruined pizza; one set of frazzled nerves; one pissed lady.

When the next tap on the door came she was ready for them.

"Stop that!" she snapped, launching herself through the doorway onto the landing. Once more stairs plunged down into darkness; once more there was no one there; once more she'd made an idiot of herself. No. No she hadn't. Those trick or treaters were going to be told exactly—EXACTLY—what she thought of them. She ran lightly down the carpeted stair, hitting light switches as she went, flooding landing after landing with light. "You come back here...what do you think you're playing at?"

She hit the light switch on the first floor to find an old man standing outside an apartment. The same old man, in fact, that she'd seen looking up at her earlier. She stared at him suspiciously for a moment, half-ready to accuse him of knocking on her door; then she noticed he leaned on a cane.

"Is there anything wrong?" he asked in a surprisingly soft voice.

"It's those damn kids..." She took a calming breath. "I'm sorry, it's just that some children have been playing rather annoying games."

"Ah," he said, "they would do that." Then he gave a little smile that caused his eyes to dwindle into two glassy specks in his face. "It's the time of year I'm afraid."

"I know...Halloween. But they don't trick or treat. They just knock on the door and run like hell."

He gave a whispery chuckle. "A local custom. Whitby has a variation of Halloween; it's called Mischief Night."

"Mischief Night." She sighed. "I figure that gives kids a license to do exactly that."

"Precisely. It's great fun as a child but tiresome when you're as old as I am."

"What now? They're going to spend the next five hours knocking on my door and running away before the little darlings go home to bed."

"Something like that. Do you have a car?"

"Yes, why?" She felt a sinking sensation.

"Then, I'd check it if I were you. Some children get a bit carried away. They might have let the tires down or put broken glass under them in the hope you don't notice in the morning."

"The little...." She clicked her tongue. "Thanks for the warning." She smiled. "And thank you for your concern."

"Oh, that's all right. It's only I heard you calling, and, well...I thought you might be having a bit of trouble?"

"I've managed to ruin supper and my husband's bugged out—nothing I can't handle."

"Well, if you should need me, I live here. Number one."

"Thank you, that's very kind." She smiled again. "And very neighborly of you."

"Not at all...goodnight, then."

"Goodnight."

Feeling a little less irritated she climbed the stairs back to her apartment. Even so, she'd have a choice word or two to say to Ben when he managed to wend his way back from whatever bar he'd wandered into. Still no joy with the TV; a snowstorm on every channel. She drummed her fingers on the armchair, ignoring the tapping on the fire-escape door to the rear and to the landing door.

"Go away. I'm a foreigner. I don't celebrate Mischief Night." She'd called out the words in a half-humorous way, but she itched to get her hands on the little brats. Now an hour had ticked away since Ben had so cheerfully bounded down the stairs promising to be back in minutes. *Damn.*

With the time creeping up to eight it was dark outside. What's more, the thick mist swamped everything in a lake of white, stained here and there with uncanny blotches of orange, marking where the streetlights lay buried. That's all. The foghorn continued its cry. A melancholy sound that rolled out across the ocean to die of loneliness somewhere in the mist.

After a while even the knocking of knucklebones on her door stopped. The brats had either gotten tired of tormenting her or they'd turned their attention to other things like—

Oh shit. The car. Damn, all it needed was for them to trash the hire-car, then life would become even less rosy than it had been over the last couple of hours. Damn, double damn, triple damn...she pulled a jacket over her sweatshirt and jeans and once more went downstairs.

❊ ❊ ❊

The instant she left the apartment block fog swallowed her. Ten paces from the apartment she couldn't see it when she looked back into that impenetrable gray wall. Nor could she see the car, even though they'd parked the thing just outside. She followed a sidewalk now wet and somehow unpleasantly greasy from the mist. Parked cars dripped as if they were stalactites in a cave; they looked as if they'd been there a thousand years.

Soon, however, she found their car. What little light filtered through this murk had turned its red livery into a morbid brown closer to the shade of congealed blood. It only took a moment to see that the car hadn't been touched; its doors were locked; no-one had wedged tacks or glass bottles under the wheels in celebration of the no doubt ancient and occult festival of Mischief Night (when everyone else in the free world were lighting candles in pumpkin heads, eating vampire bat candy and wearing funny spook masks, damn it).

Great, now her thoughts had taken on an acid quality. But she found she was no longer irritated but angry; a hot burning anger at that. Ben had played a dirty trick on her. Why the hell hadn't he come back from the supermarket yet? *Because some whore gave him the eye on Church Street....* No. That wasn't Ben's style. *He's been mugged; he's lying unconscious in one of those little streets; the cold killing him by inches....* Oh shit, why did she have to think that? Now she couldn't simply storm back to the apartment then sit drinking vodka, waiting for him to return so she could give him a piece of her mind....

He's simply missed his way, that's all, she reassured herself. It's dark; it's foggy, so foggy, in fact, you can hardly see five paces in front of you. He'll have taken a wrong turn somewhere and probably even now he's scratching his head, wondering where the hell the apartment vanished.

Ingrid zipped up her jacket then determinedly set off for the seafront, the mist snuffing out the sound of her footsteps. In fact, the mist killed all sound apart from the mournful cry of the foghorn. Even the whisper of the sea no longer reached her. And there were no people or cars about even though it couldn't have been much later than eight. Maybe they were all home protecting their property from the Mischief Night kids. She walked as quickly as she could through the mist, seeing nothing but a few slick paving slabs, while every so often dark coffin shapes lying on the sidewalk loomed toward her. At first she'd stopped, thinking 'who on earth would leave a coffin out here? Perhaps kids had broken into a funeral home and....' But no; they were only seat benches. Then again, in this near dark was it surprising her imagination played her up something rotten?

She put her head down as if charging the wall of gray in front of her; already salt deposited by the sea fog ran into her mouth with a briny sharpness; it found the burn on the back of her hand, too, causing the blister to sting like fury. God, what a night, she thought. What a damn awful night.

After walking for a few moments, the dark monolithic shapes of old houses closed in on her as she entered the narrow lane that ran down to the supermarket. Whether lights burned through windows she couldn't tell. This nightmare mist hid everything but the diffuse outline of buildings. She moved faster now, plunging down a long flight of steps between cottages that, she remembered, led to the supermarket.

"I don't believe it...I don't damn well believe it." For a moment she stood looking at the steel shutters covering the doors of the supermarket. "For crying out loud, where has he got to?" She looked round half-expecting to see Ben lying bleeding on the street. Shaking her head, she followed the road that ran steeply down to the harbor-side. No, he must be lost, that's all. If she walked along the harbor near the amusement arcades she might find him there. After all, there he'd find people who could give him directions back to Royal Crescent.

With blasts of white jetting blowing from her mouth she reached the harbor to find the tide out and an expanse of mud stretching greasily out into the mist. And so much for people being here. Pubs and cafes were shut. Amusement arcades shuttered and silent.

In fact, the whole of Whitby was silent. Apart from the foghorn that still bellowed its mournful cry. God, that sound...it felt as if it was dragging through her body like a saw blade. Didn't they ever switch the damn thing off?

She put her head down to walk on again, the mist stroking her neck with cold fingers...bone fingers that had been dead for a hundred years...a thousand years...the foghorn lowed across morbid, black mud...there, a long lost rope coiled unpleasantly eel-like...boat tracks formed many an open wound in the river-bed...abandoned lobster pots became the muddy ribs of dead children claimed by the gluttonous silt...beyond those, monstrous shadows loomed in a spectral mist that didn't reveal so much as a trace of another living human being.

She watched her passing reflection in the windows of The Dracula Experience; a hunched phantom-like figure with mist damp hair pasted down flat against her skull. And all the time the blister on her hand burned as if her flesh was being gnawed by fire ants.

That foghorn boomed so loudly it set her teeth on edge and cursed her with the thumping mother and grandmother of all headaches. Good grief, all she wanted now was to get back to the apartment, get under a hot shower then get some vodka down her throat.

She'd been walking perhaps five minutes when the road ended at a ramp. Confused, she stared at it for a moment. This led down to the sands...how had she missed the road that would take her back?

Ahead of her, the beach stretched out to be lost in that all enshrouding bleak mist. Waves of salt-air rolled with a tomb-like iciness over her, probing cold fingers through her clothes to touch her skin. She gave a great shiver that shuddered down to the marrow of her bones. That cold alone was enough to drive her back to the apartment, Ben or no Ben, but at that moment she saw a figure on the beach. Obscured by mist, she couldn't even tell if it was male or female, but there was something about the silhouette; the angle of the head....

"Ben?"

Slowly, she walked down the ramp, sensing stone slabs give way to soft yielding sand beneath her feet. "Ben?"

The figure didn't react to her voice at first. But as she walked out across the sand it turned and moved down the beach toward the still unseen ocean. She followed.

It's him...I'm sure it's him, she told herself. What on earth was he doing on the beach at night? Perhaps he had been attacked, or had fallen and struck his head; now he wandered in a confused state, looking for her.

"Ben!" This time a full-blooded shout came from her lips. The figure stopped. Looked back (she was sure he'd looked back, even though she couldn't clearly see his features in this God-awful mist). Then the figure began to walk purposefully once more.

Ingrid found herself half-running after him *(it has to be Ben; it is him; no doubt).* Soon Whitby town and its cliffs vanished behind her into the fog. Now she moved through that all but dark murk, which had the clarity of ditch water. "Ben. What's the matter?" This time her call didn't slow him, he still strode purposefully toward the water's edge.

But what water?

She could see no waves. The tide had gone way out; she could have been crossing some cold, damp desert. Every so often she'd walk across a white speckling of dead seashells, looking for all the world like tiny skulls. But there was nothing to indicate the direction she walked. She couldn't even make out the harbor wall that must run out to sea to her right.

Ahead, the figure began to vanish into the mist as it moved faster and faster away from her. *"Ben...Ben! Wait!"* A breathless panic bore down her; a pitiless weight, crushing her chest. *"Wait for me!"*

She followed the fading figure for a full five minutes, desperately trying to keep it in view. Still she hadn't reached the water's edge; what's more, she couldn't even hear the surf between the velvet dark cries of the foghorn now way, *way,* behind.

Surely the tide can't have gone this far out, could it? She must have lost her sense of direction and be walking *along* the beach, not *toward* the sea. But even as she walked, the nature of the shore changed; dark boulders emerged from the mist. They littered the beach at weirdly regular intervals. She walked by one. Perhaps eight feet long, it was oblong in shape, and closely resembled its neighbors that now surrounded her.

This was absurd; impossible; but she found herself thinking of them as being coffins hewn from stone. But what would coffins be doing lying out here on the seabed?

Passing by another, she looked more closely at it. Although erupting with a malignant growth of kelp the coffin shape was unmistakable. But coffins, hundreds of coffins on the seabed? Could this be the remains of a long sunken graveyard? After all, she remembered reading that water levels had inexorably risen around the British coast over the last few centuries, submerging whole villages. And she recalled the stone coffins at Whitby Abbey where the monks were interred. Maybe an unusually low tide had laid bare this submerged cemetery? One that had long since been stripped of its soil by ocean currents. But the coffins were of tremendous size. She pulled aside strands of weed from one of the stone caskets to reveal where the lid joined to the main body of the coffin. A scabbing crust of shellfish had formed over parts of the stone. Where the lid joined, the shells had broken as if....

She closed off the images her imagination sent oozing into her brain. Find Ben, she told herself. That's the important thing now. She walked on, the foghorn lowing with a dark and morbid intensity across the beach.

❋ ❋ ❋

Exhausted, she toiled up the same steps the long dead Bram Stoker and his long dead wife and children had climbed to their holiday apartment all those years ago. It seemed as if the mist had followed her here, it swirled up the stairwell like water flooding the building.

Too bone tired to raise her arms to switch on the lights she climbed the well of darkness to the white painted door. But where was the key? She'd swear it had been in her jacket pocket. "Well, it's gone now," she told herself wearily. "Must have dropped it."

Maybe Ben had found his way back here before her after his insane game of hide-and-seek on the beach. Yes, maybe, she thought, her spirits rising a little. There was a strip of light showing beneath the door.

Feeling a renewed burst of energy she rapped sharply on the door. Then she rapped again.

Her heart gave a leap as she heard the bolt slide back and saw the handle turn. *He's home, thank God.* She stood back as the door opened a few inches and a pair of eyes beneath a yellow fringe looked out. Strangely the eyes looked straight through her, then to the back of her and down the stairs. Then the female voice called out softly. "Ben...Ben? Is that you?"

❋ ❋ ❋

She woke with a massive thumping headache. God, what a dream...and why was she so cold?

That was the moment she opened her eyes to see them lowering the stone lid back over her, sealing her into darkness—they were singing out in their high children's voices: "Trick or treat, trick or treat, trick or treat...." Those misshapen, long drowned boys and girls with pink sea anemone eyes, starfish mouths, barnacle encrusted jaws, and brown leathery seaweed hair that spilt from their rotting skulls. Those no longer little children, suffocated by seawater, and saturated with a *post-mortem* mischief, who'd tricked her out here. And who'd laid her in the coffin with bare-bone hands.... "Trick or treat, trick or treat...." Even now she thought: *Good God, the idiots; why can't they get it right?*

Dazed from the blow on her head, she laughed deliriously: they'd got it all wrong; you only play the trick if the victim doesn't offer the treat.... All wrong...all wrong, wrong, wrong....

She still laughed (with a crimson note of hysteria) when she remembered seeing Ben lying in the stone coffin nearby with his face gouged like some pumpkin mask, the thick, white church candles driven deep into his empty eye sockets; the wicks burning with a greasy yellow flame in the damp sea-air. "They can't even get that right!" She sobbed with laughter. "The candles go *inside* the pumpkin head! Not *through* the eyes! It's all wrong. *All wrong!*" Her laughter rose into great, wailing shrieks.

And as a matter of fact, she only stopped laughing when the first wave hit the end of the stone coffin and she realized that, at long last, the tide had turned.

Halloween Memories

Christopher Golden

Was I eleven?

I don't think so. At least not quite. Let's say nine, then, though perhaps I'm erring on the side of vanity, not wanting to admit just how long I held on to the more gleefully childish parts of Halloween.

So, yes, nine.

Before I begin, though, you need to know about my mother's hand. Or, rather, her lack of one. The left. From birth she has been forced to manage with what one might call a truncated version of a left hand, dealing both with the practical impact of that loss as well as the emotional. She's done very well, thank you. Though an attorney now, in her youth she was a singer and performer whose efforts took her to Off-Broadway shows in New York.

In order to prevent audiences from being distracted by her handicap, she had one made for her. It was plastic and felt not unlike a turkey baster to the touch.

By the time I was nine—we all agreed on nine, did we not?—my mother had long since abandoned the stage. But the hand remained in my basement for me to discover it one early fall. It was a fascinating piece of equipment, particularly to one of my darkly mischievous mind set. Thus, that Halloween, when I put on my father's torn black jacket that hung to my knees and pulled my Frankenstein's Monster mask over my head, I also slipped that hand over my own....

Poor Mrs. Nye.

I lived in a suburban Massachusetts town twenty miles north of Boston, on a quiet, dead-end street with plenty of kids. My road was part of a warren of them that comprised a single, enormous middle-class neighborhood called Pheasant Hill.

Halloween on Pheasant Hill was truly something to behold. My brother and I took huge white pillowcases out before dark and began our rounds, filling up once, twice, even three times before finally settling down to fish through our booty and trade what we didn't like for things we did. If I close my eyes now I can remember the bustle of garishly costumed children roving up and down the streets in small packs.

Cabbage Night, what we called the local night of mischief and misdemeanors the evening before Halloween, had just passed. And yet we had the unmitigated gall to approach the front doors of homes we had egged or soaped the windows of or toilet-papered the trees of not twenty four hours earlier.

One house, on the far end of Briarwood Road, offered cold sodas instead of candy, and at least one Halloween was hot enough for us to be sweating in our masks and costumes. I had a devil's mask as well, but I think that came later, after the Frankenstein.

Of course there were sinister elements as well. The LaVolley mansion—which wasn't much of a mansion at all, to be honest—had shattered windows and an overgrown lot and that was our haunted house, the one we all sprinted by when we had to pass it. If we dared go down that way at all on Halloween night.

The whispers of razor-blades in apples and poison in candy. But we were foolish enough to think a wrapper that wasn't ripped meant the candy was safe to eat. We were children. And children in a time when parents thought most of those stories were just urban myths.

It didn't matter. Halloween was a glorious night. The best night of the year. When cable television came in, I could go home from trick-or-treating and watch *Halloween* or *Magic* on HBO. Conveniently, one or the other always seemed to be on that night. There were others, of course, but those are the ones I remember.

I got older, of course. Old enough, eventually, to bitterly accept that the solicitation of candy was reserved for younger children. And then older still.

But I never stopped loving Halloween. I usually take my children out trick-or-treating because I'm too dangerous to leave at home on Halloween night with my gore-drenched ghoul mask and lots of gullible little garishly-dressed neighbor kids to frighten.

Which brings me back to Mrs. Nye. What a sweet old woman she was....

I rang the bell, a group of other kids behind me. She came to the door and I was the one who yelled "trick or treat" the loudest. With a kindly smile she dropped a Zagnut and a Reese's cup in my bag. I thanked her and thrust out my hand for her to shake.

My left hand.

She shook it, of course. It came off in her hand and I shouted as if I'd been injured and she shrieked in shock and terror and dropped it on the ground.

Mrs. Nye stared at me in horror.

And I liked it.

A lot.

In-between
A Halloween poem

Ray Bradbury

Attics are awful and lovely.
You know what I mean?
Basements are low, dank, and darksome,
Halloween's buried there;
The air of the earth
Simmers slowly, gives rise
To nightmares at midnight,
The size of its shadows is awesome.
And in-between?
The house that we live in,
Sane, boring and plain,
Pictures hang straight on walls,
Here nothing appalls.
The rugs, if they misbehave,
Are twice a year taken out and beaten.
Meals are eaten three times a day
In a room where our dining,
And occasional wining with poker
With loud uncles who laugh
When the Joker is played,

Is all staid, sound and clean.
In-between, where we live, in-between,
A boy could go mad.
So, on sad days in autumn,
He takes his dry soul
Down the hole into dark
Or, pure lark on the fly,
Climbs to attic and sky,
Where the wind leans all year,
And pure fear is the stuff
That roams gardens of snuff-dust
And web, where the spider,
Soft glider of nerves,
Serves a fly for dessert
Then back down to the scene
Where the green salad waits
On dumb dining-room plates,
And nice parents whose talk
Is a chalk-screech on board.
Where the lands of the Lord
Are a Baptist morn chat
That can flatten the mind,
And sift dust in the ear
Year on Year. No wildness. No joy.
No place for a boy.
Attic, *yes*! Basement, *sure*!
There the terror is pure.
There an All Hallows grave
Can save souls that might smother
From calm dad or sweet mother.
Up! Down! That's the scene!
But—in-between?
Oh, my god. *In-between*?
Know what I mean?

GONE

Jack Ketchum

Seven-thirty and nobody at the door. No knock, no doorbell.

What am I? The wicked old witch from Hansel and Gretel.

The jack-o-lantern flickered out into the world from the window ledge, the jointed cardboard skeleton swayed dangling from the transform. Both there by way of invitation, which so far had been ignored. In a wooden salad bowl on the coffee table in front of her bite-sized Milky Ways and Mars Bars and Nestle's Crunch winked at her reassuringly—crinkly gleaming foil-wrap and smooth shiny paper.

Buy candy, and they will come.

Don't worry, she thought. Someone'll show. It's early yet.

But it wasn't.

Not these days. At least that's what she'd gathered from her window on Halloweens previous. By dark it was pretty much over on her block. When she was a kid they'd stayed out till eleven—twelve even. Roamed where they pleased. Nobody was afraid of strangers or razored apples or poisoned candy. Nobody's mother or father lurked in attendance either.

For everybody but the real toddlers, having mom and dad around was ludicrous, unthinkable.

But by today's standards, seven-thirty was late.

Somebody'll come by. Don't worry.

ET was over and NBC was doing a marathon *Third Rock* every half hour from now till ten. What *Third Rock* had to do with Halloween she didn't know. Maybe there was a clue in the Mars Bars. But *Third Rock* was usually okay for a laugh now and then so she padded barefoot to the kitchen and poured herself a second dirty Stoli martini from the shaker in the fridge and lay back on the couch and picked at the olives and tried to settle in.

The waiting made her anxious, though. Thoughts nagged like scolding parents.

Why'd you let yourself in for this, idiot?

You knew it would hurt if they didn't come.

You knew it would hurt if they did.

"You've got a no-win situation here," she said.

She was talking to herself out loud now. Great.

It was a damn good question, though.

Years past, she'd avoided this. Turned off the porch light and the lights in the living room. *Nobody home.* Watched TV in the bedroom.

Maybe she should have done the same tonight.

But for her, holidays were all about children. Thanksgiving and New Year's Eve being the exceptions. Labor Day and the President's days and the rest didn't even count—they weren't *real* holidays. Christmas. *That was Santa.* Easter. *The Easter Bunny.* The Fourth of July. *Firecrackers, sparklers, fireworks in the night sky.* And none was more about kids than Halloween. Halloween was about dress-up and *trick or treat.* And *trick or treat* was children.

She'd shut out children for a very long time now.

She was trying to let them in.

It looked like they weren't buying.

She didn't know whether to be angry, laugh or cry.

She knew it was partly her fault. She'd been such a goddamn mess.

People still talked about it. Talked about *her*. She knew they did. *Was that why her house seemed to have PLAGUE painted on the door? Parents talking to their kids about the lady down the block?* She could still walk by in a supermarket and stop somebody's conversation dead in its tracks. Almost five years later and she *still* got that from time to time.

Five years—shy three months, really, because the afternoon had been in August—over which time the *MISSING* posters gradually came down off the store windows and trees and phone poles, the police had stopped coming round long before, her mother had gone from calling her over twice a day to only once a week—she could be glad of some things, anyhow—and long-suffering Stephen, sick of her sullenness, sick of her brooding, sick of her rages, had finally moved in with his dental assistant, a pretty little strawberry blonde named Shirley who reminded them both of the actress Shirley Jones.

The car was hers, the house was hers.

The house was empty.

Five years since the less than three minutes that changed everything.

All she'd done was forget the newspaper—a simple event, an inconsequential event, everybody did it once in a while—and then go back for it and come out of the 7-Eleven and the car was there with the passenger door open and Alice wasn't. It had occurred with all the impact of a bullet or head-on collision and nearly that fast.

Her three-year-old daughter, gone. Vanished. Not a soul in the lot.

And she, Helen Teal, *nee* Mazik, went from pre-school teacher, homemaker, wife and mother to the three *p*'s—psychoanalysis, Prozac and paralysis.

She took another sip of her martini. Not too much.

Just in case they came.

By nine-twenty-five *Third Rock* was wearing thin and she was considering a fourth and final dirty martini and then putting it to bed.

At nine-thirty a Ford commercial brought her close to tears.

There was this family, two kids in the back and mom and dad in front and they were going somewhere with mom looking at the map and the kids peering over her shoulder and though she always clicked the MUTE button during the commercials and couldn't tell what they were saying they were a happy family and you knew that.

To hell with it, she thought, one more, the goddamn night was practically breaking her heart here, and got up and went to the refrigerator.

She'd set the martini down and was headed for the hall to turn out the porch light, to give up the vigil, the night depressing her, the night a total loss finally, a total waste, when the doorbell rang.

She stepped back.

Teenagers, she thought. *Uh-oh*. They'd probably be the only ones out this late. With teenagers these days you never knew. Teens could be trouble. She turned and went to the window. The jack-o-lantern's jagged carved top was caving slowly down into its body. It gave off a half-cooked musky aroma that pleased her. She felt excited and a little scared. She leaned over the windowsill and looked outside.

On the porch stood a witch in a short black cloak, a werewolf in plaid shirt and jeans, and a bug-eyed alien. All wearing rubber masks. The alien standing in front by the doorbell.

Not teenagers.

Ten or eleven, tops.

Not the little ones she'd been hoping for all night long in their ghost-sheets and ballerina costumes. But kids. *Children.*

And the night's thrill—the *enchantment* even—was suddenly there for her.

She went to the door and opened it and her smile was wide and very real.

"Trick or treat!"

Two boys and a girl. She hadn't been sure of the alien.

"Happy Halloween!" she said.

"Happy Halloween," they chorused back.

The witch was giggling. The werewolf elbowed her in the ribs.

"Ow!" she said and hit him with her black plastic broom.

"Wait right here, kids" she said.

She knew they wouldn't come in. Nobody came in anymore. The days of bobbing for apples were long over.

She wondered where their parents were. Usually there were parents around. She hadn't seen them on the lawn or in the street.

She took the bowl of candy off the coffee table and returned to them standing silent and expectant at the door. She was going to be generous with them, she'd decided that immediately. They were the first kids to show, for one thing. Possibly they'd be the *only* ones to show. But these also weren't kids who came from money. You only had to take one look to see that. Not only were the three of them mostly skin and bones but the costumes were cheap-looking mass-market affairs—the kind you see in generic cardboard packages at Walgreen's. In the werewolf's case, not even a proper costume at all. Just a shirt and jeans and a mask with some fake fur attached.

"Anybody have any preferences, candy-wise?"

They shook their heads. She began digging into the candy and dropping fistfuls into their black plastic shopping bags.

"Are you guys all related?"

Nods.

"Brothers and sister?"

More nods.

The shy type, she guessed. But that was okay. Doing this felt just right. Doing this was fine. She felt a kind of weight lifted off her, sailing away through the clear night sky. If nobody else came by for the rest of the night that was fine too. Next year would be even better.

Somehow she knew that.

"Do you live around here? Do I know you, or your mom and dad maybe?"

"No, ma'am," said the alien.

She waited for more but more evidently wasn't forthcoming.

They really *were* shy.

"Well, I love your costumes," she lied. "*Very* scary. You have a Happy Halloween now, okay?"

"Thank you." A murmured chorus.

She emptied the bowl. Why not? she thought. She had more in the refrigerator just in case. *Lots* more. She smiled and said *Happy Halloween* again and stepped back and was about to close the door when she realized that instead of tumbling down the stairs on their way to the next house the way she figured kids would always do all three of them were still standing there.

Could they possibly want more? She almost laughed. *Little gluttons.*

"You're her, right, ma'am?" said the alien.

"Excuse me?"

"You're her?"

"Who?"

"The lady who lost her baby? The little girl?"

And of course she'd heard it in her head before he even said it, heard it from the first question, knew it could be nothing else. She just needed to hear *him* say it, hear the *way* he said it and determine what was there, mockery or pity or morbid curiosity but his voice held none of that, it was flat and indeterminate as a newly washed chalkboard. Yet she felt as if he'd hit her anyhow, as though they all had. As though the clear blue eyes gazing up at her from behind the masks were not so much awaiting her answer as awaiting an execution.

She turned away a moment and swiped at the tears with the back of her hand and cleared her throat and then turned back to them.

"Yes," she said.

"Thought so," he said. "We're sorry. G'night, ma'am. Happy Halloween."

They turned away and headed slowly down the stairs and she almost asked them to wait, to stay a moment, for what reason and to what end she didn't know but that would be silly and awful too, no reason to put them through her pain, they were just kids, children, they were just asking a question the way children did sometimes, oblivious to its consequences and it would be wrong to say anything further, so she began to close the door and almost didn't hear him turn to his sister and say, *too bad they wouldn't let her out tonight, huh? too bad they never do* in a low voice but loud enough to register but at first it *didn't* register, not quite, as though the words held no meaning, as though the words were some strange rebus she could not immediately master, not until after she'd closed the door and then when finally they impacted her like grapeshot, she flung open the door and ran screaming down the stairs into the empty street.

❋ ❋ ❋

She thought when she was able to think at all of what she might say to the police.

Witch, werewolf, alien. Of this age and that height and weight.

Out of nowhere, vanished back into nowhere.

Carrying along what was left of her.

Gone.

That Smell In the Air

Alan M. Clark

Some of my earliest experiences producing creepy art were in grade school during the Halloween season. I think of Halloween as a season which begins as soon as fall is in the air and ends when the leaves are gone from the trees, or after October 31st. At Glendale Elementary School in Nashville Tennessee, we were allowed to decorate our classroom for Halloween, creating our own spooky images and sticking them up on the walls with that sticky white gum that was used instead of thumbtacks so there wouldn't be any holes left in the walls. I loved it. I was good at drawing and painting and so was depended on to create some cool, creepy stuff.

Just the color combination of orange and black can bring it all back to me. The season started with the days getting noticeably shorter, and cooler weather coming on, bringing relief from the sweltering heat and humidity of the long Tennessee summer. Then the leaves started to change and there was that smell in the air. All over town Halloween icons were dragged out of basements and attics; skeletons, witches, spider webs, etc.... These icons, made mostly of paper, plastic, and paper maché, were dusted off and set about or hung in windows, often haphazardly, adding to their grotesqueness. Pumpkins were carved into jack-o-lanterns. Pumpkin seeds were roasted. Apple cider was spiced. Ghost stories were told in the evenings outdoors as piles of leaves were burned.

Every bit of this added to the anticipation, which built every day until Halloween night, when I would be allowed to run with other kids like a demon through our neighborhoods pumped up on all that sugar, knowing we'd be going door to door, receiving candy from the friendly folks, I thought I knew who those folks were, or be run off the porches of those who had no tolerance for Halloween or children, I also thought I knew who those were too, but you never *really* knew. Truth is I had no idea what I'd find out there in the night, but I was trusted to take care of myself and get myself out of whatever trouble I got into. Most of the trick-or-treaters I knew never had any intention of doing any tricking if they didn't receive a treat, but you didn't tell folks that when you were standing on their stoop with your hand out. And, of course, on this night of nights there was also more potential for supernatural happenings than any other night of the year.

I have to credit my father, William Clark, with some of my enthusiasm for Halloween. He had an appreciation for the dark and disturbing, and somehow managed to pass this on to me at a very early age. God knows I resisted, but he was my father, and one should always love and respect one's father. Although he was a physician, he also considered himself an artist. His paintings, drawings and sculptures had always been exhibited in our home. He was quite an art lover.

With obvious glee he introduced me to the works of such cartoonists as Charles Adams, illustrators such as Edward Gorey, and he took me to see exhibits of the works of the Surrealists. His enthusiasm for dark material didn't end with two-dimensional work. He loved Tom Lehrer's disturbingly droll *Irish Ballad* about the maiden who murdered her entire family, each by a different, horrible method, but when confronted by the police could not deny the acts because she knew that lying was a sin. My father also had a fondness for Hitchcock films.

I was fortunate to have a father who enjoyed reading to his children. When I was still small enough to do so, he'd sit me on his knee and read from *Struwwelpeter* and we would look at the dreadful illustrations together and laugh. He read me dark poems, like James Whitcomb Riley's "Little Orphant Annie," and selections from such macabre collections as *Ruthless Rhymes for Heartless Homes.* He loved a good bit of black humor most of all.

My Father's father, Doctor Sam L. Clark, while head of Anatomy at Vanderbilt University back in the thirties, had employed a body snatcher to insure that the medical school had enough cadavers. He too had a dark sense of humor, doctors are funny that way, and apparently had had a similar influence on his son. I'm sure my father resisted, as I had, but my grandfather won out in the end.

Anyway, back to grade school and decorating the classroom for Halloween: I was in my element, drawing haunted houses, ghosts, cemeteries, black cats, with that particular arch to their backs that was a little difficult to perfect at first, and of course monsters.

I have always considered myself an artist, but I wasn't exactly aware of this until I was an adult and found the little blue book in which my parents had kept funny quotes from their children, at least *they* thought were funny. In it I found that when told by my kindergarten teacher that I had done a good drawing, I had responded, matter-of-factly, "Yes, I know. I'm going to be an artist." Perhaps this was because my father considered himself an artist, and I wanted to be like him.

One day, after school, when I hadn't gotten quite enough from drawing and painting monsters on paper, I looked in the mirror and something strange happened. It was like the moon was full and I was about to undergo a metamorphosis, something very much like what happened to my favorite monster, the Wolfman.

I began to paint on myself. I decided I could use oil pastels as face paint to make myself up for Halloween. My parents had given me the oil pastels for my birthday. They were oil paint pigments, some of them probably poisonous and absorbable through the skin, in the form of crayons with a minimum of oil in them so they were nice and hard and pretty good to draw with. I had to warm them up, holding them in my hand for a long time, before I could use them to draw on my skin.

The first time I tried this, the metamorphosis was indeed similar to what happened to the Wolfman. I drew fur all over my face and hands and up my arms to just under my sleeves. I gave myself a dark, wrinkled-up, growling snout and black circles around my eyes. I knew just how to make myself look really scary because I had seen the Wolfman, as well as many other popular monsters of the day, many times in *Famous Monsters* magazine and on *The Big Show*, an afternoon television program which showed mostly old black and white horror films. In the sixties monsters were everywhere, and I couldn't get enough of them.

One Halloween my father helped me become the Mummy. I used the poisonous oil pastels to make my face all cracked and wrinkled and he wrapped me in bandages from head to toe. Then we rubbed the bandages down with ashes from the fireplace to make them old and dirty. That night, as I went door to door asking for candy, my bandages slowly became more and more unraveled. That was okay, isn't that what happened to the Mummy?

I became many different monsters over the years, but I always seemed to cycle back to the Wolfman. After a while just that one day a year, Halloween, wasn't enough. I'd feel the change coming over me and then find myself sporting a heavy coat of paint on an odd evening even in the middle of the week in say...March, and then struggling to remove the stuff before school the next day. I'd use a whole jar of Ponds cold cream. My mother would have to make sure to keep a supply just for me. Even with the cold cream and several vigorous washings with soap and water, there would still be a residue of the oil pastels left on my skin. It wasn't meant to come off. Hell, it wasn't supposed to be used as make-up. I had the most colorful blackheads of any kid in school. It was only slightly embarrassing to explain why.

I never did get enough of painting and drawing Halloween images. Although I do a variety of freelance illustration work now, with subjects ranging from science fiction, mystery, young adult, and fantasy, to biology, even molecular biology, I have found, and I think publishers have found, that I am most adept at creating creepy subject matter. Because of this the majority of my work is in the Horror genre.

Now, for me, it's Halloween all year long. Even so, when fall comes and there's that smell in the air, something comes over me and I'm afraid that one day my wife might come home from work to find the Wolfman fixing her dinner.

I think I still have some of those oil pastels in an old cigar box out in the garage. They're probably pretty dried out and would take a long time to warm up in my hands.

Let's see, it's just now four o'clock, Melody gets home at 6:30, and of course, I'll have to start the spaghetti soon....

Yesterday's Witch

Gahan Wilson

Her house is gone now. Someone tore it down and bulldozed away her trees and set up an ugly apartment building made of cheap bricks and cracking concrete on the flattened place they'd built. I drove by there a few nights ago; I'd come back to town for the first time in years to give a lecture at the university, and I saw blue TV flickers glowing in the building's living rooms.

Her house sat on a small rise, I remember, with a wide stretch of scraggly lawn between it and the ironwork fence, which walled off her property from the sidewalk and the rest of the outside world. The windows of her house peered down at you through a thick tangle of oak tree branches, and I can remember walking by and knowing she was peering out at me, and hunching up my shoulders because I couldn't help it, but never, ever, giving her the satisfaction of seeing me hurry because of fear.

To the adults, she was Miss Marble, but we children knew better. We knew she had another name, though none of us knew just what it was, and we knew she was a witch. I don't know who it was told me first about Miss Marble's being a witch; it might have been Billy Drew. I think it was, but I had already guessed in spite of being less than six. I grew up, all of us grew up, sure and certain of Miss Marble's being a witch.

You never managed to get a clear view of Miss Marble, or I don't remember doing so, except that once. You just got peeks and hints. A quick glimpse of her wide, short body as she scuttled up the front porch steps; a brief hint of her brown-wrapped form behind a thick clump of bushes by the garage where, it was said, an electric runabout sat rusting away; a sudden flash of her fantastically wrinkled face in the narrowing slot of a closing door, and that was all.

Fred Pulley claimed he had gotten a good long look at her one afternoon. She had been weeding, or something, absorbed at digging in the ground, and off guard and careless even though she stood a mere few feet from the fence. Fred had fought down his impulse to keep on going by, and he had stood and studied her for as much as two or three minutes before she looked up and saw him and snarled and turned away.

We never tired of asking Fred about what he had seen.

"Her teeth, Fred," one of us would whisper—you almost always talked about Miss Marble in whispers—"did you see her *teeth*?"

"They're long and yellow," Fred would say. "And they come to points at the ends. And I think I saw blood on them."

None of us really believed Fred had seen Miss Marble, understand, and we certainly didn't believe that part about the blood, but we were so very curious about her, and when you're really curious about something, especially if you're a bunch of kids, you want to get all the information on the subject even if you're sure it's lies.

So we didn't believe what Fred Pulley said about Miss Marble's having blood on her teeth, nor about the bones he'd seen her pulling out of the ground, but we remembered it all the same, just in case, and it entered into any calculations we made about Miss Marble.

Halloween was the time she figured most prominently in our thoughts. First because she was a witch, of course, and second because of a time-honored ritual among the neighborhood children concerning her and ourselves and that evening of the year. It was a kind of test by fire that every male child had to go through when he reached the age of thirteen, or be shamed forever after. I have no idea when it originated; I only know that when I attained my thirteenth year and was thereby qualified and doomed for the ordeal, the rite was established beyond question.

I can remember putting on my costume for that memorable Halloween, an old Prince Albert coat and a papier-mache mask which bore a satisfying likeness to a decayed cadaver, with the feeling I was girding myself for a great battle. I studied my reflection in a mirror affixed by swivels to my bedroom bureau and wondered gravely if I would be able to meet the challenge this night would bring. Unsure, but determined, I picked up my brown paper shopping bag, which was very large so as to accommodate as much candy as possible, said goodbye to my mother and father and dog, and went out. I had not gone a block before I met George Watson and Billy Drew.

"Have you got anything yet?" asked Billy.

"No." I indicated the emptiness of my bag. "I just started."

"The same with us," said George. And then he looked at me carefully. "Are you ready?"

"Yes," I said, realizing I had not been ready until that very moment, and feeling an encouraging glow at knowing I was. "I can do it all right."

Mary Taylor and her little sister Betty came up, and so did Eddy Baker and Phil Myers and the Arthur brothers. I couldn't see where they all had come from, but it seemed as if every kid in the neighborhood was suddenly there, crowding around under the streetlamp, costumes flapping in the wind, holding bags and boxes and staring at me with glistening, curious eyes.

"Do you want to do it now," asked George, "or do you want to wait?"

George had done it the year before and he had waited.

"I'll do it now," I said.

I began walking along the sidewalk, the others following after me. We crossed Garfield Street and Peabody Street and that brought us to Baline Avenue where we turned left. I could see Miss Marble's iron fence half a block ahead, but I was careful not to slow my pace. When we arrived at the fence I walked to the gate with as firm a tread as I could muster and put my hand upon its latch. The metal was cold and made me think of coffin handles and graveyard diggers' picks. I pushed it down and the gate swung open with a low, rusty groaning.

Now it was up to me alone. I was face to face with the ordeal. The basic terms of it were simple enough: walk down the crumbling path which led through the tall, dry grass to Miss Marble's porch, cross the porch, ring Miss Marble's bell, and escape. I had seen George Watson do it last year and I had seen other brave souls do it before him. I knew it was not an impossible task.

It was a chilly night with a strong, persistent wind and clouds scudding overhead. The moon was three-fourths full and it looked remarkably round and solid in the sky. I became suddenly aware, for the first time in my life, that it was a real *thing* up there. I wondered how many Halloweens it had looked down on and what it had seen.

I pulled the lapels of my Price Albert coat close about me and started walking down Miss Marble's path. I walked because all the others had run or skulked, and I was resolved to bring new dignity to the test if I possibly could.

From afar the house looked bleak and abandoned, a thing of cold blues and grays and greens, but as I drew nearer, a peculiar phenomenon began to assert itself. The windows, which from the sidewalk had seemed only to reflect the moon's glisten, now began to take on a warmer glow; the walls and porch, which had seemed all shriveled, peeling paint, and leprous patches of rotting wood, now began to appear well kept. I swallowed and strained my eyes. I had been prepared for a growing feeling of menace, for ever darker shadows, and this increasing evidence of warmth and tidiness absolutely baffled me.

By the time I reached the porch steps the place had taken on a positively cozy feel. I now saw that the building was in excellent repair and that it was well painted with a smooth coat of reassuring cream. The light from the windows was now unmistakably cheerful, a ruddy, friendly pumpkin kind of orange suggesting crackling fireplaces all set and ready for toasting marshmallows. There was a very unwitchlike clump of Indian corn fixed to the front door, and I was almost certain I detected an odor of sugar and cinnamon wafting into the cold night air.

I stepped onto the porch, gaping. I had anticipated many awful possibilities during this past year. Never far from my mind had been the horrible pet Miss Marble was said to own, a something-or-other, which was all claws and scales and flew on wings with transparent webbing. Perhaps, I had thought this thing would swoop down from the bare oak limbs and carry me off while my friends on the sidewalk screamed and screamed. Again, I had not dismissed the notion Miss Marble might turn me into a frog with a little motion of her fingers and then step on me with her foot and squish me.

But here I was feeling foolish, very young, crossing this friendly porch and smelling—I was sure of it now—sugar and cinnamon and cider, and, what's more, butterscotch on top of that. I raised my hand to ring the bell and was astonished at myself for not being the least bit afraid when the door softly opened and there stood Miss Marble herself.

I looked at her and she smiled at me. She was short and plump, and she wore an apron with a thick ruffle all along its edges, and her face was smooth and red and shiny as an autumn apple. She wore bifocals on the tip of her tiny nose and she had her white hair fixed in a perfectly round bun in the exact center of the top of her head. Delicious odors wafted round her through the open door and I peered greedily past her.

"Well," she said in a mild, old voice, "I am so glad that someone has at last come to have a treat. I've waited so many years, and each year I've been ready, but nobody's come."

She stood to one side and I could see a table in the hall piled with candy and nuts and bowls of fruit and platesful of pies and muffins and cakes, all of it shining and glittering in the warm, golden glow which seemed everywhere. I heard Miss Marble chuckle warmly.

"Why don't you call your friends in? I'm sure there will be plenty for all."

I turned and looked down the path and saw them, huddled in the moonlight by the gate, hunched wide-eyed over their boxes and bags. I felt a sort of generous pity for them. I walked to the steps and waved.

"Come on! It's all right!"

They would not budge.

"May I show them something?"

She nodded yes and I went into the house and got an enormous orange-frosted cake with numbers of golden sugar pumpkins on its sides.

"Look," I cried, lifting the cake into the moonlight, "look at this! And she's got lots more! She always had, but we never asked for it!"

George was the first through the gate, as I knew he would be. Billy came next, and then Eddy, then the rest. They came slowly, at first, timid as mice, but then the smells of chocolate and tangerines and brown sugar got to their noses and they came faster. By the time they had arrived at the porch they had lost their fear, the same as I, but their astonished faces showed me how I must have looked to Miss Marble when she'd opened the door.

"Come in, children. I'm so glad you've all come at last!"

None of us had ever seen such candy or dared to dream of such cookies and cakes. We circled the table in the hall, awed by its contents, clutching at our bags.

"Take all you want, children. It's all for you."

Little Betty was the first to reach out. She got a gumdrop as big as a plum and was about to pop it into her mouth when Miss Marble said:

"Oh, no, dear, don't eat it now. That's not the way you do with tricks or treats. You wait till you get out on the sidewalk and then you go ahead and gobble it up. Just put it in your bag for now, sweetie."

Betty was not all that pleased with the idea of putting off eating her gumdrop, but she did as Miss Marble asked and plopped it into her bag and quickly followed it with other items such as licorice cats and apples dipped in caramel and pecans lumped together with some lovely-looking brown stuff, and soon all the other children, myself very much included, were doing the same, filling our bags industriously, giving the task of clearing the table as rapidly as possible our entire attention.

Soon, amazingly soon, we had done it. True, there was the occasional peanut, now and then a largish crumb survived, but by and large, the job was done. What was left was fit only for rats and roaches, I thought, and then was puzzled by the thought. Where had such an unpleasant thought come from?

How our bags bulged! How they strained to hold what we had stuffed into them! How wonderfully heavy they were to hold!

Miss Marble was at the door now, holding it open and smiling at us.

"You must come back next year, sweeties, and I will give you more of the same."

We trooped out, some of us giving the table one last glance just to make sure, and then we headed down the path, Miss Marble waving us goodbye. The long, dead grass at the sides of the path brushed stiffly against our bags, making strange hissing sounds. I felt as cold as if I had been standing in the chill night air all along, and not comforted by the cozy warmth inside Miss Marble's house. The moon was higher now and seemed—I didn't know how or why—to be mocking us.

I heard Mary Taylor scolding her little sister: "She said not to eat any till we got to the sidewalk!"

"I don't care. I want some!"

The wind had gotten stronger and I could hear the stiff tree branches growl high over our heads. The fence seemed far away and I wondered why it was taking us so long to get to it. I looked back at the house and my mouth went dry when I saw that it was gray and old and dark, once more, and that the only light from its windows was reflections of the pale moon.

Suddenly little Betty Taylor began to cry, first in small, choking sobs, and then in loud wails. George Watson said: "What's wrong?" and then there was a pause, and then George cursed and threw Betty's bag over the lawn toward the house and his own box after it. They landed with a queer rustling slither that made the small hairs on the back of my neck stand up. I let go of my own bag and it flopped, bulging, into the grass by my feet. It looked like a huge, pale toad with a gaping, grinning mouth.

One by one the others rid themselves of what they carried. Some of the younger ones, whimpering, would not let go, but the older children gently separated them from the things they clutched.

I opened the gate and held it while the rest filed out onto the sidewalk. I followed them and closed the gate firmly. We stood and looked into the darkness beyond the fence. Here and there one of our abandoned boxes or bags seemed to glimmer faintly, some of them moved—I'll swear it—though others claimed it was just an illusion produced by the waving grass. All of us heard the high, thin laughing of the witch.

A Short History of Halloween

Paula Guran

The farther we've gotten from the magic and mystery of our past, the more we've come to need Halloween. It's a festival of fantasy, a celebration of otherness, the one time each year when the mundane is overturned in favor of the bizarre, and anyone can become anyone or anything they wish. At its core, Halloween is a chance to confront our most primal fear—death—and attempt to control it or, at the very least, mock it. Ancient beliefs, religious meanings, a multitude of ethnic heritages, diverse occult traditions, and the continual influence of popular culture have combined to make Halloween a booming commercial industry as well as a beloved holiday.

Fed by phantasm and frivolity, Halloween nowadays generates a seriously spooktacular cash flow. How big has Halloween become? In the United States, only Christmas is bigger in terms of retail dollars spent. According to a 1999 survey by the International Mass Retail Association, 82% of all Americans purchase candy, costumes, decorations, and other items for Halloween. In 1999, adults age 35-44 spent about $50 on average; those age 18-24 spent $42 on average; and adults age 25-34 spent $41 on average. A yearly estimate of $5 billion in Halloween sales doesn't even include income generated by local haunted attractions or the larger commercial endeavors like those staged at Universal Studios, Disney World, and Disneyland and other regional theme parks. Nor does the total take other purchases into account: leotards, fabric or other costume-making supplies; food and liquor sales for entertaining; florist shop merchandise, balloons (at least 18% of seasonal balloon sales come at Halloween), lingerie and magic shop sales. It's also thought up to 75% of all sales in second-hand and retro clothing shops may be Halloween-related.

The essentially American holiday is now spreading to other countries. Canadians already celebrate with their neighbors to the south. England, Australia, and Japan are adopting American Halloween activities. In France, Yankee Halloween customs have become very popular in the last decade. Some French revelers point out, however, a conviction that Halloween is really Gallic in origin anyway and that America is just a jack-o-lantern come lately. Since France's ancestral Gauls were a Celtic tribe—and the largest and wealthiest at that—and Halloween's beginnings are probably Celtic...well, they have a point.

Festivals emphasizing the supernatural and death are common in almost all cultures. Modern Halloween is, at least, influenced by and probably originated with the ancient Celtic festival of Samhain. About 500-1,000 BC, the Celts—who at the time populated Ireland, Scotland, Wales, England, Brittany, and northern France—celebrated the first day of winter as their New Year. Winter began, in the climate of Northern Europe, in November. The end of summer marked radical change in the daily life of this pastoral people. The herds were brought down from the summer pastures in the hills, the best animals put to shelter, and the rest slaughtered. For the Celts, the period we now consider the end of October and start of November was a time of preparation, festival, and plenty before the coming of the long winter. As agriculture became a part of their lives, harvest time also became part of the seasonal activity. The communal celebration became known as "Samhain" (there are a number of variant spellings, including Samfuin, Samhuinn, Samain). Linguistically, the word evidently simply combines the Gaelic words "sam" for "end" and "fuin" for "summer"—End of Summer. Samhain may have just been one night—October 31—or it may have stretched out over three days—October 31, November 1, and November 2.

Although the bounty of nature and the natural change of seasons were important aspects of Samhain, it was also a festival of the supernatural. Samhain was the turning point of the year for a people who believed that even minor "turning points"—the change from one day to the next, the meeting of sea and shore—were magical. The turning of the year was the most powerful and sacred of such junctures. The worlds of the living and of the dead were very close to one another at Samhain, the veil between the two at its thinnest. The living could communicate with those who had gone beyond; the dead could visit the living. In Celtic times, the dead were not considered evil or particularly dreaded so much as consulted and honored as ancestral spirits and guardians of the wisdom of the tribe. Celtic priests, the Druids, contacted the dead in order to divine the future and make predictions for the community.

[In Halloween lore of the last two centuries or so, references are made to "Samhain" as a deity or Celtic "Lord of the Dead." There is no evidence for such a god. The fallacy seems to have arisen in the 1770s before improved translation of Celtic literary work and modern archeology. It can be traced to the writings of a Col. Charles Vallency (who, for some reason, was trying to prove that the Irish originally came from Armenia) and then was later perpetuated by Lady Jane Francesca Wilde (Oscar's mum) in her mid-nineteenth century book *Irish Cures, Mystic Charms and Superstitions*. It has gone on to be unquestioningly and inaccurately repeated in many sources over the years.]

Although possibly later developed as post-Christian mythology, the Celts may have believed in faeries or similar magical creatures. They did not believe in demons or devils, but they may well have had these not-so-nice entities to deal with. Resentful of humans taking over the world, the faerie-folk were often thought to be hostile and dangerous. During the magical time of Samhain the faeries were even more powerful than usual. Humans might be lured astray by faeries. These unfortunates would then be lost in the fairy mounds and trapped forever.

Faeries or their kind weren't the only ones causing mischief. The yearly turning point was also seen as a suspension of ordinary space and time. For order and structure to be maintained for the rest of the year, chaos would reign during Samhain. Humans indulged in cross-gender dressing, tricks, and highjinks. On the practical side, such behavior was an outlet for high spirits before the confining winter came.

We know very little of Druidic religious rituals, but we do know Samhain was one of four "Fire Festivals" of the Celts. Hearth fires were extinguished to symbolize the coming "dark half" of the year, then re-lit from Druidic fires to signify the return and continuance of life. Bonfires were also part of this observance.

Halloween can't really be considered a *direct* outgrowth of ancient Celtic practices. Other cultural elements—including various harvest festivals—eventually became part of Halloween custom. Over the centuries traditions have been both correctly and incorrectly attributed to the Celts. Sometimes this has been done with an appreciation of the ancient ways.

But, more often, cultural-centrism and historic revisionism so colored thinking that the past was unfairly interpreted. Early Christian missionaries intentionally identified contact with the supernatural as experiences originating with the Devil and inherently evil. The Druids, since they adhered to "false gods" were, therefore, worshippers of Satan. Later religious prejudice also lumped pagans in Satan worship and the resulting misinformation has been further propitiated. (For that matter, as we shall see, animosity between Catholics and Protestants resulted in the alteration of some Halloween lore.)

As with other pre-Christian practices, Samhain was eventually absorbed by the Church. In AD 609 or 610, May 13 was designated as a day to honor the Virgin Mary and the martyred saints. In the eighth century, Pope Gregory III (731-741) then fixed November 1 as the anniversary for all saints (including the martyrs). October 31 became All Hallows' Eve [Hallowmas or Halloween], the evening before All Hallows Day [All Saints Day] on November 1. (The word "hallow" was used in the Middle ages as a synonym for "saint.") Gregory IV (827-844) extended the celebration of All Hallows Day to the entire Church.

The old beliefs did not die out so easily and just honoring saints was not enough to replace the notion of a time of year when the dead could travel the earth. A more abstract holiday (on November 2) commemorating *all* the faithful departed began to be marked as early as the ninth century, although Odilo, Abbot of Cluny (d. 1048) actually instituted the date. By the end of the thirteenth century, it was accepted by the entire Church.

Not only did the Church give the holiday its popular name, it also sanctified the custom of remembering the dead on the eve on November 1. Other pagan traditions and religious practices were adapted by the Church and readapted by the people. "Soul cakes" were baked and given to the town's poor in exchange for their prayers for the dead. Eventually young men and boys went "souling" from house to house, singing and asking for food, ale and money rather than cakes. The church encouraged parishioners to dress as saints, angels and devils as part of All Saints Day. Spirits of the dead and the supernatural, now associated with evil and the devil, became something to fear. Gifts of food and drink once meant to welcome the dead were now offered to keep them away. Bonfires were now lit to frighten the devil.

On October 31, 1517 Martin Luther, intending to stir debate, posted his Ninety-five Theses on the door of the Wittenberg Castle Church. (An occasion still marked in Lutheran churches on Reformation Sunday.) The religious reformation he sparked eventually did away with the celebration of Halloween for many Europeans. Reformation Protestants did away with the observance of saints' days and without the "hallows" one can not have All Hallows' Eve.

The English, however, managed to preserve some of the secular traditions of the holiday with Guy Fawkes Day. (In 1605 a group of English Roman Catholics conspired to blow up Parliament, King James I, and his heir on November 5. They evidently hoped that in the confusion following, the English Catholics could take over the country. What came to be known as the Gunpowder Plot was foiled and in January 1606 Parliament established November 5 as a day of public thanksgiving. The day became known as Guy Fawkes Day for a conspirator who was arrested and, under torture, revealed the names of the other plotters.) Guy Fawkes Day borrowed a great many of the traditions used to mark Halloween that had fallen just six days before. Bonfires, pranks, begging, and dressing in costume became part of the occasion. In some parts of England, the festivities were virulently anti-Catholic.

In the seventeenth century, immigrants brought a variety of traditions, beliefs, customs, and superstitions to what would later become the United States of America. The Puritan influence in New England left little room for any form of Halloween. Guy Fawkes Day (and its attendant anti-Catholicism), however, was celebrated until the Revolution. The Puritans also brought their fear of witchcraft and a history of persecuting witches to the colonies. Anglican settlers in Virginia brought not only commemoration of saints days, but a typically seventeenth century English belief in the occult. Many Germans who settled in the tolerant Quaker-run state of Pennsylvania had pronounced supernatural beliefs and mystical ideas. Catholics in Maryland and other colonies retained their Halloween-connected religious traditions. Spanish Catholic influence was felt in Florida. African slaves imported a belief in an active spirit world into the southern colonies.

Post-revolutionary America saw the popularization of harvest "play parties." These community get-togethers were non-religious and—unlike similar task-oriented fall convenings for sorghum-making, corn husking, apple picking and paring, and the like—were just for fun. The early autumn parties often featured fortune-telling games played with apples and nuts (both seasonally plentiful) and the telling of spooky tales. A tradition of mischief-making on the night of October 31 was common in some communities as well.

Almost 7.4 million new immigrants from all over the world came to the United States between 1820 and 1870 and each nationality brought its own traditions and customs. In the early nineteenth century, Cubans and Haitians fleeing unrest in the Caribbean strengthened the Voudoun culture in the South and mixed new mythologies of the dead, witchcraft, and divination into the Halloween cauldron. Spanish and Mexican Catholic traditions of the Day of the Dead were strong in the Southwest. But the Irish had the greatest influence by far on the overall celebration of

American Halloween. (From 1825 to 1845, Irish famines drove 700,000 Irish Catholics to the U.S. Another 300,000 entered between 1847 and 1854.)

In County Cork, All Hallows was marked with a mummers' procession of young men claiming to be followers of "Muck Olla" (a boar from Irish folk tales). Led by Lair Bhain (white mare) who wore a horse's head and white robes, the group went from house to house noisily beseeching householders to impart food, drink, or money in return for a promise of prosperity in the coming year. Similar masquerades were popular in other Irish locales.

Young Irish women and girls marked the night with various methods of telling the future. The divinations most commonly foretold the identity of future spouses or one's destiny in love.

Irish villagers had used carved-out turnips and occasionally beets—abundant in late autumn—to make cheap lanterns with which to light their way as the evenings darkened toward winter. (The term "jack-o-lantern" first appeared in print in 1750. It referred to a night watchman or a man carrying a lantern.) Some say these vegetable lights were carved or painted with scary faces to frighten the spirits away on Halloween. In the U.S. the pumpkin took the place of the turnip.

By the 1880s upper and middle class Victorian Americans thought of Halloween as a quaint holiday brought to America by genteel English. This seems to have been the result of the popular fiction and articles in children's and ladies' periodicals of the day. They downplayed Irish Catholic connections and provided social tips on entertaining. Although they also downplayed death and magic, they reveled in divination—especially that involving romance. Parlor games (such as bobbing for apples, jumping over candle sticks and the like) and Halloween parties were intended for Victorian adults, not children. Halloween was seen as an occasion for matchmaking more than fright. Ghost stories in the ladies' magazines became less involved with ghosts and more inclined to be tales of love with mildly Gothic trappings.

By the beginning of the twentieth century, middle class Halloween became more of a children's holiday full of harmless amusements. Parties, scavenger hunts and other games became the focus. Scary and eerie elements were sanitized into safe, folkloric fun.

Among the lower classes, however, Halloween remained a night of rough mischief. It became an increasingly destructive way for poor city dwellers to vent their frustrations. By the 1920s vandalism was no longer confined to tipping over outhouses and soaping windows. Severe property damage, fires, and cruelty to animals and people became all too common. Local civic groups mobilized to deal with the "Halloween problem." Various charitable and community activities—raking leaves, neighborhood clean-ups, property improvements—were organized with young participants treated to parties as a reward. Children were encouraged to go door to door and receive treats instead of making trouble. By the 1930s these "beggar's nights" were practiced all over the country. The "trick-or-treat" greeting first appeared in print in 1939.

But vandalism and destruction—particularly in crowded urban areas like Detroit, Chicago, New York—continued to grow throughout the 30s. Halloween was already endangered in some areas when World War II made such activities even more seriously frowned upon. The Chicago City Council banned Halloween for the duration of the war, substituting "Conservation Day" in its stead. Single-minded community intolerance of wasteful destruction and vigilance curtailed vandalism in other communities. Although some communities did away with officially sanctioning Halloween, most saw the holiday as an opportunity for morale-building. Even though some festivities were altered due to war shortages, substitutions and innovation made for wartime Halloween celebrating.

After the war, civic leaders continued their campaigns for "safe and sane" Halloween activities. Halloween became, more and more during the 40s and 50s, a holiday for children to enjoy rather than one for pranksters. In the 50s, the impetus moved back to school and family activities. Trick-or-treating became a nationwide custom. Its implied threat became less and less a reality in most communities; in others the "tricks" were relegated to a Mischief Night and the "treats" to Halloween itself.

By the 1960s, when most Americans were no longer particularly frightened by supernatural entities, a new element arose: the fear of sadistic or deranged adults intent on harming children. These "urban legends" were originally given impetus by incidents with some truth, but no real malicious intent. In the mid-sixties, the fear was of poisoned candy. In 1967 the focus became the threat of razors and sharp objects hidden in apples (and later candy). In 1973-74, completely unfounded rumors of Satanic cults plotting to kidnap and sacrifice children on Halloween arose. These new legends altered Halloween celebrations. Trick-or-treat was banned entirely in some areas; safety factors and "safe" festivities were stressed.

Some conservative fundamentalist Christian groups also began to come out against celebrating Halloween in the 70s. Ironically, many churches had, in the 30s, 50s and 60s, sponsored "wholesome" community Halloween activities. Some of the anti-Halloween propaganda from these groups also tended toward anti-Catholicism. In the 90s some public schools reacted to parental concerns about Halloween—sometimes linked to promoting violence and violent images—by substituting "Harvest Festivals" for Halloween celebrations.

In some parts of the world, All Saints' Day and All Souls' Day are still important days of religious observance and in the U.S. there is still something of a Christian religious aspect to the holiday as marked by Roman Catholics, Anglicans, and Episcopalians. Modern Wiccans and other neopagans consider Samhain a major holiday. But Halloween as we now know it is a secular holiday with no religious significance for most. One organization, The Halloween Association, even promotes the change of the celebration of Halloween to the last Saturday in October, citing practical, safety, and merchandising advantages.

In many ways, modern Halloween has actually become two separate celebrations. One is child-oriented and evolves around masquerade, parties, family-oriented events (hayrides, not-very-scary haunted houses, and pumpkin patches), and trick-or-treating—even if the latter is sometimes restricted, adult-controlled, and made entirely "safe." At the same time, many of the negative myths that arose in the previous three decades were, by the end of the 90s, beginning to be debunked by the media.

Halloween marketing began to shift toward adults in the 70s. By 1980, a quarter of adults aged 18 to 40 wore costumes; by 1986, it was around 60%. Halloween is now the third biggest "party day" (after New Year's and Super Bowl Sunday) of the year. Adults celebrate it not only at home, but in the work environment and retail and entertainment outlets.

Haunted attractions—from local charity-run haunted locations to more extravagant for-profit attractions and even major commercial theme parks—now number in the thousands. Although some cater to youngsters, most are aimed at scaring teens and young adults. There are now "virtual haunted houses" online and hundreds of Web sites—ranging from mild to intense. Many homes are decorated with Halloween lights and displays.

You'll also now find educational events with a Halloween theme—

parks, zoos, museums, and nature study facilities educating both adults and children about traditionally scary creatures likes owls, spiders, snakes and bats; ghost-tours related to historic locations and events; some older cemeteries even use Halloween as an excuse to nurture an appreciation of history. "Trick or Treat for UNICEF" is no longer the only charitable event using Halloween for a good cause. There are blood drives with vampires, programs to collect used costumes to allow homeless and disadvantaged children to dress up for the holiday, balls to raise funds for AIDS research, and more.

Fall celebrations of life and death are common in most cultures. The way modern folks relate to the dead, the supernatural, their fears, and their futures has changed. For Americans, Halloween has manifested itself as an important—if still unofficial—holiday. We are just now beginning to seriously investigate its history and antecedents even as we adapt it to an ever-changing society and devise new traditions and customs with which to celebrate. What we do at Halloween—and what it does for us—varies from individual to individual and group to group depending on our beliefs, backgrounds, sexual orientation, even employment.

There are certain rites of passage associated with Halloween as well. As we progress through different stages in life, we relate to Halloween in different ways. The day comes when we are "too old" for trick-or-treat, but that may mean we are ready for more adult activities. Like the Victorians, young and single adults often mix the modern equivalent of "matchmaking" with Halloween celebration. As we become parents ourselves, we pass on traditions, give out the treats, and make the costumes: we become responsible for supplying some of the magic ourselves. At the same time, we discover we still have a need to be, for just one night, something other than what we usually are. Instead of becoming gatekeepers for a new generation, some adults extend the fantasy of Halloween far past the perimeters of age.

Whatever its history, Halloween is anything but a dead tradition. It is, perhaps, more alive and more meaningful now than ever before.

The Last Halloween

Poppy Z. Brite

From the earliest Halloween I can remember (two or three years old, dressed as the Cat in the Hat, trick-or-treating in our New Orleans apartment complex with my mother pulling my giant wagonload of candy behind me) to the year I was ten, Halloween was the greatest and most magical holiday of all. If you're reading this book, odds are you've also read Ray Bradbury's *The Halloween Tree*, and I certainly can't top his descriptions so I won't even try—but that's how it was. Dark mystery and the smell of singeing pumpkinflesh. Swirling dry leaves maybe swept along in the wake of passing ghosts. The feeling that, on this one night, absolutely anything could happen.

As I say, I was ten. My mother and I had moved to North Carolina by this time, so the air had the snap and tang that Halloween air ought to have. Earlier in the week, I'd won a prize for "Ugliest Jack O'Lantern" at a pumpkin-carving contest by adding green candlewax warts to my jack's leering face, so I was riding especially high on the Halloween season.

My friend Terry and I had long since booked each other for trick-or-treating. This was the first year either of us had been allowed to go without a trailing parent. I dressed as a devil, with a red leotard, red tights that didn't quite match the leotard, plastic horns, a yarn-and-construction paper tail I'd fashioned for myself, and one of those little pitchforks they throw from Mardi Gras floats, maybe two feet long. Terry, who was beginning to pull ahead of me in the coolness department and already had feathered hair, dressed as Farrah Fawcett-Major's character Jill from *Charlie's Angels*. We thought we were a pretty clever combo, an angel and a devil. This could be heaven or this could be hell.

We were about halfway through the neighborhood when we crossed a yard containing a large weeping willow tree. As we passed beneath the canopy of the tree branches, two big boys stepped out of the darkness. They were at least twelve or thirteen, and were wearing hooded sweatshirts instead of costumes. One of them showed us a handful of Black Cat firecrackers and a book of matches. "Give us your candy," said the other one, "or we're gonna blow you up with these firecrackers."

"Go to hell," said Terry. She's a lesbian human-rights lawyer in New York now, but even back then she was always the tough one.

"Go get your own candy," I said.

"Why should we when we can get yours? Come on, give it up." The other big boy grabbed for my bag of candy and got my pitchfork handle instead. It separated from the red plastic fork part with a little popping sound. I tried to grab it back, but his arms were about twice as long as mine.

"Give it back to her!" said Terry. She was tough, but not tough enough. The first boy struck a match. In our rational minds, we must have known that a handful of Black Cat firecrackers could not blow us up, but we were beyond sensible thought. We fled the overhang of the willow tree, dashed through the puddle of the streetlight, and banged on the nearest door. The woman who answered it said the boys were probably long gone and would not come outside to look for them and (I hoped) recover my pitchfork handle.

Terry and I were both crying a little, but we could not allow a couple of sixth-grade thugs to completely ruin our Halloween. More importantly, to go home now might be to admit that we weren't old enough to trick-or-treat without parents after all. For the rest of the night, I was a devil without a pitchfork.

At most, there are only a couple of years between being old enough to trick-or-treat without parents and being too old to trick-or-treat altogether. The next year, Terry ditched me to go out with a group of popular girls, and I had to do my trick-or-treating with a lesser friend. The year after that I didn't go at all.

Since then, I've done many things to try to recapture the magic of my early Halloweens: big house parties, Ecstasy, costuming in the French Quarter. But nothing ever comes remotely close to the magic of those Halloweens between two and ten. The closest I can come is to try to recreate that magic for other kids. I can barely tolerate kids the rest of the year, but when Halloween comes, I decorate my house and do up little bags of candy and sit out on the porch with zombie makeup and a real skull. The kids who do come seem to enjoy it, but there are fewer of them every year. Parents don't like their kids taking candy from strangers anymore.

A couple of years ago, the mean eighteen-year-old who used to live in his parents' house next door came drunkenly onto my porch and smashed my jack o'lantern, then threatened to kick my ass when I told him to get off my property. For a moment I felt as powerless as that ten-year-old red devil under the willow tree. Then I went inside and called the cops, who arrested him. I guess there are a few advantages to growing up.

Mask Game

John Shirley

"Neva has a new Halloween game she wants us to play at the party," said Donny.

Juno looked across the room at her younger brother. "Say what, scrubster?"

Donny was barely thirteen. He surprised everyone in the family room by chiming in about the Halloween party, because he didn't seem to be paying attention to them at all; he was staring so fixedly into the Sega Dreamcast game he seemed in another room, another world; his fingers clicked the controller; his hands jabbed it in the air, his shoulders wrenched this way and that, as if these contortions could help his Killflyer safely pass the ice-spikes hurtled by the enraged Living Mountains.

Juno, Donny's older sister, sat with the others at the breakfast table on the tile floor beyond the stained carpet of the Dreamcast-dominated family room. On wicker chairs around the kitchen table were Donny's wearily obese Mom; Juno and her best friend Linda; and Linda's always-smiling Dad, Mr Carpenter...Mr Carpenter was "a heavily medicated soccer Dad", according to Linda.

Juno looked at her brother, saw him flying, in his mind and on-screen, into the box of the videogame....

One of those weird feelings of unwanted scale came into Juno's mind again: she seemed to see Donny in the box of the TV screen, and the box was like a little puppet theatre in which he zipped around in a toy spaceship, shooting things; and that box was inside the box of the Family room, next to the box of the kitchen, both in the box of the split-level house, which was in a grid of such house-boxes, in the Southerton suburb of Sacramento, in the middle of California, on the coast of North America—in her mind, she could see it all from space, the planet a ball in space: the boxes stuck to the big ball, the big ball itself hanging, in her imagination, in some vast transparent box that astronomers had failed to discover because they weren't supposed to, because....

Stop.

Dizzy, Juno pulled her mind back, and focused on the kitchen table; the crumbs of breakfast, the bowl of chips, the homely, comfortingly ordinary faces of her family and her friend Linda.

Donny was muttering something, again about masks for the Halloween party. *Focus on that.*

"So you're, like, in on this Halloween party committee all of a sudden, scrubster?" Juno asked, fishing in the bowl for a taco chip that hadn't gotten limp by sitting out all night. "Ugh. Mom these chips are, like, blue food."

"Then throw them in the trash and put out some fresh, Juno," Mom said, distractedly looking at Donny.

He was still staring into the screen, jerking his body around in a burlesque of the trajectory of his Killflyer. He made it past the beetling visages of the Living Mountains, muttering, "Aw riiiiight," and flew on into the Jurassic Swamplands, where he began to systematically strafe the Village of the Swamp People.

"You have to kill people in some village, in that game?" Mom asked, frowning. "They look like, you know, innocent bystanders...."

Juno thought: *Like you'd do anything about it even if he had to torture them to death for points....*

"You get more points," Donny said, "if the people in the village have *weapons.* But yeah you kill everybody, if you want enough points to get the Annihilator.... You can't really win unless you get the Annihilator.... Yeah uh Neva, anyway, said...shit...flew too low...."

"Neva said 'shit'?" Juno asked, pretending innocence. Linda giggled.

"You two watch your language," Mom said. Grunting, she heaved herself up, out of her chair: a big woman, she'd lost enough weight so that she didn't have to use a cane anymore, but she still breathed through her mouth when she moved. She looked at her watch—a tiny silver strip of watch on a big pink slab of arm—and decided it was close enough to lunchtime; she got her Slimfast from the fridge and drank it down hungrily.

"Neva said that uh, she...shit! Every time I come to this swamp part, their stupid trained dino-gator's vomiting those acid bombs...He always—whoa, gottim!... Neva said she had a game she wanted to play with the kids at the party and she...she had prepared for it, for, like, months, and made special masks for everyone. Everyone's got their own mask. Kinda weird but that's what she said.... That little kid keeps escaping into the woods.... Now I've gotta use my nuker on the woods to kill him...."

"She made the masks by hand?" Mr Carpenter asked. He snapped his fingers in admiration. "*Gee*, that's great, I'd love to see them." He was a chiropractor, who'd retired after losing a lawsuit with a patient.

Something about spinal adjustments and strokes. Mr Carpenter's receding blond hair was going grey, but he still had a little ponytail, tied in the back; a head that seemed slightly too long and narrow for his wide shoulders.

"She worked on it for *months*?" Juno asked. "The girl's, like, obsessed!"

"Rully," Linda said. "That's like so...." Her voice trailed off.

Linda was stocky like her dad, with that same long chin. Not as pretty as Juno; not as brave about expressing herself.

"Oh I think spending that long perfecting a craft to get it right, that's marvelous," said Linda's dad, as both Juno and Linda had known he would. "The masks must be *great*."

"That's right," Mom said. "I don't know how we all lost touch with craftsmanship and caring about doing things right. I'm not saying I'm much better. In the 70s, I guess, we were having too much fun to think about getting some skills that mattered. Me, I mean—not you, Frank."

Mr Carpenter nodded pleasantly.

Juno thought: *Mom's always saying things are screwed up, and then saying she's no better. But she starts out judging everything anyway—then she judges herself.*

Breathing through her mouth, Mom labored around the kitchen, dumping out the old chips, putting new chips in the big earthenware bowl. "Mo-om," said Juno, as soon as she was sure her Mom had already done it. "I would've got those. I was going to."

Donny went on, barely audible: "Yuh, Neva said...said she wanted us to wear these special masks...and...she...." He broke off, for a long moment, staring at the screen, as it loaded another level. "...wants to show us how to play the game...tonight.... Oh, *sweet*: Next level is Killfrenzy.... Yeah she's coming tonight to...to...."

"Uh, *riiiiiight*, Donny," Juno said. She and Linda exchanged looks. It was like Donny was a Mynah bird, just repeating something.

Mom made one of her frustrated noises, a kind of low growling, and went to the videogame—and surprised Juno by shutting it off. Donny looked at her in outraged shock. "I hadn't *saved* yet!"

"Tough," Mom said, "I'm sick of you doing all that video-killing and not participating in...in...family stuff."

"What—stuff like Halloween? Where we can, like, pretend to be Jason or Freddie and carry toy knives with fake blood on em and stuff? *That's* not violence? Shit I was just about to—"

"Watch your language, buddy-boy! Now tell me what your cousin Neva was going to do with the masks. We're trying to plan the evening. We want to do something together as a family this year."

"Neva?" Donny brushed some lank brown hair out of his eyes and blinked at her. "Neva was going to do what?"

"You were just saying you'd talked to Neva?"

"Like, a month ago—she didn't say anything about masks. You could've warned me before you switched off the game so I coulda saved. Now I have to replay that level."

"That's, like, such a tragedy, losing your saved videogame," Juno said, dripping sarcasm. "It's tragic if you're a retard, I mean." She stared. "*God*, Donny you haven't even got any *pants* on—running around in a shirt and underwear...."

"That's just disrespectful," Linda said. "I have to say. None of my business but...I mean...Ex*cuse* me? It's like he's all...."

"Why're you looking at my ass, Linda?" Donny jeered, unfolding his long, bare legs to get up. He stalked angrily out, going down to his room; to his computer. He liked to walk out on things, on people, to make a point. The picture of Eminem on the back of his T-shirt glared a reproach at them, as if 'getting Donny's back', all the way down the stairs. Slim Shady's printed-on face receded into the shadows of the downstairs hall.

"Donny's being such a butt-head," Juno said. "Like, he'll just not tell us now about Neva because he's mad."

"Boys are confused, at his age, pretty easily," said Mr Carpenter, always the conciliator. "He'll be fine."

Juno wondered what Mr Carpenter would say, instead, if he hadn't been taking his Paxil.

They heard the faraway sound of the Internet connecting in Donny's room and almost immediately the muted chiming of Instant Messages, one after another, as the Buddy List told his friends he was once more in their shared digital world.

⁂

Wearing only a bra and panties and feeling a little sick from the cooking smells of instant dinners coming up through the grate in the floor, Juno was standing in her bedroom-closet door with Linda, trying to decide what to put on. She was supposed to wear some artsy-craftsy mask that her weird cousin Neva had made, tonight—made for them without even asking them all first—and since she didn't know what mask she would have she didn't know what costume to put together to go *with* the mask.

"Some, like, tights—black tights and a leotard, that'd go with any mask. You look cute in tights anyway," Linda was saying. Linda took a fashion-design course and was good with design software. She was into pictures, into color and texture, like her Mom had been.

"I'm putting on weight, I can't wear tights," Juno said.

"You are so *not* putting on weight."

Juno whispered: "I'm scared I'll end up like...." She glanced at the door.

"You have more your dad's metabolism, from what your doctor said that time," Linda said, abstractedly, riffling the outfits hanging in the closet. "How about this?"

Then the doorbell rang, and the tightness started in her stomach: it was her dad.

"JU-noooo!" her mom called, from downstairs. "Your dad's here!"

Dad was bringing her half-brother, six-year-old Little Mick, over for the party, probably because Dad was going to some office Halloween thing with his wife. He worked for UniNet, where they were supposed to be "just like a family" and their CEO was heavy into having "family holidays" and it was so weird how that was like her Mom lately, too. Mom was on a 'family togetherness' kick. Like that would make up for Dad being married to some skinny lawyer bitch.

"Yeah, I'll put on my Danskins for now, I guess," Juno said. She took the tights off the shelf inside the closet, next to the hanging clothes, and drew them on, then shrugged and wriggled into a matching scoop-necked leotard; black Danskins. If Russell came over, it'd be worthwhile to wear clinging things.

She contemplated herself in the mirror, smoothing out wrinkles in the stretchy fabric; Linda pulled up on the elastic for her, from behind.

"Yow, easy, I might want to have babies some day."

Linda giggled and the two looked critically at Juno: her long, wavy brown hair; her tortoise-shell berette flipping it just a little to one side; her pert, angular face; the deep-set green eyes she got from her dad; nails painted glossy-black. The nails were already good for Halloween, no reason to change that. But the almost painted-on Danskins—you could see her nipples...oh so what, Mom couldn't object to something she wore for dancing being too sexy. Mostly her objections were just noise anyway.

"DON-neeee! JU-noooo!"

Juno exchanged a sigh with Linda and they went downstairs.

❋ ❋ ❋

Mick was orbiting his dad, trailing one hand on his dad's legs as he circled him, making an *RRRRR* sound. Dad, still wearing his tieless suit, was tall, gangly, with a wide, easily-smiling mouth and lots of flashing white teeth; glinting green eyes.

Mick stopped dead-still, his small round face beaming up at Donny when he came slouching into the front hall. "Donny!" Mick shrilled. "Can we play Killforces?"

"Yuh, sure— split screen, dude. Hi Dad."

"Hi Donny," Dad said. "So, are thirteen year old guys allowed to have any fun on Halloween?"

"Yuh sure, whatever. We're, like, having a party or something." Donny trailed Mick into the family room.

"You give Mick a chance to win!" Dad yelled after them, smiling. He pretended to gawk up at Juno as she descended the stairs. "Who's this terribly skinny vision in black?"

"Oh right like I'm so skinny." She made herself go to him for The Hug.

It was hard to be mad at him, after six years, especially with him trying so hard when he came over. But it was hard to hug him too. She *wanted* to hug him—*and* she wanted to push him away; and the tug-of-war made that tight, sick feeling in her guts when he came to visit.

He let her go. "So what's up tonight? Hi Linda!" He waved at Linda, who sat on a step halfway down.

"Hi Mr Weiss."

"Um—we're not doing much," Juno said, relieved to be able to step back; to hug herself, instead. "Neva...cousin Neva...is coming over...bringing some masks...."

"Cousin Neva?" He shrugged. "I can't keep up. Time marches on. And so must I." He kissed her cheek. She let him. He grinned down at her—holding her shoulders cupped in his big hands for a moment, looking into her face.

Did he *have* to have that it's-all-good expression, when he didn't live with them? Like it was so *good* to be not married to her Mom.

He squeezed her shoulders gently, once, and turned to go—then turned back long enough to check: "Oh—I think your mom has Mick's costume. He insists on wearing the same one from last year for trick or treating. Should still fit, one more time. Donny and Linda's dad are taking him...?"

"Yep, that's the plan, Dad."

"That's a done deal, then. Okay kids—Happy Halloween." He blew Juno a kiss, waved to Linda and then he was gone, closing the door softly, swiftly, behind him.

❋ ❋ ❋

Russell, the jerk, didn't come. He would have some good excuse, he always did, and he'd been careful not to promise. They weren't really going steady, after all. One blowjob didn't make him her boyfriend. Don't try to date somebody that popular, Linda had warned her, and she'd been right, as much as Juno hated to admit it.

Her friend Marcy *couldn't* come—she was volunteering to help run some dance at her Catholic school. They were really lame, the dances at that school, they played, like, Britney Spears, not even Vitamin C, but it was a place to meet the boys from St Anthony's. Dandridge couldn't come, he was doing some DJ thing somewhere. Atesha and Ahmed had made excuses so lame that Juno couldn't even remember what they were. They knew what Mrs Wiess's Halloween parties were like.

So it was just Linda, and Mr Carpenter—Linda's dad— after he got back with Donny and Little Mick, and Mom, and Mom's sister Laura—Laura was a nervously active, medium-sized woman with her rusty hair up in a bun and pants that were way too tight for her big derriere—and Juno. Later, Granddad Morrisey, Mom's father, was supposed to come over. Thrill. Granddad was deadly dull when he wasn't bitching. Some Halloween party.

It was after dark and they were in the living room, doing busywork to avoid the discomfort of having to wait for anything like a real party to start. Laura had set out punch and cookies and put on music: *Classics from the Crypt*. Mom had Linda and Juno putting up the Halloween decorations she'd bought at The Big Halloween Store, a discount place that rented a space at the mall for a month out of the year. Juno grimaced at the decorations: Cut-outs of clichéd witches, trite ghosts, hackneyed werewolves, stereotyped Frankenstein monsters; bright chirpy images printed on cereal-box cardboard. "What I hate," said Juno, "is how they make the 'monsters' in Halloween decorations all happy and jolly and grinning and...like they're trying to make you feel they couldn't *really* hurt you. Don't want to *scare* the kids on Hallo-*ween*...."

"Or piss off the Fundamentalists—the fascist scrubs—" said Linda, whose Mother, Lupe, had been rather a political activist with the Catholic Workers, before she'd died. Lupe had died of an embolism, six years before. "If you make Halloween stuff scary they think it's...it's...you know...."

Juno pushed a tack through a ghost's eye. "Like...demonic?"

The doorbell rang. Juno got the door, and there was Neva, and things were instantly more interesting. Neva had her jet-black hair in long, rank dreadlocks; she had some kind of white coloring on her lips, not lipstick, more like white paint, so that they were dead white, and the same on her eyelids; her nose was doubly pierced by little emerald and ruby studs, her ears quadrupally hooped. Her heart-shaped face was pretty but abjectly solemn; her black eyes were like polished onyx. When she blinked, the bone-white to onyx flash was sometimes startling.

But her smile put Juno at ease. "Cousin *Juno!*" Neva said, reaching out to press Juno's hand; and Juno saw a flash of the shiny brass stud piercing Neva's tongue, in the dead center of that laughing, open-mouthed smile. "I haven't seen you since you were so little...and now you're bigger than me!"

It was true: Neva was probably in her twenties, but she was a small woman, a well-turned but pixieish shape, no more than five-foot-one. She wore flat-white, a sleeveless, sash-belted shift like something the servant girl would wear in a movie about ancient Rome; the cloth was sewn, here and there, with runes. She wore an antique silver armlet of a snake biting its own tail, and a really old, worn-out pair of sandals. Neva hesitated in the doorway as Juno frankly stared at her, forgetting her peevishness about the mask game, beginning to appreciate Neva's style.

"Whoa, nice toe-nails," Juno said. Neva's toenails were alternately black and white. "Black and white and—"

"—and black and white and black and white!" Neva laughed. Her voice both soft and husky, and her laugh was infectious so that Juno found herself laughing too. "And you've got all black fingernails, Juno!

If you do a hand-stand next to me, just right, some piano player may stroke his fingers on the ends of us. I know just which octave I am too...."

What a weird-ass little thing to say, Juno thought.

"Well do come *in,* for heaven's sake, Neva!" Mom called, from the sofa where she was watching Linda put up black and orange crepe paper. "Juno, you're making her stand out there!"

"Sorry...." Juno closed the door behind Neva who stood on the carpet, looking around, smiling like the Mona Lisa at their decorations. "Very...nice." She put down a large satiny black bag—the kind of material that was black and gold both, depending on how it shifted around in the light. The bag was full, its contents covered in a coarse white cloth. Neva gazed benignly at Mom. "Good to see you, Judith!"

Mom looked at Neva with slightly narrowed eyes, her head tilted. "Um.... You too, Neva."

"Are those the masks you made?" Juno asked, looking at the bag. She was embarrassed, suddenly, by the party, and her family—Neva was so cool, so confident, and she found she wanted to know her better.

What did Neva *do* for a living? Juno couldn't remember.

She remembered something about Neva doing...what? Going off to school somewhere? Studying art in Europe or something? She must have: she was so effortlessly exotic.

"Yes, those are the masks," said Neva. "Oh! That music—'Night on Bald Mountain'. I like that composition."

"It's *Classics from the Crypt*," Laura said. She was stringing unnecessary crepe.

"Is that what it is? I'll bet it's much quieter in a crypt than that," said Neva.

Linda and Juno laughed. Laura turned and blinked at Neva in confusion, then managed a chuckle.

"Have some punch!" Mom said. "You can have the grown up punch with the white wine in it.... Laura would you get her some punch?"

Neva dutifully went to stand by the transparent plastic punchbowl, to wait for her drink. The bowls were on the folding table, covered with black construction paper, they'd set up against the wall. With exquisite care, Laura ladled out a wax paper cup of wine and Hawaiian Punch from the "grown up bowl". Juno got herself some punch from the other bowl—a mix of canned juices with some orange slices floating in it.

"Mmm, thanks." She sipped at the cup, her eyes darting from one person to the next, and around the room. "Delightful. Lovely."

Mr Carpenter had taken Donny and Little Mick out trick-or-treating. Mick was Batman; Donny had decided he wanted to make his own mask design with Halloween makeup—he'd ended up with scribbles on his face, and what looked like unreadable graffiti.

The doorbell rang; Laura let Granddad Morrisey in, on his aluminum cane that sprouted into four legs near the bottom; scowling, nodding, shuffling. "Thank you, Laura. Kids, how ya doing, there. Judith. Where's Little Mick?"

"Trick or treating, Dad. I've got your water heating...." Laura took his arm, and slowly escorted him into the kitchen for the instant coffee and Oreos he always had when he arrived.

The trick or treating commenced. Neva stood near the punch, watched Juno and Linda take turns answering the door, offering the bowl of miniature Snickers and Mars bars and Baby Ruths to kids wearing store-bought masks of Freddie and Pikachu; to kids in green monster makeup their parents had put on them by hand. Some kids had the wailing-ghost masks associated with the *Scream* movies; others the grinning *Scream*-parody mask from *Scary Movie*. Now and then groups of large black kids, most of them looking like they were at least fifteen, came to the door and mumbled, "Trickertreat"; they usually didn't bother with masks. Linda gave them candy.

Mom, in turn, watched Neva—Mom's gaze wandered from Neva's dreadlocks to her piercings, to the eyes that seemed so familiar and so unfamiliar...

...And watching Neva, Mom ruminatively ate mini-Mars Bars from a sack, one after another, forgetting her diet, accumulating a pile of discarded candy bar wrappers.

Neva drifted over to the lamp table, beside Mom, where the wrappers were piling up and ran her fingers through the crinkly pile. "Like a heap of autumn leaves...."

"You can sit on the couch, you know, or a chair, hon," Mom said

"I need to stand for a while. But thank you."

She *needs* to stand? Juno thought.

Still gazing at Neva, Mom put a mini-Mars bar down half eaten, and sat up a little straighter in excitement. "I remember.... Gosh—you've grown so much, Neva...."

"Oh I wish I'd grow some more! I'm so damnedly short. But you get used to it. It gives you a more realistic sense of scale." She looked at Juno.

Mom cocked her head at this, considering it, frowning. Juno looked at Neva for a moment, some half-memory of what might've been a dream stirring in her...and then turned away and emptied another family-size bag of Halloween-candy into the trick-or-treat bowl.

Laura came in long enough to change the music to Disco Inferno; she did a few dance steps in place, at the stereo—it was disco music but she was doing an Irish folk dance, with her arms straight at her side. She'd taken lessons. She did all her dancing that way—she said Michael Flatley proved you could Irish-dance to anything.

Neva stared at Laura a moment, then drifted up beside Juno to watch as a disparate batch of masked kids came to the door at once—two Wolverines from the *X-Men* movie, one Mystique from the same movie, one fourteen-year-old boy with *The Crow* makeup, one Fairy Princess—not long out of diapers—with sparkles on her cheeks, holding her dad's hand; one *Scary Movie* mask.

"Some masks speak so deeply, Juno—but some drip onto our faces from the glass screens...and some only mock us from dreams we forgot we had," Neva murmured.

Juno looked at her, thinking: *What was that? Something from some lame community college drama class?* "When are you going to show us the masks you brought, Neva?"

"Soon as the trick-or-treating dies out," Neva said, going to stand by the punch table again. She'd stayed there most of the evening, so far, but hadn't drunk anything else.

"This one coming up the sidewalk'll be one of the last groups... around here they stop around ten...."

Neva was gazing out the open door, at the beacon of the moon in the black sky. As if drawn, she walked across the room to Juno again, her gaze seamlessly on the moon. "It's not quite full, tonight. It's waxing. Growing."

"Yeah. The moon's really pretty tonight. It's so bright."

"It's *awesome*," Linda said, coming to join them. "It's all...." Her voice trailed off, as usual; they gazed together into the night sky, each with the moon in her mind's eye.

Then another group of kids came, yelling trick or treat in a listless, off-hand kind of way, accidentally knocking over potted plants as they came up the walk and not stopping to right them.

The doorbell stopped ringing about ten-thirty and, soon after, Neva closed the front door and said, "Time for the Mask Game."

❋ ❋ ❋

Granddad Morrisey was in the barcalounger, Donny, his makeup smeared—scowling and put-upon—was seated on the floor between Grandad and Laura who sat stiffly on a kitchen chair she'd brought into the living room. Donny was eating Halloween candy from a plastic orange trick-or-treat bag he'd brought back with him. Juno and Linda sat on the two arms of the overstuffed chair across from the sofa, under the painting of a troubador singing up to a Spanish girl on a balcony. Little Mick was playing Gameboy, half curled up on the chair between them; he had lost his beloved Batman mask somewhere in a park, occasioning a minor crisis; but he'd forgotten about it when Donny pressed the Gameboy on him to quiet him down.

Mr Carpenter was leaning on the back of a turned-around kitchen chair, rocking its front legs off the floor, humming to himself while gazing vaguely at the plaster light-bulb-lit jack-o-lantern in the front window. Mom had wanted a family session to carve real jack-o-lanterns, this year, but the kids had all made excuses, and the pumpkins were rotting, unmarked, on the back porch.

"Could we put on music?" Donny was saying. "And for once could we listen to something I like, something that's good for Halloween? There's that song 'Kim'—"

Juno groaned, "Not Eminem, please God."

"Juno come on, it's Hallo-*ween* stuff—it's a scary story about this guy who kills this girl and tells his daughter it's all just a game but he's getting the kid to help dump her in the lake.... It's just like a horror movie...."

"It's his sick fantasy about murdering his wife—*that*'s not Halloween—"

"Actually," Neva said, mildly, as she took the cloth covering off the masks in the sack. "I agree with Donny, I have heard that song and it is a Halloween story, very much. But music right now would be distracting...we have storytelling of our own to do with the help of the masks...." With a mask gazing empty-eyed from her hand, she straightened up and announced with just the right air of mystery: "For now commences our Halloween Mask Game!"

And she went counter-clockwise, passing out masks, one to each.

The masks were like glazed papier-mâché— but it wasn't paper, exactly. It was more like crushed straw, Juno thought, looking at the back: Some kind of fibrous plant. The front was beautifully painted, and shaped; they were human faces—familiar faces—not monsters. The workmanship was indeed of a quality beyond merely professional. It was "the art of the hands."

"Can I have that one...?" Juno asked, pointing at a mask of an old woman.

"No, I'm sorry, that one is mine," Neva said sweetly, huskily. "Each has his own mask. Try yours on—it should fit quite well to your features...."

Juno took her own mask: it was a mask of her mom's face, not a mocking caricature, just Mom younger than now, more slender. Juno hesitated, not quite wanting to put it on.

With a deeply-etched scowl, Granddad was staring at his own mask—which stared sightlessly back from his trembling, blue-veined hands. He grunted, and shook his head. The mask was a parody of his own face—much younger. "Me in Korea," he said. "About that time...stationed in Korea...the Forty-second...I was thirty-two."

Mom gazed at her own mask. "Why that's my mother, rest her soul.... They really are beautifully made. I...it gives me such a funny feeling....

You know, I should have done another art course.... People give up on them so easily, when they try to take classes, and...I guess I did too. I wish I'd done some more art classes...like Lupe—but she was so good at them...."

At the mention of Lupe, Mr Carpenter glanced at Mom, then looked quickly back at the mask in his hands.

"Oh yes," Laura said, "Lupe was very talented. You know, I'd have to be talented at something to really want to learn it—an art, I mean. I...I wanted to do more dancing but I didn't think I had...." She broke off, seeming embarrassed, as if she'd exposed herself.

"Mine's not like the others," Mick said, tossing his Gameboy aside to take his mask. "It doesn't have a face and it's madea something else. "

"It is made of something different! You're a wise boy!" said Neva, all charming encouragement as she pulled his Batman shirt off over his head, so that he was bare chested. "It doesn't have much of a face yet, but just wait. We need at least one real honest monster on Halloween." She put the mask gently on his face and began to....

What is she *doing?* Juno wondered.

The mask had started out without any real character to it; just a generic face. She was shaping the mask, under her fingers, as she spoke. "The other masks are made of something similar to paper, and they're fixed in one shape by a glaze. This one is of a kind of special, stiff cloth that's very adjustable.... It can be changed...."

As her fingers worked over the mask, it took shape, suggesting a werewolf. Not any particular werewolf; not Lon Chaney Jr, nor the Wolfen. Not Eddie Munster. But it was more or less, thought Juno, what Little Mick would look like if he turned into some kind of wolfboy.

"There—you're a wolfman!" Neva said, clapping her hands, just once.

"You go on now, and be a werewolf, boy! Explore that! Go see in the mirror of the bathroom what it looks like!"

"Ow-WOOO!" Mick howled, to nervous laughter. His eyes sparkled at the attention; at everyone looking at him and laughing. Then he ran down the hall to the bathroom to look in the mirror.

The laughter died down as everyone looked at their masks. "After you've had a good look at them, put the mask on," Neva said.

Everyone obediently put their masks on, except Granddad Morrisey.

There was no string, no rubber band on the back of the mask—the top of the mask curved back into a kind of cap that held the mask on the head, and against the face. It clung to her face with such unnatural steadiness, she took it off and put it back on a couple of times, just to reassure herself that she *could* take it off.

Weird ideas get into your head at Halloween, she thought.

Every mask fit perfectly, so far as Juno could see. How had Neva done that, without measuring everyone? Juno found she was afraid to ask.

"Whoa-hey—like a glove!" Laura said, giggling faintly. Laura's own mask was an image of herself as a child of about twelve.

"No, it's some kind of mean joke," Granddad said, staring at his mask. Even as he said, "I won't put it on"...he put it on.

"You just *did* put it on, Granddad," Donny said.

"I won't put it on," Granddad said again, his voice muffled from behind his mask.

Juno started to laugh—then realized there was no humor in Granddad Morrisey's voice. He wasn't kidding.

Linda's mask was of her mother, Juno guessed—Lupe, a pretty woman, half-Latino.

Linda's dad, Mr Carpenter asked, jovially, "How d'I look?"

"Like yourself, but younger," Mom said.

"What I want is the other way around—to be younger, but myself, Judith," he said, chuckling.

Donny's mask looked like his dad—but younger. "We're...we're all each other," he said, "or...the same but younger or...."

"Not you, you're not someone here," said Juno. "And Mom is *her* mom—and you're Dad." For some reason, the remark seemed to hang in the air, as if it wasn't through releasing all its meaning.

"But who are you, Neva?" Laura asked, as Neva put on her own mask.

"I'm a grandmother crone," said Neva. "Any grandmother crone—one of this family's ancestors, perhaps, or someone alive, it doesn't matter." Her mask was a very old woman's face, but not a witch—more like a matriarch, smiling softly but also determined, firm in her convictions.

Looking at Neva in her mask, it was difficult to remember her original face.

Neva was switching off the lights, one by one, lastly the ones in the living room, making darkness fall across the room like an old-fashioned "wipe" in an old fashioned movie.. No one objected—this was a Halloween party.

"Maybe we should have candles," Laura said tentatively. "I could get some. I think there's some in the garage...." Her masked face, in the shadows, seemed a frightened child—though the mask's expression hadn't seemed frightened before she'd put it on.

"We don't need candles, we have the moon herself," Neva said, and she pulled the bottom of the front window shade to make it snap up—so that suddenly moonlight flooded into the room. It only brought a little clarity, but it changed the character of the room. And Neva turned to them and intoned, with more simple declaration of conviction than drama:

"The waxing moon—a moon pregnant with Harvest...." Even in this faint light the edge of the mask Neva wore could be seen—yet the features almost moved as she spoke. The visage of an elderly matriarch was so archetypally pure it made Juno shudder. "...Tonight there are solar flares, you know—" Neva went on. "—and so the moon is even brighter than normal, reflecting the petulant fury of the sun with its own lunar flares. We forget that moonlight is reflected sunlight—sunlight that has been stolen by the moon, and re-directed; this very light you see here—" She lifted her hand so that it was bathed in moonlight. "This light on my hand first struck the surface of the moon, before it struck my hand—it struck the filmy coating of moondust there, the cratered hills of the moon—and it bounced off that moonscape, and came here, to us—to all of us in this room.... But it has in it still something of the dead dust of those bleak, shadow-etched craters...and something else—a power we can use...."

"Gosh she's good at that, isn't she?" Mr Carpenter chuckled. But there was a quaver, the faintest quaver, of uncertainty in his voice.

"I knew it," Juno whispered to Linda, "she's been taking drama or something."

Linda suppressed a snigger. But Juno was far from certain that Neva was dramatizing. Even when she said something poetic, she seemed so unaffected, so definite about it all, as if she were speaking of the weather, or the stock market.

"Now each of you knows who your mask is," Neva said, turning to them, silhouetted against the tarnished silver of the moonlit window. "To play the game, you need only listen to the mask and it will tell you what your part is, and how to play the role.... Now stand you up, all of you...you too, Donny.... Yes, and you too, Clarence...." Clarence was Granddad Morrisey's first name. "Good.... Now we stand here, facing one another...and we each take a step back, and as we do we step back from the people we pretended we were before, and into the masks...into the people who are these masks, the masks who are these people...."

Playing along—or perhaps caught up in some kind of eternity-touched ritual of solemnity they couldn't articulate—they each took a step back...out of the pool of moonlight....

They stepped back all at once....

Each masked face receding into the shadows so that only the faintest moonlit sketches of the masks remained, hanging unsupported, like bodiless spectres, in the dim reaches of the room....

❋ ❋ ❋

Little Mick kept going back to the mirror in the bathroom. The room was lit only by a night-light in the wallplug next to the mirror.

He'd stand on the toilet lid and gaze into the dark glass. And every time he looked at the face he saw reflected there—the mask like an angry dog, to him who'd never seen a wolf—the face seemed a little more powerful, more independent. But he never felt scared of it—it was not like the face was some monster.

Every time he looked at the face, it seemed more like him—like Mick Weiss....

After each mirror-look he would get down on the floor, and go prowling about the bathroom, growling, swaying his head from side to side; sometimes chuckling in wonder at the good feeling the growling and skulking gave him. He snarled at some plastic family-size bottles of bubble bath and conditioner on the edge of the tub—and struck out at them with his clawed, furred hands—and knocked them into the tub, where the hollow ring of their bouncing sounded like frightened yelping.

He went to the mirror one more time—and then the mask was finished, somehow. It hadn't been finished till that moment.

He climbed down and began to prowl down the hall...and into the kitchen, then out the back door, into the cool night air.

❋ ❋ ❋

"What...do we do now?" came Laura's voice, a little angry, from the darkness.

"Listen..." came Neva's voice urgently. "...just try not to think about anything, even if only for a second or two, and listen, and you'll hear what you should say...what the mask you're wearing wants to say."

Then they heard Grandad Morissey speak, and saw him step out of the shadows, into the moonlight, without his cane. He was still an old, bent figure, but he was moving easily now, and his voice seemed a little younger—though you could hear the age in it too. It was as if he were doing an uncanny mimicry of himself as a young man.

"Judith, get your heinie in here!"

Juno watched in fascination as her Mom stepped into the moonlight. A big shape—with that young, more slender woman's face: the mask of Judith's mother, Juno's deceased grandmother.

But Mom wasn't in character yet. "Dad...? Gosh you're so.... Are you all right? I'm not sure about this game...."

"Listen to the mask, Judith," Neva prompted. "Even if it doesn't speak in words, it will guide you. Give it a chance and something miraculous may come!" There was something about Neva's voice that seemed to come from within each of them, in that moment. It seemed to say that something precious would be lost if they didn't play the game. So persuasive was Neva's own voice, in that moment, that all of them

listened intently to the silence that preceded the murmur of their masks, and the drama began to unfold....

"Yes, Daddy?" Judith's voice, younger—and then Juno realized it had come from *her.* She found herself stepping into the light—as her Mother stepped back into the shadows. She'd spoken in her Mother's voice, saying what her mask wanted her to say.

"You going to marry this fella, Judith?" Granddad Morrisey asked.

Juno...the mask of Judith...answered, hesitantly: "I expect so...But Daddy I...."

"You're not sure? You're not sure you're pregnant? You're not sure he knocked you up?"

Juno falling into it now...hearing the words even as she spoke them. "Daddy...." She found she was crying.

Juno wanted to shout for Neva to stop this. But she couldn't. Like the others, she was carried inexorably along—she was watching it all from some distant part of herself....

Then Laura, the twelve-year-old Laura, stepped up; the mask spoke: "Daddy—stop it. She couldn't help it. He was too much for her. He sent her poetry every day. She had to."

"Had to!" He laughed sadly, contemptuously. "Laura—no I see you're in danger of becoming exactly what your sister is. You're in her shadow! I will not spawn a family of whores!"

"Clarence!" It was Juno's Mom—in her mother's mask. Her mother's voice. "I won't have you speaking to the girl like that."

"She has to learn what life is, it's time, goddammit!" His voice shook with emotion. "This world is pitiless! It is without pity, without mercy! I saw it! I saw them butcher women and children in Korea—refugees they were, who wanted only to escape from the Communists. But the South thought they might have infiltrators among them, and the order went out, and they were butchered like sheep! That's the kind of world this is—there is no pity in it. Women who lay themselves down to be used will be destroyed! People will see them as whores!"

"Clarence—this is a foul way to talk around Laura...."

"Talk? I won't talk to her! I'll *show* her!" Still raging, he stepped over to Laura and slapped her, hard, across the face. The mask she wore didn't budge from its place. Laura staggered and covered her eyes, and went to her knees. "That's how the world treats whores—better get used to it!"

(Strange, Juno thought, how the moonlight seemed to spotlight one, then the other, as the drama unfolded....)

Juno—as her Mom—pulled him away from Laura. "You're hurting her for what I did!"

"Really, Clarence!" His wife's outrage was palpable—but ineffectual. Juno's Mom as Grandma, Clarence's wife.

"You will marry that slick son of a bitch or you'll get twice that and more! And I'll see to it he marries you, you may depend on it!"

"Daddy—I don't think he really loves me. It was like he was...he was practicing on me.... You said I could go to college. But I'd be a housewife if I...."

"You should have thought of that before you opened your dirty little legs!" He backed away, shaking, into the shadows, the mask fading from sight. "...your dirty...little legs...before you opened...your dirty...little legs...."

The moonlight seemed to dim on Juno and Laura and Mom—and to increase near Neva, as she emerged from the shadows. "As time passes," intoned the old woman of Neva's mask, with simple conviction, "it pulls things this way and that—they move in one direction and they're pulled in another, and they resist and yet they submit, and in the struggle comes their shape; and so a tree becomes gnarled, a vine becomes tangled, a face becomes imprinted with selfishness, or kindness.... And time pulls, and tugs against us, and we're shaped by the struggle with time, and the world...."

The moonlight shifted, like shafts of light underwater as clouds boil and the surface roils, and Juno seemed to see another room, in her mind's eye; another place: She saw Donny approaching her, wearing his father's face, speaking in a voice that was his own, but with an adult resonance—a voice that went with the mask he was wearing. His mask didn't move its lips, yet it seemed to take on shadings, emphasis in light and shadow that underscored the words of the drama; as all the masks did.

"...but, a chiropractor, Judith?" the mask of Dad said to Juno—who wore, who was, the mask of her Mom. Juno as Judith.

"He made me feel like something again...he called me every day...."

"You weren't something already?" The voice, only a little too high, of a man, filtered through the mask of that man, coming from the body of a boy. (There was no way Donny could make this stuff up on his own, thought Juno, in some distant part of herself). "You were a wife, a mother. You've got Juno, and Donny now...."

"He said.... I wanted to learn something, to be something.... I could be an acupuncturist maybe...."

"What the hell is that?"

"It's this new thing—it's not new, it's ancient but it's sort of new to us—from China—"

"Forget it, I don't care, for God's sake. Good Lord above, couldn't he have paid for a motel room? The cheap prick."

Juno...Judith...was weeping. "I'm so sorry...sorry about you finding us like that....We got carried away."

"And you wanted to be 'something'—like Lupe? She had a gallery show. What good did it do her, he cheated on her anyway."

"She's so caught up in her career.... She hasn't got much time for him...."

"Oh yeah, I feel *so* fucking sorry for him. I feel sorry for our kids—that's who I feel sorry for."

"Look, I've told him I won't see him again...."

"Then you won't have either one of us."

"What?"

"You heard me. I've already packed. I'm gone. There's a lady who's interning for my attorney...you should see the way she smiles at me. If I were free...."

"You've walked out on me before...."

"And came back? Not this time."

"But you enjoy it so much—walking out on people. You even walked out on your kids when they forgot Father's Day. When I reminded them, they wanted to take you out to dinner—but you used the excuse to play golf...."

"You think I enjoy this break up? I won't enjoy being separated from my kids—or paying you child support, for Chris'sakes...And the alimony.... Oh no. But I'll enjoy not having to wonder what I'll find in my bed when I come home...."

He turned and walked out of the moonlight.... Donny as Dad walked out....

Judith...Juno...tried to follow—and a door slammed in her face, though there was no door in that wall.

Then Mom—as her own Mom, Grandmother Morrisey—stepped out of the shadows, and said, "Judith? Go after him. This isn't right."

"I deserve it, Mother," said Juno—said Juno as her Mom. "I deserve it."

"This is hurting me, Judith. I don't want to go out this way...."

"What are you talking about?"

"I'm not sure—I'm getting a second opinion. You'd better take me to Kaiser to get the results.... Oh Judith I don't want to die with you kids breaking up like this...."

"And that's my fault too, I guess...I don't know...I don't know...."

✻ ✻ ✻

Little Mick had pulled off his clothing, his shoes, and, taking a feral joy in the cool October air on his skin, crouched ankle deep in the Gunderson's koi pond, snarling, swiping at the blotchy black and gold goldfish.

The moonlight seemed to infuse the fish with a glowing energy.... Swipe, splash, he had one—but it slithered and flopped back into the pond before he could leap onto it. He could hear—and almost taste—the blood pumping through its frightened heart. He went all statue-still, to make them think he'd gone. The rippling water slowly quieted, and his face came into reflective focus in the pond at his feet—the triumphantly bestial, powerful face that he was now.

He lifted his head as he heard a muted yowl from the back porch. He moved slowly, carefully, on hind legs and all fours by turns, out of the pond and across the back yard toward the glass doors of the back porch.... The cat made a growl of warning—which only drew him more quickly toward it....

He could see the ghostly-white outline of the cat against the glass—a white cat. His other self, unmasked, knew its name, and sometimes played with it. He couldn't remember its name, and he didn't care about *playing*. Mick was hungry, achingly hungry. He could smell the warm life of the cat from here. He set himself....

✽ ✽ ✽

The moonlight had tripped away and returned, time had passed, and now Frank Carpenter was emerging from the shadows, wearing his mask, putting his hand on Juno's arm. Only it was Juno's mom he was touching, in their drama—Judith Weiss, Juno's mask.

"If Lupe won't let go...we can't really fight that...." said Juno, through the mask of her Mom.

"She's Catholic. She tries to be so modern, with her Catholic Worker crowd—but she's just another Catholic," Frank said.

"I just want to know—if she were out of the picture, if she were gone—"

"She's fallen in love with someone, Frank? She wants to marry someone else?"

"In any sense. If Lupe were gone—you'd marry me, Judith?"

"I'd do anything for you, Frank. You're all I have."

"That sounds like it's me by default, Judith. That's why you'd do anything for me? Because you couldn't be without...someone?"

"No, no—I mean—you're everything to me. Of course I'd marry you if she...if she left or whatever."

The room darkened; the darkness lingered; there was muffled sobbing. Juno almost came back to control of herself. But then some unseeable hand dialed up the reflected glamor of the moon, and a lunatic spotlight caught Linda in the mask of her Mother, Lupe—and her Dad, Frank Carpenter, in the mask of himself, a little younger. Only the mask seemed to have aged a little. It was Frank Carpenter six or seven years ago. He was approaching Linda, who was curled up on the sofa, wearing the mask of her mother Lupe. "Frank?" asked Linda as Lupe, sleepily. "Is that you?"

"Lupe.... Did you think it over? You said you'd think it over...."

She stretched, yawning, though her mouth couldn't be seen under the mask. "I prayed over it, anyhow. I spoke to Father Devsky. I just can't in good conscious say yes to a divorce. And what's come between us, I mean, really? Infidelity, Frank. If you're screwing someone else, how can you say you're working on your marriage? No, I can't do it. I can't live with a divorce. Look, I couldn't sleep last night and I finally managed to take a nap...Let's talk later."

"I'll let you sleep," came Mr Carpenter's voice, from behind the mask.

As Juno breathlessly watched, from that dim place faraway behind her own mask, Mr Carpenter seemed to struggle within himself—or with the mask. He reached up toward the mask, as if about to take it off. His hands froze. His shoulders trembled. Then his reach changed direction: he reached for the pillow behind Linda's head, pulled it out from under her head as she—as Lupe—shouted in protest, just once, before he pressed the pillow over her face, holding her down; she flailed; her feet kicked.

"I'll let you sleep," Mr Carpenter said again hoarsely.

Juno tried to drag leaden limbs across the room to stop him.... She managed a few steps....

But then Little Mick burst the drama apart. He ran into the livingroom, naked and streaming blood....

Vomiting blood as he came; then wailing....

The electric lights coming back on. The room flooding with artificial light....

The smeared mask falling away from him, falling into fibrous streamers, so that they could see the gobbets of red-sticky white fur rimming his mouth like a hideous parody of a beard; fur gore-pasted to his own baby teeth; blood-soaked fur vomiting up to splatter the very center of the caramel-colored carpet.

Mr Carpenter stood up straight—freed now, to pull his mask away—and he threw it aside.

Linda sat up, unhurt, pulling her own mask away—

Mom lumbered toward Mick but she hadn't taken her mask off yet and he screamed and floundered back, falling, scrambling across the floor to get away from her; from the disorienting mock of Judith's face.

She flung the mask aside and went ponderously to her knees beside him, scooped him up though he were her own child.

"Oh Mick—what happened...?"

"What happened to all of us?" Donny asked wonderingly, tossing his mask aside.

Juno was looking for Neva.

The front door was open. Neva was gone; her bag was gone too.

Juno went to the porch and shouted for her. She walked out to the sidewalk, and looked up and down the street, and saw no one but a carful of laughing, drunken teenagers weaving down the cross street, on their way to a newspaper article.

⁂ ⁂ ⁂

Juno was lying on her back in the bottom bunk, looking through the window at the gibbous moon; the moon shattering and reforming, breaking and becoming whole between the brown, shedding leaves as the big tree in the back yard surged in the night wind. Juno was hoping that alien sense of connectedness to cosmic scale would come back, if she looked at the moon—usually it scared her, but now it made her feel like she didn't have to be part of this family....

Linda was sleeping in the top bunk that Mick slept in when he was visiting his half-siblings. Naturally Linda wouldn't stay at Mr Carpenter's house anymore; wouldn't stay in a room with him, her own dad. Mick had gone back to his mom and dad, the next morning—washed and numb and quiet.

An insomniac old man had seen a small, masked boy running naked through the yards, Halloween night; the naked boy had snarled at some little girl, and chased her, and rooted through her dropped candy bag, finding nothing he wanted; then he'd leaped a fence and splashed through a goldfish pond; and he'd trapped and killed a cat with his hands and the sharp edge of a garden stone. No one knew who the boy was—except here.

Juno thought about the others. Granddad Morrisey had been hospitalized with a stroke the very next day, at five a.m.; he was lingering in critical care. He was not expected to linger long. Laura was selling all her things, and claimed she was moving to Ireland. She'd always wanted to live in Ireland, though she was not in the least Irish.

Juno sat up, thinking about checking the doors again. Make sure they were locked.

Mom had had the locks changed, because of Frank Carpenter. He had threatened her, when she'd gone to the police and said she wanted to testify. She signed a paper saying that Frank Carpenter had told her that he'd killed his wife, Lupe; that she'd been afraid to speak out till now.

Linda's dad had been arrested, put up the bond, and now as far as they knew he was alone in his own house, though Linda thought he might jump bail.

Now, Linda's voice floated out of the darkness. "Juno...?"

"I thought you were asleep."

"Sort of for a while. But sometimes when I start...you know...."

"Drifting off?"

"Yeah, I—feel the...the thing...."

"The mask?"

"Yeah. I can feel it on my face."

"We burned the masks," Juno said, though she knew what Linda meant.

"It's just a feeling—it's sort of a dream. And then I feel I'm my mom...and my dad is...."

Juno didn't finish that one for her. She could hear Linda's soft weeping. After a while, Juno said, "Linda...chill. Mom says you can always stay with us."

"I can't stay here all that long.... I don't want to. Your mom *knew*."

"She didn't tell him to kill Lupe. She never, like, said to do it. She told me everything—she said she didn't know he was going to do that shit."

"But she didn't turn him in when he told her."

"She was afraid they'd take her kids away, because she was even half way mixed up in it.... I mean, serious, why do you think Mom got so fat? She didn't used to be like that. She was so neurotic about the whole thing, she was just freaked—but she couldn't talk about it. It was like she had to hide it under...just *more body*, or something. And—your dad just kept saying, 'I did it for you, I did it for you' and she couldn't tell him to go away, he was so...dependent on her somehow...but she stopped, you know.... She wouldn't...."

"Don't say it. I don't want to think about my...about him and your mom...."

"I know. Especially now."

They were quiet for a few moments. The wind rattled the window; the moonlight falling on the floor shifted nervously.

"Juno.... Did you guys ever find Neva?"

"No. Linda—there's something I haven't told you. Mom didn't want me to talk about this...Linda...." It was hard to tell because it was hard to accept. It sounded like a lie. But it was true. "Linda...*we don't have a cousin Neva.* We never did. When we heard her name, we were all...it was like we sort of remembered her...we pictured her at the family things, you know, Thanksgiving or something...we, like, saw her in our memories? But it was all like...something was suggesting it to us...Linda—we never heard of Neva before Halloween. Neva is some kind of...Linda? Are you listening?"

Silence.

"Linda?"

"She's asleep, Juno. She won't wake till morning, now."

Oh no.

The voice had come from the window. Neva was sitting on the dresser, her head haloed by the tossing gold of the moon, her legs primly crossed. Dressed exactly as she had been on Halloween.

"It wasn't a costume...." Juno murmured.

"No. Juno. I've come here to—"

"What did you do to Mick?"

"Don't shout, Juno, you'll wake your mom. I only gave Mick the experience he wanted—and I showed him something special. He has seen the Beast that all men live with; the bestial god they share their bodies with; the one they must contend with if they are to climb the hidden staircase. But few choose to climb it. Mick, now, will climb it—because he has seen, he has known the Beast, and he cannot forget it.... You were afraid he was going to become some kind of...what? One of those who murders for pleasure?"

"You made him a psychokiller...or...the beginning of one."

"I have seen what will become of him; or more accurately what he will choose to become. He has seen his dark self, and this will give him awareness; and he will one day climb the staircase. He will be a leader, and lead people away from the thing he met that night...."

"Neva...Are you...?"

"Yes. I'm really here. You and I are here together. You called me, after all."

"I did not."

"You did. You called me, Juno. You have that power—you have that natural connectedness to the cosmic, to the real source of Life—you're like me...and you it was who really made the mask game possible. You knew somehow what Frank had done to Lupe. And to your Mother. You felt it. You knew about the sickness in your family, and the masks behind the masks behind the masks...."

"Just, like—get away from my house."

"Juno—You knew, and *you called me*. Now I'm calling you, Juno. You try to be one of these haunters of malls, these ghosts in chatrooms. But you don't belong there. You're more substantial than that. You were my best friend, and my lover, once, and you will be again, if you choose...it's all a matter of choice...Linda will be all right. Your mom will take care of her. All you have to do is listen to what the night has to say.... Just listen...to the silence between breath, between heartbeats...just listen, and know.... And ask yourself—'What do I really want?'"

In the morning, Mom found Linda, deeply asleep, and smiling, dreaming sweetly. But they never did find Juno. She didn't even leave a note.

❋ ❋ ❋

Two years, like twists on roots, shaped by impulse and resistance; by time and struggle.

It was Halloween, in Portland, Oregon, just after sunset. The smallest trick or treaters were already going from door to door, holding their mothers' hands.

Mr Stroud was the only one carving the pumpkin on the porch with a kitchen knife. He couldn't get the kids interested. He was listening to the radio he'd set up in the window, the classic rock station's Jimi Hendrix marathon, and watching the sidewalk; expecting visitors. So he saw the two young women walking up toward him from half a block away. Yes, they were turning in at the walk to the front door, coming up between the juniper hedges.

So one of them—the darker one maybe in the slave girl costume—that must be cousin Neva, from the letter Angela had gotten. He should have looked for her picture in the photo album like he'd intended to. Never got around to it. Maybe she was one of his half-sister Doreen's kids.

I'm a voodoo child, voodoo child....

And that other one was her friend, Juno. The two of them were supposed to teach the family a new Halloween game.

Well. What the hell. It would be good to do something different, this year.

Criswell Conquers The Alien Elvis-'Nappers

Tom Piccirilli

Our pug, the Amazing Criswell, is named after the notoriously inaccurate silver-haired psychic and Ed Wood cast regular who recited that key phrase from *Plan 9 from Outer Space*, asking the audience, "Can your mind stand the shocking truth?"

Maybe some of us can and some of us can't. I have a poster with that quote on it in the family room which I often look at just waiting for the day when I can't answer the question the way I'd like to respond to it. Horror writers live with little fears like that. It keeps them on edge, and often that edge is where they find the incentive for their next story.

Criswell, though, lies on the futon and gazes out from beneath his wrinkled brow, staring at the poster with what appears to be a frightening amount of retrospection. You'd have to see a pug up close to understand just how human its contemplative glare can be. Criswell's bulging eyes are always lit with a fiery intensity, head upright and barrel chest poised for a deep breath, as though he's hinging on each of our words, always waiting to abruptly lunge and charge. He'd have fit in well rushing at the heels of Custer's flag-carrier.

As such, the Amazing Criswell is an eccentric enough dog at the best of times, much less when dressed up in a blue doggie sweater that doesn't fit him and a red cape with the letters *SP* on it, surrounded by several hundred people and other similarly outfitted pets.

Moving from New York to Estes Park, Colorado was an especially difficult transition even for a suburbia-born boy like myself. I met my girlfriend Michelle online in a writers chat room, fell madly in love over the course of our two-year courtship, and unwilling to let our commitment peter out or slam the wall the way that most long-distance relationships end, I finally made the plunge that took me two thousand miles from the only home I'd ever known.

Estes Park is a small mountain town of about 5000 year-round residents, fraught with hills, dirt roads receding into open forest areas, and herds of wild elk and deer wandering about. Like most small American towns it's a gateway—in this case, the gateway to the Rocky Mountain National Park. And I learned they do Halloween a bit differently here.

In my Long Island neighborhood we had to go door to door in small groups of three or five kids. We'd knock and face the dark windows and drawn drapes of houses whose owners were either at work when we called or else were hiding from us with their televisions off, trying hard not to make a sound.

I think part of the reason I became a horror writer in the first place is because I wanted to make up all the hair-raising details and incidents we never had at Halloween. The mysterious and hushed legends of the swamp bottoms, secrets hidden in shuttered rooms, the house on the hill with the hag answering, and all the stuff of myth and tradition. We had none of it except in our October dreams.

Since it's logistically impossible for children in Estes Park to trick-or-treat door to door, the town's Halloween custom is to keep the downtown shops open late into the night and have the shopkeepers hand out candy. The main street through town, Elkhorn Avenue, is shut down for a few blocks by cross-parked fire engines. Costumed kids, pets, families and couples stroll in the middle of the street having something of a community party.

My first Halloween in Colorado, Michelle made herself up as J. O'Barr's *The Crow*, replete with black leather coat and clown face. She'd spent hours designing a little superman outfit for Criswell, and he looked a little lost walking around in it. I was the proverbial party pooper in jeans and jacket as we strolled down the hill from our place and went to embrace All Hallow's Eve.

We walked Criswell among the other trick-or-treaters, where he sniffed at plenty of people's cuffs and skirts and barked at other dogs, including a pug outfitted in witch's apparel, complete with black pointy hat. Maybe he knew it would only take one glance at that for Michelle to say, "Oh, he'd look so cute in that!" His already buggy eyes bugged-out further and I had to take him aside and whisper, "Don't worry, we won't let that happen." He seemed too wary to fully believe me.

Even my dog had a history full of superstitious antiquity. Pugs, or Foo dogs, are named for the Chinese Foo monkey which they resemble. Bulging eyes, wide blunt faces, tiny noses without any snout. In Chinese mythology they are bringers of good luck and are capable of warding off evil spirits. Their distinctive characteristic faces have a dragon-like quality on Foo dog statues. Perhaps because of this, in the mid-Sixteenth century the word "pug" was also taken to mean demon, sprite, and imp. The most unusual costume we saw that night was of the Headless Horseman, on horseback, riding through town carrying his jack-o'-lantern head on his saddle. Kids squealed and parents made sure they got their pictures taken with him. We walked the length of Elkhorn and up towards the historic Stanley Hotel, made famous as the Overlook Hotel in Stephen King's *The Shining* and where the 1997 mini-series based on the novel was filmed.

The masquerade ball was in progress, thrown for those who had paid to stay over the entire weekend. We wandered around the hotel grounds for a time, watching the costumed guests arriving: Lestat and Louis were on hand, King Henry the VIII, drag queens in wedding gowns—and what Halloween would be complete without Sinead O'Connor wrapped in the arms of the Pope?

The Stanley Hotel is alleged to be haunted, and the management keeps a written file of all such intriguing tales. You can ask to read it and even track down the folks who've signed their names swearing the stories are true. Most of the narratives have been written by employees. Michelle worked as a hostess and bartender at the Stanley Hotel for over two years and had heard a lot of the yarns firsthand. How the piano player, who'd never performed "Danny Boy" before, was told by a widow that the ghost of her recently deceased husband stood behind him while he played, listening to the song. How a chef claimed to have seen a spectral child at the foot of his bed who slowly vanished before his eyes.

The hotel is still being remodeled, which apparently Mr. Stanley, dead for sixty years, isn't too happy about. A shuttle driver who once took me back from Denver International says that he'll never step foot inside the hotel. According to him, one of his passengers claimed to have spent a night on the fourth floor and briefly chatted with the ghost, who appeared sitting at the foot of the bed.

As a horror writer and a generally curious person I'm always on the lookout for any experience that might be tinged with the supernatural.

In thirty-five years though, I've never so much as seen a flitting shape out of the corner of my eye or heard odd noises in the deep of night that might be phantasmal footprints parading around the living room or down a creaking hallway.

Michelle on the other hand, though she remains a skeptic, has mentioned a couple of occurrences that spooked her pretty well in the past: once, as a teenager, shortly after she'd relocated to Estes Park, she found a note in her locked dormitory room written in a nearly illegible (ghoulish?) scrawl claiming that no harm would ever come to her and that she was under (divine?) protection. Another time she swears she saw the figure of a woman walk into the ladies room of the restaurant she currently works at, and, following directly behind the woman, found that she had disappeared.

And then there are the tunnels.

They lead from the Stanley Hotel parking lot to an area underneath the stage in the ballroom, the same stage where Stephen King danced in zombie-face while playing the hideous band leader Gage Creed in *The Shining* mini-series. Michelle had met King during the filming and hoards her signed copies of *Pet Sematary* and *Carrie* with an inappropriate amount of glee, I think.

The fourth floor of the Stanley Hotel is where most of the sightings and bizarre events have taken place, but Michelle, despite her penchant for wandering the hotel just waiting for something to scare the hell out of her, never had any paranormal experiences. But she swears the tunnels give her vibes. At one end is a small opening, used as a break room or smokers room for employees. Once, she and a co-worker were alone in the room and heard high-heeled footsteps coming down the tunnel towards them. They continued chatting, waiting for the unseen person to join them, but no one entered. After a moment, Michelle checked and saw that nobody was there.

So I was all for it, clambering around down there in a space that wasn't all that different from the unfinished basement of the ancient house we rent. Criswell didn't much mind either, so long as we constantly fed him doggie treats. He would've much preferred bologna, his favorite food, which is also the only word he'll immediately come to attention for. Shout, "Bologna!" and he'll snap to attention and trek to death's door for a slice of Oscar Mayer.

He marched into the dim tunnel completely oblivious to demonic forces, angelic presences, dead folks a'walking or the fact that Stephen King got the impetus for one of the most important and startling novels of all time in a room just a few feet above our heads (the Stanley Hotel sells Room 217 keys in their gift shop for $12.99 a pop).

The Amazing Criswell led, and I trudged on into darkness, with my painted Crow lady at my side. Cue the eerie music, plenty of violins and pipe organ toccatas. About halfway down the tunnel Criswell began to bark wildly. That didn't bother me much since he barks at everything and nothing, either vying for attention or because he wants water or simply to inform us that he really wanted out of that stupid sweater.

Michelle whispered to me, "Listen."

"What is it?"

"Shh. Listen."

Silhouettes of two bald figures in trench coats appeared at the far end of the tunnel, backlit and throwing shadows all along the length of the ceiling. Criswell kept going and I stopped short trying to get a hold of his leash. I looked up again and saw tremendous black oval eyes glowering steadily at me. No expression, no change of those lightly green-tinted features. Criswell can crank when he's in the mood, his stubby legs carrying him on, as he reached maximum speed and lifted off. Twenty pounds of pug power, aided and abetted by the aerodynamic cape, flew through the air like a guided missile, a solid mass of muscle that slammed into the figures and toppled them both in a move so perfect it might've been choreographed by Buster Keaton.

They screamed "Augugh!"—which I mistakenly took for an alien war cry. Criswell growled and wrestled with the edges of their coats, those piranha-like teeth of his digging in good. In defense, they vainly attempted to beat him off with the cardboard signs they were carrying. One read *GIVE US CANDY OR ELSE...* and the other boasted... *WE'LL NEVER BRING ELVIS BACK.*

"Keep it away! Get it off!" one shouted.

"What the hell is it!" the other added.

"Augh!"

"Get 'em, Criswell!" I yelled, pointing. "Bologna! Bologna!"

"Don't say that!" Michelle told me.

"But they've got Elvis!"

"They don't have Elvis."

"Well, they say they do."

Michelle grabbed the dog and calmed the alien Elvis-'nappers while I listened to the first strains of the swinging big band above playing "Stomping at the Savoy." Granted, it would've been more appropriate to hear "Heartbreak Hotel" or "Harum Scarum" at that particular moment, but writers will take whatever soundtrack they can get.

We might not have seen the ghost of Mr. Stanley or received any helpful messages or dire warnings from beyond the grave—and I still don't have any signed King books—but at least on that dark Halloween night as the evil forces gathered, the super pug managed to mete out a small dose of justice in the name of that other King.

1942

Jack Cady

I was ten years old in '42, and trapped in the German-Lutheran wilderness of small town Indiana. That Halloween still lives because threats of Hell spouted from every pulpit, while true fires of Hell rose above coal and wood-burning chimneys; and a real ghost walked.

In October of '42 our town lay stunned as Hitler, having leveled Europe, marched on Russia. The Battle of Stalingrad thundered; bloodstained symbol of an adventure that would eventually cost a million, six hundred thousand lives. However, that many people, and more, were already dead before the Nazi thrust.

In that Indiana town, where lived many third and fourth generation Germans, our people wisely concentrated their fears and hatreds on Japan. The Rape of Nanking had worked its way into local thought. Bataan had fallen, and government censorship could not conceal the Bataan Death March. Nor could censors hide the battle of the Java Sea. Government news hawks made much of the Battle of the Coral Sea, but its turn-around-significance would not be understood for years. Jimmy Doolittle led a raid on Tokyo, lost men (of whom some were captured and executed as war criminals). Attu and Kiska in the Aleutians fell to Japan; and Japan took Correigidor.

Difficult memories, these. It is also difficult to separate feelings about WWII from those of localized wars that have happened since. America would lose 33,529 of her people in Korea, above 60,000 in Vietnam; but in this war 406,000 were lost; and that in a nation of 100 million (today we are 267 million).

In that small town, Halloween usually progressed with boring predictability. Kids went costumed, soaped windows, and youths 16 years and up tipped over outhouses (yes, many people still had outhouses). Occasionally, while stealing pumpkins to smash on porches, a miscreant would run into a farmer who carried a shotgun filled with rock salt. The blast tore the salt to dust, and the dust bored beneath skin so that the unlucky target 'scratched where it didn't itch' for weeks. But all of that, as I say, was 'ordinarily'.

On this Halloween there were sixteen-year-olds, but few eighteen year olds, and almost no twenties. Those not in the Army were in the Navy, or the Army Air Corps; and it is with the Air Corps, and a piano, and a witch, that this story begins:

My family's across-the-street-neighbor-lady lives in memory as The Widow, for her last name is lost. She was only a little dumpy, wore plain house dresses, and had become reclusive.

She had a son, Darrell, age eighteen, and a daughter, Janine. When he was alive, Darrell made model airplanes that really flew. During my growing-up, and because of the airplanes, he was one of my heroes. He went to war; an early casualty, his bomber blown to bits with no survivors. There was a gold star on her front window.

During that war, families with sons in the service hung small flags in their windows. A white star on a blue field meant a man still serving. A gold star meant a man, dead. Some houses had both kinds.

To a ten-year-old, Janine seemed ancient, but I now know she could not have been more than twenty. Even in that small town, where—if anybody thought about art they felt threatened—it was known that Janine was a musical prodigy. On soft summer nights, with windows open, she would play ballads instead of classical exercises. Neighbors gathered on porches, watched lightning bugs, and listened to the best musical renditions that most of them would ever hear. After Darrell was killed there were no more ballads, and the music became subdued.

The witch was Mrs. Lydia Kale. She was, it was rumored, nothing but a fearful old country woman moved to town shortly after WWI; angry and bitter from a life spent in a place so small that people walked to church. No one knew why she came. No one cared.

To a ten year old she meant fright. Most people, I believe, remember at least one 'mean lady' from their childhoods, but Mrs. Lydia Kale really was mean. She would grab a child, shake and mutter. She would even send curses when a kid passed on the sidewalk. She insulted preachers (no one else dared), and she intimidated adults.

She remains a crazed figure, dressed as dark as night wings. Her hair did not flow in the wind; nothing like that. Her hair was as white as her clothes were black, and her hair was worn in a tight knot at the back of her head. No one knew what she hated most.

These, then, were the players in that Halloween when, dressed in an old bed sheet and wearing a 'funny face' (our name for mask) I embarked after a warning:

"Do not," my mother said, "go to any house with a gold star." She was adamant.

What does a ten-year-old know? More, I think, than I believed when I sat down to write this small tale. I remember stepping into a windblown, leaf-blown night—7 p.m. but midnight dark—with dry leaves scurrying.

Something was wrong with the night. Other kids trotted past, laughing and whooping. Older kids hid in shadows, soaping windows, or suddenly appearing as they tried to scare each other. A normal Halloween, but something was wrong with the night.

I could not get in motion. I sat on a step at the side of the house feeling 'wrong'. An adult would say that he felt depressed, perhaps beleaguered. Children did not then know such words.

I could feel balsa wings fight the wind, rise, and rise higher.

There came music in the wind, but only gradually. Janine, when at that keyboard, found comfort beyond religion, beyond philosophy. The music began as light finger exercises and light runs, the kind of practice that lifts wings.

They were, brother and older sister, somehow together. I don't know, and never will, if Janine knew what was happening. I do know that for what seemed a long time I sat waiting. The balsa planes rose into the wind, the rubber bands that drove them somehow never unwinding. They flew and flew. Music lifted them; and Darrell was no more than a moving shadow.

I finally understood that it was Darrell. He moved out there in the night, standing in his own yard amidst gusts of wind, flying airplanes. I could, but vaguely, see him. I could feel him.

And what the hell did I know about death? All I knew was that Darrell would not hurt me. But he was supposed to be gone. Lost, somewhere in the South Pacific.

I hope Janine knew. I think Janine knew. Because of what happened.

There was music in the wind, a ghost in the wind, and so who needed a witch? And besides, Mrs. Lydia Kale was a daytime witch who never stepped outdoors at night.

Her clothes were black. Only her white hair was a trace of her slow movement through the wind. It came to me that Mrs. Lydia Kale must be very, very old. Music, or Darrell, pulled her forward. Wind, only strong enough to scatter leaves, seemed to press her back. She had to walk a short block, and yet it took awhile.

Twenty-five years before, back in WWI, our nation had lost 116,000 sons. Tales of that war still covered the town. And, Mrs. Lydia Kale walked slow.

It was a night of shadows. On the darkened back porch, and facing the yard where Darrell flew his planes, The Widow appeared. She moved timidly. The Widow was but a dumpy form, a darker shadow among shadows. The music did not crescendo, but began to rise. Some sort of fury, or anger, or sorrow propelled the music; but Janine was already a master. She had it under control.

The shadows came together, but gradually. Mrs. Lydia Kale walked along the sidewalk, while in the yard the planes rose. I think she saw nothing. I think she wanted to see nothing. The Widow stepped from the back porch, moving slowly to the sidewalk. In that dark night the two forms came together. I could only see the white hair of Mrs. Lydia Kale. It seemed, to a child, that there was but one person out there, white-haired.

I do not know why Darrell appeared, and can't say exactly when he left. Mystery lived in the night, and the two women who seemed to have become only one woman, stood silent. From the house the music became, for a few moments, tender. That must be when Darrell left.

And when the music began to weep it filtered through the night, through wind, and across the street to ten year old ears. The three women held the night, or pressed it back. The young woman wept above her keyboard, wept with her keyboard. The two older women simply held each other and wept.

Out of The Dark

David B. Silva

I'd never told Evelyn about the Halloween of '49. By the time you reach what they like to sugar coat as "your golden years" you've got a whole treasure chest of stories saved up. Some of 'em you've told so many times that folks turn toward the heavens for a sign of release before you even have the first sentence out. Others you know you'll never tell because those are the shameful stories of your life. You'd just as soon forget you were ever that bastard of a person in the first place. And still others...well, others you save for a moment that's just ripe for the telling.

It would have been hard to imagine a riper time than that Halloween night.

We hadn't seen many trick-or-treaters out wandering about. 'Course, times had changed since I was a boy. Kids had to be more careful these days. Those that we had seen were mostly of the tiny tot variety, barely old enough to hold their plastic, hollowed-out jack-o'-lanterns and keep their balance while climbing the porch steps. Cute enough, the lot of them, though I didn't care much for them Pokemon outfits. I remembered a few years back when Batman had become popular again. He walked a little more on the dark side than the Batman I remembered growing up, but at least he was American. This Pokemon stuff....

"It used to be more fun," Evelyn said.

"Halloween?"

She nodded, losing herself somewhere out beyond the candle-lit pumpkin heads lining our walkway. The evening had been unseasonably warm for late October—something we both appreciated more than we might had Evelyn not been feeling bad lately—but it was beginning to cool now. She bundled up the cotton-knit sweater a little tighter around her shoulders. I was proud of her, I do say. She had fought her way through two bouts of pneumonia that year, and they had taken quite a toll on her. "When I was a little girl, I used to go out with my sister and a few friends. No adults. Just us girls. We'd go around the block, and maybe another block over, two if we hurried. Mama would take after us with a yard stick if we weren't back home within the hour, but she trusted the world enough to let us go. Now...now...."

She let the thought hang in the air for me to finish, and I did just that, though I finished it in my own head. *It's not Halloween anymore.* After nearly thirty-five years of being married, you learned where your wife's thoughts were taking her, even when she wasn't up to telling you. This time out, though, the thought belonged to both of us. It *wasn't* Halloween anymore. The magic was gone. The unknown...the surprise...the pure pleasure of being frightened when you never would have thought it possible...they were all gone. I thought I had a pretty good idea why they were gone, too.

"I think I know what you mean," I said.

We agreed in silence, the way people do when they've been together as long as we had, then I watched as the top of a head poked up from the other side of the picket fence that bordered our front lawn. It belonged to a little girl, not yet out of first grade by the size of her. That little head bobbed up and down along the fence until she finally rounded the corner and came down the walkway wearing a shiny, store-bought costume of one of them crudely-drawn, flat-like-a-postage stamp Pokemon characters. The girl came up the steps with some difficulty, and when she was finally standing on the porch, I heard a man's voice call out from the street. "What do you say?"

"Trick or treat."

Evelyn leaned forward in her chair, her face warm with a smile. She hadn't smiled much of late. Hadn't had good reason, I guessed. "Oh, my. What are you supposed to be?"

"*Togeeepeee*," the girl said.

I admit, I didn't know what the hell a *Togeeepeee* was—still don't, and that three-pointed head, with its Kool-Aid pitcher body didn't help none—but it was definitely one of them Pokemon characters.

Evelyn scooped up a handful of candy from the bowl sitting on the table between us and dropped it into the little girl's shopping bag. There were another three or four bags of candy, maybe more, sitting unopened on the kitchen counter in the house. Evelyn always bought more than we needed. Just in case there might be a run of trick-or-treaters. "You never know," she said.

But I knew.

The little girl started down the porch steps.

From the street, the man's voice rang out again. "What do you say?"

"Thank you."

"You're welcome," Evelyn said. I could tell she wanted to add something to that, and I thought it was probably something of a warning.

Something like: *you make sure your daddy checks that candy now before you eat any*. We feel better when we toss out our little cautions. I don't know why that is, though I suppose it's because we feel like we're showing how much we care. I know that's part of why I nag after Evelyn all the time, even though it drives her half batty.

The girl met up again with her father, who took her hand and walked her past the edge of the front yard, down the block to the next house.

"Wasn't she adorable?" Evelyn said.

"That she was."

A breeze stirred up, just long enough to make the candles inside the pumpkins angry, and put a little life back into the holiday. In the distance, I could hear the laughter of children. Beneath the laughter, and much closer, there was another sound. An eerie, low-pitched howl that reminded me of hot sleepless nights.

"What's that?" Evelyn asked.

"The children?"

"No, that other sound. Hear it?"

I heard it, and I knew what it was.

"I want to tell you something," I said. I had been holding onto the reins of my Halloween story for some fifty-odd years, always assuming it was one of those stories that would never be told. But I knew I couldn't hold onto it any longer. Things had changed, and the itch was driving me crazy. I wasn't sure how much of the story I should tell—in a way, the ending was still open—but I knew I had to tell Evelyn something. She deserved to hear at least something. "It happened when I was just a boy, and to this day I've never told another living soul. Never had to. Never thought it was right. Not until now. The thing is...I don't want to scare you while I'm at it. So you can tell me right now to put it back where it belongs if that's what suits you. Or...if you want to hear enough to get an idea, I'll go ahead and you can tell me to stop along the way if you start to feeling you've heard enough for one outing. It's up to you, Sweet Pea."

Evelyn grinned. Mostly curious, I gathered, though I thought there might be the tiniest sliver of concern in her eyes. "You can't leave it at that. Not unless you want me to lie awake nights, wondering."

We folks are a naturally curious lot. We like to hear our stories about other folks, living in other places, in other times. And by the other end of the match, we like to hear ourselves talk whenever we get the chance. No harm in that. If someone's gotta do the talking, it helps that someone else is willing to do the listening. I was pleased that I had caught her interest. Maybe more pleased by the idea that after all our years together I still had a story or two in me that she hadn't already heard a half-a-dozen times.

"It happened in '49," I said. "Halloween."

"Um-hum." Evelyn nodded, and settled comfortably into her chair. The low-pitched, none-too-happy wail had died down some. Enough so you weren't bothered by it much.

"I was ten. This was a short time after my mother had suffered her second stroke. Only a week or so after. Maybe less. I don't remember exactly. The doctor's orders had confined her to bed, and the stroke, which had shut down the left side of her body like a strike of lightning, had done a fine job of making sure she stayed there."

"I'm sorry," Evelyn said.

"No need. It was a long time ago. But I don't mind admitting I was scared she was going to die. Death was on his way, I imagined. You could count on it. Just as sure as you could count on the tax man to show up on your doorstep when you could least afford to pay him. I had his picture already forming in my head. You know, this ten-year-old's idea of Death. This huge black shadow, all fancied up in a dark robe with wings instead of arms. Swooping down out of the night sky like a hungry hawk. Scooping up my mother's soul and carrying her away. That's the way it seemed to settle into my mind. Death was this ill-famed comic book character. The kind of character you'd dress up as on Halloween, because that's what Halloween was all about. A celebration of Death. Death's birthday, so to speak."

Evelyn adjusted her sweater. Her face was pale, her eyes dark. She looked exhausted. The most recent bout of pneumonia had wrung her dry. Some days it was all the strength she could muster just to get herself out of bed and down to the kitchen for breakfast.

"Cold?"

"No, I'm all right."

"We can go inside if you'd like."

"No. It's early still." There hadn't been a trick-or-treater since the little girl in the Pokemon outfit, and it was anyone's guess if we'd see another one tonight. She closed her eyes. "Go on with your story."

I reached across the table, took her hand, and kissed it. "The world's a different place when you're ten. We forget that. We forget what it's like to believe in magic coin boxes, and Uncle Ned's stories about buried treasure and the boogeyman. Anything can happen when you're ten. Anything."

I heard another rise of that low-pitched wail and looked to Evelyn to see if she had heard it, too. Apparently she hadn't. "I guess it was that ten-year-old's imagination that got me thinking about my mother. If I could capture Death, I thought, then maybe that would keep him from taking her. Well, everything started to fall into place after that. It was Halloween. What better time to make the acquaintance of Death hisself? And I remembered the old steamer trunk my father kept in the attic. He kept his Air Force uniform from the war in there, along with some old newspaper clippings and some other stuff that I have to confess I don't remember now. My sister cleaned it out after his death, and I never saw any of those things again. Back then, though, I emptied out what was there, then fought the trunk down the stairs to my mother's room, where I set it up next to her bed.

"The stroke had been a cruel one. It had made it so's she couldn't get around, but that wasn't all it had done to her. It had made it so's she couldn't talk none, either. So I told her what I was up to, without a word coming back at me about how none of it made a lick of sense and would never work in a million years even if I prayed on it for a month or two. I told her the plan, and I told her that if it all worked out the way it was supposed to, then everything was going to be all right. She would start feeling better again and things would be the way they were before."

With her eyes still closed, Evelyn smiled. I imagined she found the whole idea rather amusing.

"I know. I know. It sounds rather foolish now."

"No it doesn't. It sounds brave of you."

"I don't know about brave," I said. "Desperate, maybe. Anyways, I took a ruler out of my father's desk and some twine from a drawer in the kitchen. Then I rigged the trunk so all I had to do was give the twine a little tug, the ruler would pop out, and the lid would snap shut faster than the jaw of an old gator. That would be that, I told myself. Death would be out of business. 'Course, I still had to figure a way to get him into the trunk in the first place."

"No small task, I imagine," Evelyn said.

"No small task at all." I watched three more kids of the tiny-tot variety come down the sidewalk and start up our walkway. All boys, I decided from their costumes, though I suppose you can't really tell when the costume is a ghost. "Looks like we've got company."

Evelyn opened her eyes and sat up. A new smile grew across her face.

"Trick or treat!"

"Oh, my," she said, reaching into the bowl of candy. "What do we have here? A ghost. And a policeman. And a magician."

She filled their bags, and two of three kids said thank you as they went back down the porch steps on their way to meet up with their mothers, who were waiting at the curb. As they disappeared from sight, Evelyn settled back into her chair again. "What did you dress up as?"

"When I was ten? A hobo. I wore an old pea coat that belonged to my uncle, and a night cap, and my father smeared my face with burnt cork."

"Bet you were cute."

"Adorable."

She laughed, and as had happened so often of late, the laughter turned to a cough. It took an effort on her part to bring it back under control again. When she did, she smiled, her eyes watery, and went on as if nothing had happened. "So...what did you do about Mr. Death?"

"You sure you're up for this?"

"I think I can muster enough strength to listen to a story."

I nodded, not fully believing her, and went on about my telling because I knew better than to argue with her. "I gave a lot of thought to how to go about getting him into the box. It seemed to me that getting him into my mother's room was the easy part. He was already hanging around in the shadows, I imagined. Waiting. Sniffing at the stale stench of her pending passing. That's what Death did, I decided. That's what drew his attention. The stench in the air. He breathed that stench the way you and I breathe oxygen. For his very survival.

"Then I remembered Cecil, my friend's cat. It had died of one of them cat diseases you're always hearing about, distemper or feline leukemia, I don't remember exactly what the hell it was. But the day before last, my friend Steven and I had buried the cat in his back yard, under an oak. Just two days before. And I thought, what better way to interest Death than by offering up something that still carried that stench on it."

"Please tell me you didn't," Evelyn said.

"Mind you, it was no picnic. That cat stunk to high heaven. Only a couple of days in the dirt and things were already sliding around on its bones like it was broiled chicken."

"You can skip the gory details, if you don't mind."

"I don't. Not at all. They aren't important anyway. Not as important as the rest of it, that is. All you really need to know, I suppose, is that it worked."

Evelyn had never quite settled back into her chair after the last three trick-or-treaters had left. Her eyes were wide, and there was a hint of a smile at the corner of her mouth. I could tell she thought I was pulling her leg. "I'm not one of the neighborhood kids, Manny."

"I swear it's true. I never went trick-or-treating that night. I sat in the corner of her room, dressed up like a hobo, and I held onto one end of that twine like it was the only thing keeping me from sinking in quicksand. That's the way I had it in my head. I was going to catch Death, and my mother was going to live forever."

I took a miniature Hershey's bar out of the bowl, unwrapped it, and popped it into my mouth. "Around nine o'clock, my father came upstairs to say goodnight. I heard the floorboards creaking as he climbed the steps, and I managed to close the steamer trunk and sit on it before he entered the room. I don't think he even noticed the trunk. If he did, he didn't let on none. He noticed the smell, though. 'What the hell died in here?' he said, opening the bedroom window.

"He sat on the bed, next to my mother and held her hand for awhile. Then eventually, he kissed her on the forehead and stood up. 'You watching over her tonight?' I said that I was. 'That's good,' he said. He had been sleeping downstairs in the living room since her second stroke. He said it was because he tossed and turned too much and it bothered her, but I think it was really because he was as scared of losing her as I was."

Evelyn yawned. It was getting late now, already a bit past nine. Late enough that we shouldn't be getting anymore trick-or-treaters. Sometimes, we'll get a few stragglers, usually the older kids who shouldn't be out trick-or-treating at all, but I didn't imagine even they would be out tonight. This wasn't like most Halloweens. The guest of honor was missing.

"I'll make this fast," I said.

"No need. I'm fine."

"I'll make it fast anyway," I said. "Death arrived sometime around midnight. I had been fighting against sleep for what seemed like forever, but the moment he was in the room, I felt the goose flesh break out in a little jig on my arms, and I came wide awake. He rolled through the open door like a bank of morning fog slipping over the mountains. Hugging the floor. Not making a sound. Darker than the creosote baked to the back of the wood stove. Darker than the shadows themselves as I remember it. He slipped around the foot of her bed, then suddenly he was standing over her. Two red eyes glowing beneath the shadow of his hood, the faint outline of his naked skull barely visible.

Death.

Standing right in front of me.

"He seemed not to notice me at all, but he did notice the smell of that dead cat. He raised his head in the air, taking in the scent like a wild animal, then he followed it across the bed sheets covering my mother, to the edge of the mattress, where he stopped and sniffed the air again. He didn't move for a bit, and I thought that was probably the end of it, that was as close as he was going to come. Then suddenly he swooped down on the trunk like a hawk dropping out of the sky and I had him. I tugged on the twine. The lid dropped into place. And I had him."

"Death," Evelyn whispered.

"Death."

She let out a sigh, and it seemed to me she was probably enjoying herself some, whether or not she was willing to lend any credence to the story. At the same time, there was a sparkle in her eyes, and I took it upon myself to assume it was a sparkle of interest. "What did you do with him?"

"Well, I guess the short of it is...I let him go." I didn't like this particular part of the telling, because it was the part that still troubled me. But you get to a certain point in a story and there's no turning back. Not if you ever want anyone to listen to you again. "He was Br'er Rabbit I suppose you could say, and the world outside that trunk was his briar patch. He promised me if I let him out he would fix it so my mother would die of natural causes."

"And you were ten years old...."

"And I believed him," I said heavily. "The way I saw it, natural causes meant she was going to get to live to be an old woman. It meant going to bed one night when you were in your nineties and not waking up the next morning. That's all I wanted. I just wanted her to live a long life. It never occurred to me that natural causes meant just about everything short of murder. So I opened the trunk, and Death came gliding out like he was that Leonardo kid in that movie, like he was king of the world.

"She died that night. Sometime after I went to bed and before my father came upstairs with her breakfast the next morning. The doctor said it was her heart. It just gave out on her. But I knew what had really happened. Death had come waltzing back into that room just tickled all over with himself, and he'd taken my mother, and I'd allowed as he could do it."

Evelyn reached across the table and took my hand. The joy had gone out of her eyes, replaced with a pity that I didn't much care for. That didn't mean she believed all of the story, least wise not the part about Death hisself, but I think she believed that I *believed.* And I think she believed I was still carrying around the guilt for it. In that, I suppose she was right.

"It wasn't your fault."

But it was my fault.

Death had done his sales pitch and I had bought it for all it was worth.

It *was* my fault.

"Getting late," I said. I stood and stretched, my joints breaking into a chorus of pops and crackles. It was terrible being old. I didn't have the slightest hankering to start over as a teenager again, I can assure you of that. But there were times when I wished I could go back and start my life with Evelyn over again. They had been the best of my years. "That's enough storytelling for one Halloween."

I helped her to her feet, and when she reached for the candy bowl I told her to leave it. "In case some stragglers come by. I'd just as soon not have to clean rotten eggs off the windows in the morning. Besides, you bring that stuff into the house and I'm liable to start picking through it."

Once we were inside, Evelyn finally admitted to feeling tired.

"Go on up to bed," I said. "I'll clean up the dinner dishes and be up in a few minutes."

She kissed me. "'Night."

"'Night."

I stacked the dishes in the sink, added some soap, and let the water run. It was the sound of the water I thought I was hearing when that low-pitched howl started up again. I turned off the faucet, listened and realized what it was. It was a sound that made me want to cover my ears. Mournful. Despairing.

Then I heard Evelyn call out for me, and I knew she had followed it.

I climbed the stairs, paused a moment outside our bedroom door with the misplaced hope that maybe I'd been wrong. But of course, I hadn't. She'd followed that wail right up to the attic.

By the time I reached the top of the steps, I found her pressed so tight against the wall she could have stopped a leak. Across the room, my father's old steamer trunk was doing a little two-step, dancing around the floor on its brass-plated corners like a chicken dancing on a hot plate.

The wail began to wind down.

Evelyn looked at me, wide awake again, with fear in her eyes now. "What did you do?"

"You don't want to know, Sweet Pea."

"It's him, isn't it?"

I nodded.

"You said you let him go."

"You do something and it works, it gets a little easier the next time out," I said. If she'd doubted my story before, she had no doubts now. 'Course it didn't hurt any having that old trunk flopping around on the floor like a fish out of water. "I'm not letting him out this time, either. He can stay right where he is as far as I'm concerned. For the rest of eternity for all I care. It's where he belongs."

"You gotta let him out," Evelyn said. "You keep him locked in the trunk, folks are gonna stop dying."

"I believe that's pretty much the idea."

She shook her head, one hand holding onto an exposed stud to help her keep her balance. The blood had emptied from her face, and I didn't think it had anything to do with her being scared. She was tired was all. More than tired. "I know it sounds like a dream come true, Manny, but you can't fool yourself with this. You got a nightmare is what you got. How long you think it'll be before we run out of food? How long before the majority of folks out there are too old to care for themselves? You're tossing a wrench into the works and folks are gonna suffer because of it. That something you want for yourself? Too old for your own good?"

"All I want is you."

"Then let me have my self-respect," Evelyn said. "Let Death come when he comes. That's the way it's always been. It's the way it's supposed to be. I don't want it any different for me."

I guess I didn't want it any different for *me*, either. I told her as much, and she seemed pleased to hear it. Then I had her stand behind me, because I didn't want Death popping out of that old trunk and coming face-to-face with her right off the bat. If that happened, I figured he was just as likely to take her as not. He wasn't going to be none too happy after being boxed up for the last day or so.

I flipped the lock, raised the lid.

Death, that same blacker-than-black figure I'd once seen hovering over my mother, rose up out of the trunk right alongside the stench of the dead chicken I'd put in there to lure him. He moved around the edges of the room like a shadow on the walls—gaining his bearings, I supposed—then discovered the attic steps, and followed them down and on out of the house.

That was that.

For the second time in my life, I'd given Death his release.

❋ ❋ ❋

Evelyn, bless her heart, died less than six months later, after another bout with pneumonia weakened her to the point where she just didn't have the fight in her anymore. She died at Mercy Medical, the third day of her stay there, a little after midnight. I was with her when she died, right at her bedside, holding her hand.

'Course I wasn't the only one in the room. Death was there, too. I'd known he was coming. Evelyn and I had talked about him on occasion when she was feeling her worse. "Just leave him be," she'd said. "You promise?" I crossed my heart and hoped to die, which I knew I would want to do if I ever lost her. It was no easy chore watching him steal that last breath from her, but I let him do it because that's the way Evelyn had wanted it.

When he was done, his attention moved from her to me like the second hand on a clock. "You can see me."

I nodded.

"I remember you. The trunk." He crept across the bed—right over Evelyn's body, which made me sick—and we came face-to-face, so damn close I could smell that godawful stench on his breath. He laughed. "You know what I think I'll do with you? I think I'll let you live forever."

He laughed again. Then he was a shadow on the wall again, racing around the edges of the room.

"See how you like it, my friend," he said.

Then he was gone.

Halloween's come around again.

The months without Evelyn have been the worst months of my life, there's no denying that. I think about her just about every minute of every day. The way a thirsty man thinks about water, I suppose. I know it's foolish living in the past like that. There's no bringing her back now. Too late for that. And I wouldn't have done it any different. I did it the way Evelyn wanted it done. I tell myself that almost as often as I think about her. Then I start in to thinking that maybe it won't be long and I can join up with her again. And I remind myself what Death said about me living without no end.

'Course you do something and it works, it gets a little easier the next time out.

Maybe another Halloween without its guest of honor wouldn't be such a bad thing.

Who knows? Maybe I could make a little deal with Death.

Pumpkins and Circumstance

Robert Morrish

This is a story about how good things do, sometimes, come to those who wait. And how, rather suddenly and unexpectedly, Halloween, 1999 came to embody that sentiment for me.

Looking back, Halloween had always been, well, a little *disappointing* to me. When I was a child, still desperately wanting to believe in witches, ghosts, and their ilk, I always hoped that on that night, of all nights, perhaps I would see something out of the ordinary, something supernatural or other-worldly, something that would give substance to my dreams and fears. If nothing else, maybe at least a glimpse of Charlie Brown's Great Pumpkin.

But such was not to be. The Halloweens of my youth were ultimately unfulfilling in that regard, if not in the copious amounts of candy that were acquired.

As I grew older, my high hopes for Hallow's eve evolved into something very different, hinging upon a quest for highlight-reel levels of debauchery. But despite my best efforts, I usually went home feeling as though something was lacking.

Although I'm painting a rather bleak picture, there *were* certainly a few notable nights along the way.... For example:

1978 - After an ill-advised Halloween involving eggs, spray paint, and a full-blown melee, the police paid a visit to me at my parents' house the next day. As one might imagine, my parents were none too pleased about this—although, fortunately, no further trouble ever came of it.

1984 - As dusk crept up, my friends and I decided at the last minute to forego a Peoples' Express (Remember them? The cattle-call airline?) flight to New York, and instead embarked on a canoe trip down Ann Arbor's rain-swollen Huron River, a memorable journey inspired by various illicit substances. We borrowed the canoe from a friend who, as she came to realize our state, grew increasingly worried about our safety. The look of concern on her face when she handed us the paddles and asked if we knew how to use them was not lessened when one of my friends responded, in all seriousness, "sure, the big end goes in the water." Several hours later, as we drifted through a deep fog, laying back in the canoe in order to pass beneath a bridge (the water level was high!), we heard a deep rumbling and a mournful cry. Moments later, a train rushed through, passing directly over our heads, seemingly just inches away. It was quite a moment.

1987 - I attended my first genre-oriented event, the World Fantasy Convention, held over Halloween weekend in Nashville, TN. The event still lingers in my mind, partially because it was my first opportunity to socialize with like-minded folk, and also because I've only been to two more conventions since.

1989 - On October 17th, I was in San Pedro (in the greater Los Angeles area), trying to watch the World Series while a moving company loaded up all of my worldly possessions for a move to the San Francisco Bay area. At 5:04 p.m., the Loma Prieta earthquake struck, a 7.1 jolt that delayed the World Series, caused more than $7 billion dollars in damage, and killed at least 62 people. There was no escaping the fact: I was moving into a Federal Disaster Area. Nonetheless, there was no turning back. My girlfriend and I went ahead with the move, taking up residence in the house we had earlier rented, despite the fact that it had no running water (and still didn't six weeks later, when we moved out). When Halloween came, two weeks after the quake, many of the grim and shaken survivors in our mountain community were ready for any excuse to cut loose. There was a certain desperation infusing the large party we attended that year; a mad light dancing behind the eyes of many of the revelers, the image of which refuses to fade from memory.

1997 - Less than 48 hours removed from fairly significant surgery, I ventured out on a blind date. The date apparently went fairly well, although I don't remember much about it.... Apparently, it's true what they say—one really shouldn't mix alcohol and painkillers.

Despite these occasional memorable moments, for me Halloween remained, on par, an underwhelming occasion. The disappointment I had felt regarding Halloween in my youth lingered through my young adult years. In essence, Halloween always seemed to lack the sense of *magic* that I felt should be associated with it. Despite my attempts to find or attain something special on that night, it inevitably wound up seeming like just another, pretty ordinary night.

But that perception would eventually change. The events that would lead to a change in my feelings toward Halloween began on May 19th, 1999.

I've always looked upon whirlwind courtships with a certain amount of incredulity. How could one dive headlong into such a tenuous, even risky, proposition? How could one ever be so sure, so trusting, so carefree, all in such a short period of time? My rather dim view of full-speed-ahead, throw-caution-to-the-wind romances was probably particularly pronounced after my first marriage, which was preceded by a relatively leisurely two-year courtship, crashed and burned. After all, if the results of a more traditional engagement couldn't be trusted, how could I ever possibly believe in the foundation of a relationship that was seemingly rushed?

But then something happened. Then I met Kaya.

We were brought together through the machinations of a mutual friend. Within days of meeting, it was apparent to both of us where we were headed. At the risk of sounding exceedingly trite, we just *knew*.

I asked her to marry me in July, and once we started discussing prospective dates for the ceremony, one in particular kept shouldering its way to the forefront—Halloween. It had always been Kaya's favorite holiday, and my interest in Halloween and all things dark and mysterious is obvious from a glance at my bookshelves.

We thus undertook, from a standing start, a mad rush to pull together, in less than three months' time, a ceremony for approximately one hundred people. We were fortunate to line up a fantastic venue, both in terms of physical location—a nearby mountain winery, with sweeping views of the Santa Clara valley—and in terms of emotional significance. We had been there twice together previously, and the first occasion happened to be the date on which I first used the dreaded (to a bachelor) "L word" with her, while the second occasion happened to be the day on which I initially met her mother (who we hadn't yet told that we were getting married) and Kaya crowned that occasion by uttering an unexpected proposal to *me*, in front of her slightly shell-shocked mother. Anyway, enough of the sappy stuff.

We plunged ahead with the planning and despite the inevitable headaches, all went relatively smoothly; much better than we had any right to hope for. One of the highlights of the preparations was the writing of the invitations which, in a feverish fit of alliteration, declared:

> "But once year comes All Hallows' Eve, a night for fear,
> phantoms, and frolic
> Join our band of ghouls, goblins, and a groom; banshees,
> broomsticks, and a bride
> At twilight the ceremony shall commence, followed by runes,
> revelry, and revenants beneath the light of the moon"

Although I tend to shudder when I look at that prose now, I think the invitations did manage to capture the sense of fun and mischieviousness that we intended to convey—and which we hoped the evening itself would inspire.

Our Samhain Sabbath Hallow's Eve wedding opened with a bagpiper playing the highland pipes—fitting, since the historical purpose of the piper was to act as a battle-lead, to call the banshees and ghosts to join the march.

We wrote our own vows, modified from the Middle English ceremony, and launched the ceremony with an invocation to any spirits that might be lingering in the vicinity. Any vestiges of solemnity that clung to the proceedings were dispelled when the closing line was uttered: "Mensch, you may kiss your wench."

In the spirit of the occasion, invitees had been advised that masks were encouraged and costumes were optional, and most complied, resulting in an event that resembled a costume ball or Mardi Gras party more than any traditional wedding.

Unlike the bride and groom at most ceremonies, we stayed late into the evening, virtually closing down the venue with the last of our closest friends and family. The capper came when we discovered that my wife's Aunt Bobbie, who had helped us immeasurably by quickly dismantling and packing away all our various props and materials, had inadvertently snagged our overnight bags as well, and driven off with them.

We thus spent our wedding night (at a nearby hotel) with naught but our wedding finery. The next morning, we staggered through the painfully bright Monday-morning streets of Saratoga, California, dressed in tuxedo and wedding dress, respectively, desperately in search of coffee (although it was a lovely little hotel, their coffee was nothing to write home about, and we were in need of high-octane product). Needless to say, we received our share of strange looks. These minor morning-after tribulations, however, did nothing to detract from the enchantment of the prior evening, memories of which will likely linger forever.

So it took the better part of four decades, but that sense of Halloween magic, which I had so long sought and which had so consistently eluded me, was finally embraced.

HEAVY SET

Ray Bradbury

The woman stepped to the kitchen window and looked out. There in the twilight yard a man stood surrounded by barbells and dumbbells and dark iron weights of all kinds and slung jump ropes and elastic and coiled-spring exercisers. He wore a sweat suit and tennis shoes and said nothing to anyone as he simply stood in the darkening world and did not know she watched.

This was her son, and people called him Heavy Set.

Heavy Set squeezed the little bunched, coiled springs in his big fists. They were lost in his fingers, like magic tricks, then they reappeared. He crushed them. They vanished. He let them go. They came back.

He did this for ten minutes, otherwise motionless.

Then he bent down and hoisted up the one-hundred-pound barbell, noiselessly, not breathing. He motioned it a number of times over his head, then abandoned it and went into the open garage among the various surfboards he had cut out and glued together and sanded and painted and waxed, and there he punched a punching bag easily, swiftly, steadily, until his curly golden hair got moist. Then he stopped and filled his lungs until his chest measured 50 inches, and stood, eyes closed, seeing himself in an invisible mirror poised and tremendous, 220 muscled pounds, tanned by the sun, salted by the sea wind and his own sweat.

He exhaled. He opened his eyes.

He walked into the house, into the kitchen and did not look at his mother, this woman, and opened the refrigerator and let the arctic cold steam him while he drank a quart of milk straight out of the carton, never putting it down, just gulping and swallowing. Then he sat down at the kitchen table to examine the Halloween pumpkins.

He had gone out earlier in the day and bought the pumpkins and carved most of them and did a fine job: they were beauties and he was proud of them. Now, looking childlike in the kitchen, he started carving the last of them. You would never suspect he was thirty years old, he still moved so swiftly, so quietly, for a large action like hitting a wave with an uptilted and outthrust board, or here with the small action of a knife, giving sight to a Halloween eye. The electric light bulb filled the summer wildness of his hair, but revealed no emotion, except this one intent purpose of carving, on his face. There was all muscle in him, and no fat, and that muscle waited behind every move of the knife.

His mother came and went on personal errands around the house and then came to stand and look at him and the pumpkins and smile. She was used to him. She heard him every night drubbing the punching bag outside, or squeezing the little metal springs in his hands, or grunting as he lifted his world of weights and held them in balance on his strangely quiet shoulders. She was used to all these sounds even as she knew the ocean coming in on the shore beyond the cottage and laying itself out flat and shining on the sand. Even as she was used, by now, to hearing Heavy Set each night on the phone saying he was tired to girls and saying no, no he had to wax the car tonight or do his exercises to the eighteen-year-old boys who called.

She cleared her throat. "Was the dinner good tonight?"

"Sure," he said.

"I had to get special steak. I bought the asparagus fresh."

"It was good," he said.

"I'm glad you liked it, I always like to have you like it."

"Sure," he said, working.

"What time is the party?"

"Seven-thirty." He finished the last of the smile on the pumpkin and sat back. "If they all show up—they might not show up—I bought two jugs of cider."

He got up and moved into his bedroom, quietly massive, his shoulders filling the door and beyond. In the room, in the half dark, he made the strange pantomime of a man seriously and silently wrestling an invisible opponent as he got into his costume. He came to the door of the living room a minute later licking a gigantic peppermint-striped lollipop. He wore a pair of short black pants, a little boy's shirt with ruff collar, and an Eton cap. He licked the lollipop and said, "I'm the mean little kid!" and the woman who had been watching him laughed. He walked with an exaggerated little child's walk, licking the huge lollipop, all around the room while she laughed at him and he said things and pretended to be leading a big dog on a rope. "You'll be the life of the party!" the woman cried, pink-faced and exhausted. He was laughing now, also.

The phone rang.

He toddled out to answer it in the bedroom. He talked for a long time and his mother heard him say Oh For Gosh Sakes several times and finally he came slowly and massively into the living room looking stubborn. "What's wrong?" she wanted to know.

"Aw," he said, "half the guys aren't showing up at the party. They got other dates. That was Tommy calling. He's got a date with a girl from somewhere. Good grief."

"There'll be enough," said his mother.

"I don't know," he said.

"There'll be enough for a party," she said. "You go on."

"I ought to throw the pumpkins in the garbage," he said, scowling.

"Well you just go on and have a good time," she said. "You haven't been out in weeks."

Silence.

He stood there twisting the huge lollipop as big as his head, turning it in his large muscular fingers. He looked as if at any moment now he would do what he did other nights. Some nights he pressed himself up and down on the ground with his arms and some nights he played a game of basketball with himself and scored himself, team against team, black against white, in the backyard. Some nights he stood around like this and then suddenly vanished and you saw him way out in the ocean swimming long and strong and quiet as a seal under the full moon or you could not see him those nights the moon was gone and only the stars lay over the water but you heard him there, on occasion, a faint splash as he went under and stayed under a long time and came up, or he went out sometimes with his surfboard as smooth as a girl's cheeks, sandpapered to a softness, and came riding in, huge and alone on a white and ghastly wave that creamed along the shore and touched the sands with the surfboard as he stepped off like a visitor from another world and stood for a long while holding the soft smooth surfboard in the moonlight, a quiet man and a vast tombstone-shaped thing held there with no writing on it.

In all the nights like that in the past years, he had taken a girl out three times one week and she ate a lot and every time he saw her she said Let's Eat and so one night he drove her up to a restaurant and opened the car door and helped her out and got back in and said There's the Restaurant. Solong. And drove off. And went back to swimming way out, alone. Much later, a girl was half an hour late getting ready and he never spoke to her again.

Thinking all this, remembering all this, his mother looked at him now.

"Don't just stand there," she said. "You make me nervous."

"Well," he said , resentfully.

"Go on!" she cried. But she didn't cry it strong enough. Even to herself her voice sounded faint. And she did not know if her voice was just naturally faint or if she made it that way. She might as well have been talking about winter coming; everything she said had a lonely sound. And she heard the words again from her own mouth, with no force: "Go on!"

He went into the kitchen. "I guess there'll be enough guys there," he said.

"Sure, there will," she said, smiling again. She always smiled again. Sometimes when she talked to him, night after night, she looked as if she were lifting weights, too. When he walked through the rooms she looked like she was doing the walking for him. And when he sat brooding, as he often did, she looked around for something to do which might be burn the toast or overfire the steak. She made a short barking faint and stifled laugh now, "Get out, have a good time." But the echoes of it moved around in the house as if it were already empty and cold and he should come back in the door. Her lips moved: "Fly away."

He snatched up the cider and the pumpkins and hurried them out to his car. It was a new car and had been new and unused for almost a year. He polished it and jiggered with the motor or lay underneath it for hours messing with all the junk there, or just sat in the front seat glancing over the strength and health magazines, but rarely drove it. He put the cider and the cut pumpkins proudly in on the front seat, and by this time he was thinking of the possible good time tonight, so he did a little child's stagger as if he might drop everything, and his mother laughed. He licked his lollipop again, jumped into the car, backed it out of the gravel driveway, swerved it around down by the ocean, not looking out at this woman, and drove off along the shore road. She stood in the yard watching the car go away. William, my son, she thought.

It was seven-fifteen and very dark now; already the children were fluttering along the sidewalks in white ghost sheets and zinc-oxide masks, ringing bells, screaming, lumpy paper sacks banging their knees as they ran.

William, she thought.

They didn't call him William, they called him Heavy Set and Sammy which was short for Samson. They called him Butch and they called him Atlas and Hercules. At the beach you always saw high school boys around him feeling his biceps as if he were a new sports car, testing him, admiring him. He walked golden among them. Each year it was that way. And then the eighteen-year-old ones got to be nineteen and didn't come around so often and then twenty and very rarely and then twenty-one and never again, just gone, and suddenly there were new eighteen-year-olds to replace them, yes, always the new ones to stand where the others had stood in the sun, while the older ones went on somewhere to something and somebody else.

William, my good boy, she thought. We go to shows on Saturday nights. He works on the high-power lines all day, up in the sky, alone, and sleeps alone in his room at night, and never reads a book or paper or listens to a radio or plays a record, and this year he'll be thirty-one. And just where, in all the years, did the thing happen that put him up that pole alone and working out alone every night? Certainly there had been enough women, here and there, now and then, through his life. Little scrubby ones, of course, fools, yes, by the look of them, but women, or girls, rather, and none worth glancing at a second time. Still, when a boy gets past thirty...? She sighed. Why, even as recently as last night the phone had rung. Heavy Set answered it, and she could fill in the unheard half of the conversation, she had heard thousands like it in a dozen years:

"Sammy, this is Christine." A woman's voice. "What you doing?"

His little golden eyelashes flickered and his brow furrowed, alert and wary. "Why?"

"Tom, Lu, and I are going to a show, want to come along?"

"It better be good!" he cried, indignantly.

She named it.

"That!" he snorted.

"It's a good film," she said.

"Not that one," he said. "Besides, I haven't shaved yet today."

"You can shave in five minutes."

"I need a bath, and it'd take a long time,"

A long time, thought his mother, he was in the bathroom two hours today. He combs his hair two dozen times, musses it, combs it again, talking to himself.

"OK for you." The woman's voice on the phone. "You going to the beach this week?"

"Saturday," he said, before he thought.

"See you there, then," she said.

"I meant Sunday," he said, quickly.

"I could change it to Sunday," she replied.

"If I can make it," he said, even more quickly. "Things go wrong with my car."

"Sure," she said. "Samson. Solong."

And he had stood there for a long time, turning the silent phone in his hand.

Well, his mother thought, he's having a good time now. A good Halloween party, with all the apples he took along, tied on strings, and the apples, untied, to bob for in a tub of water, and the boxes of candy, the sweet corn kernels that really taste like autumn. He's running around looking like the bad little boy, she thought, licking his lollipop, everyone shouting, blowing horns, laughing, dancing.

At eight, and again at eight-thirty and nine she went to the screen door and looked out and could almost hear the party a long way off at the dark beach, the sounds of it blowing on the wind crisp and furious and wild, and wished she could be there at the little shack out over the waves on the pier, everyone whirling about in costumes, and all the pumpkins cut, each a different way, and a contest for the best homemade mask or makeup job, and too much popcorn to eat and—

She held to the screen doorknob, her face pink and excited, and suddenly realized the children had stopped coming to beg at the door. Halloween, for the neighborhood kids anyway, was over.

She went to look out into the backyard.

The house and yard were too quiet. It was strange not hearing the basketball volley on the gravel or the steady bumble of the punching bag taking a beating. Or the little tweezing sound of the hand squeezers.

What if, she thought, he found someone tonight, found someone down there, and just never came back, never came home. No telephone call. No letter, that was the way it could be. No word. Just go off away and never come back again. What if? What if?

No! she thought, there's no one, no one there, no one anywhere. There's just this place. This is the only place.

But her heart was beating fast and she had to sit down.

The wind blew softly from the shore.

She turned on the radio but could not hear it.

Now, she thought, they're not doing anything except playing blindman's bluff, yes, that's it, blind tag, and after that they'll just be—

She gasped and jumped.

The windows had exploded with raw light.

The gravel spurted in a machine-gun spray as the car jolted in, braked and stopped, motor running. The lights went off in the yard. But the motor still gunned up, idled, gunned up, idled.

She could see the dark figure in the front seat of the car, not moving, staring straight ahead.

"You—" she started to say, and opened the back screen door. She found a smile on her mouth. She stopped it. Her heart was slowing now. She made herself frown.

He shut off the motor. She waited. He climbed out of the car and threw the pumpkins in the garbage can and slammed the lid.

"What happened?" she asked. "Why are you home so early—?"

"Nothing." He brushed by her with the two gallons of cider intact. He set them on the kitchen sink.

"But it's not ten yet—"

"That's right." He went into the bedroom and sat down in the dark.

She waited five minutes. She always waited five minutes. He wanted her to come ask, he'd be mad if she didn't, so finally she went and looked into the dark bedroom

"Tell me," she said.

"Oh, they all stood around," he said. "They just stood around like a bunch of fools and didn't do anything."

"What a shame."

"They just stood around like dumb fools."

"Oh, that's a shame."

"I tried to get them to do something, but they just stood around. Only eight of them showed up, eight out of twenty, eight, and me the only one in costume. I tell you. The only one. What a bunch of fools."

"After all your trouble, too."

"They had their girls and they just stood around with them and wouldn't do anything, no games, nothing. Some of them went off with the girls," he said, in the dark, seated, not looking at her. "They went off up the beach and didn't come back. Honest to gosh." He stood now, huge, and leaned against the wall, looking all disproportioned in the short trousers. He had forgotten the child's hat was on his head. He suddenly remembered it and took it off and threw it on the floor. "I tried to kid them. I played with a toy dog and did some other stuff, but nobody did anything. I felt like a fool, the only one there dressed like this, and them all different, and only eight out of twenty there, and most of them gone half an hour. Vi was there. She tried to get me to walk up the beach, too. I was mad by then. I was really mad. I said no thanks. And here I am. You can have the lollipop. Where did I put it? Pour the cider down the sink, drink it, I don't care."

She had not moved so much as an inch in all the time he talked. She opened her mouth.

The telephone rang.

"If that's them, I'm not home."

"You'd better answer it," she said.

He grabbed the phone and whipped off the receiver.

"Sammy?" said a loud high clear voice. He was holding the receiver out on the air, glaring at it in the dark. "That you?" He grunted. "This is Bob." The eighteen-year-old voice rushed on. "Glad you're home. In a big rush, but—what about that game tomorrow?"

"What game?"

"What game? For cri-yi, you're kidding. Notre Dame and SC!"

"Oh, football."

"Don't say Oh Football like that, you talked it, you played it up, *you* said—"

"That's no game," he said, not looking at the telephone, the receiver, the woman, the wall, nothing.

"You mean you're not going? Heavy Set, it won't be a *game* without you!"

"I got to water the lawn, polish the car—"

"You can do that Sunday!"

"Besides, I think my uncle's coming over to see me. Solong."

He hung up and walked out past his mother into the yard. She heard the sounds of him out there as she got ready for bed.

He must have drubbed the punching bag until three in the morning. Three, she thought, wide awake, listening to the concussions. He's always stopped at twelve, before.

At three-thirty he came into the house.

She heard him standing just outside her door.

He did nothing else except stand there in the dark, breathing.

She had a feeling he still had the little-boy suit on. But she didn't want to know if this were true.

After a long while the door swung slowly open.

He came into her dark room and lay down on the bed, next to her, not touching her. She pretended to be asleep.

He lay face up and rigid.

She could not see him. But she felt the bed shake as if he were laughing. She could hear no sound coming from him, so she could not be sure.

And then she heard the squeaking sounds of the little steel springs being crushed and uncrushed, crushed and uncrushed in his fists.

She wanted to sit up and scream for him to throw those awful noisy things away. She wanted to slap them out of his fingers.

But then, she thought, what would he do with his hands? What could he put in them? What would he, yes, what would he do with his hands?

So she did the only thing she could do—she held her breath, shut her eyes, listened, and prayed, Oh God, let it go on, let him keep squeezing those things, let him keep squeezing those things, let him, let him, oh let, let him, let him keep squeezing...let...let....

It was like lying in bed with a great dark cricket.

And a long time before dawn.

YEAR OF THE WITCH

William F. Nolan

I was twelve that year, and enjoying a carefree life in Kansas City with Don Miller and Jack Morgan, my two closest buddies. Don was kind of shortish and red-haired, with a ton of freckles. Jack was tall and thin as a bean stalk, with dark eyes and a great smile. We'd play Cowboy-and-Indians in Troost Park, shoot marbles "for keeps" in Don's driveway, attend the Freddy Fox matinees at the Isis Theatre, break old whiskey bottles with bricks at the corner lot, swap issues of super-hero comics (we liked Dollman the best because that little guy could really kick butt), and hide out in the treehouse we'd built in Jack's backyard. (We were hiding from an army of terrible purple aliens from Mars who were invading the Earth, starting with our neighborhood.)

In early October of that year I made my folks proud by winning first place in the big, all-class spelling bee at my grade school. I even beat out Joanne Haake from seventh grade, which nobody had ever been able to do before.

Anyhow, Don and Jack and I had special plans for Halloween. Three blocks from our neighborhood, on Paseo, there was this old vacant, boarded-up house that other kids at school swore for sure was haunted. A long time ago, the story went, a scuzzy old witch moved into the house and cast awful spells on anybody who came near her, so people stayed clear of the place. She finally got into trouble with the law by luring little kids into her house with raisin cookies and then boiling them (the kids) in a big pot for supper. After her meal, only tiny bones remained. According to the story, the cops broke in one night and shot her in the heart. After that, the house was boarded up and left to rot.

But she didn't go away. Her ghost lived upstairs on the second floor, and if you crouched in the yard next door and listened hard, you could hear scary thumping noises up there. It was the witch, all right, and that was a known fact.

So that year, when I was twelve, Jack and Don and I decided to challenge the witch-ghost on Halloween. It took a lot of courage for us to do what we planned, but we'd all double-dared each other to face the ghost that night, so of course we *had* to go. You can't chicken out on a double-dare.

We didn't tell our parents or anybody else. It was our secret. For us, there wasn't going to be any going from house to house for trick-or-treats. And that night we wouldn't go to bed with stomach aches, or have our own brown paper sacks filled to the top with all kinds of candy sold at Radaker's Market. Nosiree, not *this* Halloween.

So on Halloween night there we were, all dressed in costumes our Moms had bought for us. I was a pirate, Jack was a clown, and Don was a scarecrow. (Straw kept falling out of his pants.) We tossed away our unused candy sacks and trudged up the long hill to Paseo.

At last we reached the witch house. We stood close together in the weedy, abandoned front yard and stared at the place. It towered above us like a dark castle. We strained our ears, but could hear no ghost noises.

"Maybe she's sleeping," Jack said hopefully.

"Naw, ghosts don't sleep," Don said.

"How do *you* know?" Jack demanded. "You don't know nothin' about ghosts!"

"Do, too!" said Don. "I read up in a book about them. The book said ghosts just float round all the time. They don't sleep."

"Yeah," I chimed in. "They just keep floating around."

"I got me a bad feeling in the pit of my stomach," said Jack. "What if she don't like us coming into her place? What if she tries to kill us?"

"The book said ghosts can't kill people," Don said authoritatively. "They're made out of stuff that's sorta like smoke. They don't have real bodies like us."

Jack shook his head. "I just got me a bad feeling," he repeated. "We shoulda gone trick-or-treating."

"Fooey!" I said. "You're chicken. You're *scared* to go inside."

"Am not!" Jack muttered, but his denial wasn't very convincing.

"Well, *I'm* not afraid," declared Don. "Let's do it."

The truth was, we were all plenty scared, but you can't go back on a double-dare.

Slowly, we moved up the weathered porch steps to the front door. It was nailed shut.

"Over here," I said, after shuffling carefully along the dark porch. "Look! This window's got a loose board. We can get in here."

So we did.

There was a full moon that night and it cast eerie yellow light over the sheeted furniture in the living room. An oil painting of some old

Civil War guy in a blue uniform was hanging over the fireplace. He had big whiskers and mean eyes.

"C'mon," I whispered. "We gotta head upstairs."

Our images rippled past us in a dusty wall mirror as we moved into the hall that faced the main stairway.

Suddenly, horribly...a *thump* from the second floor!

We all gasped.

"That's her!" Don's voice was quavery. "She's up there for sure."

"I'm leaving!" said Jack, but I caught him firmly by his clown collar.

"No, you aren't," I said. "We're all in this together—like the Three Musketeers."

"Maybe Jack's right," said Don, losing more straw as his body shook. "Maybe this wasn't such a great idea."

"No chickening out," I said, pushing them forward. "Up we go."

We crept up the creaking stairs. Creak...step...creak...step... creak...step...all of us huddled close together, our eyes bugged, our hearts beating in unison like Indian tom-toms.

We were within three steps of the top when Jack yelled: "Yikes!"

The ghost had suddenly popped into sight. It was a tall pale figure in gray rags who shook a bony finger at us and shouted: "How *dare* you come into my house! Curse you! Curse the lot of you!"

That's all it took. We tumbled crazily down the stairs, reached the open window, and got the hell out of there.

A week later things started going bad. Don's parents received a letter from Illinois telling about how Don's grandpa, on his Mom's side, had fallen into the town ravine in Waukegan and died of a heart attack. That meant Don's Dad had to take over the old man's lumber business, so the whole family moved to Illinois and I never saw Don again.

Bad things kept happening. An old-fashioned horse-drawn ice wagon serviced our block in those days and, just a week after Don's family left for Waukegan, Jack slipped on a pile of horse manure in the street and broke his ankle. The local doctor set it, but it didn't mend right, so Jack's parents took him to a special hospital in St. Louis to get it fixed. They never came back to K.C., and that was the end of my friendship with Jack. A new family, who only had girls, moved into Jack's house and soon after they took down his backyard treehouse. Suddenly I had no one left to help me defend our neighborhood from Martians.

Then, without warning, I couldn't spell anymore. I just lost the ability overnight. Finished dead last in the next spelling bee at school.

"It was the witch," I told my Dad. "She put a curse on the three of us, and that's why I can't spell anymore."

My folks never believed in ghosts or curses so they failed to share my view of things. They blamed my spelling lapse on "stubborn laziness," which my Mom was sure I'd inherited from my father's side of the family. (She never liked my Dad's relatives.)

Two months later Dad brought me the morning paper and pointed out a news article. "Read that," he ordered.

The article said that the body of an unidentified woman, probably somewhere in her late eighties, had been found dead on the second floor of a vacant house on 3625 Paseo. She was a hobo who, unknown to anyone in the neighborhood, had been living in the house for approximately the past three years.

"You see," said Dad, "there's your explanation. No witch. No ghost. Just a poor lady down on her luck."

I didn't argue with him, but I was certain he was wrong. I know a ghost when I see one, and that awful figure at the top of the stairs was no hobo. She was an honest-to-God witch.

Why did Don's grandpa fall into the ravine? Why did Jack slip on the horse manure? Why did I suddenly lose my ability to spell?

I knew it was the curse. The curse that old gray witch put on us. And I double-dare you to prove me wrong.

Where Julie Went: A Halloween Memory

Michael Cadnum

Every Halloween it was getting worse, the kids torching the eucalyptus, setting fire to the patio furniture. If you stayed home you had kids on the roof, peeing in the rain gutters, writing on the porch screens. If you went away they rolled the trash cans, but they tended to strike where there was an audience. So it seemed like a good plan to go out to the trailer near Victorville, in the high-desert Mojave, and survive Halloween out under the bright stars.

But when we got to the acreage, a plot of desert land up against the hills, yucca trees and cactus, the gate was chained and locked. The right-of-way easement I shared with the Ralston Purina alfalfa plot to the west allowed equal access, but there I was at twilight on Halloween, faced with a Yale lock on a vinyl-sheath chain that was wrapped around the metal frame of the chain link gate.

The tire iron in the Camry was a little thing about this big, and the gun I carried was a custom double-barrel from the shop on New Bond Street, London, the right barrel rifled for deer and the other smooth bore for not-deer. A gun comes in handy out there. You get mourning doves the size of sandwiches and sometimes you get maverick Hereford steer who have been living on creosote and haven't seen a human for a long time.

I pulled the car around and backed it up against the gate, having no faith I could reverse the V-6 through the barrier. I let the tires spin craters, the car grinding against the fence, causing minor damage on the bumpers, which are plastic anyway. I was trying to push through, not smash into it at any velocity as they do in movies, and which I have never seen anyone do in life. Then I gave up and got the gun.

I put the two barrels up against the chain in its vinyl tubing, and I wasn't all that surprised at the big noise. And I was temporarily too deaf to hear any little noises that might have been going on right after.

It did blow the chain out, but I was embarrassed at doing what was basically yet another movie thing and not thinking out a real-life way to get through the gate. On the way up to the trailer, driving the two lane dirt track through the drift dunes, I saw what I saw. I didn't know what it was and I didn't like to look at it, and I kept driving, all the way up to the little old Air Stream two-wheeler, dwarfed by the air conditioner hanging on its side.

I went inside and made Hershey's instant milk chocolate like we always did. Heated water on the butane stove, two cups, and stirred in the cocoa, but then the water petered out. I really didn't want to go out there, having seen what I had, but if the pump lost its prime you are never going to get even a steady drip out of the new Haws faucet and stainless steel setup I'd installed that summer.

It was past the hay-growing season, and the alfalfa land was fallow, but sometimes the Rainbirds come on anyway, year round, just asserting authority, pluming the air with water. So I wasn't surprised when I heard pattering gazing the aluminum skin of the trailer. Only when the noises continued to the door and pounded did I think that this wasn't really water. And then when the trailer moved.

It shifted just a little, like the time a bear tested out the doors on that Sentra I drove to Alaska, and now I was feeling my pockets for shotgun shells and wondering how come I didn't have a normal .38 magnum, like my neighbor down there in the Low Mojave, a retired biscuit plant manager with a cabin nine miles toward Victorville, past the Roy Rogers museum. My friend wouldn't go out to get the mail without three or four pounds of ordnance on his hip. All I had was a hand-made, one-of-a-kind gun, which to tell you the truth I only kept ammunition for the left barrel for anyway.

I waited for the shuddering of the entire vehicle to cease and then, after a long spell of quiet, I opened the door, and ran down into the night, holding the gun the way you do when you know it's just weight now, without anything to shoot. I got into the four-door and drove home and got back in San Bernardino before midnight.

I went to bed.

I got up the next morning, and you know that feeling. The whole world, it seems like, has finally gone off Day Light savings time and the feeling on November 1 is pure autumn, even with the drought hard and only the really fanatically deciduous liquid amber going colorful. Some Trick or Treaters had written in soap all over the porch screens, which are old and black with rust and make a satisfactory surface for a bar of Ivory. Nothing really bad, just a big penis and a yelling mouth, something illegible, although I had to set the screens out on the crab grass and use the hose to wash them.

And even then, with cold water, you'd be surprised how hard it is. Then I decided to report the thing I'd seen, and the sheriff's department said they would come out. You know how it always takes so long for everything to be made clear in movies, how sometimes you don't even know at first is this a naked-people movie or a family going on a trip. This was quick. They said an irrigation specialist out checking the sprinkler pipes had found that thing on the empty hay field at dawn. The sheriffs took me to the headquarters out by Baseline Road, where San Bernardino County stretches from there all the way to the Nevada state line.

And you know how you think they must have a little curtain they part, leave open, and then shut, or else have a video camera, let you take a look and then not look. Well, they didn't have such arrangements right then, it was just here you go, unzipping that body bag which in those days was like a garment bag, with a big Talon zipper down the side. And I said that's what I saw going out into the field, with a piece of chain or slug in her. That's what I saw and couldn't look at, and now I am so glad I called.

Boo

Richard Laymon

The last time I ever went out trick or treating, it was with my best friend Jimmy and his sisters, Peggy and Donna. Peggy, Jimmy's kid sister, had a couple of her little friends along, Alice and Olive. There was also Olive's older brother, Nick. Donna, Jimmy's older sister, was in charge.

We all wore costumes except Donna.

Being sixteen, Donna thought of herself as too old for dressing up so she went as herself in a plaid chamois shirt, blue jeans and sneakers.

Peggy wore a Peter Pan outfit. When I saw her in the green elf outfit and feathered cap, I said, "Peter Pan!" She corrected me. "Not *Peter* Pan, *Peggy* Pan."

One of her little friends, I don't remember whether it was Olive or Alice, sported a tutu and a tiara and carried a wand with a star at one end. The other girl wore a store-bought E.T. costume. Or maybe she was Yoda. I'm not sure which.

Nick, I remember. All of fourteen, he was a year older than Jimmy and me. He was supposed to be a Jedi warrior. He wore black coveralls, a black cape and black galoshes. No mask, no helmet. We only knew he was a Jedi warrior because he told us so. And because he carried a "light saber," pretty much a hollow plastic tube attached to a flashlight.

Jimmy was "the Mummy." Earlier that night, Donna and I had spent ages wrapping him up in a white bedsheet that we'd cut into narrow strips. We kept pinning the strips to Jimmy's white longjohns. It took forever. It would've driven me nuts except for Donna. Every so often, she gave Jimmy a poke with a pin just to keep things interesting. We finally got it done, though, and Jimmy made a good-looking mummy.

My costume was easy. I was Huck Finn. I wore a straw hat, an old flannel shirt and blue jeans. I had a length of clothesline over one shoulder, tied at the ends to a couple of my belt loops to look like an old rope suspender. As a final touch, I had a corncob pipe that my dad let me borrow for the night.

So that was our group: who we were and how we were dressed that night.

Jimmy and me, Donna and Peggy, Alice and Olive and Nick.

Seven of us.

Except for Donna, we carried paper bags for our treats. Donna carried a flashlight. For the most part, she took up the rear. She usually didn't even go to the doors with us, but waited on the sidewalk while we rang doorbells, yelled "Trick or treat!" and held out our bags to receive the goodies.

For the first couple of hours that night, everything went along fine. If you don't count Nick going on occasional rampages, bopping us on the heads or prodding us in the butts with his light saber, proclaiming, "The Dark Side rules!" After a while, Jimmy's bandages started to come off and droop. At one point, ET (or Yoda) fell down and skinned her knee and spent a while bawling. But nothing major went wrong and we kept on collecting loot and roaming further and further into unknown territory.

It was getting very late when we came to a certain house that was not at all like the others on its block. Whereas they were brightly lighted and most had jack-o'-lanterns on their porches, this house was utterly dark. Whereas their shrubbery and lawns were neatly trimmed, this house seemed nearly lost in a jungle of deep grass, wild foliage and brooding trees. It also seemed much older than the other houses on the block. Three stories high (not two like its neighbors) and made of wood (not brick), it looked as if it belonged to a different century.

The houses on both sides of the old one seemed unusually far away from it, as if whoever'd built them had been afraid to get too close.

Though Nick usually ran from house to house without returning to the sidewalk, cutting across lawns and brandishing his light saber with Peggy and Olive and Alice chasing after him, this time he thought better of it. All four of them came back to the sidewalk, where Jimmy and I were walking along with Donna.

"What's with *that* house?" Nick asked.

"It's *creepy-eepy-eepy*," said either Olive or Alice, whichever one was the fairy godmother princess ballerina.

"It doesn't look like anyone lives there," Donna said.

"Maybe like the Munsters," I said.

"I think maybe we should skip this one," Donna said.

"Hey, no," Jimmy protested. "We can't skip this one. It's the best one yet!"

I felt exactly the same way, but I never could've forced myself to disagree with Donna.

She shook her head, her bangs swaying across her brow. "I really don't like the looks of it. Besides, it'd be a waste of time. Nobody's there. You won't get any treats. We might as well just...."

"You never know," Jimmy interrupted. "Maybe they just forgot to turn their lights on."

"I think Donna's right," I said. "I don't think anyone's there."

Jimmy shook his head. By this time, all the "bandages" had slipped off his head. They dangled around his neck like rag necklaces. "If somebody *does* live in a place like that," he said, "wouldn't you wanta meet him? Or her. Maybe it's a creepy old woman. Just imagine. Like some crazy old witch or hermit or something, you know?"

For a while, we all just stood there and stared at the dark old house—what we could see of it through the bushes and trees, anyway, which wasn't much.

Looking at it, I felt a little shivery inside.

"I think we should just go on," Donna said.

"You're in charge," Jimmy muttered. He'd been ordered by his parents to obey Donna, but he sounded disappointed.

She took a deep breath and sighed. It felt good to watch her do that.

"It's *probably* deserted," she said. Then she said, "Okay, let's give it a try."

"All RIGHT!" Jimmy blurted.

"This time, I'll lead the way. Who else wants to come?"

The three girls jumped up and down, yelling, "Me! I do! Me! Me-me-me!"

Nick raised his light saber and said, "I'll come and protect you, Princess Donna."

"Any trouble," I told him, "cut 'em to ribbons with your flashlight."

"Take *that*!" He jabbed me in the crotch.

He didn't even do it very hard, but the tube got me in the nuts. I grunted and gritted my teeth and barely managed not to double over.

"Gotcha!" Nick announced.

Donna bounced her flashlight off his head. Not very hard, but the bulb went dark and Nick yelped, *"OW!"* and dropped his light saber and candy bag and grabbed the top of his head with both hands and hunched over and walked in circles.

"Oh, take it easy," she told him. "I barely tapped you."

"I'm gonna *tell!*" he blurted.

"Tell your little ass off, see if I care."

The ballerina fairy-godmother princess gasped.

ET or Yoda blurted, "Language!"

Little sister Peggy Pan almost split a gut, but seemed to know she shouldn't laugh at Nick's misfortune so she clamped a hand across her mouth.

Jimmy, more concerned about my fate than Nick's, patted me on the back and asked, "You okay, man?"

"Fine," I squeezed out.

Donna came closer. Looking me in the eyes, she said, "Did he get you bad?"

I grimaced and shrugged.

"Right in the nads," offered Jimmy.

I gave him a look.

Instead of killing him, as intended, my look seemed to inspire him. "Donna's a certified life guard, you know. All that first aid training. Want her to take a look?"

"Shut up!" I snapped at him.

"Stop it, Jimmy," she said.

"How'd you like to have her kiss...."

I punched his arm. He yelled, *"Hey!"* and grabbed it.

"Okay, okay," Donna said. "Everybody calm down. No more hitting. How are you doing, Matt?" she asked me.

"Okay, I guess."

"Nick?" she asked.

He was standing nearby, gently touching the top of his head. "I've got a bump."

"Well, that's too bad, but you asked for it."

"Did not."

Donna said, "You busted my damn flashlight."

Jimmy and I laughed. So did Peggy Pan.

ET or Yoda blurted, "Language!"

"You shouldn't go around whumping people on the head," Nick explained. "You can cause 'em brain damage."

"Not you!" Jimmy said. "You haven't got one."

"That's enough," Donna said. "Come on, are we gonna check out this house or aren't we?" Without even waiting for a response, she stepped off the sidewalk and started trudging toward the creepy old place.

I went after her, hurting. Each step I took, it felt like a little hand was squeezing one of my balls. But I didn't let it stop me and it seemed to pretty much go away by the time we reached the porch stairs.

Donna stopped and turned around. She still held the flashlight in one hand, though it wasn't working anymore. With her other hand, she put a finger to her lips.

In a few moments, everyone was standing in front of her, motionless and silent.

Donna took the forefinger away from her lips. She pointed it at each of us, counting heads the way a school bus driver does before bringing a bunch of kids back from a field trip. Done, she whispered, "Okay, six."

"Seven," I said.

She turned her head toward me. The moon was full, so I could see her face pretty well. She raised her eyebrows.

"You," I whispered.

"Ah. Okay. Right." In a somewhat louder voice, she said, "Okay, there're seven of us right now. Let's hope and pray there're *still* seven when we get back to the street."

Her words gave me the creeps.

One of the girls made a whiny sound.

"I wanna go back," said one of them. Maybe the same one who'd whined. I don't know whether it was Alice or Olive. It wasn't Peggy Pan, though.

Peggy Pan whispered, "Wussy."

Jimmy chuckled.

And I saw the look on Donna's face and realized she was trying to psych us out.

Not *us*, really. *Them*.

Nick had made her mad, and she wasn't exactly tickled by Alice or Olive, either, so she figured to make life a little more interesting for them.

"If anybody wants to go back and wait for us on the sidewalk," she said, "that's fine. It'd probably be a good idea. No telling what might happen when we go up and ring the doorbell."

One of the girls whined again.

"You're just trying to scare us," Nick said. In the full moon, I could see the sneer on his face. "Can't scare a Jedi," he said.

Donna continued, "I just think...everyone needs to know the score. I wasn't planning to mention it, but...I've heard about this house. I know what happened here. And I happen to know it *isn't* deserted."

"Yeah, sure," Nick said.

Lowering her voice, Donna said, "A crazy man lives here. A crazy man named...Boo. Boo Ripley."

I almost let out a laugh, but held it in.

"Boo *who*?" Jimmy asked.

I snorted and gave him my elbow.

"Ow!"

"Shhh!" Donna said. "Want Boo to hear us?" She looked at the others, frowning slightly. "When he was only eight years old, Boo chopped up his mom and dad with a hatchet...and ate 'em. Gobbled 'em up! Yum yum!"

"Did not," Nick said.

"I wanna go home!"

"Shut up," Nick snapped.

"But Boo was a *little* boy back then. And his mom and dad were very large. Even though he gobbled them day and night, night and day, there was always more that needed to be eaten. Well, Boo's mom was a real cat lover. She had about a dozen cats living in the house all the time and stinking it up, so finally Boo started feeding his folks to the cats. Day and night, night and day, Boo and the cats ate and ate and ate. At last, they managed to polish off the last of Boo's mom and dad. And you know what?"

"What?" asked Peggy Pan. She sounded rather gleeful.

"I don't wanna hear!" blurted tutu girl.

"Knock it off, pipsqueak," Nick snapped at her.

"Boo and the cats," Donna said, "enjoyed eating the mom and dad so much that they lost all interest in any other kind of food. From that time forth, they would only eat people. Raw people. And you know what?"

"What?" asked Peggy Pan and I in unison.

"They still live right here in this house. Every night, they hide in the dark and watch out the windows, waiting for visitors."

"You're just making this up," Nick said.

"Sure I am."

"She *isn't*, man," said Jimmy.

"They're probably up in the house right this very minute watching us, licking their lips, just *praying* we'll climb the stairs and go across the porch and ring the doorbell. Because they're *very* hungry and you know what?"

"WHAT?" asked Peggy Pan, Jimmy and I in unison.

In a low, trembling voice, Donna said, "The food they love most of all is...." Shouting *"LITTLE GIRLS LIKE YOU!"* she lunged toward Alice and Olive.

They shrieked and whirled around and ran for their lives. Yoda or ET waved her little arms overhead as she fled. The fairy dancer whipped her magic wand as if swatting at bats. One of them fell and crashed in the weeds and started to cry.

Nick yelled, "Fuck!" and ran after them, his light saber jumping.

"Language!" Jimmy called after him.

Donna brushed her hands together. "Golly," she said. "What got into *them*?"

"Can't imagine," I said.

"What a bunch of wussies," said Peggy Pan.

"I can't *stand* that Nick," said Jimmy. "He is *such* a shit."

"Language," Donna told him.

We laughed, all four of us.

Then Donna said, "Come on, gang," and trotted up the porch stairs. We hurried after her.

And I'll always remember trotting up those stairs and stepping onto the dark porch and walking up to the door. Even while it was happening, I knew I would never forget it. It was just one of those moments when you think, *It doesn't get any better than this.*

I was out there in the windy, wonderful October night with cute and spunky little Peggy Pan, with my best buddy Jimmy, and with Donna. I was in love with Donna. I'd fallen in love with her the first time I ever met her and I'm in love with her to this day and I'll love her the rest of my life.

That night, she was sixteen and beautiful and brash and innocent and full of fun and vengeance. She'd trounced Nick and done quite a number on Alice and Olive, too. Now she was about to ring the doorbell of the creepiest house I'd ever seen. I wanted to run away screaming myself. I wanted to yell with joy. I wanted to hug Donna and never let her go. And also I sort of felt like crying.

Crying *because* it was all so terrifying and glorious and beautiful—and because I knew it wouldn't last.

All the very best times are like that. They hurt because you know they'll be left behind.

But I guess that's partly what makes them special, too.

"Here goes," Donna whispered.

She raised her hand to knock on the door, but Jimmy grabbed her wrist. "That stuff about Boo and the cats," he whispered. "You made it up, didn't you?"

"What do you think?"

"Okay." He let go of her hand.

She knocked on the door.

Nothing.

I turned halfway around. Beyond the bushes and trees of the front yard, Nick and the two girls were watching us from the sidewalk.

Donna knocked again. Then she whispered, "I really don't think anyone lives here anymore."

"I hope not," I whispered.

Donna reached out and gave the screen door a pull. It swung toward us, hinges squawking.

"What're you *doing*?" Jimmy blurted.

"Nothing," said Donna. She tried the main door. "Damn," she muttered.

"What?" I asked.

"Locked."

Oh, I thought. *That's* too bad.

The wooden door had a small window at about face level. Donna leaned forward against the door, cupped her hands by the sides of her eyes, and peered in.

Peered and peered and didn't say a word.

"Can you see something?" Jimmy asked.

Donna nodded ever so slightly.

"What? What's in there?"

She stepped back, lowered her arms and turned her back to the door and said very softly, "I think we'd better get out of here."

Peggy Pan groaned.

Jimmy muttered, "Oh, shit."

I suddenly felt cold and shrively all over my body.

We let Donna take the lead. Staying close behind her, we quietly descended the porch stairs. At the bottom, I thought she might break into a run. She didn't, though. She just walked slowly through the high weeds.

I glanced back at the porch a couple of times. It was still dark. Nobody seemed to be coming after us.

Entering the shadows of some trees near the middle of the lawn, Donna almost disappeared. We all hurried toward her. In a hushed voice, Jimmy said, "What did you see?"

"Nothing really," she said.

"Yes you did," Peggy Pan insisted.

"No, I mean...." She stopped.

The four of us stood there in the darkness. Though we weren't far from the sidewalk where Nick and the girls were waiting, a high clump of bushes blocked our view of them.

"Okay," Donna said. "Look, this is just between us. They ran off, so they've got no right to hear about it, okay?"

"Sure," I said.

Peggy Pan nodded.

Jimmy whispered, "They'll never hear it from me."

"Okay," Donna said. "Here's the thing. It was *really* dark in the house. I didn't see anything at first. But then I could just barely make out a stairway. And something was *on* the stairway. Sitting on the stairs part-way up, and it seemed to be staring straight at me."

"What was it?" Peggy Pan whispered.

"I'm not really sure, but I think it was a cat. A white cat."

"So?" Jimmy asked.

I felt a little letdown, myself.

"I think it was sitting on someone's lap," she said.

"Oh, jeez."

Peggy Pan made a high-pitched whiny noise. Or maybe that was me.

"He was wearing dark clothes, I think. So I really couldn't see him. Or her. All I could see was this darkness on the stairs."

"How do you know it was even *there*?" Jimmy asked.

"The cat was white."

"So?"

"Someone was petting it."

"Let's get outa here," Jimmy said.

Donna nodded.

"Remember, not a word to Nick or Alice or Olive. We'll just say nothing happened."

We all agreed, and Donna led us through the trees. Out in the moonlight, we walked around the clump of bushes and found Nick and the girls waiting.

"So what happened?" Nick asked.

We shrugged and shook our heads. Donna said, "Nothing much. We knocked, but nobody was home."

Smirking, he said, "You mean *Boo* and his *cats* weren't there?"

Donna grinned. "You didn't *believe* that story, did you? It's *Halloween*. I made it up."

Nick scowled. The ballerina fairy godmother princess looked very relieved, and Yoda or ET sighed through her mask.

"Good story," I said.

"Thanks, Matt," said Donna.

"Can we still trick or treat some more?" Peggy Pan asked.

Donna shrugged. "It's getting pretty late. And we're a *long* way from home."

"Please?" asked Peggy Pan.

Her little friends started jumping and yelling, *"Please? Please-please-please? Oh, please? Pretty please?"*

"How about you, Nick?"

"Sure, why not?"

"Guys?" she asked Jimmy and me.

"Yeah!"

"Sure!"

"Okay," Donna said. "We'll go a little longer. Maybe just for a couple more blocks."

"Yayyy!"

The girls led the way, running up the sidewalk to the next house—a *normal* house—cutting across its front lawn and rushing up half a dozen stairs to its well-lighted porch. Nick chased them up the stairs. Jimmy and I hurried. By the time the door was opened by an elderly man with a tray of candy, Jimmy and I were also on the porch, Donna waiting at the foot of the stairs.

We were back to normal.

Almost.

We hurried from house to house, reached the end of the block, crossed the street and went to the corner house on the next block. It was just after that house, when we met on the sidewalk and headed for the next house, that Donna, lagging behind, called out, "Hang on a minute, okay? Come on back."

So we all turned around. As we hurried toward the place where Donna was waiting on the sidewalk, she raised her hand, index finger extended, and poked the finger at each of us. Like a school bus driver counting heads before starting home from a field trip.

She finished.

"Seven," she said.

"That's right," I said as I halted in front of her.

"Seven not including me," she said.

I whirled around and there was Jimmy the woebegone mummy dangling loose strips of sheet, some of which by now were trailing on the sidewalk. There was Nick the Jedi warrior with his light saber. And Peggy Pan and the ballerina fairy princess godmother and Yoda or ET and—

bringing up the rear but only a few paces behind the girls—*someone else.*

He carried a grocery bag like any other trick or treater, but he was bigger than the girls, bigger than Nick, bigger than any of us. He wore a dark cowboy hat and a black raincoat and jeans. Underneath his hat was some sort of strange mask. I couldn't tell what it was at first. When he got closer, though, I saw that it seemed to be made of red bandannas. It covered his entire head and neck. It had ragged round holes over his eyes, a slot over his mouth.

I had no idea where he'd come from.

I had no idea how long he'd been walking along with us, though certainly he'd shown up sometime *after* we'd left the dark old house.

Is *that* where he joined us? I wondered.

Speaking in his direction, Donna said, "I don't think we *know* you." Though she sounded friendly and calm, I heard tension in her voice.

The stranger nodded but didn't speak.

The girls, apparently noticing him for the first time, stepped away from him.

"Where'd you come from?"

He raised an arm. When he pointed, I saw that his hand was covered by a black leather glove.

He pointed behind us. In the direction of the dark old house...and lots of other places.

"Who are you?" Donna asked.

And he said, "Killer Joe."

Alice and Olive took another step away from him, but Peggy Pan stepped closer. "You aren't gonna kill us are you?" she asked.

He shook his head.

"Cool costume," Jimmy said.

"Thanks," said Killer Joe.

"So who are you really?" Donna asked.

Killer Joe shrugged.

"How about taking off the mask?" she said.

He shook his head.

"Do we *know* you?" Jimmy asked.

Another shrug.

"You wanta come along trick or treating with us?" Peggy Pan asked.

He nodded. Yes.

Donna shook her head. No. "Not unless we know who you are." Her voice no longer sounded quite so calm or friendly. She was speaking more loudly than before. And breathing hard.

She's scared.

And she wasn't the only one.

"I'm sorry," she said, "but you'll either have to let us see who you are or leave. Okay? We've got little kids here, and...and we don't know who you are."

"He's Killer Joe," Nick explained.

"We know," Jimmy said.

"But he's all by himself," Peggy Pan said. "He shouldn't have to go trick or treating all by himself." She stepped right up to him and took hold of a sleeve of his raincoat and tilted her head back.

"Peggy," Donna said. "Get away from him. Right now."

"No!"

Killer Joe shrugged, then gently pulled his arm out of Peggy's grip and turned around and began to walk away very slowly, his head down.

And I suddenly figured this was some poor kid—a *big* and possibly somewhat weird kid, granted—but a kid nevertheless without any friends, trying his best to have fun on Halloween night, and now he was being shunned by us.

I actually got a tight feeling in my throat.

Peggy Pan, sounding desolate, called out, "Bye, Killer Joe!"

Still walking away, head still down, he raised a hand to acknowledge the girl's farewell.

"Come on back!" Donna called.

He stopped walking. His head lifted. Slowly, he turned around and pointed to himself with a gloved hand.

"Yeah, you," Donna said. "It's all right. You can come with us. But we *are* almost done for the night."

Killer Joe came back, a certain spring in his walk.

Though he never removed his strange and rather disturbing bandanna mask and never told us who he was, he stayed with us that night as we went on from house to house, trick or treating.

Before his arrival, we'd been on the verge of quitting and going home. But even though he rarely spoke—mostly just a gruff "Trick or treat" when people answered their doors—he was so strange and friendly and *perky*, we just couldn't seem to quit.

This had been going on for a while and I was about to follow the bunch toward another house when Donna called softly, "Matt?"

I turned around and went back to her.

She took hold of my forearm. In a quiet voice, she said, "What do you think of this guy?"

"He's having a great time."

"Do you trust him?"

I shrugged.

"I don't," Donna said. "I mean, he could be *anyone*. I think it's very weird he wouldn't take off his mask. I'm afraid he might be up to something."

"Why'd you let him come with us?"

She shrugged. "Guess I felt sorry for him. Anyway, he's *probably* fine. But how about helping me keep an eye on him, okay? I mean, he might be after the girls or something. You just never really know."

"I'll watch him," I promised.

"Thanks." She gave my arm a squeeze. "Not that we'd be able to do anything much about it if he *does* try something."

"I don't know," I said. "I know one thing, I won't let him do anything to Peggy. Or you."

She smiled and squeezed my arm again. "Sure. We'll let him have Alice and Olive."

"But we'll *encourage* him to take Nick."

Donna laughed. "You're terrible."

"So are you," I said.

After that, I joined up with the rest of them and kept a close eye on Killer Joe as we hurried from door to door.

Sometimes, he touched us. He gave us friendly pats. But nothing more than what a buddy might do. I started to think of him as a buddy, but warned myself to stay cautious.

Finally, Donna called us all over to her. She said, "It's *really* getting late, now. I think we'd better call it quits for the night."

Sighs, moans.

"Just one more house!" the girls pleaded. *"Please, please, just one more house? Pretty please?"*

"Well," said Donna. "Just one more."

Olive and Alice went, *"Yayyyyy!"*

Killer Joe bobbed his masked head and clapped his hands, his gloves making heavy *whopping* sounds.

We all took off for our final house of the night. It was a two-story brick house. Its porch light was off, but one of the upstairs windows glowed brightly.

All of us gathered on the porch except Donna, who waited at the foot of the stairs as she often did.

Peggy Pan rang the doorbell. Olive and Alice stood beside her, and the rest of us stood behind them. I was between Mummy Jimmy and Killer Joe.

Nobody came to the door.

Peggy jabbed the button a few more times.

"Guess nobody's home," I said.

"Somebody *has* to be!" said Peggy. "This is the last house. Somebody *has* to be home."

Olive and Alice started shouting, *"Trick or treat! Trick or treat! Open the door! Trick or treat!"*

Killer Joe stood there in silence. He seemed to be swaying slightly as if enjoying some music inside his head.

"Maybe we'd better give it up," Jimmy said.

"No!" Peggy jabbed the doorbell some more.

Suddenly, the wooden door flew open.

We all shouted: *"TRICK OR TREAT!"*

An old woman in a bathrobe blinked out at us.

"Don't any of you kids know what time it is?" she asked. "It's almost *eleven o'clock*. Are you out of your *minds*, ringing people's doorbells at this hour?"

We all stood there, silent.

I felt a little sick inside.

The old woman had watery eyes and scraggly white hair. She must've been eighty. At least.

"Sorry," I muttered.

"Well, y'oughta be, damn kids."

"Trick or treat?" asked Peggy Pan in a small, hopeful voice.

"NO! NO FUCKING TRICK OR TREATS FOR ANY OF YOU, YOU BUNCHA FUCKIN' ASSHOLES! NOW GET THE FUCK OFF MY PORCH!"

That's when Killer Joe reached inside his rain coat with one hand and jerked open the screen door with his other.

If the door had been locked, the lock didn't hold.

The woman in the house yelled, *"HEY, YOU CAN'T...!"*

Killer Joe lurched over the threshold and the woman staggered backward but not fast enough and I glimpsed the hatchet for just a moment, clutched in Joe's black leather glove, and then he swung it forward and down, chopping it deep into the old woman's forehead.

That's all I saw.

I think I saw more than most. Then all of us were running.

We were about a block away and still running, some of the girls still screaming, when I did a quick head count.

Seven.

Including Donna.

Not including Killer Joe.

Joe had still been in the house when we ran off.

We never saw him again. He was never identified, never apprehended.

That was a long time ago.

I never again went trick or treating after that. Neither did Donna or Jimmy or Peggy. I don't know about Nick and Alice and Olive, and don't care.

Now I have a kid of my own. I hate for her to miss out on the strange and wonderful and frightening joys of dressing up and going house to house on Halloween night.

Trick or treating....

Sometimes, what happens on Halloween is as good as it gets.

Sometimes not.

Judy agrees.

"What the hell," she said, "let's go with her, show her how it's done."

Judy's not Donna, but...she's terrific in her own ways and I have my memories.

A Halloween Memory,
Age Four, Hawaii, 1961

Douglas Clegg

When I was four years old, I lived with my family in Hawaii; I have especially vivid memories from this time, but only in moments, like a camera's snapshot, but with sixty seconds of movement. I remember my hostility toward one of the nursery school teachers, and my love of one of the other ones; and I remember riding my father's shoulders on some trip through a garden, watching my mother, who was as beautiful as the garden itself, walk ahead of us; I remember how I'd go to the ocean with my father, lugging my large plastic fish and my black cat puppet; he'd show me how to body surf, although I doubt I ventured more than a foot out from shore. But one of the most distinct memories—and it's as if it just happened, even though this took place around 1961, was the Halloween night when I saw a witch.

At four, there isn't a lot to remember beyond specific details, so I'll begin with those. We had a lanai with a straw mat hanging down, and my godmother was visiting. My godmother and my mother always seemed to have adventures together, which they took me on (once I went to a movie with the two of them and they told me to look down at my lap, full of gumdrops, during the movie. I did as I had been told, but for a second, I looked up and saw a man sticking a hypodermic needle into a bikini-clad woman's foot, right under the heel. I never looked up at the movie again). But my memory of my first Halloween is my most vivid—my first conscious Halloween, where I knew Halloween and knew it was something special, and felt it in the air and in the stories the other kids told.

It was Halloween night, and I had heard the legends of witches and goblins and mummies. The enjoyable, enthusiastic terror was in me as I went out to the backyard and looked up at the sky.

There, flying across the face of the moon, was a witch, astride a broomstick.

Now, I knew even at four that this wasn't something you were supposed to tell grown-ups. I'm fairly sure I kept it to myself. The witch was shadowy, but she definitely rode a broom.

As a four-year-old, this didn't seem that out of the ordinary. I fully expected it on Halloween night.

I remember nothing else of that night, and I can't quite recall other Halloweens as a child, except for a few parties, a few collections for UNICEF, a few masks that smothered me as I trudged with a jack-o-lantern flashlight from house to house; my last year of trick-or-treating, in which I could only go to a couple of houses before heading off with my older brothers and sister and my father to a local football game, all the while thinking how much I'd rather be trick-or-treating with friends.

The image of that witch on her broom stayed with me for years.

We moved to Connecticut sometime after Halloween—I'm not sure how long after, but by the time I entered kindergarten, I was out of Hawaii. But each Halloween, I would go outside and look up at the sky and wonder if I'd see a witch or two again. I never did. But I always will believe that flying witches exist.

In fact, I'm certain that I clung to that memory for many years, and, at least until puberty struck with its unwanted lightning, I kept the secret of what I had seen. I felt I was protecting the witch. Well, I knew it was foolish. There were, after all, no such things as witches. And flying on brooms?

The witch never came back, but I have to tell you: it was enough. You only need to see the witch once, on her broom, sweeping the sky, to understand both what Halloween is about, and to understand how the world is never enough for someone who has seen the magic. I know there are people who will tell me that witches don't do that, or witches don't exist, or that kids have wild imaginations and that the magic isn't real like that. But no one can convince me that at four I didn't see what I know I saw.

I have not gotten too far from that little boy, standing barefoot in his swimming trunks, crew cut, brown eyes soaking up the night with all its wonder and possibilities; his brothers and sister gone out to trick-or-treat, his mother and godmother and father and godfather in the house or nearby; geckos running along the walls; the Hawaiian darkness as mysterious as the legends and stories that boy must have heard; and it's not just any night, but a magic night, a night that is like no other; a night when any and all things were possible.

Why do I have a feeling that I'll see her again, my good omen for future life? She's an assurance that what those around me tell me is true about the world is not everything, is not all true, is not the complete wisdom of the world; why do I feel that one Halloween night, perhaps in another forty years, I'll see her flying across the moon, and will let her sweep me alongside her? Maybe then I'll ride the night and the moon and the sky before the Day of the Dead comes my way, and some little kid will look up and see us on the broom against the moon and will grow into someone who believes that there is no end to what the world can dream up.

Fellini and Halloween

Ray Bradbury

This is not a favorite Halloween memory, it is a sad one. I often wonder why people wander around shouting to one another, "Happy Halloween!" It is not supposed to be happy. We celebrate it with a certain amount of fervor and excitement, but at its core it is about those who have gone on ahead of us; one day for all souls and one day for all saints.

This memory will be about Federico Fellini, who became my friend 25 years ago. Maggie and I enjoyed a wonderful week with him in Rome and I continued a correspondence with him and saw him a few years before his death.

Halloween has always been one of my special holidays. I've enjoyed it, while at the same time realizing what I have said about the essence of the holiday. It has always been my practice, along with my children, to decorate the house and, at one time or another, invite people in for a Halloween party, including a Dixieland Jazz band.

On Halloween six years ago I decorated the house and cut pumpkins, but by noon I received the terrible news on television that Federico Fellini had died that day in Rome. All of a sudden, in the words of a poem I wrote a while back, Death had lost its charm for me. I went around the house, collected the pumpkins and threw them in the trash, took down the decorations, locked the front door and turned out the lights. For the first time in fifty years I did not greet people at the door to see what costumes they were wearing, to hear what they had to say. Thus, at the core of this special evening, the lights went out and I sat with my thoughts, remembering Federico.

Halloween has never quite come back for me since then. Time has passed, but his special talent I've always felt should never have been removed from the world. If anything this coming Halloween I will celebrate his Spirit and remember him with love.

Masks

Douglas E. Winter

For the past two hours, Danny had waited. He had waited in his bedroom, hoping that Daddy would come home, hoping that the knocking at the front door would stop, hoping that she would leave for groceries—and that maybe, just maybe, she would leave forever. But he knew that none of these things would happen—that downstairs, curled upon the embroidered couch, the woman who called herself Mommy was waiting, too. She was waiting for the creatures to come, for the knocking to begin again. She would reluctantly part from the television set and answer the door, and those stupid kids would stand out there on the porch, whining through their cheap plastic masks. They would pretend to frighten her, and she would pretend to be frightened, but everybody knew they were just begging for candy. It made him sick—and in a way, it made him scared.

Danny had waited in his bed, looking at the wall. Indiana Jones stared back at him, eyes glazed but amused: "What are we doin' here, kid?" On the poster, Indiana looked just like Danny's father; and everybody said that Danny and his father looked so much alike. Danny had put on his checked flannel pajamas, and over them, his father's old Army fatigue shirt. The shirt tented around him, reaching almost to his knees; he tried to imagine himself camouflaged, Indiana Jones lying in ambush for the next band of masked invaders. But when he pulled on his mask, he felt no different—he was still Danny Martin, not some make-believe character ready to prowl the neighborhood in search of treats. The woman downstairs didn't understand; she didn't even listen when he tried to explain. So he had waited for his father, waited for the knocking to end, waited for Halloween to be over.

Danny had waited, watching the poster on his wall bleakly as Indiana's face seemed to wrinkle with age, shadows shifting as the night breeze tickled the trees outside his window.

He had waited, but he couldn't stop feeling like a baby. Just what she had called him. A baby. Ten years old and can't even go out trick-or-treating with his little brother on Halloween.

"But I don't feel like it."

Her eyes, those freezing blue eyes, had widened, and he knew that he had broken the final strand of her thin-corded patience.

"Don't feel like it? I'll tell you something I don't feel like, young man. I don't feel like listening to backtalk. I don't feel like listening to you at all. Just five days ago I spent a good ten dollars of my money...

Daddy's money

"...on this mask that you just *had* to have, and now what do I get for it? 'I don't feel like it.' And your brother's got to go with somebody...

Tommy Niebur's mother is taking him

"but you don't feel like it. Well, I don't feel like you. So go to your room—no dinner, no television, no nothing. I don't want to see you till morning. Have you got that?"

"Yeah."

"What?"

"Yes."

"Yes, what?"

He couldn't say that word—he wouldn't say that word, that hated word. But he had to, didn't he?

"Yes, Mommy."

He walked past her, heading for the stairs. "Can I say something?"

"One thing, and you'd better not...."

"Is Daddy coming home tonight?"

"I told you, and if you'd been paying any attention you would know, that Daddy has to work very late. He has a court appearance in Philadelphia tomorrow, and he may not even come home tonight. Now get to your room."

He turned away. Deron was standing at the top of the stairs, eavesdropping as usual. And wearing that stupid Darth Vader outfit, like it was a brand new idea or something.

Danny stomped up the stairs, whispering to his brother as he passed: "Bring me some candy."

"Why should I?" Deron's shrill voice seemed to whistle through the black plastic face; it sounded like Michael Jackson's impression of James Earl Jones. "You're too old...remember?"

Danny went straight to his bedroom and slammed the door, hard. And that was when he began to wait, at first half-hoping that she would storm after him, but then settling in, listening patiently for the opening garage door that would signal the arrival of his father, back from another endless day at work. But he heard only the knocking at the front door, the giggling voices, the stupid shouts of "trick or treat," the rustling of paper sacks. He could imagine the greedy, grabbing hands, hungrily taking the packages given away by the woman downstairs.

The woman who pretended to be his mother.

✱ ✱ ✱

His father had promised to be home on Halloween. He had promised. Danny remembered what had happened when he had missed Deron's birthday party—he was late, at work, as usual. The next morning, Deron was still pouting; his bottom lip seemed to have turned inside out. He was slowly spooning his bowl of Rice Krispies into a thick mush.

"Tell you what," Dad had said. "Halloween's just about three weeks away. We'll have ourselves another party then—and there's no way I'm going to miss that."

Deron's eyes seemed to light up a little.

"No way," Dad repeated. "Is that a deal?"

Then Deron seemed to think real hard. "Can...can I be Darth Vader?"

"Again?" Dad had groaned. He reached over the newspaper and stuck his finger into Deron's soupy Rice Krispies, took a taste and yelled "Yuck!"

Deron smiled and began to shovel the Rice Krispies into his mouth. "But it's really good yuck," he said, and began to laugh. Soon everyone was laughing—even Janice. Danny could tell that everything was going to be okay.

"We're gonna party," Dad had said. "And wait 'til you see the mask that I've got for Halloween. Real booga-booga stuff."

Danny saw Janice roll her eyes, reaching for a cigarette. Her smile seemed suddenly false. Grow up, he imagined her thinking. Next thing you know, he'll want to go trick-or-treating....

Dad was a real nut for masks. He had lined one bookshelf of his study with them. His favorite was probably a tiny plastic mask of some superhero called The Phantom, which he claimed was part of the first Halloween costume he had ever worn when he was a kid. "I was cool as a moose," he would say. "Back in the bad old, sad old Fifties." But he also had an expensive glow-in-the-dark latex mask that fit over his whole head, not just the face; Daddy said it had been designed by some guy named Don Post especially for that movie *Halloween III*. Danny didn't know whether that was true or not, because Daddy never let him see those kind of movies when they came on HBO; but if Daddy said it was true, it had to be true.

Just like when Daddy said he would be home for Halloween.

❋ ❋ ❋

The woman downstairs had lied; she knew that Daddy was coming home tonight. Just thinking about her made him angry. If he had to call that woman "Mommy" one more time, he knew he would puke. Her name was Janice something-or-other, Janice Martin now, and she had moved in here—right into Mom's house—just six months after his mother had gone away.

His real mother was named Melanie, and his father, when he talked of her at all, would say that she had "gone away." But dead was what he meant. His real Mommy was dead.

The first time that Danny had seen an actual funeral was on television, when that Princess Grace lady had died. He remembered sitting with his mother—his real mother—and watching these handsome people filing into a gigantic cathedral. It seemed like they had come to worship that big coffin. His mother had laughed a little when he told her that, but mostly she had cried; he remembered that quite clearly. And one other thing: they had had fried chicken that night for dinner.

He had wanted fried chicken on the day of his mother's funeral, but his father had taken him and Deron to Burger King instead. He should have known that this funeral would be different; she wasn't a princess, just his Mommy. There was no television, no church, no people in fancy clothes. Reverend Lowe, some chubby, smiling guy that his father knew, gave the service in a place called Iwry's Funeral Home. Until Johnny Sheldon showed up with his mother, Danny didn't know anybody—there were just these men in grey suits from Daddy's office, and ladies who looked liked they wanted to cry but couldn't quite understand why. Through it all, his father had sat next to him, in the front row of seats. Deron sat with a Spiderman coloring book at his other side. His father's eyes were wet, unfocused, looking at the people, the flowers, the floor, the ceiling, the walls—everywhere except that long box standing just a few feet away. Once Danny thought he heard him say something, but it wasn't meant for Danny. Maybe it wasn't meant for anyone. Only after Reverend Lowe had talked a long, long time about love and shepherds and dust and taking away, did Daddy finally lean over to Danny and whisper: "Come on. It's time to say goodbye to your mother."

It was too late. Danny had said his goodbyes three nights before, while lying in bed, staring into a night without stars. He had wanted a star to wish upon—to wish he may, to wish he might, to wish there were no hospitals, no emergency rooms, no ambulances that screamed through the night with their payload of sick mothers, taking them away to die. But there was only darkness out there.

So when his father pulled him forward, and boosted him up to peek inside the coffin, he really had nothing to say, nothing to do but cry for the wish that could never come true. And then he saw, to his horror, that the thing inside the box was not his mother.

It had her hands, folded against her chest; it was wearing her clothes.

But it was not her face, not really. She had never worn her hair that way, she had never smiled that way. Her face had been painted, pushed, twisted...into a mask.

"It's not my Mommy!" he had screamed. And he had lunged away from that horrible face, his father stumbling beneath the sudden shift of weight, nearly dropping him. Deron, cowering behind his father, started to cry, and Danny could hear the sudden rush of voices in the room, the coughs, the whispers, the words, repeated over and over

not my Mommy

until Reverend Lowe lurched forward, stiff-necked in his white collar, grasping at Danny's flailing hands. He screamed again, and his father staggered backward several steps; when he looked into his father's eyes, so close and yet so distant, he saw tears pooling, then falling down his cheeks even as he glanced back into the wooden box with the crazy hope that his son's words were true.

His father seemed to crumple into Aunt Rita, who had appeared out of nowhere to gather Danny into her arms, rushing him from the room, away from the voices, away from the box. In the hallway outside, she made him drink a cup of Seven-Up. It was warm and made him belch. Then she led him to a small room; there was a picture of Jesus on the wall, a water cooler, and a cot. And Aunt Rita gently spread him along the cot, kissed his forehead and held his hand. She told him the story about the cat in the hat. She told him the story about green eggs and ham. She started to sing something, and Danny fell asleep.

It was six months later—Danny was sure of that, because he had worked it out after overhearing one of Daddy's lawyer friends at the wedding reception—that Daddy brought that woman home for dinner. This was Janice, Daddy said. She was a secretary at the law firm where he worked. She had been oh-so-helpful when things had gone wrong, when the ambulance had come, when Mommy had...gone away. After a while, Daddy had said, "Janice is going to be your new Mommy." That was the one time—the only time that Danny knew of—that his father had lied.

Janice looked like one of those girls on the Clairol commercials—always smiling and tossing her hair from side to side. She was younger than Daddy—a lot younger—and she would call Danny and Deron her "little brothers" when people came over to visit.

She put mayonnaise on Danny's ham sandwiches even though he told her that he didn't like mayonnaise.

"It's good for you," she said.

She made Danny sit far away from the television set, where he couldn't see and hear as well as he could close up.

"You'll hurt your eyes," she said.

She made him go to bed at the same time as Deron, even though he was four years older.

"You need a good night's sleep," she said.

And she made him call her "Mommy," when she wasn't his mother—when she knew she wasn't his mother.

"You've got a new Mommy now," she said.

Daddy didn't seem to notice. Danny had tried to tell him once, but his father didn't understand. Maybe it was because he didn't have much time.

Danny usually saw his father about forty-five minutes a day—fifteen minutes in the morning, over a hectic breakfast where everyone battled for the newspaper, and then just before bedtime, when his father, who ate dinner at the office, would straggle in, looking very tired. He would pour himself a drink, then hunker down in front of the television set. And Janice would hover over him, shooing Danny and Deron off to bed.

October Dreams

Daniel Michael Martin, Sr. worked in one of those Washington, D.C. law firms with a bunch of names ("Dewey, Cheetham & Howe," Daddy would joke); he was something called a litigator, which a younger Danny had thought might have something to do with crocodiles until his father explained that not all lawyers went to court, and that those who did tended to call themselves litigators. But whatever it was that Daddy really did, he seemed to do it all of the time—every night, Saturdays, even Sundays. He wanted to "make partner," he had told Danny.

"Which means I have to dig my own grave before I can sleep in it." Daddy had laughed. Danny wasn't sure if he was really trying to be funny. Things had gotten worse lately; his father worked longer and harder—and he drank more when he came home at night. If he came home.

❋ ❋ ❋

Why didn't she answer the door?

Danny seemed to awaken with the sudden sound of knocking. It had been quiet for so long; he had waited for two hours that seemed longer than any movie he had ever seen. There were so many memories that they seemed to run together like a dream. Had he fallen asleep?

He shook his head, rubbed at his eyes. The knocking downstairs sounded like the shots of a distant cannon. He imagined the front door caving in, ten-foot tall gorillas pawing into the living room, dragging Hefty Bags stuffed to the brim with helpless trick-or-treaters.

"Hey!" he called. "Janice?" But she wasn't in the living room; peeking from his doorway, he could see the sofa, the rocking chair, the right half of the television. He could just make out the curly hair that crowned the head of Magnum, P.I. And Magnum was smooching with some blond girl who looked like she really liked having her face scrubbed down with that Brillo Pad moustache. The music was mushy—and loud. Maybe Janice hadn't heard him calling.

Maybe she hadn't even heard the knocking.

Danny started down the stairs, slowly at first, but nearly running as the knocking began again.

"Hello?" He knew he was in trouble; she was in the kitchen or the bathroom or somewhere, and when she found him scouting around outside of his room, she would whale him good—like that time she took a belt to him when he broke the china teapot.

But somebody had to answer the door. What if it was Jamie and Rick out there, standing in the cold, knowing that Danny was inside and not answering? They'd soap the windows or dump over the trash cans—or, knowing Jamie, maybe even slash the tires on the station wagon.

So Danny quickly went to the door, steeling himself for the whiny cries of "trick or treat" and a sea of E.T. masks.

But when he opened the door, no one was there.

❋ ❋ ❋

"Janice?"

On the low table between the front door and the adjacent hall closet sat a straw basket filled with Janice's gift-wrapped goodies, ready for the next wave of costumed creeps. As Danny closed and locked the front door, he thought about swiping one of the packages. He wondered what was inside.

Mom used to have the neatest things for Halloween treats—candy apples and taffy strings and popcorn balls that she made with a little help from Danny and Deron...and Daddy. He giggled, remembering

Daddy, hands all brown and gooey with molasses, chasing Mom around the kitchen, walking out of kilter like a drunken Frankenstein's monster.

And Mom would buy other stuff, too—especially Danny's favorite candy, Mars Bars.

That alone was enough to prove that Janice wasn't his mother. She didn't buy him Mars Bars; she didn't believe in candy.

"It's bad for your teeth," she said.

So she made something up, all by herself, while Danny and Deron were at school. She had wrapped her stuff in little packages, strangled with orange and black ribbons, like spooky Christmas presents. She gave them to the trick-or-treaters, but didn't offer any to Danny or Deron. She didn't even tell them what it was.

Looking at the basket now, Danny wasn't sure that he wanted to know. The packages he had seen earlier in the evening were precise little rectangles—brownies or fudge, he guessed. But these were odd lumps; he thought, for no reason, that they might be bags of mud. Or maybe half-chewed apples. When he prodded one with his finger, he felt warmth; the paper, and whatever was beneath the paper, seemed to give with a wet sigh. He pulled his finger back as if he had touched a white-hot burner, then wiped it along the leg of his pajamas.

He would wait for Deron to come home, and if the little brat didn't give him some candy—hopefully a Mars Bar—well, he'd sneak into his room later, and lift something.

He noticed the little clock beside the basket; the red digits blinked 10:24.

He had waited longer than he thought—a lot longer. He must have fallen asleep. Deron ought to be home by now....

Daddy ought to be home by now.

He went back upstairs.

❋ ❋ ❋

Deron's room was a shambles, as usual. In the dark, the floor was like an obstacle course; Danny stumbled over schoolbooks, side-stepped a knapsack, jumped over a pile of clothes. He kicked shoes aside, almost stepped squarely on top of a G.I. Joe assault vehicle. Didn't Deron know about drawers? Trying to get that kid to clean up after himself was like trying to get him to brush his teeth. "Old Yeller" was what Daddy called him. Gross was a better word.

"Deron?"

For a moment, Danny thought that his brother was curled in bed, asleep; then he saw that it was only a trick of shadows on the rumpled sheets.

Satisfied that no one was there, Danny started back toward the hall. That was when he saw, in the faint swathe of light angling through the doorway, Darth Vader's face peering out from a pile of dirty t-shirts.

So Deron was back from spooking the neighbors and begging for candy. Funny, though, that he should leave his precious mask in the middle of the floor.

What a slob.

"Deron?"

No answer. Nothing. Not a word.

"Deron? Come on, Deron." *You little shit*, he wanted to add. But that was when the knocking began again.

Danny sprinted into the hall, toward the stairs, glancing into the study and the guest bathroom as he ran. Nobody there. Then he was down the stairs, two and three at a time.

When he slid to a stocking-footed stop on the landing, the knocking had stopped. He pulled the security chain aside; it swung, jangling, away from its mounting.

"Boo!" he screamed, yanking the door open.

There was no one there.

He eased out onto the doorstep. It was cold, and his toes curled on the icy concrete. The wind was rising, whistling in the night and scattering twisted leaves across the lawn.

"Jamie!" he called. "Jamie and Rick! I know it's you! It's gettin' late, you punks! You better get on home, or your momma's gonna get you!"

He stalked back into the house, slamming the door, fumbling the chain lock back into place with his cold, stiff hands. Then, for good measure,

your momma's gonna get you

he slipped the dead bolt into place. Home for the night, locked up tight. He grinned with relief. His father's Toyota had been parked in the driveway, right next to the station wagon. Maybe Deron was too little to remember

There's no way...

but Danny remembered. His father had promised

no way I'm gonna miss that

and he hadn't forgotten his promise. He hadn't lied. He was home, and we were

gonna party.

❋ ❋ ❋

Danny tried the living room first; he switched off the television set just before Magnum closed down another case. Then he checked the kitchen.

Nothing seemed to have changed. The light above the oven glowed. A folded magazine and three placemats decked the table. The door to the basement was open slightly, just as he remembered it from hours before. The thin gap showed only darkness—no one in the basement.

"Dad?" He moved on down the hall, toward the study, flipping light switches as he went. The study was dark; Danny fingered the goose-necked lamp on his father's desk.

"Dad?" A briefcase lay open on the desk chair. Paper, pens, thick file folders. On the desk was a suitcoat. But Danny couldn't remember what his father had been wearing that morning when he left for work.

"Dad?" Danny thought he heard something. A leak. The drip of a faucet.

Something wet.

He looked up, saw the row of masks smiling down on him from the middle bookshelf. But something was wrong; something was missing, or changed. There was the impish plastic Phantom mask on the far left, its black and purple paint scratched and scarred. At the far right sat the Don Post skull, literally grinning its teeth out. In between were ghoulies and ghosties and gremlins and....

gonna party

something different, something he didn't really like to look at for very long, something that looked like the twisted face of a pig that had been

booga-booga

stuffed with the head of a boy. A human ear seemed to squeeze out from the left pink ear of the pig, and the left eye dangled on a red, bulbous stalk. Yellowish teeth protruded donkey-like from the mouth, dripping ropes of blood and saliva.

For a moment Danny's stomach cramped; his mouth tasted like bad cider. The pig-boy mask made him feel awful; it was

real booga-booga stuff

and he didn't want to touch it. He didn't want to be near it. He didn't want to be in the same room with it.

Then he thought he heard the mask drip—thought that it was really leaking blood and spit. When the knocking came again, he jumped; it was as if a cold hand had slid across his neck and pinched his ear.

The knocking came once. Twice. Three times.

Daddy was home. His car was here, his briefcase was here, his coat was here. His

real booga-booga stuff

mask was here.

So where was Daddy—and Deron? Were they out trick-or-treating? Then why didn't they have their masks?

The knocking stopped.

And started again.

Once. Twice. Three times.

He didn't move, hoping that someone else would answer the door. But the house was silent...except for the dripping. And the knocking.

They're outside, he suddenly realized. They went outside without a key. They're outside on the porch, knocking for me to let them in.

Once. Twice. Three times.

"I'm coming, Dad!" he yelled. He was nearly laughing, nearly crying, and his voice cracked as he ran down the hallway. "Hold your horses! I'm coming!"

But when he opened the front door, no one was there.

He shut the door gently, backing away from it, fighting the tears that poured freely down his cheeks. And he called for her then. She was home. She had to be home. She wouldn't leave him; she hadn't gone away.

He called for her. The word tore at his throat, but he called for her.

"Mommy?"

He hung the chain, homed the deadbolt.

"Mommy?"

The knocking came again.

Danny stared at the front door; the sound didn't seem right—it didn't seem to be coming from outside. He took a deep breath. He wiped his forearm across his eyes and nose, dabbing away the tears. Then he yanked the chain lock away, for the final time.

"All right," he said. "All right. You want to come in? Well, come on. Come on in." And he twisted the deadbolt—it gave with the crackle of a splintering branch—and stepped back.

He heard a metallic gasp as a doorknob turned; his eyes widened as he saw that the brass knob of the front door had not moved. It was the sharp click that drew his eyes from the front door, across the basket of secret Halloween treats, to the adjacent hall closet; its doorknob was rotating ever so slowly, a crack of darkness appearing to its left, expanding, yawning outward as the closet door opened, offering up the enticing darkness within. Danny faced the closet, and he started to speak, but then she came, out of the shadows, out of the closet, and into his world. In her hand, she was holding something that looked like his Indiana Jones mask; but it had hair, real hair, she was holding it by its hair.

At first, he didn't know her. But when the bright lights met her upturned face, he recognized her eyes.

At least he recognized her eyes.

She had taken off her Mommy mask.

Stanley Wiater

I can no longer recall most of the names of those at the party, even though there were only a handful of us who formed a circle around the body in Jimmy Cook's cellar that night.

Halloween night.

October 31, 1969.

Actually I do recall the exact number: seven. I remember because it was the minimum you would think was required for having a decent party—especially one without parental supervision. Not that we were exactly caged animals back then—as honor roll sophomores and juniors, the most dangerous delacies at hand were unfiltered cigarettes and bottles of cheap beer liberated from our unsuspecting parents' basement refrigerators or dank storage rooms.

What we were involved in that night called for seven warm bodies, more or less paired off male alongside female to make it work. It was a new party game that had no formal name, although Bonnie O'Brien, a vivacious blonde cheerleader (and yet one of the smartest girls in the entire school) called it "hypnotic levitation."

Whatever it was called, it was something different...and hopefully maybe even a little bit forbidden.

Something that, like the always disreputable Ouija Boards and Tarot Cards, was making the rounds for teenagers with more than just a passing interest in the occult. Kids like us who knew who Lovecraft was (both the writer and the rock group), or who had read the entire *The Lord of the Rings* partially because so few would even bother to try. We already suspected this game of "levitation" was just a nifty old trick; similar to those turn-of-the-century mediums who could raise heavy tables from the floor using only the slightest touch of their fingertips.

Besides the drinking and the flirting, carrying out that trick was our focus that chilly Halloween night—on seeing if we could accomplish the impossible. We were all too old to go trick or treating, and though a few of us in attendance had their driver's license, I recall only one of us could afford a used car.

So Bonnie herself instructed us in this wild idea of "hypnotic levitation"—in which a full grown person could be lifted bodily from the floor by others who used only their stiffly extended index fingers to accomplish this amazing feat. There was of course nothing truly supernatural about it—yet it was nevertheless a strange sight to behold if you'd never seen it performed. Just the idea that any of us—in a set group of six—could lift up over our heads anyone who was "hypnotized" made it for me a most memorable night indeed.

So memorable, in fact, that I later composed a short article entitled "How to Perform Hypnotic Levitation" and submitted it to FATE magazine. Amazingly enough they published it the following year—my first piece as a professional writer in a national magazine. I was even featured on the cover! (I gave Bonnie—who showed us how to perform the trick—co-credit on the byline, though in spite of my romantic hidden agenda, she still never thought of me as other than like a brother or a cousin.)

❋ ❋ ❋

Just as memorable an incident occurred later that night in this small rural farmtown of Hadley, Massachusetts. Like most small towns, there were a few deserted homes built in Hadley in the previous century reputed to be haunted. It seemed only logical on Halloween to go pay our respects to one—and perform our rite of hypnotic levitation there. Happily squeezing ourselves into one vehicle, we soon arrived at a large old house on a dairy farm that was supposed to be deserted—and of course haunted.

But as fate would have it, no sooner than did we attempt to gain entry through an unlocked door or window, when—BOOM!!— there was the unmistakable roar of a shotgun being discharged near our parked car.

Wouldn't you know it—the dumb old farmer who owned the property was wise enough to figure that there would be kids all too primed and ready to get into trouble on this chilly October night. Smarter by far than a group of half-drunk, giddy teenagers in picking the most obvious night of the year to go trespassing on posted land. And his shotgun blast in the air was all the warning we fearless ghost hunters needed to hightail it out of there and find a quieter, less potentially deadly setting for our no-longer-child, but not-yet-adult Halloween games. Like down in Jimmy Cook's panel-lined and lava lamped basement.

Looking back, it still makes for a damn fine memory to connect that Halloween party with the eventual sale of my first "true story of the strange and unknown." The one that started my career as a writer who would always love the dark the most.

And at least I linked that pretty cheerleader's name with mine forever in print, so she would always have something of me in case she is ever asked to relate her favorite Halloween memory....

A Redress for Andromeda

Caitlín R. Kiernan

Where the land ends and the unsleeping, omnivorous Pacific has chewed the edge of the continent ragged, the old house sits alone in the tall grass, waiting for Tara. She parks the rental car at the edge of the sandy dirt road and gets out, stares towards the house and the sea, breathing the salt and the night, the moonlight and all the wine- and applecrisp October smells. The wind whips the grass, whips it into tall waves and fleeting troughs the way it whips the sea, and Tara watches the house as the house watches her. Mutual curiosity or wary misgiving, one or the other or both, and she decides to leave the car here and walk the rest of the way.

There are a few other cars, parked much closer to the house, though not as many as she expected, and the porch is burning down in a mad conflagration of jack-o'-lanterns, a hundred candle-glowing eyes and mouths and nostrils, or that's how it looks to her, anyway. Walking along the sandy road as it curves towards the ocean and the tall, gabled house with its turrets and lightning rods, that's how it looks; the house besieged by all those carved and flaming pumpkins and she takes her time, walks slow, listening to the wind and the sea slamming itself against the headland. The wind colder than she expected and all she's wearing is a white dress, one of her simple shirtwaist dresses fashionable forty or forty-five years ago, a dress her mother might have worn when she was a girl; the white dress with its sensible cuffs and collars, and black espadrilles on her feet, shoes as simple as the dress because that's what Darren said. *It isn't a masquerade, nothing like that at all. Just be yourself*, but she wishes she'd remembered her coat. It's in the passenger seat of the rental car and she thinks about going back for it, and then decides she can stand the chill as far as the front door.

She knows a little about this house, but only because Darren told her about it; never much of a geek for architecture herself, even old houses with stories like this one has. The Dandridge House, because the man who built it in 1890 was named Dandridge and back in the sixties it was one of those places that hippies and occultists liked to haunt, someplace remote enough and out of sight and nobody to notice if you sacrificed a farm animal now and then. Darren told her ghost stories, too, because a house like this has to have ghost stories, but she took two Xanax on the drive up from Monterey and they've all run together in her head.

Not much farther before a sandy walkway turns off the sandy road, a rusty mail box on a post that's fallen over and no one's bothered to set it right again, and Tara follows the path towards the wide, pumpkincrowded porch that seems to wrap itself all the way around the house. Her shoes are already full of sand, sand between her toes, and she stops and looks back towards her car, all by itself at the edge of the road and now it seems a long way back.

There's a black-haired woman sitting on the porch steps, smoking a cigarette and watching her, and when Tara smiles the woman smiles back at her. "You must be Tara," the woman says and holds out her hand. "Darren said that you would be late. I thought someone should wait out here for you, a friendly face in the wilderness, you know."

Tara says thank you and shakes the woman's hand and this close, the jack-o'-lanterns seem very, very bright; hurt her eyes after the night and she squints at them and nods for the woman on the steps of the house.

"You didn't have any trouble finding us?" the woman asks and "No," Tara says. "No trouble at all. Darren gives good directions."

"Well, it's not as if there's much of anything else out here," and she releases Tara's hand and glances past all the jack-o'-lanterns towards the cliffs and the sea. "Just keep going until there's nowhere left to go."

"Who carved all these things? There must be a hundred of them," Tara says, pointing at one of the jack-o'-lanterns, and the woman on the steps smiles again and takes another drag off her brown cigarette, exhales smoke that smells like cloves and cinnamon.

"One hundred and eleven, actually," she says. "They're like birthday candles. One for every year since the house was built. We've been carving them for a week."

"Oh," Tara says because she doesn't know what else to say. "I see."

"You should go on inside, Tara," the woman says. "I expect they'll be waiting. It's getting late," and Tara says nice to meet you, we'll talk some more later, something polite and obligatory like that, and then she steps past her towards the front door, past and between the grinning and grimacing and frowning pumpkin faces.

"Yes, she's the one that I was telling you about last week," Darren is saying to them all, "The marine biologist," and he laughs and Tara shakes someone else's hand, all these pale people in their impeccable black clothes and she feels like a pigeon dropped down among the crows. Not a masquerade, not a costume party, but she could have at least had the good sense to wear black. A tall, painfully-thin woman with a thick French accent touches the back of her hand, her nails the brownred color of seaweed, and she smiles as gently as the woman out on the porch.

"It's always so nice to see a new face," the French woman says. "Especially when it's such a fine and splendid face." The woman kisses the back of Tara's hand, and then Darren's introducing her to a short, fat man wearing an ascot the color of a stormy summer sky.

"Ah," he says, and shakes Tara's hand so forcefully it hurts. "A scientist. That's grand. We've had so few scientists, you know." She isn't sure if his accent is Scots or Irish but it's heavy, like his face. Jowls and wide, thin lips and the man looks more than just a little like a frog, she thinks.

"We've had doctors, yes, lots and lots of doctors. Once we had a neurologist, even. But I've never thought doctors were quite the same thing. As scientists, I mean. Doctors aren't really much more than glorified mechanics, are they?"

"I never thought of it that way," Tara says, which isn't true, and she manages to slip free of the fat man's endless, crushing handshake without seeming rude, glances at Darren, hoping that he can read the discomfort, the unease, in her eyes.

"If you'll all please excuse us for a moment," Darren says, so she knows that he has seen, that he understands, and he puts one of his long arms around her shoulders. "I need to steal her away for just a few minutes," and there's a splash of soft, knowing laughter from the little crowd of people.

He leads her from the front parlor towards what might have once been a dining room, and Tara's beginning to realize how very empty the house is. The way it looked from the outside, she expected the place to be full of antiques, perhaps neglected antiques gone just a bit shabby, a threadbare and discrepant mix of Edwardian and Victorian, but still, she thought that it would be furnished. These rooms are almost empty, not even carpets on the floors or drapes on the tall windows; the velvet wallpaper is faded and torn in places, hanging down in strips here and there like a reptile shedding its skin. And no electricity, as far as she can tell, just candles and old-fashioned gaslight fixtures on the walls, warm and flickering light held inside frosted crystal flowers.

"They can be somewhat intimidating at first, I know that," Darren says. "It's a pretty close-knit group. I should have warned you," and she shakes her head, smiles and no, it's fine, she says, it's not a problem.

"They were probably as anxious about your being here," he says and rubs his hands together in a nervous way, glances back towards the crows milling about in the parlor, whispering among themselves. *Are they talking about me?* she wonders. *Are they asking each other questions about me?* and then Darren's talking again.

"I trust you didn't have any trouble finding the house? We had someone get lost once," he says and "No," she says. "Finding the house was easy. With all those jack-o'-lanterns, it's almost like a lighthouse," and she thinks that's probably exactly what it would look like to a ship passing in the night, fishermen or a tanker passing on their way north or south, an unblinking lighthouse perched high on the craggy shore.

"That's one of the traditions," Darren says, brushes his long black bangs away from his face. Not exactly a handsome face, something more honest than handsome, something more secretive, and the reason she finds him attractive buried somewhere inside that contradiction.

"One of the traditions? Are there many others?"

"A few," he says. "I hope all this isn't freaking you out."

"No, it isn't," and she turns her head towards a window, the moonlight shining clean through the glass, shining white off the sea. "Not at all. It's all very dignified, I think. Not like Halloween in the city. All the noisy drunks and drag queens, those gaudy parades. I like this much better than that. I wish you'd told me to wear black, though," and he laughs at her then.

"Well, I don't think it's funny," she says, frowning slightly, still watching the moon riding on the waves, and he puts a hand on her arm. "I must stick out like a sore thumb."

"A bit of contrast isn't a bad thing," Darren says, and she turns away from the window, turns back towards him, his high cheekbones and high forehead, his long, aquiline nose, and eyes that are neither blue nor green.

"I think you need a drink," he says and Tara nods and smiles for him.

"I think maybe I need two or three."

"That can be arranged," and now he's leading her back towards the crows. A few of them turn their heads to see, dark eyes watching her, and she half expects them to spread wide, black wings and fly away.

"They'll ask you questions," and now Darren's almost whispering, hushed words meant for her and no one else. "But don't ever feel like you have to tell them anything you don't want to tell them. They don't mean to be pushy, Tara. They're just impatient, that's all." And she starts to ask what he means by that exactly, impatient, but then she and Darren are already in the parlor again; the small and murmuring crowd opens momentarily, parts long enough to take them in, and then it closes eagerly around them.

An hour later, after a string quartet, Bach and Chopin and only one piece that she didn't recognize, and now the musicians are carefully returning their sleek instruments to black violin and viola cases, cases lined in aubergine and lavender silk.

"It really isn't very fair of you, Mr. Quince," someone says and Tara turns around and it's the dapper fat man with the bluegray ascot, the man who's either Irish or Scottish. "The way you're keeping her all to yourself like this," and he glances past her to Darren, then, coy glance, and the man smiles and rubs at his short, salt-and-pepper beard.

"I'm sorry. I wasn't aware," Darren says and he looks at Tara, checking to be sure it's okay before leaving her in the man's company; but he seems harmless enough, as eccentric as the rest, certainly, but nothing threatening in that eccentricity. He has a walking stick topped with a silver dolphin, and she thinks that he's probably gay.

"Oh, I think we'll be fine," she says and Darren nods once and disappears into the crowd.

"I am Peterson," the man says, "Ahmed Peterson," and then he kisses the back of her hand the same way that the tall French woman did earlier. The same peculiar formality about him, about all of them, manners that ought to come across as affected but don't somehow.

"Quince tells us that you're a marine biologist," he says, releases her hand, and stands very straight but he's still a few inches shorter than Tara.

"An ichthyologist, actually," she says. "I do some work at the aquarium in Monterey, and teach at Cal State. That's where I met Darren."

"Marvelous," Peterson beams. "You know, my dear, I once came across an oarfish, a great, long, spiny thing, stranded on the shingle at Lyme Regis. The fellow I was with thought sure we'd found ourselves a sea serpent."

"I saw an oarfish alive off the coast of Oregon about ten years ago, when I was still a graduate student," she tells him, happy to be swapping fish stories with the fat man, starting to relax, feeling less like an outsider. "We estimated it at almost twenty feet."

"Ah, well, mine was smaller," he says, sounding a little disappointed, perhaps, and then there's a jolting, reverberating noise and Tara turns to see that one of the women is holding up a small brass gong.

"Oh my," the fat man says. "Is it really that late already? I lost track," and then Darren's standing next to her again.

"What's happening?" she asks and "You'll see," he replies, takes her hand and slips something cold and metallic into her palm, a coin or a token.

"What's this?" and "Just hang onto it," he says. "Don't lose it. You'll need it later." So, *it's a game*, she thinks. *Yes, it must be some sort of party game.*

And now everyone is starting to leave the parlor. She lets Darren lead her and they follow the others, file down a narrow hallway to a locked door near the very back of the house; behind the door are stairs winding down and down and down, stone steps that seem to have been cut directly from the native rock, damp stone walls and some of the guests have candles or oil lanterns. She slips once and Darren catches her, leans close, whispers in her ear and his breath is very faintly sour.

"Watch your step," he says, "It's not much farther, but you wouldn't want to fall," and there are cool gusts of salty air rising up from below, not the sort of air she'd expect from a cellar at all; cool air against her skin, but tainted by an oily, fishy odor, low tide sort of a smell, kelp and dying starfish trapped in stagnant tidal pools.

"Where the hell are we going?" she asks him, not bothering to whisper, and a woman with a conch shell tattooed on her forehead turns around and looks at her with a guarded hint of disapproval, and then she turns away again.

"You'll see," Darren whispers, and she realizes that there's something besides the salty darkness and the light from the candles and lanterns, a softer yellowgreen glow coming from somewhere below; chartreuse light that gets a little brighter with every step towards the bottom of the stairway.

And now, if Darren were to ask again whether or not she was getting freaked out, now she might say yes, now she might even tell him she really should be going, that it was late and she needed to get back to the city. Papers to grade or a test to write for her oceanography class, anything that sounded plausible enough to get her out of the house and onto the pumpkinlittered porch, back down the path to her rented car. The stars overhead instead of stone, but he doesn't ask again, and the chartreuse light grows brighter and brighter and in a few more minutes they've come to the bottom.

"No one ever understands at first," Darren says. He has one hand gripped just a little too tightly around her left wrist, and she's about to tell him that it hurts, about to ask him to let go, when Tara sees the pool and forgets about everything else.

There's a sort of a boardwalk at the bottom of the stairs, short path of warped planks and rails and pilings gone driftwood soft from the alwaysdamp air, from the spray and seawater lapping restless at the wood. The strange light is coming from the water, from the wide pool that entirely fills the cavern at the foot of the stairs, light that rises in dancing, fairy shafts to play across the uneven ceiling of the chamber. Tara's stopped moving and people are having to step around her, all the impatient crows grown quiet and beginning to take their places on the boardwalk, no sound now but the hollow clock, clock, clock of their shoes on the planks and the waves splashing against the pier and the limestone walls of the sea cave.

Like they've all done this thing a hundred, hundred times before, and she looks to Darren for an explanation, for a wink or a smile to tell her this really *is* just some odd Halloween game, but his bluegreen eyes are fixed on the far end of the boardwalk and he doesn't seem to notice.

"Take me back now," she says, "I don't want to see this," but if he's heard her it doesn't show on his face, his long, angular face reflecting the light from the pool and he has the awed and joyous expression of someone witnessing a miracle. The sort of expression that Hollywood always gives a Joan of Arc or a Bernadette, eyes of someone who's seen God, she thinks, and then Tara looks towards the end of the boardwalk again. And the crowd parts on cue, steps aside so she can see the rocks jutting up from the middle of the pool, from whatever depths there are beneath her feet, stacked one upon the other as precarious as jackstraws. The rocks and the thing that's chained there, and in a moment she knows that it's seen her, as well.

"When I was five," she says, "When I was five I found a sea turtle dead on the beach near Santa Cruz," and she opens her hand again to stare at the coin that Darren gave her upstairs.

"No, dear," Ahmed Peterson says. "It was an oarfish. Don't you remember?" and she shakes her head, because it wasn't an oarfish that time. That time it was a turtle, and the maggots and the gulls had eaten away its eyes.

"You must be mistaken," the fat man says again and her coin glints and glimmers in the yellowgreen light, glints purest moonlight silver in her palm. She doesn't want to give it away, the way all the others have already done. Maybe the only thing that's left and she doesn't want to drop it into the water and watch as it spirals down to nowhere, see-saw descent towards the blazing deep, and she quickly closes her hand again. Makes a tight fist and the fat man huffs and grumbles and she looks up at the moon instead of the pool.

"You may not have lived much under the sea," he says, and "No, I haven't," Tara confesses, "I haven't."

"Perhaps you were never even introduced to a lobster," he says.

She thinks about that for a moment, about brown claws boiled orange, jointed crustacean legs on china plates, and "I once tasted — " but then she stops herself, something she isn't supposed to say, she's almost certain.

"No, never," Tara whispers.

And the sea slams itself against the cliffs below the house, the angry sea, the cheated sea that wants to drown the world again. Darren is lying in the tall grass and Tara can hear a train far away in the night, its steamthroat whistle and steelrazor wheels, rolling from there to there and she traces a line in the dark with the tip of one index finger, horizon to horizon, sea to sky, stitching with her finger.

"She keeps the balance," Darren says, and Tara knows he's talking about the woman on the rocks in the cave below the house. The thing that was a woman, once, and "She stands between the worlds," he says. "She watches all the gates."

"Did she have a choice?" Tara asks him and he's pulling her down, into the grass, the sea of grass washed beneath the harvest moon. He smells like fresh hay and pumpkin flesh, nutmeg and candy corn.

"Do saints ever have choices?"

And Tara's trying to remember, if they ever have, when Ahmed and the woman with the conch-shell tattoo lean close and whisper the names of deep-sea things in her ears, rushed and bathypelagic litany of fish and jellies, squid and the translucent larvae of shrimp and crabs.

Saccopharynx, Stylephorus, Pelagothuria, Asteronyx.

"Not so *fast*," she says. "Not so fast, *please*."

"You can really have no notion, how delightful it will be," sings

Ahmed Peterson, and then the tattooed woman finishes for him, "When they take us up and throw us, with the lobsters, out to sea."

It's easier to shut her eyes and lie in Darren's arms, hidden by the merciful, undulating grass; "The jack-o'-lanterns?" he says again, because she asked him why all the jack-o'-lanterns, and "You said it yourself, Tara. Remember? A lighthouse. One night a year, they rise and we want them to know we're watching."

"Beneath the waters of the sea, Are lobsters thick as thick can be— They love to dance with you and me. My own and gentle Salmon."

"It hurts her," Tara says, watching the woman on the rocks, the lady of spines and scales and the squirming podia sprouting from her distended belly.

"Drop the coin, Tara," Darren murmurs, and his voice is urgent, but not unkind. "Drop the coin into the pool. It helps her hold the line."

Drop the coin, the coin, the candy in a plastic pumpkin grinning basket.

"The reason is," says the Gryphon, who was a moment before the woman with the conch on her forehead, "that they *would* go with the lobsters to the dance. So they got thrown out to sea. So they had to fall a long, long way."

Trick or treat.

And the Mock Turtle, who was Ahmed Peterson, glares at the Gryphon; "I never went to him," he huffs. "He taught Laughing and Grief, they used to say."

"Someone got lost," Darren whispers. "We had to have another. The number is fixed," and the blacksalt breeze blows unseen through the concealing grass; she can't hear the train any longer. And the moon stares down at them with its single swollen, jaundiced eye, searching, and dragging the oceans against the rocks.

It will find me soon, and what then?

"Drop the coin, Tara. There's not much time left. It's almost midnight," and the woman on the rocks strains against her shackles, the rusted chains that hold her there, and cold corroded iron bites into her pulpy, cheesewhite skin. The crimson tentacles between her alabaster thighs, the barnacles that have encrusted her legs, and her lips move without making a sound.

"They're rising, Tara," Darren says, and now he sounds scared, and stares down into the glowing water, the abyss below the boardwalk that's so much deeper than any ocean has ever been. And there *is* movement down there, she can see that, the coils and lashing fins, and the woman on the rock makes a sound like a dying whale.

"There is another shore, you know, upon the other side."

"*Now*, goddamnit," Darren says, and the coin slips so easily through her fingers.

"Will you, won't you, will you, won't you, will you join the dance...."

She watches it sink, taking a living part of her down with it, drowning some speck of her soul. Because it isn't only the woman on the rock that holds back the sea; it's all of them, the crows, and now she's burned as black as the rest, scorched feathers and strangled hearts, falling from the sun into the greedy maelstrom.

And the moon can see her now.

"I told them you were strong," Darren whispers, proud of her, and he wipes the tears from her face; the crows are dancing on the boardwalk, circling them, clomp clomp clomp, while the woman on the rock slips silently away into a stinging, anemone-choked crevice on her island.

"Will you, won't you, will you, won't you, won't you join the dance?"

❋ ❋ ❋

Tara wakes up shivering, lying beneath the wide gray sky spitting cold raindrops down at her. Lying in the grass, the wind and the roar of the breakers in her ears, and she lies there for a few more minutes, remembering what she can. No recollection of making her way back up the stairs from the sea cave, from the phosphorescent pool below the house. No memory of leaving the house, either, but here she is, staring up at the leaden sky and the faint glow where the sun is hiding itself safe behind the clouds.

Someone's left her purse nearby, Darren or some other thoughtful crow, and she reaches for it, sits up in the wet grass and stares back towards the house. Those walls and shuttered windows, the spires and gables, no less severe for this wounded daylight; more so, perhaps. The bitter face of anything that has to keep such secrets in its bowels, that has to hide the world's shame beneath its floors. The house is dark, all the other cars have gone, and there's no sign of the one hundred and eleven jack-o'-lanterns.

She stands and looks out to sea for a moment, watches a handful of white birds buffeted by the gales, whitecaps, and *Next year*, she thinks, next year she'll be here a week before Halloween to help carve the lighthouse faces, and next year she'll know to dress in black. She'll know to drop the silver coin quickly and turn quickly away.

One of the gulls dives suddenly and pulls something dark and wriggling from the seething, stormtossed ocean; Tara looks away, wipes the rain from her eyes, rain that could be tears, and wet bits of grass from her skirt, and then she begins the walk that will carry her past the house and down the sandy road to her car.

The Santa of Halloween

Richard Laymon

When I was a kid growing up in the suburbs of Chicago in the fifties, the first snowfall of the year always seemed to come on the night of our church's Halloween party. I don't remember much of the party itself, except perhaps that we bobbed for apples. Afterwards, though, as we walked back to where we'd parked the car, the soft pale snow would come drifting down through the streetlights.

This was usually a week or more before Halloween and the snow that fell that night never lasted long but it was very special while it fell. And it was always gone by the time Halloween arrived.

When I was a kid, it never snowed on Halloween. Halloween night was usually brisk and windy, leaves blowing along the streets and across the front yards of houses. There was always a smell of burning in the air. Smoke from the leaves that had been recently piled along the street curbs and lit on fire, smoke from neighborhood fireplace chimneys, the sweet smoke of jack-o'-lantern lids being scorched by the candle flames beneath them, and the acrid smell of burnt cork that often blackened our faces as we walked through the night.

Burnt cork was the preferred makeup, at least for my brother and I. Though Boy Scouts, we were never quite prepared for Halloween's arrival. Bob and I fervently looked *forward* to Halloween, but there often seemed to be confusion in our household as to *when* Halloween would arrive. When the evening for trick or treating finally came, we were rarely ready for it.

The refrain of the day seemed to be, "What're ya gonna wear trick or treating?"

"What're ya gonna be?"

"What're ya gonna go as?"

The answer generally went, "I donno, how 'bout you?"

When it came to last-minute costume choices for boys, hobos and pirates generally carried the night. To "go as" either, all we needed were some old clothes: a stick and bundle and one of Dad's old hats for a hobo; a bandanna and one of Mom's hoop earrings for a pirate. Hobos and pirates both required belts made of rope. And, of course, burnt cork on our faces.

We always had corks around the house, but I'm not sure where they came from. My parents didn't drink wine in those days—we lived in a duplex with a teetotaling maiden great-aunt and her cousin, a member of the Women's Temperance Union. Though the origin of the corks is a mystery to me, one could always be found somewhere in the house.

All set to go out trick-or-treating, Bob and I waited while Mom set the end of a cork on fire. She would let it blaze for a while, then blow it out and apply hobo or pirate smudges to our faces. The cork felt warm (sometimes *too* warm) and stiff, and made dry whispery sounds against our skin, and smelled of burn.

While we often went out as hobos or pirates (though never at the same time) our costumes were sometimes less make-shift.

Now and then, we went trick or treating in masks or costumes bought at stores. Lone Ranger type masks felt scratchy and smelled of fabric. Rubber masks smelled like the inside of a tennis ball. After a while, they became wet with condensation and clung to the face almost like real skin—*someone* else's skin. They felt hot. The elastic string that went behind the head to hold the masks on made your ears hurt after a while, and pulled at your hair.

Masks also obstructed the vision. If you wore glasses (as I did), you had special troubles. Most masks didn't fit on over them very well. If you did manage to wear your glasses underneath the mask, the lenses would fog up in half a minute.

Glasses or no glasses, Halloween masks added a "blind-man's-bluff" excitement to trick or treating. You bumped into your friends and strangers. You tripped on cracks in the sidewalk. You stumbled off stairs and curbs. You walked in front of cars. And you could never be quite sure who was walking beside you.

In those days in the neighborhood where I grew up, falls and collisions caused by impaired vision were probably the greatest peril we faced on Halloween. Parents rarely accompanied anyone old enough to walk, so long as there were older brothers or sisters to lead the way. While the kids roamed the night unsupervised, most parents remained home to answer the door and give out treats.

Usually, I went trick or treating with my brother and three or four friends. In addition to our costumes, each of us carried a grocery bag for the goodies we intended to collect. One or two of us usually brought along flashlights. We never brought eggs to throw. As I recall, we never even brought soap for soaping windows.

We were "good kids."

Starting on our own block, we hurried from house to house, rushed up the stairs of porches or stoops (often stumbling), and rang the doorbell. When the doors opened, we shouted, "Trick or treat!" We had no intention, however, of "tricking" anyone.

Not that it would've been necessary. If people were home, they usually opened the door and dropped goodies into our bags and said, "My, don't *you* look nice!" or "What are *you* supposed to be?" or, "Ooo, aren't *you* the scary one!" Then we would call out "Happy Halloween!" and run off for the next house.

With each house we visited, our bags grew heavier. Apples and oranges were the heaviest treats and also, for most of us, the least desirable. We also received homemade cookies or brownies usually wrapped in a table napkin tied at the top with a ribbon, miniature Hershey bars, several varieties of bubble gum including sometimes those wonderful cigars that might've passed for the real things except for being pink, Hershey kisses in shiny silver foil, small packs of white candy cigarettes with red tips, wads of taffy, and always at least one pair of bright red shiny wax lips.

The wax lips were a great favorite. We never quite knew whether to wear them or eat them. Therefore, we did both. First we spent some time wearing them, mincing about and batting our eyelashes. Then we ate them. While eating the lips, I always found myself wondering whether they were *meant* to be eaten. They tasted like sweet candles.

Sometimes people dropped coins into our bags. We rarely received much—a few pennies here and there—but always gathered enough change to give our swinging, weighty bags a pleasant jingle as we hurried down the sidewalks and jumped off curbs and fell in streets.

Though we started our trick or treating at houses close to home, we soon moved on to different blocks. We roamed farther and farther away, venturing into areas where those who dwelled in the homes were strangers.

It was always later in the night by then. Our bags were heavy. Store bought costumes, made of flimsy and smelly plastic, were torn here and there. Some of us now wore our masks perched atop our heads, at least until we mounted a porch to ring a doorbell. The burnt cork on the faces of hobos and pirates was runny and smeared from sweat. Only the most hardy of pirates still wore his earring. Ears hurt from mask strings. Feet were sore. Hands ached from carrying treat-heavy bags.

And the neighborhood was beginning to feel ominous.

"Think we better start back?"

"Nah. We still got time."

"I donno, it's awful late."

"Let's give it one more block."

"Does anyone know where we are?"

"We just gotta go back the way we came."

"What if we run into *big* kids?"

We'd *heard* what the big kids do to smaller kids they catch trick or treating. Though it had never happened to us, we'd been told they sometimes threw eggs. Or they stole the candy bags. We'd even heard of tales of the big kids using tortures such as the "Indian burn" or the "pink belly," both of which were much dreaded by me and my friends...though we weren't above applying them to each other.

"If anything goes wrong, we run like heck."

Not being among the fastest of our group, that solution never held much appeal for me.

"Maybe we oughta start back."

"One more block."

"But what if...?"

"Chickie chickie chickie."

Those final few blocks were always the best. We were tired and aching, making our way deeper into unknown territory, our time running out. More and more of the houses had no lights on. Jack-o'-lanterns wore dark faces, their candles snuffed by the wind or burnt out.

At any moment, we might be attacked by a savage pack of older kids. At any door, we might encounter a stranger with more on his mind than handing out candy.

We'd heard stories.

Stories about men with furniture made of bones, lampshades made of skin, livers of little kids sizzling in skillets on the kitchen stove.

Also, our parents had warned us in vague ways of men who "do things" to boys and girls. I was never told exactly what they did. If it was too awful for adults to talk about, though, it had to be horrible.

What could be more horrible than getting skinned alive and eaten and made into furniture?

I didn't want to know.

In a way, though, I did.

And I approached each strange house with a mixture of terror and excitement. The older and darker the house, the better.

On that last block at the tag end of a Halloween night when I was a boy, we came to the oldest and darkest house of all.

"Let's try this one!"

"Are you nuts?"

"Come on!"

"Nobody's gonna answer the door anyhow."

"I don't think anybody's home."

"I don't think anybody even *lives* there."

"The joint's a wreck."

"We oughta forget it."

"Maybe we oughta start back now."

"Chickie chickie chickie."

"Mom and Dad're gonna kill us."

"No they won't."

"Will too."

"It *is* pretty late."

"We'll make this the last one."

"Promise?"

"Scout's honor."

And so we walked through the tall grass and climbed the wooden stairs. The porch floor creaked under our shoes. Our bags rustled and jingled. Then we were standing motionless in front of the screen door.

"I don't know about this."

"Yeah, we oughta get outa here."

"Chickens." He rang the doorbell.

"Hey, look."

We could see in. On the other side of the screen door, the main door seemed to be standing wide open.

"Oh, jeez."

"Shhh."

Inside the house, at the end of a long dark corridor, a trembling glow appeared.

"Oh, jeez."

A man stepped into the corridor, a candle in one hand. I don't remember what he looked like. I don't remember anything about him...except how much he frightened us.

Nobody called out "Trick or treat."

We whirled around and ran. We ran for blocks and blocks and he didn't get his clutches on any of us.

He was probably just a regular guy.

For just a moment, however, he *was* the boogyman coming down the corridor to get us.

In his house he had furniture of bones, lampshades of skin, livers on the skillet. He was one of those most evil and horrifying of monsters who "did things" to boys and girls.

If we hadn't been so quick to run....

No telling what he might've done to us.

Unspeakable things.

Or perhaps he would've dropped candy into our bags and wished us a Happy Halloween.

We'll never know.

But I do know this.

He blessed that special Halloween with a treat far better than candy—better than Hershey kisses or pink bubble gum cigars or ruby red wax lips—he gave me a deep thrill of terror.

A boogyman, if only in our hearts.

The Santa of Halloween.

The Circle

Lewis Shiner

For six years they'd been meeting on Halloween night here at Walter's cabin, and reading ghost stories to each other. Some of the faces varied from year to year, but Lesley had never missed one of the readings.

She'd come alone this year, and as she parked her Datsun at the edge of the graveled road she couldn't help but think of Rob. She'd brought him to the reading the year before, and that night they'd slept together for the first time. It had been nearly two months now since she'd heard from him, and the thought of him left her wavering between guilt and sadness.

Her shoes crunched on pine needles as she dodged the water droplets dripping from the trees overhead. The night was colder than she had expected, the chill seeping quickly through her light jacket.

She hopped onto the porch of the cabin and rapped on the door. Walter's wife, Susan, answered it. "Come in," she said. "You're the first one."

"It's cold out there," Lesley said.

"Isn't it? Tea's ready. Sit down and I'll bring you a cup."

Lesley had barely settled by the fireplace when the others began to trickle in. Some of them had books, others had manuscripts, most of them also had wine or beer. All of them wrote, several of them professionally, and about half the stories each year had been written for the occasion.

Lesley hadn't felt up to writing one herself this year. In fact she hadn't felt up to much of anything since she and Rob had broken up. His bitterness had hurt her badly, and she was hoping that something would happen tonight to pull her back out of herself.

She hoped it would be the way it used to, when the stories had been chilling and the nights had been damp and eerie, and they'd gotten themselves so scared sometimes that they hadn't gone home until daylight.

They'd been younger, then, of course. Now that they were all closing in on thirty they seemed to be more afraid of election results and property taxes than they were of vampires and werewolves.

About nine-thirty Walter stood up and ceremonially lighted the candelabra over the fireplace. The other lamps were turned off, and Walter stood for a moment in the flickering candlelight. He looked a bit like an accountant in his sweater and slacks, with his horn-rimmed glasses and his neatly trimmed mustache.

"Well," he said, clearing his throat. "I think we're all here. Before we get started, we've got something unusual I wanted to tell you about. I got this in the mail last week." He held up a large manila envelope. "It's from Rob Tranchin, in Mexico."

Lesley felt a pang again. "Did he...." she blurted out. "Did he say how he is?"

She felt all the eyes in the room turning on her. The others had never liked Rob all that well, had only put up with him for her sake. While all of them dabbled in the occult, Rob was the only one who had ever taken it seriously, and on more than one occasion he'd had shouted arguments with some of them on the subject.

"I, uh, can't really tell," Walter said. "There was a note inside, but it didn't say much. Just said that he's written a story for us and that he wanted somebody to read it at tonight's, uh, gathering. It's not very long, I took a quick glance at it, so if nobody minds I'll just draw a card for Rob and one of us can read it when that turn comes around."

Behind Lesley, Brian muttered, "I hope it's not some more of that occult shit of his," but there was no formal objection.

Walter took the ace through eight from a deck of cards and shuffled them, then let each of the others draw for a turn. Brian had the ace and read "Heavy Set" by Bradbury. Walter followed with a new story that he'd just sold, another Halloween story, and the chill seemed to creep in through the windows. Lesley read a piece from Beaumont and even gave herself shudders.

Then Susan took a turn, her straight blonde hair and pale skin looking cold and waxen in the candles' flicker. Everyone shifted nervously as she finished, and Lesley thought happily that it was really happening again. We've done it, she thought. We've gotten ourselves so worked up that we're ready to believe anything.

"It's Rob's turn," Walter said quietly. "Anyone want to do the honors?"

When no one else spoke up, Lesley said, "I will."

I'm still carrying him, she thought as she took the envelope from Walter. Without wanting to, she finished the thought: someone has to. Poor childish Rob, with his tantrums and his grandiose dreams. How long would he keep haunting them?

She took the manuscript out of the envelope. It was handwritten on some kind of ragged paper that looked like parchment. She recognized the scrawled printing, despite the peculiar brownish ink he'd used.

She glanced at her watch, then went back to the manuscript. "It's called 'The Circle,'" she said.

She began to read.

"'For six years they'd been meeting on Halloween night, here at the cabin by the lake, and reading ghost stories to each other.'"

Lesley looked up. Something about the story was making her nervous, and she could see that same unease on the shadowy faces around her.

"'Some of the faces varied from year to year, but a central group remained the same. They had a lot in common—they played their games with each other, went to movies together, and sometimes they went to bed with each other.'"

Lesley felt a blush starting up her neck. She might have known he would do something like this to embarrass her. He'd been so jealous of the few stories she'd sold, and when she'd tried to offer him some advice he'd blown up. That had been the first quarrel, and he'd come back to it again and again, more bitter each time, until finally he'd left for Mexico.

Well, I'm the one reading this thing, she thought. If it gets any more personal, I'll just stop.

"'Together,'" she read, "'they'd decided that the supernatural was fit material for stories on Halloween, and not much else. Thus they, in their infinite wisdom, were not prepared for what happened to them that Halloween night.

"'The leader of the circle got a story in the mail that week. It was written by someone he had known, but never really considered a friend. Because of his beliefs, he didn't recognize the power that lay in the pages and in the ink that the story was written on. And so he accepted the challenge to read the story aloud that Halloween.

"'They met at the cabin and read their stories, and then they began to read the story by the man who was not with them anymore. And as soon as they began to read it, a heavy mist settled down around the cabin.

"'It was like a fog, but so thick you could almost feel it squeeze between your fingers. It carried the salt smell of an ocean that shouldn't have been there, and everywhere it touched, the world ceased to exist.'"

Lesley's mouth had gone dry. She was leaning forward to pick up her teacup when she saw the window.

"Oh my God...." she whispered.

Beyond the window was a solid mass of white.

They all stared at the fog outside the window.

Guy and his new girlfriend Dana had been sitting under the window, and they'd moved into the center of the room. "What is it?" Dana asked. Her voice had a tremor in it that made Lesley even more frightened than before.

"It's called fog," Brian sneered. "Haven't you ever seen fog before?" He started for the door. "Look, I'll show it to you."

"Don't—" Lesley started, but her throat caught before she could finish the sentence.

The candlelight glinted off Brian's moist lips and oily hair. "What's the matter with you guys? What are you afraid of?"

He jerked the door open.

The fog lay outside like a wall of cotton wool. The edge of it, where the door had been, was as smooth as if it had been cut with a razor. Not even the thinnest wisp tried to reach through the doorway.

"See?" Brian said, sticking his arm into it. "Fog." Lesley saw his nose wrinkle, and then she smelled it herself. It was a salty, low-tide odor like dead fish.

"Yuck," Brian said. He took a step toward the porch of the cabin, lost his balance, and caught himself by gripping the molding on either side of the door. "What the hell—?"

He extended one leg as far as it would go, then lay down and reached out into the fog. "There's nothing there."

"I don't like this," Susan said, but no one was listening to her.

"No porch," Brian said, "no ground, nothing."

Almost imperceptively they all began to move closer to the fireplace.

"Close the door," Walter said calmly, and Brian did as he was told. "Lesley, what's the next line of the story?"

"'With the fog came the sound of the wind. It howled and screamed, but the air never moved and the fog lay heavy over the cabin.'"

The noise began.

It started as a low whistle, then built into a moaning, shrieking crescendo. It sounded less like a wind than a chorus of human voices, frightened and tortured out of their minds.

"Stop it!" Susan screamed. "Stop it, please make it stop!" Walter put his arms around her and held her head to his chest. She began to sob quietly.

They were now a circle in fact, a tight circle on the floor in front of the fireplace, knees touching, eyes searching each other's faces for some sign of understanding.

"What is it?" Dana cried. She was nearly shouting in order to be heard. "Where's it coming from?"

Lesley and Walter looked at each other, then Lesley's gaze dropped to the floor.

"It's that story, isn't it?" Dana said, her voice so high it was starting to crack. "Isn't it?"

"It must be," Walter said. His voice was so low that Lesley could barely hear it over the howling outside. "Rob must have found something in Mexico. A way to get back at us."

"This isn't happening," Brian said. "It's not. It can't be."

"It is," Walter said, raising his voice over the wind. "Pretending it isn't real is not going to help." Susan whimpered, and he held her tighter to his chest. "Look, we've all read stories like this. Some of us have written them. We all get irritated when people refuse to accept what's happening to them. How long is it going to take for us to admit what's happening here?"

"All right," Brian said. "It's real. What do we do?"

Lesley said, "The paper and ink. Rob said they were special. In the story."

"Why don't we just burn the damned thing?" Brian said, "We should have done that in the first place." As if in answer, the wind roared up to a deafening volume.

"No," said Walter. He waited until the noise subsided again and added, "What if we burn it and trap ourselves here? If only we knew how it ends."

"That's easy enough," Brian said. He reached across and took the papers from Lesley's unresisting fingers.

"No!" Walter shouted, lunging at him, but Brian had already flipped over to the last page.

"We all die," he said, handing the story back to Lesley. "Not very well written, but pretty gruesome." His levity failed completely. The wind was so loud it seemed to Lesley that the walls should have been shaken to pieces.

"Ideas?" Walter said. "Anybody?"

"I say burn it," Brian said again. "What can happen?"

"Rewrite it," Lesley said.

"What?" Walter asked. Lesley realized that the awful noise had swallowed her words.

"Rewrite it!" she repeated. "Change the ending!"

"I like it," Walter said. "Guy?"

He shrugged. "Worth a try. Anybody got a pen?"

"No," Lesley said. "I don't think that'll work."

"Why not?"

"I think," she said, "it's written in blood."

She knew it was up to her. It was like belling the cat—her idea, her responsibility. Before any of the others could stop her, she got a safety pin out of her purse and jabbed it into the index finger of her left hand.

She rolled the point of the pin in the droplet of blood, then tried to draw an *X* across the bottom of the page she'd been reading from. The point of the pin wouldn't hold enough. Finally she just wiped her finger across it, and then did the same thing on the last two pages.

"Now," she said. "What do I write?"

They all sat and looked at each other while the ghost wind shrieked at them.

"How about, 'Everything returned to normal,'" Guy said.

"What's normal?" Brian asked.

"He's got a point," Walter admitted. "We may need to be more specific."

"Not too specific," Lesley said. "I've only got so much blood."

No one laughed.

"Okay," Walter said. "Does anybody know what time Lesley started reading?"

"I checked," Lesley said. "It was about eleven-eighteen."

"All right. How about, 'Everything returned to the way it had been at eleven-eighteen that night?'"

There were nods all around. "Go for it," Guy said.

This time Lesley had to use the pin. It was slow going, but she finally got the words scrawled across the bottom of the page.

The wind continued to scream.

"Read it," Walter said.

Lesley's hands were shaking. Come on, she told herself, you didn't lose that much blood. But she knew it wasn't that. What if she read it and it didn't work? She couldn't stand that horrible, shrill noise much longer.

From the back of her mind a grim thought began to nag at her. What were the gruesome things the story said happened to them?

Let it work, she prayed. Let everything be the way it had been. Just exactly the way it had been.

"'Everything,'" she read, her shaking voice barely topping the roar of the wind, "'returned to the way it had been at eleven-eighteen that night.'"

It was quiet.

The night was clear and cold, and water dripped from the trees to the layer of pine needles on the ground.

Lesley looked at her watch. It was 11:18.

"It's called 'The Circle,'" she said.

She began to read.

"First Of All, It Was October..."

An Overview of Halloween Films

Gary A. Braunbeck

"A goblin lives in our house, in our house, in *our* house,
A goblin lives in *our* house, all the year 'round..."

—Traditional Children's Halloween rhyme

And if you're like the rest of we Halloween *afficionados*, said goblin lurks in your video cabinet, or in well-preserved laser disc sleeves, or resides quietly in a DVD case until October rolls 'round and it's time to bring out the fright flicks.

This is not to imply that we wait exclusively for Halloween to watch horror movies, far from it; October just gives us an iron-clad, no-arguments, "It's-that-time-of-year" excuse to watch them almost non-stop because, well, It's Our Favorite Holiday. After all, what would Christmas be without Scrooge and Charlie Brown, right? Same applies to Halloween: if you don't have your Michael Myers or vampires or witches or

Ichabod Crane, why bother with the pumpkins or candy? Can I get an *Amen?*

So it's Halloween, and all the candy's been handed out and the kids are back home; the masks are off (if not the rest of the costume), the goodies are scattered on the floor just waiting to be gobbled, and everyone's stoked on sugar and the atmosphere of the season; the dry whisper of dead leaves skittering across the front porch sounds more and more like the bony fingers of the dead scratching at the door, and as the darkness bleeds over the street, the time for Scary Movies is at hand.

You can almost taste the candy corn at this point, can't you?

So you reach for the first movie (after all, you're not going to watch just *one* now, are you?) in the media of your preference and get ready to load it into its respective player.

The question is: *Which* movies to watch?

In what follows, I have attempted to gather together every Halloween-themed or-related movie that I know in hopes of offering you and yours a wide variety of frights for that Most Special Night of the Year. I do not claim that this list is all-inclusive. Undoubtedly someone out there will know of at least a dozen short subjects, three Indies, or nine obscure Italian horror films that deal with the theme of Halloween, for example, and will call me on their exclusion; if you know of Halloween films *other* than those I talk about, let us know, and perhaps we'll do an update in a future issue of *Cemetery Dance.* But it does contain *every* Halloween-related film that I have found. I have excluded nothing here; you've got Great movies, Good ones, So-So movies, Just Okay ones, Bad ones, and Those So Foul You Dare Not Speak Their Names.

I thought it was important to establish some very specific criteria for these movies, simply because there are films not listed here which, admittedly, would be perfect Halloween viewing (*The Exorcist, The Sixth*

Sense, Exorcist III, Pumpkinhead, Scream, Manhunter, Sorcerer, Silence of the Lambs, Fright Night and *Seconds* to name a handful), but they do not have any direct connection to Halloween aside from being first-rate horror films.

I needed more than that here, so (for those of you who are interested) here is the criteria I used for the films which are included here.

In order for a movie to make this list, it had to possess at least three of the following elements and/or qualities:

1) Its story had to take place on or around Halloween;

2) If not set on or around Halloween, its story had to take place in October, as well as contain at least one traditional Halloween element (see next) necessary to the story;

3) It had to contain some of the usual trappings associated with Halloween—goblins, ghosts, witches, vampires, monsters/demons, dark woods, an abundance of bright-eyed jack-o'-lanterns, skulls and skeletons galore, haunted houses, masked madmen, people in macabre costumes (you get the idea)—and said trapping(s) had to be essential to some element of the story, not just window-dressing;

4) A sense of humor was a big plus—after all, when everything's said and done, Halloween should be *fun;*

5) In some—but by no means *all*—cases, it had to be appropriate for family viewing, because the holiday is (and should be) mostly about children having a grand old spooky time, and parents being able to enjoy it with them;

6) It had to be *accessible*, meaning easily found: it wouldn't do a lot of good to go on at length about a wonderful Halloween movie that you can't locate at the local video store or Media Play or order on-line;

AND (lest we overlook the obvious)

7) It had to be *scary* (and I gave some of these movies a *lot* of leeway

on this last point; in some instances, I settled on them having simply a *spooky scene* or *creepy moment*).

At the end of this piece you'll find a list of movies that are appropriate for younger viewers, along with recommendations for Halloween night Double Features.

That said, let's get to the movies themselves—and what better way to begin with than with a pair of movies based on works by the man who, if Halloween hadn't already existed, might very well have invented it: Ray Bradbury.

***Something Wicked This Way Comes* (1983):** Before the Disney Studios became our Dark Overlord of the Tried and True Repackaged for the Undiscriminating, they produced this handsome, reverent, and extremely well-acted adaptation of what many consider to be Bradbury's masterpiece. For admirers of the book, the results will be familiar; for those who have never read this magnificent and important novel, it is—like the film adaptation of Peter Straub's *Ghost Story*—a severely watered-down, though atmospherically precise, short-hand representation of a work that remains best experienced on the printed page.

Which is not to say that *Something Wicked* is a bad movie; in fact, there is much here to please admirers of the novel—particularly the sterling performances of Jason Robards and Jonathan Pryce.

There are three major problems with the movie: one is that the filmmakers—who obviously had great love and respect for the novel—perhaps had a little *too* much reverence for the work; this is not so much an *adaptation* of the book as it is an *appreciation*; it's as if they were not so much trying to capture the actual essence of the novel as they were their fond memories of the book: this isn't the novel, it's the way they *remember* the novel as being.

The second problem is, of course, Disney. One has the feeling while watching this movie that director Jack Clayton *(The Innocents, The Lonely Passion of Judith Hearn)* had a Disney executive breathing down his neck the entire time saying, "Not *too* scary right here...not *too* covertly erotic there, gotta keep the audience in mind...this is *Disney*, after all." *Something Wicked* comes *this close* on countless occasions to delivering the real goods that the viewer, after a while, becomes frustrated at how many punches are pulled—or in this case, frights filtered. (There are exceptions to this; the initial appearance of Dark's Pandemonium Shadow Show's parade in downtown Greentown—where Dark is trying to find Jim Nightshade and William Halloway—is genuinely eerie; the confrontation in the library where Dark tempts Charles Halloway with a second chance overpowers with its dazzling balance of terror and poignancy; and the sequence where Jim and Will are attacked by an army of spiders in Jim's bedroom at night is truly nightmarish.)

The third problem—and I'm almost hesitant to say this—is Bradbury's screenplay. Over the years, I have come to the conclusion that most authors who also happen to be screenwriters should never attempt to adapt their own work. William Goldman—the god of screenwriters—has written some brilliant original screenplays, and performed miracles when adapting others' novels; but when it comes to adapting his own work, Goldman inevitably flounders (case in point: *Magic,* where he somehow managed to reduce one of the best psychological horror stories ever written into an expanded episode from *Dead of Night*; had it not been for the superb performances from Anthony Hopkins, Ed Lauter, and the late Burgess Meredith, the movie would have stayed with you about as long as a rerun of *What's Happening?*).

The same happens with *Something Wicked.* The Bradbury who wrote the screenplay was not the same man who wrote the novel over a quarter-century previous. I would not be so arrogant as to guess why, but as I watched this movie again recently, I couldn't help but notice that it's much more sentimental than the novel—almost downright treacly in places. It's almost as if Bradbury had opted to emphasize the more poignant aspects of the novel rather than the horrific.

Still, *Something Wicked* succeeds overall, thanks to the performances (Pryce is an absolute spellbinder in his soft-spoken interpretation of Dark), first-rate production design (Greentown and the Pandemonium Show look *exactly* as you've imagined they would), an appropriately lush score by James Horner that is both eerie and glorious, and, as an added bonus, Stephen Burum's dreamlike cinematography, which knows when and how to blur focus or radically shift an angle in order to disorient or agitate the viewer. Then there's the carousel finale, which is true movie magic. The movie is worth seeing for this sequence alone.

Though not the classic it could have been, *Something Wicked This Way Comes* is nonetheless an affectionate, respectful, well-acted and—at times—dazzlingly scary variation on one of *the* classic novels in American literature (genre be damned). Adults will admire its craftsmanship, kids will love the Pandemonium Show's assortment of oddities and weird goings-on. You could do much, much worse than include it on your Halloween viewing list.

The second—and surprisingly more successful—adaptation of a Bradbury work is the 1993 animated version of ***The Halloween Tree***. I say "surprising" because it was made for television by the *Scooby-Doo* folks themselves, Hanna-Barbera Productions. Written by Bradbury and directed by Mario Piluso, *The Halloween Tree* is the best adaptation of a Bradbury work I've ever seen, and perhaps a lot of it has to do with the fact that the novel itself isn't very long, and so easily leant itself to a fully-realized film version.

In case you're not familiar with the story (and shame on you if that's the case), it concerns itself with a group of young friends running to meet their friend Pipkin at the haunted house outside town; there they encounter the huge and cadaverous Mr. Moundshroud. As Pipkin scrambles to join them, he is swept away by a dark Something, and Moundshroud leads the children on the tail of a kite through time and space to search the past for their friend and the meaning of Halloween. After witnessing a funeral procession in ancient Egypt, cavemen discovering fire, Druid rites, the persecution of witches in the Dark Ages, and the gargoyles of Notre Dame, they catch up with the elusive Pipkin in the catacombs of Mexico, where each friend gives one year from the end of their life to save Pipkin's.

It's a wonderfully atmospheric and evocative tale, full of chills and laughter, but while it entertains it also offers an almost-scholarly lesson on the history of Halloween, as well as a powerful statement about the strength of friendship and the heroism of sacrifice. All without ever climbing onto a soapbox.

All of that is to be found in the movie.

Though the quality of the hand-drawn animation never breaks any new ground (it is only slightly better than your average Saturday morning cartoon fest), the HB animators have to be given credit for keeping the look of the movie as close as possible to Joseph Mugnaini's marvelous black and white drawings for the book. From the time Moundshroud shows up until the last, touching scene, *The Halloween Tree* strives toward—and mostly achieves—a decidedly surrealist (if two-dimensional) visual scheme.

But the quality of the animation never detracts from the wonder, joy, and creepiness of the story itself. The movie moves at a swift pace, barely stopping to catch its breath, and the voice characterizations are excellent, especially Leonard Nimoy's colorful turn as Moundshroud. What's more, Bradbury himself provides the voice of the narrator, and his presence—his wonderfully musical, somewhat melancholy, age-worn but still very childlike baritone—gives *The Halloween Tree* the measure of genuine emotional depth that *Something Wicked* only flirted with from a distance.

You can find *The Halloween Tree* in most video stores. It's offered under the Cartoon Network's label and will set you back all of ten dollars. Buy it, watch by yourself or with a room full of mesmerized children; either way, it's one to treasure.

And thank you, Mr. Bradbury.

Now we go from the intense quietude of Bradbury to the equally intense quirkiness of Tim Burton, our other double-honoree. You all know the movie I'm talking about.

Even if you found some of its unabashedly grotesque visual elements a little too dark and over the top, what cannot be denied is that 1993's ***The Nightmare Before Christmas*** is a genuine original; the type of movie you haven't seen before (or since, in my opinion).

Based on a story by Tim Burton (adapted by the late Michael McDowell and written for the screen by Caroline Thompson) *Nightmare* takes place in a fairytale world where each holiday has its own special land. Opening in Halloween Town, it concerns itself with Jack Skellington, the Pumpkin King, who finds that he's become bored with scaring people. Through a series of coincidences worthy of the best of the Brothers Grimm, Jack finds the entrance to Christmas Town and decides that he'd like to give this Santa thing a try.

But I'm sort of preaching to the choir here by recapping the story; you know it well enough. Suffice to say that there is not one second in this marvelous film that isn't a stunner. The animators (supervised here by Eric Leighton) have created some of the most breathtaking stop-action since the days when Ray Harryhousen and Willis O'Brien were inventing the craft. Each character moves with a fluid grace that most live-action actors don't possess—and nowhere is this more evident than in the spectacular opening number, "Welcome to Halloween Town," a brilliantly-conceived and -staged production number that plays like a macabre variation on *The Music Man*'s "76 Trombones." I lost count of how many characters' bodies were based on geometric shapes, with a hatchet in the head or an extra set of legs added for good measure.

Here, as in *The Halloween Tree,* the voice characterizations are first-rate, with a special nod going to Chris Sarandon's *(Fright Night)* performance as Jack; he gives the character a touching note of wistfulness that works as a lovely counterpoint to much of the bizarre events surrounding him, like a child who knows that everything around it is just a bad dream that will soon be over.

There are some spectacular sequences in the movie. My two favorites are the sequence where Jack, decked out in full Santa garb and flying through the night in Santa's sleigh, is fired upon by military missles; the other—and easily the movie's most hysterical sequence—involves Christmas morning, as children all over the world open their gifts to find snakes, severed limbs, and monsters of the jump-out-of-the-box-and-gobble-your-face variety; the childrens' confused reactions to their gifts, and their parents' panic-in-the-streets screams of horror, will bring a tear to the eye of even the most jaded cynic while Danny Elfman's best score to date—a joyous mixture of Bernard Herrmann and Vince Guiraldi—keeps giving the viewer musical winks, just to remind you it's all in good fun.

Many have made note that the director, Henry Selick (*James and the Giant Peach*) seemed to have been purposefully imitating Burton's directorial style, but I think that's an injustice to his fine work here; Selick's direction is smooth and crisp, and never pulls a muscle drawing attention to itself. As he did in *James*, Selick is content to let the story take main focus, and his style is a bit more streamlined than Burton's sometimes self-conscious visual acrobatics. (Note this: I think both are fine directors. Burton, in particular, brings to his movies a world-view that is, methinks, completely unique in American cinema, so don't walk away from this thinking that I hate Burton movies, okay?)

The Nightmare Before Christmas ranks with *The Halloween Tree* as one of the Must-See movies on this list. Some of it may be a little too grotesque for very young children, so if you're a parent use your own judgment; but I think this modern-day masterpiece is perfect Halloween viewing for the entire family.

Next we come to a story that is justifiably regarded as an American Halloween classic, *The Legend of Sleepy Hollow.* There have been, at last count, five film versions of this timeless Washington Irving tale, dating all the way back to a 1921 silent short starring John Barrymore—a film that is no longer in existence due to the deterioration of its film stock, I'm saddened to tell you. The four which remain (and I'm focusing on the American versions because those are the ones I'm aware of), are from 1949, 1979, 1986, and, most recently, Tim Burton's 1999 revisionist version starring Johnny Depp and Christina Ricci, as well as a gallery of instantly recognizable character actors (Jeffrey Jones, Michael Gough, and the great Christopher Lee) in key supporting roles.

Disney's 1949 animated adaptation of Irving's story, narrated by Bing Crosby, remains loyal to its source material, providing all the humor and terror you'd expect, but the real star here is the animation. Deeply colored, richly layered, and with a painstaking eye for even the most minute detail (check out the way the muscles in the Headless Horseman's hands twitch whenever he makes a fist, or how his horse's nostrils flare madly even when it's in the background), this movie is proof-positive of just how lazy Disney animators have become in this digital age. Any single frame of this movie could be frozen and turned into a painting that would reveal new details upon repeated viewings—as does the movie itself. Like the old saying goes, They Don't Make 'Em Like This Any More. (An exception might be 1999's superb *The Iron Giant*, which combined the best of hand-drawn and computer-generated animation, but I digress.)

The 1979 TV movie offers little more than it has to, save for Jeff Goldblum's endearing, self-deprecating performance as Ichabod Crane. The 1986 version, filmed by Showtime for *Shelly Duvall's Tall Tales and Legends*, is visually striking and well-made, but wears out its welcome all too soon, thanks to Ed Begley Jr.'s excruciatingly whiny interpretation of Ichabod; he's like watching water drip, only without the interesting visuals. Better by far is the terrific Charles Durning's turn as a town father; Durning seems to be the only performer on hand who's in the spirit of things. Watch this one only if the others aren't available. Trust me on this.

Aside from the 1949 Disney version, my pick for the best adaptation of this story is Tim Burton's 1999 *Sleepy Hollow*—a wildly uneven but ultimately nightmarish re-thinking of Irving's story that tries to be all things at once—murder mystery, ghost story, gothic nightmare, conspiracy film, dark comedy, and love story—and, much to my surprise, succeeded in everything it attempted to do.

I say "surprise" because the combination of Tim Burton and in-your-face grue seemed to me a tricky proposition at best. Burton, to my mind, was better suited to such whimsical fare as *Edward Scissorhands* and *Beetlejuice* (even his Oscar-winning *Ed Wood* managed to whitewash much of its subject's seamier character traits in favor of paying tribute to an absolutely talentless man whose love for movies far exceeded his abilities to make them; the exception here was the treatment of Bela Lugosi's poverty and drug addiction, which Burton unflinchingly examined, and it created a dichotomy in tone which made *Ed Wood* a memorable, loving, but ultimately uneven movie for me).

So, the marriage of Burton and graphic violence had me, to say the least, skeptical. But—like Blake Edwards' magnificent *S.O.B.*—the radical shifts in tone here are a plus; Burton never gives you the chance to tire of any one particular element. Perhaps his most inspired move in the making of *Sleepy Hollow* was to intentionally copy the look of the old Hammer horror movies; cinematographer Emmanuel Lubezki won an Oscar for his magnificent work here, and deservedly so, as did the team of production-design wizards who built the town of Sleepy Hollow from the ground up; the result is a gothic hamlet whose architecture is at once Dickensian and Geiger-like, a seamless blend of the man-made and organic. When Depp, as Ichabod Crane, first walks into Sleepy Hollow, Burton takes his time showing us the village; it's his way of visually warning us that the tone of the rest of the movie—like the look of the buildings themselves—is not going to be what we're expecting. Nightmare stalks the dreamscape here, and never retreats too far into the shadows.

In Burton's version, Crane is no longer a school teacher but a New York Police constable, a young upstart whose constant questioning of his superior's methods of crime investigation earns him a fast trip upstate to investigate a series of gruesome beheadings.

Depp is marvelous as Crane, making him a somewhat prudish, humorless stick-in-the-mud whose outwardly cold demeanor masks his inner buffoon—who shows himself all too soon, much to the confusion of the town fathers. *Sleepy Hollow* marks the third time Depp and Burton have worked together, and if Burton were to decide to cast Depp (a frighteningly talented actor) in every movie he makes from now on, that's fine by me. It's all too rare that an actor and director so beautifully compliment one another—think of Sean Connery's films with Sidney Lumet, or Robert De Niro and Martin Scorsese, or the late Burt Lancaster and John Frankenheimer, and you'll have some idea of what I'm talking about—and when the magic is there, you don't mess with it. Burton and Depp don't mess with it here, and the result is one of Depp's most charming and full-bodied performances, the kind of performance Oscars *should* go to.

The screenplay (by Andrew Kevin Walker, with uncredited assistance from Tom Stoppard) crackles with literate dialogue and terrific character touches, but almost collapses toward the end when it becomes clear that Everything Is Going To Be Explained—a necessary evil when dealing with conspiracies and murder mysteries. (The movie also goes so far—as Francis Coppola did in *Bram Stoker's Dracula*—to provide a backstory for its central character; in this case, Christopher Walken plays the Horseman as a mercenary addicted to violence; he's appropriately over-the-top, and meets with a Just End...or so you think.) It's to everyone's credit that this penchant for tying up all loose ends does not ultimately harm the movie.

Sleepy Hollow has some genuinely jolting bursts of graphic violence—I lost count of how many heads are chopped off during its running time—which earned the film its solid "R" rating. But for as much violence as the film contains—and there's plenty—none of it is gratuitous, nor does Burton dwell on it for the sake of shock; the horseman thunders down on a victim, his heavy sword is unsheathed (accompanied by a nerve-wracking sound effect), and the head is chopped in a spinning blur of blood and bone fragments. Each beheading is shown in quick, graphic detail, but Burton never repeats himself visually with any two murders; each is unique to its victim, each one is new, each one is more and more shocking—no easy feat in horror.

It also contains what is hands-down the most spectacular, horrifying, and masterful sequence Burton has ever done, one that should remove any doubts from your mind that Burton will someday take his place among the list of Great American Directors; a no-holds-barred, grab-onto-something scene where the Horseman traps the entire town inside the church and—even though he cannot enter because the church is on hallowed ground—manages to raise his death-toll, anyway. This breathtaking sequence had me on the edge of my seat, and I'm a bit of a hard-case when it comes to being frightened at horror movies; this sequence builds with near-operatic grandeur, culminating in a moment that is equal parts *Die Hard*, gruesome slapstick, and classic *Grand Guignol*. If you're going to re-tell an American classic, *this* is the way to do it.

So spectacular is this sequence that you're left wondering how Burton's going to top it. In truth, he doesn't, but the final, frenetic chase and battle between Crane and the Horseman (which ends with a moment of grotesquerie that will make even the most jaded horror film fan squirm) nearly equals it, and for my money, that's good enough.

Yes, *Sleepy Hollow* flirts with disaster in its wild shifts of tone, but it never loses its footing, thanks to Burton's masterful hand.

Besides, how can you quibble about a movie that so effortlessly makes you laugh and cringe in the same moment so consistently? Add *Sleepy Hollow* to the Must-See list.

By this time you're probably wondering when I'm going to get to John Carpenter's ***Halloween***.

The answer is now—but I'm not going to spend too much time on it, and I'll tell you why.

I think it's safe to say that if you're reading this, if you purchased this book, odds are you've already seen it. Several times. And it's a film that only gets better upon repeated viewings.

Working with a budget that would make that of *The Blair Witch Project* look like Bruce Willis's salary, and using a mostly then-unknown cast (with the exception of the late Donald Pleasence, wonderfully intense and somewhat daffy here), Carpenter fashioned a modern-day version of the Bogeyman bedtime story, with healthy doses of sex and violence thrown into the mix. The result is what some consider the granddaddy of all Halloween horror movies. It also (like Friedkin's *The Exorcist* and Hopper's *Easy Rider)* spawned countless imitations that nearly destroyed the genre, and whose ill effect on the way horror is widely regarded still holds the genre down in the gutter, regardless of what we tell ourselves. (But that's another argument for another venue.)

What cannot be denied is that *Halloween* is an outright screamer, the type of scary movie where you're going to jump at least half a dozen times before the credits roll. Filmed as if it were some soft-focus love story, *Halloween* actually achieves the fairy-tale feel it's going for—and nowhere in the movie is this more evident than in the scene where Michael Myers kills a young man who's just finished having sex with his girlfriend by impaling him on a kitchen pantry door with a butcher's knife. Myers takes his hand away and stands back, staring at the young man whose feet dangle a good two feet above the floor. Carpenter cuts to a long shot, showing both Myers and the body in silhouette, the body in darkness, Myers looking almost ethereal as he's bathed in moonlight streaming in through a window. Crucifixion symbolism aside, what gives this moment its quiet power is what happens in the moment before Carpenter cuts away: Myers tilts his head slightly to the side, as if examining a work of art he's just finished. It's a moment that is both chilling and somehow sweet, because you realize then that Myers is still very much a child who looks upon what he's just done not as murder, but as creating something that gives back to him some of the childhood he lost in the asylum. There's a certain twisted beauty to the moment, and it crystalizes, methinks, Carpenter's intentions as a film maker here; that this type of psycho-on-the-loose story can achieve a level of craftsmanship that viewers aren't expecting; it's as if both he and Myers are simultaneously looking at their creation and thinking, "Huh, whatta you know: this stuff can be done *artfully*."

If only that kind of thinking had carried over into the sequels.

We all know that, with the exception of *Halloween 3: The Season of the Witch* all of the sequels fell into the same tired formula: horny slacker teens are stalked by Michael Myers, Donald Pleasence screams that Myers is "pure evil" and so must be destroyed, horny slacker teens are cornered by Myers, many die, but a few emerge alive, thinking Myers is dead but he isn't, and the lazy groundwork for the next sequel is laid as the credits roll and Carpenter's now-classic theme reminds us of the beauty of the original.

Yawn.

Even the final film in the series, *Halloween: H20*, by far the best-acted movie in the bunch, eventually fell victim to terminal *Scream*-iness, copying that movie's structure nearly all the way down the line; sure,it had some clever touches here and there, but it was so determined to cash in with Wes Craven's new-found audience that it lost its own tenuous identity early on. Had Jamie Lee Curtis not been in it, it could have been just another *I Still Know What You Screamed Last Halloween* clone.

It purported to be the Last Word in slasher films; it emerged as little more than a minor footnote.

No, if you're going to watch any of the sequels, then I would recommend—with more than a few reservations—*Halloween 3: The Season of the Witch,* not because it's a particularly good movie (it isn't), but because this in-name-only sequel strove to stand out from the crowd, and this it does with a vengeance.

Originally slated to be scripted by Nigel Neale (creator of the *Quatermass* series), whose script was, for reasons that are still unclear, rejected, this entry in the series was written and directed by Tommy Lee Wallace and is based on the gloriously and unapologetically depraved conceit that a billionaire madman (Dan O'Herlihy), leader of a group of modern-day Druids, plans to kill 50 million children on Halloween with special, deadly masks. Made at the height of the gore-hungry 80s, this film leaves nothing to the imagination; there are crushed skulls and splattered brains galore. No one is safe in this movie, especially children—and that's where my strongest reservation comes in; it's one thing to base all suspense on the threat of harm to children, it's another thing altogether when the gruesome death of a child is played for sensationalistic effect, as it is here in what is surely one of the lowest points in the history of horror films.

Still, I had to give it credit for sticking to its dehumanizing guns; it moves quickly, it has a genuinely horrifying idea at its center, it's a much better made film than you'd expect, and there's the plus of O'Herlihy's wonderfully dark-humored performance; if there's anything to recommend seeing this movie, it's O'Herlihy; suave, menacing, and seemingly classy, his rich baritone voice, when he explains his plans, nearly sings with bloody glee; he is so enchanted by the idea, and O'Herlihy is so good, that you almost want to see him get away with it.

Almost.

Balancing humor and horror is no simple task; one slip, and the whole thing can come crashing down around you in a tasteless, offensive heap. Not that I'm against tastelessness or offensive humor; witness the classic *The Loved One*, a blacker-than-black comedy that, now some thirty-odd years old, is still considered too potent and tasteless by many people. I think it's a hoot, and always will.

Enough: both humor and horror are subjective, so take these next few films with a grain of salt and panic.

To illustrate the old comic's adage that "Timing is everything," I submit to you our next Halloween movie, 1999's unjustifiably trashed ***Idle Hands***. This clever and gleefully tasteless black comedy's release coincided with the numbing, heart-breaking tragedy of the Littleton shootings, and as a result, I think that's why people stayed away from it in droves.

(Note: I am in no way trying to trivialize the unspeakable horror of what happened in Littleton by blaming *Idle Hands*' box-office and critical failure on it; the nation was sickened by what happened, as well it should have been, and my heart broke for the victims and their families. But if you'll recall, there was a backlash against everything from video games to horror novels to the Goth culture as people tried to find someone or something to Blame, some way to Make Sense of the Senseless, and *Idle Hands*, because of the timing of its release, fell into the line of sight. Timing was its enemy—why go to see a *horror comedy* about kids killing kids when the blood-drenched, serious-as-hell *reality* of kids killing kids is all over the news? Hopefully, my point has been made clear. Back to the movie.)

Idle Hands tells the story of pothead slacker Anton (Devon Sawa) who discovers one Halloween that his hand has become possessed by a demon. It makes him kill his two friends (Elden Henson and *Buffy, the Vampire Slayer*'s Seth Green) and grab innocent passersby in most inappropriate ways. Devon hacks off his hand, only to discover that it's going after his girlfriend to drag her soul to hell. Enlisting the help of a Druid priestess (Vivica Fox), as well as his now-undead friends, Devon sets out to do battle with his hand and save his girlfriend's soul (as well as her bodacious bod, as is pointed out more than once).

The sight of Seth Green, undead and doing various heroics with a spike in his head, is good for many laughs, as is Sawa's physical performance as he battles with his hand. (I was reminded on several occasions of Steve Martin's brilliant turn in Carl Reiner's *All Of Me*). There is some truly inspired slapstick here, and Sawa takes some pratfalls that Buster Keaton would have approved of.

Sure, everything about *Idle Hands* is over the top, but if you've got a strong stomach and aren't easily offended, you'll find that the movie—while sloppily made and often obvious and juvenile in its humor—offers a gory good time. You'll enjoy yourself, despite everything. Just don't look at yourself too closely in the mirror for a couple of days afterward, okay?

The same can be said of 1991's ***Ernest Scared Stupid***, where the eternally pea-brained Ernest P. Worrell accidentally releases a demon from its tomb and sets into motion the fruition of a 200 year-old curse that threatens to destroy his home town.

Would *you* want your town's fate in Ernest's hands?

Written and directed by John C. Cherry III, *Ernest Scared Stupid* never purports to be anything more than a silly, goofy, no-brainer, live-action Halloween cartoon for kids; if you watch this movie with that in mind, you'll find (as I did when my then-5 year-old nephew asked me to watch it with him on video) yourself laughing almost constantly as Ernest—good-natured, sweet, doesn't-have-the-brains-God-gave-an-ice-cube Ernest—tries everything he can think of to trick the demon back into its tomb. Depleting his reserve of wit in about four minutes, Ernest is reduced to a series of incredible slapstick schemes—one of the funniest involves a bulldozer and the great line, "Eat metal, booger-lips!"

The effects are pretty good, and though it contains its share of prerequisite fart-and-snot jokes, *Ernest Scared Stupid* has an unbound, happy innocence to it that is absolutely infectious, largely due to the late Jim Varney's performance as Ernest.

Though by no means a fine actor, Varney was nonetheless a gifted mimic, and Ernest P. Worrell is undoubtedly his most memorable character, one who can take his place in American pop culture (like it or not) alongside the likes of Forrest Gump and Gomer Pyle, U.S.M.C. Not a brain in sight, but heart to spare.

And if you pay attention, you'll find some surprisingly clever in-jokes for horror movie buffs. Some are fairly obvious (*Night of the Living Dead, The Shining, Pet Sematary*), but others (*The Haunting, Hell House, Carnival of Souls,* and—blink and you'll miss it—the film version of Peter Straub's *Ghost Story)* are more subtle, and give the movie that little extra something that you're going to be wishing for.

Speaking of in-jokes, you'll find a few good ones in 1990's ***Spaced Invaders***, starting with its plot line: some befuddled Martians (who make Ernest P. Worrell look like Carl Sagan) who are out to "...kick some earthling butt," overhear a radio rebroadcast of Orson Welles' *War of the Worlds* one Halloween and mistake it for genuine invasion orders. They land to find they were sorely mistaken and, finding their ship in need of repairs, must learn to work with the earthling children who befriend them. What follows is the usual predictable complications as the kids try to pass the aliens off as friends of theirs who are too shy to take off their costumes, and of course the aliens turn into cuddly-wuddly little bags of cuteness that you immediately want to step on, but it's harmless fun...though for adults, it'll wear out its welcome after the first twenty-five minutes. Still, young children will enjoy it.

For a much better treatment of aliens-at-Halloween, go to your cabinet and take out the copy of 1982's ***E.T. The Extra-Terrestrial*** that I know you own. Don't deny it. You cried at the end, you know you did, and how many times did you repeat the classic line, "E.T. phone home!"? More than you're willing to admit. The Halloween element of this still-wonderful movie works well in the overall story, and provides several good laughs along the way. Though FX technology has moved forward by leaps and bounds since everybody's favorite alien first appeared on screen, this movie has lost none of its magic or wonder in the last 18 years. A Halloween movie for the whole clan.

As is Don Knotts' finest hour on the screen; yes, I'm talking about 1965's ***The Ghost and Mr. Chicken.*** In it, Knotts (never more nervous or funnier) plays Luther Heggs, a reporter for the local newspaper who stumbles upon a 20-year old murder mystery at the old Simmons house where, it is said, the ghost of the murdered victim still haunts the halls, looking for justice. Wide-eyed at the idea of becoming a hotshot hero, Luther agrees to spend the night alone in the Simmons house. The result is by turns funny, scary (thanks in large part to Vic Mizzy's church organ theme), and funnier still as Luther nearly jumps out of his skin at every little sound or meaningless shadow.

No one, and I mean *no one*, flips out better than Don Knotts. The man can simply just stand there *trying* to look cool and you'll laugh your head off. You might do well to have a tank of oxygen handy when you watch this one, because in places you'll be laughing so hard you might pass out from lack of air. Knotts' wonderful performance makes Luther an accidental hero that you can really root for.

Far less successful in the laughs-and-poignancy department is the lamentable ***Hocus Pocus*** (Disney, 1993). This dreadful movie is made watchable only by Cathy Najimy and *Sex and the City*'s Sarah Jessica Parker, both of whom use their considerable comedic abilities to rise above an obvious, poorly-written script (by—hold on—Neil Cuthbert and Mick Garris, of all people). Top-billed Bette Midler chews the scenery in a manner worthy of Joan Crawford, and the garish makeup turns this into more of an outright freak show than I'm sure Disney intended. The result is a grotesque and numbingly un-funny "comedy" whose central story—about three executed witches who suddenly find they've been dropped right into the middle of the 20th century—had some real possibilities; in fact, the story flirts with some substance when the witches start to realize there's not a lot of difference between the way they were treated 300 years ago and the way most women are treated today, but like every other instance of depth that rears its unwanted head, it soon is drowned under a tidal wave of overblown effects, ham-fisted acting, and deafening music. Still, I suppose there's a certain morbid fascination to be had here; the movie is just so jaw-droppingly *awful* that it must be seen in order to be mocked at the level it deserves.

Not so with 1998's underrated ***Practical Magic***, adapted from Alice Hoffman's bestseller and enthusiastically directed by actor Griffin Dunne *(After Hours, An American Werewolf in London)*. It concerns a pair of sisters (Sandra Bullock and Nicole Kidman, neither ever more charming or sexy than they are here), both desecended from a long line of white witches, whose family suffers from a 100-year old curse: any man they fall in love with is destined to die. Sally (Bullock) remains in their hometown, marries, has a daughter, and loses her husband in a freak accident; Gillian (Kidman), the wilder of the two, gets mixed up with an abusive boyfriend who she ends up killing (with Sally's accidental assistance) in self-defense. Enter detective Aidan Quinn to investigate said boyfriend's death, and the sparks between him and Sally start to fly. *Then* the dead boyfriend returns in the form of a demon, and it's up to the sisters and their aunts (Dianne Weist and the wonderful Stockard Channing) to band together and, with the help of other women (of the non-witch variety) from the town, do battle with the demon and, if they win, lift the curse.

It's all done with great flair and compassion, with healthy doses of humor, and a gallery of sterling performances. It also has a lot to say about how modern-day witchcraft is still totally misunderstood by the world at large, how individual faith can indeed move mountains (or banish demons), how families must come together at times of crisis, and—probably the film's most important point—how the sisterhood of women remains abused and underestimated by the male of the species.

Practical Magic never gets preachy, despite its loaded agenda; its goal is first and foremost to entertain its audience, and that it accomplishes in spades. There's also a sweetly magical coda to the movie that leaves you feeling, well...*pretty good* about the human condition. And despite some of the violence—mostly that which is directed at Gillian by her monstrous boyfriend—this movie emerges with its solidly romantic heart intact. Watch this one after the kids have been put to bed.

The last entry in our witch section *has* to be 1999's surprise phenomenon, ***The Blair Witch Project.*** You all know the story: "In October of 1994, three student film makers...." Cha-cha-cha. I won't spend a lot of time on this because, to date, it's been debated and analyzed and talked to death.

This largely improvised film is by turns fascinating, irritating, and incredibly scary—a testament to the power of cumulative terror. Heather Donahue, Joshua Leonard, and especially Michael Williams give remarkable performances, and though the movie would have been more effective had it been 15-20 minutes shorter, it nonetheless remains one of the most nerve-wracking horror movies in recent memory. It's crude, sloppy, oppressively atmospheric, and ultimately horrifying. Say what you will about the first three-quarters of this controversial, flawed masterpiece, but the last fifteen minutes are among the most genuinely terrifying I've ever experienced...and the final, devastating image actually sent chills down my spine. Watch this one late, late at night, with all the lights out.

Okay, we're now starting to get toward the bottom of the barrel, so pardon me if I don't spend too much time on this next batch of Halloween movies.

The Clown Murders (1983). A posh Halloween party turns deadly when some folks fake a kidnapping to ruin a friend's business deal. *Very* minor entry in the slasher genre, though it does boast a good performance by the late John Candy in a rare non-comedic role.

Wacko (1983). Andrew "Dice" Clay stars in a *Halloween* spoof whose sole laugh comes from a lawnmower decapitation. The best performance in the movie is given by a cat. You have been warned.

Trick or Treat (1986). Nerdy high school boy raises the spirit of dead heavy metal star to help him exact revenge on those who mock him. Energetic to a fault, thanks to actor Charles Martin Smith's (*The Untouchables, Starman)* good-humored direction, and very clever in places, though the scare factor is low. Terrific rock soundtrack.

Jack-O (1995). Uninspired story of vengeful demon unleashed by partying teens boasts a better-than-average monster, plus old footage of the late John Carradine and Cameron Mitchell cleverly incorporated into existing footage.

Frankenstein and Me (1996). A bored 12-year-old (Jamieson Boulanger, in an impressively naturalistic performance) visits a traveling carnival one Halloween and, through a nifty little slapstick sequence worthy of the Keystone Cops, comes into possession of the body of Frankenstein's monster when it falls off the truck as the carnival is leaving. What follows is a wonderful, often Bradbury-esque examination of the power inherent in childhood imagination, and the need to keep that wonder alive, even if it means becoming an outcast. Full of dreamlike fantasy sequences, this movie is perfect family fare; fun and poignant, but never *too* scary. A real sleeper.

Demons; Demons 2 (1986, 1987). By far the most gory-drenched and violent of the films discussed here, these two films from director Lamberto Bava (*Son of Mario*), though short on character development, create unbelievable tension, and are linked by an ingenious plot device. In the first film, movie-goers gather at Halloween to watch a film about demon-raising, and become so involved in the story that several of them actually turn into the monsters they see on the screen. The doors to the theater are mysteriously locked, and the bloodbath begins as panicked patrons try to fight off the encroaching hordes from Hell while attempting to find a way out. At its best moments, this incredibly explicit film reaches Romero's level of feverish terror. Its sequel, co-scripted by none other than Dario Argento, finds the residents of an exclusive high-rise apartment building watching a documentary about the events depicted in the first film (a high-tech variation of the play-within-a-play device), and—lo and behold!—the demons step out of the television to munch on them and turn more than a few into demons, as well. The high-rise doors are mysteriously locked, and soon the tenants...you're way ahead of me, aren't you? There are several visual touches that had to be the work of Argento himself—particularly in the way much of the indoor architecture seems to become more and more organic as the horror spreads—and the pace is, if anything, even *more* relentless than in the first film. If you want good, gory, nerve-wracking horror, served up steamy and dripping, these two films are prime cut.

Revenge of the Living Zombies (1988). Or: *Hee-Haw Meets Night of the Living Dead.* Teens on a Halloween hayride encounter flesh-hungry zombies. Blood flows, nubile virgins flee into dark forests alone, chaos ensues, and you'll enjoy this grade-Z junk in spite of yourself; one of those "So-Bad-It's-Almost-Good" movies that the term "guilty pleasure" was invented for.

The Midnight Hour (1986). Made-for-television fare about group of teens who stumble (just once, wouldn't you like to see, say, the gang from, oh, *Cocoon,* do the honors?) across a vintage curse that brings back the dead. Nothing really original here, but a good sense of self-deprecating humor fuels this movie almost all the way to the end.

There are a few more Halloween movies to list, but I either haven't seen them or don't think they're worth either your time to view or mine to discuss, so I'll simply add them to the overall list, thank you very much.

Hopefully, you've found something herein that has sparked your interest for your Halloween viewing. If you're like me, you just plain old *love* scary movies any time of the year, whether watched alone, with the love of your life, or in a room full of sugar-stoked children. Halloween is a time for frights and fun for all ages, so how could I not end this list with a Halloween treat that we've all grown up with, and one that generations to come will pass along to their children?

I speak, of course, of the immortal ***It's the Great Pumpkin, Charlie Brown.*** Nearly four decades after it initially aired on CBS, this charmer has lost none of its appeal. Who can forget Snoopy's midnight crawl through the pumpkin patch or Linus's impassioned Shakespearian soliloquy about how "...the Great Pumpkin rises out of the pumpkin patch...." or—a classic line that ranks right up there with "Frankly my dear, I don't give a damn," and "If you build it, he will come," you know the line, say it with me: "I got a rock."

When in doubt, stick to the classics, you cannot go wrong. Long live the Great Pumpkin!

And long live Hallowe̊en and the movies that try, in their own way, to capture the spirit of that most marvelous holiday of the year.

❋ ❋ ❋

A List of Halloween Movies for You and Yours
(I have "starred" my personal favorites):

The Clown Murders
*The Blair Witch Project**
*Demons**
*Demons 2**
Double Double Toil and Trouble
Ernest Scared Stupid (I laughed like hell, so sue me)*
*E.T. The Extra-Terrestrial**
*Frankenstein and Me**
Frankenstein Sings...The Movie
*The Ghost and Mr. Chicken**
*Halloween**
Halloween 2
Halloween 3: Season of the Witch
Halloween 4: The Return of Michael Myers
Halloween 5: The Revenge of Michael Myers
Halloween 6: The Curse of Michael Myers
*Halloween 7: The Persecution and Assassination of Michael Myers As Performed By the Inmates of the Asylum Under the Direction of the Marquis De Sade**
Halloween H20
*The Halloween Tree**

Hocus Pocus
Idle Hands
I've Been Waiting for You
Jack-O
KISS Meets the Phantom of the Park
*The Legend of Sleepy Hollow (1949)**
The Legend of Sleepy Hollow (1979)
The Legend of Sleepy Hollow (1986)
*Sleepy Hollow (1999)**
The Midnight Hour
Night of the Demons
Night of the Demons 2
Night of the Demons 3
*The Nightmare Before Christmas**
*Practical Magic**
Revenge of the Living Zombies
*Something Wicked This Way Comes**
Spaced Invaders
Teen Alien
Trick or Treat
Trick or Treats
Wacko

Halloween Movies For Younger Viewers:

Double Double Toil and Trouble
*Ernest Scared Stupid**
*E.T. The Extra-Terrestrial**
*Frankenstein and Me**

Frankenstein Sings...The Movie
*The Ghost and Mr. Chicken**
Hocus Pocus
*It's the Great Pumpkin, Charlie Brown****
*The Halloween Tree**
*The Legend of Sleepy Hollow (1949)**
*The Nightmare Before Christmas**
Spaced Invaders
Teen Alien

Some Suggested Double Features:

Demons; Demons 2
Ernest Scared Stupid; The Ghost and Mr. Chicken
The Blair Witch Project; Practical Magic
E.T. The Extra-Terrestrial; Frankenstein and Me
Something Wicked This Way Comes; The Halloween Tree
Teen Alien; Spaced Invaders
Hocus Pocus; Double Double Toil and Trouble
The Nightmare Before Christmas; Sleepy Hollow (1999)
KISS Meets the Phantom of the Park; Trick or Treat
The Legend of Sleepy Hollow (1949); It's the Great Pumpkin, Charlie Brown
Revenge of the Living Zombies; The Midnight Hour
Jack-O; Idle Hands

And that's it for now. Hopefully the coming seasons will find us adding more worthwhile—and wonderfully wretched—movies to this list. If you've got a Halloween movie that I've omitted, please drop me a line at gbraunbeck@mindspring.com and maybe we'll get enough for a supplemental list to include in a future issue of *Cemetery Dance.*

Until then, have a great Halloween.

I'll look for you as we cower in the aisles....

Halloween Dreams

Yvonne Navarro

Costumes. Candy. The shadows cast along concrete city sidewalks by bright moonlight through tree limbs and dying leaves swaying in the wind. Crisp fall nights in a childhood long gone where the laughter of groups of children brought light to the darkness of a neighborhood street in a way that the street lamps never could.

I can't pick just one Halloween memory— in my mind, the recollections are all jumbled up, melding and leapfrogging over one another from year to year, timeless. And how could they be anything but, because I never really wanted to grow up, not at all. I remember, of course, myself—

—as a small girl, with my hand tucked securely in my older sister's as she performed her sisterly duty and took me from house to house, this in particular an eternal moment because my sister left us forever in 1981.

—as part of a group of ten-year-olds who Trick-Or-Treated in total safety in Chicago at well past eleven o'clock on a Halloween night.

—as a seventh grader invited into the home of a childless couple who served the neighborhood children hot apple cider and homemade popcorn balls every Halloween afternoon.

—as a teenager who pieced together a pumpkin outfit from bright orange felt and stuffed it with newspaper.

—at a party where someone else wore a makeshift shower rod and silver curtain and decreed himself a spaceship.

—as I wrapped my best friend's hair in tiny pieces of aluminum foil... her take on the Bride of Frankenstein.

—as I hefted an axe and wore a wedding gown bought at a resale shop then splashed with stage blood... and later raising the bottle of bubbly won as the prize in the neighborhood bar's costume contest.

—calling my elderly Uncle Garlon on October 31st every year to wish him happy birthday until the year he died of leukemia.

—made up as Countess Elizabeth Bathory in a four hundred dollar ball gown and makeup so successful that my own friends failed to recognize me in the photographs.

—putting intricately carved pumpkins and candles in every window of my first house.

—writing a heart-wrenching story called "Pumpkin Dreams," fictionalized truth, about a small boy in Chicago victimized by his mother and stepfather, my grim printed memorial to a deed that should have never happened.

—examining caricature rubber presidential masks that changed from year to year and paled in comparison only to the toothy, dripping-mouthed space aliens.

—gluing on long white fingernails with tiny black skeletons painted on them.

—always intending to wear a Lady Godiva costume... but never quite having the nerve.

—watching the children stomp again and again on the battery-powered welcome mat at my door on a Halloween afternoon just to hear it scream.

—wishing, as I became more firmly entrenched in my career, that a certain writers' convention would stop scheduling itself over the Halloween holiday so I can enjoy it along with everyone else.

Well, I guess I'm wrong. It *does* come down to just one Halloween memory—the magic of it, seen from the eyes of a child who never did, and never will, grow up.

Pay The Ghost

Tim Lebbon

Lee lost his daughter on Hallowe'en. He didn't mislay her, or leave her behind in a car park, or walk down a different aisle in a shopping centre...he lost her. One second she was there by his side, beautiful little Moll, sauntering along with a child's exaggerated gait. The next, gone. Vanished.

Taken from him forever.

Nobody saw anything. The police appealed for witnesses, distributed posters, asked a local schoolgirl to walk with Lee in a reconstruction, trying to jar memories from those in the area at the time. To no avail. They received over five hundred calls from members of the public, all of which led nowhere. For one terrible, soul destroying day, they questioned Lee. They even found one of Moll's shoes a mile from the scene, but it offered no significant clues. There was no blood staining it. This did not comfort Lee at all.

He knew how these things usually worked out. *We're treating this as a missing person inquiry*, the police said at every press conference, but in his heart Lee knew where Moll was now. Dead in a ditch. Raped. Murdered. Some fucker had taken his little girl and killed her, and they didn't even have the humanity to give an anonymous tip to tell the police where her body was buried. That would end one facet of his suffering at least.

The criminal psychologists said that this gave the kidnapper (they still used that term, never *murderer*) a sense of power.

Fucker.

Yes, Lee knew how this would end. And his wife Kate had known too. That's why she had left him eight months after the kidnapping. She...actually...blamed...him. *You should have been holding her hand, you shouldn't have let her go, there are people out there, sick people, and now one of them has...*

As if every father expected his daughter to be stolen away at every minute of the day. As if he really could have done something to prevent it.

He'd been left a hollow man.

It had happened on Hallowe'en. He remembered not because of the hype and the commercial vultures destroying the occasion, nor the reputation it held for supernatural events, and witches, demons and lost souls being abroad. He recalled it purely because of Moll's request earlier on that fateful day. *Daddy, can we pay the ghost*?

He'd never even bothered to ask her what she meant. And now, almost a year later, things were just as bad as ever.

Daddy, can we pay the ghost?

He remembered the words but not the voice that spoke them. He could conjure Moll's face to memory although sometimes, like now, he had to sit and stare at a photograph to remember every dimple, crease and curve of her expression. She was only six years old when she vanished. And he could not remember her voice.

Lee took another sip of tea. It was cold, but his hot drinks usually were by the time he came to finish them. He spent so long inside his own head that time just slipped away, and he hardly noticed the minutes, hours and days ticking off the months of his life. Someone screamed at him from the television and he glanced over the lip of the cup. Witches frolicked beneath a dead tree, leaping up to swing from skeletal branches, cackling and laughing when their noses fell off or their black wigs slipped to reveal the girlish hair beneath. A shadow crossed the screen and then there were more things in the picture, a collage of grotesque monsters, leaping and rolling and tickling and growling. The inevitable caption covered the fun, saying where and how the costumes could be bought or hired.

It was two days until Hallowe'en, a two-day countdown to the anniversary of Moll's disappearance. Lee couldn't help wondering where her body was resting, what state it was in. He started to cry but the tears acted as magnifiers, etching terrible images in his mind's eye even as he threw down the photo, tried to forget her face because he did not want to see it as he was seeing it now.

"Let me forget!" he pleaded. He did not believe in God—how could he?—but he had to talk to someone. He bent forward and picked up the photo. It was ragged from his own sweat and grease; he had held it close every day for a year. "Moll...."

There was a loud knocking at the front door. Lee looked up and his heart stuttered, but only for a second or two. It took a lot to scare him now. He stood slowly from his armchair and left the darkened sanctuary of his living room.

At the door, something remarkable happened. He felt space moving outwards from him, horizons expanding and an invisible weight lifting away from his shoulders and head. Something touched him: a thought, a feeling, a shred of optimism. It was such an alien sensation that he did not recognise it at first, but when he opened the front door it flooded through him, buoying his spirits and telling him that, somehow, everything was going to be all right.

Strange thoughts...because the thing on the doorstep shocked him rigid.

"Let me in," it whispered.

Lee could not speak.

"Let me in!" It shoved past him, glancing over its shoulder as if something worse might be following.

It was human, but other than that it bore little resemblance to anyone Lee had ever seen or imagined. It was dreadfully thin, an echo of Belsen still walking, with flesh so wasted that the skin was shiny and stretched where bones pressed out. And the skin itself was a freakish colour, an orangey hue clinging to it like juice-stains and shimmering in the changing light. It staggered instead of walked, jerking its head with a birdlike movement, scanning its surroundings.

"You have to care," it said. "You *have* to."

"Care?" Lee was still standing by the front door, unable to move, trying to understand what was happening. The flush of euphoria still echoed at the extremes of his senses, even confronted with this horror. It felt all wrong.

"You have to, you must," the thing muttered, scratching at its scalp, ragged nails scoring vivid red lines. "You used to care, you do now, you will again, you must."

"Care?" Lee said again, louder.

The thing stood in the corridor outside the kitchen. It turned and stared at Lee, and at last he knew who it was. Impossible, but he knew all the same. "Care about Moll!" it said.

"Kate...."

"I've been looking," the ruined thing that was Kate said, "I've never given up, all I've been doing is searching. Not living, just searching, four months without pause. Do you know what that can do to a heart, a soul? Can you see?"

"Oh Kate, what's happened....?" Lee moved at last. He walked to Kate with his arms held out, yet desperate not to touch her. She had blamed him and he had hated her for that, but whatever had happened to her since then—

—what could have happened to make her like this? Her hair had mostly gone, the flesh all but sloughed from her bones, leaving her little more than a leathery sack. The orange hue was sickness, starvation, waste.

And then, in the wan light leaking from the living room, he saw her eyes. And they were grotesque in the shrunken face, because they were full of hope.

"I don't know what he is," Kate said. She was talking of the man whom she claimed had Moll. Already, Lee was confused.

He busied himself making her a cup of tea, stealing covert glances at this thing that had been his wife. Never exactly beautiful, Kate had always been striking in her own way, her greenish eyes and bright auburn hair always turning heads. Now, she would turn heads for all the wrong reasons.

"He's not a man. Well...maybe he is, but he doesn't act like one. I don't think he eats." She grabbed Lee's arm as he set a cup on the table beside her. "What sort of a man doesn't eat, Lee?"

"When did *you* last eat?" he asked gingerly, trying to keep the look of disgust from his face. She stank. Sweat, urine, feces, the stench of the road, the aroma of dispossession. And her breath was full of death.

"I can't recall."

"Kate—"

"I don't blame you anymore, Lee," she said, her voice surprisingly strong.

"But you're sure you've found her? You know exactly where she is?"

Kate nodded.

"Have you been to the police?" Lee could not contain the excitement in his voice, and that sense of euphoria he'd felt when the first knock landed on the door rose once more. Maybe it was an omen, advance knowledge that his year of hell was over, that Moll would be back soon.

She looked up and her eyes burned. "Finding her did this to me. All the effort, the time...do you think I want to leave it up to them?"

"We can't do anything—"

"There are others, as well."

Lee frowned. "Kidnappers?"

"Children. He has a house full of them, must have been taking them for a long time. I couldn't see properly, I didn't get close enough...but there's something wrong with them...." Her shoulders shook and her head lowered, trailing wisps of hair into her tea. Lee thought she was crying, but no tears fell. It was doubtful her body could spare the moisture. "I think maybe he's a ghost."

Can we pay the ghost?

"Moll?" he said. "What's wrong with Moll?" The absurdity of this whole scene washed over him, and for a moment Lee wondered whether he was imagining it. He had not touched a drop of alcohol since Kate left him, yet ironically his own reality had been more prone to hallucination since then than ever before. And now here he was talking about his daughter—Moll, whom he'd thought of as dead for almost a year—in the present tense.

She may be alive, he thought. Kate might be right. She's mad, and ill, and she looks diseased...but she might also be telling the truth.

"I didn't get close enough to see properly," she said. "Lee, I'm so tired. I want all this over with."

"So do I. If you're right, it can be. It will be." He should call the police, he knew. Let them handle this, raid wherever it was Kate was talking about. "Will you take me there?" he asked instead.

His wife nodded. He could almost hear the muscles in her neck straining with the effort. "Soon."

"When Moll was taken...on that day...she said something to me before she went. I've never told you before. It just sounded so odd."

Kate's eyes snapped open, bright pearls in her orange sandy face.

"She said, 'Daddy, can we pay the ghost?'"

"What can that mean?" she croaked.

"I don't know. Maybe the man you saw was following us that day, pretending to be a beggar, and Moll thought the same as you...that he was something strange. And maybe she wanted to give him some money. You know what she was like, always concerned." He closed his eyes. "And perhaps that's how he took her. Appealed to her better nature...."

Kate shook her head. "I can't remember. Isn't that strange? I can't recall anything about Moll at all."

Lee set about making her some food, his mind in utter turmoil. He'd spent a year in the darkest places he could imagine, a landscape of despair and depression where only an occasional rise lifted him above the black clouds, however briefly. Now he had been snagged and boosted right into the sunlight. Given hope. If what Kate said were true and Moll was still alive, perhaps he had a future after all.

Kate ate minutely and slept, and there was nothing Lee could do to keep her awake. It was dark outside, midnight having rolled by while he cooked, and he could hear occasional shouts and infrequent explosions as kids fired premature fireworks into the frosty night.

He had lost his daughter when she was dressed as a witch—black sack cape, cardboard pointy hat, old broom—and the little pockets of her jeans were already bulging with sweets and loose change. *Trick or treat* had been the chant that night.

Daddy, can we pay the ghost? she had said.

Whether or not some ghost or madman had extracted a strange payment, Lee was sure of one thing. He would have payback. Soon.

Lee no longer worked. He'd quit his job soon after Moll's disappearance and never managed to hold down another. Some sympathy work had come his way for a while, but with his mind constantly distracted, his performance suffered. Soon even sympathy was not enough to buy him employment, and people forgot. That was one of the most terrible, unbearable factors of all...people forgot. Their eyes claimed otherwise—not many people could meet his stare nowadays—but inside, for them, it was old news. *You're the guy who lost his daughter. Tragic. Now, let's move on.*

For Lee, every morning he woke felt like the first day without Moll.

That day before Hallowe'en was different. He took the same route along the canal and into town as he used most days, usually just to clear the cobwebs and try to take his mind elsewhere. Sometimes he would stand next to the canal, open his mouth and exhale, ready to jump in and sink. He'd never been stupid enough. He'd never been brave. On this occasion, however, not everything existed to haunt him. He saw a mother walking with her child and hoped he would do that again with Moll. The dirty waters held no allure for him any more, in fact he found the idea of harming himself repulsive. How could he leave Moll without a daddy? Her mother was close to death, so what sort of a parent would he be if he killed himself? A bad sort. A waste.

And another way this walk differed from all the others...he had a destination. His walk held purpose, a purpose he had never believed existed any more. He was going to find his little girl. That morning Kate had given him directions. She had been wandering for months looking for Moll, and at last she had stumbled onto a hideaway, a place on the very edge of town where strange noises and sights convinced her that something was amiss. It was a bus journey, and then a twenty minute walk past a condemned housing estate on one side, and a huge deserted business park on the other. The place, Kate said, was somewhere it should never be.

She would not tell him what the noises and sights were, and she pointedly refused to return with him. She obviously knew that, with even the slightest possibility that Moll was there, Lee would go anyway.

Almost two hours after leaving home, Lee arrived at the housing estate. At least half of the houses were boarded up and several were burned out, looking ready to tumble into ash at the slightest provocation. Those not closed up looked equally dilapidated. Windows were cracked and smashed, front doors held the sledgehammer scars of forced entries, brickwork bore the strange hieroglyphics of graffiti, combinations of mis-spelled words and crude pictures forming a distinct language of degradation and apathy and hate. Some houses were vandalised more than others, their occupants staring through dirty windows with the glassy gazes of the newly-dead. Perhaps, Lee thought, because they knew that *they* would be soon.

He skirted the estate, heading around towards the deserted business park. If he kept just outside, he thought, maybe he could stay apart from the desperate people who lived here, even try to pretend he was not like them at all. A group of men stood smoking against a wall, following him with blank, bland eyes. A woman pushed a pram up and down kerbs, never slowing, never seeming to notice how much its frame was bouncing and shaking. Her expression remained the same even when her child started to scream. Lee wanted to go to her, point out what she was doing, but that would mean crossing the line and entering the estate.

They could watch him from in there, gazes loaded with whatever accusations he chose to read into them, but he was still out here. Just passing by.

A group of kids—some no more than two or three years old—ran from an alleyway, across a patch of oil-spotted grass and back between two houses. Their cries echoed back at Lee, screams and shouts and something in between. Why couldn't you take them? he thought, hating the way his mind was working. Why take Moll, why not them?

Moll had always come to him when she was hurt or confused and he had let her down. *I never gave up hope*, Kate had told him that morning, yet he had never even *had* any hope. Dead in a ditch, he had thought. How he despised himself for that. How he despised himself for so much.

On his right, a deserted petrol station. The pumps were long since gone, the shop a shattered remnant of what it had once been. Even the graffiti had been smashed down.

To the left of the petrol station, a path leads across to the business park, Kate had said.

Lee found the path, leading behind a retaining wall and across an area of heavy undergrowth. As he started along the trail, he wondered what Kate had seen and heard.

Keep going until you reach the burned out car on your left.

And there it was, an old Escort resting on grotesquely melted and reset tyres, its exposed metal skeleton half rusted away.

*Pass the car, aim for the big hanger-like building...*it was a furniture warehouse, now it only houses bats and cats and drop-outs.

Lee eased himself past the car's sharp edges, brushing aside the heavy arms of spiked bushes as he looked for the warehouse. He'd gone a hundred paces before he saw a hint of white to his right. He moved that way for a while and mounted a small rise from where he could see the old warehouse, white paint stripped and covered with a decade of bird shit.

Look to your left, towards the electricity pylon. You'll see the house. Quite old and grand, as if it was there way before the estate and the business park. I expect it was. Way before.

Lee could see no house.

Someone screamed, high pitched and angry. It could have been a fox, he thought, as a shiver played with his spine. Just a fox crying out, but it was daylight and it sounded like a kid, so much like a little girl crying bitterly for the father who had deserted her, never really believing that he would come to rescue her after so long. Something dashed in front of him, rustling one bush and disappearing behind another.

He froze, heart thumping. He could not bear the thought of coming to grief now, not so near to seeing Moll once more.

Definitely no house. He stood on tiptoes and scanned across towards the pylon, sweeping his gaze left as far as the roofs of the housing estate, and right again all the way to the hulking form of the warehouse. No roof above the bushes, no walls standing proud, nothing to indicate that there had ever been an old house here at all. He went over Kate's directions in his mind, closed his eyes for just a second before the scream erupted again.

It could be Moll. Now, so near, it could be Moll.

Lee ran into the bushes, aiming roughly towards the pylon. In places it looked as though a path snaked between the small trees, but then it would vanish and the only signs of humanity were heaps of refuse here and there, old tyres, stacks of newspapers soaked into congealed masses. The scream came again from his right, and he changed direction to find it. Undergrowth whipped at his body and face. He felt a sudden coolness on his cheek and realised he had been cut, the blood bathing his skin, his flesh open to the day. He tasted the blood as he ran, and the scream came from behind him.

He spun around and tried to orient himself. The pylon was behind him now, and try as he might he could not see the warehouse. It should be to his left, but even though he strained and hauled on the branches of a small tree, he could not lift himself high enough to see it. Either he had passed the house or he had not yet gone far enough to find it. He started towards the pylon once more.

Something cracked to his left, a heavy foot snapping a dead twig. Then the same sound came from his right, and again behind him, and he ran blindly through the bushes and shrubs, eyes half closed against the clutching branches, face stinging as they struck at him again, opening new cuts. Blood dripped from his chin and he wondered if it was the land bleeding him, drawing blood because it needed a strange sustenance of its own—

The first he knew of the ditch was when he stumbled into it. He closed his eyes and tried to tuck in his limbs, but he struck the stump of a dead tree and went spinning and flailing. The breath was knocked from him as he hit bottom, landing in something soft yet sharp, like butter laced with glass.

He opened his eyes and instantly regretted it. In those first few seconds he wished so much that could not be un-wished later, no matter how hard he tried: he wished that Kate had never come to him; that she had not mentioned Moll; that they had found his daughter's body a year ago instead of leaving him in limbo, only to be plucked up and given hope and then faced with this...this....

Carnage. It was a word he had heard used many times but he never truly understood its meaning. And now here it was. A human carnage, a waste-ground of ruined parts. Some bits he could identify, even though most of the skin had been burnt away and the flesh melted into horrifically sculpted shapes. Here and there a smear of fat held the impressions of the heavy raindrops that had cooled this burning pit. A skull sat atop a pile of bones, hair gone, eyeballs shrivelled beans in their sockets. Lee touched it and the bone crumbled under the featherweight of his fingertips. Other bones powdered as he scrambled to his feet, giving up a fine dust, a rich stink and a gritty feel at the back of his throat.

All of the bones were small.

He tried to scream but he had lost his voice.

He was covered. He had slithered into the trench on a sheen of burned bodies, their fats and juices lubricating his way. Beneath his feet the ground squelched. The air was thick with the stink of the pit. A greasy smoke still hung around the pale roots of the plants lining its edges, and sick warmth radiated from the bare earth walls.

Lee tried to scream again but the indrawn breath scraped at his throat. He gagged, leaned over and puked, closing his eyes so that he did not see what his vomit was mixing with around his feet.

Moll!

Lee forced himself to look around, the guilt of the past year providing the stimulus. Was she here? Was his daughter here, killed and burned, or perhaps burned alive? There was no way he could tell, nothing to distinguish one body from another, let alone identify them.

Small bones.

He found his voice at last and screamed, and it seemed to Lee—as he scrabbled at the slick ditch walls, staggered through the undergrowth, heading in any direction away from the pit—that his scream was echoed all around by others. They could have been his own terrified shouts bouncing back at him, but they sounded out of time, higher pitched, like a mocking impersonation of children by someone who had never had them.

Eventually he found his way back to the road, pushing his way through a hedge not far from the old petrol station. He ran past the estate, meeting the stares of its inhabitants. They could not frighten him any more. *Look after your children*, he wanted to scream at them, *keep them inside, there's a monster and I don't know its name*! But he could not catch his breath, and he was sure that they would ignore him anyway.

Back into town, a bus trip where he was the centre of disgusted attention—his clothes stank, he had rusty brown stains on his face, the blood both his own and that of others—and then he arrived home.

It was late afternoon. By now Lee's senses had calmed down to merely panicked, and he could smell and feel what he had found. He so wished that Kate had told him about the pit.

"Moll!" she screeched as he opened the front door. She came at him, a haggard shadow skimming along the hall wall.

He caught her by the shoulders. "No Moll," he said, "and no house."

Her manic eyes widened even more, dwarfing her shrunken face. She touched his cheeks and looked at his clothes, sniffed. "But you found the burning pit? The way back to the other place? They've used it already, they must have tested it, oh God, not Moll—"

"I have to shower," he said very precisely. "We have to tell the police." He moved her gently to one side and closed the front door, but on the second stair he sank to his knees and began to weep. Tears came, real tears, for the first time in months. He had previously thought he had cried himself dry, and that a desert bitterness was all that could replace his grief.

"Did you see or hear anything else?" Kate asked.

"Screams."

"Moll, do you think?"

Lee shrugged. The tears stung the cuts on his cheeks and forehead and chin. "I don't know. I can't remember the sound of her voice."

Lee sat with a cup of cold tea in front of him. Kate was trying to prepare food, but her ragged breathing and constant groans told him that she would be at the point of collapse very soon. He did not care. He stared at the fresh scratches on his hands and listened to his wife slowly dying nearby, but all he could see was the pit coated with charred and melted remains. The bones...they had been so small....

"She's there!" Kate said. "I tell you, she's there in the house. He hasn't burned her yet, I know it."

"There is no house—"

"I'll take you, we'll go there and see. Tomorrow. We'll go tomorrow."

"Tomorrow...." Lee trailed off. Tomorrow was Hallowe'en, a year to the day since Moll had been lost.

"Maybe only I can find it." She spoke slowly now, easing herself into the chair next to Lee and touching his arm with stick fingers.

Lee shook his head. "Have to call the police. So many bodies...."

"You haven't yet."

He could say nothing. She was right. He should have called them but he could not. Not while there was the remotest chance that Kate was right, that only she could find the house. Maybe he had not been looking hard enough, maybe he had not believed that Moll could still be here in this world with them, not suffering somewhere in the next. Perhaps all it took was faith.

"Tomorrow...." Lee said, resting his head on his arms. He closed his eyes and Moll popped into his mind instantaneously, her wild laugh when he was tickling her, the frown she had copied from him. Then he imagined her shouting and tried to hear her voice, but it was still lost to him. Tears squeezed from his closed eyes. He felt Kate wiping them from his cheek.

Daddy, can we pay the ghost?

Lee snapped awake but the voice had gone already, fled with the dregs of his dreams. His neck and back ached, his arms had gone to sleep and flopped onto his lap like the limbs of a corpse. It was morning. "Kate!"

He heard her approach along the corridor...and when she arrived in the kitchen he could not help but let out a gasp. His wife looked even worse than she had yesterday, if that were possible. Her skin, previously a subtle orange from malnutrition and exposure to the elements, was now a rusty gold. It clung to her protruding bones like Clingfilm. The remainder of her hair had fallen out. She had lost several more teeth during the night.

"I haven't slept," she said, "in six weeks."

So much had changed. So much had been distorted and knocked

out of joint over the past year. But for a few brief seconds in Lee's memory it was just him and Kate again, young lovers, dreamers, selfish in their love but knowing they had all to give when the time came. And the time had come and gone, been stolen away. Events ruled, not emotions.

"Oh Kate," he said, "I loved you so much."

"We had better go and find Moll." Each word was an effort.

"I'll carry you," he said.

Kate shook her head. "People will stop us. I know what I look like. Wait until later, and they'll think...." She sobbed dryly, rubbing her big eyes with one gnarled hand. "They'll think I'm dressed for Hallowe'en."

"I can't wait—"

"We have to."

Lee looked desperately at the clock, saw that it was late morning already and resigned himself to a long few hours.

Outside, it had started to rain.

They did not talk much that afternoon. Lee was preparing in his own way, though he found it difficult to concentrate on anything other than Moll. Her smile, her walk, her laughing mouth, but not her voice. He had lost that and no amount of hope could recover it. Only the real thing...the real voice...would make it live for him again.

Darkness fell. By five o'clock the witches, ghosts and demons of the neighbourhood were abroad, knocking on doors and laughing and running and singing and screaming.

Lee led Kate out along the street, forcing a smile for passers-by as they stared at her, their eyes widening in admiration at the effort she had put into the haggard-old-witch routine. The world around him felt as alien as ever, as far removed as it had been on the first day that Moll went missing. The people he saw meant no more to him than pictures in a book.

They reached the estate and walked around to the old petrol station. They were both soaked to the skin and the rain never let up for one instant. Kate wheezed and moaned and coughed, and every now and then they had to stop for her to sit down, her knees popping and bones grinding each other where joints were worn away. But she never once complained. She had been looking for a long time—*Do you know what that can do to a heart, a soul? Can you see?*—and now that the end was in sight she was drawing on unknown veins of energy and determination.

The estate presented an eerie scene. Lights flickered in many of the houses, even those boarded up or gutted by fire, but the streets were virtually deserted. An occasional shadow flitted from one alley to the next, but there were no children trick or treating, no gangs of kids throwing eggs at windows or splashing cars with flour and water, no drunken teenagers using this particular night as an excuse to cause even more chaos and ruin and pain to those around them. It was almost totally silent. Lee tried to convince himself that the shimmering lights in most of the houses were from television screens, but he was sure that they were candles.

"Here," Kate said as they walked alongside the petrol station. It was dark behind the retaining wall, but she moved unerringly, hardly needing light to find her way. Lee wondered just how many times she had come this way before she realised that she would need his help to go the final step.

She's mad, he thought suddenly, driven insane by our loss, she's leading me on a wild goose chase....

But there was the pit. And Moll's words in the voice he could not hear: *Daddy, can we pay the ghost?*

"Here," Kate said again, turning, twisting left and right between trees and bushes, past the gutted car. "Here....and around here...." He followed because she knew where she was going, and he was lost already. If she left him now—or collapsed and died—it would take him hours to get out of here.

"Can you see him?" Kate asked quietly.

"Who?" It was very dark; he could make out only the vague outlines of trees and bushes around them.

"Him. The one from the house. He's with us."

Lee shuddered, reached out and rested a hand on Kate's shoulder, an involuntary need for contact. Then he looked around. "I can't see," he whispered. He tried to believe it was the rain making him cold.

"To the left."

She spoke without turning her head, but Lee had to look. There were bush-shadows hulking against the sky, something taller that must have been a tree, pattering with falling raindrops...nothing else.

"Nothing!" he hissed.

"What are you?" Kate suddenly shouted.

Lee jumped. Something small scurried through the bushes with a startled squeal.

"A revenant," a voice said from the night. "A guide, but not for you." It moved as it spoke, as if its owner were circling them, but that was not possible. They were surrounded by trees and bushes, none of which were being disturbed other than by the rains. In fact the voice was so quiet that Lee thought he may well have imagined it, a chance combination of raindrops and expectation and rustling leaves forming sense from usual chaos.

"One that you paid...handsomely."

"Oh my God!" Lee hissed.

"Just keep going," Kate said, "he's spoken to me before."

"What did he say?"

He felt her shoulder stiffen beneath his hand, then she moved on and he was forced to follow. "Kate?"

"All sorts of things," she responded, not answering him at all.

"Oh Daddy," it whined in imitation of a little girl's voice, "can we pay the ghost, Daddy?"

"What have you done—"

"Ignore it!" Kate said sharply. "It's trying to bait you, make you lose yourself. I know the way, but however hard you hold onto me you'll never get there if you let it distract you."

"How do you know all this?"

She whispered, so quietly that Lee may have misheard her in the rain. "Been trying to find this place for a long time."

They continued on through the dark, and now Lee had a real sense that there was something there with them, walking in the same direction but unconcerned at trees or branches, or unseen holes ready to snap their ankles. And sometimes the voice came from the dark, so quiet and blended with the rain that it seemed little more than memory.

"Such a sweet girl," it whispered, "tasty and whole." A flurry of something leaving a tree to their left. "And her voice, so grown-up when she screams for those who deserted her." The haunting bark of a fox in the distance, or perhaps not a fox at all. "Ahhh yes...her poor voice."

Lee did his best to ignore what was said. He wondered if Kate could hear the same words, or whether her torments were personal to her. He kept one hand on her shoulder and the other in his jacket pocket, curved around the haft of the kitchen knife, the only weapon he had thought to bring.

Kate stopped suddenly. The house seemed to have appeared from nowhere. At the same instant as Lee saw it silhouetted against the clouds, the voice vanished back into the hiss of rain.

"This wasn't here yesterday."

"It's always been here."

"What about the pit? Where's the pit?"

"You really want to see that place again? I bypassed it. Brought us here, not there."

Lee let go of Kate and went to a window, trying in vain to see inside. "No lights on. Deserted."

"Don't you ever sit in the dark?" she rasped. Then her shadow slid to the ground as if the earth itself were consuming her, and a terrible rattle came from her throat.

Lee ran to his wife and picked her up, shocked at how light she was. He held her slumped across both arms. In the darkness her features were hidden from him. There was a glint in her half-open eyes...but she could easily have been dead.

He heard a noise through the downpour, a whisper as if water gently flowing between rocks. He held his breath and stood very still, glancing over his shoulder at the house as he did so. Its dark windows looked back. A hanging gutter gave it an expression of bored irony. He noticed for the first time that it had only windows, no doors, as if once inside there was no escape.

The noise increased in volume. It came from back in the bushes, perhaps the way they had just come, perhaps not. Lee was too disorientated to decide for sure.

"Kate!" he whispered, shaking his wife very gently. She groaned but did not wake.

He could stay here until morning, wet and tired and frightened, while Moll perhaps sat inside this strange house. He could try to find his way back to the road. Or he could investigate the noise...the noise that was louder than ever and which, he was certain, was composed of individual voices mumbling and whispering to each other, or to themselves.

He stared at the house. No, it was deserted. Whatever Kate had said about sitting in the dark, this house was empty. He could feel the building itself watching him, but no one from inside. And besides: no doors. That was freakish. He did not want to stay here on his own.

He slung Kate over his left shoulder and set off through the rain. His right hand closed around the knife handle and slipped it from his jacket. As he walked the rain lessened and the moon peered from between storm clouds. It was as he stared at the ground to avoid holes or dips that he became aware that he was following a large trail of footprints. Most of them were very small.

Through the bushes, closing in on the sound, Kate murmuring and twitching on his shoulder, the knife singing as the occasional raindrops hit it...Lee realised at last where he was going.

From the shelter of a clump of trees he saw the people, dozens of them, standing and staring down into the pit. They were the inhabitants of the estate, some shifting from foot to foot, others simply standing and staring. They all seemed to be on their own. He followed their gaze and could not help uttering a terrified gasp.

The pit was full of children.

Some were sitting, others standing. There must have been twenty toddlers and teens in there, crying and hugging, sometimes staring blankly at the earth wall or the sky far above them.

"Kate!" Lee said, shaking his wife, letting her slip unceremoniously to the ground. He held the knife before him, shaking now, trying to realise the consequence of all this, struggling to piece together what was happening. His wife stirred in the mud.

"Come to pay the ghost?" a voice said in his ear. He spun around but there was no one there, only shadows. When he looked back towards the pit everything had changed. They were all looking at him. Even the children.

Even Moll.

"Oh my God!" he gasped, stumbling from the cover of bushes and into the faint moonlight. Nobody moved to stop him, and he ran to the edge of the pit, staring down at his daughter where she stood with her back against the earth wall. She looked up at him but did not smile. She did not seem to recognise him.

"You bastards!" he shouted, brandishing the knife, sweeping it in slow clumsy arcs to keep the people at bay. They had closed around him while he was looking at Moll. To get out now...to reach Kate and freedom...he would have to fight his way through them. "What have you done to her? What are you doing?" He was screaming and crying at the same time, strengthened by rage and weakened by a terrible sense of hopelessness, born of the realisation that she had been here all along. He had given her up on the day she disappeared, yet a year later, here she was.

He held out his hand to Moll. "Come on, darling. Come on. Daddy's here, I've come to take you home." He kept glancing back, but none of the silent people seemed ready to attack him. They simply stood and watched, eyes wide, shifting slightly as if impatient for something to happen.

The air stank of petrol. There were hay bales and dead ferns in the pit with the children. One of the kids seemed to have no legs, another shivered on the ground, bald and emaciated...and Lee was certain that in the shadows, even more dreadful mutilations hid themselves away.

"Leave her," a voice said.

Lee looked around but none of the people seemed to have spoken. He waved the knife at them.

"Leave her alone," the voice said again, "you've lost her."

"That's my daughter in there!" he screamed, and a shape manifested itself before him. It came from the darkness and formed a shadow, and when its eyes and mouth opened they reflected no moonlight.

"Not for a long while now," it said.

Children whimpered behind and below him. Somewhere a flame popped into being, and an excited ripple passed through those gathered there. The final drops of rain hissed as they hit the naked flame.

Lee's anger burst out. He slashed at the figure, lunging and stabbing and slicing with the kitchen knife. Even as he did so a sense of unreality grabbed him, the realisation that he was actually trying to kill someone...and this was aggravated when the knife found nothing but air.

The shape shifted, came towards Lee and actually seemed to touch him, a coolness far more deep-felt than mere temperature, a black, engulfing cold that touched his lungs and heart and spine with its gossamer fingers. "You can leave....now."

"Me," Kate said from behind the assembled people. "Me, use me. Please." The watchers stepped aside to let her pass. She slithered through the mud, pushing with her feet and pulling with her hands, unable to stand but finding motion like the reptile cast out from the garden.

"Kate, Moll's here, Moll's in the pit!"

"Put me in," she said, "please, me instead."

"You're not a child," the voice breathed. "A child's flesh burns better."

"I found you," Kate shouted, her strength surprising Lee. "That must count for something."

"Determination and love," the shadow whispered. "And...well, you've been due to us for some time now."

"Please," Lee pleaded, tears blurring his image of the moonlit night and the shadow that hovered there before him. "My daughter...please."

"Your wife...."

"Yes, yes!" Kate gasped, squirming forward once more, touching Lee once on the ankle before tumbling into the pit. She cried out as she struck the bottom, the tears continuing as Moll knelt gingerly beside her.

"Honey," Kate said. But her daughter stood and turned away.

The shadow laughed, a horrid sound. "Take your child that has forgotten you."

"You have to let these kids go...." The futility of what he was asking for struck Lee then. He was talking to a ghost. He was outnumbered. He should have gone to the police, although he was certain they would have never found this place. There was something odd about it, something removed from the norm...the trees and bushes seemed unconcerned that there was a ghost in their midst, one with human consorts.

"There will be a fire," the shadow said. "If you would avoid the flames, take her now."

One of the silent watchers kicked over a barrel of petrol and let it run into the trench. The children stirred, Kate began to pray.

"Moll," Lee said, holding out his hand, never once taking his eyes from the shadow shifting before him. Kate must have boosted her from the trench, using whatever final reserves of energy she could find to save her daughter and doom herself. Moll's hand closed around his fingers, he pulled, and his lost daughter was with him once more.

"Let them go," he said pathetically, knowing that there was nothing he could do.

"It's our turn to go home to the other world," one of the people said.

And that was when Lee realised that their eyes reflected nothing; no moonlight, no glimmer from the naked flame. Nothing.

"Run, Lee! Run, Moll! Before it changes its mind!"

Lee hoisted Moll up and she clung to his shoulders, her legs resting on his hips. She did not say anything. He so wanted to hear her voice, but he wanted to live as well. He wanted all of them to live.

He stared at the people—the things—from the estate and saw that there was no help there. They were completely in thrall to the shadow.

"Kate—"

"I'm dead anyway, Lee," she sobbed from the pit. "You've seen me. Take Moll. Save one, it's better than none at all."

So Lee ran along the edge of the trench, constantly expecting to be tripped by an unseen foot or pushed by one of the motionless watchers. Soon he was in the bushes, Moll clinging to him and burying her face in his neck. He could not imagine what she had witnessed or been through over the past year, but she obviously did not want to see any more. He felt her body heat pressing through his wet clothes, her breath on his skin, her hair tickling his face, and he could not believe that he had ever given up hope.

The night sky lit up behind them. There were screams, searing screams, but they did not last for very long. He could not help turning around to look, to see...people leaping across the pit, some falling into the flames, screeching with delight as they found their way home, wherever home was to them. And a shadow before the flames, guiding the dispossessed into the other-worldly fire.

Lee fled, running into bushes and trees, stumbling, falling, expecting to feel hands on his shoulders or around his ankles at any minute. Moll grunted and whined when he fell, but said nothing. A shadow loomed, moonlight reflecting from sharp teeth...but it was only the burned out car.

As Lee emerged onto the road with his stolen daughter clinging to him, the fire reflecting from the clouds had dimmed to almost nothing.

Lee lost his wife on Hallowe'en. He knew...he *prayed*...that she was never coming back.

He also lost any pride, dignity or humanity he should have regained by rescuing his daughter, and any feeling that there was more to it than this. There was not. There was life and death and everything bad in between...like leaving children burning in a ditch to save himself.

Lee found Moll's mutilation: her tongue had been sliced out just after she had been taken, so he could never remember his daughter's voice. She did not attempt to communicate with him by any other means. He guessed that during her year trapped in that out-of-the-way house, some of those doomed children he had left behind had become her friends.

Halloween 25

Kim Newman

Thursday, October the 31st, 1974

I am fifteen, live in a village in Somerset with my parents and sister, go to school in a nearby town (Bridgwater) and have started to keep a fragmentary diary. I am in the middle of writing a novel. On this day, which falls in the middle of a half-term holiday, I begin 'Chapter 11' in rough. The novel was later lost, mercifully to judge by the prose in the diary. I have also begun to keep lists of books read (I was in a Lovecraft phase) and films seen (mostly on television).

Friday, October the 31st, 1975

I am at Bridgwater College, beginning to study for A levels. The sociology class is me and nine girls. 'History was less soporific than yesterday, did okay in sociology test, dinner was ordinary.' After lessons, I hang about with Brian Smedley and Eugene Byrne, whom I've known since we all started at secondary school in 1970. We're all going in our own separate directions, but keep coming back together for 'projects.'

Sunday, October the 31st, 1976

'Chopped wood.' I also write an essay for my course, and am so impressed that a girl (Hazel Thompson) telephoned me that I mention it in my diary. She wants to know about sociology homework but we also have a conversation about the Iliad (?!). I am in the middle of reading *The Fifth Mayflower Book of Black Magic Stories*, edited by Michel Parry. On television, I watch *10 Rillington Place*.

Monday, October the 31st, 1977

I am living on campus at the University of Sussex, and trying to see every film shown for everyone else's course. Today, I sleep late and see a couple of movies—*Native Son* for a black studies course, and *Some Like It Hot*, a student film society screening held in a bar called the Crypt (next year, I'll take over this strand of programming from Tom Tunney, whom I still know). I go to the Crypt with Jo Bartlett, who lives down the corridor in the student accommodation. Afterwards, we go to someone's birthday party downstairs in the hall. It says something about the profile of Halloween in the UK that it isn't a holiday-themed bash.

Tuesday, October the 31st, 1978

I am living in a bed-sit in Brighton, and commuting to the campus. Today, I work at home on an essay on John Ford's *My Darling Clementine* for an American Cinema course. I also read Arthur Conan Doyle's *The Land of the Mist*, least-known of the Professor Challenger stories, and watch *Hammersmith is Out* on television.

Wednesday, October the 31st, 1979

I hang around campus, chatting to various people—Susan Rodway and David Cross, both of whose names I borrowed in my novel, *Jago*—in the common room of the School of English and American Studies, or sitting in the library reading Harry Harrison in preference to Kierkegaard (I'm doing a course called Modern European Mind). The Student Union Film Society's Halloween presentation is *Dougal and the Blue Cat.*

Friday, October the 31st, 1980

I'm back in Somerset, but am about to move to a bed-sit in East Molesey, near London. I have a degree but no prospects of employment. I have to go into Bridgwater to visit the bank and the post office, 'to arrange finances for my leaving', and buy a coach ticket. I am reading *100 Great Science Fiction Short Short Stories*, edited by Isaac Asimov, Martin Harry Greenberg and Joseph D. Olander.

Saturday, October the 31st, 1981

Though I'm still living in East Molesey, today I am back in Bridgwater, getting a band (Club Whoopee) together with Brian Smedley. I have been writing plays which are being produced at the Bridgwater Arts Centre under our Sheep Worrying Enterprises label. Today, we have an early read-through of *Deep South*, a Southern gothic melodrama that would eventually be staged during the worst snows of several decades.

Sunday, October the 31st, 1982

'A quiet Halloween at home', it says here. By now, I am selling film reviews to the *Monthly Film Bulletin* and submitting fiction to *Interzone* magazine (who are encouraging me). The band is having a hard time, since Brian and I have brought in our old friend Rod Jones, who is just breaking up with Lynne, the best singer in the group. One of them has to go, and as it happens we don't last long anyway with or without either of them. I watch *From Russia With Love* on the black and white portable television in my bed-sit.

Monday, October the 31st, 1983

I am no longer a dole claimant, having a couple of regular film freelance gigs and a stipend to grind out 'films of' books for a strange publisher that went bankrupt before publishing anything but my first book, *Nightmare Movies*. I take the train from East Molesey to Central London and spend the day in cinemas: seeing *Kramer vs Kramer* (I am doing a book on Dustin Hoffman) in a West End place happy to show three-year-old films, then *Exposed* and *The House on Sorority Row* (re-titled *House of Evil* in Britain) at a preview theatre in Wardour Street. Halloween is starting to make an impression in the UK: I take Susannah Hickling, who was in the plays (and now edits *Reader's Digest*), out for an Italian meal after the movie, and the waitress is dressed as a witch.

October Dreams

Wednesday, October the 31st, 1984

I am living with an old hippie and his punk son, and whatever strays they take on from time to time, in a flat in Muswell Hill, and work a notional day a week for *City Limits*, then a London listings magazine. Today, I do my bits of work for them—capsule reviews, a column about late-night films—and have lunch with Faith Brooker, the editor at NEL who bought *Ghastly Beyond Belief* from Neil Gaiman and me. In the evening, a crowd of us—Steve Jones, Jo Fletcher, Neil, Julian Petley—get together in the squat-like flat to watch a very blurry video of Michael Mann's *The Keep*, which didn't get a proper UK release. We all hated it (Julian fell asleep). We also sit through Al Adamson's *The Female Bunch*, which happens to be on the tape.

Thursday, October the 31st, 1985

I'm still in Muswell Hill. Today, I'm in the middle of writing 'Thirty Years in Another Town', a multi-part article on Italian exploitation movies for the *Monthly Film Bulletin*. I have time to read a couple of novels: John Halkin's *Slime*, Jim Thompson's *Pop. 1250*.

Friday, October the 31st, 1986

One of my chores at *City Limits* was to go to see films no one dared press-show, usually in their first week at the Cannons Panton Street or Swiss Centre (off Leicester Square); today, it is *The Future is Woman*. In the evening, by a coincidence unnoted until I sat down to write this, I see *The Keep* again, on 16mm at the notoriously uncomfortable Gothique Film Society in Holborn (support feature: Bela Lugosi in *Murder By Television*). I've warmed up to Mann's film over the years.

Saturday, October the 31st, 1987

I live in Crouch End now, sharing a flat with another journalist, just a street over from where Peter Straub and Clive Barker used to live. For the first time in my life, I go to a Halloween party, thrown by Lisa Tuttle at her flat in Harrow. A bunch of people—Rob Holdstock, Garry Kilworth, Chris Evans, Faith Brooker, Meg Davis, Dave Garnett, Martin Rowson—read aloud ghost stories written for the occasion. This is a tradition that has been going for a while, though it is discontinued when Lisa moves to Scotland. Garry sells his story to Rob for an anthology, mine (*'Mrs Vail'*) later turns up in *The Dedalus Book of Femmes Fatales* and one of my collections. I eat a lot of Lisa's Texas chili, and Meg has to look after me.

Monday, October the 31st, 1988

The day after the London World Fantasy Convention. In the evening, Gollancz throws a party for Rob Holdstock and Terry Pratchett in a London club accessible only through the world's thinnest passageway. After a weekend of relative sobriety (last night, I had a launch party for *Horror: 100 Best Books*), I get drunk and, while eating after the party with Dave Tamlyn (another schoolfriend, now in the book trade), stagger to the basement toilet of Pizza Hut to be sick.

Tuesday, October the 31st, 1989

Another of Lisa's ghost story parties. Colin Greenland and John Brosnan, who have both moved into the old house where Lisa's flat is, add stories. This time, I didn't write something especially but read *'The*

Man Who Collected Barker'. People laugh. I am careful about the chili.

Wednesday, October the 31st, 1990

I'm doing a regular early morning film review slot on Channel 4 television, and have a lunch meeting with the producer I'd later fall out with and one of the many researchers I would work with. I have a tea date at Fortnum & Mason's with two girls I have met working in television—a mad blonde woman called Janet and my former make-up artist Cindy. I take Cindy to a Halloween signing at Forbidden Planet for a couple of Steve Jones anthologies, one of which I'm in. Conrad Hill, an old-time *Pan Book of Horror Stories* contributor who was a friend of my parents in the 1970s, is amazed at me turning up seventeen years later and in the business. I have published my first novel (*The Night Mayor*) and am working on more. My Halloween reading: Cedric Belfrage's *The American Inquistion 1945-1960.*

Thursday, October the 31st, 1991

I am hauled out of bed at 4.00 to be taken by minicab to the ITN studios, where I do the TV show. After a couple of years, it's coming to the end of the run. Susan, my current researcher, is a saint, but the series editor is evil incarnate. Within a week, he will discover that he is called 'Imelda Marcos' behind his back, and I won't be finishing the series. Producers and directors snipe at each other, and everyone is thinking of their next job. In the evening, it's a holiday-themed press show of *Freddy's Dead: The Final Nightmare*.

Saturday, October the 31st, 1992

I do a signing—with Graham Joyce and Freda Warrington—to promote my fourth novel, *Anno Dracula*. This means sitting around the Conservatory, a London wine bar near Forbidden Planet, drinking and signing the odd hardback book as people either try to cadge free copies or promise to read it when it comes out in paperback. Through the night, *The Vault of Horror*, a TV documentary I worked on is transmitted on BBC-2; this introduces the UK's first horror host, originally incarnated as Dr Walpurgis, for whom I will write three seasons of material.

Sunday, October the 31st, 1993

Hung over after a champagne tea yesterday to launch *Anno Dracula* in paperback. My diary entry for the Saturday is much more interesting, but those are the breaks.

Monday, October the 31st, 1994

I am in New Orleans, just after the World Fantasy Convention. I hang around with Steve Jones and Jo Fletcher, buying things, and have a meal with the guy who sang 'If You Want to Be a Bird' in *Easy Rider* and now makes allegations it would be unwise to publish about the New Orleans DA Kevin Costner played in JFK.

Tuesday, October the 31st, 1995

I own my own flat, in a converted police station in Islington. Today,

I am in Norwich, which is less interesting than New Orleans, lecturing about Stephen King to Pam Cook's cinema course. On the train there and back, I read Norman Longmate's *If Britain Had Fallen* and Jay Russell's *Celestial Dogs*.

Thursday, October the 31st, 1996

I juggle work on the novel *Life's Lottery*, a (still-unmade) film script from *Anno Dracula* and the final collaborative story (with Eugene Byrne) of the series that would come out as *Back in the USSA*. I have a Chinese meal with Mike Hodges, director of *Get Carter* amd *Flash Gordon*, a friend rather than a movie person, whom I met at a film festival in Portugal and always quotes back the vicious review line ('die rather than see this film') I gave his *Morons From Outer Space*.

Friday, October the 31st, 1997

Another London World Fantasy Convention. I have to get up early for a slow-starting panel. The evening's party is held by HarperCollins, and involves a complicated river trip that winds up with a drunken crowd abandoned at a dock and Dave Langford climbing over railings to escape. Graham Joyce tries hard to impress Muriel Gray, but his Leicester lines don't play in the Big City.

Saturday, October the 31st, 1998

I finish a rough draft of the story that will be published as *'Angel Down, Sussex'*. I promise in my diary to pay more attention to characterisation in the polish.

Sunday, October the 31st, 1999

A fucking car alarm goes off in the street in the middle of the night, forcing me to get up and watch a movie (*The Wanderers* on DVD). If one of the things has been ringing for over a minute, it should be legal to steal (or burn) the car.

Buckets

F. Paul Wilson

Halloween—1985

"My, aren't you an early bird!"

Dr. Edward Cantrell looked down at the doe-eyed child in the five-and-dime Princess Leia costume on his front doorstep and tried to guess her age. A beautiful child of about seven or eight, with flaxen hair and scrawny little shoulders drawn up as if she were afraid of him, as if he might bite her. It occurred to him that today was Wednesday and it was not yet noon. Why wasn't she in school? Never mind. It was Halloween and it was none of his business why she was getting a jump on the rest of the kids in the trick-or-treat routine.

"Are you looking for a treat?" he asked her.

She nodded slowly, shyly.

"Okay! You got it!" He went to the bowl behind him on the hall table and picked out a big Snickers. Then he added a dime to the package. He wanted it to become a Halloween tradition over the years that

Dr. Cantrell's place was where you got dimes when you trick-or-treated. He thrust his hand through the open space where the screen used to be. He liked to remove the storm door screen on Halloween; it saved him the inconvenience of repeatedly opening the door against the kids pressing against it for their treats; and besides, he worried about one of the little ones being pushed backward off the front steps. A lawsuit could easily follow something like that.

The little girl lifted her silver bucket.

He took a closer look. No, not silver—shiny stainless steel, reflecting the dull gray overcast sky. It reminded him of something, but he couldn't place it at the moment. Strange sort of thing to be collecting Halloween treats in. Probably some new fad. Whatever became of the old pillowcase or the shopping bag, or even the plastic jack-o-lantern?

He poised his hand over the bucket, then let the candy bar and dime drop. They landed with a soft *squish*.

Not exactly the sound he had expected. He leaned forward to see what else was in the bucket but the child had swung around and was making her way down the steps.

Out on the sidewalk, some hundred feet away along the maple-lined driveway, two older children waited for her. A stainless steel bucket dangled from each of their hands.

Edward shivered as he closed the front door. A new chill seemed to fill the air. Maybe he should put on a sweater. But what color? He checked himself over in the hall mirror. Not bad for a guy looking fifty-two in the eye. That was Erica's doing. Trading in the old wife for a new model twenty years younger had had a rejuvenating effect. Also it made him work at staying young looking—like three trips a week to the Short Hills Nautilus Club and watching his diet. He decided to forego the sweater for now.

He almost made it back to his recliner and the unfinished *New York Times* when the front bell rang again. Sighing resignedly, he turned and went back to the front door. He didn't mind tending to the trick-or-treaters, but he wished Erica were here to share door duty. Why did she have to pick today for her monthly spending spree at the Mall? He knew she loved Bloomingdale's—in fact, she had once told him that after she died she wanted her ashes placed in an urn in the lingerie department there—but she could have waited until tomorrow.

Two boys this time, both about eleven, both made up like punkers with orange and green spiked hair, ripped clothes, and crude tattoos, obviously done with a Bic instead of a real tattooer's pen. They stood restlessly in the chill breeze, shifting from one foot to the other, looking up and down the block, stainless steel buckets in hand.

He threw up his hands. "Whoa! Tough guys, ay? I'd better not mess around with the likes of—!"

One of the boys glanced at him briefly, and in his eyes Edward caught a flash of such rage and hatred—not just for him, but for the whole world—that his voice dried away to a whisper. And then the look was gone as if it had never been and the boy was just another kid again. He hastily grabbed a pair of Three Musketeers and two dimes, leaned through the opening in the door, and dropped one of each into their buckets.

The one on the right went *squish* and the one on the left went *plop*.

He managed to catch just a glimpse of the bottom of the bucket on the right as the kid turned. He couldn't tell what was in there, but it was red.

He was glad to see them go. Surly pair, he thought. Not a word out of either of them. And what was in the bottom of that bucket? Didn't look like any candy he knew, and he considered himself an expert on candy. He patted the belly that he had been trying to flatten for months. More than an expert—an *aficionado* of candy.

Further speculation was forestalled by a call from the hospital. One of his postpartum patients needed a laxative. He okayed a couple of ounces of milk of mag. Then the nurse double-checked his pre-op orders on the hysterectomy tomorrow.

He managed to suffer through it all with dignity. It was Wednesday and he always took Wednesdays off. Jeff Sewell was supposed to be taking his calls today, but all the floors at the hospital had the Cantrell home phone number and they habitually tried here first before they went hunting for whoever was covering him.

Edward was used to it. He had learned ages ago that there was no such thing as a day off in OB-Gyn.

The bell rang again, and for half a second Edward found himself hesitant to answer it. He shrugged off the reluctance and pulled open the door.

Two mothers and two children. He sucked in his gut when he recognized the mothers as long-time patients.

This is more like it!

"Hi, Doctor Cantrell!" the red-haired woman said with a big smile. She put a hand atop the red-haired child's head. "You remember Shana, don't you? You delivered her five years ago next month."

"I remember you, Gloria," he said, noting her flash of pleasure at having her first name remembered. He never forgot a face. "But Shana here looks a little bit different from when I last saw her."

As both women laughed, he scanned his mind for the other's name. Then it came to him:

"Yours looks a little bigger, too, Diane."

"She sure does. What do you say to Doctor Cantrell, Susan?"

The child mumbled something that sounded like "Ricky Meat" and held up an orange plastic jack-o-lantern with a black plastic strap.

"That's what I like to see!" he said. "A real Halloweeny treat holder. Better than those stainless steel buckets the other kids have been carrying!"

Gloria and Diane looked at each other. "Stainless steel buckets?"

"Can you believe it?" he said as he got the two little girls each a Milky Way and a dime. "My first three Halloween customers this morning carried steel buckets for their treats. Never seen anything like it."

"Neither have we," Diane said.

"You haven't? You should have passed a couple of boys out on the street."

"No. We're the only ones around."

Strange. But maybe they'd cut back to the street through the trees as this group entered the driveway.

He dropped identical candy and coins into the identical jack-o-lanterns and heard them strike the other treats with a reassuring rustle.

He watched the retreating forms of the two young mothers and their two happy kids until they were out of sight. This is the way Halloween should be, he thought. Much better than strange hostile kids with metal buckets.

And just as he completed the thought, he saw three small, white-sheeted forms of indeterminate age and sex round the hedge and head down the driveway. Each had a shiny metal bucket in hand.

He wished Erica were here.

He got the candy bars and coins and waited at the door for them. He had decided that before he parted with the goodies he was going to find out who these kids were and what they had in their little buckets. Fair was fair.

The trio climbed to the top step of the stoop and stood there waiting, silently watching him through the eyeholes of their sheets.

Their silence got under his skin.

Doesn't anybody say "Trick or treat" anymore?

"Well, what have we here?" he said with all the joviality he could muster. "Three little ghosts! The Ghostly Trio!"

One of them, he couldn't tell which, lisped a timid, "Yeth."

"Good! I like ghosts on Halloween! You want a treat?"

They nodded as one.

"Okay! But first you're gonna have to earn it! Show me what you've got in those buckets and I'll give you each a dime and a box of Milk Duds! How's that for a deal?"

The kids looked at each other. Some wordless communication seemed to pass between them, then they turned and started back down the steps.

"Hey, kids! Hey, wait!" he said quickly, forcing a laugh. "I was only kidding! You don't have to show me anything. Here! Just take the candy."

They paused on the second step, obviously confused.

Ever so gently, he coaxed them back. "C'mon, kids. I'm just curious about those buckets, is all. I've been seeing them all day and I've been wondering where they came from. But if I frightened you, well, hey, I'll ask somebody else later on." He held up the candy and the coins and extended his hand through the door. "Here you go."

One little ghost stepped forward but raised an open hand—a little girl's hand—instead of a bucket.

He could not bear to be denied any longer. He pushed open the storm door and stepped out, looming over the child, craning his neck to see into that damn little bucket. The child squealed in fright and turned away, crouching over the bucket as if to protect it from him.

What are they trying to hide? What's the matter with them? And what's the matter with me?

Really. Who *cared* what was in those buckets?

He cared. It was becoming an obsession with him. He'd go crazy if he didn't find out.

Hoping nobody was watching—nobody who'd think he was some sort of child molester—he grabbed the little ghost by the shoulders and twisted her toward him. She couldn't hide the bucket from him now. In the clear light of day he got a good look into it.

Blood.

Blood with some floating bits of tissue and membrane lay maybe an inch and a half deep in the bottom.

Startled and sickened, he could only stand there and stare at the red, swirling liquid. As the child tried to pull the bucket away from him, it tipped, spilling its contents over the front of her white sheet. She screamed—more in dismay than terror, it seemed.

"Let her go!" said a little boy's voice from beside him. Edward turned to see one of the other ghosts hurling the contents of its bucket at him. As if in slow motion, he saw the sheet of red liquid and debris float toward him through the air, spreading as it neared. The warm spray splattered him up and down and he reeled back in revulsion.

By the time he had wiped his eyes clear, the kids were half way down the driveway. He wanted to chase after them but he had to get out of these bloody clothes first. He'd look like a homicidal maniac if someone saw him running after three little kids looking like this. Arms akimbo, he hurried to the utility room and threw his shirt into the sink.

Why? his mind cried as he tried to remember whether hot or cold water set a stain. He tried cold and began rubbing at the blood in the blue oxford cloth.

He scrubbed hard and fast to offset the shaking of his hands. What a horrible thing for anyone to do, but especially children! Questions tumbled over each other in confusion: What could be going through their sick little minds? And where had they gotten the blood?

But most of all, Why me?

Slowly, the red color began to thin and run, but the bits of tissue clung. He looked at them more closely. Damn if that doesn't look like....

Recognition triggered an epiphany. He suddenly understood everything. He now knew who those children were—or at least who had put them up to it—and he understood why. He sighed with relief as anger flooded through him like a cleansing flame. He much preferred being angry to being afraid.

He dried his arms with a paper towel and went to call the cops.

⁂ ⁂ ⁂

"Right-to-Lifers, Joe! Has to be them!"

Sgt. Joe Morelli scratched his head. "You sure, Doc?"

Edward had known the Morelli family since Joe's days as a security guard at the Mall, waiting for a spot to open up on the Short Hills police force. He'd delivered all three of Joe's kids.

"Who else could it be? Those little stainless steel buckets they carry—the ones I told you about—they're the same kind we use in D-and-C's, and get this: We use suction now, but used to use those buckets in abortions. The scrapings from the uterus slid down through a weighted speculum into a bucket just like those."

And it was those bloody scrapings that had been splattered all over him.

"But why you, Doc? I know you do abortions now and then—all you guys do—but you're not an abortionist per se, if you know what I'm saying."

Edward nodded, not mentioning Sandy. He knew Joe's youngest daughter's pregnancy two years ago was still a touchy subject. She'd been only fifteen but Edward had taken care of everything for Joe with the utmost discretion. He now had a devoted friend on the police force.

A thought suddenly flashed through Edward's mind:

They must know about the women's center! But how could they?

It was due to open tomorrow, the first of the month. He had been so careful to avoid any overt connection with it, situating it down in Newark and going so far as to set it up through a corporate front. Abortions might be legal, but it still didn't sit well with a lot of people to know that their neighbor ran an abortion mill.

Maybe that was it. Maybe a bunch of sicko right-to-lifers had connected him with the new center.

"What gets me," Joe was saying, "is that if this is real abortion material like you say, where'd they get it?"

"I wish I knew." The question had plagued him since he had called the police.

"Well, don't you worry, Doc," Joe said, slipping his hat over his thinning hair. "Whatever's going on, it's gonna stop. I'll cruise the neighborhood. If I see any kids, or even adults with any of these buckets, I'll I-D them and find out what's up."

"Thanks, Joe," he said, meaning it. It was comforting to know a cop was looking out for him. "I appreciate that. I'd especially like to get this ugly business cleared up before the wife and I get home from dinner tonight."

"I don't blame you," he said, shaking his head. "I know I wouldn't want Marie to see no buckets of blood."

✻ ✻ ✻

The trick-or-treaters swelled in numbers as the afternoon progressed. They flowed to the door in motley hordes of all shapes, sizes, and colors. A steady stream of Spocks, Skywalkers, Vaders, Indiana Joneses, Madonnas, Motley Crues, Twisted Sisters, and even a few ghosts, goblins, and witches.

And always among them were one or two kids with steel buckets.

Edward bit his lip and repressed his anger when he saw them. He said nothing, did not try to look into their buckets, gave no sign that their presence meant anything to him, pretended they were no different from the other kids as he dropped candies and coins into the steel buckets among the paper sacks and pillow cases and jack-o-lanterns, all the while praying that Morelli would catch one of the little bastards crossing the street and find out who was behind this bullshit.

He saw the patrol car pull into the drive around 4:00. Morelli finally must have nailed one of them. About time! He had to leave for the women's center soon and wanted this thing settled and done with.

"No luck, Doc," Joe said, rolling down his window. "You must have scared them off."

"Are you crazy?" His anger exploded as he trotted down the walk to the driveway. "They've been through here all afternoon!"

"Hey, take it easy, Doc. If they're around, they must be hiding those buckets when they're on the street, because I've been by here about fifty times and I haven't seen one steel bucket."

Edward reined in his anger. It would do no good to alienate Joe. He wanted the police force on his side.

"Sorry. It's just that this is very upsetting."

"I can imagine. Look, Doc. Why don't I do this: Why don't I just park the car right out at the curb and watch the kids as they come in. Maybe I'll catch one in the act. At the very least, it might keep them away."

"I appreciate that, Joe, but it won't be necessary. I'm going out in a few minutes and won't be back until much later tonight. However, I do wish you'd keep an eye on the place—vandals, you know."

"Sure thing, Doc. No problem."

Edward watched the police car pull out of the driveway, then he set the house alarm and hurried to the garage to make his getaway before the doorbell rang again.

❋ ❋ ❋

THE
MIDTOWN WOMEN'S
MEDICAL CENTER

Edward savored the effect of the westering sun glinting off the thick brass letters over the entrance as he walked by. Red letters on a white placard proclaimed "Grand Opening Tomorrow" from the front door. He slipped around the side of the building into the alley, unlocked the private entrance, and stepped inside.

Dark, quiet, deserted. Damn! He'd hoped to catch the contractor for one last check of the trim. He wanted everything perfect for the opening tomorrow.

He flipped on the lights and checked his watch. Erica would be meeting him here in about an hour, then they would pick up the Klines and have drinks and dinner at the club. He had just enough time for a quick inspection tour.

So clean, he thought as he walked through the waiting room—the floors shiny and unscuffed, the carpet pile unmatted, the wall surfaces unmarred by chips or finger smudges. Even the air smelled new.

This center—*his* center—had been in the planning stages for three years. Countless hours of meetings with lawyers, bankers, planning boards, architects and contractors had gone into it. But at last it was ready to go. He planned to work here himself in the beginning, just to keep overhead down, but once the operation got rolling he'd hire other doctors and have them do the work while he ran the show from a distance.

He stepped into Procedure Room One and looked over the equipment. Dominating the room was the Rappaport 206, a state-of-the-art procedure table with thigh and calf supports on the stirrups, three breakaway sections, and fully motorized tilts in all planes—Trendelenberg, reverse Trendelenberg, left and right lateral.

Close by, the Zarick suction extractor—the most efficient abortion device on the market—hung gleaming on its chrome stand. He pressed the ON button to check the power but nothing happened.

"It won't work tonight," said a child's voice behind him, making him almost scream with fright.

He spun around. Fifteen or twenty kids stood there staring at him. Most were costumed, and they all carried those goddamn steel buckets.

"All right!" he said. "This does it! I've had just about enough! I'm getting the police!"

He turned to reach for the phone but stopped after one step. More kids were coming in from the hall. They streamed in slowly and silently, their eyes fixed on him, piercing him. They filled the room, occupying every square foot except for the small circle of space they left around him and the equipment. And behind them he could see more, filling the hall and the waiting room beyond. A sea of faces, all staring at him.

He was frightened now. They were just kids, but there were so damn many of them. A few looked fifteen or so, and one looked to be in her early twenties, but by far most of them appeared to be twelve and under. Some were even toddlers! What sort of sick mind would involve such tiny children in this?

And how did they get in? All the doors were locked.

"Get out of here," he said, forcing his voice into calm, measured tones.

They said nothing, merely continued to stare at him.

"All right, then. If you won't leave, I will! And when I return—" He tried to push by a five-year old girl in a gypsy costume. Without warning she jabbed her open hand into his abdomen with stunning force, driving him back against the table.

"Who are you?" This time his voice was less calm, his tones less measured.

"You mean you don't recognize us?" a mocking voice said from the crowd.

"I've never seen any of you before today."

"Not true," said another voice. "After our fathers, you're the second most important man in our lives."

This was insane! "I don't know *any* of you!"

"You should." Another voice—were they trying to confuse him by talking from different spots in the room?

"Why?"

"Because you killed us."

The absurdity of the statement made him laugh. He straightened from the table and stepped forward. "Okay. That's it. This isn't the least bit funny."

A little boy shoved him back, roughly, violently. His strength was hideous.

"M-my wife will be here s-soon." He was ashamed of the stammer in his voice, but he couldn't help it. "She'll call the police."

"Sergeant Morelli, perhaps?" This voice was more mature than the others—more womanly. He found her and looked her in the eye. She was the tall one in her early twenties, dressed in a sweater and skirt. He had a sudden crazy thought that maybe she was a young teacher and these were her students on a class trip. But these kids looked like they spanned all grades from pre-school to junior high.

"Who are you?"

"I don't have a name," she said, facing him squarely. "Very few of us do. But this one does." She indicated a little girl at her side, a toddler made up like a hobo in raggedy clothes with burnt cork rubbed on her face for a beard. An Emmett Kelly dwarf. "Here Laura," she said to the child as she urged her forward. "Show Dr. Cantrell what you looked like last time he saw you."

Laura stepped up to him. Behind the make-up he could see that she was a beautiful child with short dark hair, a pudgy face, and big brown eyes. She held her bucket out to him.

"She was eleven weeks old," the woman said, "three inches long, and weighed fourteen grams when you ripped her from her mother's uterus. She was no match for you and your suction tube."

Blood and tissue swirled in the bottom of her bucket.

"You don't expect me to buy this, do you?"

"I don't care what you buy, Doctor. But this is Sandra Morelli's child—or at least what her child would look like now if she'd been allowed to be born. But she wasn't born. Her mother had names all picked out—Adam for a boy, Laura for a girl—but her grandfather bullied Laura's mother into an abortion and you were oh-so-willing to see that there were no problems along the way."

"This is absurd!" he said.

"Really?" the woman said. "Then go ahead and call Sergeant Morelli. Maybe he'd like to drive down and meet his granddaughter. The one you killed."

"I killed no one!" he shouted. "No one! Abortion has been legal since 1974! Absolutely legal! And besides—she wasn't really alive!"

What's the matter with me? he asked himself. I'm talking to them as if I believe them!

"Oh, yes," the woman said. "I forgot. Some political appointees decided that we weren't people and that was that. Pretty much like what happened to East European Jews back in World War Two. We're not even afforded the grace of being called embryos or fetuses. We're known as 'products of conception.' What a neat, dehumanizing little phrase. So much easier to scrape the 'products of conception' into a bucket than a person."

"I've had just about enough of this!" he said.

"So?" a young belligerent voice said. "What're y'gonna do?"

He knew he was going to do nothing. He didn't want to have another primary grade kid shove him back against the table again. No kid that size should be that strong. It wasn't natural.

"You can't hold me responsible!" he said. "They came to me, asking for help. They were pregnant and they didn't want to be. My God! *I didn't make them pregnant!"*

Another voice: "No, but you sure gave them a convenient solution!"

"So blame your mothers! They're the ones who spread their legs and didn't want to take responsibility for it! How about *them*?"

"They are not absolved," the woman said. "They shirked their responsibilities to us, but the vast majority of them are each responsible for only one of us. You, Doctor Cantrell, are responsible for all of us. Most of them were scared teenagers, like Laura's mother, who were bullied and badgered into 'terminating' us. Others were too afraid of what their parents would say so they snuck off to women's medical centers like this and lied about their age and put us out of their misery."

"Not all of them, sweetheart!" he said. He was beginning to feel he was on firmer ground now. "Many a time I've done three or four on the same woman! Don't tell me they were poor, scared teenagers. Abortion was their idea of birth control!"

"We know," a number of voices chorused, and something in their tone made him shiver. "We'll see them later."

"The point is," the woman said, "that you were always there, always ready with a gentle smile, a helpful hand, an easy solution, a simple way to get them off the hook by getting rid of us. And a bill, of course."

"If it hadn't been me, it would have been someone else!"

"You can't dilute your own blame. Or your own responsibility," said a voice from behind his chair. "Plenty of doctors refuse to do abortions."

"If you were one of those," said another from his left, "we wouldn't be here tonight."

"The *law* lets me do it. The Supreme Court. So don't blame me. Blame those Supreme Court justices."

"That's politics. We don't care about politics."

"But I believe in a woman's right to control her own life, to make decisions about her own body!"

"We don't care what you believe. Do you think the beliefs of a terrorist matter to the victims of his bombs? Don't you understand? This is *personal*!"

A little girl's voice said, "I could have been adopted, you know. I would've made someone a good kid. But I never had the chance!"

They all began shouting at once, about never getting Christmas gifts or birthday presents or hugs or tucked in at night or playing with matches or playing catch or playing house or even playing doctor—

It seemed to go on endlessly. Finally the woman held up her bucket. "All their possibilities ended in here."

"Wait a goddam minute!" he said. He had just discovered a significant flaw in their little show. "Only a few of them ended up in buckets! If you were up on your facts, you'd know that no one uses those old D-and-C buckets for abortions anymore." He pointed to the glass trap on the Zarick suction extractor. "This is where the products of conception wind up."

The woman stepped forward with her bucket. "They carry this in honor of me. I have the dubious distinction of being your first victim."

"You're not *my* victims!" he shouted. "The law—"

She spat in his face. Shocked and humiliated, Edward wiped away the saliva with his shirt sleeve and pressed himself back against the table. The rage in her face was utterly terrifying.

"The *law*?" she hissed. "Don't speak of legalities to me! Look at me! I'd be twenty-two now and this is how I'd look if you hadn't murdered me. Do a little subtraction, doctor: 1974 was a lot less than twenty-two years ago. I'm Ellen Benedict's daughter—or at least I would have been if you hadn't agreed to do that 'D-and-C' on her when she couldn't find a way to explain her pregnancy to her impotent husband!"

Ellen Benedict! God! How did they know about Ellen Benedict? Even *he* had forgotten about her!

The woman stepped forward and grabbed his wrist. He was helpless against her strength as she pressed his hand over her left breast. He might have found the softness beneath her sweater exciting under different circumstances, but now it elicited only dread.

"Feel my heart beating? It was beating when your curette ripped me to pieces. I was only six weeks old. And I'm not the only one here you killed before 1974—I was just your first. So you can't get off the hook by naming the Supreme Court as an accomplice. And even if we allowed you that cop-out, other things you've done since '74 are utterly abominable!" She looked around and pointed into the crowd. "There's one! Come here, honey, and show your bucket to the doctor."

A five- or six-year-old boy came forward. He had blond bangs and the biggest, saddest blue eyes the doctor had ever seen. The boy held out his bucket.

Edward covered his face with his hands. "I don't want to see!"

Suddenly he felt his hands yanked downward with numbing force and found the woman's face scant inches from his own.

"*Look*, damn you! You've seen it before!"

He looked into the upheld bucket. A fully formed male fetus lay curled in the blood, its blue eyes open, its head turned at an unnatural angle.

"This is Rachel Walraven's baby as you last saw him."

The Walraven baby! Oh, God, not that one! How could they know?

"This little boy is how he'd look now if you hadn't broken his neck after the abortifacient you gave his mother made her uterus dump him out."

"He couldn't have survived!" he shouted. He could hear the hysteria edging into his voice. "He was pre-viable! Too immature to survive! The best neonatal ICU in the world couldn't have saved him!"

"Then why'd you break my neck?" the little boy asked.

Edward could only sob—a single harsh sound that seemed to rip itself from the tissues inside his chest and burst free into the air. What could he say? How could he tell them that he had miscalculated the length of gestation and that no one had been more shocked than he at the size of the infant that had dropped into his gloved hands. And then it had opened its eyes and stared at him and my God it had looked like it was trying to breathe! He'd done late terminations before where the fetus had squirmed around awhile in the bucket before finally dying, but this one—!

Christ!, he remembered thinking, what if the damn thing lets out a cry? He'd get sued by the patient and be the laughing stock of the staff. Poor Ed Cantrell—can't tell the difference between an abortion and a delivery! He'd look like a jerk!

So he did the only thing he could do. He gave its neck a sharp twist as he lowered it into the bucket. The neck didn't even crack when he broke it.

"Why have you come to me?" he said.

"Answer us first," a child's voice said. "Why do you do it? You don't need the money. Why did you kill us?"

"I told you! I believe in every woman's right to—"

They began to boo him, drowning him out. Then the boos changed to a chant: "*Why? Why? Why? Why?*"

"Stop that! Listen to me! I told you why!"

But still they chanted, sounding like a crowd at a football game: "*Why? Why? Why? Why?*"

Finally he could stand no more. He raised his fists and screamed. "All right! Because I can! Is that what you want to hear? I do it because I *can!*"

The room was suddenly dead silent.

The answer startled him. He had never asked himself why before. "Because I can," he said softly.

"Yes," the woman said with equal softness. "The ultimate power."

He suddenly felt very old, very tired. "What do you want of me?"

No one answered.

"Why have you come?"

They all spoke as one: "Because today, this Halloween, this night...*we* can."

"And we don't want this place to open," the woman said.

So that was it. They wanted to kill the women's center before it got started—*abort it*, so to speak. He almost smiled at the pun. He looked at their faces, their staring eyes. They mean business, he thought. And he knew they wouldn't take no for an answer.

Well, this was no time to stand on principle. Promise them anything, then get the hell out of here to safety.

"Okay," he said, in what he hoped was a meek voice. "You've convinced me. I'll turn this into a general medical center. No abortions. Just family practice for the community."

They watched him silently. Finally a voice said, "He's lying."

The woman nodded. "I know." She turned to the children. "Do it," she said.

Pure chaos erupted as the children went wild. They were like a berserk mob, surging in all directions. But silent. So silent.

Edward felt himself shoved aside as the children tore into the procedure table and the Zarick extractor. The table was ripped from the floor and all its upholstery shredded. Its sections were torn free and hurled against the walls with such force that they punctured through the plasterboard.

The rage in the children's eyes seemed to leak out into the room, filling it, thickening the air like an onrushing storm, making his skin ripple with fear at its ferocity.

As he saw the Zarick start to topple, he forced himself forward to try to save it but was casually slammed against the wall with stunning force. In a semi-daze, he watched the Zarick raised into the air; he ducked flying glass as it was slammed onto the floor, not just once, but over and over until it was nothing more than a twisted wreck of wire, plastic hose, and ruptured circuitry.

And from down the hall he could hear similar carnage in the other procedure rooms. Finally the noise stopped and room one was packed with children again.

He began to weep. He hated himself for it, but couldn't help it. He simply broke down and cried in front of them. He was frightened. And all the money, all the plans...destroyed.

He pulled himself together and straightened his spine. He would rebuild. All this destruction was covered by insurance. He would blame it on vandalism, collect his money, and have the place brand new inside of a month. These vicious little bastards weren't going to stop him. But he couldn't let them know that.

"Get out, all of you," he said softly. "You've had you're fun. You've ruined me. Now leave me alone."

"We'll leave you alone," said the woman who would have been Ellen Benedict's child. "But not yet."

Suddenly, they began to empty their buckets on him, hurling the contents at him in a continuous wave, turning the air red with flying blood and tissue, engulfing him from all sides, choking him, clogging his mouth and nostrils.

And then they reached for him....

❋ ❋ ❋

Erica knocked on the front door of the center for the third time and still got no answer.

Now where can he be? she thought as she walked around to the private entrance. She tried the door and found it unlocked. She pushed in but stopped on the threshold.

The waiting room was lit and looked normal enough.

"Ed?" she called, but he didn't answer.

Odd. His car was out front. She was supposed to meet him here at five. She'd taken a cab from the mall—after all, she didn't want Ginger dropping her off here; there would be too many questions. The silence was beginning to make her uneasy.

She glanced down the hallway. It was dark and quiet.

Almost quiet.

She heard tiny little scraping noises, tiny movements, so soft that she would have missed them if there had been any other sound in the building. It seemed to come from the first procedure room. She stepped up to the door and listened to the dark. Yes, they were definitely coming from in there.

She flipped on the light...and felt her knees buckle.

The room was red—the walls, the ceiling, the remnants of the shattered fixtures, all dripping with red. The clots and the coppery odor that saturated the air left no doubt in Erica's reeling mind that she was looking at blood. But on the floor—the blood-puddled linoleum was littered with countless shiny, silvery buckets. The little rustling sounds were coming from them. She saw something that looked like hair in a nearby bucket and took a staggering step over to see what was inside.

It was Edward's head, floating in a pool of blood, his eyes wide and mad, looking at her. She wanted to scream but the air clogged in her throat as she saw Ed's lips begin to move. They were forming words but there was no sound, for there were no lungs to push air through his larynx. Yet still his lips kept moving in what seemed to be silent pleas. But pleas for what?

And then he opened his mouth wide and screamed—silently.

My Favorite Halloween Memory

Owl Goingback

I didn't get to experience Halloween until I was six years old. I had heard of the holiday, had even read of it in a story about Clifford the big red dog, but I had never gotten to share in the festivities until then.

Perhaps my parents finally thought that, if I was old enough to attend first grade in a public school, I was old enough to take part in the rituals of Halloween. Maybe they felt sorry for me, as I sat alone in our mobile home, on a lonely stretch of country road where no one ever visited. Perhaps they just grew tired of my heavy sighs, frowns, tears, and long faces.

Whatever the reason, in the autumn of 1965, my mother bought for me my very first Halloween costume. The costume consisted of a thin jumpsuit and a cheap plastic mask, the kind they still sell today in department stores throughout the country. I would have preferred dressing up as a werewolf, or a vampire, or even a spooky ghost, but the costume presented to me was that of an evil genie. It really didn't look like a genie at all. The face was a mismatched creation, part ghost and part monster, while the image printed on the suit featured a lot of colored smoke and a misshapen bottle. It wasn't a great costume, but it was mine and I loved the silly thing. Hell, for two weeks leading up to Halloween, I practically lived in it, removing it only long enough so I could go to school. I even slept in my costume, donning the suit in place of pajamas and keeping the mask on a dresser beside my bed.

Living in the country made it impossible to go trick-or-treating close to home. The houses were just too far apart to make it safe, and there were animals traveling the roads at night that could easily eat a six-year-old boy: big mean dogs, wild foxes, and herds of rabbits with nasty attitudes. And you sure as hell didn't want to go knocking on doors in the country. Chances were, if you did, you would end up picking buckshot out of your butt for a week. Farmers are funny people, and most of them want to be left alone. Makes no difference if it's Halloween, or Christmas Eve.

Knowing that trick-or-treating in the country was out of the question, my mother drove me into town to do a little candy gathering. Once there, I proceeded down one dark street after another, searching for tasty treats to rot my teeth. I still recall the sights, sounds, and smells of that night: costumed children scampering like spiders down moonlit streets, excited laughter floating on the crisp, October air, dogs barking, the smell of apples and popcorn balls, and the sticky sweet taste of cotton candy. I also remember sweating heavily in my evil genie costume, barely able to see out of the tiny eyeholes in the mask.

I must have shouted "trick-or-treat" a million times that evening, holding out my plastic jack-o-lantern for tasty morsels and sweet treats. Most of the people I panhandled gladly gave me a treat, but some would ask for a trick in return. Having little talent in those days, I relied on a simple poem to get me through those tough performances. It wasn't Shakespeare, but it always paid off.

The tiny town I visited that night didn't have a haunted house, but the Jaycees did sponsor a Halloween parade for all the children. They also put on a free cookout, giving out hot dogs and soft drinks to all the kids in costumes. I was so proud to be a part of that parade, marching along in my evil genie costume, trying to look fierce for all the people watching along the sidelines. I don't know how fierce I really was, but I must have done a good job because I was rewarded with a hot-dog for my efforts.

Ah, those Jaycees hot-dogs, how I truly loved them. Cooked slowly over an open fire, blackened to just the right degree, the perfect thing to balance out a night of too much candy corn and licorice whips. Still in my costume, with my mask flipped up, I stood in line with the other children, eagerly waiting for a hot dog to be handed to me. I didn't need mustard, or ketchup, because my tastes were simpler in those days. All I needed was a plain, old fashioned weenie, trapped inside a golden bun.

I remember how that hot-dog looked when it was handed to me. I remember how it smelled. And I still remember to this day how hard I cried when it slipped out of the bun and fell to the parking lot pavement. There it lay, naked and soon to be stepped on, having fallen to the ground before I could even get a single bite.

Hearing my wail of grief, my mother rushed over to me to see what was the matter. I explained what had happened, pointing a trembling finger at the lost hot-dog. Knowing that my first Halloween was about to be ruined, my mother acted quickly. She cut into the line of waiting children, explaining to one of the volunteers about the tragedy of my hot-dog. The man was sympathetic to my plight, supplying my mother with a new hot-dog to replace the one I had lost.

Wiping the tears from my tiny eyes, I took the second hot-dog from my mother. I held it carefully and brought it slowly to my lips. I was about to take the first bite, when the second hot-dog also slipped out of its bun and fell to the ground. I was speechless. Two hot-dogs I had received, and two hot-dogs lay on the pavement. Untouched by human lips. Not a tooth mark on them.

Less than happy with my inability to hold onto a hot-dog, my mother decided it was time we called it a night. I was loaded into the back seat of the car, and strapped into place, while my mother drove back to our tiny mobile home in the country. On the way home I snacked on candy, apples, and popcorn balls, and spoke of the night's adventure. My very first night of trick-or-treating had been a smashing success, and my plastic orange pumpkin was nearly filled with assorted treats. Still, there was a great sadness in my heart. Laying beside me on the car seat were two empty hot-dog buns, a painful reminder that, on an eve that was all hallow, I had no weenie.

Needles and Razor Blades

Dennis Etchison

The kids on my street loved Halloween.

It was a chance to scare and be scared. We planned our costumes, homemade except for the masks, in a kind of competition to see who could look the most horrible. There were cheapjack outfits for sale but they weren't very good and anyway you'd be afraid of running into another kid dressed exactly the same, which was no fun at all. We searched joke shops and out-of-the-way stores for the most unusual mask, then talked our parents into buying it as the centerpiece for this year's creation, adding the weirdest clothes and props we could find. Old bedsheets worked if everything else failed—you could always be a ghost or wrap yourself up like a mummy, and if you still had your favorite masks from years past you might want to mix-and-match or even lose the mask entirely and make your face up with fake scars and blood like a corpse or an accident victim. The idea, of course, was to be as disgusting as possible, and if your folks shook their heads and turned away because you were too nauseating to look at, that was the greatest. Kids love to make their parents sick to their stomachs, the sicker the better.

We carried brown paper bags and covered as many blocks as we could before we had to stop off at home to empty them out. That was the other part of the competition: to see who got the most candy. One year I set a personal record with four big bags full, more than my best friend Robert Covington, whose mother was too nervous to let him go out of the neighborhood. The next day we'd count the take, Tootsie Rolls and jellybeans and cookies and miniature candy bars, then play with our stash like Scrooge McDuck. Before we could eat it the grownups had to check everything to be sure it was safe. There were rumors about bad people who put razor blades or needles in apples or popcorn balls, and anything that looked homemade was automatically suspect. Years later I learned that this was a widespread urban myth, but in our town we believed it, though no one knew who those bad people were or where they lived.

The worst thing about Halloween was growing up.

When were you too old for trick-or-treating? It was hard to be sure. The last year before adolescence I tried to have it both ways. I dressed as a ghost in a sheet with my best rubber skull mask, set up a stand in the front yard and handed out candy to the little kids who came by, hoping to give them a scare. It was safer that way but it was also sadder, at least for me. There were no more oranges or apples or popcorn balls that might hide poison or needles or razor blades, but there was no sense of danger, either. And that was the point of Halloween. When the danger went away so did the fun. Which may have something to do with why John Carpenter's *Halloween* was such a success with teenagers, and why I started going to as many horror movies as I could and eventually tried to write that sort of thing myself. It was a way of recapturing the feeling, or some part of it, the only way I had left.

Orchestra

Stephen Mark Rainey

And how shall we play without him?" Jacob Kravitz grumbled. "He's the only one who knows the music well enough to conduct!"

"Well," sighed Bert Hoffman, "we will *have* to find someone else. One does not cancel the Halloween program after all the work we've done!"

"By the way, what happened to him?"

"That's what I'm saying—he is just gone! No one has seen him since he left the auditorium last Friday. His car is gone, but they say everything in his house is still there. All his clothes. His valuables. Everything. Why can't *you* conduct?"

"Pah! I'm no conductor. I've never lifted a baton in my life."

"You could conduct in your sleep!"

"Get out. Besides, who would you put on first violin? Jennings?"

"He's as good as you."

"Never!"

The elderly pair fell silent, occasionally casting annoyed looks at one another. A shower of golden leaves wafted down on their heads as a draught of chilly Lake Michigan wind shook the trees in Lincoln Park. Across the sidewalk, an exceptionally broad man settled onto a bench, the wooden planks uttering an annoyed groan beneath him. A willowy 12-year old would have been hard-pressed to find space beside him.

"Oy," sighed Kravitz. "There are only two weeks to the performance. Who would learn Vaughn-Williams, Hovhaness, and Sibelius and do what we must do with it? In two weeks? So, are the police suspecting foul play?"

"Police only suspect foul play when they have blood and a body. Weintraub is off with some young vixen."

"He is 74 years old! A vixen would kill him."

Across the way, the very large man chuckled at Kravitz's remark and lit a cigarette, which looked more like a lollipop stick in his massive fingers. Kravitz shuddered at the grotesque way the fat man sucked on the filter with his slick, pursed lips.

"So why not you?" pressed Hoffman. "You know the music better than anyone. You are the concertmaster!"

"I play the violin! I do not conduct! Plus, don't forget, I also man the organ in *Sinfonia Antarctica!* Who else could do *that?*"

"Pah!"

"Paaaah!"

Kravitz noticed the man across the sidewalk watching them with apparent amusement. "You know," he said in a much quieter voice, "Weintraub has a son in Philadelphia, and a daughter in Aurora. Has anyone thought to let them know their father has gone missing?"

"How would I know? The police, I'm sure, have contacted the family."

"You said the police think he's with a vixen."

"That doesn't mean he isn't dead."

"What *shtuss.*"

"It's cold and I'm going home. I think we're going to have to draft someone from the ranks, it's as simple as that. You're the senior man. The choice must be up to you."

"If it were my choice, I would cancel the Halloween program. I would cancel Halloween. It's a stupid holiday—as if it even qualifies to be a holiday," Kravitz sighed.

"Ah. You are capable of making an intelligent remark. However, the point remains unanswered."

The two men rose from their bench and started up the sidewalk toward the park entrance. Kravitz paused before the large man, who gave him an affable grin and took a long drag on his cigarette.

"Those things are going to kill you," Kravitz growled.

In a surprisingly light, silky voice, the heavy man replied, "The cigarettes will not kill me." And he drew back his slick lips in a wide smile, revealing a row of polished, white teeth.

Kravitz shook his head and turned away, pulling his coat tighter against the increasing gale. Hoffman sent him a knowing glance before bowing his head against the wind. *Damned old bastard.* Hoffman knew well enough that he refused to conduct because, as a violinist, he did not have to step into the spotlight; he only had to play in the company of his fellow musicians, where he could thoroughly disregard everything in that field of blackness beyond the stage lights.

Stage fright. Pure and simple. Standing at the forefront with a baton, he would choke. And he could not bear such failure in front of an audience.

He and Hoffman parted ways on Lincoln Avenue, each heading back to their respective homes, Kravitz to the north, Hoffman to the south. They had known each other for more years than either could remember, and both had known Weintraub, conductor *in absentia*, for the almost fifteen years they had been playing with the Chicago Cosmopolitan Symphony Orchestra—a grandiose title for an only slightly organized company of talented amateurs.

Terrible that such a fine man could vanish under such mysterious circumstances.

By the time Kravitz reached the door of his ancient apartment building on Belden, the streetlights had begun flickering on and the temperature had dropped from barely tolerable to insufferable. Even pulling open the heavy door hurt his joints, and when the blast of warm air from the foyer washed over him, it not only broke the chill, it stifled him.

Halloween performances...what a stupid tradition.

❋ ❋ ❋

At three-thirty the following afternoon, Jacob Kravitz found himself jarred from a light doze by the buzzing of his doorbell. *"Momzer,"* he muttered; he had not meant to fall asleep in his recliner. He planned to meet Hoffman for dinner—an almost nightly ritual—at five-thirty. But who would be at the door now? Too early for Hoffman, too late for the mailman.

"Yes?" he barked into the intercom by the front door.

"Hello," came a silky voice, slightly distorted by static. "I have come to speak with you about the orchestra. I understand you are in need of a conductor. My name is John Hanger."

"The orchestra? Why have you come to me?"

"I spoke to a secretary at your office and she recommended I speak with you."

Kravitz chuckled. The symphony's only office was the den of cellist Luther Corcoran's house; the secretary would no doubt have been his wife. "Come up, third floor." He pressed the buzzer to admit his visitor through the front door.

After what seemed an inordinate amount of time, Kravitz heard a heavy creaking on the stairs outside his door. Never one to take chances, he peered curiously through the peephole and saw a familiar figure appear on the landing: the huge gentleman from the park bench yesterday. *Momzer* indeed. Shrugging off an inexplicable twinge of discomfort, he opened the door.

"Good afternoon," said John Hanger. The huge man held out a swollen hand, which Kravitz took hesitantly. He had expected a clammy grip, but the handshake was firm and dry.

"Come in," Kravitz said, motioning for the man to enter. John Hanger pulled off an overcoat the size of a parachute, which Kravitz took and hung on the coat rack behind the door. The big man looked to be in his early fifties, with very close-cropped, gray-flecked brown hair and wide—seemingly unblinking—blue eyes. "I recognize you from the park. I don't allow smoking in my apartment."

"That's quite all right, sir. Anyway, I'm led to understand you would be the gentleman to speak to about the position of conductor."

Kravitz motioned for Hanger to sit down on the couch. As the giant settled awkwardly into the plush upholstery, Kravitz sat back in his recliner. "I'm led to understand the same thing. It's my job by default, I suppose. I helped found the symphony many years ago and now they all see me as their grandfather. So what on earth brings you looking for a conducting job?"

"The playbills in the park for your upcoming performance caught my notice. And I couldn't help overhearing your conversation yesterday.

As sad as it is for someone you obviously care about to go missing, it's also apparent that canceling a performance you've worked so hard on would be an equally terrible tragedy."

"Quite, quite," Kravitz said with a nod. "I take it you have conducting experience?"

"Music is one of my passions, Mr. Kravitz. I have worked with many orchestras in my time, though I confess it has been many, many years. I used to be friends with Dimitri Mitropoulos. I'm sure you are familiar with his work with the New York Philharmonic. I also understand you are to be performing *Tapiola*, by Sibelius. A most fitting 'fantasy' piece for Halloween, I might say. But I once had the honor of meeting Sibelius himself on a visit to Finland, just before his death, in the late fifties."

Studying his guest with an appraising eye, Kravitz said, "You must have been quite young at the time!"

Hanger chuckled. "I am no doubt older than you might think. But my appreciation for music began at a very young age. You might also find it interesting that I made the acquaintance of the composer Ralph Vaughn-Williams, in England, quite a number of years ago. His ballet, *Job*, is one of my favorites—as is *Sinfonia Antarctica.*"

"You sound like a well-traveled man."

"I have spent time in almost every civilized nation on earth, and some not so civilized. I carry in here," he tapped his forehead, "the musical history of the entire world. As I said, music is my greatest passion. To be perfectly candid, I have been away from Chicago for a long time. To conduct an orchestra such as yours—and on Halloween, which I confess is a meaningful time to me—would be a great honor."

Kravitz groaned inwardly at the man's apparent reverence for the pagan "holiday."

"I assume that you are willing and able to provide some references?"

"I can provide you with a full list of credentials. However, it is my hope that you will merely allow me to audition for you. At the next rehearsal of your symphony, I would like to have the honor of conducting. And, after you have had the opportunity to evaluate my performance, should you have any reservations whatsoever, I will understand and withdraw my application."

Kravitz clicked his tongue. "Sounds fair enough. We are supposed to have a rehearsal tomorrow night at the Park East. Mind you, since Mr. Weintraub disappeared, no one has yet made the decision whether or not to continue on schedule. And, you must understand, there is always the possibility that there has merely been some unfortunate miscommunication, and our regular conductor will be available to perform."

"That would be fortunate indeed."

"Very well, Mr. Hanger," Kravitz said, almost surprised at himself. "I will contact the members of the symphony to let them know that tomorrow's rehearsal is on. And you may have your audition."

The huge man's face split into an almost revoltingly wide grin, the lips shining wetly in the afternoon sunlight. "Thank you ever so much, Mr. Kravitz. I assure you...you will not be disappointed!"

* * *

The very idea of such a huge man holding a baton and conducting nearly two-score musicians seemed almost absurd, but as John Hanger expertly drew the musical notes in the air with the simple tool, Jacob Kravitz marveled at the dexterity in those monstrous paws. The giant barely glanced at the sheets of music on the stand before him; most of the time he kept his eyes closed, as if reading the notes mentally. As Kravitz played the opening *détaché* notes of *Tapiola* on his ancient violin, which had been hand-made by his own grandfather, he could watch only Hanger's baton.

My God, this man was a better conductor than Weintraub could have ever dreamed of becoming!

Kravitz immediately felt a pang of regret at having thought derisively of his old friend. Yet his fellow musicians had instantly perceived the energy and passion the huge man positively radiated, and responded to him with unprecedented vigor. As the dark notes of the Sibelius tone poem rose in volume and intensity, punctuated by deep rolls of the kettle drum, Kravitz could see an infectious enthusiasm for the music glowing on the faces of the players.

The Park East was empty except for the orchestra and its new conductor. The stage belonged to them two nights a week until the performance—which was now less than two weeks away. Beyond the stage, the auditorium hid in darkness, and here in the island of light, Kravitz felt secure and in his own element. When the rows of plush chairs were filled (the Park East had the charm of a semiformal theater as opposed to a grand concert hall), he would hardly know the difference, for the stage lights created a comfortable dividing wall between the musicians and their audience.

Kravitz was able to give his fingers a few moments' respite as the woodwinds section, led by his capable friend Bert Hoffman, huffed and cavorted through the second passage of the Sibelius opus. Arthritis had begun working its painful effect on Kravitz's joints; as yet it had not affected his playing, but he could foresee the dreaded day when forming the notes on the fingerboard and even holding the bow could cause him considerable difficulty. But these grim thoughts were quickly dispelled by the zeal that the conductor spread through his charges. When Kravitz again lifted the bow and drew it across the strings, he was certain he had never heard such perfection emanating from his own instrument.

Hanger had already led them through a wonderful rendition of the third movement of Hovhaness's moody and mystical *Symphony of Light*—a piece that Kravitz could play blindfolded, since the orchestra played it every Halloween. The finale would be Movements 3, 4 and 5 of Vaughn-Williams *Sinfonia Antarctica*, a magnificent, if dark-toned tribute to the Scott expedition to the South Pole. Long and difficult, it would present Kravitz an opportunity to shine, for he had himself written the arrangement for the Chicago Cosmopolitan Symphony, adapting many of the traditional parts meant for brass and woodwinds to the strings, simply because the orchestra barely had enough of a horn section to do the piece justice. As *Tapiola* finally wound to its close, Hanger cast Kravitz a knowing look, as if to say, *I expect from you the very best you have ever delivered.*

And deliver he did. Following a brief break for refreshment, the orchestra began anew, and Kravitz's fingers moved as they had not since he was a young man in his prime. Accompanying the rich tones of the oboes, clarinets and French horns, Kravitz's string section played the most powerful, harmonious notes he had ever heard rushing forth from the instruments' chests.

And as the music built to a crescendo, Kravitz simply turned in his chair to the electronic organ set up just behind him. And with visions in his head of the icy wilderness of the southernmost continent—from McMurdo Sound, over Victoria Land, past the monumental peaks of Mt. Markham and Mt. Kirkpatrick, across the Beardsmore Glacier to the South Pole itself—he fingered the keyboard of the organ to fashion chords, produced electronically, whose resonance seemed to rival the pipe organs of Europe's most splendid cathedrals. He simply could not believe the music that he and his fellow players were producing with their own hands.

And when it was all done, Kravitz slumped in his chair, thoroughly and utterly exhausted, yet exhilarated to his soul. At the front of the stage, John Hanger merely laid his baton on the stand before him, bowed curtly to his orchestra—yes, *his*—and said in his soft, silky voice, "I thank you all so much. I hope to have the opportunity to perform with you again."

Without so much as another look toward Kravitz, Hanger lumbered off stage left, wiping his hands briefly on the pants of his well-pressed, obviously personally tailored suit. With a renewed burst of energy, Kravitz sprang from his seat and followed after him, catching him on the stairs that led into the darkness beyond the stage.

"Mr. Hanger," he called, his voice seeming little more than a whisper. The giant turned slowly around, his gaping blue eyes reflecting the stage lights like cold lanterns. His pursed mouth again spread into an unbelievably wide grin.

"I would like to shake you by the hand, Mr. Hanger." Kravitz extended his, and it was clasped firmly but gently by the other's great paw. "That was the finest performance I have ever attended, much less been a part of. Your skills are exceptional indeed. And I would like to offer you the part of conductor for our symphony."

"Why, Mr. Kravitz," Hanger beamed. "It would be my honor."

"Come to my house tomorrow afternoon and we can discuss whatever details may be necessary. You realize, of course, that we are amateurs, and we see very little, if any, financial remuneration."

"Of course, Mr. Kravitz. I was aware of this from the beginning. As you have probably realized, money is of little concern to me. I desire this opportunity strictly for personal satisfaction."

"Of course. Again, sir, you have my admiration for a wonderful, and need I say, successful audition."

John Hanger chuckled. "It did go well, didn't it. Until tomorrow, then, Mr. Kravitz." He once again clasped hands with Kravitz, and then, with surprising speed for one of such stature, disappeared into the darkness. A moment later, a rectangle of light appeared at the far end of the theatre, and the huge silhouette materialized there briefly as he exited. Then, the darkness was again complete.

As Kravitz stared after him, he clicked his tongue, thinking that tonight's rehearsal had indeed been an audition, not by John Hanger for the orchestra, but quite the other way around.

❋ ❋ ❋

The next two weeks passed uneventfully. If an investigation were being made into the disappearance of Stanislaus Weintraub, it was progressing either slowly or not at all. The orchestra rehearsed its two nights each week with John Hanger in confident command of the music and personnel. Indeed, for the first time in years, each session drew 100 percent attendance from the members. And finally, Halloween night arrived with Jacob Kravitz feeling exuberant and more confident than he could ever remember.

Yet, at the back of his mind, a strange, ambiguous cloud lingered, that he felt could somehow be traced to the very presence of John Hanger, the mysterious man who appeared only at rehearsals, never accompanying any of the more socially-active players who went to nosh afterwards. Hanger presented only the most dignified and courteous face to his new friends, as he insisted on calling the musicians; but those cold blue eyes gave Kravitz the idea that something possibly unwholesome lurked deep inside that massive skull.

"So, what *does* anyone know of this man's background, other than what he's told us?" he asked Bert Hoffman as they shared bagels and coffee in Kravitz's apartment on that afternoon of All Hallow's Eve. "He says Chicago is his home, and he's obviously traveled the world. Such an odd, solitary fellow. I'd say he's probably lonely, wouldn't you?"

"How the hell would I know?" muttered Hoffman. "You never asked him for any of his so-called credentials. It's a little late for that now, though, eh? Even *you* wouldn't be that rude."

"Of course not. I'm just curious, that's all."

Hoffman was thumbing through the pages of the *Chicago Tribune* and finally exclaimed, "Aha!" He handed the paper over to Kravitz with a smug little smile. Sandwiched between advertisements for a pair of local haunted houses—both of which lauded themselves as the world's largest—was a small display ad for the Chicago Cosmopolitan Orchestra's concert that evening. There had been a very brief notice about it in the Friday entertainment insert, proclaiming it as a landmark achievement for the amateur company. But that was about the extent of the advance publicity; advertising was an expensive proposition. Most of the orchestra's audience consisted of long-time aficionados and those who had heard word-of-mouth promotion by the company's friends, relatives, and the musicians themselves.

As Kravitz pushed the paper aside, his eye was drawn to a small headline that read, "Body of Missing Man Found on North Shore." A sudden cold chill swept over him as, for a moment, he thought he saw the name "Weintraub" amid the text. But upon scanning it further, he saw he was mistaken. The individual in question was named "Weinberg."

Almost morbidly curious, he began reading the article:

> A body, identified by police as Isaac P. Weinberg, was discovered Friday A.M. by a boater in Belmont Harbor. Weinberg, 64, of Skokie, had been reported missing almost four months ago by neighbors when he failed to respond to numerous attempts to contact him. According to a police spokesman, the body was found floating in the water in a badly decomposed condition, indicating it had been exposed to the elements for a period of days or possibly weeks.
>
> Friends of the victim maintain that Weinberg was somewhat reclusive, but a respectable gentleman with no known enemies. Investigators had been probing his disappearance, with few leads, since June.

There was more to the article, but Kravitz felt no compulsion to finish it. Certainly, in a city the size of Chicago, this kind of terrible thing must happen with uncomfortable frequency. But Belmont Harbor was not far away. Not far away at all.

"Bad story," Hoffman grumbled, seeing Kravitz's dismayed expression. "I'm sure *that* isn't what happened to Weintraub. He's out living his second childhood. That would be just like him, wouldn't it?"

"Yeah, sure," Kravitz said half-heartedly. "He's always had a childish streak in him."

"Worse than yours, even."

"I have only sophisticated streaks."

"Pah!"

"Paaah!"

The two ate their bagels and sipped coffee in silence for a time, and finally Kravitz noticed that it was going on four o' clock. The concert started at eight, and the musicians were to be at the Park East by six-thirty to set-up and make a final run-through of a few difficult passages. Never one to procrastinate, Kravitz began making overtures to rid himself of his guest.

"Look at the hour. Off with you. You're already running short of time to dress yourself."

"I can be ready in ten minutes."

"Nonsense. You're worse than an old woman. Go, already. Go. Go."

"All right, I'll go. You obviously need that much time for yourself. I should hate to be responsible for you coming to the concert looking like something the cat threw up."

"You're still here."

"You've lost your mind, old man. I'm long gone."

"See you tonight."

"Till then."

"Happy Halloween."

"Get out!"

⁂

The tuxedo felt stiff and constricting, yet once he began playing he was able to lose himself in the music; even the heavy, uncomfortable jacket could not hamper his performance. The complex but eerily melodious notes of the Hohvanness symphony flowed from his violin as if by magic, with scarcely any effort on his part. His instrument, which had been played first by his grandfather, then his father before him, had become a mere amplifier, the physical device for producing the music in his soul.

At the forefront stood John Hanger, a behemoth in tux and tails, the sheer formality of his attire somehow ascribing dignity to his ungainly, massive form. As in rehearsal, he stood with eyes closed, his hands in constant, refined motion, his baton directing the musicians with precision and passion. Beyond, in the great field of darkness, Kravitz could sense the presence of the audience, unseen but for an occasional stirring of black within black: a non-threatening entity as long as the stage lights maintained the wall of separation.

The audience had been unbelievable, in the words of his friend Hoffman. "The house is almost full," he'd said just before the curtain opened. "We've never played before such a crowd!"

Indeed, as the strings wove their magical spell into the darkness, Kravitz could feel all those pairs of eyes watching him and his companions with a greater intensity than usual. But rather than intimidating him, those presences combined with Hanger's own, drawing out yet more feeling from his violin strings. When the Hovhaness movement drew to its close, the applause that rang from the darkness overwhelmed him. He had never heard such a clamor from an audience!

The Sibelius opus began to a hushed crowd, and as in rehearsal, the notes flowed from Kravitz's bow and strings with a kind of disembodied life. The knowledge that there were now other souls being touched by its dark, haunting beauty brought an almost physical pleasure, the music caressing him and loving him, responding ardently to the touch of his bow. He occasionally added a flourish by plucking the strings *pizzicato,* creating a whole new texture to the sound.

Hanger had called the music appropriate for the holiday; but then, that was precisely why it had been selected for the event. Out there—in the audience—the listeners were awestruck. Perhaps there *was* a spirit in the season that complemented this music unlike any other, Kravitz thought. Any conscious resistance to that idea had by now melted away.

And finally came the huge, majestic Vaughn-Williams symphony. A crackling energy charged the concert hall, like the moments before a lightning strike. Kravitz could not recall ever experiencing anything similar during a performance; furthermore, he could read the same feeling in the faces of all the players around him. Next to him, the youthful but typically impassive face of Bryan Jennings beamed with uncustomary excitement, proving to Kravitz that this was indeed a phenomenon, catalyzed by the mesmerizing power of the giant at the front of the stage.

Now and again, John Hanger's eyes would open and focus on Kravitz's own, as if to convey some secret to him; that all of this, somehow, was meant for Jacob Kravitz and no other. *Ridiculous,* he thought, trying to dismiss such an egotistical notion. But as he played on, automatically now, Kravitz concentrated only on the movements of the conductor, watching his every gesture and glance.

John Hanger never once opened his eyes except to cast him that same look of confidence, as if he, at first violin, were the only player in the entire orchestra worth a moment of the maestro's notice.

As the crescendo rose, and Kravitz turned to play the organ keys that would send thunder through the hall, reflecting the splendor of the great ice peaks of the Antarctic wilderness, Hanger's eyes burned at him. And suddenly, all the magic of the moment dissolved into tremors of apprehension; a sense of underlying wrongness, a reinforcement of his first impression that, somewhere behind Hanger's cold blue eyes, an unknowable darkness lurked.

And then it was over. The music ended, and the unseemly feeling dissolved into dreamlike, hazy memory. The audience rose and the conductor bowed, and applause shook the walls of the auditorium until Kravitz thought his eardrums could take no more. The house lights came up and he could see them: all those bodies, all those hands beating together in a frenzied chorus of unconditional gratitude—surely out of proportion to the reality of the performance itself!

Now, his only remaining fear was that of being exposed to the audience; that peculiar sensation of stage fright that tortured him, yet lured him time and again to play to those who would come to witness.

Then, John Hanger was holding out his hand to him, beckoning him to take a bow. *But why?* He was just a violinist, an accomplished, yet undistinguished component of the orchestra as a whole. But next to him, young Bryan Jennings was clapping and smiling at him, and over in the brass section, Bert Hoffman's face positively glowed, his hands adding measurably to the thunderous applause. What had he done? He had only played the violin, as it was meant to be played. Nothing extraordinary there.

Yet the audience would not release him from his obligation. Finally, he bowed low, never understanding why, only realizing that this formality was required of him, and the hundreds of eyes in the hall would never release him until he had satisfied their expectations. He knew he should be pleased. Honored. Flattered. Yet he felt only bewilderment.

Finally it was over. The curtain closed, the lights dimmed, and the orchestra was sequestered behind its shield of heavy fabric.

"Jacob!" cried Bert Hoffman, rushing up to him. "I've never heard such magic coming from those strings before! What a show! What hands! You have surpassed yourself!"

"I...I just played," he managed, smiling broadly in spite of himself. "The entire orchestra was brilliant. No one can be singled out."

"Perhaps," Hoffman said. "Except for him." He pointed to the giant who still stood at the front of the stage with his head lowered, apparently gathering his breath.

Around them, the musicians had begun packing their instruments amid rounds of congratulations to one another. Kravitz placed his own violin carefully into its battered but sturdy case and shook hands with his friend. "I will meet you later," he said. "I must have a word with our illustrious conductor."

"Very well. We will *tsimis* tomorrow, no?"

"Sure, sure." Kravitz picked up his case and approached John Hanger rather tentatively, almost afraid of disturbing the great man in his reverie. But he finally cleared his throat and the cold blue eyes opened. The huge face split into one of those impossible grins.

"Mr. Kravitz," purred the silky voice. "You were magnificent. Magnificent! It is hard to believe you are playing with a group of local amateurs. Did you miss your calling by never joining a professional, touring symphony?"

"You're too kind," he replied softly. "But I have never seen anyone conduct with such intensity, such style. And you seem to have made a special effort to encourage me. *Only* me. Why would this be?"

"I merely wished to convey my appreciation, Mr. Kravitz. No one else here has exhibited such finesse, or such devotion to the music. You truly do love the strings."

"I can't deny that."

"Mr. Kravitz, I would be honored if you would come to my home to share a toast with me. I have wine, brandy...whatever you prefer."

"That's kind of you. I have never even inquired—do you live nearby? I don't have a car."

"I live very near here. An easy walk, and the night air will do us both good." He withdrew a handkerchief from his tuxedo jacket and wiped his brow—the most mundane of gestures, which, to Kravitz, seemed an almost reassuring affirmation of the giant's humanity. "The air seems very close here. I hope I didn't overexert myself."

"All these bodies generated some heat. I have never seen it so packed. You yourself made quite the impression on the audience, I'm sure."

Hanger nodded, a mere shade beneath arrogance. "I am always compelled to give my best. Now, will you accept my offer of a drink? I confess.... I would appreciate the company."

Kravitz remembered his own assertion that Hanger must be a lonely man. No doubt he wished to share his success with someone. Who more natural than the one who had made the greatest contribution—at least in his own mind? "All right," he said with a little smile. "It would be my pleasure."

"One moment, and we shall be off."

Kravitz gave him a little bow and waited while the big man lumbered away, most likely to freshen himself. This was the opportunity, he thought; he could freely ask some questions about John Hanger's background without seeming to pry. He would merely be showing friendly curiosity about a professional colleague with whom he might be working on a regular basis.

A few moments later, Hanger returned and beckoned Kravitz to accompany him. As they left via the rear stage door, he noticed the big man's unblinking, blue eyes. They seemed alight with anticipation, and Kravitz once again felt a little twinge of uneasiness about this leviathan of a man. He could hardly change his mind now without appearing hopelessly ill-mannered. Besides, others in the orchestra knew who he was with. Surely, this uneasiness was as foolish as his stage fright.

He heard a few childish giggles somewhere nearby. Looking toward the sidewalk on Lincoln, he saw several youngsters dressed as devils, ghosts, and witches, all carrying bags of their evening's treats, laughing and making their way up the street.

It was after ten o'clock. Wasn't it too late to be out trick-or-treating?

Swallowing hard, he clicked his tongue, tucking his vague suspicions into the dark corners of his mind, telling himself that, after such a promising show as tonight, John Hanger's foremost consideration would be making sure his prized violinist would be around for many more performances to come.

* * *

The first thing Kravitz saw as he entered the almost absurdly tiny basement apartment was a small Star of David etched above the door frame. The flat was merely an efficiency with a single bed (hardly large enough for such a man, he thought), a kitchenette littered by a few clean but haphazardly stacked dishes, a large reclining chair and a cloth-covered dining table. Tall bookshelves—filled to overflowing—made up one wall; the one window facing the street was barred and dingy, covered by a yellowing diaphanous drape. There was no television or stereo or any other modern electronic equipment that he might have expected from an audiophile.

The whole place seemed quite out of character for the man. Given the giant's cultured manner and expensive dress, Kravitz would have expected little less than opulence.

Hanger politely took Kravitz's coat and hung it from a peg on the wall next to the front door. "Would you care for a glass of wine? Or would you prefer a brandy?"

"A brandy, I think," Kravitz replied uncomfortably. The big man took a decanter from a shelf next to the refrigerator and poured a polite portion into two large snifters. "Are you Jewish, Mr. Hanger?" he asked at last.

"No, I am not a Jew, Mr. Kravitz. However, I have what you might call a certain history with the Children of Israel." Kravitz almost started at the epithet. "I have a unique appreciation for the antiquity of the culture, for the civilization whence the modern Jewish community sprang. You are not Orthodox, I take it."

Kravitz chuckled. "No, I fear I have not been so faithful over the course of my adult life. I suppose I have regrets in this regard. But then, who doesn't?"

"You came from the old country originally?"

"I was born in Milwaukee. To some, that is the old country."

Hanger laughed and sipped his brandy. Kravitz took a swallow of his own. It was sweet and delicious, the burn in his throat quick and numbing. The giant then struck a match, and Kravitz feared he was going to light one of his filthy cigarettes. But instead, Hanger turned to a small table next to his recliner and lit a short black candle that gave off the scent of cinnamon and honeysuckle.

"I suspect, Mr. Kravitz, that you are bewildered by my living quarters. I am sure you must have had different expectations."

Somewhat taken aback, Kravitz could only nod. "Well, I am not one to judge."

"No, of course not." Hanger drained his snifter and poured another. Without asking, he took Kravitz's and refilled it as well. "This is merely one of many places I use for shelter. I move about as my needs change. I shall no doubt be seeking a new abode in the near future."

"Your travels," Kravitz said with a weak nod. He had begun to feel lightheaded—moreso than he would have expected from a single snifter of brandy. "But surely, you plan to perform with the orchestra again, don't you?"

"There will be more performances."

At the distant reaches of his perception, Kravitz heard a dull roar building, like a train approaching through a long tunnel. He slid into one of the chairs at the dining table. "I'm sorry, Mr. Hanger. Suddenly I feel a bit discombobulated."

"Yes."

The cold blue eyes were now glaring at him, curiously, appraisingly. The whole room seemed to blur, with only the huge silhouette remaining in partial focus. "What...what's going on?"

"You are soon to have your shining moment, Mr. Kravitz. The performance of a lifetime. The performance that will be your legacy. *Jew.*"

A horrible chill passed down Kravitz's spine. But his limbs had frozen, and the thunder in his head increased with every beat of his heart. "Hanger...you have poisoned me!"

From the cavernous chest rose something between a laugh and a growl. "Poison? Oh, no, Mr. Kravitz. Merely an anesthetic to facilitate your conveyance to your new stage. In a few moments, you will feel nothing. Rest easy, my friend. The drug itself is quite harmless."

Kravitz's lungs struggled for air; the room began to spin and the roaring now drowned all other sound. As he tried to stop the mad reeling, he gazed at the tiny frame bed in the corner. It was too small for such a giant, and it was not bowed in the middle, as it should have been had John Hanger ever so much as lain there. Surely, that bed had never been used—not by this man.

He tried to speak Hanger's name, but nothing escaped his lips, not even a whisper. He saw blazing, golden eyes, and grotesque, pursed lips spreading into a grin that split the huge face from cheek to cheek, exposing a row of teeth that ended in razor sharp points.

A living, blazing jack-o'-lantern face moving steadily closer to his own....

The last thing he remembered was the smooth, silky voice of the maestro breaking through the thunder and whispering in his ear, *"Shalom."*

❋ ❋ ❋

Jacob Kravitz slipped back into consciousness to the sound of muted, almost melodious moaning coming from somewhere nearby. His eyes fluttered open, but darkness replaced darkness, and he could feel only frigid air around him. As his nerves began to reactivate, he realized he was lying on his back on some cold, rough surface—*stone,* he thought. And the first moan he'd heard was joined by another, then another. Low, masculine voices, weary and full of pain, those uttering them quite unseen and possibly as incognizant of their surroundings as he.

His throat felt dry and raw, but after gathering a lungful of air, he finally managed to utter, "Hello? Where am I?"

A moment later a weak voice replied, "Who is that?"

"Tell me where I am," he groaned.

"I don't know," came the low whisper. "Who are you?"

"I am Jacob Kravitz."

"Kravitz! My God, my God, it's me. Weintraub."

"Weintraub!" He could feel his energy beginning to return little by little. He tried to move his arms but found them pinioned by something cold and unyielding. *Steel.* "Stan, what is this place?"

A familiar, chilling, silky voice now rose out of the darkness. "My friends," it purred. "The Children of Israel. Welcome to your new stage."

"Hanger!"

"An adopted name, but feel free to use it. I have known many names. But the soul has only one name, and mine, both soul and name, have been preserved for eternities that you could not imagine. There are many of you here now...all collected by my own hand. Tonight, you shall make a joyful noise, as decreed by the very word of the Lord, your God. Tonight, on the very night that glorifies those who were once proclaimed false. This night, now so ironically termed 'hallowed.'" A low chuckle wafted through the darkness. "It *shall* be a hallowed evening."

"What kind of madness is this?" whispered Kravitz.

A pair of cold blue eyes appeared in the darkness, disembodied, gleaming. "The madness of so many centuries, Mr. Kravitz. I was a King in Moab, until my rightful place was usurped by the Children of Israel. And I was persecuted for the worship of false gods, and driven out of my homeland. And when I sought to reclaim what was mine, I enlisted the services of the sorcerer, Balaam, only to be betrayed when he himself became a servant of Israel's arrogant Father. And seeing this, my friends, those who *I* worship granted me the means to avenge myself upon our mutual enemy—through those such as yourself."

"Balak," hissed Kravitz. "You refer to the story of Balak."

"For an unorthodox man, you know your scripture, Jacob Kravitz. The name of this soul is indeed Balak...Jew. And this soul has passed through the ages, in many guises, allying itself to those who would smite Israel's children, and their Father Jehovah. Soon, my friends, you will learn the truth of that which was once called false."

From somewhere far away, the faintest flickering gleam, possibly from torches or candles, illuminated the walls of whatever chamber enclosed them, walls of rough-hewn stone that rose into pure darkness far above. They could only be underground, Kravitz thought—but *where? How?* Bound on a slab next to him, he saw the withered, naked form of his friend Weintraub, his head rolling slowly back and forth. Beyond the old conductor, he could see the pale shapes of countless other bodies, splayed on stones just as he was.

Before he could speak, a deep vibration passed through the slab beneath him, then another. A heavy booming...like great footsteps shuddering through the earth, reverberating through the chamber. And in his field of vision, far above, something began to take form; a tall, spindly shape, something inhuman but walking, with cold eyes of blue like those of John Hanger...but so much larger, burning icily high above.

More heavy vibrations followed, and a sulfurous, fetid odor washed over Kravitz as more of the half-seen silhouettes appeared in the darkness around him. The low voice of John Hanger now chanted, "Ia, ia, gh'nagh ngai agkha nyem r'lyea...*selah!*"

As the terrible stench swirled through the air, infiltrating Kravitz's lungs, he heard Hanger say, "The breath of the Old Ones shall keep you alive and aware for countless days, much in the way it has preserved my own life. Our respective fates, however, shall be very different. In the days of Moab, there were special punishments meted out by the Children of Israel to worshippers of false gods. Now, in keeping with your faith, the *true* Gods shall mete out that same punishment to you."

In the flickering light, Kravitz saw John Hanger's huge silhouette appear above him, standing on a raised dais. The great arms rose as if to conduct, and a moment later Kravitz heard a familiar voice cry out nearby; Stan Weintraub. He turned his head to see a vague shadow swirl down from above and encircle his old friend's arms like the legs of a monstrous spider. A burst of flame erupted in the air above Weintraub's prone figure, and suddenly he loosed a scream of raw and pure agony. A long gash had opened in his chest, and a thick stream of hot sparks fell from the fireball into the bloody wound. The spidery shadows quickly encircled the mutilated torso, closing the gash. The stench of charred flesh soon mixed with the sulfurous odor of demon's breath.

"The Children of Israel sewed burning coals into deep cuts in the bodies of my people, as punishment for their faith. And so it shall be for all of you—for time immeasurable. Now, my friends... let the orchestra play." The blue eyes of John Hanger—Balak—gazed deeply into Kravitz's. "*This,* my friend," he said softly, "is truly to be your finest performance."

As a fireball suddenly burst into life above Kravitz's head, he saw a spidery shadow forming around it, slowly lowering itself toward him. He saw the maestro lift his arms and draw the first musical note in the air as, all through the darkness, the chorus of agonized screams began.

Jacob Kravitz's voice soon rose above the rest, in a virtuoso solo, while the cold blue eyes of the Moabite Gods gazed rapturously at him from high above. For the first time in all his years of performing, his fears of failing in front of his audience were quickly, wholly forgotten.

Halloween Companion Piece

David B. Silva

Halloween was still Halloween when I was a kid. Your mother helped you make your costume, which was usually something along the lines of a cowboy or a hobo or maybe a ghost, and homemade baked goods were just as likely to end up in your sack as candy bars. There were no X-Ray machines checking for pins or needles back then. You knew your neighbors. You went out trick-or-treating with a few friends. And your parents never gave a thought to the possibility that you might not come back safe and sound.

I was eight this particular Halloween, and I had spent all eight years of my life in the same neighborhood. The streets were narrow and uneven. There were no sidewalks. No streetlights. Trees overshadowed nearly every square inch of the three-block area. The houses were small and individually distinctive, often set back from the road in such a manner that you couldn't be sure of the exact layout.

I was with my sister, who was a year younger than me, and two friends who were my age. We had covered the usual territory in record time, and for the first time in my Halloween experience, we decided to break the rules and see what we could gather from the next block over.

Right around the corner sat an old colonial-style house. White. Huge pillars. An overrun front yard. Vines coursing the walls. Paint peeling. All of it illuminated by nothing more than a few porch lights from the houses across the street. An eight-year-old's perfect idea of a haunted house.

There was one other thing of note. Sitting on the concrete porch just outside the front door was a huge bowl of candy.

These people had gone out for the evening and they had left a bowl of candy behind, nearly hidden in the shadows, trusting that the first kid brave enough to cross the barren front yard in the dark to reach the bowl would be honorable enough not to empty all the candy in a single shot. We each did our best to cajole and shame the others into going for it, but none of us wanted to try it alone. Finally, we agreed to brave it together. Courage comes easier when you're part of a crowd. That was the first lesson I learned that day. The other lesson, which was the more important of the two, was that sometimes rules are rules for a reason. We had no business wandering around an area we were unfamiliar with.

Crossing the yard turned out to be far less frightening than we had made it out to be. Emptying the bowl of candy, however, was a different story. This was a long time ago in my life, so I have to confess that I'm not sure how much of it is what really happened and how much belongs to an eight-year-old's imagination. Either way, I was the one who ended up being elected to do the actual candy-snatching.

The bowl sat on a small table on the porch, next to the front door of the house, under a narrow, slatted window. I stepped up on the concrete landing, looking back to my friends for encouragement, then staring down at the bowl of candy. It wasn't the best stuff, as I remember it—a lot of hard candies, with some Pez mixed in—but the bowl was brimming. I reached out and grabbed a handful that couldn't have held another piece if my life depended on it, started to drop it all into my bag, and....

The window slats flipped open.

They made a glass-against-glass rattling sound that in my mind could have just as easily been the rattling of bones.

I froze. Then a hand reached out from between two slats. It wasn't a human hand, at least what I remember of it wasn't human. It was dark and scaly, with thick, long nails that had been filed to a point. The hand flailed in the air as if it were blindly trying to find me.

I let out a scream that finally got my feet moving.

I'm not sure any of the others ever saw the hand, but they ran right alongside me, back around the corner, back into familiar territory, where we finally felt safe enough to stop and catch our breaths again.

To this day, I don't know if someone was just playing a Halloween prank or if I imagined something that was never there. I do know that I never went back to that house again, and I wouldn't go back there today if you paid me.

EYES

Charles L. Grant

The leaves were gone when the wind returned past sunset, and there was nothing left to do but help the empty branches claw at the sky. An unlatched gate fought its brown-rusted hinges. An empty silver trash can toppled off the curb, its lid clattering pinwheel until it struck the rear bumper of a small truck at the corner. A shutter banged open, slammed shut, and froze. Curtains trembled. Shadows walked. Streetlamps grew brittle, hazed white light without a promise of warmth. The only traffic signal in town swayed like a hanged man, tugging at its guy wires until it flared just red.

And the leaves on the ground, here raked into piles and there untouched and turning brown, hunched and spun madly into man-high dervishes that slammed against hedges, exploded against porches, crested off sidewalks into the windshields of passing cars. They hissed and crackled, their edges age-sharp and stinging, and when they swept past lighted windows they were hunting bats enraged.

Ron turned his back against the leaf-woven wind and waited for the gust to pass him by. The collar of his black trench coat was snapped up in back and folded out in front, the gold-buckled belt cinched tight around his waist. All he needed, he thought, was the hat Bogart wore, and someone would surely ask him how to get to Casablanca. As it was, the length of his brown hair tangled around his ears, poked needles at his eyes, and there was no sense brushing it back because the wind was still there.

He didn't mind it. Standing out here, in the cold, in the dark, made him feel as if he were stalking a killer, or a spy, or a warlock determined to conquer the world with mad spells. It certainly made for better copy than saying he was just waiting for his son. He grinned to himself. He walked a few paces to the corner and leaned back against the rear fender of a red pickup. In the gutter was the dented metal lid of a trash can, and he almost picked it up before he shrugged and changed his mind.

A gust made him squint, a cat's scream made him jump.

C'mon, Paulie, he urged, it's getting cold out here.

The houses that surrounded him were well lighted and old, comforting in their size and the people who lived there. And it was curious, he thought, how tomorrow they would be transformed into birthplaces of goblins. Of witches. Of burnt-cork hobos out foraging for a candy meal. Even now, as he looked around, he could see the holiday trimmings: stalks of maze taped to storm doors, cardboard cutouts of ghosts on the windows, a basket of polished apples, black cats hissing.

And the eyes.

As he pushed away from the truck and paced up the street, he could see the eyes watching. Orange eyes, flickering eyes, winking in the wind. Jack-o'-lanterns balanced on porch railings and perched on front stoops, hiding from the cold in the split of a curtain, staring out from a child's bedroom on the second floor, behind the trees. He didn't mind the black cats and the hags and the monsters; he didn't mind the trick-or-treating or the UNICEF brigades; and he didn't even mind the cold jagged grins the pumpkins gave him as he passed. Knowing grins. Dead grins. He didn't mind them much at all.

The eyes, on the other hand, gave him the creeps.

They were up there looking out, looking down, and they saw him.

Paulie knew.

Two years ago Ron was holding his son's hand, and they walked through an Indian summer night to fill the paper bag with candy. They passed several of the boy's schoolmates, all of them greeting him with muffled laughter, with jeers behind his back. Paulie didn't care as long as his father held his hand. And Ron didn't care as long as Paulie knew that some people were cruel when faced with something different, something they were too young, or too insecure, or too stupid, to understand.

It happened every year, each Halloween since Paulie had been old enough to get into his costume and walk with him door to door.

But five years ago, when Paulie was nearing ten, a group of teenagers laughing their way from one house to another began following them, making rude comments until Ron could take no more. He'd turned and faced them, his hands in fists, out where the kids could see them.

"Very brave," he'd said, and the laughter faded as the teenagers huddled, one girl carefully studying the sky. "Very brave."

"Ah, c'mon, Mr. Ritter, we were only kidding."

"No," he'd said, "don't tell me, tell my son."

Paulie had tugged at his hand, wanting to leave, clearly afraid.

"No, you tell my son you think he's funny. Go ahead, tell him to his face."

They muttered, shuffled feet, finally turned and walked away. None of them looked back, and Ron filled his lungs with the warm night air.

"Daddy?"

"It's okay, pal, it's okay."

At the corner a boy suddenly whipped around and lifted his middle finger, and Ron reacted before his mind caught up—he broke into a sprint, dropping the paper bag on the sidewalk as the sprint became a charge. The boy gaped, and turned too late. Ron grabbed his shoulders and shoved him hard into a hedge, grabbed his denim jacket in one hand, pulled him close and smiled.

The eyes widened in fear.

Ron slammed a fist into his stomach and shoved him back again. When the boy doubled over, Ron put a knee to his chin and stepped back to avoid the blood from the split lip and the slashed gums. Then he glared at the rest of them, some ready to run, two ready to fight.

"Go ahead," he invited, still smiling. "Go ahead. And when you're done with me you can beat up on the retard."

One of them, a girl, caught a gasp behind a palm.

"Hey," Ron said, "that's what you're thinking, right? The kid's a retard. He looks funny, walks funny, maybe dribbles a little when he tries to talk. A clown, right? No problem. He can't hurt you."

"Mister, that's not fair."

He nodded. "You're right, little girl. It isn't fair at all, but you don't have the slightest idea what I'm talking about. Not the slightest idea in hell." Then he'd spun around and hooked the fallen boy by the collar, yanked him to his feet, and virtually thrown him at his friends. "Clean him up," he ordered in disgust. "Clean the bastard up; he's a disgrace to this town."

As he returned to his son, poor Paulie standing all alone in the middle of the sidewalk, holding the paper bag his father had dropped, his Batman cape limp, his store-bought costume not quite fitting, Ron began to cry. He was glad he'd hit the kid; for years he'd wanted to do something like that and every time the urge took shape every convention in the book had stopped him, had held him; he'd long since stopped telling Irma because she thought it was childish. Hell, maybe it was, but it sure felt great. In the morning he'd probably get a call from the police, and his wife would shake her head sadly and wonder why he didn't stop and *think*. But he felt good, and there was no way at all he could explain that to Irma.

"Wrong, Daddy," the boy had said then, surprising Ron to a halt. He looked down at the blue eyes, innocent, almost blank, and saw the disappointment. "Wrong, Daddy, wrong."

Over and over for the rest of the night until he'd finally lost his temper and dragged the boy home, refusing him any of his candy until the next day. But it was less at his son than at himself that his anger had flared—by hitting that punk he had contradicted everything he'd tried to teach Paulie from the time he could understand.

The following year he bought the pumpkin.

A dog chained in a backyard began howling and barking. Leaves caught in a storm drain stirred and rustled under the wind. A large dead beetle lay in the middle of the sidewalk, and his heel crunched the hard shell before he could avoid it. The temperature dropped, and his breath began to fog. The gutters were black with shadows. A woman laughed. The stars waited. The slow-dying grass began to grey with early frost.

And the eyes.

The houses went dark, but the candles were still burning, and the eyes brightened and dimmed and watched him pass through the black, dressed in black, avoiding their looks from over there on the rocker, and over there on the mat, and over there on the brick house at the corner where they gathered on the roof like the angry souls of waiting cats.

He shuddered, and watched his feet stepping over the cracks and around shadow-puddles that weren't puddles at all. An empty pack of cigarettes was kicked to one side. A bottle cap squashed flat looked too much like a penny. He adjusted his collar more snugly around his neck and slipped his hands into his pockets, pursing his lips to try a silent whistle, failing, and grinning self-consciously as if someone had seen him.

The street rose slightly and the houses began to drift apart, longer stretches between yards, higher screens of dark shrubs. By the time he reached the top he was beginning to breathe heavily, and scolded himself for smoking too much when he knew what was coming, when he knew he'd need the wind. Another grin, this one mocking—wind, stamina, strong legs, what the hell. Paulie wouldn't care.

The trouble had been the pumpkin.

He'd come home that year with the great thing in his arms, his cheeks puffed with exertion as he staggered into the kitchen and thumped it on the table. Irma was settled in the front room, knitting, scowling, telling him with her eyes that the boy didn't know what was going on and she thought he was being silly, perhaps even cruel. But Paulie had danced, a clumsy shuffle on the tiled floor that made Ron smile a little sadly. Then he spread out the newspapers, brought out the knife and ladle, and with a running commentary spiked with bad jokes, he hollowed out the pumpkin. He tried not to seem nervous, but this was the first time he'd ever done it and he wanted Paulie to believe his father knew it all.

Paulie sat in his chair, chin in his hands, eyes on the knife and the ladle and the seeds on the paper. A faint line of saliva glinted on his chin. He was pale.

With a felt-tip pen Ron drew the gap-toothed mouth, the triangle nose, and with his tongue between his lips, tried to make the eyes straight. He knew they had to be triangular as well, but somehow they wouldn't work, and when he felt his patience going he shrugged to Paulie and decided to start in by carving the mouth first.

Paulie wanted to help.

Ron denied him gently.

Paulie pouted and frowned, shaking the table to unsteady his hand.

At the nose, the knife slipped and cut Ron slightly on the thumb. Paulie's eyes widened in fascination and fright, but his father didn't yell, didn't shout. He gnawed his lower lip and took up the knife again. A smile to show that everything was fine, don't worry, I'll live, and he carved the first eye—slowly, grunting to himself, finally shoving the thick piece free into the pumpkin. A grin of satisfaction, and the second one was done.

"Try, Daddy?"

He shook his head. "Son, you know better. This knife is too sharp. Besides, I'm already finished."

"Try!"

"Paulie, no. A pumpkin's like a person, it has only two eyes."

Paulie scowled, then lunged across the table to snatch the knife away and began stabbing at the pumpkin's finished face. Ron grabbed his wrist and squeezed until the boy whimpered, squeezed until the knife clattered to the floor.

The pumpkin fell from the table, hit its side, and shattered.

"Try," Paulie sobbed, wiping his face with the backs of his hands.

"Two eyes, you stupid brat! You only get two goddamned eyes!"

"Wrong, Daddy."

He felt like crying himself, suddenly threw his arms around the boy and hugged him, rocked him, told him he was sorry but there were things going on, in the house and at work, that'd he'd never understand. He didn't mean to take it out on the one person who couldn't fight back.

"Wrong, Daddy, wrong."

Then Paulie had plunged his hands into the wreckage and pulled out the triangle wedges poked from the eyes. He stood and held them to his face, grinned, and marched away. Ron lunged for him, and succeeded only in giving him a slight shove through the doorway. Blinded by the pumpkin shards, Paulie tripped over the loose edge of the rug and struck his head on the dining room table. There wasn't much blood. There didn't have to be blood.

The corner had gone straight into his eye.

Just beyond the top of the street rise, the church reached out of the dark ground, a black silhouette cut from the sky in spite of the moon. It was small, steepled, set back from the sidewalk behind a low picket fence. There was no parking lot; parishioners used the streets and walked up the flagstone path to the dark oak double doors. On either side, maple and elm looked as high as the belfry; in the back was the graveyard.

Ron stopped at the far corner of the fence and looked around, checking for cars, checking for snoops. All he saw, however, at the bottom of the rise were yellow flecks blinking furiously as the wind moved the branches, the yellow eyes watching him though they faced the other way. He was alone. He stared past the church to the fieldstone wall, the chained iron gate, the headstones and mausoleums and spread-winged angels that marked the homes of the dead. He couldn't see Paulie's grave from here, but that didn't matter. He visited it once a month, could find it blind if he had to, and he apologized to his son for not giving him longer life, for not having the money for the doctors who might have saved him.

The blunt wedge of pumpkin had been driven almost to his brain.

Well, tomorrow's the big day, he said heartily, silently, rolling his shoulders to drive off the cold. He hoped that Paulie couldn't sense his resignation; what would you like to be this year, son? Space things are pretty big, robots and spacemen and stuff like that.

Orange eyes.

No clouds this year, just lots and lots of stars. I don't think it'll rain like it did last time. Of course, the leaves have all fallen, but you can't have everything, right, Paulie? Right?

Orange eyes in the graveyard.

Maybe good old Batman again, what do you say? I still have all the things in your bedroom. I could iron the cape a little, wash the rest of it and throw it in the dryer before I go to bed, and since you'd have to wear a sweater, it's so cold, you'd look like you had more muscles than anybody in town.

Orange eyes, moving.

Well, you let me know, okay, son? Let me know. I'll be waiting.

His cheeks puffed, and he blew white into the black, sniffed once, and turned back down the hill. The town below was silent. The wind had died. The moon was gone behind a cloud that drove back the stars.

His heels were loud now on the pavement, and the brush of his trench coat against his legs annoyed him. He was cold; he'd done his duty, and he was cold. He'd gone to his son as he promised he would when the boy lay dying in his arms, and he had told him what it would be like on Halloween this year. Four years in a row, and he wondered how long he'd have to keep this up before his nightmares left him.

Paulie writhing and screaming on the dining room floor, his hands clamped against his eye, and the slow red trickle of blood between his fingers. Paulie gulping for air as the ambulance took him. Paulie trying to speak as he was wheeled into surgery.

Paulie dying. Paulie dead.

Irma had left him two weeks later, sobbing that she wanted no part of a man who had killed his child.

He reached the first house and paused to wipe a hand across his brow. He closed his eyes for a moment, then looked back over his shoulder.

Orange eyes, moving.

There was a pumpkin in the middle of the sidewalk.

There was a pumpkin squatting in the middle of the road.

All right, Paulie, he thought, stop fooling around.

He moved more quickly, the incline giving him speed and making him colder as the night parted and let him through, let him pass by the eyes in the windows, on the porches, on the roofs, by the eyes glittering and flickering and winking on the lawns, and in the street, and on the pavement behind him.

No shadows; no shadows at all.

I didn't mean it, Paulie, he thought; I was just kidding.

His house had no porch, only a concrete stoop. The pumpkin he kept there had never had a candle, never had a flashlight. The way kids were these days, he knew he'd be lucky if it lasted through the holiday before somebody smashed it. He opened the door and looked behind him. At the eyes. In the yard.

Paulie, damn it!

He closed the door and leaned against it, unbuckling the belt and pulling off his coat. It fell, and he didn't touch it. He stumbled wearily down the hall and into the kitchen, sat at the table and stared at the kettle on the stove. A pumpkin seed lay on the floor by his shoe. He nudged it aside, then cracked his knuckles, rubbed his face, and took a deep breath until he thought he was calm.

Then he focused on the newspaper spread open before him and suddenly decided he'd go to a movie.

He smiled.

A movie. God, it had been months since he'd been in an honest-to-god theater, had popcorn and soda, and stayed for the second show; years since he'd done anything he hadn't done with Paulie. It might be a good thing; hell, it would be a damned good thing. Of course he would still visit the grave and still go though the ritual, but there was no sense sacrificing the rest of his life by living in the past. No sense at all. So a movie it would be. He reached for the paper, soggy and stained orange, and turned the pages gingerly until he found what he wanted. His finger slipped down the column to check the times and the titles, his lips moving as he read, and the lights went out.

The kitchen was dark.

Except for the eyes.

The eyes in the window, and the eyes in the front room; the eyes on the staircase, and the eyes on the stove.

And the eyes in the shadow that came through the back door, triangular eyes, orange and flickering.

The paper turned to ash and flaked to the table, without a spark, without a sound.

"Paulie."

Wrong, Daddy, wrong.

"Paulie, for god's sake."

Do it, Daddy.

Eyes on the ceiling, eyes on the table.

He thought about telling Paulie to go to hell, sighed, and rose stiffly, still cold and tired. He walked to the doorway and looked back with a sigh.

"Paulie, I'm getting awfully sick of doing this every year."

Daddy, try.

"God*damn*, I said I was sorry."

Every Halloween the same damn thing; every Halloween the screaming, and the bleeding, and the agony until dawn, every year the day in bed until it was over and he had eleven months left to get himself ready again. Every year eleven months to think about running, and knowing he couldn't because Paulie wouldn't let him.

Daddy!

"Paulie," he said, suddenly licking his lips, "Paulie, you *are* going to help me, right? I mean, you're not—"

Try, Daddy. Try.

He took a deep breath, and threw himself at the table, turning his head to catch the corner just right.

Eyes.

Ugh! Good Grief! R.I.P. Pepe Lopez, Charlie Brown!

Kelly Laymon

Over the past year, I have watched the destruction of my favorite Halloween memory.

According to the family photo albums, it appears as though I made my first trip to Lopez Ranch when I was two. Eighteen years later, while I was a junior in college, I watched as it was reduced to a pile of dirt. From November to September, Lopez Ranch was just a fruit and nut market where all of your popcorn, cookie, and cheetoh needs could be met. It was located in a limbo between Marina del Rey and Culver City, not far from the Ballona Lagoons and the Los Angeles International Airport. The area surrounding Lopez Ranch is still reasonably undeveloped, but corporations are working hard at changing that.

Across the street from Lopez Ranch was Howard Hughes's personal runway and airport. Motion picture companies and housing developments are currently turning his hangars into studios and expensive beach housing. Behind Lopez Ranch sat a piece of Old Hollywood; a Republic Pictures soundstage, complete with the giant eagle logo painted on it. It has been gutted recently as well.

For those folks who attended Lopez Ranch during the "off season," there were some fun attractions to entertain the kiddies. Old Pepe Lopez had Chango the Savage Gorilla and some baby rattlers caged up on the property. Pepe kept Chango in a wooden box, and his only connection to the outside world was a tiny slot in the box covered by a flap of cardboard. When a brave ranchgoer dared to lift the flap, which had a Scotch Tape hinge at the top, and look at Chango the Savage Gorilla, he'd see...himself. (It was a mirror.) And the baby rattlers who lounged in a hay-lined crate were of the plastic pink and blue pastel variety. Corny? Hell yeah!

Each year, the Great Pumpkin rises out of the pumpkin patch that he thinks is the most sincere. He's gotta pick this one! He's got to! I don't see how a pumpkin patch could be more sincere than this one. You can look around and there is not a sign of hypocrisy. Nothing but sincerity as far as the eye can see.

—Linus

But come October, Pepe Lopez would pull out all the stops. The relatively nondescript market and its few amusing attractions exploded into a Halloween wonderland....

To begin with, Pepe filled the field with pumpkins and hung black and orange flags over the parking lot. He also rolled out the nine-foot high hollow ceramic pumpkin with an open nose, mouth, and eyes for kids to climb through.

He also opened a petting zoo, of which I was never particularly fond.

There aren't really any great memories for me on this one. I have a well-defined idea of fun, which has never included frolicking with barnyard animals, receiving a handful of green pellets of grass mush from the farm vending machine, and feeding it to the animals and getting my hand slimed.

When it came to decorations, Pepe Lopez's specialty was life-sized stuffed cloth dummies. The dummies all wore overalls or jumpsuits, a straw hat, and a spooky mask. Pepe's masks of choice were not cartoon characters or other recognizable figures, but masks resembling the faces of hideously deformed hobos. Some of them were identified by the faded block lettering of a black permanent marker on the upper left-hand corner of the costume. Two of these dummies sat in a kitchen scene near the baby rattlers and were marked as being Pepe Lopez and Mrs. Lopez. (Instead of overalls, Mrs. Lopez wore a messy flower print dress with her creepy mask. Her mask was accompanied by a wig with long hair put up in a bun.) There were two other dummies scattered around the grounds. One hideous hobo sat at the helm of a tractor, while the other opted for an army tank.

Pepe Lopez would also pull back the curtain on the entrance to his haunted house.

Okay, so it wasn't exactly a curtain at the haunted house's entrance. It was more of a garbage bag. And come to think of it, the haunted house was actually a tool shed.

So, Pepe Lopez would draw back the garbage bag and let us look through his poorly lit tool shed. Inside that tool shed, Pepe had arranged old roller coaster cars and miniature ferris wheels containing an odd mixture of Mickey Mouse and Tweety dolls and the Lopez signature dummies, who looked an awful lot like Leatherface from *The Texas Chainsaw Massacre*. It was an amusing mix.

On rare occasions, if it had been a very good year, Lopez would invest three bucks in a new mask for one of the dummies and trace over their names to darken the writing and make it more legible.

In addition to the annual visits to Lopez Ranch, I ended up attending Loyola Marymount University, which is located on a hill across the street from Lopez Ranch and overlooks both Lopez Ranch and the Howard Hughes airport. During the month of October, I often took detours from my usual route to and from school to drive past Lopez Ranch and look at the decorations. Plus, from the bluff adorned with the giant white letters "LMU", I would keep an eye on Lopez Ranch. Although I never had any trouble finding it, the fluttering orange and black flags always gave it away during that one month of the year.

Ohhhh! You didn't tell me you were gonna kill it! Ohhhhhh!

—Linus

Last summer, the Lopez Ranch market closed and the parking lot was converted into a used car dealership. I began to worry.

"It's only temporary," I'd bitch to my parents. "The market's closed, but it's still there. It better be open for Halloween! It's just gotta!"

As the month of October approached, the used car dealership showed no signs of packing up shop. I kept an eye on what was going on from the bluff and frequent passes in my vehicle.

With the beginning of the Halloween season and the month of October, Target and the supermarkets shifted into high gear for Halloween, carrying pumpkins, bags of candy corn, the year's popular plastic costumes with plastic masks, and those snap-'em green glow lights. At Lopez Ranch, nothing shifted into high gear for Halloween.

During the first week of October I drove past Lopez Ranch early one morning on my way to school and saw that the windows and doors of the market were boarded up.

You heard about the fury of a woman scorned, haven't you? Well, that's nothing compared to the fury of a woman who has been cheated out of tricks-or-treats.

—Linus

Which pales in comparison to the fury of a woman who is witnessing the destruction of a family-owned and sincere pumpkin patch/Halloween wonderland, the last of its kind.

The week of Halloween rolled around and there was no Lopez Ranch. Although the market was closed and Lopez Ranch was clearly a goner, the large black "Lopez Ranch" sign still hung over the entrance to the used car dealership, and the great big pumpkin still sat at the back of the empty patch. No pumpkins, no haunted house, and no orange and black flags. The Great Pumpkin would not be rising up out of this sincere pumpkin patch on Halloween night with his bag of toys for all the children of the world.

In the early hours of some weekday morning of Halloween week, I stopped at what was left of Lopez Ranch. I parked my car, got out, and walked around the remains.

I had been out with a friend the week before. I drove her past the ranch and, in an expletive-laced rant, explained the history of Lopez Ranch in all of its kitschy Los Angeles glory.

She taunted me with just seven words. "You know, luncheon meat ruins paint jobs," she said.

I perked up. "Really?" I asked.

"Peels the paint off."

All of this crossed my mind as I stood in the parking lot of Lopez Ranch during the week of Halloween. As I looked at that lonely great big pumpkin, I realized that I had quite an arsenal in my vehicle.

At a moment's notice, armed with road flares, a semi-automatic handgun, Scotch Tape, smelling salts, scissors, fireworks, staples, knives, tennis balls, and glue, I can be ready for just about any kind of shit to go down. I also took into account that antennaes snap and windows shatter. However, in my short little life, I have managed to run afoul of PETA, the NAACP, the teacher's union of Los Angeles, and the Los Angeles Superior Court. Somewhere, an agency has a file on me and is ready to use it. I'll never be able to be cross-examined by Johnny Cochran or become a big tobacco whistle blower. I opted not to add a count of vandalism to this rapidly growing file. I don't need to become completely official and earn a police record *yet.*

Lopez Ranch was clearly a place from a bygone era. With historic diners, movie theaters, amusement parks, drive-ins, and bowling alleys meeting untimely demises left and right, especially here in Los Angeles, Pepe Lopez's number was bound to come up one day.

For a little kid, Lopez Ranch was an exciting place to visit. It was a place where kids could go to get their pumpkins and have a good fun time year after year. Plus, it was my favorite kind of fun, that tacky and cool throwback to the fifties kind of fun. The large road that ran in front of Lopez Ranch felt like it should have been Route 66.

From now on, I suppose we'll have to buy our pumpkins at the grocery store. That should be a hell of a lot of fun. When I walk through the chilled fruit and vegetable aisle, I can pick a few pumpkins up off the black and white checkered tile floor and toss them into the cart before moving on to the tabloid-lined check-out lanes.

Since last Halloween, the used car dealership has moved on. The "Lopez Ranch" sign, the market, and the tool shed/haunted house are gone. Somewhere along the way, Chango the Savage Gorilla, the baby rattlers, the inhabitants of the tool shed, and the riders of the tanks and tractors went by the wayside too. Something surely happened to the great big pumpkin too.

Lopez Ranch is now a giant patch of dirt encircled by a wooden wall covered with posters for *Gladiator*.

I'm not sure what business will take over the property. Since the nearest ones are a distant two miles away, it will probably turn into a Target, a Best Buy, or a Costco. That's what everything that gets torn down around here turns into. If it turns into a Starbucks, I'll apply for a job. Since those clerks have signed documents testifying that they won't heat up the pasteries they serve, a toasting accident is out of the question.

However, I'm sure I could think of something damaging to do with a biscotti, a scone, and some hot foam.

I'm doomed! One little slip like that can cause the Great Pumpkin to pass you by. Oh Great Pumpkin! Where are you?

—Linus

It's the Great Pumpkin, Charlie Brown. Dir. Bill Melendez. Wri. Charles M. Schulz. Videocassette. Paramount Pictures Home Video. 1994.

Simon Clark

In Britain, the period round the end of October and early November is Christmas's oh so dark cousin with a cluster of weird festivals. For children, the excitement starts mounting late October when they start building bonfires in time for Bonfire night on November 5 when human effigies are burnt. Before that, of course, is Halloween, and Mischief Night on November 4 (generally, that is, but there are regional variations). One of the tricks on Halloween night was to do a Black Magic. This involved breaking open a firecracker onto the ground then dropping a lighted match onto the little pile of gunpowder and, hey presto, there's the 'Black Magic' flash and puff of smoke. When I was eleven I was doing this with a friend who'd managed to acquire an unfeasibly large amount of firecrackers. Happily, he broke open around a hundred or so until he had a large mound of gunpowder there on the street. Boasting that he was going to create the 'Black Magic' flash to end 'Black Magic' flashes, he waited until a sizeable audience of kids surrounded him. Then with a flourish he dropped a lighted match onto the mountain of gunpowder. Now the moral of this story is 'don't mess with fireworks', because even though Andy (let's call him Andy to spare this now top-flight executive further embarrassment) even though he sparked up the biggest flash-cum-fireball in the village, he managed (without so much as scorching the tip of his nose) to singe off every single hair on his head. For the next few weeks he had to constantly wear a woolly hat to hide his bald head—even in class. So, kids, don't try this at home!

Deathmask

Dominick Cancilla

At the threshold of Alice's house stood a little boy not more than two, holding out a tiny treat sack. He was dressed in a darling little ladybug outfit, spring antennae sticking up from his curls, and his mother stood just behind him, all smiles. Alice could barely remember when her own daughter, this summer's poster child for rebellion and body piercing, had been so adorable.

When the boy said his little "Trick or tweet," Alice's heart melted. She knelt to put herself at the boy's level. "Here you go, sweetie," she said. His eyes followed the candy bar from the bowl in her hands to his treat bag.

"Thank you," the boy said, unprompted, before turning and running past his mom toward the steps.

The boy's mother shared a broad grin before chasing after her charge. Now *that* was what Halloween was supposed to be about—little kids playing dress-up, not teenagers in realistic gore, not eight-year-olds who'd been dressed by their parents as some political figure. When Alice was a girl, everyone had still been so full of Vietnam that any chance to completely forget gore and politics was happily embraced. Now, even her own daughter didn't keep the holiday the way she should.

Alice had tried to talk Brandy into staying home with her, watching something scary in-between trick-or-treaters. But Brandy had put on a fit about her *friends.* "But my *friends* are going out, and *everyone* will be at the party, and *nobody* stays home on Halloween." Which seemed to sum up Alice in Brandy's eyes—not a friend, not anyone, no one. And after that the girl had had the gall to ask to borrow the car or be driven to the party—ha!

Some thanks. After all the years Alice had taken Brandy around the block for her tricks and treats before the babysitter came, she was suddenly too big to spend Halloween with her mother. Brandy hadn't even shown a glimmer of interest in the wonderful scarecrow costume Alice had rented for her.

Apparently, dressing like a slut was what passed for a costume in Brandy's crowd these days. She'd painted her face up, showed a lot of cleavage, and put on a skirt that barely hid her ass. She'd worn garter belts and stockings stolen from the back of Alice's dresser. Alice hadn't worn those in years, not since her husband died, but the fact that they were hers made her protests sound ineffectual even to her own ears. Not that anything she said would have made a difference.

Brandy was probably going trick or treating, too, even though she knew her mother disapproved. Or *because* her mother disapproved. When Alice was a girl, anyone who wanted to trick or treat after the age of thirteen was being a baby. Now you were lucky if they stopped at twenty.

Across the street, a small mob of Ninjas and movie tie-ins giggled up the Braner's driveway. Alice had zoned out for a moment—she wondered how long she'd been standing there like an idiot with her bowl of candy, mentally berating the world but seeing none of it. She might as well have hung a "just take one" sign around her own neck.

Even after she'd returned to reality, Alice had been so intent on the activity at the Braner's that the shadow standing between her and the street seemed to appear from the nothingness at the bottom of the lawn. "What are you looking at?" Alice called out, more to hide her own embarrassment than in anger at whoever it was that stood watching her. She followed this with an unrepentant, "Well?" when no answer came.

Alice couldn't make out much of the intruder—what with the Braner's porch light behind it and the lawn's centerpiece orange tree masking her own—but she saw enough to know it was a teenager. No younger child would be unaccompanied even if precociously tall, and a true adult would surely be behaving in a more sensible manner.

Whomever it was, he didn't seem to be doing anything but standing and staring. Either he was a shy trick-or-treater (and well he should be at that age) or was just trying to get on her nerves.

"I'm not waiting here forever," Alice said to no response. Then, with an exaggerated sigh of exhausted patience, "Fine." She closed herself behind the front door in dismissal.

Alice slammed the candy bowl on the entry table and headed back to the living room where the television beckoned. It was amazing how one idiot could ruin a perfectly good holiday. The boy had been wearing a robe or shroud—something long and shapeless, anyway—and standing still like that was probably supposed to be intimidating. What a jerk. Alice dropped onto the sofa, put her bare feet up on the coffee table. She'd rented the *Hookrape* trilogy as a treat for Brandy, since that series—along with all the *Halloweens, Hellraisers, Screams, Nightmares,* and *Fridays*—had always been on the household *verboten* list. But Brandy had not only preferred to go out rather than stay home for a horror marathon with Mom, she'd admitted to having seen *Hookrape I* and *II* at a friend's house and sneaking out for *HR-3D* under the guise of going Christmas shopping.

Well, to hell with her then. The movies were disgusting, not Alice's cup of tea at all, but she was determined to have Halloween with or without Brandy.

The tape was paused to show a woman's tight belly, bulging with violation. Alice tapped the remote on the arm of the chair beside her, calling up the squeal of a woman barely restraining a scream as she fought not to move.

The doorbell rang a few minutes later, just as victim three of film two was breathing her last. Alice paused the picture on a staring eye perfectly framed by the shadow of a hook.

With the TV silent, Alice could hear a decent size group milling about outside as she got up from the couch. The bell rang again. "Hang on," Alice called out. She gathered up the bowl and opened the door.

Two video game characters, a super hero, two Disney princesses, and a professional wrestler said their trick-or-treats and held open sacks in demand. Alice played her part for each in turn: "There you are—There you are—How about a 'Thank you' from you?—Here you go—There you are."

She was down to the last of the batch—a kindergarten-age girl in a tiara and a blue dress that said "Sleeping Beauty" across the front—when she noticed the robed figure beneath the orange tree. Alice froze, holding a candy bar over the girl's bag but not dropping it in.

"Trick or treat?" the girl asked again, recapturing Alice's attention.

The girl's mother, half way up the walk, looked a little concerned about the delay. Alice formed a quick plan. "Can you do me a big favor princess?" she said to the girl, trying to sound extra nice. "Give that silly man under a tree a big kick on your way back to Mommy. Will you do that for Auntie Alice?"

The girl frowned, looked back toward her mother, shook her head. When Alice gently insisted, she took a step backward.

Alice put a hand on the girl's shoulder. "No, wait. Look at the man. See the stupid man?"

"What do you think you're doing?" The mother hurried up the walk behind her child; the little girl began to cry.

"We were just having a little talk." Alice stood up, nodded toward the teenager while keeping her eyes on the mother's reddening face. "I wanted to warn her about the strange man under the tree."

The woman scooped up her child before turning to look in the direction Alice had indicated. "You ought to be put away," she said, cattily, and hurried off.

The children who had accompanied the little princess were milling about the sidewalk, waiting for their friend and escort. With dismay, Alice saw that what the corner of her eye had taken for the annoying stranger was just the silhouette of the tallest boy wed to the apple tree's shadow. The coward had fled the moment Alice showed any backbone, before the mother had a chance to see him. Typical.

Well, it made Alice feel a bit better to have chased him away, even if in the short term it left her looking like a bit of a dope. She closed the front door—a bit too hard, perhaps—and returned to her movie.

❋ ❋ ❋

Alice watched her movie, refusing to dwell on her increasing annoyance.

She wasn't going to let this turn into some pathetic "my worst Halloween ever" story. If Brandy wanted to run off with friends instead of showing a little loyalty, well then to hell with her. When years went by, her friends were all dead or in jail, and each piercing without permission was another reason she couldn't get a decent job, well, then she'd see.

It would have been different if Craig were still around. He'd have known what to do. None of the men Alice had dated since his death had been able to hold a candle to him, but that hadn't stopped her from trying. All the late evenings, all the drunken indiscretions overlooked, all the false shows of affection wasted trying to rebuild their family—all, in the end, for Brandy's benefit. And the only word of appreciation Brandy had ever uttered for her mother's untiring effort was a curse.

So this was what it had come to. That jerk on the lawn—probably one of Brandy's asshole friends, trying to draw her out so they could have a good laugh at her expense. Alice wondered if they'd given up the game for good.

Hitting pause on the remote Alice got up from the couch. Stupid as it was, a little bit of her was going to be bothered until she knew for certain the boy in the shroud hadn't returned. There was a lull between treaters—it was getting late in any case—so she had no convenient excuse to go to the door. A peek through curtains would have to do.

Around the corner to the front hall, Alice contemplated her choice of windows. The living room overlooked the lawn, but its windows had Venetian blinds and Alice didn't think she could peek through them without rattling the works. The kitchen window had the same problem. The front door had no peephole and its glass was heavily frosted, leaving the small curtained windows to either side of it—windows that were practically *made* for sneaking a peek through.

Her resolve to use a small window lasted until the moment just before her finger brushed the curtain.

What was she pussyfooting around for? What did she care if the practical-joking idiot knew she was looking for him? If he was out there he was just going to stand about looking menacing, but they wouldn't expect her at the door until more treaters rang. Bursting out now might catch the bastard with his pants down, might even catch some of his partners in crime out of their hiding places.

Alice liked that idea.

She slowly turned the doorknob until she felt the lock disengage, and then, prepared with the most pissed-off look she could muster, she whipped open the door and stepped out.

It was Alice's height and covered in blood. A short length of twig stuck out where the left eye should have been; its head was misshapen, as if by a massive bow. From between a checkerboard of missing and bloodied teeth, the short stump of a bitten-off tongue waggled around a word incomprehensible. Its dark, shapeless robe was wet with gore.

And it was standing on the porch, not two feet away.

Alice screamed. She stepped back, caught a heel on the threshold of her own home, and sprawled backwards, her head meeting the entry linoleum with a loud *crack*. Her vision blurred but only long enough for her to fear unconsciousness. Then she was watching with too-clear eyes as the horror began to bend, reaching out to her.

As tea rushes to the spout as its pot is tilted, so the drip of blood from the hideous face became a stream as it lowered. It was only with the first damp splat against her bare toe that Alice remembered she could move.

Curling her legs, Alice kicked out—not at the gruesome figure but at the edge of the open door beside her. She caught it on the first try, sending the door slamming shut. Fearful imagination showed her a bloodied hand wedged against the doorjamb or that horrible face smashing through the frosted glass, but no such thing came to pass. There was not even a thud of contact or moment of resistance before the door slammed and the latch clicked home.

The doorknob was self locking, for all the good that flimsy thing would do. She needed to get up, to reach the deadbolt and chain, but her legs, which had served her so well just a moment before, betrayed her completely and all she could do was lie panting on the cold floor.

When someone knocked on the door, she almost screamed. She hadn't been lying long—seconds at most—so whomever was there had to have seen her assailant, but there'd been no screams or excited words, which meant they had to be in on the joke.

"Go away," Alice yelled when the knock came again. She raised herself to her elbows, her head swimming with pain.

A muffled mini-chorus of "Trick-or-treat" came through the door.

"Go the hell away! Get out of here before I call the police!" she yelled, loud enough to make her own head throb. "Haven't you done enough already?"

Shapes through the frosted glass milled, then shrank away. There was a wet, muffled thump and giggles mixed with running feet—one of the brats had ruined Alice's carefully carved Jack-o-lantern.

Alice got up. Her hands still shook when she locked the door and as she hesitated over switching off the porch light. With the light off, there would be no more trick-or-treaters, but it would also be difficult for her to see the front of the house since the street lights were neither near nor particularly powerful.

She finally settled on leaving the porch light as it was. She could always ignore the door, and there was no reason to put herself in an island of darkness when someone was so obviously set on harassing her all night.

It was difficult to turn her back to the front door, but Alice did it. She headed back to the living room.

Being so upset had been foolishness, incredible foolishness. Alice felt like an old woman, frightened by a parlor trick. It had been makeup of course—damned good makeup, she had to give him that, but makeup just the same. Seriously, what else could it be? Anyone that smashed up would have better things to do than hang around on the lawn. And despite the costume, Alice had recognized the gore-covered face. She couldn't place it at the moment, but it tickled at her mind. She'd get it. Surely, one of Brandy's asshole friends. Alice might have guessed it was that boy Brandy was seeing, but the zombie or whatever it was didn't have ten pounds of crap pierced into its head. The rest of the party was probably hiding in the bushes, waiting to laugh at her or pelt her with water balloons or rotten eggs.

The TV was still on, its picture still. Alice clicked it off. She just wasn't in the mood any more. Fact of the matter was, regardless of how she berated herself she had been pretty damned frightened for a moment there. And she couldn't get the horrible face out of her mind.

A knock at the door; Alice ignored it.

Something clattered against the front window—a stick perhaps?—and Alice jumped half out of her skin. Well that was it, that was just enough. She wasn't going to let herself be made prisoner in her own home. If they were going to spend so much time and energy trying to upset her, then she was damned well going to make them pay for the pleasure. If Alice was being harassed, then that was a matter for the police. And if some teenager had to spend Halloween in jail with his face all made up, then so be it.

The phone, a portable, was in its cradle on the wall in the front room. Alice went through the kitchen to avoid the entry.

The phone was hung at one edge of the Venetian blinds, but Alice easily resisted what little temptation she had to peek through them. Even so, as she picked up the handset she swore she saw movement through the gaps between string and slat. Probably just treaters passing by. Probably just her imagination.

Alice took a couple of steps back from the window and dialed 911. This would show them. This would show the brats. Flashing lights would flush them from their hiding places with their rotten eggs and rotten attitudes. If Brandy was going to hang around with such a crowd—

Someone was speaking in Alice's ear.

"Yes, yes," Alice said. She'd lost herself in thought again and missed the operator's greeting. Well, whatever. This was 911, not confession—Alice didn't have to stand on ceremony.

"What is the nature of your emergency?" the man on the phone asked.

"I'm being harassed," Alice said. "There's a young man in an absolutely horrible costume. First he would stand out at the edge of my lawn and just stare, trying to get me out of the house, I think. Then he came up to the door, practically knocked me over, he was trying to grab me when I slammed the door in his face. He got blood, fake blood of course, everywhere. And I doubt he's alone."

She absently looked down and noticed that there was no stain on her foot where the blood had dripped. How was that—

"—soon as possible." The operator finished a sentence Alice had largely missed.

"What was that?" Alice demanded.

"We'll send an officer as soon as possible, Ma'am."

"'As soon as possible?' I need this taken care of immediately, don't you understand."

"Yes Ma'am, but we're very busy tonight and—"

"Jesus!" Alice thumbed the phone off with a huff, raised her eyes to find something to vent her frustration on, and found herself looking straight into a face covered in blood.

The hideous figure—from the lawn, from the porch—was standing not five feet away. A trail of blood pointed from its feet to the wall behind it. And now that she faced it in the front room's ample light, Alice could not believe that she was looking at a costume, no matter how hard she tried to convince herself of it.

This was how a deer felt in a car's headlights.

This was what they meant when they said panic brings time to a crawl.

So many details Alice saw as the corpse approached. Long hair, just like Alice's but shaved at the temples. A bloodied silver charm hanging from a ribbon around its torn throat. The hint of a young woman's figure beneath the shroud. Alice was struck blind with clarity.

"Go away!" Alice yelled, finding her voice.

The corpse took another step. "Mathah? Pleth Mathan?" it said with ruined mouth.

Alice took a step back, two, dropped the phone and held out empty hands, pushing the air. "Go *away*!"

The phone rang. Alice screamed.

But by the time she fell silent and dared to open her eyes, the horror was gone.

The phone stopped ringing; the answering machine clicked on, said its peace. And then: "Ms. Blake? Hello? Is anyone there?"

Alice just stood, still. There was no blood on the floor. No footprints; no trail.

"This is Dr. Westin at St. Joseph's Hospital. If someone's there, please pick up."

Where the corpse had stood, something lay on the floor. Alice bent, reached for it. The motion was stiff, as if she were feeling her age for the first time.

"Uh, Ms. Blake, I need to speak with you as soon as possible. It's about your daughter. There's been an accident, a traffic accident, and I need to speak with you. It's very serious. Please call the hospital immediately." He left a number.

It was Brandy's ribbon, the satin one she wore around her neck. The charm was clean now, a tiny silver heart. And engraved on the heart, in perfect pinpoint cursive, it said "Mom".

Halloween Frights

Kristine Kathryn Rusch

Halloween has always been the most disappointing holiday for me. I feel as if the holiday has consistently promised and failed to deliver.

Oh, there were highlights. When I was really, really little—younger than seven, perhaps as young as four—my father had a colleague who devised a haunted house in his garage. At the time, my father worked at an exclusive college in Iowa, and most everyone connected with that college had money. This house was at the end of a long lane filled with trees, and the house was huge.

The haunted house had the typical stuff—peeled grape eyeballs, cold spaghetti intestines, and lots of teenagers jumping out of shadows and saying "boo!"—but I had never experienced anything like it before. These people gave out a prize for Best Costume, but we didn't find out until we kids compared notes the next day that we all got Best Costume prizes. By then, it didn't matter. Only that puff of importance that had come at the moment of the prize, and the wonderful feeling that someone had noticed.

Just after my seventh birthday in June, we moved to Northern Wisconsin. Planning for Halloween was still important. I remember many costume discussions, and begging, pleading, maybe even bribing my mother to sew me something special instead of buying the same store-bought items everyone else had. (In those dark days, there were only a few mass-produced Halloween costumes.) She never did, although once she got a neighbor to make me a princess costume.

The year of the princess costume (when I was about 9 and becoming quite girly) was important because on October 28th, it snowed. Halloween dawned clear and cold, so cold that I had to wear my parka over my princess costume, and I had to wear boots instead of my pretty pink slippers. Even my cone-shaped hat with its long net veil had to be worn over a stocking cap.

The weather turned all of us into flashers. Trick-or-treat was accompanied by requests from the grown-ups to see our costumes, so we'd unzip the winter jackets, open them real fast, and close them again.

No glamour, no scary looks, no nothing. Just candy tossed into our little pumpkin carriers. Candy and homemade caramel apples and all kinds of forbidden Fritos products from the guy who lived two blocks over. He worked for Frito Lay and got them for free. He was as cool as his next door neighbor, the dentist, was uncool. That damn dentist gave out toothbrushes every year.

Halloween got worse as I got older. Some crazy idiot who lived half a block away from me put razorblades in apples, and fortunately we all found them before eating them. He got arrested. Most people stopped giving out really good goodies then. They settled for the prepackaged stuff, like candy bars, which all the parents inspected with magnifying glasses (you think I'm kidding. I'm not.) before we could even touch them.

And then there was the matter of belief.

I don't know how old I was—maybe ten, but still in grade school—when one of my teachers decided to do Halloween in a big way. For the entire month of October, she had us study the origin of the holiday, read scary stories, perform poetry aloud, and prepare for our big Halloween party.

The origin stories—about the fact that the ghouls and ghosties wandered the night, only to disappear on November 1, All Saints Day, fired my imagination. I was convinced I'd see a ghost on Halloween.

The poetry didn't help. That was the year we memorized "The Cremation of Sam McGee" by Robert Service, which was particularly appropriate because it was a story-poem about being cold. In fact, the ghost of good old Sam, who freezes to death, is happy when his body is put into the furnace of that old barge. He says it's the first time he's been warm in months.

Halloween in Northern Wisconsin was always cold. Always. That snow from princess-year was common. It made trudging around in hopes of free candy a somewhat taxing experience.

But the poems that really got to me were written by James Whitcomb Riley. He wrote a lot of funny, scary poetry suited to kids. And the most memorable, even for me now, is one called, "The Goblins Will Getcha If You Don't Watch Out."

By October 29th of that year, I felt a lot like the Cowardly Lion—"I do believe in spooks! I do believe in spooks!"—but unlike my long-tailed friend, I wasn't afraid of those spooks. I wanted to see one. Banshees, goblins, wee beasties—I wanted to see them all. And in the nice, safe way that the holiday promised. They'd be there on All Hallow's Eve, and they'd be gone by morning.

Well, that year, we had our Halloween party. There was fog in our classroom, but it was caused by dry ice. There were monsters, but they were only teachers in costume. And there were flying ghosts, but they were only sheets bunched up and tied with rubber bands.

So I had hope that I might see something when I trick or treated. I trudged out into the snow—dressed like a belly dancer this time (a costume I borrowed from the university's theater department)—a parka covering my bare arms and midriff, and the same damn boots digging through the snow.

There were other ghosts and goblins and monsters with plastic faces—all wearing parkas and carrying little pumpkin baskets. And there were some Big Kids who, rumor had it, were going to beat up on all us little kids. Not to mention that crazy apple guy who had gotten out of jail and whose house was lit like an orange and black Christmas tree. Parents hurried us away from that place.

In the nearby park that night, two teenage girls got raped. And near the high school, a man got sprayed with mace although I never did learn why. The Frito guy had moved, leaving only the dentist, and then as we were halfway through our trudge, it started to snow—big, wet flakes that soaked through the parka onto my bare skin.

A month-long build-up—and nothing.

After that, I constantly found myself searching for the monsters. I wanted to see a ghost. I liked being scared in a safe environment. I started reading collections like *Alfred Hitchcock's Stories to Read with the Lights On* (aptly named) and watching cheesy movies of the week, which, in those days, were mostly about Satan taking over girl's schools or the Devil taking over a town or Beelzebub taking over the world's elite.

The books and movies provided some scary moments, but they were clearly fiction. I read gothics too, and tried to be all wispy and passive in hopes that some dark brooding hero would take me to a moor (whatever that was) so that I could be mistress of his haunted house. As I got older, and gave up trick-or-treating, I went to haunted houses, first sponsored by the school, then by a local radio station, and then by some commercial outfit that specialized in them for a while.

Sure, the haunted houses had scary moments—things brushing your face in the dark, big menacing creatures jumping out at you, fake spiders falling on your head—but those were "gotcha!" moments. I was searching for the real thing. A real haunt, a real spook, a real ghost.

I never found it. Not on Halloween, anyway.

Years later, at the moment my grandmother died, I thought I felt her brush my cheek. My father, after death, haunted me in nightmares for nearly a year. And for six months after one of my cats died, I would see her curled up in her usual places. (Another of my cats saw her too, and his hackles would rise every time, then he'd go sniff the spot, always walking around the curved body of the ghost cat.)

As I've gotten older, I've come to realize that there are things in this world that we can't explain. Moments when the hair rises on the back of your neck for no discernable reason, moments when a puff of cold air is menacing. Those moments can't be called upon at will, and few people will believe you when you say that you've experienced one.

In that way, Halloween is still a cheat to me, a month of buildup that ends in laughter and candy instead of good-natured thrills and chills.

But Halloween is different now. No children come to my door, even though I dutifully buy candy every year. They trick-or-treat at the mall, in the safe confines of a well-lit environment, parents and grown-ups watching their every move.

Because the monsters did start to come out on Halloween, right toward the end of my trick-or-treat days. The razor blade guy in my neighborhood was a copycat. There had been a number of razor blade incidents in larger cities just the year before. Children were getting snatched on Halloween or beaten or worse. Those horrors were just beginning. And over time, the simple innocence of begging door-to-door became as scary a prospect for parents as taking a child to a drug-infested park and leaving him there.

Those weren't the kinds of frights I wanted on Halloween. I wanted a white see-through face to pop up in an upstairs window, a shimmery shadowy shape to appear in a dark corridor. I wanted to see a corpse sit up in a barge on Lake LaFarge and be thankful to be warm. I wanted to outrun those goblins that were gonna get me if I didn't watch out.

Some Witch's Bed

Michael Marshall Smith

An Autumn Town, always in late afternoon with the light just gone and replaced by orange lamplight glow; warm air in streets dark with trees and rustling with leaves which have not yet fallen. A hazy town, with a roof just over the tops of the branches, a town that covers the country, the planet; always the same, a neighborhood that goes on forever and is everything in all dimensions and all futures. And quiet always, in this Halloween dream, as if everyone is inside, though they are not. Everyone is elsewhere, somewhere, but not here. The fullness you feel is that of streets forever empty. Everyone is different, a part of this place, as you are tonight, but not for long.

A boy. A boy who has agreed to live in a house down one of these streets, a house of slanting light and utter silence. A boy until recently young, who thinks of his parents often and can picture them in their lives. A boy who comes home every afternoon and wanders a silent house, and then goes to the room hung with fabrics where the light is darker, and sleeps there, in some witch's bed. He wakes in the morning and goes, and knows that she has been there in the warmth, and that she wants him to come back, though he has never seen her. Sometimes he finds notes, but nothing has been written on them. Sometimes too he hears voices, hears them as feelings. They tell him he's not safe in this house, that he should not be sleeping here, in some witch's bed. He knows the voices are good, and mean well, but he does not fear what they fear, whatever that may be.

And so he does come back, every night, in this long October of his youth. He lets himself in and sits alone in silent rooms, surrounded by an evening world in which nothing moves. He doesn't know if he will look back as an adult and see this time as wise, or even if he is safe. But he knows she wants him, in her distant and intangible way, and so he sleeps in her bed. This woman, this witch, is his first love, is a secret adulthood which has finally come. He will never tell of it, much less boast, but it is making him different. His features already seem a little more defined, his nose more in proportion with the rest of his face. There will always be a hidden drawer in his heart, at the back of which will be a space, and in it will be this time. The long quiet streets, the front lawn offerings and tableau. The golden treacle of the light and the sense, the knowledge, that things can begin and end at once, that nothing comes without something else passing, that tricks always come wrapped in treats.

He will never forget her, and some part of him will never leave, no matter where the rest of his life takes him. And he will never see or hear her—unless perhaps he saw her once, when it seemed to him out of the corner of his eye that there were candles lit round the bed, and that a woman with long black hair lay on it in a gown, staring at the ceiling. When he turned to look he saw the bed was empty, and there were no candles.

But he will come again tomorrow. And the next day.
Until he is grown.

Cyanide and Pixie Stix

Wayne Allen Sallee

It wasn't that long ago I lived in Chicago, taking the elevated train into and back from the Loop each weekday. You live in a routine, you get to recognize sights and smells on an almost subliminal basis; anyone from out of town need only assume that the subway entrances smell of sweat and sewage even during the harshest months, but there are sweeter smells from factories and warehouses that share the same blocks with tenement apartments.

At Ashland Avenue, the train stops just across the river from the Holsum bread factory, and when the doors slide open on a summer morning, it's as if a blowsy woman wearing just the right amount of perfume sashayed down the aisle. Further west where the blue line bisects the Eisenhower, the Pan Candy factory makes its presence known. Southwest, where the streets hump the train yards near Marquette Park, there's the Nabisco cookie factory and the old joint where they still make Tootsie Rolls. It's this last place where I'm reminded of the smell of death.

Walking from the train to my home, the smell from the confectionery smokestacks is intoxicatingly sweet, and I think of Pixie Stix, a brand name candy from my youth, long paper tubes of powdered sugar in pastel-colored offerings of lime and cherry. In the early eighties, when I would be walking the same route home after college, immersed in espionage novels or wondering if I had it in me to write stories instead of poetry, Jack Malvides became "the man who murdered Halloween."

At least, that was his nickname to the television audiences; ever since "Killer Clown" John Wayne Gacy was arrested, catch-name killers were big in Chicago. Jack Malvides killed his seven year-old son in a heinous way, poked a hole in his boy's Halloween stash and slipped some cyanide in. Difficult? No way, as the still unknown deviate who killed seven people with tainted Tylenol capsules, or the investigating cops and coroners, could attest to.

The cyanide was powder, just like the Pixie Stix. I think the candy company also made little candy buttons you could peel off of butcher paper. Malvides banked on an insurance scam against the makers of the product but that plan went bust mostly because he acted too shifty, or shiftless, depending on who was making the comparisons between grieving father and that of cunning murderer. So the police eventually wore him down, but the boy was still dead And his death, in turn, gave birth to the stigma of the one day a year that a kid can get free goodies from neighborly strangers (or strange neighbors) and yet die choking on lime green vomit.

I hadn't even been thinking about writing horror fiction at that time. If anything I was being deluded by the grand-scale confusion that Robert Ludlum and Frederick Forsythe created in each new conspiracy. I would not write "A Field Near Grayslake" or "Rapid Transit" until the following spring. A part of me believes the death of Bobby Malvides allowed me to slowly desensitize my prose, which I did all that winter, culminating with my poem about spring for my senior year workshop, about a dog romping through a field with part of a woman's skull in his jaws.

And as I said, there is an intensity to certain smells just as there is *deja vu* to a recurring image. I can smell copper in my sleep, to wake from some dream of an imagined fiend, with blood in my nostrils and my jaw numb from clenching. Twenty years later and everybody is desensitized by life itself. Every other day there's some kid shooting up a school or random bombings by some idiot with an agenda.

I can still visualize what Pixie Stix felt like, the paper tearing away, the bitter powder on my tongue. Most times, it is the scent from the Tootsie Roll factory that provides the catalyst. But as the years pass, I find it increasingly hard to recall a Halloween afternoon filled with children, without adult supervision, dumping piles of candy together on a living room floor and dividing the spoils.

THE TRICK

Ramsey Campbell

As October waned Debbie forgot about the old witch: she didn't associate her with Halloween. Halloween wasn't frightening. After the long depression following the summer holidays, it was the first night of winter excitements: not as good as Guy Fawkes' Night or Christmas, but still capable of excluding less pleasant things from Debbie's mind—the sarcastic teacher, the gangs of boys who leaned against the shops, the old witch.

Debbie wasn't really frightened of her, not at her age. Even years ago, when Debbie was a little kid, she hadn't found her terrifying. Not like some things: not like her feverish night when the dark in her bedroom had grown like mold on the furniture, making the familiar chair and wardrobe soft and huge. Nor like the face that had looked in her bedroom window once, when she was ill: a face like a wrinkled monkey's, whose jaw drooped as if melting, lower and lower: a face that had spoken to her in a voice that sagged as the face did—a voice that must have been a car's engine struggling to start.

The witch had never seized Debbie with panic, as those moments had. Perhaps she was only an old woman, after all. She lived in a terraced house, in the row opposite Debbie's home. People owned their houses in that row, but Debbie's parents only rented the top half of a similar building. They didn't like the old woman: nobody did.

Whenever the children played outside her house she would come out to them. "Can't you make your row somewhere else? Haven't you got a home to go to?" "We're playing outside our own house," someone might say. "You don't own the street." Then she would stand and stare at them, with eyes like gray marbles. The fixed lifeless gaze always made them uneasy; they would dawdle away jeering.

Parents were never sympathetic. "Play somewhere else, then," Debbie's father would say. Her parents were more frightened of the witch than she was. "Isn't her garden awful," she'd once heard her mother saying. "It makes the whole street look like a slum. But we mustn't say anything, we're only tenants." Debbie thought that was just an excuse.

Why were they frightened? The woman was small, hardly taller than Debbie. Boys didn't like to play near her house in case they had to rescue a football, to grope through the slimy nets, tall as a child, of weeds and grass full of crawlers. But that was only nasty, not frightening. Debbie wasn't even sure why the woman was supposed to be a witch.

Perhaps it was her house. "Keep away from my house," she told nearby children when she went out, as though they would want to go near the drab unpainted crumbling house that was sinking into its own jungle. The windows were cracked and thick with grime; when the woman's face peered out it looked like something pale stirring in a dirty jar. Sometimes children stood outside shouting and screaming to make the face loom. Boys often dared each other to peer in, but rarely did. Perhaps that was it, then: her house looked like a witch's house. Sometimes black smoke that looked solid as oil dragged its long swollen body from the chimney.

There were other things. Animals disliked her almost as much as she disliked them. Older brothers said that she went out after midnight, hurrying through the mercury-vapor glare towards the derelict streets across the main road; but older brothers often made up stories. When Debbie tried to question her father he only told her not to be stupid. "Who's been wasting your time with that?"

The uncertainty annoyed her. If the woman were a witch she must be in retirement; she didn't do anything. Much of the time—at least, during the day—she stayed in her house: rarely answering the door, and then only to peer through a crack and send the intruder away. What did she do, alone in the dark house? Sometimes people odder than herself would visit her: a tall thin woman with glittering wrists and eyes, who dressed in clothes like tapestries of lurid flame: two fat men. Tweedledum and Tweedledee draped in lethargically flapping black cloaks. They might be witches too.

"Maybe she doesn't want anyone to know she's a witch," suggested Debbie's friend Sandra. Debbie didn't really care. The old woman only annoyed her, as bossy adults did. Besides, Halloween was coming. Then, on Halloween morning—just when Debbie had managed to forget her completely—the woman did the most annoying thing of all.

Debbie and Sandra had wheeled their prams to the supermarket, feeling grown-up. On the way they'd met Lucy, who never acted her age. When Lucy had asked, "Where are you taking your dolls?" Sandra had replied loftily, "We aren't taking our *dolls* anywhere." She'd done the shopping each Saturday morning since she was nine, so that her mother could work. Often she shopped in the evenings, because her mother was tired after work, and then Debbie would accompany her, so that she felt less uneasy in the crowds beneath the white glare. This Saturday morning Debbie was shopping too.

The main road was full of crowds trying to beat the crowds. Boys sat like a row of shouting ornaments on the railing above the underpass; women queued a block for cauliflowers, babies struggled screaming in prams. The crowds flapped as a wind fumbled along the road. Debbie and Sandra maneuvered their prams to the supermarket. A little girl was racing a trolley through the aisles, jumping on the back for a ride. How childish, Debbie thought.

When they emerged Sandra said, "Let's walk to the tunnel and back."

She couldn't be anxious to hurry home to vacuum the flat. They wheeled their laden prams towards the tunnel, which fascinated them. A railway cutting divided the streets a few hundred yards beyond the supermarket, in the derelict area. Houses crowded both its banks, their windows and doorways blinded and gagged with boards. From the cutting, disused railway lines probed into a tunnel beneath the main road—and never reappeared, so far as Debbie could see.

The girls pushed their prams down an alley, to the near edge of the cutting. Beside them the remains of black yards were cluttered with fragments of brick. The cutting was rather frightening, in a delicious way. Rusty metal skeletons sat tangled unidentifiably among the lines, soggy cartons flapped sluggishly, a door lay as though it led to something in the soil. Green sprouted minutely between scatterings of rubble.

Debbie stared down at the tunnel, at the way it burrowed into the dark beneath the earth. Within the mouth was only a shallow rim, surrounding thick darkness. No: now she strained her eyes she made out a further arch of dimmer brick, cut short by the dark. As she peered another formed, composed as much of darkness as of brick. Beyond it she thought something pale moved. The surrounding daylight flickered with

Debbie's peering; she felt as though she were being drawn slowly into the tunnel. What was it, the pale feeble stirring? She held on to a broken wall, so as to lean out to peer: but a voice startled her away.

"Go on. Keep away from there." It was the old witch, shouting from the main road, just as if they were little kids. To Debbie she looked silly: her head poked over the wall above the tunnel, as if someone had put a turnip there to grimace at them.

"We're all right," Sandra called impatiently. "We know what we're doing." They wouldn't have gone too near the cutting: years ago a little boy had run into the tunnel and had never been seen again.

"Just do as you're told. Get away." The head hung above the wall, staring hatefully at them, looking even more like a turnip.

"Oh, let's go home," Debbie said. "I don't want to stay here now, anyway."

They wheeled their prams around the chunks that littered the street. At the main road the witch was waiting for them. Her face frowned, glaring from its perch above the small black tent of her coat. Little more of her was visible, scuffed black snouts poked from beneath the coat, hands lurked in her drooping sleeves: one finger was hooked around the cane of a tattered umbrella. "And keep away from there in the future," she said harshly.

"Why, is that your house?" Debbie muttered.

"That's where she keeps her bats' eyes."

"What's that?" The woman's gray eyebrows writhed up, threatening. Her head looked like an old apple, Debbie thought, with mold for eyebrows and tufts of dead grass stuck on top. "What did you just say?" the woman shouted.

She was repeating herself into a fury when she was interrupted. Debbie tried not to laugh. Sandra's dog Mop was the interruption; he must have jumped out of Sandra's back yard. He was something like a stumpy-legged terrier, black and white and spiky. Debbie liked him, even though he'd once run away with her old teddy bear, her favorite, and had returned empty-mouthed. Now he ran around Sandra, bouncing up at her: he ran towards the cutting and back again, barking.

The witch didn't like him, nor did he care for her. Once he had run into her grass only to emerge with his tail between his legs, while she watched through the grime, smiling like a skull. "Keep that insect away from here, as well," she shouted.

She shook her umbrella at him: it fluttered dangling like a sad broomstick. At once Mop pounced at it, barking. The girls tried to gag themselves with their knuckles, but vainly. Their laughter boiled up; they stood snorting helplessly, weeping with mirth.

The woman drew herself up rigidly; bony hands crept from her sleeves. The wizened apple turned slowly to Sandra, then to Debbie. The mouth was a thin bloodless slit full of teeth: the eyes seemed to have congealed around hatred. "Well, you shouldn't have called him an insect," Debbie said defensively.

Cars rushed by, two abreast. Shoppers hurried past, glancing at the woman and the two girls. Debbie could seize none of these distractions: she could only see the face. It wasn't a fruit or vegetable now, it was a mask that had once been a face, drained of humanity. Its hatred was cold as a shark's gaze. Even the smallness of the face wasn't reassuring; it concentrated its power.

Mop bounced up and poked at the girls. At last they could turn; they ran. Their prams yawed. At the supermarket they looked back. The witch hadn't moved; the wizened mask stared above the immobile black coat. They stuck out their tongues, then they stalked home, nudging each other into nonchalance. "She's only an old fart," Debbie dared to say. In the street they stood and made faces at her house for minutes.

It wasn't long before Sandra came to ask Debbie to play. She couldn't have vacuumed so quickly, but perhaps she felt uneasy alone in the house. They played rounders in the street, with Lucy and her younger brother. Passing cars took sides.

When Debbie saw the witch approaching, a seed of fear grew in her stomach. But she was almost outside her own house: she needn't be afraid, even if the witch made faces at her again. Sandra must have thought similarly, for she ran across the pavement almost in front of the witch.

The woman didn't react: she seemed hardly to move. Only the black coat stirred a little as she passed, carrying her mask of hatred as though bearing it carefully somewhere, for a purpose. Debbie shouted for the ball; her voice clattered back from the houses, sounding false as her bravado.

As the witch reached her gate Miss Bake from the flats hurried over, blue hair glinting, hands fluttering. "Oh, have they put the fire out?"

The witch peered suspiciously at her. "I really couldn't tell you."

"Haven't you heard?" This indifference made her more nervous; her voice leapt and shook. "Some boys got into the houses by the supermarket and started a fire. That's what they told me at the corner. They must have put it out. Isn't it wicked, Miss Trodden. They never used to do these things. You can't feel safe these days, can you?"

"Oh yes, I think I can."

"You can't mean that, Miss Trodden. Nobody's safe, not with all these children. If they're bored, why doesn't someone give them something to do? The churches should. They could find them something worth doing. Someone's got to make the country safe for the old folk."

"Which churches are those?" She was smirking faintly.

Miss Bake drew back a little. "All the churches," she said, trying to placate her. "All the Christians. They should work together, form a coalition."

"Oh, them. They've had their chance." She smirked broadly. "Don't you worry. Someone will take control. I must be going."

Miss Bake hurried away, frowning and tutting; her door slammed. Shortly the witch's face appeared behind the grimy panes, glimmering as though twilight came earlier to her house. Her expression lurked in the dimness, unreadable.

When Debbie's father called her in, she could tell that her parents had had an argument; the flat was heavy with dissatisfaction. "When are you going trick-or-treating?" her mother demanded.

"Tonight. After tea."

"Well, you're not. You've got to go before it's dark."

The argument was poised to pounce on Debbie. "Oh, all right," she said grumpily.

After lunch she washed up. Her father dabbed at the plates, then sat watching football. He fiddled irritably with the controls, but the flesh of the players grew orange. Her mother kept swearing at food as she prepared it. Debbie read her love comics, and tried to make herself invisible with silence. Through the wall she could hear the song of the vacuum droning about the flat in the next house.

Eventually it faded, and Sandra came knocking. "You'd better go now," Debbie's mother said.

"We're not going until tonight."

"I'm sorry, Sandra, Debbie has to go before it's dark. And you aren't to go to anyone we don't know."

"Oh, why not?" Sandra protested. Challenging strangers was part of the excitement. "We won't go in," Debbie said.

"Because you're not to, that's why."

"Because some people have been putting things in sweets," Debbie's father said wearily, hunching forward towards the television. "Drugs and things. It was on the News."

"You go with them," her mother told him, worried again. "Make sure they're all right."

"What's stopping you?"

"You'll cook the tea, will you?"

"My mother might go," Sandra said. "But I think she's too tired."

"Oh God, all right, I'll go. When the match is finished." He slumped back in his armchair; the mock leather sighed. "Never any bloody rest," he muttered.

By the time they began it was dark, after all. But the streets weren't deserted and dimly exciting; they were full of people hurrying home from the match, shouting to each other, singing. Her father's impatience tugged at Debbie like a leash.

Some of the people they visited were preparing meals, and barely tolerant. Too many seemed anxious to trick them; perhaps they couldn't afford treats. At a teacher's house they had to attempt impossible plastic mazes which even Debbie's father decided irritably that he couldn't solve—though the teacher's wife sneaked them an apple each anyway. Elsewhere, several boys with glowing skulls for faces flung open a front door then slammed it, laughing. Mop appeared from an alley and joined the girls, to bounce at anyone who opened a door. He cheered Debbie, and she had pocketfuls of fruit and sweets. But it was an unsatisfying Halloween.

They were nearly home when Mop began to growl. He balked as they came abreast of the witch's garden. Unwillingly Debbie stared towards the house. The white mercury-vapor glare sharpened the tangled grass; a ragged spiky frieze of shadow lay low on the walls. The house seemed smoky and dim, drained of color. But she could see the gaping doorway, the coat like a tent of darker shadow, the dim perched face, a hand beckoning. "Come here," the voice said. "I've got something for you."

"Go on, be quick," hissed Debbie's father.

The girls hesitated. "Go on, she won't bite you," he said, pushing Debbie. "Take it while she's offering."

He wanted peace, he wanted her to make friends with the old witch. If she said she was frightened he would only tell her not to be stupid. Now he had made her more frightened to refuse. She dragged her feet up the cracked path, towards the door to shadow. Dangling grasses plucked at her socks, scraping dryly. The house stretched her shadow into its mouth.

Fists like knotted clubs crept from sleeves and deposited something in Debbie's palm, then in Sandra's: wrapped boiled sweets. "There you are," said the shrunken mouth, smiling dimly.

"Thank you very much." Debbie almost screamed: she hadn't heard her father follow her, to thank the woman. His finger was trying to prod her to gratitude.

"Let's see if you like them," the witch said.

Debbie's fingers picked stiffly at the wrapping. The paper rustled like dead grass, loud and somehow vicious. She raised the bared sweet towards her mouth, wondering whether she could drop it. She held her mouth still around the sweet. But when she could no longer fend off the taste, it was pleasant: raspberry, clear and sharp. "It's nice," she said. "Thank you."

"Yes, it is," Sandra said.

Hearing her voice Mop, who had halted snarling at the far end of the path, came racing between the clattering grasses. "We mustn't forget the dog, must we," the voice said. Mop overshot his sweet and bounced back to catch it. Sandra made to run to him, but he'd crunched and swallowed the sweet. They turned back to the house. The closed front door faced them in the dimness.

"I'm going home now," Sandra said and ran into her house, followed by Mop. Debbie found an odd taste in her mouth: a thick bitter trail, as if something had crawled down her throat. Just the liquid center of the sweet: it wasn't worth telling her father, he would only be impatient. "Did you enjoy yourself?" he said, tousling her hair, and she nodded.

During the meal her tongue searched for the taste. It was never there, nor could she find it in her memory: perhaps it hadn't been there at all. She watched comedies on television: she was understanding more of the jokes that made her parents laugh. She tricked some little girls who came to the door, but they looked so forlorn that she gave them sweets. The street was bare, deserted, frosted by the light: the ghost of its daytime self. She was glad to close it out. She watched the screen. Colors bobbed up, laughter exploded; gaps interrupted, for she was falling asleep. "Do you want to go to bed?" She strained to prove she didn't but at last admitted to herself that she did. In bed she fell asleep at once.

She slept uneasily. Something kept waking her: a sound, a taste? Straining drowsily to remember, she drifted into sleep. Once she glimpsed a figure staring at her from the doorway—her father. Only seconds later—or so it seemed at first—she woke again. A face had peered in the window. She turned violently, tethered by the blankets. There was nothing but the lighted gap which she always left between the curtains, to keep her company in the dark. The house was silent, asleep.

Her mind streamed with thoughts. The mask on the wizened apple, the skull-faced boys, the street flattened by the glare, her father's finger prodding her ribs. The face that had peered in her window had been hanging wide, too wide. It was the melting monkey from when she was little. Placing it didn't reassure her. The house surrounded her, huge and unfamiliar, darkly threatening.

She tried to think of Mop. He ran barking into the tunnel—no, he chased cheekily around the witch. Debbie remembered the day he had to run into the witch's garden. Scared to pursue him, they had watched him vanish amid the grass. They'd heard digging, then a silence: what sounded like a pattering explosion of earth, a threshing of grass, and Mop had run out with his tail between his legs. The dim face had watched, grinning.

That wasn't reassuring either. She tried to think of something she loved, but could think of nothing but her old bear that Mop had stolen. Her mind became a maze, leading always back to the face at her window. She'd seen it only once, but she had often felt it peering in. Its jaw had sagged like wax, pulling open a yawning pink throat. She had been ill, she must have been frightened by a monkey making a face on television. But as the mouth had drooped and then drawn up again, she'd heard a voice speaking to her through the glass: a slow deep dragging voice that sagged like the face, stretching out each separate word. She'd lain paralyzed as the voice blurred in the glass, but hadn't been able to make out a word. She opened her eyes to dislodge the memory. A shadow sprang away from the window.

Only a car's light, plucking at the curtains. She lay, trying to be calm around her heart. But she felt uneasy, and kept almost tasting the center of the burst sweet. The room seemed oppressive; she felt imprisoned. The window imprisoned her, for something could peer in.

She crawled out of bed. The floor felt unpleasantly soft underfoot, as if moldering in the dark. The street stretched below, deserted and glittering; the witch's windows were black, as though the grime had filled the house. The taste was almost in Debbie's mouth.

Had the witch put something in the sweets? Suddenly Debbie had to know whether Sandra had tasted it too. She had to shake off the oppressively padded darkness. She dressed, fumbling quietly in the dark. Squirming into her anorak, she crept into the hall.

She couldn't leave the front door open, the wind would slam it. She tiptoed into the living-room and groped in her mother's handbag. Her face burned; it skulked dimly in the mirror. She clutched the key in her fist and inched open the door to the stairs.

On the stairs she realized she was behaving stupidly. How could she waken Sandra without disturbing her mother? Sandra's bedroom window faced the back yard, too far from the alley to pelt. Yet her thoughts seemed only a commentary, for she was still descending. She opened the front door, and started. Sandra was waiting beneath the streetlamp.

She was wearing her anorak too. She looked anxious. "Mop's run off," she said.

"Oh no. Shall we look for him?"

"Come on, I know where he is." They muffled their footsteps, which sounded like a dream. The bleached street stood frozen around them, fossilized by the glare; trees cast nets over the houses, cars squatted, closed and dim. The ghost of the street made Debbie dislike to ask, but she had to know. "Do you think she put something funny in those sweets? Did you taste something?"

"Yes, I can now." At once Debbie could too: a brief hint of the indefinable taste. She hadn't wanted so definite an answer: she bit her lip.

At the main road Sandra turned towards the supermarket. Shops displayed bare slabs of glazed light, plastic cups scuttled in the underpass. How could Sandra be so sure where Mop had gone? Why did Debbie feel she knew as well? Sandra ran past the supermarket. Surely they weren't going to—But Sandra was already running into an alley, towards the cutting.

She gazed down, waiting for Debbie. White lamps glared into the artificial valley; shadows of the broken walls crumbled over scattered bricks. "He won't have gone down there," Debbie said, wanting to believe it.

"He has," Sandra cried. "Listen."

The wind wandered groping among the clutter on the tracks, it hooted feebly in the stone throat. Another sound was floated up to Debbie by the wind, then snatched away: a whining?

"He's in the tunnel," Sandra said. "Come on."

She slipped down a few feet; her face stared over the edge at Debbie. "If you don't come you aren't my friend," she said.

Debbie watched her reach the floor of the cutting and stare up challengingly; then reluctantly she followed. A bitter taste rose momentarily in her throat. She slithered down all too swiftly. The dark deep tunnel grew tall.

Why didn't Sandra call? "Mop! Mop!" Debbie shouted. But her shouts dropped into the cutting like pats of mud. There might have been an answering whine; the wind threw the sound away. "Come on," Sandra said impatiently.

She strode into the tunnel. The shadow hanging from the arch chopped her in half, then wiped her out entirely. Debbie remembered the little boy who had vanished. Suppose he were in there now—what would he be like? Around her the glistening cartons shifted restlessly; their gaping tops nodded. Twisted skeletons rattled, jangling.

Some of the squealing of metal might be an animal's faint cry; perhaps the metal was what they'd heard. "All right," Sandra said from the dark, "you're not my friend."

Debbie glanced about hopelessly. A taste touched her mouth. Above her, ruins gleamed jaggedly against the sky; cartons dipped their mouths towards her, torn lips working. Among piled bricks at the edge of the cutting, a punctured football or a crumpled rag peered down at her. Unwillingly she walked forward.

Darkness fell on her, filling her eyes. "Wait until your eyes get used to it," Sandra said, but Debbie disliked to keep them closed for long. At last bricks began to solidify from the dark. Darkness arched over her, outlines of bricks glinted faintly. The rails were thin dull lines, shortly erased by the dark.

Sandra groped forward. "Go slowly, then we won't fall over anything," she said.

They walked slowly as a dream, halting every few feet to wait for the light to catch up. Debbie's eyes were full of shifting fog which fastened very gradually on her surroundings, sketching them: the dwindling arch of the tunnel, the fading rails. Her progress was like a ritual in a nightmare.

The first stretch of the tunnel was cluttered with missiles: broken bottles crunched underfoot, tin cans toppled loudly. After that the way was clear, except for odd lurking bricks. But the dark was oppressively full of the sounds the girls made—hasty breathing, shuffling, the chafing of rust against their feet—and Debbie could never be sure whether, amid the close sounds and the invisibility, there was a whining.

They shuffled onward. Cold encircled them, dripping. The tunnel smelled dank and dusty; it seemed to insinuate a bitter taste into Debbie's mouth. She felt the weight of earth huge around the stone tube. The dimness flickered forward again, beckoning them on. It was almost as though someone were coaxing them into the tunnel with a feeble lamp. Beneath her feet bricks scraped and clattered.

The twilight flickered, then leapt ahead. The roundness of the tunnel glistened faintly; Debbie could make out random edges of brick, a dull hint of rails. The taste grew in her mouth. Again she felt that they were being led. She didn't dare ask Sandra whether the light was really moving. It must be her eyes. A shadow loomed on the arch overhead: the bearer of the light—behind her. She turned gasping. At once the dimness went out. The distant mouth of the tunnel was small as a fingernail.

Its light couldn't have reached so far. Something else had illuminated their way. The taste filled her mouth, like suffocation; dark dripped all around her; the distant entrance flickered, dancing. If she made for the entrance Sandra would have to follow. She could move now, she'd only to move one foot, just one, just a little. Sandra screamed.

When Debbie turned—furious with Sandra: there was nothing to be scared of, they could go now, escape—shadows reached for her. The light had leapt ahead again, still dim but brighter. The shadows were attached to vague objects, of which the nearest seemed familiar. Light gathered on it, crawling, glimmering. It had large ragged ears. It was her old lost teddy bear.

It was moving. In the subterranean twilight its fur stirred as if drowned. No, it wasn't the fur. Debbie's bear was covered with a swarm that crawled. The swarm was emerging sluggishly from within the bear, piling more thickly on its body, crawling.

It was a lost toy, not hers at all. Nothing covered it but moisture and unstable light. "It's all right," she muttered weakly. "It's only someone's old bear." But Sandra was staring beyond it, sobbing with horror.

Farther in, where dimness and dark flickered together, there was a hole in the floor of the tunnel, surrounded by bricks and earth and something that squatted. It squatted at the edge; its hands dangled into the hole, its dim face gaped pinkly. Its eyes gleamed like bubbles of mud.

"Oh, oh," Sandra sobbed. "It's the monkey."

Perhaps that was the worst—that Sandra knew the gaping face too. But Debbie's horror was blurred and numbing, because she could see so much. She could see what lay beside the hole, struggling feebly as if drugged, and whining: Mop.

Sandra staggered towards him as if she had lost her balance. Debbie stumbled after her, unable to think, feeling only her feet dragging her over the jagged floor. Then part of the darkness shifted and advanced on them, growing paler. A toy—a large clockwork toy, jerking rustily: the figure of a little boy, its body and ragged sodden clothes covered with dust and cobwebs. It plodded jerkily between them and the hole, and halted. Parts of it shone white, as if patched with flaking paint: particularly the face.

Debbie tried to look away, to turn, to run. But the taste burned in her mouth; it seemed to thread her with a rigid frame, holding her helpless. The dim stone tube was hemmed in by darkness; the twilight fluttered. Dust crawled in her throat. The toy bear glistened restlessly. The figure of the little boy swayed; its face glimmered, pale, featureless, blotchy. The monkey moved.

Its long hands closed around Mop and pulled him into the hole, then they scooped bricks and earth on top of him. The earth struggled in the hole, the whining became a muffled coughing and choking. Eventually the earth was still. The squat floppy body capered on the grave. Thick deep laughter, very slow, dropped from the gaping face. Each time the jaw drooped lower, almost touching the floor.

Another part of the dark moved. "That'll teach you. You won't forget that," a voice said.

It was the witch. She was lurking in the darkness, out of sight. Her voice was as lifeless now as her face had been. Debbie was able to see that the woman needed to hide in the dark to be herself. But she was trapped too efficiently for the thought to be at all reassuring.

"You'd better behave yourselves in the future. I'll be watching," the voice said. "Go on now. Go away."

As Debbie found she was able to turn, though very lethargically, the little boy moved. She heard a crack; then he seemed to shrink jerkily, and topple towards her. But she was turning, and saw no more. The taste was heavy in her. She couldn't run; she could only plod through the close treacherous darkness towards the tiny light.

The light refused to grow. She plodded, she plodded, but the light held itself back. Then at last it seemed nearer, and much later it reached into the dark. She plodded out, exhausted and hollow. She clambered numbly up the bank, dragged her feet through the deserted streets; she was just aware of Sandra near her. She went into her room, still trudging. Her numb trudge became the plodding of her heart, her slow suffocated gasps. She woke.

So it had been a dream, after all. Her mouth tasted bitter. What had awakened her? She lay uneasily, eyelids tight, trying to retreat into sleep; if she awoke completely she'd be alone with the dark. But light flapped on her eyelids. Something was wrong. The room was too bright and flickering. Things cracked loudly, popping; a voice cried her name. Reluctantly she groped to the window, towards the blazing light.

The witch's house was on fire. Flames gushed from the windows, painting smoke red. Sandra stood outside, crying "Debbie!" As Debbie watched, bewildered, a screaming blaze appeared at an upstairs window, jerking like a puppet; then it writhed and fell back into the flames. Sandra seemed to be dancing, outlined by reflected fire, and weeping.

People were unlocking doors. Sandra's mother hurried out, and Debbie's father. Sandra's mother fluttered about, trying to drag the girl home, but Sandra was crying "Debbie!" Debbie gripped the sill, afraid to let go.

More houses were switched on. Debbie's mother ran out. There was a hasty discussion among the parents, then Debbie's father came hurrying back with Sandra. Debbie dodged into bed as they came upstairs; the witch's house roared, splintering.

"Here's Sandra, Debbie. She's frightened. She's going to sleep with you tonight." Shadows rushed into the room with him. When Sandra took off her dressing-gown and stood holding it, confused, he threw it impatiently on the chair. "Into bed now, quickly. And just you stay there."

They heard him hurrying downstairs, Sandra's mother saying, "Oh God, oh my God," Debbie's' mother trying to calm her down. The girls lay silent in the shaking twilit room. Sandra was trembling.

"What happened?" Debbie whispered. "Did you see?"

After a while Sandra sobbed. "My little dog," she said indistinctly.

Was that an answer? Debbie's thoughts were blurred; the room quaked. Sandra's dressing-gown was slipping off the chair, distracting her. "What about Mop?" she whispered. "Where is he?"

Sandra seemed to be choking. The dressing-gown fell in a heap on the floor. Debbie felt nervous. What had happened to Mop? She'd dreamed—Surely Sandra couldn't have dreamed that too. The rest of the contents of the chair were following the dressing-gown.

"I dreamed," Debbie began uneasily, and bitterness filled her mouth like a gag. When she'd finished choking, she had forgotten what she'd meant to say. The room and furniture were unsteady with dimming light. Far away and fading, she heard her parents' voices.

Sandra was trying to speak. "Debbie," she said, "Debbie." Her body shook violently, with effort or with fear. "I burned the witch," she said. "Because of what she did."

Debbie stared in front of her, aghast. She couldn't take in Sandra's words. Too much had happened too quickly: the dream, the fire, her own bitter-tasting dumbness, Sandra's revelation, the distracting object that drooped from the chair—But until Sandra's dressing-gown was thrown there, that chair had been empty.

She heard Sandra's almost breathless cry. Something dim squatted forward on the chair. Its pink yawning drooped towards the floor. Very slowly, relishing each separate word, it began to speak.

OCTOBER!

Ed Gorman

I don't imagine it holds up well but at the time—I was eighteen or so—it was the best short story I'd ever written.

The title was "The Better Goblin" and it concerned a Halloween night when a bunch of tough teenage boys went trick or treating as a lark (too cool to do it any other way).

The chill, dark street was filled with tots dressed up as Draculas, Frankensteins, Aliens (this was back in the late Fifties).

But there was a far "better"—i.e., serious and truly dark—goblin loose that night. And it was to be found within some of the boys themselves.

A rather grotesquely overweight girl invited several of them up to the shabby apartment where she lived with her drunken father. She said she'd have sex with all of them.

Now, everybody knew the girl was disturbed in certain obvious ways. In class—everybody went to the same school—she'd suddenley have violent sobbing spells and would have to rush from the room. She ate so loudly that she sat alone in the cafeteria and would sometimes talk out loud to herself. And upon occasion she was known to offer guys oral sex in somewhat public places.

By now, as you've probably guessed, the story I wrote was essentially true. I'd lived down the street from the girl for many years but didn't really know anything about her except that I felt miserable for her, the way other kids picked on her. They humiliated her every chance they got.

I wasn't completely innocent (I rarely am). From time to time—we never knew its source—she'd come into a little money and invite guys up to her place for beers. (Her father spent most of his time in taverns.) I stole her old man's whiskey (I was an active alcoholic by age fifteen), I stole money from her purse, and I even lifted a lot of her comic books. What I didn't do was make fun of her. I guess I was enough of a freak myself to know what it was like to be taunted.

"Gang bangs" were a big thing in that era. I'm not sure why. Even though I knew several people who'd been in reform school and prison, even though I was friends with at least one very pretty neighborhood girl who was turning tricks at fifteen, I never actually knew anybody who'd participated in a gang bang. And I didn't want to, really. I was a romantic. I definitely wanted—craved—sex. But I also wanted romance. Gang bangs were about as far away from romance as you could get.

That Halloween night, six or seven of my friends gang-banged her. A couple of us just sat on the steps that ran up the side of the old house and drank our beer and smoked our cigarettes. She didn't object to the gang bang. She laughed about it afterwards, in fact. But she changed. Not immediately but over the winter semester of our junior year. Stopped coming to school. Didn't show up at the hang-out places to invite us up for beers. Then she left her old man and moved across town and started working at this department store. And took up with this guy who was like fifty or something. A year later he beat her to death. With his fists. Drunk, of course. Manslaughter was what he plead to. Every day of my life I see people on the street and they just break my heart. I sense where they've been. Where they're going. They've never known a moment's peace or joy, shambling on down the sidewalk in their sorrow. The girl was one of them.

So that became the theme of my story. That there are goblins far more dangerous and dehumanizing than the mythic ones. "Better" goblins, if you will.

By now, I've long forgotten the story.

But I'll never forget the girl.

Porkpie Hat

Peter Straub

Part One

If you know jazz, you know about him, and the title of this memoir tells you who he is. If you don't know the music, his name doesn't matter. I'll call him Hat. What does matter is what he meant. I don't mean what he meant to people who were touched by what he said through his horn. (His horn was an old Selmer Balanced Action tenor saxophone, most of its lacquer worn off.) I'm talking about the whole long curve of his life, and the way that what appeared to be a long slide from joyous mastery to outright exhaustion can be seen in another way altogether.

Hat did slide into alcoholism and depression. The last ten years of his life amounted to suicide by malnutrition, and he was almost transparent by the time he died in the hotel room where I met him. Yet he was able to play until nearly the end. When he was working, he would wake up around seven in the evening, listen to Frank Sinatra or Billie Holiday records while he dressed, get to the club by nine, play three sets, come back to his room sometime after three, drink and listen to more records (he was on a lot of those records), and finally go back to bed around the time day people begin thinking about lunch. When he wasn't working, he got into bed about an hour earlier, woke up about five or six, and listened to records and drank through his long upside-down day.

It sounds like a miserable life, but it was just an unhappy one. The unhappiness came from a deep, irreversible sadness. Sadness is different from misery, at least Hat's was. His sadness seemed impersonal—it did not disfigure him, as misery can do. Hat's sadness seemed to be for the universe, or to be a larger than usual personal share of a sadness already existing in the universe. Inside it, Hat was unfailingly gentle, kind, even funny. His sadness seemed merely the opposite face of the equally impersonal happiness that shone through his earlier work.

In Hat's later years, his music thickened, and sorrow spoke through the phrases. In his last years, what he played often sounded like heartbreak itself. He was like someone who had passed through a great mystery, who *was passing* through a great mystery, and had to speak of what he had seen, what he was seeing.

2

I brought two boxes of records with me when I first came to New York from Evanston, Illinois, where I'd earned a B.A. in English at Northwestern, and the first thing I set up in my shoebox at the top of John Jay Hall in Columbia University was my portable record player. I did everything to music in those days, and I supplied the rest of my unpacking with a soundtrack provided by Hat's disciples. The kind of music I most liked when I was twenty-one was called "cool" jazz, but my respect for Hat, the progenitor of this movement, was almost entirely abstract. I didn't know his earliest records, and all I'd heard of his later style was one track on a Verve sampler album. I thought he must almost certainly be dead, and I imagined that if by some miracle he was still alive, he would have been in his early seventies, like Louis Armstrong. In fact, the man who seemed a virtual ancient to me was a few months short of his fiftieth birthday.

In my first weeks at Columbia I almost never left the campus. I was taking five courses, also a seminar that was intended to lead me to a Master's thesis, and when I was not in lecture halls or my room, I was in the library. But by the end of September, feeling less overwhelmed, I began to go downtown to Greenwich Village. The IRT, the only subway line I actually understood, described a straight north-south axis which allowed you to get on at 116th Street and get off at Sheridan Square. From Sheridan Square radiated out an unimaginable wealth (unimaginable if you'd spent the previous four years in Evanston, Illinois) of cafes, bars, restaurants, record shops, bookstores, and jazz clubs. I'd come to New York to get a MA in English, but I'd also come for this.

I learned that Hat was still alive about seven o'clock in the evening on the first Saturday in October, when I saw a poster bearing his name on the window of a storefront jazz club near St. Mark's Place. My conviction that Hat was dead was so strong that I first saw the poster as an advertisement of past glory. I stopped to gaze longer at this relic of a historical period. Hat had been playing with a quartet including a bassist and drummer of his own era, musicians long associated with him. But the piano player had been John Hawes, one of *my* musicians—John Hawes was on half a dozen of the records back in John Jay Hall. He must have been about twenty at the time, I thought, convinced that the poster had been preserved as memorabilia. Maybe Hawes' first job had been with Hat—anyhow, Hat's quartet must have been one of Hawes' first stops on the way to fame. John Hawes was a great figure to me, and the thought of him playing with a back number like Hat was a disturbance in the texture of reality. I looked down at the date on the poster, and my snobbish and rule-bound version of reality shuddered under another assault of the unthinkable. Hat's engagement had begun on the Tuesday of this week—the first Tuesday in October—and its last night took place on the Sunday after next—the Sunday before Halloween. Hat was still alive, and John Hawes was playing with him. I couldn't have told you which half of this proposition was the more surprising.

To make sure, I went inside and asked the short, impassive man behind the bar if John Hawes were really playing there tonight. "He'd better be, if he wants to get paid," the man said.

"So Hat is still alive," I said.

"Put it this way," he said. "If it was you, you probably wouldn't be."

3

Two hours and twenty minutes later, Hat came through the front door, and I saw what he meant. Maybe a third of the tables between the door and the bandstand were filled with people listening to the piano trio. This was what I'd come for, and I thought that the evening was perfect. I hoped that Hat would stay away. All he could accomplish by showing up would be to steal soloing time from Hawes, who, apart from seeming a bit disengaged, was playing wonderfully. Maybe Hawes always seemed a bit disengaged. That was fine with me. Hawes was *supposed* to be cool. Then the bass player looked toward the door and smiled, and the drummer grinned and knocked one stick against the side of his snare drum in a rhythmic figure that managed both to suit what the trio was playing and serve as a half-comic, half-respectful greeting. I turned away from the trio and looked back toward the door. The bent figure of a light-skinned black man in a long, drooping, dark coat was carrying a tenor saxophone case into the club. Layers of airline stickers covered the case, and a black porkpie hat concealed most of the man's face. As soon as he got past the door, he fell into a chair next to an empty table—really fell, as if he would need a wheelchair to get any farther.

Most of the people who had watched him enter turned back to John Hawes and the trio, who were beginning the last few choruses of "Love Walked In." The old man laboriously unbuttoned his coat and let it fall off his shoulders, onto the back of the chair. Then, with the same painful slowness, he lifted the hat off his head and lowered it to the table beside him. A brimming shotglass had appeared between himself and the hat, though I hadn't noticed any of the waiters or waitresses put it there. Hat picked up the glass and poured its entire contents into his mouth. Before he swallowed, he let himself take in the room, moving his eyes without changing the position of his head. He was wearing a dark grey suit, a blue shirt with a tight tab collar, and a black knit tie. His face looked soft and worn with drink, and his eyes were of no real color at all, as if not merely washed out but washed clean. He bent over, unlocked the case, and began assembling his horn. As soon as "Love Walked In" ended, he was on his feet, clipping the horn to his strap and walking toward the bandstand. There was some quiet applause.

Hat stepped neatly up onto the bandstand, acknowledged us with a nod, and whispered something to John Hawes, who raised his hands to the keyboard. The drummer was still grinning, and the bassist had closed his eyes. Hat tilted his horn to one side, examined the mouthpiece, and slid it a tiny distance down the cork. He licked the reed, tapped his foot twice, and put his lips around the mouthpiece.

What happened next changed my life—changed me, anyhow. It was like discovering that some vital, even necessary substance had all along been missing from my life. Anyone who hears a great musician for the first time knows the feeling that the universe has just expanded. In fact, all that happened was that Hat had started playing "Too Marvelous For Words," one of the twenty-odd songs that were his entire repertoire at the time. Actually, he was playing some oblique, one-time-only melody of his own that floated above "Too Marvelous For Words," and this spontaneous melody seemed to me to comment affectionately on the song while utterly transcending it—to turn a nice little song into something profound. I forgot to breathe for a little while, and goosebumps came up on my arms. Half-way through Hat's solo, I saw John Hawes watching him and realized that Hawes, whom I all but revered, revered *him*. But by that time, I did, too.

I stayed for all three sets, and after my seminar the next day, I went down to Sam Goody's and bought five of Hat's records, all I could afford. That night, I went back to the club and took a table right in front of the bandstand. For the next two weeks, I occupied the same table every night I could persuade myself that I did not have to study—eight or nine, out of the twelve nights Hat worked. Every night was like the first: the same things, in the same order, happened. Half-way through the first set, Hat turned up and collapsed into the nearest chair. Unobtrusively, a waiter put a drink beside him. Off went the pork-pie and the long coat, and out from its case came the horn. The waiter carried the case, pork-pie, and coat into a back room while Hat drifted toward the bandstand, often still fitting the pieces of his saxophone together. He stood straighter, seemed almost to grow taller, as he got on the stand. A nod to his audience, an inaudible word to John Hawes. And then that sense of passing over the border between very good, even excellent music and majestic, mysterious art. Between songs, Hat sipped from a glass placed beside his left foot. Three forty-five minute sets. Two half-hour breaks, during which

Hat disappeared through a door behind the bandstand. The same twenty or so songs, recycled again and again. Ecstasy, as if I were hearing *Mozart* play Mozart.

One afternoon toward the end of the second week, I stood up from a library book I was trying to stuff whole into my brain—*Modern Approaches to Milton*—and walked out of my carrel to find whatever I could that had been written about Hat. I'd been hearing the sound of Hat's tenor in my head ever since I'd gotten out of bed. And in those days, I was a sort of apprentice scholar: I thought that real answers in the form of interpretations could be found in the pages of scholarly journals. If there were at least a thousand, maybe two thousand, articles concerning John Milton in Low Library, shouldn't there be at least a hundred about Hat? And out of the hundred shouldn't a dozen or so at least begin to explain what happened to me when I heard him play? I was looking for *close readings* of his solos, for analyses that would explain Hat's effects in terms of subdivided rhythms, alternate chords, and note choices, in the way that poetry critics parsed diction levels, inversions of meter, and permutations of imagery.

Of course I did not find a dozen articles that applied a musicological version of the New Criticism to Hat's recorded solos. I found six old concert write-ups in the *New York Times*, maybe as many record reviews in jazz magazines, and a couple of chapters in jazz histories. Hat had been born in Mississippi, played in his family band, left after a mysterious disagreement at the time they were becoming a successful "territory" band, then joined a famous jazz band in its infancy and quit, again mysteriously, just after its breakthrough into nationwide success. After that, he went out on his own. It seemed that if you wanted to know about him, you had to go straight to the music: there was virtually nowhere else to go.

I wandered back from the catalogues to my carrel, closed the door on the outer world, and went back to stuffing *Modern Approaches to Milton* into my brain. Around six o'clock, I opened the carrell door and realized that *I* could write about Hat. Given the paucity of criticism of his work—given the virtual absence of information about the man himself—I virtually had to write something. The only drawback to this inspiration was that I knew nothing about music. I could not write the sort of article I had wished to read. What I could do, however, would be to interview the man. Potentially, an interview would be more valuable than analysis. I could fill in the dark places, answer the unanswered questions—why had he left both bands just as they began to do well? I wondered if he'd had problems with his father, and then transferred these problems to his next bandleader. There had to be some kind of story. Any band within smelling distance of its first success would be more than reluctant to lose its star soloist—wouldn't they beg him, bribe him, to stay? I could think of other questions no one had ever asked: who had influenced him? What did he think of all those tenor players whom he had influenced? Was he friendly with any of his artistic children? Did they come to his house and talk about music?

Above all, I was curious about the texture of his life—I wondered what his life, the life of a genius, tasted like. If I could have put my half-formed fantasies into words, I would have described my naive, uninformed conceptions of Leonard Bernstein's surroundings. Mentally, I equipped Hat with a big apartment, handsome furniture, advanced stereo equipment, a good but not flashy car, paintings...the surroundings of a famous American artist, at least by the standards of John Jay Hall and Evanston, Illinois. The difference between Bernstein and Hat was that the conductor probably lived on Fifth Avenue, and the tenor player in the Village.

I walked out of the library humming "Love Walked in."

4

The dictionary-sized Manhattan telephone directory chained to the shelf beneath the pay telephone on the ground floor of John Jay Hall failed to provide Hat's number. Moments later, I met similar failure back in the library after having consulted the equally impressive directories for Brooklyn, Queens, and the Bronx, as well as the much smaller volume for Staten Island. But of course Hat lived in New York: where else would he live? Like other celebrities, he avoided the unwelcome intrusions of strangers by going unlisted. I could not explain his absence from the city's five telephone books in any other way. Of course Hat lived in the Village—that was what the Village was *for*.

Yet even then, remembering the unhealthy-looking man who each night entered the club to drop into the nearest chair, I experienced a wobble of doubt. Maybe the great man's life was nothing like my imaginings. Hat wore decent clothes, but did not seem rich—he seemed to exist at the same oblique angle to wordly sucess that his nightly variations on "Too Marvelous For Words" bore to the original melody. For a moment, I pictured my genius in a slum apartment where roaches scuttled across a bare floor and water dripped from a rip in the ceiling. I had no idea of how jazz musicians actually lived. Hollywood, unafraid of cliche, surrounded them with squalor. On the rare moments when literature stooped to consider jazz people, it, too, served up an ambiance of broken bedsprings and peeling walls. And literature's bohemians—Rimbaud, Jack London, Kerouac, Harte Crane, William Burroughs—had often inhabited mean, unhappy rooms. It was possible that the great man was not listed in the city's directories because he could not afford a telephone.

This notion was unacceptable. There was another explanation—Hat could not live in a tenement room without a telephone. The man still possessed the elegance of his generation of jazz musicians, the generation that wore good suits and highly polished shoes, played in big bands, and lived on buses and in hotel rooms.

And there, I thought, was my answer. It was a comedown from the apartment in the Village with which I had supplied him, but a room in some "artistic" hotel like the Chelsea would suit him just as well, and probably cost a lot less in rent. Feeling inspired, I looked up the Chelsea's number on the spot, dialed, and asked for Hat's room. The clerk told me that he wasn't registered in the hotel. "But you know who he is," I said. "Sure," said the clerk. "Guitar, right? I know he was in one of those San Francisco bands, but I can't remember which one."

I hung up without replying, realizing that the only way I was going to discover Hat's telephone number, short of calling every hotel in New York, was by asking him for it.

5

This was on a Monday, and the jazz clubs were closed. On Tuesday, Professor Marcus told us to read all of *Vanity Fair* by Friday; on Wednesday, after I'd spent a nearly sleepless night with Thackeray, my seminar leader asked me to prepare a paper on James Joyce's "Two Gallants" for the Friday class. Wednesday and Thursday nights I spent in the library. On Friday I listened to Professor Marcus being brilliant about *Vanity Fair* and read my laborious and dimwitted Joyce paper, on each of the five pages of which the word "epiphany" appeared at least twice, to my fellow-scholars. The seminar leader smiled and nodded throughout my performance and when I sat down metaphorically picked up my little paper between thumb and forefinger and slit its throat. "Some of you students are so *certain* about things," he said. The rest of his remarks disappeared into a vast, horrifying sense of shame. I returned to my room, intending to lie down for an hour or two, and woke up ravenous ten hours later, when even the West End bar, even the local Chock Full O' Nuts, were shut for the night.

On Saturday night, I took my usual table in front of the bandstand and sat expectantly through the piano trio's usual three numbers. In the middle of "Love Walked In" I looked around with an insider's foreknowledge to enjoy Hat's dramatic entrance, but he did not appear, and the number ended without him. John Hawes and the other two musicians seemed untroubled by this break in the routine, and went on to play "Too Marvelous For Words" without their leader. During the next three songs, I kept turning around to look for Hat, but the set ended without him. Hawes announced a short break, and the musicians stood up and moved toward the bar. I fidgeted at my table, nursing my second beer of the night and anxiously checking the door. The minutes trudged by. I feared he would never show up. He had passed out in his room. He'd been hit by a cab, he'd had a stroke, he was already lying dead in a hospital room—just when I was going to write the article that would finally do him justice!

Half an hour later, still without their leader, John Hawes and other sidemen went back on the stand. No one but me seemed to have noticed that Hat was not present. The other customers talked and smoked—this was in the days when people still smoked—and gave the music the intermittent and sometimes ostentatious attention they allowed it even when Hat was on the stand. By now, Hat was an hour and a half late, and I could see the gangsterish man behind the bar, the owner of the club, scowling as he checked his wristwatch. Hawes played two originals I particularly liked, favorites of mine from his Contemporary records, but in my mingled anxiety and irritation I scarcely heard them.

Toward the end of the second of these songs, Hat entered the club and fell into his customary seat a little more heavily than usual. The owner motioned away the waiter, who had begun moving toward him with the customary shot glass. Hat dropped the porkpie on the table and struggled with his coat buttons. When he heard what Hawes was playing, he sat listening with his hands still on a coat button, and I listened, too—the music had a tighter, harder, more modern feel, like Hawes' records. Hat nodded to himself, got his coat off, and struggled with the snaps on his saxophone case. The audience gave Hawes unusually appreciative applause. It took Hat longer than usual to fit the horn together, and by the time he was up on his feet, Hawes and the other two musicians had turned around to watch his progress as if they feared he would not make it all the way to the bandstand. Hat wound through the tables with his head tilted back, smiling to himself. When he got close to the stand, I saw that he was walking on his toes like a small child. The owner crossed his arms over his chest and glared. Hat seemed almost to float onto the stand. He licked his reed. Then he lowered his horn and, with his mouth open, stared out at us for a moment. "Ladies, ladies," he said in a soft, high voice. These were the first words I had ever heard him speak. "Thank you for your appreciation of our pianist, Mr. Hawes. And now I must explain my absence during the first set. My son passed away this afternoon, and I have been...busy...with details. Thank you."

With that, he spoke a single word to Hawes, put his horn back in his mouth, and began to play a blues called "Hat Jumped Up," one of his twenty songs. The audience sat motionless with shock. Hawes, the bassist, and the drummer played on as if nothing unusual had happened—

they must have known about his son, I thought. Or maybe they knew that he had no son, and had invented a grotesque excuse for turning up ninety minutes late. The club owner bit his lower lip and looked unusually introspective. Hat played one familiar, uncomplicated figure after another, his tone rough, almost coarse. At the end of his solo, he repeated one note for an entire chorus, fingering the key while staring out toward the back of the club. Maybe he was watching the customers leave—three couples and a couple of single people walked out while he was playing. But I don't think he saw anything at all. When the song was over, Hat leaned over to whisper to Hawes, and the piano player announced a short break. The second set was over.

Hat put his tenor on top of the piano and stepped down off the bandstand, pursing his mouth with concentration. The owner had come out from behind the bar and moved up in front of him as Hat tip-toed around the stand. The owner spoke a few quiet words. Hat answered. From behind, he looked slumped and tired, and his hair curled far over the back of his collar. Whatever he had said only partially satisfied the owner, who spoke again before leaving him. Hat stood in place for a moment, perhaps not noticing that the owner had gone, and resumed his tip-toe glide toward the door. Looking at his back, I think I took in for the first time how genuinely *strange* he was. Floating through the door in his grey flannel suit, hair dangling in ringlet-like strands past his collar, leaving in the air behind him the announcement about a dead son, he seemed absolutely separate from the rest of humankind, a species of one.

I turned as if for guidance to the musicians at the bar. Talking, smiling, greeting a few fans and friends, they behaved just as they did on every other night. Could Hat really have lost a son earlier today? Maybe this was the jazz way of facing grief—to come back to work, to carry on.

Still it seemed the worst of all times to approach Hat with my offer. His playing was a drunken parody of itself. He would forget anything he said to me; I was wasting my time.

On that thought, I stood up and walked past the bandstand and opened the door—if I was wasting my time, it didn't matter what I did. He was leaning against a brick wall about ten feet up the alleyway from the club's back door. The door clicked shut behind me, but Hat did not open his eyes. His face tilted up, and a sweetness that might have been sleep lay over his features. He looked exhausted and insubstantial, too frail to move. I would have gone back inside the club if he had not produced a cigarette from a pack in his shirt pocket, lit it with a match, and then flicked the match away, all without opening his eyes. At least he was awake. I stepped toward him, and his eyes opened. He glanced at me and blew out white smoke. "Taste?" he said.

I had no idea what he meant. "Can I talk to you for a minute, sir?" I asked.

He put his hand into one of his jacket pockets and pulled out a half pint bottle. "Have a taste." Hat broke the seal on the cap, tilted it into his mouth, and drank. Then he held the bottle out toward me.

I took it. "I've been coming here as often as I can."

"Me, too," he said. "Go on, do it."

I took a sip from the bottle—gin. "I'm sorry about your son."

"Son?" He looked upward, as if trying to work out my meaning. "I got a son—out on Long Island. With his momma. " He drank again and checked the level of the bottle.

"He's not dead, then."

He spoke the next words slowly, almost wonderingly. "Nobody—told—me—if—he—is." He shook his head and drank another mouthful of gin. "Damn. Wouldn't that be something, boy dies and nobody tells me? I'd have to think about that, you know, have to really *think* about that one."

"I'm just talking about what you said on stage."

He cocked his head and seemed to examine an empty place in the dark air about three feet from his face. "Uh huh. That's right. I did say that. Son of mine passed."

It was like dealing with a sphinx. All I could do was plunge in. "Well, sir, actually there's a reason I came out here," I said. "I'd like to interview you. Do you think that might be possible? You're a great artist, and there's very little about you in print. Do you think we could set up a time when I could talk to you?"

He looked at me with his bleary, colorless eyes, and I wondered if he could see me at all. And then I felt that, despite his drunkenness, he saw everything—that he saw things about me that I couldn't see.

"You a jazz writer?" he asked.

"No, I'm a graduate student. I'd just like to do it. I think it would be important."

"Important." He took another swallow from the half pint and slid the bottle back into his pocket. "Be nice, doing an *important* interview."

He stood leaning against the wall, moving further into outer space with every word. Only because I had started, I pressed on: I was already losing faith in this project. The reason Hat had never been interviewed was that ordinary American English was a foreign language to him. "Could we do the interview after you finish up at this club? I could meet you anywhere you like." Even as I said these words, I despaired. Hat was in no shape to know what he had to do after this engagement finished. I was surprised he could make it back to Long Island every night.

Hat rubbed his face, sighed, and restored my faith in him. "It'll have to wait a little while. Night after I finish here, I go to Toronto for two nights. Then I got something in Hartford on the thirtieth. You come see me after that."

"On the thirty-first?" I asked.

"Around nine, ten, something like that. Be nice if you brought some refreshments."

"Fine, great," I said, wondering if I would be able to take a late train back from wherever he lived. "But where on Long Island should I go?"

His eyes widened in mock-horror. "Don't go nowhere on Long Island. You come see me. In the Albert Hotel, Forty-Ninth and Eighth. Room 821."

I smiled at him—I had guessed right about one thing, anyhow. Hat did not live in the Village, but he did live in a Manhattan hotel. I asked him for his phone number, and wrote it down, along with the other information, on a napkin from the club. After I folded the napkin into my jacket pocket, I thanked him and turned toward the door.

"Important as a mother-fucker," he said in his high, soft, slurry voice.

I turned around in alarm, but he had tilted his head toward the sky again, and his eyes were closed.

"Indiana," he said. His voice made the word seem sung. "Moonlight in Vermont. I Thought About You. Flamingo."

He was deciding what to play during his next set. I went back inside, where twenty or thirty new arrivals, more people than I had ever seen in the club, waited for the music to start. Hat soon reappeared through the door, the other musicians left the bar, and the third set began. Hat played all four of the songs he had named, interspersing them through his standard repertoire during the course of an unusually long set. He was playing as well as I'd ever heard him, maybe better than I'd heard on all the other nights I had come to the club. The Saturday night crowd applauded explosively after every solo. I didn't know if what I was seeing was genius or desperation.

❋ ❋ ❋

An obituary in the Sunday *New York Times*, which I read over breakfast the next morning in the John Jay cafeteria, explained some of what had happened. Early Saturday morning, a thirty-eight year old tenor saxophone player named Grant Kilbert had been killed in an automobile accident. One of the most successful jazz musicians in the world, one of the few jazz musicians known outside of the immediate circle of fans, Kilbert had probably been Hat's most prominent disciple. He had certainly been one of my favorite musicians. More importantly, from his first record, *Cool Breeze,* Kilbert had excited respect and admiration. I looked at the photograph of the handsome young man beaming out over the neck of his saxophone and realized that the first four songs on *Cool Breeze* were "Indiana," "Moonlight in Vermont," "I Thought About You," and "Flamingo." Sometime late Saturday afternoon, someone had called up Hat to tell him about Kilbert. What I had seen had not merely been alcoholic eccentricity, it had been grief for a lost son. And when I thought about it, I was sure that the lost son, not himself, had been the important motherfucker he'd apothesized. What I had taken for spaciness and disconnection had all along been irony.

Part Two

1

On the thirty-first of October, after calling to make sure he remembered our appointment, I did go the Albert Hotel, room 821, and interview Hat. That is, I asked him questions and listened to the long, rambling, often obscene responses he gave them. During the long night I spent in his room, he drank the fifth of Gordon's gin, the "refreshments" I brought with me—all of it, an entire bottle of gin, without tonic, ice, or other dilutants. He just poured it into a tumbler and drank, as if it were water. (I refused his single offer of a "taste.") I frequently checked to make sure that the tape recorder I'd borrowed from a business student down the hall from me was still working, I changed tapes until they ran out, I made detailed back-up notes with a ballpoint pen in a stenographic notebook. A couple of times, he played me sections of records that he wanted me to hear, and now and then he sang a couple of bars to make sure that I understood what he was telling me. He sat me in his only chair, and during the entire night stationed himself, dressed in his pork-pie hat, a dark blue chalk-stripe suit, and white button-down shirt with a black knit tie, on the edge of his bed. This was a formal occasion. When I arrived at nine o'clock, he addressed me as "Mr. Leonard Feather" (the name of a well-known jazz critic), and when he opened his door at six-thirty the next morning, he called me "Miss Rosemary." By then, I knew that this was an allusion to Rosemary Clooney, whose singing I had learned that he liked, and that the nickname meant he liked me, too. It was not at all certain, however, that he remembered my actual name.

I had three sixty-minute tapes and a notebook filled with handwriting that gradually degenerated from my usual scrawl into loops and wiggles that resembled Arabic more than English. Over the next month, I spent whatever spare time I had transcribing the tapes and trying to decipher my own handwriting. I wasn't sure that what I had was an interview. My carefully-prepared questions had been met either with evasions or blank, silent refusals to answer—he had simply started talking about something else. After about an hour, I realized that this was his interview, not mine, and let him roll.

October Dreams

After my notes had been typed up and the tapes transcribed, I put everything in a drawer and went back to work on my MA. What I had was even more puzzling than I'd thought, and straightening it out would have taken more time than I could afford. So the rest of that academic year was a long grind of studying for the comprehensive exam and getting a thesis ready. Until I picked up an old *Time* magazine in the John Jay lounge and saw his name in the "Milestones" columns, I didn't even know that Hat had died.

Two months after I'd interviewed him, he had begun to hemorrhage on a flight back from France; an ambulance had taken him directly from the airport to a hospital. Five days after his release from the hospital, he had died in his bed at the Albert.

After I earned my degree, I was determined to wrestle something useable from my long night with Hat—I owed it to him. During the first weeks of that summer, I wrote out a version of what Hat had said to me and sent it to the only publication I thought would be interested in it. *Downbeat* accepted the interview, and it appeared there about six months later. Eventually, it acquired some fame as the last of his rare public statements. I still see lines from the interview quoted in the sort of pieces about Hat never printed during his life. Sometimes they are lines he really did say to me; sometimes they are stitched together from remarks he made at different times; sometimes, they are quotations I invented in order to be able to use other things he did say.

But one section of that interview has never been quoted, because it was never printed. I never figured out what to make of it. Certainly I could not believe all he had said. He had been putting me on, silently laughing at my credulity, for he could not possibly believe that what he was telling me was literal truth. I was a white boy with a tape recorder, it was Halloween, and Hat was having fun with me. He was *jiving* me.

Now I feel different about his story, and about him, too. He was a great man, and I was an unwordly kid. He was drunk, and I was priggishly sober, but in every important way, he was functioning far above my level. Hat had lived forty-nine years as a black man in America, and I'd spent all of my twenty-one years in white suburbs. He was an immensely talented musician, a man who virtually thought in music, and I can't even hum in tune. That I expected to understand anything at all about him staggers me now. Back then, I didn't know anything about grief, and Hat wore grief about him daily, like a cloak. Now that I am the age he was then, I see that most of what is called information is interpretation, and interpretation is always partial.

Probably Hat was putting me on, jiving me, though not maliciously. He certainly was not telling me the literal truth, though I have never been able to learn what was the literal truth of this case. It's possible that even Hat never knew what was the literal truth behind the story he told me—possible, I mean, that he was still trying to work out what the truth was, nearly forty years after the fact.

2

He started telling me the story after we heard what I thought were gunshots from the street. I jumped from the chair and rushed to the windows, which looked out onto Eighth Avenue. "Kids," Hat said. In the hard yellow light of the streetlamps, four or five teenage boys trotted up the Avenue. Three of them carried paper bags. "Kids shooting?" I asked. My amazement tells you how long ago this was.

"Fireworks," Hat said. "Every Halloween in New York, fool kids run around with bags full of fireworks, trying to blow their hands off."

Here and in what follows, I am not going to try to represent the way

Hat actually spoke. I cannot represent the way his voice glided over certain words and turned others into mushy growls, though he expressed more than half of his meaning by sound; and I don't want to reproduce his constant, reflexive obscenity. Hat couldn't utter four words in a row without throwing in a "motherfucker." Mostly, I have replaced his obscenities with other words, and the reader can imagine what was really said. Also, if I tried to imitate his grammar, I'd sound racist and he would sound stupid. Hat left school in the fourth grade, and his language, though precise, was casual. To add to these difficulties, Hat employed a private language of his own, a code to ensure that he would be understood only by the people he wished to understand him. I have replaced most of his code words with their equivalents.

It must have been around one in the morning, which means that I had been in his room about four hours. Until Hat explained the "gunshots," I had forgotten that it was Halloween night, and I told him this as I turned away from the window.

"I never forget about Halloween," Hat said. "If I can, I stay home on Halloween. Don't want to be out on the street, that night."

He had already given me proof that he was superstitious, and as he spoke he glanced almost nervously around the room, as if looking for sinister presences.

"You'd feel in danger?" I asked.

He rolled gin around in his mouth and looked at me as he had in the alley behind the club, taking note of qualities I myself did not yet perceive. This did not feel at all judgmental. The nervousness I thought I had seen had disappeared, and his manner seemed marginally more concentrated than earlier in the evening. He swallowed the gin and looked at me without speaking for a couple of seconds.

"No," he finally said. "Not exactly. But I wouldn't feel safe, either."

I sat with my pen half an inch from the page of my notebook, uncertain whether or not to write this down.

"I'm from Mississippi, you know."

I nodded.

"Funny things happen down there. Back when I was a little kid, it was a whole different world. Know what I mean?"

"I can guess," I said.

He nodded. "Sometimes people disappeared. They'd be *gone*. All kinds of stuff used to happen, stuff you wouldn't even believe in now. I met a witch-lady once who could put curses on you, make you go blind and crazy. Another time, I saw a mean, murdering son of a bitch named Eddie Grimes die and come back to life—he got shot to death at a dance we were playing, he was *dead*, and a woman went down and whispered to him, and Eddie Grimes stood right back up on his feet. The man who shot him took off double-quick and he must have kept on going, because we never saw him after that."

"Did you start playing again?" I asked, taking notes as fast as I could.

"We never stopped," Hat said. "You let the people deal with what's going on, but you gotta keep on playing."

"Did you live in the country?" I asked, thinking that all of this sounded like Dogpatch—witches and walking dead men.

He shook his head. "I was brought up in town, Woodland, Mississippi. On the river. Where we lived was called Darktown, you know, but most of Woodland was white, with nice houses and all. Lots of our people did the cooking and washing in the big houses on Miller's Hill, that kind of work. In fact, we lived in a pretty nice house, for Darktown—the band always did well, and my father had a couple of other jobs on top of that. He was a good piano player, mainly, but he could play any kind of instrument. And he was a big, strong guy, nice-looking, real light-complected, so he was called Red, which was what that meant in those days. People respected him."

Another long, rattling burst of explosions came from Eighth Avenue. I wanted to ask him again about leaving his father's band, but Hat once more gave his little room a quick inspection, swallowed another mouthful of gin, and went on talking.

"We even went out trick or treating on Halloween, you know, like the white kids. I guess our people didn't do that everywhere, but we did. Naturally, we stuck to our neighborhood, and probably we got a lot less than the kids from Miller's Hill, but they didn't have anything up there that tasted as good as the apples and candy we brought home in our bags. Around us, people made instead of bought, and that's the difference." He smiled at either the memory or the unexpected sentimentality he had just revealed—for a moment, he looked both lost in time and uneasy with himself for having said too much. "Or maybe I just remember it that way, you know? Anyhow, we used to raise some hell, too. You were *supposed* to raise hell, on Halloween."

"You went out with your brothers?" I asked.

"No, no, they were—" He flipped his hand in the air, dismissing whatever it was that his brothers had been. "I was always apart, you dig? Me, I was always into my own little things. I was that way right from the beginning. I play like that—never play like anyone else, don't even play like myself. You gotta find new places for yourself, or else nothing's happening, isn't that right? Don't want to be a repeater pencil." He saluted this declaration with another swallow of gin. "Back in those days, I used to go out with a boy named Rodney Sparks—we called him Dee, short for Demon, 'cause Dee Sparks would do anything that came into his head. That boy was the bravest little bastard I ever knew. He'd wrassle a mad dog. And the reason was, Dee was the preacher's boy. If you happen to be the preacher's boy, seems like you gotta prove every way you can that you're no Buster Brown, you know? So I hung with Dee, because I wasn't any Buster Brown, either. This is when we were eleven, around then—the time when you talk about girls, you know, but you still aren't too sure what that's about. You don't know what *anything's* about, to tell the truth. You along for the ride, you trying to pack in as much fun as possible. So Dee was my right hand, and when I went out on Halloween in Woodland, I went out with *him*."

He rolled his eyes toward the window and said, "Yeah." An expression I could not read at all took over his face. By the standards of ordinary people, Hat almost always looked detached, even impassive, tuned to some private wavelength, and this sense of detachment had intensified. I thought he was changing mental gears, dismissing his childhood, and opened my mouth to ask him about Grant Kilbert. But he raised his glass to his mouth again and rolled his eyes back to me, and the quality of his gaze told me to keep quiet.

"I didn't know it," he said, "but I was getting ready to stop being a little boy. To stop believing in little boy things and start seeing like a grown-up. I guess that's part of what I liked about Dee Sparks—he seemed like he was a lot more grown-up than I was, shows you what my head was like. The age we were, this would have been the last time we went out on Halloween to get apples and candy. From then on, we would have gone out mainly to raise hell. Scare the shit out of little kids. But the way it turned out, it was the last time we ever went out on Halloween."

He finished off the gin in his glass and reached down to pick the bottle off the floor and pour another few inches into the tumbler. "Here I am, sitting in this room. There's my horn over there. Here's this bottle. You know what I'm saying?"

I didn't. I had no idea what he was saying. The hint of fatality clung to his earlier statement, and for a second I thought he was going to say that he was here but Dee Sparks was nowhere because Dee Sparks had died in Woodland, Mississippi, at the age of eleven on Halloween night. Hat was looking at me with a steady curiosity which compelled a response. "What happened?" I asked.

Now I know that he was saying *It has come down to just this, my room, my horn, my bottle*. My question was as good as any other response.

"If I was to tell you everything that happened, we'd have to stay in this room for a month." He smiled and straightened up on the bed. His ankles were crossed, and for the first time I noticed that his feet, shod in dark suede shoes with crepe soles, did not quite touch the floor. "And, you know, I never tell anybody everything, I always have to keep something back for myself. Things turned out all right. Only thing I mind is, I should have earned more money. Grant Kilbert, he earned a lot of money, and some of that was mine, you know."

"Were you friends?" I asked.

"I knew the man." He tilted his head and stared at the ceiling for so long that eventually I looked up at it, too. It was not a remarkable ceiling. A circular section near the center had been replastered not long before.

"No matter where you live, there are places you're not supposed to go," he said, still gazing up. "And sooner or later, you're gonna wind up there." He smiled at me again. "Where we lived, the place you weren't supposed to go was called The Backs. Out of town, stuck in the woods on one little path. In Darktown, we had all kinds from preachers on down. We had washerwomen and blacksmiths and carpenters, and we had some no-good thieving trash, too, like Eddie Grimes, that man who came back from being dead. In The Backs, they started with trash like

Eddie Grimes, and went down from there. Sometimes, our people went out there to buy a jug, and sometimes they went there to get a woman, but they never talked about it. The Backs was *rough*. What they had was *rough*." He rolled his eyes at me and said, "That witch-lady I told you about, she lived in The Backs." He snickered. "Man, they were a mean bunch of people. They'd cut you, you looked at 'em bad. But one thing funny about the place, white and colored lived there just the same—it was *integrated*. Backs people were so evil, color didn't make no difference to them. They hated everybody anyhow, on principle." Hat pointed his glass at me, tilted his head, and narrowed his eyes. "At least, that was what everybody *said*. So this particular Halloween, Dee Sparks says to me after we finish with Darktown, we ought to head out to The Backs and see what the place is really like. Maybe we can have some fun.

"The idea of going out to The Backs kind of scared me, but being scared was part of the fun—Halloween, right? And if anyplace in Woodland was perfect for all that Halloween shit, you know, someplace where you might really see a ghost or a goblin, The Backs was better than the graveyard." Hat shook his head, holding the glass out at a right angle to his body. A silvery amusement momentarily transformed him, and it struck me that his native elegance, the product of his character and bearing much more than of the handsome suit and the suede shoes, had in effect been paid for by the surviving of a thousand unimaginable difficulties, each painful to a varying degree. Then I realized that what I meant by elegance was really dignity, that for the first time I had recognized actual dignity in another human being, and that dignity was nothing like the self-congratulatory superiority people usually mistook for it.

"We were just little babies, and we wanted some of those good old

Halloween scares. Like those dumbbells out on the street, tossing firecrackers at each other." Hat wiped his free hand down over his face and made sure that I was prepared to write down everything he said. (The tapes had already been used up.) "When I'm done, tell me if we found it, okay?"

"Okay," I said.

3

"Dee showed up at my house just after dinner, dressed in an old sheet with two eyeholes cut in it and carrying a paper bag. His big old shoes stuck out underneath the sheet. I had the same costume, but it was the one my brother used the year before, and it dragged along the ground and my feet got caught in it. The eyeholes kept sliding away from my eyes. My mother gave me a bag and told me to behave myself and get home before eight. It didn't take but half an hour to cover all the likely houses in Darktown, but she knew I'd want to fool around with Dee for an hour or so afterwards.

"Then up and down the streets we go, knocking on the doors where they'd give us stuff and making a little mischief where we knew they wouldn't. Nothing real bad, just banging on the door and running like hell, throwing rocks on the roof, little stuff. A few places, we plain and simple stayed away from—the places where people like Eddie Grimes lived. I always thought that was funny. We knew enough to steer clear of those houses, but we were still crazy to get out to The Backs.

"Only way I can figure it is, The Backs was *forbidden*. Nobody had to tell us to stay away from Eddie Grimes' house at night. You wouldn't even go there in the daylight, 'cause Eddie Grimes would get you and that would be that.

"Anyhow, Dee kept us moving along real quick, and when folks asked us questions or said they wouldn't give us stuff unless we sang a song, he moaned like a ghost and shook his bag in their faces, so we could get away faster. He was so excited, I think he was almost shaking.

"Me, I was excited, too. Not like Dee—sort of sick-excited, the way people must feel the first time they use a parachute. Scared-excited.

"As soon as we got away from the last house, Dee crossed the street and started running down the side of the little general store we all used. I knew where he was going. Out behind the store was a field, and on the other side of the field was Meridian Road, which took you out into the woods and to the path up to The Backs. When he realized that I wasn't next to him, he turned around and yelled at me to hurry up. *No,* I said inside myself, *I ain't gonna jump outta this here airplane, I'm not dumb enough to do that.* And then I pulled up my sheet and scrunched up my eye to look through the one hole close enough to see through, and I took off after him.

"It was beginning to get dark when Dee and I left my house, and now it was dark. The Backs was about a mile and a half away, or at least the path was. We didn't know how far along that path you had to go before you got there. Hell, we didn't even know what it was—I was still thinking the place was a collection of little houses, like a sort of shadow-Woodland. And then, while we were crossing the field, I stepped on my costume and fell down flat on my face. Enough of this stuff, I said, and yanked the damned thing off. Dee started cussing me out, I wasn't doing this stuff the right way, we had to keep our costumes on in case anybody saw us, did I forget that this is Halloween, on Halloween a costume *protected* you. So I told l him I'd put it back on when we got there. If I kept on falling down, it'd take us twice as long. That shut him up.

"As soon as I got that blasted sheet over my head, I discovered that

I could see at least a little ways ahead of me. The moon was up, and a lot of stars were out. Under his sheet, Dee Sparks looked a little bit like a real ghost. It kind of glimmered. You couldn't really make out its edges, so the darn thing like *floated.* But I could see his legs and those big old shoes sticking out.

"We got out of the field and started up Meridian Road, and pretty soon the trees came up right to the ditches alongside the road, and I couldn't see too well any more. The road seemed like it went smack into the woods and disappeared. The trees looked taller and thicker than in the daytime, and now and then something right at the edge of the woods shone round and white, like an eye—reflecting the moonlight, I guess. Spooked me. I didn't think we'd ever be able to find the path up to The Backs, and that was fine with me. I thought we might go along the road another ten-fifteen minutes, and then turn around and go home. Dee was swooping around up in front of me, flapping his sheet and acting bughouse. *He* sure wasn't trying too hard to find that path.

"After we walked about a mile down Meridian Road, I saw headlights like yellow dots coming toward us fast—Dee didn't see anything at all, running around in circles the way he was. I shouted at him to get off the road, and he took off like a rabbit—disappeared into the woods before I did. I jumped the ditch and hunkered down behind a pine about ten feet off the road to see who was coming. There weren't many cars in Woodland in those days, and I knew every one of them. When the car came by, it was Dr. Garland's old red Cord—Dr. Garland was a white man, but he had two waiting rooms and took colored patients, so colored patients was mostly what he had. And the man was a heavy drinker, *heavy* drinker. He zipped by, goin' at least fifty, which was mighty fast for those days, probably as fast as that old Cord would go. For about a second, I saw Dr. Garland's face under his white hair, and his mouth was wide open, stretched like he was screaming. After he passed, I waited a long time before I came out of the woods. Turning around and going home would have been fine with me. Dr. Garland changed everything. Normally, he was kind of slow and quiet, you know, and I could still see that black screaming hole opened up in his face—he looked like he was being tortured, like he was in Hell. I sure as hell didn't want to see whatever *he* had seen.

"I could hear the Cord's engine after the tail lights disappeared. I turned around and saw that I was all alone on the road. Dee Sparks was nowhere in sight. A couple of times, real soft, I called out his name. Then I called his name a little louder. Away off in the woods, I heard Dee giggle. I said he could run around all night if he liked but I was going home, and then I saw that pale silver sheet moving through the trees, and I started back down Meridian Road. After about twenty paces, I looked back, and there he was, standing in the middle of the road in that silly sheet, watching me go. Come on, I said, let's get back. He paid me no mind. Wasn't that Dr. Garland? Where was he going, as fast as that? What was happening? When I said the doctor was probably out on some emergency, Dee said the man was going *home*—he lived in Woodland, didn't he?

"Then I thought maybe Dr. Garland had been up in The Backs. And Dee thought the same thing, which made him want to go there all the more. Now he was determined. Maybe we'd see some dead guy. We stood there until I understood that he was going to go by himself if I didn't go with him. That meant that I *had* to go. Wild as he was, Dee'd get himself into some kind of mess for sure if I wasn't there to hold him down. So I said okay, I was coming along, and Dee started swooping along like before, saying crazy stuff. There was no way we were going to be able to find some little old path that went up into the woods. It was so dark, you couldn't see the separate trees, only giant black walls on both sides of the road.

"We went so far along Meridian Road I was sure we must have passed it. Dee was running around in circles about ten feet ahead of me. I told him that we missed the path, and now it was time to get back home. He laughed at me and ran across to the right side of the road and disappeared into the darkness.

"I told him to get back, damn it, and he laughed some more and said I should come to *him*. Why? I said, and he said, Because this here is the path, dummy. I didn't believe him—came right up to where he disappeared. All I could see was a black wall that could have been trees or just plain night. Moron, Dee said, look down. And I did. Sure enough, one of those white things like an eye shone up from where the ditch should have been. I bent down and touched cold little stones, and the shining dot of white went off like a light—a pebble that caught the moonlight just right. Bending down like that, I could see the hump of grass growing up between the tire tracks that led out onto Meridian Road. He'd found the path, all right.

"At night, Dee Sparks could see one hell of a lot better than me. He spotted the break in the ditch from across the road. He was already walking up the path in those big old shoes, turning around every other step to look back at me, make sure I was coming along behind him. When I started following him, Dee told me to get my sheet back on, and I pulled the thing over my head even though I'd rather have sucked the water out of a hollow stump. But I knew he was right—on Halloween, especially in a place like where we were, you were safer in a costume.

"From then on in, we were in No Man's Land. Neither one of us had any idea how far we had to go to get to The Backs, or what it would look like once we got there. Once I set foot on that wagon-track I knew for sure The Backs wasn't anything like the way I thought. It was a lot more primitive than a bunch of houses in the woods. Maybe they didn't even have houses! Maybe they lived in caves!

"Naturally, after I got that blamed costume over my head, I couldn't see for a while. Dee kept hissing at me to hurry up, and I kept cussing him out. Finally I bunched up a couple handfuls of the sheet right under my chin and held it against my neck, and that way I could see pretty well and walk without tripping all over myself. All I had to do was follow Dee, and that was easy. He was only a couple of inches in front of me, and even through one eye-hole, I could see that silvery sheet moving along.

"Things moved in the woods, and once in a while an owl hooted. To tell you the truth, I never did like being out in the woods at night. Even back then, give me a nice warm barroom instead, and I'd be happy. Only animal I ever liked was a cat, because a cat is soft to the touch, and it'll fall asleep on your lap. But this was even worse than usual, because of Halloween, and even before we got to The Backs, I wasn't sure if what I heard moving around in the woods was just a possum or a fox or something a lot worse, something with funny eyes and long teeth that liked the taste of little boys. Maybe Eddie Grimes was out there, looking for whatever kind of treat Eddie Grimes liked on Halloween night. Once I thought of that, I got so close to Dee Sparks I could smell him right through his sheet.

"You know what Dee Sparks smelled like? Like sweat, and a little bit like the soap the preacher made him use on his hands and face before dinner, but really like a fire in a junction box. A sharp, kind of bitter smell. That's how excited he was.

"After a while we were going uphill, and then we got to the top of the rise, and a breeze pressed my sheet against my legs. We started going downhill, and over Dee's electrical fire, I could smell wood smoke. And something else I couldn't name. Dee stopped moving so sudden, I bumped into him. I asked him what he could see. Nothing but the woods, he said, but we're getting there. People are up ahead somewhere. And they got a still. We got to be real quiet from here on out, he told me, as if he had to, and to let him know I understood I pulled him off the path into the woods.

"Well, I thought, at least I know what Dr. Garland was after.

"Dee and I went snaking through the trees—me holding that blamed sheet under my chin so I could see out of one eye, at least, and walk without falling down. I was glad for that big fat pad of pine needles on the ground. An elephant could have walked over that stuff as quiet as a beetle. We went along a little further, and it got so I could smell all kinds of stuff—burned sugar, crushed juniper berries, tobacco juice, grease. And after Dee and I moved a little bit along, I heard voices, and that was enough for me. Those voices sounded angry.

"I yanked at Dee's sheet and squatted down—I wasn't going any farther without taking a good look. He slipped down beside me. I pushed the wad of material under my chin up over my face, grabbed another handful, and yanked that up, too, to look out under the bottom of the sheet. Once I could actually *see* where we were, I almost passed out. Twenty feet away through the trees, a kerosene lantern lit up the grease-paper window cut into the back of a little wooden shack, and a big raggedy guy carrying another kerosene lantern came stepping out of a door we couldn't see and stumbled toward a shed. On the other side of the building I could see the yellow square of a window in another shack, and past that, another one, a sliver of yellow shining out through the trees. Dee was crouched next to me, and when I turned to look at him, I could see another chink of yellow light from some way off in the woods over that way. Whether he knew it not, he'd just about walked us straight into the middle of The Backs.

"He whispered for me to cover my face. I shook my head. Both of us watched the big guy stagger toward the shed. Somewhere in front of us, a woman screeched, and I almost dumped a load in my pants. Dee stuck his hand out from under his sheet and held it out, as if I needed *him* to tell me to be quiet. The woman screeched again, and the big guy sort of swayed back and forth. The light from the lantern swung around in big circles. I saw that the woods were full of little paths that ran between the shacks. The light hit the shack, and it wasn't even wood, but tar paper. The woman laughed or maybe sobbed. Whoever was inside the shack shouted, and the raggedy guy wobbled toward the shed again. He was so drunk he couldn't even walk straight. When he got to the shed, he set down the lantern and bent to get in.

"Dee put his mouth up to my ear and whispered, Cover up—you don't want these people to see who you are. Rip the eyeholes, if you can't see good enough.

"I didn't want anyone in The Backs to see my face. I let the costume drop down over me again, and stuck my fingers in the nearest eyehole and pulled. Every living thing for about a mile around must have heard that cloth ripping. The big guy came out of the shed like someone pulled him out on a string, yanked the lantern up off the ground, and held it in our direction. Then we could see his face, and it was Eddie Grimes. You wouldn't want to run into Eddie Grimes anywhere, but The Backs was the last place you'd want to come across him. I was afraid he was going to start looking for us, but that woman started making stuck pig noises, and the man in the shack yelled something, and Grimes ducked back into the shed and came out with a jug. He lumbered back toward the shack and disappeared around the front of it. Dee and I could hear him arguing with the man inside.

"I jerked my thumb toward Meridian Road, but Dee shook his head. I whispered, Didn't you already see Eddie Grimes, and isn't that enough for you? He shook his head again. His eyes were gleaming behind that sheet. So what do you want, I asked, and he said, I want to see that girl. We don't even know where she is, I whispered, and Dee said, All we got to do is follow her sound.

"Dee and I sat and listened for a while. Every now and then, she let out a sort of whoop, and then she'd sort of cry, and after that she might say a word or two that sounded almost ordinary before she got going again on crying or laughing, the two all mixed up together. Sometimes we could hear other noises coming from the shacks, and none of them sounded happy. People were grumbling and arguing or just plain talking to themselves, but at least they sounded normal. That lady, she sounded like *Halloween*—like something that came up out of a grave.

"Probably you're thinking what I was hearing was sex—that I was too young to know how much noise ladies make when they're having fun. Well, maybe I was only eleven, but I grew up in Darktown, not Miller's Hill, and our walls were none too thick. What was going on with this lady didn't have anything to do with fun. The strange thing is, Dee didn't know that—he thought just what you were thinking. He wanted to see this lady getting humped. Maybe he even thought he could sneak in and get some for himself, I don't know. The main thing is, he thought he was listening to some wild sex, and he wanted to get close enough to see it. Well, I thought, his daddy was a preacher, and maybe preachers didn't do it once they got kids. And Dee didn't have an older brother like mine, who sneaked girls into the house whenever he thought he wouldn't get caught.

"He started sliding sideways through the woods, and I had to follow him. I'd seen enough of The Backs to last me the rest of my life, but I couldn't run off and leave Dee behind. And at least he was going at it the right way, circling around the shacks sideways, instead of trying to sneak straight through them. I started off after him. At least I could see a little better ever since I ripped at my eyehole, but I still had to hold my blasted costume bunched up under my chin, and if I moved my head or my hand the wrong way, the hole moved away from my eye and I couldn't see anything at all.

"So naturally, the first thing that happened was that I lost sight of Dee Sparks. My foot came down in a hole and I stumbled ahead for a few steps, completely blind, and then I hit a tree. I just came to a halt, sure that Eddie Grimes and a few other murderers were about to jump on me. For a couple of seconds I stood as still as a wooden Indian, too scared to move. When I didn't hear anything, I hauled at my costume until I could see out of it. No murderers were coming toward me from the shack beside the still. Eddie Grimes was saying *You don't understand* over and over, like he was so drunk that one phrase got stuck in his head, and he couldn't say or hear anything else. That woman yipped, like an animal noise, not a human one—like a fox barking. I sidled up next to the tree I'd run into and looked around for Dee. All I could see was dark trees and that one yellow window I'd seen before. To hell with Dee Sparks, I said to myself, and pulled the costume off over my head. I could see better, but there wasn't any glimmer of white over that way. He'd gone so far ahead of me I couldn't even see him.

"So I had to catch up with him, didn't I? I knew where he was going—the woman's noises were coming from the shack way up there in the woods—and I knew he was going to sneak around the outside of the shacks. In a couple of seconds, after he noticed I wasn't there, he was going to stop and wait for me. Makes sense, doesn't it? All I had to do was keep going toward that shack off to the side until I ran into him. I shoved my costume inside my shirt, and then I did something else—set my bag of candy down next to the tree. I'd clean forgotten about it ever since I saw Eddie Grimes' face, and if I had to run, I'd go faster without holding onto a lot of apples and chunks of taffy.

"About a minute later, I came out into the open between two big old chinaberry trees. There was a patch of grass between me and the next stand of trees. The woman made a gargling sound that ended in one of those fox-yips, and I looked up in that direction and saw that the clearing extended in a straight line up and down, like a path. Stars shone out of the patch of darkness between the two parts of the woods. And when I started to walk across it, I felt a grassy hump between two beaten tracks. The path into The Backs off Meridian Road curved around somewhere up ahead and wound back down through the shacks before it came to a dead end. It had to come to a dead end, because it sure didn't join back up with Meridian Road.

"And this was how I'd managed to lose sight of Dee Sparks. Instead of avoiding the path and working his way north through the woods, he'd just taken the easiest way toward the woman's shack. Hell, I'd had to pull him off the path in the first place! By the time I got out of my sheet, he was probably way up there, out in the open for anyone to see and too excited to notice that he was all by himself. What I had to do was what I'd been trying to do all along, save his ass from anybody who might see him.

"As soon as I started going as soft as I could up the path, I saw that saving Dee Sparks' ass might be a tougher job than I thought—maybe I couldn't even save my own. When I first took off my costume, I'd seen lights from three or four shacks. I thought that's what The Backs was—

three or four shacks. But after I started up the path, I saw a low square shape standing between two trees at the edge of the woods and realized that it was another shack. Whoever was inside had extinguished his kerosene lamp, or maybe wasn't home. About twenty-thirty feet on, there was another shack, all dark, and the only reason I noticed that one was, I heard voices coming from it, a man and a woman, both of them sounding drunk and slowed-down. Deeper in the woods past that one, another grease-paper window gleamed through the trees like a firefly. There were shacks all over the woods. As soon as I realized that Dee and I might not be the only people walking through The Backs on Halloween night, I bent down low to the ground and damn near slowed to a standstill. The only thing Dee had going for him, I thought, was good night vision—at least he might spot someone before they spotted him.

"A noise came from one of those shacks, and I stopped cold, with my heart pounding away like a bass drum. Then a big voice yelled out, *Who's that?*, and I just lay down in the track and tried to disappear. *Who's there?* Here I was calling Dee a fool, and I was making more noise than he did. I heard that man walk outside his door, and my heart pretty near exploded. Then the woman moaned up ahead, and the man who'd heard me swore to himself and went back inside. I just lay there in the dirt for a while. The woman moaned again, and this time it sounded scarier than ever, because it had a kind of a chuckle in it. She was crazy. Or she was a witch, and if she was having sex, it was with the devil. That was enough to make me start crawling along, and I kept on crawling until I was long past the shack where the man had heard me. Finally I got up on my feet again, thinking that if I didn't see Dee Sparks real soon, I was going to sneak back to Meridian Road by myself. If Dee Sparks wanted to see a witch in bed with the devil, he could do it without me.

"And then I thought I was a fool not to ditch Dee, because hadn't he ditched me? After all this time, he must have noticed that I wasn't with him any more. Did he come back and look for me? The hell he did.

"And right then I would have gone back home, but for two things. The first was that I heard that woman make another sound—a sound that was hardly human, but wasn't made by any animal. It wasn't even loud. And it sure as hell wasn't any witch in bed with the devil. It made me want to throw up. That woman was being *hurt*. She wasn't just getting beat up—I knew what that sounded like—she was being hurt bad enough to drive her crazy, bad enough to kill her. Because you couldn't live through being hurt bad enough to make that sound. I was in The Backs, sure enough, and the place was even worse than it was supposed to be. Someone was killing a woman, everybody could hear it, and all that happened was that Eddie Grimes fetched another jug back from the still. I froze. When I could move, I pulled my ghost costume out from inside my shirt, because Dee was right, and for certain I didn't want anybody seeing my face out there on *this* night. And then the second thing happened. While I was pulling the sheet over my head, I saw something pale lying in the grass a couple of feet back toward the woods I'd come out of, and when I looked at it, it turned into Dee Sparks' Halloween bag.

"I went up to the bag and touched it to make sure about what it was. I'd found Dee's bag, all right. And it was empty. Flat. He had stuffed the contents into his pockets and left the bag behind. What that meant was, I couldn't turn around and leave him—because he hadn't left me after all. He waited for me until he couldn't stand it any more, and then he emptied his bag and left it behind as a sign. He was counting on me to see in the dark as well as he could. But I wouldn't have seen it all if that woman hadn't stopped me cold.

"The top of the bag was pointing north, so Dee was still heading toward the woman's shack. I looked up that way, and all I could see was a solid wall of darkness underneath a lighter darkness filled with stars. For about a second, I realized, I had felt pure relief. Dee had ditched me, so I could ditch him and go home. Now I was stuck with Dee all over again.

"About twenty feet ahead, another surprise jumped up at me out of darkness. Something that looked like a little tiny shack began to take shape; and I got down on my hands and knees to crawl toward the path when I saw a long silver gleam along the top of the thing. That meant it had to be metal—tar paper might have a lot of uses, but it never yet reflected starlight. Once I realized that the thing in front of me was metal, I remembered its shape and realized it was a car. You wouldn't think you'd come across a car in a down-and-out rathole like The Backs, would you? People like that, they don't even own two shirts, so how do they come by cars? Then I remembered Dr. Garland speeding away down Meridian Road, and I thought *You don't have to live in The Backs to drive there.* Someone could turn up onto the path, drive around the loop, pull his car off onto the grass, and no one would ever see it or know that he was there.

"And this made me feel funny. The car probably belonged to someone I knew. Our band played dances and parties all over the county and everywhere in Woodland, and I'd probably seen every single person in town, and they'd seen me, too, and knew me by name. I walked closer to the car to see if I recognized it, but it was just an old black Model T. There must have been twenty cars just like it in Woodland. Whites and coloreds, the few coloreds that owned cars, both had them. And when I got right up beside the Model T, I saw what Dee had left for me on the hood—an apple.

"About twenty feet further along, there was an apple on top of a big old stone. He was putting those apples where I couldn't help but see them. The third one was on top of a post at the edge of the woods, and it was so pale it looked almost white. Next to the post one of those paths running all through The Backs led back into the woods. If it hadn't been for that apple, I would have gone right past it.

"At least I didn't have to worry so much about making noise once I got back into the woods. Must have been six inches of pine needles and fallen leaves underfoot, and I walked so quiet I could have been floating—I've worn crepe soles ever since then, and for the same reason. You walk *soft*. But I was still plenty scared—back in the woods there was a lot less light, and I'd have to step on an apple to see it. All I wanted was to find Dee and persuade him to leave with me.

"For a while, all I did was keep moving between the trees and try to make sure I wasn't coming up on a shack. Every now and then, a faint, slurry voice came from somewhere off in the woods, but I didn't let it spook me. Then, way up ahead, I saw Dee Sparks. The path didn't go in a straight line, it kind of angled back and forth, so I didn't have a good clear look at him, but I got a flash of that silvery-looking sheet way off through the trees. If I sped up I could get to him before he did anything stupid. I pulled my costume up a little further toward my neck and started to jog.

"The path started dipping *downhill*. I couldn't figure it out. Dee was in a straight line ahead of me, and as soon as I followed the path downhill a little bit, I lost sight of him. After a couple more steps, I stopped. The path got a lot steeper. If I kept running, I'd go ass over teakettle. The woman made another terrible sound, and it seemed to come from everywhere at once. Like everything around me had been *hurt*. I damn near came unglued. Seemed like everything was *dying*. That Halloween stuff about horrible creatures wasn't any story, man, it was the way things really were—you couldn't know anything, you couldn't trust anything, and you were surrounded by *death*. I almost fell down and cried like a baby boy. I was lost. I didn't think I'd ever get back home.

"Then the worst thing of all happened.

"I heard her die. It was just a little noise, more like a sigh than anything, but that sigh came from everywhere and went straight into my ear. A soft sound can be loud, too, you know, be the loudest thing you ever heard. That sigh about lifted me up off the ground, about blew my head apart.

"I stumbled down the path, trying to wipe my eyes with my costume, and all of a sudden I heard men's voices from off to my left. Someone was saying a word I couldn't understand over and over, and someone else was telling him to shut up. Then, behind me, I heard running—heavy running, a man. I took off, and right away my feet got tangled up in the sheet and I was rolling downhill, hitting my head on rocks and bouncing off trees and smashing into stuff I didn't have any idea what it was. Biff bop bang slam smash clang crash ding dong. I hit something big and solid and wound up half-covered in water. Took me a long time to get upright, twisted up in the sheet the way I was. My ears buzzed, and I saw stars—yellow and blue and red stars, not real ones. When I tried to sit up, the blasted sheet pulled me back down, so I got a faceful of cold water. I scrambled around like a fox in a trap, and when I finally got so I was at least sitting up, I saw a slash of real sky out the corner of one eye, and I got my hands free and ripped that hole in the sheet wide enough for my whole head to fit through it.

"I was sitting in a little stream next to a fallen tree. The tree was what had stopped me. My whole body hurt like the dickens. No idea where I was. Wasn't even sure I could stand up. Got my hands on the top of the fallen tree and pushed myself up with my legs—blasted sheet ripped in half, and my knees almost bent back the wrong way, but I got up on my feet. And there was Dee Sparks, coming toward me through the woods on the other side of the stream.

"He looked like he didn't feel any better than I did, like he couldn't move in a straight line. His silvery sheet was smearing through the trees. *Dee got hurt, too*, I thought—he looked like he was in some total panic. The next time I saw the white smear between the trees it was twisting about ten feet off the ground. *No,* I said to myself, and closed my eyes. Whatever that thing was, it wasn't Dee. An unbearable feeling, an absolute despair, flowed out from it. I fought against this wave of despair with every weapon I had. I didn't want to know that feeling. I couldn't know that feeling—I was eleven years old. If that feeling reached me when I was eleven years old, my entire life would be changed, I'd be in a different universe altogether.

"But it did reach me, didn't it? I could say *no* all I liked, but I couldn't change what had happened. I opened my eyes, and the white smear was gone.

"That was almost worse—I wanted it to be Dee after all, doing something crazy and reckless, climbing trees, running around like a wild man, trying to give me a big whopping scare. But it wasn't Dee Sparks, and it meant that the worst things I'd ever imagined were true. Everything was dying. You couldn't know anything, you couldn't trust anything, we were all lost in the midst of the death that surrounded us.

"Most people will tell you growing up means you stop believing in Halloween things—I'm telling you the reverse. You start to grow up when you understand that the stuff that scares you is part of the air you breathe.

"I stared at the spot where I'd seen that twist of whiteness, I guess trying to go back in time to before I saw Dr. Garland fleeing down Meridian Road. My face looked like his, I thought—because now I knew that you really *could* see a ghost. The heavy footsteps I'd heard before suddenly cut through the buzzing in my head, and after I turned around and saw who was coming at me down the hill, I thought it was probably my own ghost I'd seen.

"Eddie Grimes looked as big as an oak tree, and he had a long knife in one hand. His feet slipped out from under him, and he skidded the last few yards down to the creek, but I didn't even try to run away. Drunk as he was, I'd never get away from him. All I did was back up alongside the fallen tree and watch him slide downhill toward the water. I was so scared I couldn't even talk. Eddie Grimes' shirt was flapping open, and big long scars ran all across his chest and belly. He'd been raised from the dead at least a couple of times since I'd seen him get killed at the dance. He jumped back up on his feet and started coming for me. I opened my mouth, but nothing came out.

"Eddie Grimes took another step toward me, and then he stopped and looked straight at my face. He lowered the knife. A sour stink of sweat and alcohol came off him. All he could do was stare at me. Eddie Grimes knew my face all right, he knew my name, he knew my whole family—even at night, he couldn't mistake me for anyone else. I finally saw that Eddie was actually afraid, like he was the one who'd seen a ghost. The two of us just stood there in the shallow water for a couple more seconds, and then Eddie Grimes pointed his knife at the other side of the creek.

"That was all I needed, baby. My legs unfroze, and I forgot all my aches and pains. Eddie watched me roll over the fallen tree and lowered his knife. I splashed through the water and started moving up the hill, grabbing at weeds and branches to pull me along. My feet were frozen, and my clothes were soaked and muddy, and I was trembling all over. About half way up the hill, I looked back over my shoulder, but Eddie Grimes was gone. It was like he'd never been there at all, like he was nothing but the product of a couple of good raps to the noggin.

"Finally, I pulled myself shaking up over the top of the rise, and what did I see about ten feet away through a lot of skinny birch trees but a kid in a sheet facing away from me into the woods, and hopping from foot to foot in a pair of big clumsy shoes? And what was in front of him but a path I could make out from even ten feet away? Obviously, this was where I was supposed to turn up, only in the dark and all I must have missed an apple stuck onto a branch or some blasted thing, and I took that little side trip downhill on my head and wound up throwing a spook into Eddie Grimes.

"As soon as I saw him, I realized I hated Dee Sparks. I wouldn't have tossed him a rope if he was drowning. Without even thinking about it, I bent down and picked up a stone and flung it at him. The stone bounced off a tree, so I bent down and got another one. Dee turned around to find out what made the noise, and the second stone hit him right in the chest, even though it was his head I was aiming at.

"He pulled his sheet up over his face like an Arab and stared at me with his mouth wide open. Then he looked back over his shoulder at the path, as if the real me might come along at any second. I felt like pegging another rock at his stupid face, but instead I marched up to him. He was shaking his head from side to side. *Jim Dawg,* he whispered, *what happened to you?* By way of answer, I hit him a good hard knock on the breastbone. *What's the matter?* he wanted to know. *After you left me,* I say, *I fell down a hill and ran into Eddie Grimes.*

"That gave him something to think about, all right. Was Grimes coming after me, he wanted to know? Did he see which way I went? Did Grimes see who I was? He was pulling me into the woods while he asked me these dumb-ass questions, and I shoved him away. His sheet flopped back down over his front, and he looked like a little boy. He couldn't figure out why I was mad at him. From his point of view, he'd been pretty clever, and if I got lost, it was my fault. But I wasn't mad at him because I got lost. I wasn't even mad at him because I'd run into Eddie Grimes. It was everything else. Maybe it wasn't even him I was mad at.

"*I want to get home without getting killed*, I whispered. *Eddie ain't gonna let me go twice.* Then I pretended he wasn't there any more and tried to figure out how to get back to Meridian Road. It seemed to me that I was still going north when I took that tumble downhill, so when I climbed up the hill on the other side of the creek I was still going north. The wagon-track that Dee and I took into The Backs had to be off to my right. I turned away from Dee and started moving through the woods. I didn't care if he followed me or not. He had nothing to do with me any more, he was on his own. When I heard him coming along after me, I was sorry. I wanted to get away from Dee Sparks. I wanted to get away from everybody.

"I didn't want to be around anybody who was supposed to be my friend. I'd rather have had Eddie Grimes following me than Dee Sparks.

"Then I stopped moving, because through the trees I could see one of those grease-paper windows glowing up ahead of me. That yellow light looked evil as the devil's eye—everything in The Backs was evil, poisoned, even the trees, even the air. The terrible expression on Dr. Garland's face and the white smudge in the air seemed like the same thing—they were what I didn't want to know.

"Dee shoved me from behind, and if I hadn't felt so sick inside I would have turned around and punched him. Instead, I looked over my shoulder and saw him nodding toward where the side of the shack would be. He wanted to get closer! For a second, he seemed as crazy as everything else out there, and then I got it: I was all turned around, and instead of heading back to the main path, I'd been taking us toward the woman's shack. That was why Dee was following me.

"I shook my head. No, I wasn't going to sneak up to that place. Whatever was inside there was something I didn't have to know about. It had too much power—it turned Eddie Grimes around, and that was enough for me. Dee knew I wasn't fooling. He went around me and started creeping toward the shack.

"And damndest thing, I watched him slipping through the trees for a second, and started following him. If he could go up there, so could I. If I didn't exactly look at whatever was in there myself, I could watch Dee look at it. That would tell me most of what I had to know. And anyways, probably Dee wouldn't see anything anyhow, unless the front door was hanging open, and that didn't seem too likely to me. He wouldn't see anything, and I wouldn't either, and we could both go home.

"The door of the shack opened up, and a man walked outside. Dee and I freeze, and I mean *freeze*. We're about twenty feet away, on the side of this shack, and if the man looked sideways, he'd see our sheets. There were a lot of trees between us and him, and I couldn't get a very good look at him, but one thing about him made the whole situation a lot more serious. This man was white, and he was wearing good clothes—I couldn't see his face, but I could see his rolled up sleeves, and his suit jacket slung over one arm, and some kind of wrapped-up bundle he was holding in his hands. All this took about a second. The white man started carrying his bundle straight through the woods, and in another two seconds he was out of sight.

"Dee was a little closer than I was, and I think his sight line was a little clearer than mine. On top of that, he saw better at night than I did. Dee didn't get around like me, but he might have recognized the man we'd seen, and that would be pure trouble. Some rich white man, killing a girl out in The Backs? And us two boys close enough to see him? Do you know what would have happened to us? There wouldn't be enough left of either one of us to make a decent smudge.

"Dee turned around to face me, and I could see his eyes behind his costume, but I couldn't tell what he was thinking. He just stood there, looking at me. In a little bit, just when I was about to explode, we heard a car starting up off to our left. I whispered at Dee if he saw who that was. *Nobody*, Dee said. Now, what the hell did that mean? Nobody? You could say Santa Claus, you could say J. Edgar *Hoover*, it'd be a better answer than Nobody. The Model T's headlights shone through the trees when the car swung around the top of the path and started going toward Meridian Road. *Nobody I ever saw before,* Dee said. When the headlights cut through the trees, both of us ducked out of sight. Actually, we were so far from the path, we had nothing to worry about. I could barely see the car when it went past, and I couldn't see the driver at all.

"We stood up. Over Dee's shoulder I could see the side of the shack where the white man had been. Lamplight flickered on the ground in front of the open door. The last thing in the world I wanted to do was to go inside that place—I didn't even want to walk around to the front and look in the door. Dee stepped back from me and jerked his head toward the shack. I knew it was going to be just like before. I'd say no, he'd say yes, and then I'd follow him wherever he thought he had to go. I felt the same way I did when I saw that white smear in the woods—hopeless, lost in the midst of death. *You go, if you have to*, I whispered to him, *it's what you wanted to do all along.* He didn't move, and I saw that he wasn't too sure about what he wanted any more.

"Everything was different now, because the white man made it different. Once a white man walked out that door, it was like raising the stakes in a poker game. But Dee had been working toward that one shack ever since we got into The Backs, and he was still curious as a cat about it. He turned away from me and started moving sideways in a straight line, so he'd be able to peek inside the door from a safe distance.

"After he got about half way to the front, he looked back and waved me on, like this was still some great adventure he wanted me to share. He was afraid to be on his own, that was all. When he realized I was going to stay put, he bent down and moved real slow past the side. He still couldn't see more than a sliver of the inside of the shack, and he moved ahead another little ways. By then, I figured, he should have been able to see about half of the inside of the shack. He hunkered down inside his sheet, staring in the direction of the open door. And there he stayed.

"I took it for about half a minute, and then I couldn't any more. I was sick enough to die and angry enough to explode, both at the same time. How long could Dee Sparks look at a dead whore? Wouldn't a couple of seconds be enough? Dee was acting like he was watching a goddamn Hopalong Cassidy movie. An owl screeched, and some man in another shack said *Now that's over*, and someone else shushed him. If Dee heard, he paid it no mind. I started along toward him, and I don't think he noticed me, either. He didn't look up until I was past the front of the shack, and had already seen the door hanging open, and the lamplight spilling over the plank floor and onto the grass outside.

"I took another step, and Dee's head snapped around. He tried to stop me by holding out his hand. All that did was make me mad. Who was Dee Sparks to tell me what I couldn't see? All he did was leave me alone in the woods with a trail of apples, and he didn't even do that right. When I kept on coming, Dee started waving both hands at me, looking back and forth between me and the inside of the shack. Like something was happening in there that I couldn't be allowed to see. I didn't stop, and Dee got up on his feet and skittered toward me.

"*We gotta get out of here*, he whispered. He was close enough so I could smell that electrical stink. I stepped to his side, and he grabbed my arm. I yanked my arm out of his grip and went forward a little ways and looked through the door of the shack.

"A bed was shoved up against the far wall, and a woman lay naked on the bed. There was blood all over her legs, and blood all over the sheets, and big puddles of blood on the floor. A woman in a raggedy robe, hair stuck out all over her head, squatted beside the bed, holding the other woman's hand. She was a colored woman—a Backs woman—but the other one, the one on the bed, was white. Probably she was pretty, when she was alive. All I could see was white skin and blood, and I near fainted.

"This wasn't some white-trash woman who lived out in The Backs—she was brought there, and the man who brought her had killed her. More trouble was coming down than I could imagine, trouble enough to kill lots of our people. And if Dee and I said a word about the white man we'd seen, the trouble would come right straight down on us.

"I must have made some kind of noise, because the woman next to the bed turned halfways around and looked at me. There wasn't any doubt about it—she saw me. All she saw of Dee was a dirty white sheet, but she saw my face, and she knew who I was. I knew her, too, and she wasn't any Backs woman. She lived down the street from us. Her name was Mary Randolph, and she was the one who came up to Eddie Grimes after he got shot to death and brought him back to life. Mary Randolph followed my Dad's band, and when we played roadhouses or colored dance halls, she'd be likely to turn up. A couple of times she told me I played good drums—I was a drummer back then, you know, switched to saxophone when I turned twelve. Mary Randolph just looked at me, her hair stuck out straight all over her head like she was already inside a whirlwind of trouble. No expression on her face except that look you get when your mind is going a mile a minute and your body can't move at all. She didn't even look surprised. She almost looked like she *wasn't* surprised, like she was expecting to see me. As bad as I'd felt that night, this was the worst of all. I liked to have died. I'd have disappeared down an anthill, if I could. I didn't know what I had done—just be there, I guess—but I'd never be able to undo it.

"I pulled at Dee's sheet, and he tore off down the side of the shack like he'd been waiting for a signal. Mary Randolph stared into my eyes, and it felt like I had to pull myself away—I couldn't just turn my head, I had to *disconnect.* And when I did, I could still feel her staring at me. Somehow I made myself go down past the side of the shack, but I could still see Mary Randolph inside there, looking out at the place where I'd been.

"If Dee said anything at all when I caught up with him, I'd have knocked his teeth down his throat, but he just moved fast and quiet through the trees, seeing the best way to go, and I followed after. I felt like I'd been kicked by a horse. When we got on the path, we didn't bother trying to sneak down through the woods on the other side, we lit out and ran as hard as we could—like wild dogs were after us. And after we got onto Meridian Road, we ran toward town until we couldn't run any more.

"Dee clamped his hand over his side and staggered forward a little bit. Then he stopped and ripped off his costume and lay down by the side of the road, breathing hard. I was leaning forward with hands on my knees, as winded as he was. When I could breathe again, I started walking down the road. Dee picked himself up and got next to me and walked along, looking at my face and then looking away, and then looking back at my face again.

"*So?* I said.

"*I know that lady,* Dee said.

"Hell, that was no news. Of course he knew Mary Randolph—she was his neighbor, too. I didn't bother to answer, I just grunted at him. Then I reminded him that Mary hadn't seen his face, only mine.

"*Not Mary*, he said. *The other one.*

"He knew the dead white woman's name? That made everything worse. A lady like that shouldn't be in Dee Sparks' world, especially if she's going to wind up dead in The Backs. I wondered who was going to get lynched, and how many.

"Then Dee said that I knew her, too. I stopped walking and looked him straight in the face.

"*Miss Abbey Montgomery*, he said. *She brings clothes and food down to our church, Thanksgiving and Christmas.*

"He was right—I wasn't sure if I'd ever heard her name, but I'd seen her once or twice, bringing baskets of ham and chicken and boxes of clothes to Dee's father's church. She was about twenty years old, I guess, so pretty she made you smile just to look at. From a rich family in a big house right at the top of Miller's Hill. Some man didn't think a girl like that should have any associations with colored people, I guess, and decided to express his opinion about as strong as possible. Which meant that we were going to take the blame for what happened to her, and the next time we saw white sheets, they wouldn't be Halloween costumes.

"He sure took a long time to kill her, I said.

"And Dee said, *She ain't dead.*

"So I asked him, What the hell did he mean by that? I saw the girl. I saw the blood. Did he think she was going to get up and walk around? Or maybe Mary Randolph was going to tell her that magic word and bring her back to life?

"*You can think that if you want to,* Dee said. *But Abbey Montgomery ain't dead.*

"I almost told him I'd seen her ghost, but he didn't deserve to hear about it. The fool couldn't even see what was right in front of his eyes. I couldn't expect him to understand what happened to me when I saw that miserable...that *thing*. He was rushing on ahead of me anyhow, like I'd suddenly embarrased him or something. That was fine with me. I felt the exact same way. I said, *I guess you know neither one of us can ever talk about this*, and he said, *I guess you know it, too*, and that was the last thing we said to each other that night. All the way down Meridian Road Dee Sparks kept his eyes straight ahead and his mouth shut. When we got to the field, he turned toward me like he had something to say, and I waited for it, but he faced forward again and ran away. Just ran. I watched him disappear past the general store, and then I walked home by myself.

"My mom gave me hell for getting my clothes all wet and dirty, and my brothers laughed at me and wanted to know who beat me up and stole my candy. As soon as I could, I went to bed, pulled the covers up over my head, and closed my eyes. A little while later, my mom came in and asked if I was all right. Did I get into a fight with that Dee Sparks? Dee Sparks was born to hang, that was what she thought, and I ought to have a better class of friends. *I'm tired of playing those drums, Momma,* I said, *I want to play the saxophone instead.* She looked at me surprised, but said she'd talk about it with Daddy, and that it might work out.

"For the next couple days, I waited for the bomb to go off. On the Friday, I went to school, but couldn't concentrate for beans. Dee Sparks and I didn't even nod at each other in the hallways—just walked by like the other guy was invisible. On the weekend I said I felt sick and stayed in bed, wondering when that whirlwind of trouble would come down. I wondered if Eddie Grimes would talk about seeing me—once they found the body, they'd get around to Eddie Grimes real quick.

"But nothing happened that weekend, and nothing happened all the next week. I thought Mary Randolph must have hid the white girl in a grave out in The Backs. But how long could a girl from one of those rich families go missing without investigations and search parties? And, on top of that, what was Mary Randolph doing there in the first place? She liked to have a good time, but she wasn't one of those wild girls with a razor under her skirt—she went to church every Sunday, was good to people, nice to kids. Maybe she went out to comfort that poor girl, but how did she know she'd be there in the first place? Misses Abbey Montgomerys from the hill didn't share their plans with Mary Randolphs from Darktown. I couldn't forget the way she looked at me, but I couldn't understand it, either. The more I thought about that look, the more it was like Mary Randolph was saying something to me, but what? *Are you ready for this? Do you understand this? Do you know how careful you must be?*

"My father said I could start learning the C-melody sax, and when I was ready to play it in public, my little brother wanted to take over the drums. Seems he always wanted to play drums, and in fact, he's been a drummer ever since, a good one. So I worked out how to play my little sax, I went to school and came straight home after, and everything went on like normal, except Dee Sparks and I weren't friends any more. If the police were searching for a missing rich girl, I didn't hear anything about it.

"Then one Saturday I was walking down our street to go to the general store, and Mary Randolph came through her front door just as I got to her house. When she saw me, she stopped moving real sudden, with one hand still on the side of the door. I was so surprised to see her that I was in a kind of slow-motion, and I must have stared at her. She gave me a look like an X-ray, a look that searched around down inside me. I don't know what she saw, but her face relaxed, and she took her hand off the door and let it close behind her, and she wasn't looking inside me any more. *Miss Randolph,* I said, and she told me she was looking forward to hearing our band play at a Beergarden dance in a couple of weeks. I told her I was going to be playing the saxophone at that dance, and she said something about that, and all the time it was like we were having two conversations, the top one about me and the band, and the one underneath about her and the murdered white girl in The Backs. It made me so nervous, my words got all mixed up. Finally she said *You make sure you say hello to your Daddy from me, now*, and I got away.

"After I passed her house, Mary Randolph started walking down the street behind me. I could feel her watching me, and I started to sweat. Mary Randolph was a total mystery to me. She was a nice lady, but probably she buried that girl's body. I didn't know but that she was going to come and kill *me*, one day. And then I remembered her kneeling down beside Eddie Grimes at the roadhouse. She had been *dancing* with Eddie Grimes, who was in jail more often than he was out. I wondered if you could be a respectable lady and still know Eddie Grimes well enough to dance with him. And how did she bring him back to life? Or was that what happened at all? Hearing that lady walk along behind me made me so uptight, I crossed to the other side of the street.

"A couple days after that, when I was beginning to think that the trouble was never going to happen after all, it came down. We heard police cars coming down the street right when we were finishing dinner. I thought they were coming for me, and I almost lost my chicken and rice. The sirens went right past our house, and then more sirens came toward us from other directions—the old klaxons they had in those days. It sounded like every cop in the state was rushing into Darktown. This was bad, bad news. Someone was going to wind up dead, that was certain. No way all those police were going to come into our part of town, make all that commotion, and leave without killing at least one man. That's the truth. You just had to pray that the man they killed wasn't you or anyone in your family. My Daddy turned off the lamps, and we went to the window to watch the cars go by. Two of them were state police. When it was safe, Daddy went outside to see where all the trouble was headed. After he came back in, he said it looked like the police were going toward Eddie Grimes' place. We wanted to go out and look, but they wouldn't let us, so we went to the back windows that faced toward Grimes' house. Couldn't see anything but a lot of cars and police standing all over the road back there. Sounded like they were knocking down Grimes' house with sledge hammers. Then a whole bunch of cops took off running, and all I could see was the cars spread out across the road. About ten minutes later, we heard lots of gunfire coming from a couple of streets further back. It like to have lasted forever. Like hearing the Battle of the Bulge. My momma started to cry, and so did my little brother. The shooting stopped. The police shouted to each other, and then they came back and got in their cars and went away.

"On the radio the next morning, they said that a known criminal, a Negro man named Edward Grimes, had been killed while trying to escape arrest for the murder of a white woman. The body of Eleanore Monday, missing for three days, had been found in a shallow grave by Woodland police searching near an illegal distillery in the region called The Backs. Miss Monday, the daughter of grocer Albert Monday, had been in poor mental and physical health, and Grimes had apparently taken advantage of her weakness to either abduct or lure her to The Backs, where she had been savagely murdered. That's what it said on the radio—I still remember the words. *In poor mental and physical health. Savagely murdered.*

"When the paper finally came, there on the front page was a picture of Eleanore Monday, a girl with dark hair and a big nose. She didn't look anything like the dead woman in the shack. She hadn't even disappeared on the right day. Eddie Grimes was never going to be able to explain things, because the police had finally cornered him in the old jute warehouse just off Meridian Road next to the general store. I don't suppose they even bothered trying to arrest him—they weren't interested in *arresting* him. He killed a white girl. They wanted revenge, and they got it.

"After I looked at the paper, I got out of the house and ran between the houses to get a look at the jute warehouse. Turned out a lot of folks had the same idea. A big crowd strung out in a long line in front of the warehouse, and cars were parked all along Meridian Road. Right up in front of the warehouse door was a police car, and a big cop stood in the middle of the big doorway, watching people file by. They were walking past the doorway one by one, acting like they were at some kind of exhibit. Nobody was talking. It was a sight I never saw before in that town, whites and colored all lined up together. On the other side of the warehouse, two groups of men stood alongside the road, one colored and one white, talking so quietly you couldn't hear a word.

"Now I was never one who liked standing in lines, so I figured I'd just dart up there, peek in, and save myself some time. I came around the end of the line and ambled toward the two bunches of men, like I'd already had my look and was just hanging around to enjoy the scene. After I got a little past the warehouse door, I sort of drifted up alongside it. I looked down the row of people, and there was Dee Sparks, just a few yards away from being able to see in. Dee was leaning forward, and when he saw me he almost jumped out of his skin. He looked away as fast as he could. His eyes turned as dead as stones. The cop at the door yelled at me to go to the end of the line. He never would have noticed me at all if

Dee hadn't jumped like someone just shot off a firecracker behind him.

"About half way down the line, Mary Randolph was standing behind some of the ladies from the neighborhood. She looked terrible. Her hair stuck out in raggedy clumps, and her skin was ashy, like she hadn't slept in a long time. I sped up a little, hoping she wouldn't notice me, but after I took one more step, Mary Randolph looked down and her eyes hooked into mine. I swear, what was in her eyes almost knocked me down. I couldn't even tell what it was, unless it was pure hate. Hate and pain. With her eyes hooked into mine like that, I couldn't look away. It was like I was seeing that miserable, terrible white smear twisting up between the trees on that night in The Backs. Mary let me go, and I almost fell down all over again.

"I got to the end of the line and started moving along regular and slow with everybody else. Mary Randolph stayed in my mind and blanked out everything else. When I got up to the door, I barely took in what was inside the warehouse—a wall full of bulletholes and bloodstains all over the place, big slick ones and little drizzly ones. All I could think of was the shack and Mary Randolph sitting next to the dead girl, and I was back there all over again.

"Mary Randolph didn't show up at the Beergarden dance, so she didn't hear me play saxophone in public for the first time. I didn't expect her, either, not after the way she looked out at the warehouse. There'd been a lot of news about Eddie Grimes, who they made out to be less civilized than a gorilla, a crazy man who'd murder anyone as long as he could kill all the white women first. The paper had a picture of what they called Grimes' 'lair,' with busted furniture all over the place and holes in the walls, but they never explained that it was the police tore it up and made it look that way.

"The other thing people got suddenly all hot about was The Backs.

Seems the place was even worse than everybody thought. Seems white girls besides Eleanore Monday had been taken out there—according to some, there was even white girls living out there, along with a lot of bad coloreds. The place was a nest of vice, Sodom and Gomorrah. Two days before the town council was supposed to discuss the problem, a gang of white men went out there with guns and clubs and torches and burned every shack in The Backs clear down to the ground. While they were there, they didn't see a single soul, white, colored, male, female, damned or saved. Everybody who lived in The Backs had skedaddled. And the funny thing was, long as The Backs had existed right outside of Woodland, no one in Woodland could recollect the name of anyone who had ever lived there. They couldn't even recall the name of anyone who had ever gone there, except for Eddie Grimes. In fact, after the place got burned down, it appeared that it must have been a sin just to say its name, because no one ever mentioned it. You'd think men so fine and moral as to burn down The Backs would be willing to take the credit, but none ever did.

"You could think they must have wanted to get rid of some things out there. Or wanted real bad to forget about things out there. One thing I thought, Doctor Garland and the man I saw leaving that shack had been out there with torches.

"But maybe I didn't know anything at all. Two weeks later, a couple things happened that shook me good.

"The first one happened three nights before Thanksgiving. I was hurrying home, a little bit late. Nobody else on the street, everybody inside either sitting down to dinner or getting ready for it. When I got to Mary Randolph's house, some kind of noise coming from inside stopped me. What I thought was, it sounded exactly like somebody trying to scream while someone else was holding a hand over their mouth. Well, that was plain foolish, wasn't it? How did I know what that would sound like? I moved along a step or two, and then I heard it again. Could be anything, I told myself. Mary Randolph didn't like me too much, anyway. She wouldn't be partial to my knocking on her door. Best thing I could do was get out. Which was what I did. Just went home to supper and forgot about it.

"Until the next day, anyhow, when a friend of Mary's walked in her front door and found her lying dead with her throat cut and a knife in her hand. A cut of fatback, we heard, had boiled away to cinders on her stove. I didn't tell anybody about what I heard the night before. Too scared. I couldn't do anything but wait to see what the police did.

"To the police, it was all real clear. Mary killed herself, plain and simple.

"When our minister went across town to ask why a lady who intended to commit suicide had bothered to start cooking her supper, the Chief told him that a female bent on killing herself probably didn't care *what* happened to the food on her stove. Then I suppose Mary Randolph nearly managed to cut her own head off, said the minister. A female in despair possesses a godawful strength, said the Chief. And asked, wouldn't she have screamed if she'd been attacked? And added, couldn't it be that maybe this female here had secrets in her life connected to the late savage murderer named Eddie Grimes? We might all be better off if these secrets get buried with your Mary Randolph, said the Chief. I'm sure you understand me, Reverend. And yes, the Reverend did understand, he surely did. So Mary Randolph got laid away in the cemetery, and nobody ever said her name again. She was put away out of mind, like The Backs.

"The second thing that shook me up and proved to me that I didn't know anything, that I was no better than a blind dog, happened on Thanksgiving day. My daddy played piano in church, and on special days, we played our instruments along with the gospel songs. I got to church early with the rest of my family, and we practiced with the choir. Afterwards, I went to fooling around outside until the people came, and saw a big car come up into the church parking lot. Must have been the biggest, fanciest car I'd ever seen. Miller's Hill was written all over that vehicle. I couldn't have told you why, but the sight of it made my heart stop. The front door opened, and out stepped a colored man in a fancy grey uniform with a smart cap. He didn't so much as dirty his eyes by looking at me, or at the church, or at anything around him. He stepped around the front of the car and opened the rear door on my side. A young woman was in the passenger seat, and when she got out of the car, the sun fell on her blond hair and the little fur jacket she was wearing. I couldn't see more than the top of her head, her shoulders under the jacket, and her legs. Then she straightened up, and her eyes lighted right on me. She smiled, but I couldn't smile back. I couldn't even begin to move.

"It was Abbey Montgomery, delivering baskets of food to our church, the way she did every Thanksgiving and Christmas. She looked older and thinner than the last time I'd seen her alive—older and thinner, but more than that, like there was no fun at all in her life anymore. She walked to the trunk of the car, and the driver opened it up, leaned in, and brought out a great big basket of food. He took it into the church by the back way and came back for another one. Abbey Montgomery just stood still and watched him carry the baskets. She looked—she looked like she was just going through the motions, like going through the motions was all she was ever going to do from now on, and she knew it. Once she smiled at the driver, but the smile was so sad that the driver didn't even try to smile back. When he was done, he closed the trunk and let her into the passenger seat, got behind the wheel, and drove away.

"I was thinking, *Dee Sparks was right, she was alive all the time.* Then I thought, *No, Mary Randolph brought her back, too, like she did Eddie Grimes. But it didn't work right, and only part of her came back.*

"And that's the whole thing, except that Abbey Montgomery didn't deliver food to our church, that Christmas—she was travelling out of the country, with her aunt. And she didn't bring food the next Thanksgiving, either, just sent her driver with the baskets. By that time, we didn't expect her, because we'd already heard that, soon as she got back to town, Abbey Montgomery stopped leaving her house. That girl shut herself up and never came out. I heard from somebody who probably didn't know any more than I did that she eventually got so she wouldn't even leave her room. Five years later, she passed away. Twenty-six years old, and they said she looked to be at least fifty."

4

Hat fell silent, and I sat with my pen ready over the notebook, waiting for more. When I realized that he had finished, I asked, "What did she die of?"

"Nobody ever told me."

"And nobody ever found who had killed Mary Randolph."

The limpid, colorless eyes momentarily rested on me. "Was she killed?"

"Did you ever become friends with Dee Sparks again? Did you at least talk about it with him?"

"Surely did not. Nothing to talk about."

This was a remarkable statement, considering that for an hour he had done nothing but talk about what had happened to the two of them, but I let it go. Hat was still looking at me with his unreadable eyes. His face had become particularly bland, almost immobile. It was not possible to imagine this man as an active eleven-year-old boy. "Now you heard me out, answer my question," he said.

I couldn't remember the question.

"Did we find what we were looking for?"

Scares—that was what they had been looking for. "I think you found a lot more than that," I said.

He nodded slowly. "That's right. It was more."

Then I asked him some question about his family's band, he lubricated himself with another swallow of gin, and the interview returned to more typical matters. But the experience of listening to him had changed. After I had heard the long, unresolved tale of his Halloween night, everything Hat said seemed to have two separate meanings, the daylight meaning created by sequences of ordinary English words, and another, nightime meaning, far less determined and knowable. He was like a man discoursing with eerie rationality in the midst of a surreal dream—like a man carrying on an ordinary conversation with one foot placed on solid ground and the other suspended above a bottomless abyss. I focused on the rationality, on the foot placed in the context I understood; the rest was unsettling to the point of being frightening. By six-thirty, when he kindly called me "Miss Rosemary" and opened his door, I felt as if I'd spent several weeks, if not whole months, in his room.

Part Three

1

Although I did get my M.A. at Columbia, I didn't have enough money to stay on for a Ph.D., so I never became a college professor. I never became a jazz critic, either, or anything else very interesting. For a couple of years after Columbia, I taught English in a high school, until I quit to take the job I have now, which involves a lot of travelling and pays a little bit better than teaching. Maybe even quite a bit better, but that's not saying much, especially when you consider my expenses. I own a nice little house in the Chicago suburbs, my marriage held up against everything life did to it, and my twenty-two year old son, a young man who never once in his life for the purpose of pleasure read a novel, looked at a painting, visited a museum, or listened to anything but the most readily available music, recently announced to his mother and myself that he has decided to become an artist, actual type of art to be determined later, but probably to include aspects of photography, video tape, and the creation of "installations." I take this as proof that he was raised in a manner that left his self-esteem intact.

I no longer provide my life with a perpetual sound track (though my son, who has moved back in with us, does), in part because my income does not permit the purchase of a great many compact discs. (A friend presented me with a CD player on my forty-fifth birthday.) And these days, I'm as interested in classical music as in jazz. Of course, I never go to jazz clubs when I am home. Are there still people, apart from New Yorkers, who patronize jazz nightclubs in their own home towns? The concept seems faintly retrograde, even somehow illicit. But when I am out on the road, living in airplanes and hotel rooms, I often check the jazz listings in the local papers to see if I can find some way to fill my evenings. Many of the legends of my youth are still out there, in most cases playing at least as well as before. Some months ago, while I was in San Francisco, I came across John Hawes' name in this fashion. He was working in a club so close to my hotel that I could walk to it.

His appearance in any club at all was surprising. Hawes had ceased performing jazz in public years before. He had earned a great deal of fame (and undoubtedly, a great deal of money) writing film scores, and in the past decade, he had begun to appear in swallow-tail coat and white tie as a conductor of the standard classical repertoire. I believe he had a permanent post in some city like Seattle, or perhaps Salt Lake City. If he was spending a week playing jazz with a trio in San Francisco, it must have been for the sheer pleasure of it.

I turned up just before the beginning of the first set, and got a table toward the back of the club. Most of the tables were filled—Hawes' celebrity had guaranteed him a good house. Only a few minutes after the announced time of the first set, Hawes emerged through a door at the front of the club and moved toward the piano, followed by his bassist and drummer. He looked like a more successful version of the younger man I had seen in New York, and the only indications of the extra years were his silver-gray hair, still abundant, and a little paunch. His playing, too, seemed essentially unchanged, but I could not hear it in the way I once had. He was still a good pianist—no doubt about that—but he seemed to be skating over the surface of the songs he played, using his wonderful technique and good time merely to decorate their melodies. It was the sort of playing that becomes less impressive the more attention you give it—if you were listening with half an ear, it probably sounded like Art Tatum. I wondered if John Hawes had always had this superficial streak in him, or if he had lost a certain necessary passion during his years away from jazz. Certainly he had not sounded superficial when I had heard him play with Hat.

Hawes, too, might have been thinking about his old employer, because in the first set he played "Love Walked In," "Too Marvelous For Words," and "Up Jumped Hat." In the last of these, inner gears seemed to mesh, the rhythm simultaneously relaxed and intensified, and the music turned into real, not imitation, jazz. Hawes looked pleased with himself when he stood up from the piano bench, and half a dozen fans moved to greet him as he stepped off the bandstand. Most of them were carrying old records they wished him to sign.

A few minutes later, I saw Hawes standing by himself at the end of the bar, drinking what appeared to be club soda, in proximity to his musicians but not actually speaking with them. Wondering if his allusions to Hat had been deliberate, I left my table and walked toward the bar. Hawes watched me approach out of the side of his eye, neither encouraging nor discouraging me. When I introduced myself, he smiled nicely and shook my hand and waited for whatever I wanted to say to him.

At first, I made some inane comment about the difference between playing in clubs and conducting in concert halls, and he replied with the noncommital and equally banal agreement that yes, the two experiences were very different.

Then I told him that I had seen him play with Hat all those years ago in New York, and he turned to me with genuine pleasure in his face. "Did you? At that little club on St. Mark's Place? That sure was fun. I guess I must have been thinking about it, because I played some of those songs we used to do."

"That was why I came over," I said. "I guess that was one of the best musical experiences I ever had."

"You and me both." Hawes smiled to himself. "Sometimes, I just couldn't believe what he was doing."

"It showed," I said.

"Well." His eyes slid away from mine. "Great character. Completely otherwordly."

"I saw some of that," I said. "I did that interview with him that turns up now and then, the one in *Downbeat*."

"Oh!" Hawes gave me his first genuinely interested look so far. "Well, that was him, all right."

"Most of it was, anyhow."

"You cheated?" Now he was looking even more interested.

"I had to make it understandable."

"Oh, sure. You couldn't put in all those ding-dings and bells and Bob Crosbys." These had been elements of Hat's private code. Hawes laughed at the memory. "When he wanted play a blues in G, he'd lean over and say, 'Gs, please.'"

"Did you get to know him at all well, personally?" I asked, thinking that the answer must be that he had not—I didn't think that anyone had ever really known Hat very well.

"Pretty well," Hawes said. "A couple of times, around '54 and '55, he invited me home with him, to his parents' house, I mean. We got to be friends on a Jazz at the Phil tour, and twice when we were in the South, he asked me if I wanted to eat some good home cooking."

"You went to his home town?"

He nodded. "His parents put me up. They were interesting people. Hat's father, Red, was about the lightest black man I ever saw, and he could have passed for white anywhere, but I don't suppose the thought ever occurred to him."

"Was the family band still going?"

"No, to tell you the truth, I don't think they were getting much work up toward the end of the forties. At the end, they were using a tenor player and a drummer from the high school band. And the church work got more and more demanding for Hat's father."

"His father was a deacon, or something like that?"

He raised his eyebrows. "No, Red was the Baptist minister. The reverend. He ran that church. I think he even started it."

"Hat told me his father played piano in church, but...."

"The reverend would have made a hell of a blues piano player, if he'd ever left his day job."

"There must have been another Baptist church in the neighborhood," I said, thinking this the only explanation for the presence of two Baptist ministers. But why had Hat not mentioned that his own father, like Dee Sparks's, had been a clergyman?

"Are you kidding? There was barely enough money in that place to keep one of them going." He looked at his watch, nodded at me, and began to move closer to his sidemen.

"Could I ask you one more question?"

"I suppose so," he said, almost impatiently.

"Did Hat strike you as superstitious?"

Hawes grinned. "Oh, he was superstitious, all right. He told me he never worked on Halloween—he didn't even want to go out of his room on Halloween. That's why he left the big band, you know. They were starting a tour on Halloween, and Hat refused to do it. He just quit." He leaned toward me. "I'll tell you another funny thing. I always had the feeling that Hat was terrified of his father—I thought he invited me to Hatchville with him so I could be some kind of buffer between him and his father. Never made any sense to me. Red was a big strong old guy, and I'm pretty sure a long time ago he used to mess around with the ladies, reverend or not, but I couldn't ever figure out why Hat should be afraid of him. But whenever Red came into the room, Hat shut up. Funny, isn't it?"

I must have looked very perplexed. "Hatchville?"

"Where they lived. Hatchville, Mississippi—not too far from Biloxi."

"But he told me—"

"Hat never gave too many straight answers," Hawes said. "And he didn't let the facts get in the way of a good story. When you come to think of it, why should he? He was *Hat.*"

After the next set, I walked back uphill to my hotel, wondering again about the long story Hat had told me. Had there been any truth in it at all?

2

Three weeks later I found myself released from a meeting at our Midwestern headquarters in downtown Chicago earlier than I had expected, and instead of going to a bar with the other wandering corporate ghosts like myself, made up a story about having to get home for dinner with visiting relatives. I didn't want to admit to my fellow employees, committed like all male business people to aggressive endeavors such as raquetball, drinking, and the pursuit of women, that I intended to visit the library. Short of a trip to Mississippi, a good periodical room offered the most likely means of finding out once and for all how much truth had been in what Hat had told me.

I hadn't forgotten everything I had learned at Columbia—I still knew how to look things up.

In the main library, a boy set me up with a monitor and spools of microfilm representing the complete contents of the daily newspapers from Biloxi and Hatchville, Mississippi, for Hat's tenth and eleventh years. That made three papers, two for Biloxi and one for Hatchville, but all I had to examine were the issues dating from the end of October through the middle of November—I was looking for references to Eddie Grimes, Eleanore Monday, Mary Randolph, Abbey Montgomery, Hat's family, The Backs, and anyone named Sparks.

The Hatchville *Blade*, a gossipy daily printed on peach-colored paper, offered plenty of references to each of these names and places, and the papers from Biloxi contained nearly as many—Biloxi could not conceal the delight, disguised as horror, aroused in its collective soul by the unimaginable events taking place in the smaller, supposedly respectable town ten miles west. Biloxi was riveted, Biloxi was superior, Biloxi was virtually intoxicated with dread and outrage. In Hatchville, the press maintained a persistent optimistic dignity: when wickedness had appeared, justice official and unofficial had dealt with it. Hatchville was shocked but proud (or at least pretended to be proud), and Biloxi all but preened. The *Blade* printed detailed news stories, but the Biloxi papers suggested implications not allowed by Hatchville's version of events. I needed Hatchville to confirm or question Hat's story, but Biloxi gave me at least the beginning of a way to understand it.

A black ex-convict named Edward Grimes had in some fashion persuaded or coerced Eleanore Monday, a retarded young white woman, to accompany him to an area variously described as "a longstanding local disgrace" (the *Blade*) and "a haunt of deepest vice" (Biloxi) and after "the perpetration of the most offensive and brutal deeds upon her person" (the *Blade*) or "acts which the judicious commentator must decline to imagine, much less describe" (Biloxi) murdered her, presumably to ensure her silence, and then buried the body near the "squalid dwelling" where he made and sold illegal liquor. State and local police departments acting in concert had located the body, identified Grimes as the fiend, and, after a search of his house, had tracked him to a warehouse where the murderer was killed in a gun battle. The *Blade* covered half its front page with a photograph of a gaping double door and a bloodstained wall. All Mississippi, both Hatchville and Biloxi declared, now could breathe more easily.

The *Blade* gave the death of Mary Randolph a single paragraph on its back page, the Biloxi papers nothing.

In Hatchville, the raid on The Backs was described as an heroic assault on a dangerous criminal encampment which had somehow come to flourish in a little-noticed section of the countryside. At great risk to themselves, anonymous citizens of Hatchville had descended like the army of the righteous and driven forth the hidden sinners from their dens. Troublemakers, beware! The Biloxi papers, while seeming to endorse the action in Hatchville, actually took another tone altogether. Can it be, they asked, that the Hatchville police had never before noticed the existence of a Sodom and Gomorrah so close to the town line? Did it take the savage murder of a helpless woman to bring it to their attention? Of course Biloxi celebrated the destruction of The Backs—such vileness must be eradicated—but it wondered what else had been destroyed along with the stills and the mean buildings where loose women had plied their trade. Men ever are men, and those who have succumbed to temptation may wish to remove from the face of the earth any evidence of their lapses. Had not the police of Hatchville ever heard the rumor, vague and doubtless baseless, that operations of an illegal nature had been performed in the selfsame Backs? That in an atmosphere of drugs, intoxication, and gambling, the races had mingled there, and that "fast" young women had risked life and honor in search of illicit thrills? Hatchville may have rid itself of a few buildings, but Biloxi was willing to suggest that the problems of its smaller neighbor might not have disappeared with them.

As this campaign of innuendo went on in Biloxi, the *Blade* blandly reported the ongoing events of any smaller American city. Miss Abigail Montgomery sailed with her aunt, Miss Lucinda Bright, from New Orleans to France for an eight-week tour of the continent. The Reverend Jasper Sparks of the Miller's Hill Presbyterian Church delivered a sermon on the subject "Christian Forgiveness." (Just after Thanksgiving, the Reverend Sparks' son, Rodney, was sent off with the blessings and congratulations of all Hatchville to a private academy in Charleston, South Carolina.) There were bake sales, church socials, and costume parties. A saxophone virtuoso named Albert Woodland demonstrated his astonishing wizardy at a well-attended recital presented in Temperance Hall.

Well, I knew the name of at least one person who had attended the recital. If Hat had chosen to disguise the name of his home town, he had done so by substituting for it a name that represented another sort of home.

But, although I had more ideas about this than before, I still did not know exactly what Hat had seen or done on Halloween night in The Backs. It seemed possible that he had gone there with a white boy of his age, a preacher's son like himself, and had the wits scared out of him by whatever had happened to Abbey Montgomery—and after that night, Abbey herself had been sent out of town, as had Dee Sparks. I couldn't think that a man had murdered the young woman, leaving Mary Randolph to bring her back to life. Surely whatever had happened to Abbey Montgomery had brought Dr. Garland out to The Backs, and what he had witnessed or done there had sent him away screaming. And this event—what had befallen a rich young white woman in the shadiest, most criminal section of a Mississippi county—had led to the slaying of Eddie Grimes and the murder of Mary Randolph. Because they knew what had happened, they had to die.

I understood all this, and Hat had understood it, too. Yet he had introduced needless puzzles, as if embedded in the midst of this unresolved story were something he either wished to conceal or not to know. And concealed it would remain; if Hat did not know it, I never would. He had deliberately obscured even basic but meaningless facts: first Mary Randolph was a witch-woman from The Backs, then she was a respectable church-goer who lived down the street from his family. Whatever had really happened in The Backs on Halloween night was lost for good.

On the *Blade's* entertainment page for a Saturday in the middle of November I had come across a photograph of Hat's family's band, and when I had reached this hopeless point in my thinking, I spooled back across the pages to look at it again. Hat, his two brothers, his sister, and his parents stood in a straight line, tallest to smallest, in front of what must have been the family car. Hat held a C-melody saxophone, his brothers a trumpet and drumsticks, his sister a clarinet. As the piano player, the reverend carried nothing at all—nothing except for what came through even a grainy, sixty-year old photograph as a powerful sense of self. Hat's father had been a tall, impressive man, and in the photograph he looked as white as I did. But what was impressive was not the lightness of his skin, or even his striking handsomeness: what impressed was the sense of authority implicit in his posture, his straightforward gaze, even the dictatorial set of his chin. In retrospect, I was not surprised by what John Hawes had told me, for this man could easily be frightening. You would not wish to oppose him, you would not elect to get in his way. Beside him, Hat's mother seemed vague and distracted, as if her husband had robbed her of all certainty. Then I noticed the car, and for the first time realized why it had been included in the photograph. It was a sign of their prosperity, the respectable status they had achieved—the car was as much an advertisement as the photograph. It was, I thought, an old Model T Ford, but I didn't waste any time speculating that it might have been the Model T Hat had seen in The Backs.

And that would be that—the hint of an absurd supposition—except for something I read a few days ago in a book called *Cool Breeze: The Life of Grant Kilbert*.

There are few biographies of any jazz musicians apart from Louis

Armstrong and Duke Ellington (though one does now exist of Hat, the title of which was drawn from my interview with him), and I was surprised to see *Cool Breeze* at the B. Dalton in our local mall. Biographies have not yet been written of Art Blakey, Clifford Brown, Ben Webster, Art Tatum, and many others of more musical and historical importance than Kilbert. Yet I should not have been surprised. Kilbert was one of those musicians who attract and maintain a large personal following, and twenty years after his death, almost all of his records have been released on CD, many of them in multi-disc boxed sets. He had been a great, great player, the closest to Hat of all his disciples. Because Kilbert had been one of my early heroes, I bought the book (for thirty-five dollars!) and brought it home.

Like the lives of many jazz musicians, I suppose of artists in general, Kilbert's had been an odd mixture of public fame and private misery. He had committed burglaries, even armed robberies, to feed his persistent heroin addiction; he had spent years in jail; his two marriages had ended in outright hatred; he had managed to betray most of his friends. That this weak, narcisstic louse had found it in himself to create music of real tenderness and beauty was one of art's enigmas, but not actually a surprise. I'd heard and read enough stories about Grant Kilbert to know what kind of man he'd been.

But what I had not known was that Kilbert, to all appearances an American of conventional northern European, perhaps Scandinavian or Anglo-Saxon, stock, had occasionally claimed to be black. (This claim had always been dismissed, apparently, as another indication of Kilbert's mental aberrancy.) At other times, being Kilbert, he had denied ever making this claim.

Neither had I known that the received versions of his birth and upbringing were in question. Unlike Hat, Kilbert had been interviewed dozens of times both in *Downbeat* and in mass-market weekly news magazines, invariably to offer the same story of having been born in Hattiesburg, Mississippi, to an unmusical, working-class family (a plumber's family), of knowing virtually from infancy that he was born to make music, of begging for and finally being given a saxophone, of early mastery and the dazzled admiration of his teachers, then of dropping out of school at sixteen and joining the Woody Herman band. After that, almost immediate fame.

Most of this, the Grant Kilbert myth, was undisputed. He had been raised in Hattiesburg by a plumber named Kilbert, he had been a prodigy and high-school dropout, he'd become famous with Woody Herman before he was twenty. Yet he told a few friends, not necessarily those to whom he said he was black, that he'd been adopted by the Kilberts, and that once or twice, in great anger, either the plumber or his wife had told him that he had been born into poverty and disgrace and that he'd better by God be grateful for the opportunities he'd been given. The source of this story was John Hawes, who'd met Kilbert on another long JATP tour, the last he made before leaving the road for film scoring.

"Grant didn't have a lot of friends on that tour," Hawes told the biographer. "Even though he was such a great player, you never knew what he was going to say, and if he was in a bad mood, he was liable to put down some of the older players. He was always respectful around Hat, his whole style was based on Hat's, but Hat could go days without saying anything, and by those days he certainly wasn't making any new friends. Still, he'd let Grant sit next to him on the bus, and nod his head while Grant talked to him, so he must have felt some affection for him. Anyhow, eventually I was about the only guy on the tour that was willing to have a conversation with Grant, and we'd sit up in the bar late at night after the concerts. The way he played, I could forgive him a lot of failings. One of those nights, he said that he'd been adopted, and that not knowing who his real parents were was driving him crazy. He didn't even have a birth certificate. From a hint his mother once gave him, he thought one of his birth parents was black, but when he asked them directly, they always denied it. These were white Mississippians, after all, and if they had wanted a baby so bad that they had taken in a child who looked completely white but maybe had a drop or two of black blood in his veins, they weren't going to admit it, even to themselves."

In the midst of so much supposition, here is a fact. Grant Kilbert was exactly eleven years younger than Hat. The jazz encyclopedias give his birth date as November first, which instead of his actual birthday may have been the day he was delivered to the couple in Hattiesburg.

I wonder if Hat saw more than he admitted to me of the man leaving the shack where Abbey Montgomery lay on bloody sheets; I wonder if he had reason to fear his father. I don't know if what I am thinking is correct—I'll never know that—but now, finally, I think I know why Hat never wanted to go out of his room on Halloween nights. The story he told me never left him, but it must have been most fully present on those nights. I think he heard the screams, saw the bleeding girl, and saw Mary Randolph staring at him with displaced pain and rage. I think that in some small closed corner deep within himself, he knew who had been the real object of these feelings, and therefore had to lock himself inside his hotel room and gulp gin until he obliterated the horror of his thoughts.

Trick-or-Read

A Reader's Guide to Halloween Fiction

Stefan Dziemianowicz

Like most holidays, Halloween means different things to different people—horror writers especially. Some, like Dorothy Macardle (author of the haunted house classic *Uneasy Freehold* [a.k.a. *The Uninvited*]), appreciate the romance conferred on the day through traditional festivities. "Hallowe'en, the time of revelry, when mysticism holds full sway and hearts are supposed to be united beneath the magic glow of dim lanterns," is how she describes the day in her short tale "The Vow on Hallowe'en" (1924). But not all of Macardle's colleagues share her evocative thoughts of October 31 as "the time of apple bobbing, fortune telling, and masking in motley raiment, the whole glamoured over by the light of wishing candles." Edith Wharton lumps All-Hallows Eve and All-Souls Day together in her eerie tale "All Souls" (1937), and bluntly describes them as "the night when the dead can walk." Not to be outdone, Bernard Taylor, in his morbid little piece of work, "Samhain"

(1991), exposes the holiday's roots in Celtic legend and characterizes it as "one of the two great witches' festivals of the year—a celebration of fire and the dead and the powers of darkness."

Between these extremes—the benign holiday given over to masquerades and celebration, the malignant night when evil is afoot—there are a good many possibilities, and the bounty of Halloween horror literature is like a trick-or-treat bag, full to bursting with all varieties of goodies: some that sugar-coat their dark centers, others as overtly nasty as a rotting apple.

It comes as no surprise that Halloween is such a special theme for horror writers in a way that no other holiday is similarly dealt with in other branches of fantastic fiction. What is Halloween, after all, but the night that the horror writer's imagination spills openly out onto the sidewalks of the world without apology, and is accepted without condemnation. Vampires rise from the grave, mummies unwind in public, all sorts of boogeymen come out of the closet, and the writer need offer no rationale for them more explanatory than "*Because it's Halloween!*"

Indeed, in the earliest stories to feature it, Halloween served little purpose other than to provide a context for strange goings on. "Ken's Mystery" (1883), by Julian Hawthorne, is a vampire tale that predates Bram Stoker's *Dracula* by fourteen years. It's set on Halloween, "the carnival-time of disembodied spirits," which proves explanation enough for the narrator's encounter with a female vampire of Irish folk legend when he walks past the old house where she was reputed to have stayed. Likewise Wharton's "All Souls," in which a woman experiences a peculiar dislocation in space and time while bedridden in a house, owing to her crossing paths with a witch on the weekend of All Souls,

Most of such early Halloween stories are conspicuously lacking in the paraphernalia by which we identify the holiday today. It's simply enough for a character to mention that it's Halloween, All Hallows, November-Eve, Samhain, or somesuch, and all but (usually) one luckless person realizes that you put your sanity, and possibly your life at peril, if you're foolish enough to go out unprotected after dark. Modern Halloween tales tend to be more finicky about the traditional emblems and trappings that are Halloween trademarks: the devil is in the details, you might say, and virtually every detail of the Halloween season has been commemorated in a modern horror tale.

Take pumpkins. No one knows who first put a jack-o-lantern in a story—William Black, in one of the first known Halloween stories, "A Hallowe'en Wraith," published in 1886, tells of a swarm of disembodied spectral souls in the night that prove to be children swinging hollowed-out *turnips* with candles in them—but it would be hard to top Thomas Ligotti's description of a man carving a jack-o-lantern in "Conversations in a Dead Language" (1989) for sheer spookiness:

> *First he carved out an eye, spearing the triangle with the point of his knife and neatly drawing the pulpy thing from its socket. Pinching the blade he slid his two fingers along the blunt edge, pushing the eye onto the newspaper he'd carefully placed next to the sink. Another eye, a nose, a howling oval mouth. Done. Except for manually scooping out the seedy and stringy entrails and supplanting them with a squat little candle of the vigil type.*

Jack-o-lanterns make neat surrogates for human beings—Ligotti's character sees them in the windows of houses lining the street and envisions "a race of new faces in the suburbs"—and many writers have depicted them as grotesque summations of evil in the human soul. Dean R. Koontz, in "The Black Pumpkin" (1986), presents a pumpkin carver whose disturbing creations accurately mirror the foulness in the people who buy them: the uglier they are, the more faithful their representation. In "Pumpkin" (1984), Robert Bloch pulls the old switcheroo on a man who remembers how terrified he was of the creepy old farmer whose house he lived near as a boy. The man tries to put his childish fears behind him by taking a pumpkin he finds on the dead farmer's property for a jack-o-lantern—and when his family comes home they find that the remains of the farmer have snatched his head in exchange. William Bankier takes the pumpkin/head idea one step further in "Unholy Hybrid" (1963): A farmer renowned for his prize pumpkins buries in his field the corpse of a woman he has murdered. "Her head was the shape of a gourd, small at the top where not much hair at all struggled to cover a thin bony forehead, then bloating and distending downward to an inflated jaw with puffed cheeks and a wide mouth that rippled when she talked and collapsed in a fat pout when she was silent"—so guess what sprouts from the soil the next autumn harvest. In Bill Pronzini's tale "Pumpkin" (1986), evil pumpkins are endowed not with human faces but human motives: anyone unfortunate enough to eat their tainted pulp becomes a sort of malevolent Johnny Pumpkinseed, dedicated to sowing their seeds and propagating the species. Alan Ryan is one of the few writers to have noticed what cover artists of mass market horror paperbacks have long known: lights in the windows on a dark night can make a house look as sinister as a leering jack-o-lantern. In "The Halloween House" (1986), he has characters who were foolish enough to enter an abandoned house on Halloween discover that the rotted interior resembles nothing so much as an overripe pumpkin that (naturally) is starting to collapse in on itself—and them.

For many writers, as for many readers, Halloween is synonymous with the tradition of trick-or-treating. The notion of a night of formally sanctioned masquerade provides horror writers with a unique angle from which to contrast the real with the imagined, the natural and the supernatural, the surface and the substance. Whitley Strieber's "The Nixon Mask" (1986) is one of the strangest of all modern Halloween stories, with its suggestion that the public persona of celebrity is something that can be donned like a Halloween mask—and become irremovably stuck in place if one is not careful. Douglas E. Winter, in his story "Masks" (1985) explores the same idea from a slightly different perspective. In this tale, the roles people play in everyday life—in their families, in their relations with one another—are worn like Halloween masks, and *un*-masking can reveal dark truths about who we are, and who we are *not*. The tantalizing mystery of who is behind a Halloween mask is the subject of A.R. Morlan's "Trick or Treat" (1986). In a deft inversion of the idea that kids usually dress up as something hideously unreal, Morlan presents a pair of trick-or-treaters whose masks are revealed to be a merciful buffer against their true features.

Most of the major entities in the supernatural hierarchy have gotten a feature role in a Halloween horror story: vampires in Edward D. Hoch's "Day of the Vampire," werewolves and zombies in Gary L. Holleman's *Howl-O-Ween* (1996), goblins in Michael McDowell's "Halloween Candy" (1988), old Scratch himself in Robert R. McCammon's "He'll Come Knocking at Your Door" (1986), and the ubiquitous ghost in August Derleth's "Hallowe'en for Mr. Faulkner" (1959; and a story that merges Halloween with its slightly British relation, Guy Fawkes Day). But of all the beings afoot on our most unhallowed evening, witches appear to hold a special place for horror writers. It's not hard to see why. Witches are among the more human looking and acting beings in the supernatural pantheon. In fact, in Bernard Taylor's darkly funny "Samhain", they're a bunch of aging, out-of-shape witch- and warlock-wannabes on the make, who use the Halloween sabbat with its naked prance around the bonfire as a means for finding the right person to satisfy their all-too-human cravings. But real witches in Halloween stories invite a good deal of miscalculation from luckless victims who mistake their garb and manners for masquerade and make-believe. In D.A. Fowler's *The Devil's End* (1992), a girl who is the lineal descendant of a witch is able to inflict supernatural vengeance on her enemies at high school in the guise of ordinary teenage rivalry. Harold Knowles, the titular victim of Robert F. Young's "Victim of the Year" (1962) is unlucky in everything but love: he has a stunning girlfriend. On October 31, guess who shows that she isn't just masquerading as a witch, and who chose him as a guinea pig for her coven sisters to practice spells on before sacrificing him at a party on Halloween night. Likewise the musician in Jeffrey Sackett's *Candlemas Eve* (1988), who is beguiled by a pair of beautiful groupies whose fey manner meshes perfectly with his satanic rock music act. Little does he know that they are original members of the Salem witch cult, summoned back to life by his teenage son during a satanic Halloween ritual no one ever believed would work. The protagonist of James Herbert's "Hallowe'en's Child" (1988) should be so lucky. In this classic of just how badly a man can misread the illusion of Halloween make-believe, the narrator is driving on a foggy Halloween night when he hits something that he takes to be a child in a trick-or-treat costume. Conscientious person that he is, he stops to help it, even though it tries to escape him in an apparent derangement caused by pain and panic. Imagine his horror to see what he has truly run down:

The cowl had dropped away as she—yes, it was a woman, at least I think it was a woman—raised her head from the road to stare with filmy yellow eyes into mine, her ravaged and rotting countenance caught in the full glare of my car's headlinghts. But it wasn't just the shock of seeing the sharp, hawked nose, swollen near its tip with a huge hardened wart from which a single white hair sprouted, the cheeks with hollows so deep they seemed like holes, the thick grey eyebrows that joined across her wrinkled forehead, the cruel, lipless mouth from which a black tongue protruded that made me throw myself away.

No, it's not those warty, hairy, ugly *human* features that we traditionally associate with witches that's upsetting—it's her prehensile, scaly *tail* that finally makes him realize this is something worse than a person in a dimestore costume.

Both Ramsey Campbell's "The Trick" (1981) and Gahan Wilson's "Yesterday's Witch" (1972) feature that standard of witch fiction, the crotchety old neighborhood woman whom all the kids think is a witch. Halloween proves them right. Campbell's witch gives out candy to her tormentors that gives them a sort of sensitivity to the supernatural no sane mortal should have. Wilson's witch gives a whole new meaning to the term "trick-or-treat": the candies she so generously loads the kids in her neighborhood with transform their bags into hopping, flopping toadlike things that literally run away with the evening.

Campbell's and Wilson's stories underscore what is undoubtedly one of the most alluring aspects of Halloween to horror writers: tricks or treats, i.e., that point where the playful and the sinister intertwine, and the simply mischievous can become indistinguishable from the hostilely malevolent. "Halloween is the one night of the year kids can play all kinds of pranks and get away with it" says the central mischief maker in David Robbins' *Prank Night* (1994), and the literature of Halloween is rife with representations of stunts that turn ugly, and evil that flourishes in an atmosphere of holiday sanctioned pranks. In Charles L. Grant's

Stunts (1990), a killer whose touch is death moves virtually unseen among the high school population of the small town of Port Richmond, New Jersey, where Halloween stunts are considered part of the teenage coming-of-age ritual. Dennis J. Higman's *Pranks* (1989) tells of one boy with a blighted soul who finds the strength of personality he otherwise lacks in his Halloween superhero get-up, and whose pranks turn from mischievous, to vengeful and ultimately murderous as the evening's fun progresses. *Prank Night* parallels the misbehavior of rambunctious, hormone-driven teenagers rampaging in the local graveyard on Halloween with the activities of a monster that rampages every 70 years or so through the aptly named town of Cemetery Ridge in search of brains to eat. Robbins' *Hell-O-Ween* (1992) describes a prank that goes horribly awry: a group of high school jocks determined to scare the class nerd bait him with the girl he secretly worships into Caverna del Diablo, a reputedly haunted cave, where they've planned a bunch of tricks to scare the daylights out of him. But their activities awaken the demon that gave the cavern its name more than a century ago, and the story turns into an old-dark-house thriller in which the kids scramble desperately—and mostly in vain—to escape the ravenous thing that begins picking them off in the dark one by one.

Halloween parties are as much a part of Halloween fiction as they are of the holiday itself. Horror writers frequently ponder the idea of a group of people gathered together in Halloween revels meant to defuse fears and propose the exact opposite: what happens if this actually concentrates horrors and gives them a focus for expression? Lisa Cantrell, in *The Manse* (1987) and its sequel *Torments* (1990), chronicles the unique history of the Manse, centerpiece of the small North Carolina town of Merrillville. Though a century old, it has been untenanted for decades and is somewhat tarnished in reputation by the unexplained deaths on its premises of several people related to the family that built it. For thirteen years in a row the local Jaycees have used the site for a Halloween funhouse, and unwittingly have empowered ghosts from the house's past through the atmosphere of fear generated in it. The thirteenth and final Halloween at the house takes place during a bitter custody battle for the property, which gives the spooks the spark they need to break forth and manifest monstrously as animate electric cables, plants with a snake-life life of their own and man-eating mirrors. David Robbins, in *Spook Night* (1995), appropriates the iconography of Washington Irving's classic short story "The Legend of Sleepy Hollow," and its Revolutionary War horror, the headless horseman, who substitutes a lit jack-o-lantern for his head. This novel is set in the Pennsylvania town of Spook Hollow, where the legendary Headless Horror stalks a high school dance, looking for the head that was removed from him during the Civil War—and occasionally relieving other people of their own for a temporary substitute. Novels of this kind invariably build momentum by depicting the communities where they are set as bubbling cauldrons where private prejudice, skeletons in personal closets, social cliquishness, and other aspects of small town life have stewed to the boiling point and are catalyzed explosively by Halloween hijinks. Richard Laymon's *All Hallow's Eve* (1986) is no exception: it juxtaposes the everyday bad manners and savage behavior of its average citizens to the brutal vengeance a teenage boy and his criminal father visit upon everyone who attends a Halloween party they have staged at an abdanoned house in their town.

Halloween games are a common part of Halloween parties, and several have become prominent fixtures in Halloween horror literature. Bobbing for apples is surely one of the more traditional Halloween games, and Ramsey Campbell's "Apples" (1986) leaves a bad taste in the reader's mouth when its young narrator, part of a gang of kids who accidentally drove a man to his death while stealing apples from his property, kneels down to chomp an apple in a tub of water at a Halloween party—and sees an apple with the man's face staring back at him! Lewis Shiner's "The Circle" (1982) is a campfire tale transplanted to the Halloween hearth: it tells of a group of people who get together every Halloween to read ghost stories to each other, and what happens when they discover they have been made characters in a story one of their group has written, and that they are trapped ineluctably in its plot as it speeds them toward a horrible fate. Halloween's Celtic origins become the stuff of games in John Coyne's *Hobgoblin* (1981), written at the height of the Dungeons and Dragons craze. The novel's title refers to a fantasy role-playing game based on Celtic legend, which the teenage protagonist plays with a determination that has begun to erode the boundaries separating the real from the made up. At a Halloween party, the power struggles and personal aggressions symbolized in the game begin to superimpose themselves upon attendees, drawing them into a world in which they are ill-equipped to survive.

But the most famous Halloween game tale, without a doubt, is Ray Bradbury's "The October Game" (1948), a story that still registers one of the nastiest shocks in all horror fiction. The game of the title has its roots in a game for children traditionally played around the Christmas fireside (if we are to believe A.N.L. Munby's like-minded story, "The Christmas Game"), which gets a room full of kids sitting in a circle in the dark passing around objects that feel like bones, hair, eyes, teeth and other body parts supposedly cut from a dead witch. The game is intended as an exercise in imagination: you can't see what you're touching, except in your mind's eye, which is stimulated by suggestive phrases chanted by the gameleader, such as "The witch cut apart, and this is her heart." Usually, as one of the smugger kids observes, the game is played with "chicken insides." Bradbury, however, complicates the fun and games with a loveless marriage and a husband who would do anything to get back at his wife—even if it means using their daughter....

Innocent child victims like the one found in Bradbury's tale are not as common in Halloween horror stories as one might think. A sense of fair play pervades this type of fiction much the way it does other subgenres of horror, and youths who come to harm often as not do so because they probe into places where they should never look, invoke things which ought never to be summoned on Halloween night—or just generally act like jerks toward their peers. One exception is David Hagberg's *Last Come the Children* (1982), in which a series of inexplicable deaths, bizarre murders and strange behavior extending from Halloween to Candlemas Eve (February 1) in a small Wisconsin town are evidence of devil worship and the imminent blood sacrifice adumbrated in the title. The most conspicuous exceptions include the novelizations of John Carpenter's film, *Halloween*, and its sequels. Curtis Richard's *Halloween* (1979), Jack Martin's *Halloween II* (1982) and Nicholas Grabowsky's *Halloween IV* (1988) all stick close to the scripts they flesh out and mesh to form a Halloween history of Michael Myers, a figure of indestructible evil incarnate, who as a soulless six-year-old killed his older sister on Halloween night and was institutionalized for life. Michael escapes 15 years later to return to his hometown in Haddonfield, Illinois, where his masked presence goes unremarked upon on Halloween night. Though his motivation changes from book to book, becoming increasingly contrived as in the movies themselves, Myers has become an archetypal figure not only in Halloween horror fiction and film but in mass culture because he devotes a considerable amount of his time to slicing and dicing teenagers whose worst crime is to show a healthy interest in sex and display typical teenage irresponsibility.

If anything, writers of Halloween horror fiction seem more interested with children embodying Halloween horrors than being imperiled by them. In Peter Straub's novella "Pork Pie Hat" (1994), a jazz musician recalls a Halloween night from his childhood that began on a note of fun when he and a friend went trick-or-treating, and ended in horror that scarred his life ever after when he strayed across the wrong side of the tracks and witnessed what appeared to be the back alley delivery of a child from a taboo union. The blood and horror of the moment that the man saw as an inexperienced young boy are still fresh in his memory, and they convey a profoundly disorienting sense of lost innocence. Other writers convey the sense of innocence corrupted that attaches naturally to Halloween—a holiday that simultaneously evokes childhood innocence *and* supernatural evil—by stocking their stories with sinister kids.

Both Basil Copper's "The Candle in the Skull" (1984) and Talmage Powell's horror-crime hybrid "The Night of the Goblin" (1981), feature cagey children who subtly manipulate the mechanisms of Halloween to get what they want from adults. The young boy in Powell's story gets rid of his mother's abusive boyfriend, while the young girl in Copper's tale disposes of an unwanted parent and, in a ghoulish twist, gets the authentic skull she wants for her Halloween decorations. Rose Rinaldi, in her tongue-in-cheek "A Perfect Halloween Night" (1986), considers how Halloween rituals change with each new generation, and the devious new opportunities that might be seized by roving gangs of modern kids who find simply dressing up as supernatural creatures not at all frightening. The kids who trick-or-treat at the home of a family-medicine practitioner in F. Paul Wilson's "Buckets" (1989) are not really sinister, but they're certainly menacing: instead of trick-or-treat bags, each carries a stainless steel bucket—which the doctor realizes too late bears an uncanny resemblance to the waste buckets he uses when performing abortions. The worst kids of all on Halloween are those who have died and literally entered into the spirit of the evening. Charles L. Grant's "Eyes" (1986), Thomas Ligotti's "Conversation in a Dead Language" and Alison Lurie's "Another Halloween" (1994) all involve children who return from the dead on Halloween night and mix with the make-believe spooks and specters, the better to haunt the adults complicit in their deaths.

Though Halloween comes with an abundance of eerie emblems and set pieces for the horror writer to pick and choose from, surely its most attractive aspect is its malleability as a theme. The one day of the year when, in a supernatural sense, anything goes, Halloween virtually invites writers to think the unthinkable and conjure all new horrors to fulfill the possibilities of the day. In *Horrorshow* (1994), David Darke (a.k.a. Ron Dee) tells of a small town convulsed by lust and madness on Halloween when the local television station plays the suppressed last program made twenty years before by a Zacherley-type monster movie host who died on the air before he could incite viewers to fulfill his satanic mission. Thomas Monteleone's "Cutty Back Sow" (1994) and Chris Curry's *Panic* (1994) both delve into relatively unexplored corners of Scottish folklore for their horrors. Curry's features particularly evil creations—greenjacks—who steal the souls of children on Halloween and pay their respects to a leader of uncommonly revolting aspect: "The monstrosity resembled a human skeleton, but with bones made of tortured bark and buckled wood. Naked white roots, like nerves, twisted through its limbs, and leaves and vines filled its chest, throbbing green tendrils that twined along its extremities like blood veins." Jack Martin (a pseudonym for Dennis Etchison) in the novelization *Halloween III: Season of the Witch* (1982) revisits the classic Celtic folklore surrounding Halloween but gives it a thoroughly modern twist: a mask maker determined to revive mythic horrors impregnates each of the millions of children's masks he has mass produced with a microchip fashioned from shards of Stonehenge that is programmed to trigger hideous transformations on Halloween evening. Other authors have fabricated entirely original monsters to add to the pantheon of Halloween fights. In Al Sarrantonio's *October* (1990), the spirit of Halloween is a prehistoric parasite that infests and infects humans with the wanton urge to murder and destroy. Its vaguely satanic appearance that sums up its innate inhumanity:

It was slug colored, reptilian. Its long, thin tail ended in a tiny, split fork. Behind its head were the merest bumps, the hint of horns. Its small, round mouth opened and closed like a gasping, prehistoric fish. Its eyes were round, slightly raised, dark, blank, like gray wens.

The eponymous entity of Douglas Clegg's *The Halloween Man* (1998) is equally revolting, a semi-human travesty that rose from a bog three centuries before. It embodies the hypocrisy, forbidden knowledge and dark secrets of the family that sired it, and its horrifying countenance bespeaks the rot within its soul : "[I]t was a mask, bloated and pulled by water and leeches and insect larvae—it was a face without eyes in its sockets, and when he opened his mouth water and leaves poured forth. Yellow jackets burst from the festering sore beneath his chin." William F. Nolan's "The Halloween Man" (1986) is cut from different cloth, but is no less horrifying: he's a child stalking fiend who "'comes slidin' along, in his rotty tattered coat, like a big scarecrow come alive, with those glowy red eyes of his, and the bag already" to steals souls that he pops out of kids with a squeeze of their heads. The titular being in Gary W. Shockley's "Skullcracker" (1999) is a refugee from the nuthouse who so sympathizes with Halloween masqueraders who seem no weirder than himself that he "lobotomy proofs" them by driving eight-inch steel spikes into their heads. But the most original of all Halloween horrors is the one that no one can put a name to because it supersedes the powers of human description. John Skipp, in "The Spirit of Things" (1986) imagines the resurgence of "the Great Dark Ones," ageless beings so repugnant to human sensibilities that our species has had to bastardize and mock their existence by turning them into the stuff of cheesey horror films and dime store Halloween masks.

A handful of writers have become so renowned for their Halloween stories that stories centered around the day constitute a sort of subspecialty within their writing. First is Robert Bloch, who in his story "The Cloak" (1939) looked behind the surface of Halloween terrors to find their playful roots. This classic tale of a man who discovers that the costume he has rented to attend an office costume party belonged to a real vampire, and who finds his grasp of social decorum slipping with every exposed neck he sees, is a perfect blend of horror and humor, generally regarded the first modern Halloween horror story. Bloch's subsequent forays into the same territory are vastly different: "Pumpkin" is an exercise is EC Comics-type grue, and "Pranks" (1986) a mix of scares and social consciousness that portrays a neighborhood where adult negligence and self-centeredness predispose to horrors worse than anything the children dress up as. The best known writer of Halloween horror fiction is without a doubt Ray Bradbury. The first of his major stories in which Halloween plays a role, "Homecoming" (1946), captures the thoughts and feelings of an alienated young boy, born mortal into a vast extended family of vampires, werewolves and other supernatural creatures, who awaits the impending Halloween family reunion with a mixture of anticipation and dread. The story is a sort of roadmap to the October Country, that lyrical terrain of childhood fears, twilight landscapes and natural supernaturalism in which a good many of Bradbury's tales are set. The childhood fascination with Halloween Bradbury so reverently evokes in his story can be found in numerous tales of Halloween for children and young adults readers, some directly inspired by his example. Ironically, the body of this branch of fiction is even larger than the adult body of Halloween stories, and includes Bradbury's own novel *The Halloween Tree* (1972), a poetic instruction manual for the understanding of Halloween and its background history and mythology. At least two of Bradbury's stories, "The October Game" and "Heavy Set" (1964) speculate on how sour youthful Halloween fantasies can turn in a world of adult realities. "Heavy Set" is one of his creepiest ventures, featuring a grown man whose continuing desire to celebrate Halloween the way he did as a child represents a grotesque emotional stunting.

Bradbury's influence on the literature of Halloween horror can be measured in the work of a number of writers who have crafted tales in the spirit of his fiction. F. Paul Wilson's "The November Game" (1991) is a psychological horror story written as a sequel and homage to "The October Game." In "Halloween Girl" (1982), Robert Grant rewrites Bradbury's classic "The Lake" as a Halloween story of first love that persists beyond the grave. Like Grant's story, Tom Monteleone's "Yesterday's Child" (1987) is a nostalgic recreation of childhood enthusiasm for Halloween in which a man benefits from his encounter with the costumed trick-or-treater he was decades before. Steve Rasnic Tem's diptych "Halloween Street" (1999) and "Trick or Treat" (1999) both are set on a fictional Halloween street, an unidentified road that parallels Bradbury's October Country and serves as the backdrop for a number of childhood adventures that capture the awe and tenuous mystery of Halloween night. But the writer who has followed most diligently in Bradbury's footsteps is Al Sarrantonio. Sarrantonio's Halloween stories "Pumpkin Head" (1982), "The Spook Man" (1982), "Bogy" (1987) and

"The Big House" (1999) are filled with characters plucked from the same pumpkin patch as Bradbury's autumn people: a child born with a grotesque jack-o-lantern face; an illusionist who shows a trick-or-treater that she is but a creature "of teeth and claws and wild red eyes;" a semi-human man who "changes shape and throws his voice" and who is the source of all the fears that make Halloween so delicious for the young; a thing in a pit that plays by animating the spooky house perched above it on Halloween evening. Tinged with "All-Souls' colors," brooded over by skies "roiled like freezing fire: orange, white, black," and galvanized by fears felt when "things dropped down from the ceiling and the corners became places you wouldn't want to back into," Sarrantonio's stories all feature Bradburyesque children whose world is an interplay of light and shadow viewed from behind a Halloween mask.

And that's as good a summation as any of the import of Halloween horror stories. They present us with a child's eye view of the world in which the scary and the magical closely abut one another, and where the tricks merge imperceptibly with the treats.

Recommended Reading List

Anthologies:
Jo Fletcher (ed.) Horror at Halloween. Pumpkin Books, 1999.
Peter Haining (ed.) Hallowe'en Hauntings. William Kimber, 1984.
Alan Ryan (ed.) Halloween Horrors. Doubleday, 1986.
Michele Slung (ed.) Murder for Halloween. Mysterious Press, 1994.
Carol-Lynn Rossel Waugh, et al. (eds.) 13 Horrors of Halloween. Avon, 1983.

Short Stories (not included in the anthologies listed above):
Robert Bloch. "Pumpkin." Twilight Zone, Nov-Dec. 1984.
Ray Bradbury. "Homecoming." Mademoiselle, Oct. 1946.
Ray Bradbury. "Heavy Set." Playboy, Oct. 1964.
Ramsey Campbell. "Tricks." Weird Tales #2, Daw, 1984.
James Herbert. "Hallowe'en's Child." The Daily Mail, Oct. 29, 1988.
Dean R. Koontz. "The Black Pumpkin." Twilight Zone, Dec. 1986.
Thomas Ligotti. "Conversations in a Dead Language." Deathrealm, Spring 1989.
Alison Lurie. "Another Halloween." Women and Ghosts, Heinemann, 1994

Michael McDowell. "Halloween Candy." Tales from the Darkside, edited by Mitchell Galin and Tom Allen, Berkley, 1986.
Thomas Monteleone. "The Cutty Black Sow." Cemetery Dance, Spring 1990.
Thomas Monteleone. "Yesterday's Child." Grue #5, 1987.
A.R. Morlan. "Trick or Treat." The Horror Show, Fall 1986.
William F. Nolan. "The Halloween Man." Night Cry, Summer 1986.
Rose Rinaldi. "A Perfect Halloween Night." Twilight Zone, Dec. 1986.
Al Sarrantonio. "The Big House." Toybox, CD Publications, 2000.
Al Sarrantonio. "Bogy." Whispers VI, edited by Stuart Schiff, Doubleday, 1987.
Al Sarrantonio. "The Spook Man." Twilight Zone, Nov. 1982.
Gary W. Shockley. "Skullcracker." Magazine of Fantasy and Science Fiction, 1999.
John Skipp. "The Spirit of Things." Twilight Zone, Dec. 1986.
Bernard Taylor. "Samhain." Final Shadows, edited by Charles L. Grant. Doubleday, 1991.
Steve Rasnic Tem. "Halloween Street." Magazine of Fantasy and Science Fiction, 1999.
Steve Rasnic Tem. "Trick or Treat." Magazine of Fantasy and Science Fiction, 1999.
F. Paul Wilson. "Buckets." Soft and Other Stories, Tor, 1989.
F. Paul Wilson. "The November Game." The Bradbury Chronicles, edited by William F. Nolan and Martin H. Greenberg, Roc, 1991.
Douglas E. Winter. "Masks." Midnight, edited by Charles L. Grant, Tor, 1985.

Novels:
Meg Elizabeth Atkins. Samain. Harper & Row, 1976.
Ann Brahms. Cloak of Darkness. Zebra, 1992.
Ray Bradbury. The Halloween Tree. Knopf, 1972.
Douglas Clegg. The Halloween Man. Leisure, 1998.
John Coyne. Hobgoblin. Putnam, 1981.
Lisa W. Cantrell. The Manse. Tor, 1987.
Lisa W. Cantrell. Torments. Tor, 1990.
Chris Curry. Panic. Pocket, 1994.
David Darke. Horrorshow. Zebra, 1994.
D.A. Fowler. The Devil's End. Pocket, 1992.
Nicholas Graboswky. Halloween IV. Critic's Choice, 1988.
Ben Greer. Halloween. Macmillan, 1978.
David Hagberg. Last Come the Children. Tor, 1982.
Dennis J. Higman. Pranks. Leisure, 1989.
Gary L. Holleman. Howl-O-Ween. Leisure, 1996.
Richard Laymon. All Hallow's Eve. NEL, 1986.
Ashley McConnell. Days of the Dead. Charter, 1992.
Jack Martin. Halloween II. Zebra, 1981.
Jack Martin. Halloween III: Season of the Witch. Jove, 1982.
Kimberley Rangel. The Homecoming. Leisure, 1998.
Curtis Richards. Halloween. Bantam, 1979.
David Robbins. Hell-O-Ween. Leisure, 1992.
David Robbins. Prank Night. Leisure, 1994.
David Robbins. Spook Night. Leisure, 1996.
Jeffrey Sackett. Candlemas Eve. Bantam, 1988.
Al Sarrantonio. October. Bantam, 1990.

A Halloween Memory

Peter Crowther

Even here in England, the pre-Halloween stores are increasingly filled with all the usual seasonal goodies—ghoulish heads, witch hats, ghost-face flashlights and, of course, no end of gruesomely gooey candies and chocolate bars to slip into the grasping hands of tiny trick-or-treaters...just like in the US. But it hasn't always been that way.

In fact, as recently (Hah!) as when *I* was a fresh-faced youngster in short pants, Halloween meant nothing at all for most Brits. I, however, was not what one might call typical of British childhood.

Being a 'Fourth of July' arrival, I suppose it was inevitable that I would follow US traditions, a situation undoubtedly fueled by my immersing myself in American TV shows and comic books, and, as time went by, in novels and stories written by American writers. Not surprisingly, references to Halloween and Thanksgiving—plus other US holidays and traditions—figured heavily in my greedy intake of words, and it wasn't long before a few careful inquiries revealed the truth: wow!

monsters and ghouls and witches and werewolves, all coming together for one special night of unbridled mayhem! Count me in!

Thus I would spend many a smoky autumn evening with friends, wandering the woodland trails of the park a half-mile from my house in the sleepy Yorkshire suburb of Headingley, watching the skies for signs of airborne broomsticks and peering into the thick bushes and trees for just a glimpse of something white- or furry-faced, its teeth gleaming. Alas, I didn't see any though I recall boasting—as did many of my contemporaries—of just such a sighting when school convened the next day.

The power of imagination was such that, at least in those simpler times, the other kids believed what I said just as unquestionably as I believed what they said. But my stories were always just a little bit denser and maybe just a little more graphic than those told by my friends, and I guess that was an early indication of what I'd end up doing for a living a few decades down the line.

Back then, of course, it was relatively easy to break through the thin veil of Universal Knowledge and Belief...and its detestable cousin, Common Sense: a lot of kids still believed in Santa Claus and the Tooth Fairy way up into their teens, so it was but a small step to accept that, on one special night of the year, the inhabitants of the local cemetery rolled back their soily covers and went for a wander, dark thoughts brooding in their worm-eaten heads.

It didn't matter that most of these folks were, back when they were alive, decent members of the community who would never have harmed so much as a hair on a kid's head. Nossir! Somewhere deep in the back of our minds, in that dusty rear room of the imagination where every creak signals something truly horrendous, it made a lot of sense that something had gotten to them on the Other Side...something that made every reanimated corpse a sworn enemy. We didn't mind that parents didn't seem to have the same concerns as we did: what did parents know, anyway. They didn't run everywhere—didn't run *any*where, in fact—and they didn't collect bubble gum cards, didn't laugh at the antics of Archie and Jughead...so it was perfectly reasonable to assume they'd got this wrong, too.

Now it's not so easy.

Kids these days take a lot of convincing about anything at all.

And so it was, one Halloween about 13 or 14 years ago, I hatched a plan to change all that...just for one night.

Nicky and I have two sons, Oliver and Timothy, 23 and 21 respectively. One of them graduated in graphic design a couple of years ago and the other graduates as an actor this summer. But 13 or 14 years ago they weren't quite so self-assured and worldly-wise as they are now.

We had always celebrated Halloween (if 'celebrated' is the correct word), even when it wasn't fashionable in Britain. There were a couple of stores that used to put out a few cheesey-looking cardboard masks and those slimy plastic spiders, but most stores were busy stocking up on Christmas cards—now, of course, the Christmas cards come out as soon as August comes to a close—but good props were hard to find. So we—or, rather, Nicky—used to construct black cloaks and hoods for Ollie and Tim, and send them out trick-or-treating (always hovering in the background to watch them in case the *real* kid-hurting monsters got to them), armed with plastic tubs to collect their spoils...most of which would come from the boys' nanna—my own mother—who lived in the apartment at the top of our house.

But that was when the children were really young.

By the time adolescence showed signs of creeping up on our sons and the first flush of testosterone began to pump, I needed something better to capture their imaginations. Something more *real.*

On this particular Halloween, we had friends staying over. The day itself fell on a Saturday, and it rolled on into a particularly Halloweeny night filled with mist and gloom and a damp cold that seeped through even the thickest clothing to eat right into the marrow of your bones.

Our houseguests were my oldest friend, Phil—we've been staunch pals since eight years old—and his wife, Yvonne and their two kids, Simon and Anna, both around the same age as our two. I'd spoken with Phil beforehand and hatched a fairly demonic plan—I tend to speak with Phil a lot: he's a doctor, and I always seek his advice when I want to kill somebody or to describe any horrible side-effects of symptoms of a condition I want to put a character through. (It's a hard life being a god.)

Anyway, Phil had gone for it, and Yvonne too, though she was a little more circumspect.

And the other two adults in the scheme had also gone for it...and they'd gone for it in a big way.

Sam and Lucy have since moved south but at the time they lived in Harrogate quite near to us. Sam was a big wheel in ICI and so, like me, with my corporate background in handling communications for the financial services industry, he was no stranger to the gentle art of lying and bullshitting that is so essential to boardroom survival. And Sam and Lucy have two boys, Johnny and Patrick, also around the same age as the other four.

The first part of the plan—there were two parts: one of them, the first one, for the consumption of everyone, and the other known only to the adults—was that we'd all gather *Chez Crowther* for a family meal plus spooky videos: but first, Phil, Sam and I would take the six kids up into the woods to look for witches and stuff.

There were, inevitably, lots of negative sounds from the kids, all of whom had long outgrown that shit (hell, they were 10 years old, or getting on that way) but, as the day went on and the sky darkened, they kind of warmed to the idea—like I said, it was starting to turn real nasty out there...so nasty it was like this was the Halloween night of them all, the one night in the history of really horrible nights that, if something were to come lumbering out of the graveyard hell-bent on tearing a kid's head off, then it would be tonight. Thus, as the pre-arranged time came for our departure, the bravado-cum-bored-acceptance that had replaced the kids' initial negativity began to dilute a little.

So far, so good.

Phil and I left my house with our four kids in the back seat, little faces staring out of the windows at the drizzle and the mist, and watching every figure marching forward-bent against the elements to make sure they didn't turn and glare at them with red-rimmed eyes...or maybe reach out a clawed hand at the car door while we were waiting at the traffic signals.

We arrived at Sam's place to find Sam and Lucy embroiled in a bit of an argument—a very well rehearsed argument—with Patrick and Johnny watching with that nervousness all kids develop when they see their parents having a disagreement. Lucy was saying that she didn't want us to take the kids out. *It's dangerous out there*, she told him. Sam, a true thespian, scoffed

scoff scoff

at this and asked her to elaborate on what she was talking about. Lucy continued with last-minute preparations for the food she was going to take around to my house and wouldn't say any more except for a beautifully-delivered *You know very well what I'm talking about.*

That was all the kids wanted to hear—or rather all they *didn't* want to hear. Hell, if one of their own parents wouldn't verbalize the danger then it was clearly something out of the ordinary—it wasn't like being knocked down by a car if you didn't look when you crossed the busy road, or falling off a wall you insisted on walking or out of a tall tree you insisted on climbing; this was something else...something evil, something that existed in that shadowy area which adults couldn't even bring themselves to talk about in front of their kids. In short, it was creatures with partly-decomposed bodies who snuck into your house and lay under your bed until you needed to take a pee so badly you thought your bladder would explode, wart-faced old crones who made stews of kids' eyeballs, and long-toothed men in swirling cloaks who could drink your body dry of fluids in the time it took to click your fingers.

Then the telephone rang and, while all six of the kids watched (still coming to terms with Lucy's obvious concerns), Sam picked up the phone and, after a couple of minutes, launched into a blazing temper with whoever was on the other end of the line. It was Sam's boss (actually, it was Nicky, calling from my house), and the word was that Sam was needed right now to go through some reports that had to be amended for Monday morning's board meeting. *Can't it wait until tomorrow, for crissakes?* Sam asked. Apparently not. And even his explanation of the event we'd planned fell on the stony corporate ears of 'the Boss'. Sam slammed the phone on the cradle, explained that he'd have to go out for a couple of hours and get this sorted but he'd be back in time to eat. Phil and I would have to take all the kids by ourselves.

Sam left the house in a stinker of a bad mood, slamming the door so hard behind him that one of the inlaid glass panels cracked from top to bottom (believe me, DeNiro could learn a lot from Sam Hay). As Sam's car engine burst into life outside, Phil and I held a muted conversation with Lucy—muted but anxiously watched and listened to by our six charges—and then, putting on a brave face, we loaded them into the car and set off for the woods.

The second part of the plan was underway.

And Sam, complete with appropriate costumery and props, was already a couple of miles ahead of us.

When we reached the pre-arranged pull-in—pre-arranged but, for the benefit of our passengers, apparently arbitrarily chosen on the spur of the moment—what had started out as the worst night of the year soon blossomed into the worst night since the last dinosaur had walked the planet.

The moon hid itself behind thick gray clouds scudding across the sky like stock car racers. Rain was coming down almost horizontally in the wind and somewhere off in the distance muted thunder rolled and crashed angrily while lightning forked to the ground...like it was looking for us.

The setting was perfect. Ours was the only car in the pull-in. Behind us, and stretching all the way to open fields, were the picturesque Harlow Car Gardens while right in front of us, and stretching for more than a mile in any direction, was the woods, a thick and frequently impenetrable collection of fir trees whose centuries of fallen pine needles had turned the ground and the single overgrown path into a spongy blanket.

The kids were less than happy at the prospect of venturing into the woods. In fact, one or two of them were expressing serious concerns that whatever might be out there on this night of nights was more than likely a match for me and Phil. The fact is there are first-graders who could mug me or Phil with little or no effort and, listening to the thunder and staring into the pitch blackness, our well-rehearsed exchange that they just might be right was a little more heartfelt in the gloom and the rain than it had been that afternoon when we had planned the conversation.

But fatherly bravado won the day and, all of us suitably (if reluctantly) decked out in coats and jackets, our hair slicked back by rain and our hands feeling like we'd got frostbite, we set off up the path to...The Old Clearing

bom ba dom dom BOM!

which, as we explained, had once been a meeting place for the witches of Harrogate and nearby Knaresborough.

And wouldn't you know it, as we came within earshot of this clearing, we could hear hammering and a frantic muttering.

One or two of our charges wanted to go back—and Phil and I were in two minds whether to continue, wondering if what we were doing constituted mental abuse—but, thinking of the glorious charge of terror we all 'enjoy' on the fairground rollercoaster, we pressed on, amidst frantic *shush*es and hissed instructions from the children. Dropping to our hands and knees, we crept up to a vantage point where we could see into the clearing.

The sight was pretty impressive, I have to say.

There before us was a small cloaked figure (Sam would never have made it as a basketball player) hanging what appeared to be skulls by the light of a small lantern onto a makeshift trellis. It was muttering to itself, its tall conical hat sloping forward each time it stooped to retrieve one of the small skulls and proceeded to nail it into place. Then, suddenly, it stopped and looked around...looked in our direction.

I whispered to Phil that maybe we should head for home.

We stood up, ensuring that a twig was snapped in the process, and the cloaked figure screeched at the top of its voice and started running at us, its hammer at the ready.

Phil and I and the kids, all of us screaming in blind terror (and, I have to say at this point, not one of us putting it on), turned and ran like hell back down the trail...with the creature in hot pursuit.

Back at the car, it was a very difficult job to calm the children and show that the figure was indeed none other than Sam, now chuckling to himself as he approached, removing his hat and pulling off quite the most evil-looking witch's face-mask I have ever seen.

After a violent but hysterical session of parent-beating—wholly deserved, I have to say—we set off back for home, first dropping Sam at his carefully concealed car so he could make his own way.

Watching the kids, in front of the reassuring glow of an open fire, telling the story to their mothers and nanna (who, having wandered down into the main house to welcome us all home, was clearly relieved that we *hadn't* been murdered by witches) was something to behold, their voices gaining in volume as each tried to out-do the others and explain just how horrible it truly was. And, perhaps best of all, there were also our own voices—Phil's, Sam's and mine—equally excited, trying to get across that magical feeling of stark terror...the feeling we tend to lose as the call of adulthood overtakes so many of us without our even realizing that it has disappeared...and despite our personal promises to ourselves that it never will.

There followed a wonderful meal, some carefully-chosen black-and-white movies on video—*The Thing* (shades of Carpenter's *Halloween*, as I recall) and *Invasion of the Body Snatchers*—and then the children went off to bed, exhausted but still excited...while the storm raged outside, seemingly trying to tear the house apart to get at the hoaxsters within.

Needless to say, bedroom doors—our own included—were left ajar to admit as much light as possible from the corridor.

Over time, particularly since Ollie and Tim moved to London a few years ago, the house has assumed even greater proportions...and it'll be worse this year: my mother died—a few weeks ago as I write this—following a brief but spunky fight against the *real* monster of the night, cancer.

But every time Halloween comes along and the air gets smoky Nicky and I hollow out our pumpkin and light it, just for the two of us...and, although I've never returned to the woods (at least, not in the dark), I always take a walk outside and look up into the night sky, forever whittling at the imagination in an attempt to make something sharp and deliciously nasty out of it. After all, it's the exotic monsters that make us forget the real ones—and driving past the cemetery gates on the morning of November 1st and seeing the graves undisturbed for another year is *still* a good feeling. Long may it remain so.